naughty bits

AN ANTHOLOGY *of* SHORT EROTIC FICTION

Love April

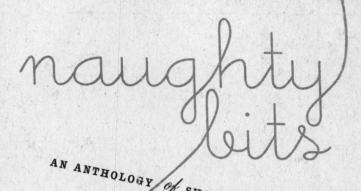

naughty bits

AN ANTHOLOGY of SHORT EROTIC FICTION

Jenesi Ash

Jina Bacarr

Eden Bradley

Jodi Lynn Copeland

Lacy Danes

Delilah Devlin

Grace D'Otare

Charlotte Featherstone

Alice Gaines

Megan Hart

Sarah McCarty

Alison Paige

Cathleen Ross

Kimberly Kaye Terry

Tracy Wolff

Spice

Recycling programs for this product may not exist in your area.

Spice

NAUGHTY BITS

ISBN-13: 978-0-373-60538-5
ISBN-10:   0-373-60538-2

CONTENTS

The Invitation

LACY DANES

YOU LEFT ME A GIFT. MY SHAKING FINGERS SLIDE ALONG the red silk ribbon and into the loop of the bow. I have never expected a gift, and you know how much I love surprises. Pinching the tail of the bow in between my thumb and forefinger, I pull the ribbon loose and slide the card from the top of the rectangular box. My stomach flutters as I ease the stiff paper from the envelope. I close my eyes as goose bumps race over my skin. What will it say? What is in the box? My hands shake and I flip the card open as I raise my eyelids to take in your words…your wishes.

My slut,
Wear this gift and meet me on the trail at dusk…the trail where we initiated our wilderness exhibitionism. Wear shorts and a shirt, an easily lifted jacket, hiking boots, no bra or panties. Bring water and a very warm blanket.
Master Eric

A hike is something I have always enjoyed and a scene in the woods something I relish. My pussy throbs as images of you handcuffing my arms around a tree and fucking my ass flood my thoughts. Yum. What could you possibly have purchased for me to wear into the woods?

I hastily grab the box and spin about, sinking down onto the chair beside the table. I slowly lift the lid to reveal a bright blue velvet bag. The sleek fabric excites me and my nipples pebble as I pull the pouch from the box. Inside is an object of heavy weight. The shape, as my fingers smooth along the outside of the bag, is of an egg with a stem and handle. A plug. I uncinch the pouch and dump the gift into my hand and grin. Chills of delight race up my neck.

A three-inch art glass plug sits in my palm. The red and black colors swirl from tip to the flanged base and in the wide stopper end, etched into the glass, are the words *Owned by E.* My heart soars and I grin. My fingernail traces each letter; they look as if you handwrote them yourself. How did you do that?

Indeed, I am yours. You own my heart and I will do all you wish of me. Running my fingers over the polished surface, the image of sliding the smooth glass into my pucker, my flesh being stretched, readying me for your onslaught, makes me quiver. I fidget in my seat as heat curls between the globes of my ass. A smile of excitement stretches my lips and I can't sit still. I can't wait to see you, and see what you have in store for me. Time I go get ready…

What lies at the end of this hike—or what I hope does—thrills me. I grin and remember your instructions as my skin tingles in excitement and arousal. I am dressed as you requested. Shorts, shirt, jacket, no bra or panties. My makeup is as you like. Red lips, eyeliner…everything done to perfection.

I feel beautiful, sexy in my short shorts and tight top. I am slightly overdone for the wilderness but know how I appear will please you, and that is all that matters to me.

I start to whistle a giddy little tune as I walk. The gravel path crunches beneath my feet as your gift tugs the skin of my bottom. The plug, snugly inserted in my ass, fills me and each step rocks the egg within me, arousing my body as I walk down the trail.

My pussy quivers remembering the last time I walked this path. Remembering you using your new crop on me, then fucking me as I trembled, floating in a euphoric haze looking out at the serene lake.

I pass the location where you kissed me on the bench, and I remember the clips tugging my sensitive nipples as we walked, talking about videos and movies we had watched, about our hometowns, and about all of our favorite foods and pastimes. We are so alike yet so opposite.

I come to the small clearing, the tree where we were caught with our pants down. I grin, wanting to relive that moment, to stay cuffed to that tree as the woman passed instead of you uncuffing me before she could see us. A small giggle bursts from my lips. God, I love to be watched, caught…it is a thrill like no other.

My feet take me deeper and deeper into the wilderness and I come to the place where our first scene was performed. You stand by the rail watching me, your blue eyes filled with intense desire, excitement. My body trembles just looking at you. Your short black hair and wicked smile. Your broad shoulders and stocky build. You are the most handsome man I know. But it goes so much beyond your looks. Your mind and your soul are what captivate me.

Your mouth quirks up as I reach your side. "Greet me properly."

My lips curl into a smile. "Yes, Master." I drop to my knees, my eyes filled with adoration never leaving yours, then smooth my hands up your thighs. My fingers trail over your zipper and slide the fly down. You stand absolutely still, hands clasped behind your back. I want to shake you, to make you moan, to lose the control you always hold in check—but I will never cross that line.

My mouth waters, wanting to take you into my sweet depths, to swallow you up and make you hard. I free your cock from the confines of your pants and press the plum-shaped tip to the soft glossed lips of my mouth. My tongue slides out and circles the head of your semifirm penis. The smell of your sex shoots straight to my wet labia, making my cunt gape with need. Saliva pools under my tongue and as I slide your prick into my mouth, the slickness slips down your cock coating you with my moisture.

You taste delicious. The salty spice of your skin tingles my taste buds and I flick my tongue against the smooth ridge of your head. The skin is loose but quickly fills, tightening over your wide penis.

I nestle your dick in my mouth then pull back out to the tip. Sliding back down your length, your crown gently touches the back of my tongue. I hesitate, afraid I may gag on your thickness, and again pull back up to the tip, swirling and gently nibbling on the rim with my teeth. You moan. The sound of your pleasure emboldens me; I want so desperately to hear more and more of that sweet delicious sound as you capture your pleasure and in turn I receive mine. Licking my lips I move back to suck the large tip deeper into my throat. To create the sensation I know you so love.

You grasp my chin. "No. Stand."

Damn.

The unyielding grip of your fingers on my jawbone washes through me and I tremble. Even the lightest touch from you on my skin makes me shake but when you firmly grasp me, my vision hazes and I begin to float in the euphoric bliss that goes back ages in time. Dominant man in control of his spirited woman. I stand without hesitation, my eyes clouded with nothing but the vision of pleasing you. Of giving you all my power to do with as you wish.

You smile at me, devotion and excitement swirling in the depths of your gaze.

God, you make my knees weak.

You lead me, your fingers entwined with mine, into the woods, away from the lake and the pretty view that we enjoyed on our first encounter. Deep into the trees we walk, neither one of us saying a word. I wonder what you have planned but know I will enjoy it no matter what it is.

We reach a set of trees that are equal in size and spread about five feet apart. There is a large grouping of boulders off to one side by which you have placed your backpack, and a flask.

"Give me your pack." You hold out your hand to me.

I hand over the bag, which contains the water and warm blanket you requested.

You grasp them in one hand and with the other you grab my hair. Tingles shoot through my scalp and you pull my lips to yours. The warmth of your mouth devours mine; the taste of

Red Bull on your tongue as it plunges in, tangling slowly, warms me to my toes. The flavor I will forever associate with you.

My nipples are pebble-hard and I groan, wanting to touch you, to feel your skin beneath my hands, but I stand absolutely still as I have been trained by you to do.

You slip my jacket from my shoulders and off of me. I shiver, but more from excitement than the cold. I only want to please you, to excite you and bring you pleasure.

You walk me to the trees. There your fingers wrap my palm and you raise my arm, placing a fur-lined cuff about my wrist. The cuff is attached to the tree by rope. You do the same with my other hand, smiling a very devious smile. God, I love that smile. It is the smile that inhabits my every dream, my every memory of us. I tug on my arms to see if I have any room for escape. The cuffs dig into the base of my hand but don't slip over.

"No escape."

"Yes, Master. You know me, I had to check." I grin at you.

You laugh as a blindfold emerges from your pocket and you slip it over my head. The soft fur underlining slides down my forehead and the last thing I see is your lips grinning at me.

Oh dear…what do you have planned?

My heart pounds and my breath hitches in my throat. I try to relax but it is impossible—my arms and legs begin to shake in anticipation of the unknown act you are about to press upon me for your pleasure, for my pleasure, for us.

Cold metal strokes my forearm, a single caress. Too quick for me to discern what it is exactly. Then the cold traces my shoulder and up my neck.

"Hold still, my slut. I wouldn't want to cut you."

Cut? The word slides panic straight to my gut.

A knife.

I inhale sharply and my body trembles involuntarily. I try to hold as still as possible as the blade traces the collar on my T-shirt, flowing like an eroticized paintbrush down between my breasts. The cold steel excites everywhere it touches.

The hem of my shirt lifts and pulls from my body. The knife reaches the place where fabric no longer is a part of me and I hear the material tear. It is a sharp knife. My stomach flips on the knowledge you could cut me at any moment. I inhale slowly and my trust in you calms my beating heart.

The knife cuts through the cotton, splitting the shirt from just below my breasts to the hem. My arms jump and shake and you pull the two tails of shirt, tearing the rest apart, exposing my breasts to the air. The difference in temperature tingles along my skin and your fingers graze my nipples. I moan, arching towards you, wanting you to pinch and suckle my peaked flesh. "Please."

"Beautiful." Your deep voice is full of love and warms my heart. "Stay still." The cool tip of the knife touches the tip of my nipple then gently flicks it. A pinprick of pain is instantly soothed by the warm wetness of your tongue swirling about the bud.

"Ahhh." My pussy throbs and my legs part trying to ease the ache sharpened by your domination. Your mouth's caress leaves my puckered tip and your hair brushes the underside of my raised arm as you duck under it. I suck in a breath as my body shakes. The knife continues…

You cut up the backside of my shirt, then slide the separated pieces up my arms and off my cuffed hands. The cool air washes my heated skin and gooseflesh rises. There is a tug on my waistband, the button pops free and the zipper falls. You push the shorts down my legs and they pool at my feet. Yes, indeed. My pussy needs you.

"Kick them free." Your voice sounds as if you have stepped quite a distance from my body.

"Yes, Master." I wiggle my feet wanting to expose my hungry wet flesh for your pleasure. My legs continue to shake as I first work one foot free, then the other and kick my shorts from my body.

I stand nude for what seems like eternity, only the cold air touching my skin. I swallow hard and wait...wait to see what it is that you wish of me.

You pull my hair back and the knife scrapes like sandpaper up my neck from nape to chin. I shake uncontrollably as you hold the blade under my chin.

Your tongue snakes into my ear, swirling the curve and then dipping into the cup. "Such a sweet thing you are. Bound and totally at my will." You pull from me and I am left panting for breath as my pussy spasms, wanting any part of you to touch the sopping wet flesh.

The cold blade traces up the inside of my thigh. I jump.

"Hold."

I stiffen, my breath tight. My muscles aching to tremble as the press travels up the inside of my leg to the crease of my buttock cheek and thigh. You hold the steel there and your other hand rubs the cheeks of my ass as if I am a skittish dog in need of a gentle hand.

The metal turns from cold to the temperature of my body. You gently slide the base of the blade over to touch my labia.

I groan, my pussy overflowing and twitching with juices. The blade slowly parts the folds of my sex, spreading the lips wide. I hold absolutely still. Your finger slides into my cunny.

I scream, my inner muscles clamping about your finger, but I don't dare move—the knife still holds my sensitive flesh. You remove your finger. The blade releases my labia and I hear you place your fingers into your mouth and suck them. My tongue traces my lips in a search for my tart flavor, but finds none.

"The best fruit this blade has opened yet." I feel the smile in your tone.

I am proud I have pleased you. A sigh of contentedness and relief presses from my lungs.

Your footfalls sound and I sag slightly on my arms allowing the rope and cuffs to support me. Your voice calls from behind me, not far, but not close. "Arch your back and display your ass to me."

I hear the rustling of tree leaves as I widen my stance and thrust my ass back in the direction of your voice.

Swoosh...

Swoosh...

"This will do quite nicely." Your tone holds a note of humor. What *this* is I have little time to consider.

Swoosh...

A long thin switch cuts across my buttocks, hard. I suck in a startled breath and tense my body, readying for the next blow.

Swoosh...

The rough wood cuts across the backs of my thighs. I cry out, half startled, half from the pain. Tears spring to my eyes, my lungs tighten and my shoulders press up to my ears as prickling heat radiates up my body to the core of me.

"Yes, indeed. Quite well. Don't you agree, my sweet?"

Heated arousal washes over me at the tone of your voice and I begin to relax. The muscles of my shoulders sag, and all the air flows out of me. "Indeed, Master."

The switch hits again, this time more gentle. The tip taps and taps my buttocks and thighs, slowly increasing in intensity and frequency. Warming my skin, readying my muscles for the more intense strokes I know will follow.

I pull on my hands. I twist against the leather cuffs that restrain me and stomp my feet. The hits get harder and closer together and I cry out, "Fuck!"

"Indeed. Take a deep breath and breathe, my love." You pull in a sharp lungful of air and I know before the sound of the switch cuts through the air this will be a harsh one. I tense, readying for the heat and pain.

Swoosh...

The switch harshly caresses my ass.

I inhale through clenched teeth, and slip...slip into that state I so crave. My muscles liquefy and peaceful calm washes over me. I stand absolutely still and quiet as a shy child, hanging in the blissful haze as the leather cuffs and rope hold me.

Swoosh...

The switch cuts again with the same harsh intensity. I moan at the heat and tingling in my ass as my pussy gushes and fevered arousal courses through me.

Swoosh...swoosh...swoosh...swoosh...

I rock and sway to each knee-weakening hit.

You stop. I hear your heavy breathing behind me. Your fingertip gently traces a welt on my ass. I lift my head just a fraction then drop it back down. Your footfalls on the dirt indicate you are coming around to the front of me. The warmth of your breath caresses my ear.

"How are you doing, my love?"

I lick my lips and swallow. "Quite well, Master."

"Exactly what I wanted to hear." Your finger traces my lips and my tongue slides out and snakes about it. "Stand up straight."

"Yes, Master."

I shift, pulling my ass in and straightening my shoulders.

The sting that hits my breasts is soothing, a sensation I know well and love. The little rubber flogger I purchased for you for our one-year anniversary. The pricking warmth of each hit sends pleasure waves straight down my stomach to my clit. The tiny hardened button throbs as you continue flogging each breast and my shoulders.

I flinch as the last changes focus to my thighs. Each hit stronger, the tips brush, sting, and arouse me.

"Part your legs."

"Yes, Master." I slide them apart and the flogger slices across my labia with a thud. I jump, suck in my breath, and quiver with pleasure as my muscles and my pussy clench.

The flogger hits again and the pleasure shoots straight to my womb. I scream as bliss grabs me and I spill juices onto the tails.

You reach in between my legs and the rubber handle pushes up into my weeping cunt. I groan. Deep. The sensation wracks my body as my pussy opens to you and your probing.

You slide the flogger back out and then in again, the tails brushing my thighs with each fuck of the handle. Your thumb rides against my clit as you push the handle deep.

The fire rushes through my body and I reach for the climax

thundering in my veins. In and out the handle goes, sliding in my slick juices. My wetness is audible. I am soaking for you.

Your thumb glides in the same relentless rhythm against my button. I tremble and my toes curl in my boots as my hips arch toward you. "Please, please, Master. May I? May I please?"

"Come for me, my love."

With your words I shatter.

My body convulsing, my pussy clenches the flogger handle in wave upon wave.

You lean in and suckle my breast. Tingles shoot through the tissue and I come again, shaking for you as I feel your lips smile against my skin.

You remove the flogger and slide the blindfold from my eyes.

I blink and stare at you, my handsome master, filled with love and devotion.

You smile. "You did very well." Your eyes are thick black pools of arousal. You walk around behind me, trailing your fingers along my stomach and side. The gentle caress on my oversensitized skin tickles and I jump and shake, pulling away from you as I giggle.

"Ticklish, eh?"

"Yes, Master." I close my eyes and try to relax the thundering in my veins.

Your finger gently traces one of the switch marks on my ass. The caress is filled with love, wonder and pride. Strange how a simple touch I can't even see expresses all of that. I know I will have the marks from this scene for days to warm my thoughts and make me smile thinking of you, of this moment, of our love.

As you slide your finger about the wide base of the glass gift in my ass, I shake. The tips of your fingers forage beneath the ridge. The press of your flesh against my slick bottom renews the arousal in my veins. My breath quickens and I whimper.

Slowly you slide the bulb-shaped plug out. My anal ring stretches over the wide part of the egg and sensation spirals hot and cold through my ass, cunt and gut. I hear a ting as the glass hits the ground.

My muscles are liquid and you place your cock at my pucker. Your hips rock forward. A tiny single push in, and my body gives way to you, yielding over your large width without hesitation.

I groan at the sensation of being filled with you, being joined in this primitive dance of us.

You moan and pull your cock back out to the tip.

Your fingers grasp my hips and you fuck me. You thrust hard; my body shakes and sways against you. My ass jiggles with each slap of your groin against my plush bottom. Each slip of you into me, you groan.

Sensations like no other overload me as your thick cock stretches me. I shake and gasp for breath. You press deep and my pussy squirts gush after gush from my core. The slick fluid slides down my legs and they tremble. My god, I want your dick in my cunt…your cunt.

You grab my hair and arch my head back. Your hips slow the rapturous pounding I so adore. Slipping from my ass, I feel you wipe your cock on something. You slide down my crack and directly spear my pussy. I suck in a pleasurable whimper. Aggressively you renew the onslaught of my cunt hole. "Oh yes. Yes, Master. Fuck me."

"Um-hum. Is this what my cunt wants?"

"Oh! Oh yes, Master."

I gush and shake violently against you in pleasure. I love the way you fuck me, the way your thick prick glides effortlessly in and out of me, joining more than our bodies. Our souls intertwine and fly.

Wanting to feel every inch of your glorious cock, I clench the muscles of my pussy about your invasion. You groan and your dick twitches within me. A telltale sign you will come soon. I grin, wanting that. To hear you cry out as you seek and find bliss.

You pull out and I gasp at the loss of you. I feel the tug of the straps on the cuffs and my arms lower. You step in front of me.

Your hand rises to my shoulder and your loving gaze caresses my face. I know what you want and I instantly drop to my knees. Your cock is glistening with my juices and steely hard. I want to taste you, your essence mixed with mine as I swallow you up.

I spit into my palms and place them on the shaft of your cock with a tight grip. Licking the tip, I slide the crown into my mouth. My body and mind are calm and languid from my flogging and thorough fucking; my muscles loose. The only thought in my mind is you; my love for you and pleasuring you so that you are in the same state of contentedness.

My lips part further and skim all the way down your cock to my hands. I slide back to the tip, my hands squeezing tight up your length in my mouth's wake. I want nothing more than to make you come, to feel you spurt deep in my mouth and drink the essence of you.

I suck your cock with vigor, pouring all my love, all my passion into the act. Your legs shake against me. Your hand snags into my hair and you begin fucking my mouth in tune with my motions.

Your cock goes deep, touching my throat again and again. You groan and the hand in my hair clenches. "I'm going to come."

I continue sucking and sucking you. I want this—I want to hear you cry out and know I was the one that caused your greatest pleasure. The smooth hot skin of your cock glides effortlessly in and out of me as saliva drizzles down my chin.

You groan, "Uh-un-uh-uh." Spurt after delicious spurt of custard slides down my throat. I swallow the tart stingy taste of you and greedily continue to suck you for more. Your hand grasps my hair and you hold me still as you slide your cock from my mouth.

You stand absolutely motionless, breathing hard. I lick my lips and swallow, then place my hands on your thighs. I gaze up at you.

Your eyes widen and you smile. "Amazing, my love." Your hand rubs my head.

A smile turns my lips, too. I have thoroughly pleased you.

"Stay right there." You turn and walk to my bag. Pulling the warm blanket out of the pack, you come back to me and hold out your hand. "Stand, my love."

I grasp your hand and you help me to stand, then wrap the blanket about me. I stare, unable to take my eyes from you. My master. I love you so intensely, more deeply than anyone before in my life. The connection we have woven together is nonesuch.

"So how was your day? Did you finish all the paperwork for

your patients?" You undo the cuffs and rope from the tree. My gaze never leaves you—your fluid, strong movements as you do even the most mundane of tasks. You are beautiful.

"Yes, I came home and then saw your gift sitting on the table." Exhaustion hits me and I start to shake once more.

"Indeed, a delicious gift, was it not?" You gather up the toys and put them in the backpack, then with it over your shoulder you walk to me.

"How did you get the words in the glass, Eric?"

"Silly. I had it specially made for you." You lean in and kiss the tip of my nose. "You are mine. Owned by E." Pride and possession flashes in your eyes.

"Indeed, you own my heart, Eric. I love you."

"I love you. You *are* mine. You did very, very well. Let's go home, get some food and cuddle." You wiggle your eyebrows and chuckle. "And of course make love again."

I giggle, and tears well in my eyes and my lower lip trembles.

You lean down, wrap your arms about me, and pick me up. "Shh."

I slump against you, content to my bones. Your strong arms about me as you carry me out of the woods stop my trembling. I feel safe. Safe to be me, who I am deep in my soul. To be vulnerable and yours.

"I will take care of you always." You kiss the top of my head.

I nuzzle into the scent of you. Your warmth surrounds me and your heart beats full of love beneath my ear. You squeeze me close and kiss my cheek. I sigh, knowing that your love for me will be forever a constant in my life.

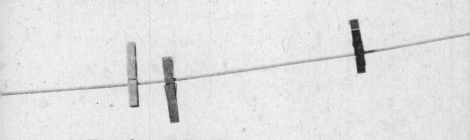

Invite Me In
DELILAH DEVLIN

YOU MUST INVITE ME IN.

I awoke from my dreams, emerging through the dark strata to find my heart pounding against my chest, soft cotton sheets tangled around my limbs. I noted the hour on my digital clock——midnight. Listened to rain pinging on the tiles of my balcony. Yes, I was awake.

Invite me in.

The voice wasn't a part of any sensual dream. I felt it like a physical caress. The rasp of his words and insistent tone slithered sinuously along my hip, wrapped around my spine, crept upward like the glide of a warm palm to lift goose bumps on my naked skin——until, at last, he whispered in my ear.

Open to me.

I recognized the deep tones and slight inflections of his indiscernible accent. I'd heard it before, several nights ago, echoing in my mind.

Even then, I'd known he was different. Never had a voice reached me without my seeking it first.

Perhaps that was the reason his dark, primal passion resonated so deeply inside me. Only, I knew that wasn't the whole truth. I shied away from the fact I found him every bit as irresistible as did the woman next door who had more men passing through her door than the Saints' locker room.

He was back—the one with the wicked kisses and silky caresses—and soon he'd be sliding into bed with her. Although why, when she'd barely satisfied him the last time, I didn't understand.

I told myself I was on a deadline, I couldn't afford to lose sleep—but her delight was palpable. What was it about him that made him such an overwhelming temptation?

Curious, I relaxed the defenses I instinctively threw up to ward off the sensations that swept through my body when people nearby began to lose themselves to passion.

For once, I waited eagerly for the intrusion of carnal thoughts drifting in the ether. I reached out, finding the slender threads of their spirits as they lifted, intertwined, and followed them back into her room. Because I could only meld with one, I chose her.

Her eagerness flooded me with heat. Already, her breasts tingled and tightened...as did mine.

He stepped closer. I knew because she inhaled sharply, dragging in the fragrance clinging to his cheeks and dampened hair. His scent, redolent with the aroma of fresh rain and heated male musk, slowly filled my nostrils.

In moments, his lips glided across her mouth, fastening to suction softly before he thrust his tongue inside. He tasted of mint and coffee, and something else I didn't recognize because he moved on too quickly, sliding his firm lips along her jaw and lower.

Her sighs deepened, her slender frame trembled. He pushed her down to the mattress and covered her, head to toe, a blanket of solid muscle and masculine heat.

Anticipation shortened our breaths and made our hearts pound faster. He reached out to snag her wrist. His thumb swept back and forth as he pushed her hand above her head and pressed it into the pillow—a silent command to submit.

Could he feel her pulse leap beneath his gently chafing thumb?

I could. My own pulse skittered, and then rushed screaming through my body to plump the folds of my sex, he brought me to the brink that fast.

Something about him drew me helplessly into her bedroom, kept me trapped beneath his long, rangy frame, my mind and body opening to the wicked delights he rained upon her warm skin.

I closed my eyes and let the fingers she trailed along his body tell me how sleek and hard his muscled back and flanks were.

When she plunged her hands into his thick hair, I learned its silky texture and length. When he leaned over her to kiss her mouth, I felt it sweep forward to brush my cheeks.

The weight of his body crushed the breath from her, and made me gasp with pleasure. The pressure of his clothed, rigid cock burrowing between her folds drew a lusty wash of liquid arousal from her body…and mine.

My legs splayed open. My knees came up to hug the sides of his hips and encourage him closer, deeper.

"Too many clothes…" Her soft words intruded…or were they mine?

A hot, hard palm cupped a naked breast; his thumb scraped a ruched nipple. I arched my back to press against his hand, demanding a rougher exploration. When his lips latched onto a nipple and drew hard, I gasped.

My hips rolled, beginning a rhythm that slowed the beats of my racing heart, and my hands fell to the pillow beside my head as I let him lead me—*no, lead us*—toward completion.

"I need you naked...*please*...inside me..." I whimpered. Already the walls of my vagina clenched and rippled, readying for his penetration.

He murmured, nuzzling my neck until I turned my head to the side to allow him to trail a wet kiss along my skin. His teeth scraped, eliciting a moan, his lips drew on my skin, suckling hard for a moment, and then I felt a sharp, piercing pain—

A scream ripped the air. Mine? Hers? My eyes slammed open in the darkness, the thread unraveling as I jackknifed upward to sit at the edge of my bed.

What the hell had just happened?

A shadow passed in front of the French doors that led to the balcony outside my bedroom. Had a cloud passed in front of the moon? My French Quarter apartment was three stories up; my fire escape ladder secured.

Invite me in!

Ice-cold terror doused the heat coursing through my body. The words hadn't been spoken aloud. This time I could be sure neither my ears nor hers had heard them. His voice echoed inside my mind—harsh and angry. The doors were glass and slender slats of wood—if he chose, he could force his way inside.

If not tonight, I'll be back tomorrow night, and the next.... You will open to me.

I sat stunned, aware of my nudity, aware of the sensual snare he'd laid on her bed... *for me.* But wasn't this what I'd secretly hoped for? A chance to experience his brand of dangerous passion for myself?

After all, I'd filtered my neighbor's activities over the months, allowing in just what I needed to fill my muse. Only with this man had I been tempted to linger and fill my well with my own lust.

He waited, as though sensing my internal battle. And what had he done? At the last moment when I'd felt him pierce her skin, I'd also felt the bloom of an orgasm, so intense it had frightened me more than the thought he might have somehow wounded her.

I reached for my thin silky robe and shrugged my arms inside, cinched the belt around my waist, and approached the doors. My stomach clenched, my body trembled—I was afraid, but also filled with a sense that this was inevitable.

As I stepped closer, I straightened my shoulders—I wasn't exactly without weapons of my own. The closer to the doors I drew, the more I gave myself over to the remnants of the simmering sensuality he'd fed me. My hips loosened and swayed, my breasts tightened, my thighs slid together and apart, building a frictional heat only one thing could assuage.

His shadow loomed, tall with broad shoulders and a narrow waist. I already knew how soft the skin was that stretched over his lean, muscled frame.

Closing my eyes for a brief moment, I turned the lock and opened the doors.

His hot, surly gaze swept over me, then locked with mine. "May I come in?" he whispered roughly.

He'd gotten me to comply with his demand, and yet he hesitated—he *needed* my permission to enter my room.

A soft rain fell, dampening his dark shirt and misting my face and the vee of skin exposed above the neckline of my robe.

I canted my head and stared at the hard edges of his face— the sharp, high cheekbones and square, stubbled jaw. His brows were furrowed, drawn in a fearsome frown as dark as the midnight hair brushing the shoulders of his cotton shirt.

Empowered by his need for me to obey, I was oddly unafraid. Staying just inside the door frame, I leaned against the edge of the door, pretending a nonchalance I was far from feeling.

"How did you get here? Fly?" I asked, turning my gaze to the five-foot span between her balcony and mine.

The corners of his lips curved upward, slight and mocking.

A frisson of alarm made me shiver. Had he? I was something *other*—was he as well?

"Stop thinking," he murmured, his hands reaching up to grip the top of the door frame. "You brought me here."

I lifted my chin. I realized that was a mistake when his gaze dropped to my lips. "I don't know what you're talking about."

As the moments stretched, my mouth grew dry, my nipples pebbled against the thin fabric sticking to my skin.

"You were with us," he said softly. "Both times. You're the only reason I returned."

I didn't pretend not to understand. "Are you angry because I peeked?"

"No...intrigued." He leaned back his head and drew a deep breath, which lifted his well-defined chest.

I'd felt the weight of all that masculine mass crushing my breasts. I licked my lips and imagined how much more powerful the sensations would be without the filter of another's body between us.

His lips twisted. "Are we going to do it out here?"

I cleared my throat. "Do what?" I asked after I'd pried my tongue loose from the roof of my dry mouth.

One dark, elegant eyebrow rose. His gaze kept its steady glare.

I straightened from the door. "Are you punishing me for intruding?"

"That's an odd way to describe the kind of pleasure I bring. Perhaps you only get off *sucking* someone else's pleasure."

Christ! He knew what I was. "Better that than taking their blood."

"We all do what we must to survive." His expression grew impossibly darker. "Invite me in."

My heart pounded harder, faster. Oh, he frightened me all right—but I was more frightened of my self. I'd learned to harness my curse, use it, control it. I lived a solitary life for a reason.

Maybe this was recompense for stubbornly distancing myself from others, letting in only what I needed, when I needed it—on my own terms.

I took a deep breath and stepped back. "Come in," I whispered.

To give him credit, he didn't immediately pounce. He let go of the door frame, shot me another all-encompassing glance and stepped past me, into my bedroom.

Once inside, he seemed to grow larger, darker. His movements, at once fluid and purposeful, drew my attention and robbed me of breath. Soon, I'd know his touch, his kisses, firsthand.

I moved to close the doors, but he glanced back and shook his head. "Let the storm inside."

I already had. His eyes, so dark and fathomless, pulled me deeper into the room. "Stop it!" I said. "No tricks. You're here— you have what you want."

A harsh, rasping laugh lifted the hairs on the back of my neck. Then before I could make up my mind whether to step closer or flee, he moved—so quickly his movements were a blur. His hands slid around my waist and he lifted me off my feet, stepping forward until the wall behind me halted his progress.

He held me up, my body inches from his, but close enough to feel the heat of his skin and his sweet breath as it washed over my face. "Decide now, succubus. Will you feed me?"

"You have the advantage. Why even ask?"

"Because I'm going to ravage you, and I want you ready— committed. I want everything you've taken."

Not just my blood? Would he take my strength as well? I trembled and leaned back against the wall, watching his mouth as it tightened.

I licked my lips, considering. I'd never shared the power of the passions I drew from others. I'd kept them, using them to fuel the stories I wove. What would it be like to release them, share them with another?

I closed my eyes for a moment. In all the months I'd lived here, no man had ever stepped inside this room. Except for a delivery boy every now and then, no one had even seen the inside of my apartment.

Yet here I was, trapped against a wall with a man towering over me, demanding I submit to his lust.

Damn, was there even a choice? I'd been lonely and alone for so long.

I made my decision, then lifted my hands to slide them over

the damp cotton covering his hard chest. "So, you intend to ravage me?" I quipped softly.

Grim satisfaction filled his stark features. His chest rose beneath my palms. His heartbeat, just beneath my fingers, hammered against his chest. "Take off your robe." But he didn't move away, just let go of my waist while he waited for me to obey, challenging me to complain with his watchful gaze.

I scowled and wriggled, sandwiched between the wall of his chest and the plaster behind me, until the robe slipped to the floor. Already, my nipples were erect, chafed into arousal by the movements that brought my breasts into contact with the fabric of his shirt. "I better not be the only one naked here."

A grin curved his lips. His hands slid between us, the backs rubbing my breasts and belly as he unbuttoned his shirt and shrugged out of it. Then he toed off his boots, one a time, while at the same time sliding down the zipper of his black pants, slowly, letting me feel the heat of his hands and belly, then the weight of his thick cock when it sprang free.

My breaths grew ragged. Cream seeped between my legs to dampen my labia and inner thighs.

His nostrils flared, no doubt picking up the proof of my arousal. When he'd managed to push down his pants and kick them to the side, we stood for a moment, skin to skin, savoring the freedom and the anticipation.

Again, I smoothed my palms upward, following the curves of his muscled arms up to his shoulders, and then I thrust my hands into his hair, combing it with my fingers as I waited for him to move.

He let me wait a long, excruciating minute while our deep

breaths rasped our chest together and apart. My knees began to shake, my belly quivered, and finally, he lifted me again, higher against the wall.

His mouth opened on the blushing skin of my chest, pressing wet kisses on the upper swell of my breasts, gliding his tongue between them, then suckling the full curve beneath.

My legs moved restlessly, until I wrapped them around his upper abdomen and squeezed. My pussy opened, sliding along his hot skin and I rolled my hips, letting him know he could hurry it up a bit and I'd have no complaints.

However, he seemed content to tease me, drawing out the pleasurable sensation of his mouth gobbling up my breasts.

"My nipples," I pleaded between clenched teeth. "Suck them! *Please.*"

He nuzzled them with his nose, licked his way around one dimpled areola without ever touching the tip, and then glided across to torture the other breast in a similar fashion.

I gripped his shoulders hard. "If I'd known you were so damn slow to take a hint, I'd have drawn you a map."

Laughter gusted against my breast, and at last, he latched his lips around one spiked tip and drew hard.

My toes curled, my hips tilted toward him, my whole body tightening as he suckled. It was almost enough. It was almost heaven.

I thrashed my head back and forth on the wall behind me before finally blurting out, "Please, enough! I need you inside me."

His teeth clamped down, nipping me gently. "When I say." But he let me slide down his body until I felt his cock nudge at my center.

My breath hitched when the blunt, velvet tip pushed against me. His size didn't surprise me. He'd stretched the inner walls of a woman who dated linebackers. But my body wasn't prepared for his girth. Hot, exquisite pressure built as he pushed. I bit my lip and begged him with my gaze to help me take him.

His eyes held mine as he slipped a hand between us and thrust his fingers through my soft curls. He parted my lust-slick folds, guided his dick into me, slowly, letting me swallow him an inch at a time, until we were both breathless and sweating.

I'm sure he was surprised by how tight I was, given what I was. He'd wanted to thrust inside, wanted to ream me with that thick cock, but he clamped his jaws tight and groaned, tunneling only so deep before withdrawing, and coming back for more.

I couldn't help the shaking that trembled along my limbs and jerked my belly against his. No more than I could help the reflexive pulsing radiating along my channel.

When his first inches grazed my inner walls, he started the slow, rhythmic push and pull, my liquid heat drenching him and easing his way. He stroked into me, sliding my body up and down the wall, an unhurried, crawling wave of motion that calmed the quivering inside me.

As I followed his powerful thrusts, friction built between his cock and my vagina in a slow-burning fire. I clenched my inner muscles around him, riding his thickly veined shaft as it moved in and out.

The ridge of his plump crown abraded the sweet spot deep inside me, the one so few men ever found, and I arched my back, surrendering to the coiling heat licking at my core. At that point, I felt a leaching away of the barrier between his mind and mine, as the passions I'd stolen began to swirl inside me and spill over to douse him in glorious heat.

A low, feral growl erupted from him and he ground inside me, deeper this time, his jaws flexing as his hips strained.

I knew there was more, knew he held back. I wondered at the strength of will he possessed to resist the crashing waves of sensuality that battered us both.

In that instant, I lost all my fear of him as a man and a vampire. He could have ravaged me and made me love it anyway, but he'd taken me slowly, with care and precision, careful not to harm or frighten me.

"It's all right," I whispered. "I can take all you want to give."

"Be quiet," he ground out. "You're so damn tight. I'm going crazy here."

"Then fuck me," I whispered in his ear. "I'm ready." *God, I'm ready.* I bit his earlobe. I squeezed hard around him as he stroked inside, released to let him withdraw, then squeezed as he rammed himself inside again. The friction was divine.

Impossibly, his cock expanded, grew longer, blunter.

"You're playing with fire," he said, ramming deeper this time.

I sucked in a jagged breath and smoothed my sweaty cheek against his shoulder. "Do me. Do me like you've never done a woman before. Give me everything."

His lips stretched in a slow, wicked smile. "Think you've seen everything?"

"I'm allowing you to fuck me against a wall, aren't I?"

"Such a baby. Don't say I didn't warn you."

Suddenly, we slid up the wall together. Alarmed, I wrapped my arms around him and gasped as his soft, wicked laughter sifted through my hair.

"Brace yourself against the wall."

I unwound my legs from his waist and let them drop. They dangled in the air. The only thing holding me up was the strength of his cock buried halfway inside me and his hard chest pressed against my breasts.

He grabbed my hands and slid my palms down and outward along the wall. I felt anchored somehow and lifted my knees to press my feet flat against the cool plaster. It was better, but I knew if he pulled away, I'd go crashing to the floor. "Nice trick," I said breathlessly.

"I'm only getting started." He kissed me, rubbing my lips hard, tangling his tongue with mine as he started to fuck in and out of me again, stroking deeper, until at last, the base of his cock was grinding into my clit.

I forgot I was suspended in the air, forgot I was at a vampire's mercy. Nothing had ever felt as decadent and delicious as the thickness gliding in and out of me, tugging at my tender, heated tissues, glistening with the liquid spilling from my body as he rolled his hips, grinding deeper, spearing my womb.

Heat coiled tighter in my core as he stroked and circled. The muscles of his back and shoulders bunched beneath my hands. Sweat slicked his skin and mine everywhere we touched. He widened his knees, nudging mine even farther apart, then gathered his body and plunged inside over and over, the thrusts deepening, sharpening.

I came apart, unraveling in a sinuous, writhing dance, driving my hips against his. I lacked rhythm, lacked any finesse, trying to fill the desperate need to stay in that moment, held onto the explosion of color and emotions that rocked me as his wild thrusts grew brutal.

He rolled us over and over, his arms encircling me to prevent me from hurting myself. My back to the wall, now his, every roll allowing his cock to slide and circle and press at a different angle each time. Flashes of the pale gray bed below and the curtains billowing inward on a breeze, interspersed with the dark shadowy ceiling. Only when he came to a halt did my orgasm finally wane, allowing me to catch my breath.

I gasped.

I was looking over his shoulder at my bed—ten feet below us.

I drew back my head and smacked it against the ceiling. "Ouch!"

His chest heaved against mine, his gaze spearing me as harshly as his cock had moments ago.

I wet my parched lips with the tip of my tongue, trying to gather my scattered wits after my trip to the moon. "That... was—" I stopped and caught my breath "—different."

"You need to expand your vocabulary. Learn some more descriptive adjectives."

I raised an eyebrow, trying to mimic his sardonic look. "Need a little praise, do you?"

He snorted. "No, I don't need any praise. I know it was good. I'm swimming in your pleasure."

I wrinkled my nose. "That was kinda crude." I wriggled against him. "You're getting a little heavy."

A mocking eyebrow rose. "Actually, love, you're on top."

"You know this doesn't make a bit of sense."

"I'm dead. The laws of physics don't necessarily apply here."

I boldly placed my hand between his legs. "Not all of you. Why didn't you come?"

"Are you complaining?"

"No, I'm just surprised," I answered, but there was that insecure part of me that wondered whether I hadn't been able to satisfy him. "I mean, you're carrying on a conversation. In my experience, men are decidedly nonverbal when they're aroused."

"Your vast experience?"

I blushed. He knew better. "Well, not so vast, I guess, unless you count…"

"Vicarious pleasures?"

"That's a nice way of putting it. Still, you didn't come. After being with her, and then me, I just thought…" His slow smile made me feel stupid, which angered me. I jutted out my chin. "Why didn't you take a bite of me? I was there for you, opening to you, ready."

"I'm not done yet. That was just to get you to relax a bit."

"I'm pinned to my ceiling. How am I supposed to relax?" However, I was strangely content.

"Sorry, are you uncomfortable?" He carefully pulled out of me, and we fell in a heap to the mattress below, bouncing once before settling.

I leaned up on my elbows and pushed back the hair falling in my face. "Not nice," I said, as I crawled off his body.

"I never claimed to be nice." His hand clamped on my thigh. "And I'm not through."

His words stopped me. As much as the arm that encircled me and dragged me down on top of him.

His cock gouged my belly as I lay over him.

"Maybe *I'm* done."

"Like I said. That first time was for you. To calm you." He

sprawled beneath me, an arm under his head, looking completely at ease, totally in control.

Already, my blood thrummed against my temple, my nipples beaded, my pussy tightened. The way his gaze bored into mine, I knew whatever wicked delights he had in store for me would probably make me cringe in embarrassment. "You know," I said, deliberately stalling, "I just realized I don't know your name."

"Do you know the names of all the people who've shared their passion with you?"

"That's different. They don't know I'm there. And I don't do it because I'm some sort of sick voyeur."

"And I don't feed my hungers just to get off."

"Neither do I!"

He lifted a finger to trail along my cheek and down my neck.

I thought I hid the little shiver of delight he elicited with that simple touch, but his mouth curved with male satisfaction. "You're dying to know what I'm going to do next."

I opened my mouth to issue a scathing denial, but he pressed his finger against my lips. "Shut up. Roll onto your back."

I swallowed, hating that he had me aching and ready to do anything he wanted, but I rolled away and lay facing the damn ceiling.

"Some sex is pure magic without any tricks," he said, coming up on his knees to crawl toward me.

Already my chest rose and fell faster, and the quivering started, something I'd never done with any other man. Not that I was still afraid.

I shook with need.

Moonlight sifted through the curtains, striking the harsh

planes of his face, illuminating his body in silver light. The ridges of his muscled chest and abdomen stood in stark relief. The length and thickness of his cock had me sucking in my breath.

His eyes trailed over my body as well, and I wondered if I'd been too lazy lately, too devoted to my writing. Spent too many late nights pounding at a keyboard instead of pounding pavement to keep my body tight and strong.

He smoothed a hand over my breasts, pausing to circle one taut nipple, then glided down my belly to trail his fingers through my curls.

One thick digit slid between my folds and I opened my legs, inviting him to play. He feathered the edges of my inner lips before thrusting the finger into my opening.

Instantly, my pussy clamped around him, making a moist sound that drew a slow smile from him.

Then he leaned low over my sex, and I knew what he was about to do would be too much, too intimate, but I couldn't force a complaint past my lips. Instead, I groaned as his tongue swept out and curled around the thin inner lips, lapping up my cream.

The flavor of me seemed to please him, but I had to know what he really felt about me, had to see myself through him.

I opened my mind, sifting through the threads until I found him.

He turned to nip my inner thigh. "I didn't give you permission."

"Please. I've never done this before."

His head lifted and his gaze locked with mine. "You can't tear away like before, if something frightens you."

"I promise."

"I'll want you to feel everything I feel."

I nodded and lay back, closing my eyes. Then I was there, with him, bending over my pussy, inhaling my fragrance, tasting the juices that slid along his tongue. I felt the tightening of his balls as his arousal spiked higher, the urgency building in his belly. How did he resist climbing over me and thrusting toward my core?

And then I couldn't think, could only follow and feel. His fingers toyed with me, two thrusting in my channel, another sliding over my hooded clit.

I gasped; my hips rolled. I opened my thighs wider and groaned when his stubbled cheek caressed my inner thigh, plunging downward to rub against the moisture coating my sex.

When he thrust another finger inside, I felt the gush of arousal greeting his entry, felt the silken walls clasp and relax to milk his hand.

He leaned closer still, and his lips closed around my clit to suck it hard into his mouth, while at the same time a thick thumb glided south and circled my anus.

"Christ, no!" I cried out, but I felt his hand shake as his excitement rose along with mine, and I surrendered, understanding he wasn't in control any longer, wasn't simply pulling strings or playing some head game with the little succubus.

He wanted me. Wanted this with me. He needed my arousal to spike with his.

When his thumb pressed inside my tight little entrance, I felt his cock jerk at the way I moaned and rolled my hips. I was out of control, beyond shame, heading straight to the precipice whether he was with me or not.

When he curved all his fingers and drove them inside me,

my bottom came off the bed, curving upward, begging him to thrust deep.

With a twist of his hand he was inside me, his knuckles scraping my walls, the ball of his fist crammed so tight and high, I keened, wailing in an agony of need. I was close.

My hands clawed at the bedding, but my vampire wasn't finished with me yet. His tongue swirled on my hard little clit, then he turned and burrowed his face into my inner thigh just to the side of my outer lips.

I felt a tingling start in his gums, then a slow glide as his incisors lengthened. I knew what he was about to do, but I lay breathless, on the edge of an orgasm I knew would thrust me beyond the strata I traveled in my dreams.

When he bit, I screamed—a strangled, choking sound cut short as soon as I tasted the blood that seeped into his mouth, mixing with my cream to coat his tongue and slide in a sensual stream down his throat.

His voice rumbled around a murmur of pleasure so great he fought the urge to thrust against the bedding and spend himself.

I wasn't nearly as strong. My body exploded, writhing against his mouth, anchored only by the hand thrust deep inside my body.

As waves of pleasure rushed over him, I understood at last the hunger that drove him. His heart slowed, his body warmed with the infusion of blood. Strength renewed, he disengaged his fangs and laved the tiny wounds he'd made, closing them completely.

When he lifted his head to catch my glance, I opened my arms.

He scooted quickly up my body, his cock sliding home inside

my slick, silken walls. I wrapped myself around him, holding him tight against my body, sharing my warmth, my sex, my stolen passions with him.

He thrust three times, and then groaned loudly in my ear. His cum bathed my channel in creamy heat. He continued to rock against me for long moments afterward.

When I could form words again, I asked, "So why were you so angry with me for being there with her?"

"You don't know?" he murmured against my shoulder. He lifted his head and sighed. "When you were drawing on her lust, you pulled me along with you. I felt everything she did. Heard everything you thought. When I bit her, I was offering you a gift."

"And I refused your gift. Sorry, I didn't understand what you wanted from me."

He cupped my face between his hands. "You do now." Again, his gaze, so dark and intense, held mine.

I dragged in a shaky breath. He'd touched me, deep inside, where no one ever had. He understood what I was, and wasn't freaked.

Then again, he was something special, too. "I still don't know your name."

One side of his beautiful mouth lifted in a wry grin. "Don't you know everything that's important?"

I shrugged my shoulders. "I'm a woman. I want shoe sizes, cell and home phone..."

"Birth date and social security number..."

"Do you have one?"

"Of course. I don't spend all my time lurking on women's balconies."

"Darn."

His thumb slid across my lower lip. "Want me to lurk on yours?"

I licked the pad of his thumb and wrinkled my nose. "You have an open invitation."

His nostrils flared and his cock twitched where it lay tucked between my legs. Soon, he'd know everything there was to know about loving a succubus.

Maybe this was the start of something. Had I found a friend? Someone to share my isolation?

I sighed, content for now to share my bed, my blood, my passion with him. But just maybe, I'd found a love of my own.

Soul Strangers

Eden Bradley

THE WARM WATER OF THE GULF OF MEXICO SWIRLS around her ankles, soothing the weariness from her bones. It had been a long drive down from Corpus Christi to Veracruz. She hadn't meant to stop here, hadn't really known where she was going; simply going was the important part.

She had wanted to be alone, and here she is, surrounded by the solitude of a nearly empty beach, populated only by a few strangers. And since they are strangers, they don't matter, don't intrude.

She has been entirely alone for three days—on the drive, then wandering this beach, taking short swims, sleeping in her hotel room. The room is really a small cottage on the beach, the sand coming right to her door, where she has to wipe her feet with a towel before going inside. Still, sand is scattered over the worn tile floor, buried deeply in the fibers of the colorful woven rugs.

The place smells of the sea, and a little of mildew and something faintly dark and exotic. She doesn't mind. She loves the scent, even the undertone of mildew; it reminds her that she's far from home, from her life. The bed, which is perhaps a bit too soft, cradles her as she sleeps at night and during her frequent daytime naps. She has been sleeping endlessly in her room here on the beach. Still, she's tired. Her limbs are filled with a languid heaviness she cannot shake. Nothing seems to energize her—not the brilliant Mexican sunsets, nor the endless hours of sleep, not even the power of the ocean.

What is it she needs?

She moves deeper into the blue-and-green water, looking out to sea where the late afternoon sun touches the tips of the waves in glinting bits of silver. The ocean surges, swells, caresses her knees, her hips, like the soft hands of a lover she has never known.

There is movement next to her and she turns to find a man standing nearby, waist-deep in water. All she can see of him is his torso, his head. Sunlight gleams off his wide, tanned shoulders, one of which is covered by an intricate tattoo, but she can't make out the design. She can see the shadowed planes of a finely muscled back, a narrow waist.

Her body gives a surprising shiver. He turns, almost as though he is aware of her looking at him, and smiles brilliantly.

She smiles back and suddenly he is moving toward her. She can see now he has a striking face, one of those faces that is beautiful and masculine at the same time. His features are a bit irregular but his jaw is strong, his mouth lush and sensual. His eyes are the color of the earth, that same deep brown she finds when digging in her small garden at home. But she doesn't want to think of home now. No, all she wants is to be here, watching this man.

His body is all hard-packed muscle and he moves with grace

through the weight of the water. He pauses several feet away. But he is still close enough that she can make out the smooth texture of his skin. Her eyes are brought back to his tattoo, which she can now see is a tiger drawn against a background of tsunami waves in classic Japanese style. She finds herself wanting to touch it.

Water seems elemental to the moment. Except that he is all earth, this man. This stranger. And when he speaks, his voice is a deep rumble that is very much of the earth.

"You're new here."

It is a statement, yet she feels the urge to answer. He's American and it seems the hospitable thing to do.

"I came the day before yesterday."

He simply nods, moves in closer. She cannot take her eyes off him. When she does glance up, his gaze is focused on her face. The sun is glaring but she can see his eyes, dark and earthy, and they make her tremble inside.

Why does she feel as though he can see right through her?

She is suddenly very much aware of the water rushing like silk between her thighs as the waves surge, then retreat. The bare skin exposed by her turquoise bikini, the same shade as the ocean out beyond the waves, makes her feel naked beneath the stranger's gaze.

She watches him. He licks his lips. She wants to kiss him so much her own mouth waters. He takes another step closer, until he is standing so near she swears she can smell the salt on his skin.

She doesn't dare move, to break the spell of this moment. They are doing nothing more than watching one another. She doesn't want to have to speak. Her whole body feels raw with yearning. She just wants to touch his skin; she doesn't want to think about why.

A wave rolls in, splashing against the small of her back. With his elemental gaze still locked on hers, she can imagine it is his hand that caresses the tender flesh there. And again, she feels as though he can see right into her, as though he knows who she is deep inside.

"Swim with me," he says.

They splash out into the waves, and he dives through them, coming up dripping, like some fantastical merman. But he *is* some fantasy creature. Her mind is making up stories about him already—erotic stories, sensual daydreams. His hands all over her naked skin, on her breasts, between her thighs. His mouth on hers, moving over her flesh…

She dips below the water to cool off. When she surfaces, smoothing her long brown hair from her face, he is right there. He puts a hand on her arm, just a small feathering of fingers she can barely feel, yet it goes through her like an electric shock. Her nipples come up hard beneath the wet fabric of her bikini. Her sex goes warm. She wants him to touch her again.

She moves closer, letting the waves bring her right up against him. His body is every bit as hard and strong as it looks. And his solid erection presses into the soft flesh of her belly.

In her mind is one word: *Yes*.

His hand grasps her shoulder, slides down her arm, and the next wave crushes them together, her breasts pressing against his hard chest. She looks up, sees his mouth, wants to kiss him still. And as though reading her mind, he lowers his head and his mouth comes down on hers.

His lips are lovely, soft, salty with the ocean. When he parts her lips and slides his tongue inside, she melts all over. Her sex grows molten with need, and she kisses him back, hungry for whatever he offers. He fills her mouth; his tongue is hot, wet. She needs more.

Pulling away, she presses her lips to his neck, slides her tongue down his throat and hears a small moan from him. Her body pulses in response. Moving her mouth, she licks the tattooed skin of his shoulder, swirls her tongue over the design there. Salt——the salt of sweat and of the sea. And something else, something almost sweet, vanilla-like, beneath the salt. Something which is simply a part of *him*. His hands go into her hair, his fingers curling, but he lets her move freely

She pulls back to see the landscape of his body, the angles and curves of him. Reaching out to touch him, she finds his nipples hard beneath her fingers. She wants to pull them, one at a time, into her mouth, and she does, while the strength of the ocean moves them around.

His hands slide down her sides and slip beneath her bathing suit top. Finding her nipples with his fingertips, he caresses, pulls, teases, until her sex is throbbing with heat. She moves back to his mouth, licks his lower lip, takes it into her mouth, sucks on it. He pinches her nipples, hard, and she breathes out, "Touch me."

His arm comes around her waist, pulling her into his body. His hand snakes down between them, beneath the water, pushes aside the edge of her bikini bottom. And delves inside, finding her swollen folds. She can hardly stand it, his touch, the warm rush of the water, the heady scent of him in her nostrils. He moves his fingertips over her clitoris, which is hard and alive and needy. He begins to rub.

She is aching, nearly hurting. Reaching beneath the water, she pulls his engorged cock from his trunks and is thrilled with the size and the weight of it. And even more with the feel of the heavy steel ring embedded just below the head. Immediately fascinated, she runs her fingertips over the cool metal, playing with the ring, tugging on it a little.

She strokes him in cadence with his hand between her thighs. He is guiding her legs with his free hand now, wrapping them around his waist, so that he is holding her, weightless, in the water.

Sensation builds. Blood pounds through her veins, her pulse beating into his mouth where it is sucking on the flesh of her throat. Her sex beats in time, a low, thrumming rhythm, matched by his pulsing cock in her hand. She loves the way he fills her palm, that she can barely wrap her fingers around him. But she doesn't want him inside her yet. She wants them to come into each other's hands first.

When he pushes a thumb inside her she almost loses it. She grasps his cock tighter, strokes harder, hangs on until she hears him moan again, feels his body tensing all over. She moves her hips into his hand, trembles as he presses onto her clit, taking her up and over the edge. Pressure is building inside her, like a vessel filled to overflowing. He moves his hand faster. Pleasure swims through her veins, through her head, overtaking her. And as her orgasm washes over her, she pumps his cock, feeling the hot rush as he comes into her palm. She shakes with the force of it, thrusts her hips, presses harder into his fingers. And he doesn't stop, stays with her, while her sex clenches, while pleasure arcs through her sex, through her body.

Her hand is sticky with his come, but soon the cleansing

ocean water washes it away, leaving her feeling a little sad. She clings to him, her sex still pulsing and warm, her breath a ragged panting in her own ears.

And all around them, the ocean moves to its own eternal rhythm.

With his fingers, he wipes her wet hair from her face. Such a tender move from a stranger, but with his softening cock still in her hand, he is hardly a stranger, is he?

They stay together in the water, letting the ocean rock them, her head against his chest, until the sky begins to streak with pink and amber. Neither seems to want to let go, to end the experience.

Finally he asks her, "Are you tired?"

"No, not tired at all." And for the first time in days, she realizes this is true. She feels the energy in her body like a banked fire he has sparked to life.

He is quiet a moment, then he whispers, so softly she can barely hear him above the pounding of the surf, the call of ocean birds, "Take me to your room."

She looks up at him, nods her head. Slowly, she unwraps her body from his, uncoiling like a long strand of seaweed, the tension gone from her body. She feels a sense of release. And yet, a new and exquisite tension is building simply from the soft tone of his voice in her ear. At the implication of what might lie ahead tonight.

He takes her hand and follows her out of the sea. On the beach, she grabs her towel from the sand, her straw hat, the book she brought along to read, but which she wasn't able to concentrate on.

Together they move across the sand. At the door to her

room she turns to look at him. His skin is beaded with water, the tips of his short, light brown hair still dripping. She offers her towel to him. He takes it, but rather than drying himself he smoothes the towel over her skin: her shoulders, down her arms, across her stomach. When he kneels to dry her calves, moving up her thighs, her sex gives a hard squeeze.

Yes...

In a moment he is on his feet again, roughly rubbing himself dry. He lifts his chin, motioning for her to open the door. She pauses, and he smiles at her.

His smile is brilliant, radiant. As beautiful as the rest of him.

She turns the knob, opens the door and they slip inside. She drops her hat and her book on a small painted table. He moves past her, looks around, then drapes the damp towel over the back of a chair. She shivers a little in the cooler air of the cottage, watching him move, the sleek motion of hard-packed muscle.

She takes a step toward him.

"Wait," he tells her. "I want to look at you. To watch you for a moment."

She stops, waits. He runs a hand down his stomach, over that narrow trail of dark hair leading from his navel and into the band of his black and red trunks. Yes, she wants to see him as well, wants to see his naked flesh, his pierced cock. Her nipples are going hard once more, the lips of her sex filling, swelling.

When he presses a hand to the front of his trunks, she can clearly see the outline of his hardening cock beneath the wet fabric.

Oh, yes...

And then he slips his trunks off and stands before her, naked.

His body is a marvel, all hard muscle and smooth, tanned skin. His cock is so beautiful, her hands ache to touch it. Her sex aches with the need to feel him inside of her. And the wicked metal ring glinting in the dying sun coming through the shuttered windows.

Her throat goes dry. Her sex goes wet. She squeezes her thighs together.

"Your turn," he says.

With his dark eyes on her, she brings her hands up to cup her breasts through her bathing suit top; she cannot wait for his touch. Her nipples are so hard they hurt. His eyes are riveted to her hands moving over her breasts, and she moves the triangles of blue fabric aside, squeezes her nipples, tugs on them, pleasure burrowing deep into her system. Everything is amplified by his brown eyes on her, by the lust clear on his face.

He moans softly. Whispers, "Beautiful."

It has been a long time since she's felt beautiful. But now, with him, she does. And it is a sort of relief she can't explain, even to herself, whispering beneath the desire.

But she doesn't need to think now. She only needs to feel.

Pulling her bikini top off, she keeps her gaze on him. His mouth has gone soft, his eyes glittering. And he is stroking his cock, his fingers moving lightly over that rigid flesh.

She has never seen anything hotter in her life.

She slides her bikini bottoms over her hips, steps out of them, takes one step closer to him. He moves toward her, stops a foot or two away.

"Touch yourself for me," he demands.

She smiles, feathers her fingers over her nipples once more before moving lower, brushing her mound. When she slips two fingers over her cleft she is soaking wet, slippery, like the sea. She can still hear it, smell that tang of salt in the air. And it is all a part of the moment—the sea moving and surging, the scent in the air. It is the power of the ocean and he is the earth, and between them is fire, building, burning.

"Put your fingers inside yourself," he tells her, and she does it, spreading her thighs a little and dipping into that wet, waiting hole.

Pleasure moves through her, at her own touch, at his dark gaze on her. At the way he takes a gasping breath and clamps his fingers over his beautiful cock.

He reaches out and takes her hand from between her thighs, raises it. His lips open and he takes her fingers into his mouth, the damp heat enveloping her.

This must be what his cock feels like, sliding into a woman. Sliding into her.

Her sex clenches.

"I need to feel you," she tells him. "I need your hands on me. Your mouth. Your cock."

"Yes," he says, his voice low, full of smoke and need.

Her hand still in his, he leads her to the bed. The sheets are mussed from her nap earlier in the day, the pillows dented. He lays her down on her back and kneels over her. She shivers, waiting.

Lowering his head, he kisses her, lightly, and she can taste her own juices on his lips. Then he is moving lower, his mouth all over her skin, sucking one rigid nipple into his mouth.

"Ah!"

She can hardly believe how close she is to coming already. Her hands go into his damp, thick hair, holding him close to her breast. He is sucking so hard it hurts. But it feels too good for her to care.

Yes, suck harder....

Pleasure, warm and sweet, washes over her body, a trail of heat from her breasts to her sex. Her clit is throbbing.

"Touch me," she says demandingly.

He moves lower and spreads her thighs wide with his hands. And then his mouth is on her, his wet, clever tongue sliding over her pussy lips, pushing inside. And she is squirming, panting. Pleasure is driving into her body, making her shudder. And when he pulls her clit into his mouth and sucks, she comes, bursting, her hips lifting up off the bed.

"Ah, yes, fuck me!"

His fingers drive into her, and pleasure coils anew in her belly, tight and hot, then crashes over her like a pummeling wave. And she shatters, coming and coming, her hips bucking into his mouth, his hand.

She is still shivering when he raises his head. He is smiling. He lifts her and moves her up on the bed, then asks her, "Condoms?"

She nods her head, but it is a moment before she can speak. "In the small silver case, next to my suitcase."

She watches as he leans over next to the bed where her open luggage sits on the floor, clothes spilling out onto the tiles. He finds the silver cosmetics case, unzips it, and after a moment of digging, pulls out the folded strand of foil packets left over from the last trip she'd taken with her ex before…

She isn't going to think of that now.

He is opening a packet with his teeth, and this seems purely sexual to her, animalistic. But perhaps that's simply because her body is still trembling with the aftershock of orgasm. Or the keen anticipation of knowing his cock will be inside her in only moments.

Yes.

He kneels over her on the bed, but before he can sheath himself she reaches up and takes the silver ring between her fingers, tugs on it.

He groans.

"It's called a Prince Albert piercing?"

"Yes."

"I've never seen one before. Not in person. Did it hurt?"

He laughs. "Yes, it hurt."

She smiles, doesn't tell him she likes knowing that for some reason.

"Will it feel different?"

"You're about to find out."

He slips the condom onto his cock, and she spreads her thighs for him.

"Yes, that's it. Wider." His voice is low, strained.

He is kneeling between her legs, and she loops them over his strong thighs. He slips one hand under her ass and pulls her up, onto his shaft, entering her.

He pauses, the head of his cock inside her, and she swears she can feel the curve of the metal ring, a lovely added texture. Her sex is pulsing with pleasure, her whole body is pulsing; a steady beat of lust centered at that point where the thick metal ring, the head of his cock, pierces her body.

She shifts, trying to take him deeper. His hand comes to her cheek, caresses her jaw, then he is holding her face a little too roughly. And he slams into her, one deep, hurting thrust.

"Oh!"

She goes loose all over, her body turning to pure liquid fire. Pleasure, pain, it's all the same as he pulls back, rams into her again. Then he is fucking her, his cock sliding in and out, hard and hurting and so damn good she is ready to come again in moments.

The first wave makes the walls of her sex clench around his swollen cock.

"So fucking tight," he murmurs.

And then he is driving harder into her, and she is coming apart, her climax pounding into her, overwhelming her. She is lost, drowning in pleasure, shaking with the force of it.

And he is still fucking her, fucking her, driving her orgasm on. Moments later he tenses, shivers, cries out as he comes, one hand gripping her ass, his nails biting deep. The other hand still holds her face, so that she is forced to look at him. And she loves the way he just comes apart, his mouth so full and soft as he groans, his eyes closed, his head falling back.

And still his hips are moving, his cock still hard somehow. And she is coming again, her body tensing, clenching. He senses what is happening, reaches down and takes her clit between his fingers, pinching, tugging. Pleasure, intense, freeing, surges through her, driving deep. And she is left panting and weak. And as sated as she has ever been in her life.

He pulls out of her and she expects him to move away. But after tugging the condom off, he rolls onto his side, pulling her close. Her head against his chest, she can hear his heart hammering beneath her ear. His body is warm. He smells more like the ocean than ever.

They sleep. When she wakes it is fully dark. She has no idea what time it is. It doesn't matter.

She slips from the bed and brings a bottle of wine—a fruity red from Chile—back to the bed, along with a plate of fruit and some pastries she bought that morning from a vendor on the beach.

Moonlight washes through the half-open shutters, blue and silver in the dark room. And she can see that he is awake, watching her.

"Hey," he says, his voice rough with sleep.

"Hey."

"Do you want me to go?"

"No. Stay here with me. Are you hungry?"

"Starving." He sits up in the bed, takes the wine from her, uncorks it and drinks from the bottle before passing it back to her.

She has set the plate on the bed, and he takes the knife she laid on the edge of the plate and peels an apple, then cuts it into pieces and offers her one. She bites into the apple, the cool sweetness filling her mouth. She follows it with a long sip of the wine. Everything seems utterly sensual to her: the fruit, the wine, the scent of sex in the air, the heat of his body next to hers. And outside the windows, the pulsing beat of the ocean crashing on the shore.

They sit on the bed and feed each other, pulling the pastry apart with their fingers. It's sweet with honey. They wash it down with the wine. And when they're both full, he pours a little of the wine on her naked skin, then licks it off until she is wet and aching, begging him to fuck her again.

He turns her onto her stomach this time, pulls her up onto her knees. She is shivering, as he uses his fingers to part her pussy lips, at the sound of a foil packet tearing.

He enters her with his fingers first, sliding right inside. She surges back onto his hand, pleasure shafting through her in long, rippling waves.

"You're so wet, so ready."

"Yes…"

He pulls his fingers from her and in a moment the head of his cock is pushing inside her. He is so big, filling her inch by inch, the ring sliding against her G-spot. His arm wraps around her waist, his other hand going into her hair, grasping tight, pulling her head up. She feels taken over, commanded. And she gives herself over to it, to him, as he begins to fuck her, moving slowly at first, then harder, faster. Pleasure seeps into her system, flooding her belly, her arms, her legs. And her sex is clenching, swollen, ready to explode.

When his hand moves down, massaging her wet cleft, pressing onto her clit, she comes, hard. Waves of pleasure wrack her body, stinging, swift as the ocean current. And she is shaking, nearly sobbing with the power of it.

She is surprised when he pulls out of her, left empty, bereft. But his hand is there, his lovely, soft fingers, pushing into her, pulling out, wiping her juices all over her pussy lips and back, over her anus. He leans in and plants wet kisses down her spine, and she arches her back, loving the sensation. She is hypersensitive all over, her skin, every part of her body, from coming so much, from his touch. He parts his lips, swirls his tongue over her lower back, and at the same time he slips one finger into her anus.

"Shh, relax," he whispers.

And she does. This is the first time that hole has been breached, but at this moment, it is utterly sensual. With his other hand he teases her clitoris into a hard nub once more. She can hardly believe her body is still able to feel pleasure. But it moves through her in a warm wash of desire, longing.

He presses his finger deeper. "Breathe," he tells her, his voice quiet, soothing. There is sex in his voice, his own desire held tight.

She does as he asks, breathing in, pulling in that scent of ocean and sex and *him*. And she is shivering once more. He moves his finger in, slides it out. She has never felt anything quite like it, a sense of fullness, and yet, she wants more.

"Fuck me. Please."

He plays her anus with his finger for another few moments, making her surge back, taking more of him in.

"Please," she begs again.

His hand moves away and she feels the head of his cock at that tightest of holes. And she is wet again, trembling with a need that rages through her. He spreads her buttocks, pushes the tip of his cock in. And at the same time, he rubs her clit in small circles with his thumb, pushes a few fingers into her sex. Pleasure, wild and keen, cuts into her like a knife. She cries out. He answers by pushing into her deeper, fingers and cock all at once. Inch by exquisite inch, telling her to breathe, to relax.

But she is already liquid all over. Liquid and wanting everything from him. Anything.

He takes it slow and it seems to go on forever, his cock working its way into her ass, his thumb circling her clit, his fingers dipping inside her.

Just when she is beginning to think he is too tentative with her, he steps up the pace, sliding in and out of her ass, her pussy, filling her, stretching her. Lovely, painful. She is dizzy with sensation, in a state of overload. But all she can do is thrust back against him, pleasure infusing her, emptying her mind. She is nothing more than these sensations, this body being fucked in every possible way. And she is loose and free in a way she has never been before.

This is what she's needed, what she's been searching for, she thinks fleetingly, even though she didn't know it until this moment.

Pleasure builds, deepens, rolls over her body in long waves. Excruciating. Sharper, heavier, until she is completely weighed down by it. She collapses on the bed, but he is still fucking her, relentless, his hand working her mercilessly. She is coming again, shards of pure pleasure stabbing into her. She is sobbing, crying out, shaking so hard her teeth are clattering together. Coming so hard she can't think of anything at all but the exquisite sensations moving through her body, a body which no longer belongs to her, but to *him*.

He tenses, growls, pumps into her ass. And it hurts, his pumping cock——and to know that it's over, this experience.

He lies on top of her. He is shivering as hard as she is. He wipes the tears from her cheek, doesn't say a word. They lie together for a long time, and at some point, they sleep.

Dawn comes as it always does on the Veracruz beach, with an edge of chill to the otherwise warm and sultry air. But he is warm beside her, the sound of his breath a quiet sigh.

She lies on her back, remembers why she needed to leave Corpus Christi. Remembers her broken heart, which is no longer broken.

Her stranger has healed her, somehow. He is like some

magical creature, except that the physical reality of him is all too real——his sleeping form next to her, the lovely ache in her body.

As she watches him, his eyes open. They are that same elemental brown. He is so much of the earth, and of the water. She reaches out, runs her fingertips over the waves tattooed behind the tiger on his shoulder. Yes, he is of the water, too. Their time together is made up of the elements and suddenly she needs to be back in the water with him. She feels desperate, a little sad.

"Come with me," she whispers.

He nods, sits up, runs a hand over his stubbled jaw. Smiles at her. And she knows everything is all right again.

She takes his hand and leads him, naked, out onto the beach and down to where the surf crashes on the sand. The sun is just coming over the horizon, an arc of fire in the deep, silvery sky.

They move together into the water, and it is soothing, womblike. The waves surge, wash away, caressing her skin, her naked sex. He pulls her deeper, until the water is waist-high. He holds her there, moves his hand between her thighs, pushes his fingers inside her. She spreads for him, reaches down to torment his cock. She runs her fingers over the cool metal of the ring piercing the head of his cock, tugs on it.

He moans, buries his face in her hair, pushes his cock into her hand. And they float in the water as they did that first time. Only yesterday, and yet it seems a million miles away.

He works her with his hand, fingers deep inside her, his thumb pressing on her clitoris. His hips thrust into her fisted hand, her fingers tight around his beautiful cock. They move together, breathe together, long, gasping pants as they build toward climax.

Pleasure, swift and sure, thrums through her body, taking her higher and higher. And the warm ocean all around them, rocks them, the wild scent of it in her nostrils.

As her body begins that first lovely clench, he murmurs, "I'm coming."

"Yes," she answers.

And their bodies buck and writhe with desire unleashed, as wild as the sea. His come floods her hand, hot and thick as honey, while she comes apart. Loose and shivering, her climax moves through her like the waves, rolling, thunderous. As powerful as the tides moving on the earth.

She wraps her legs around his waist. He kisses her cheek, her forehead. And they stay there while the sun comes up, burning golden, then pink, then finally a white glow in the deep blue sky. They are quiet as the world around them awakens, the seabirds sweeping in over the waves. All she can hear is the ocean and the sound of his breath in her ear.

He pulls back finally, watches her face quietly for a moment. Then he says, "I'm leaving today, heading down to Cozumel to do some diving."

"I hear it's very beautiful there."

"It is." He pauses. "Come with me."

She smiles, shakes her head. "I can't. I need to go home. Need to get back to…my life. Deal with some things." She only realizes as she says it that it's true.

He nods. "Do you even want to know my name?"

"No. I'm sorry but…"

"It's all right."

"You're not angry?"

"What about this time with you is there to be angry about?"

He reaches out, runs a finger down her cheek. "You're like something out of a dream. Maybe it's meant to be this way. Dream time."

"Yes."

That's it exactly. He understands.

A wave crests, splashes against them. She blinks the water from her eyes, looks up at him. He leans in and licks the salty water from her lower lip, smiling. His eyes have a languid cast to them, but they are still dark, bottomless. And still seem to see right through her, into her soul. She shivers again, but this time it is not physical pleasure but something deeper.

He knows her; she is sure of it. And it is both comforting and terrifying at the same time. It is why they are here together, as though a force that is far beyond them both has determined that this moment should be.

She won't question it further. Whatever else may happen doesn't matter. She is satisfied with knowing this much.

Gilt and Midnight
Megan Hart

YESTERDAY AND LONG AGO, IN A KINGDOM FAR FROM here but right next door, there lived a handsome young man and his equally beautiful young wife. She had hair the color of sunshine, eyes like a summer sky and skin like rich cream. Her name was Ilina, and the young man loved her more than anything else in the world.

Ilina, for her part, loved her handsome young husband. Pitor was strong, with muscled arms and legs that had no trouble chopping wood or building fences. His hair, the color of the forest's deepest shadows, hung to his shoulders in ripples like silk, and his eyes shone like the night sky littered with stars.

If Ilina had one small wish, it was that Pitor could be as satisfied with their humble cottage and plot of land as she was, but though her husband worked long and hard, he hated the labor that brought them their food and the roof above their heads. No matter how Ilina tried to soften the small rooms with her handwoven tapestries or delicately embroidered pillows, night after night Pitor looked around their home with dissatisfaction on his face.

"I love you," she told him. "No matter if we eat on gold and silver or on wooden trenchers, Pitor, I love you."

But Pitor would not be satisfied, no matter what Ilina did. And each day when he came home from chopping wood in the forest, he grew angrier and more sullen. Nothing Ilina did could move him to smile.

A time of drought and misfortune came upon the land. Pitor had to travel farther and farther into the woods to find trees he could chop for profit, until at last one day he'd traveled so far he couldn't make it home before dark. Though he ached to return to his beloved Ilina and knew she would worry for his safety, he knew how foolish traveling in the dark would be. He made himself a small camp and prepared to spend the night. He dared not even burn one small portion of the wood he'd gathered, for not only would it be taking food from Ilina's mouth to use the wood he intended to sell, but the risk of deadly fire in the dry forest was too great. Instead, he pulled his cloak around himself and hunkered down, unable even to sleep lest a beast attack him in the night.

Nevertheless, weariness overtook him, and Pitor's eyes closed. He dreamed of his love, of her touch and of her kiss, and woke with his cock straining the front of his trousers.

"Ah, sweet," said a voice from the shadows. "What a prize you hold between your legs. How I long for a man to fill me up with what you've got."

Convinced he was dreaming, Pitor sat up with a shake of his head. Laughter curled like smoke from the darkness. A woman stepped from behind a tree. The sight of her sent fear and desire coursing through him in equal amounts, and Pitor sprang to his feet, his hatchet ready to defend against her.

"You know me?" The woman's dark hair swirled around her face.

Pitor's breath heaved. The closer she stepped the more aroused he became, until all he could think of was satisfying the carnal urges flooding him.

The woman was upon him, astride him, before he knew how to object.

"Who are you?" he cried, stricken, for he'd never been unfaithful to his wife before.

"You don't need to know."

He turned and was on her before she could escape, the blade of his ax to her throat, but she only laughed. To his shame, his cock twitched and rose at the sound of it. She reached between them to grab and stroke him fully erect.

"You should be better satisfied with what you have, woodsman, else you lose it all. Let me show you what you could have."

Pitor jerked away from her and lowered the ax. "I love my wife."

The woman stood, her eyes flashing in a face still covered with shadows. "Come with me and be my love, and we will walk the forest as monarchs."

He shook his head. "No!"

She tilted her head. "No? Then fuck me once with that sweet prick, and I'll reward you for your efforts."

Pitor's hand trembled. "No reward you could offer me would be enough for me to betray my wife."

"Not even the life of your child?"

Pitor gasped aloud. "I have no children!"

Ilina had lost several pregnancies at great harm to her health. He knew she still longed for a babe, but he hoped for her sake she wouldn't catch again. The woman in front of him clucked her tongue to the roof of her mouth.

"Fuck me, and your child will never know hunger, nor poverty. How is that for a reward, and for so simple a task? One your body craves already?"

"You can promise me that?"

"That and more," promised the woman, and Pitor was lost.

As he sank into her warm, slick flesh, Pitor groaned, "Ilina!"

"Ah, yes," said the woman atop him, the woman who smelled and felt so familiar now.

Pitor groaned again as ecstasy swept him. "Ilina!"

The woman slowed her movements, rocking against him. She bent to whisper in his ear. "I am your Ilina, if you so desire."

Pitor's hands gripped her hips as he thrust inside her, over and over, until his seed boiled out of him and he fell back, spent. The woman laughed and withdrew, leaving him cold in the night air. Pitor blinked, stunned at how she'd once again become a stranger.

"Don't travel so far from home, next time," she advised, and was gone, leaving Pitor to return to his wife.

She had meant to keep it secret from him until she knew for sure the babe grew inside her without difficulty, but Ilina didn't regret telling Pitor about the child their love had planted, because the moment she did, the gloom and anger Pitor had allowed to overtake him vanished.

For months, Pitor returned each night to his Ilina with a smile as bright as diamonds. He made sure to bring her the finest fruits they could afford, even forsaking his own hunger to provide his wife with the best delicacies to tempt her failing appetite. Still, as Ilina's belly swelled, the rest of her withered. She kept a smile on her face, though, while the babe inside her wriggled and squirmed.

The midwife was not pleased with the way the babe had stolen so much of Ilina's strength. "It's not right," she told Pitor when Ilina had fallen into an exhausted, feverish sleep. "The labor has begun, but it's not progressing. They're killing her."

"They?" Pitor, white-faced and sick, clutched his hands together and tore his gaze from his wife long enough to look at the midwife.

"Your wife is carrying twins." The midwife said no more when Ilina woke and began to scream.

Ilina's daughter was born in blood and sweat and screams, and the midwife placed her into Pitor's arms at once while she sought to stanch the flow of crimson from between Ilina's legs. Pitor held the squirming, naked infant and watched his wife die in front of him, and then he handed the child to the midwife and left the cottage.

She found him in the garden, the place where his beloved Ilina had spent so many hours tending to her flowers. The midwife had cleaned and wrapped the child, who lay quiet in her arms, but when she offered the babe to her father, Pitor turned his face.

"Take them away."

The midwife, a goodhearted woman who had seen many births and deaths but none so surprising as this one, offered the child again. "There is only one. I was wrong."

She had never been wrong before and was uncertain if she was truly wrong now. One child had been born, yes, but the girl was unlike other babies. The midwife pulled the blankets away from the child's face to show Pitor, who would not look.

"See," the midwife said. "Her eyes? Her hair?"

Pitor shook his head. "My wife is dead. Take that creature away."

The midwife looked into the face of the sleeping infant. The hair was silver gilt on one half of her head and black as grief on the other. The child's eyes were the same; one pale blue and the other a deep, midnight black. Two faces...yet one.

"What do you want me to do with it?" asked the midwife quietly.

"I don't care," said Pitor. "You can kill it, for all I care. Now go away, and let me bury my wife."

So the midwife crept away into the night, the bundle in her arms, and left the man to take care of the woman he'd loved so well.

The midwife, who had already raised more than her share of babies, did not want to raise another. Not even one that cooed so prettily or waved its dainty hands in the air. One that didn't cry like other babies, but wept only from its dark eye and never from the pale.

The midwife's husband, who was as good a man as the midwife was a woman, did not want to raise any more children either. "I'm too old to start over," he complained. "We've done even with dandling our grandchildren on our knees and wait now only for them to bring us their children to love. Why do we need to adopt some ragamuffin child?"

The midwife did not disagree. "I'll take her to the noblewoman on the hill. She has long yearned for a child of her own and has had none. Maybe she will adopt this one."

So thus it was the unnamed babe with the mismatched eyes went to live in the large stone house on the hill.

* * *

The noblewoman, who was not nearly as beautiful as Ilina but whose husband loved her just as dearly, called her new daughter Miracula because of the miraculous way in which she'd been brought to them. Never was a child more cosseted and pampered, or more loved, than little Mira was by her adopted mother and father.

By the time she reached womanhood, Mira had become known as the most beautiful girl in all the land. Her hair flowed down to the backs of her knees in ripples of silver on one side and ink on the other To any who looked upon her perfect features, the different colors of her eyes only enhanced the thick darkness of her lashes, the crimson of her lips and the sweet pink blush of her cheeks. Her body had grown lush and firm, with rounded breasts and buttocks, and hips just right for a man's hands to hold

Her father's fortune only made her all the more desirable, but though many sought the hand of the nobleman's adopted daughter, none were allowed to court her.

"She is a child, still." insisted her father to her mother, who knew better but didn't wish to disagree. "She's not ready to be married, to go off and leave us."

"Someday," said the noblewoman, patting her husband's hand, "she will have to."

For though she loved her daughter very much, the noble-woman knew how it was to be a young woman without a suitor, and how her daughter must long for the time when she could be courted as all the other young women were.

"They only want her money," grumbled the nobleman. "They seek her fortune as much as they do her heart."

"That, too, might be true," said the noblewoman. She looked out the window to where Mira walked in the garden, alone. "But someday, my husband, we won't be able to keep her to ourselves any longer. Won't it be better if we've chosen a husband for her? One who won't take our beloved daughter too far from us?"

The nobleman thought of this, but harrumphed and gar-rumphed and would not give in.

And in the garden, Mira bent to smell the flowers, all alone.

Winter stole across the world like an illicit lover, taking the light and leaving darkness behind. Inside the stone house on the hill, there was food and drink aplenty, and warmth and all manner of entertainments. The nobleman and his wife hosted friends from near and far to help relieve the lethargy of the cold season.

Mira, no longer the child her father wanted her to be, wished the house were silent instead of filled with the shouts of card-players and the snuffle of hounds. She preferred the scent of snow to the savory smells of roasting fowl and baking bread. She even liked running through the now-dead garden, though it left her shivering, better than sitting in front of the blazing fireplace wrapped in a goose-down cloak. Only the year before she had longed for these long nights with a house full of company; the twelve months that had passed had turned her into someone new. Now, though her parents gestured for her to join them and their guests, she snuck away down dark and chilly corridors to find a place in the attic to sit alone.

She blew on the frost-covered windows to look down to the barren gardens below. They weren't empty, as she'd expected them to be. Footprints marred the smooth whiteness of snow-covered plots. And in the corner by the gate, a huddled figure clawed at the ground. Mira watched it scrabble in the vegetable plot. Perhaps seeking the remains of a gourd or something else? Had some poor vagrant stolen into her garden to look for food?

Pity moved her, and Mira left the attic to sneak past the rooms full of merrymakers. She crept to the garden without shoes or even a cloak to keep her warm, so intent was she on finding out who she'd seen from her window above. The snow bit at her toes and the wind gnawed her fingertips, but it was nothing compared to what the traveler must have felt.

"You must come inside," she insisted to the scarf-covered face. She couldn't tell even if the visitor was a man or a woman, so bundled and wrapped in layers was the figure. "Get warm. Have something to eat."

When they went inside, however, Mira's father was not pleased at his daughter's kindhearted gesture. There was no room at his table for a beggar, be it woman or man. Not even in his kitchen, not even to eat the scraps unfit for dogs, and he made the bundled visitor go back into the snow even before it had time to unwrap one of its many cloaks.

"Father—" Mira protested, but the nobleman wouldn't hear her plea.

"I will go," said the beggar, whose face was still hidden. "But you should know who you've turned away."

The guests who'd gathered around the scene gasped when the beggar pushed back its coverings to reveal the face of a beautiful, if cruel-eyed, woman. Everything about her was dark. Her eyes, hair, even the blush of her lips and tongue were dark rather than red. She looked around at them all before settling her eyes upon Mira.

"Your daughter has far better manners than you, old man," said the dark fairy. "She will be your salvation, as she tried to be mine."

The nobleman was too smart to try to beg forgiveness from the dark fairy. "Don't take her!"

The dark fairy laughed; in the garden the flowers shivered beneath their blanket of snow. "I don't want her, old man. Just as you would like nobody else to want her either."

"Please," begged the noblewoman, stepping forward. She was no less wise than her husband, but women know the ways to deal with one another and the dark fairy was still a woman. "Please don't punish our daughter because of our foolishness."

The dark fairy laughed. "Worry not, lady. I won't make your daughter hideous to the eye, nor make it so toads fall from her lips with each word. No, lady, I shall grant your daughter a gift, instead, for the generosity she attempted to show me. And in giving her the gift, I shall punish you."

The dark fairy clapped her hands and the guests drew back as one, each hoping not to draw her attention. The dark fairy smiled and waved her hand. Her veil of cloaks and scarves fluttered.

"You shall be desired," she told Mira. "And you shall desire."

"That's it?" cried the nobleman, perhaps not so wise as he believed himself to be. "That's the curse?"

The dark fairy drew her hood back over her face and opened the door. Snow swirled inside and melted on the floor. The gathered company shivered in unison.

"Until your daughter finds completion, old man, you will

slowly lose everything you have. Pray hope she finds it before you are beggared and must rely upon the unkindness of strangers."

With that, the dark fairy was gone.

The nobleman reached out his hand to Mira, who didn't take it. Nor did she reach for her mother, who wept with fists pressed to her mouth. Mira looked around the room, at the men and women gathered there, and something swelled inside her that she'd never felt before.

Heat flared inside her belly and lower, between her thighs. She pressed a hand to herself there, and the other to the swell of her breasts where more heat rose. She bit back a gasp at the look one of her father's friends was giving her. His eyes burned dark with an emotion she couldn't name, but that she felt echoed in her own.

Then she knew what it was, that fierceness, that burning, that flush on her skin and the flare in her gaze.

Desire.

It began at once.

Without regard to her parents or the guests assembled in their hall, Mira went to the man staring at her and let him put his mouth on her. Nobody stopped her. Nobody said a word when he took her by the elbow and led her upstairs and rid her of her virginity. Her mother wailed and her father gnashed his teeth, but neither of them stopped it.

Neither of them could stop it.

Mira's first lover was not handsome, but he was bold, and he fucked her so thoroughly that first time she couldn't walk the next day. Yet despite the hours of intercourse, the kisses he rained over her body, the things he did to her, she didn't feel complete. In fact, when it was finally over and her lover stole away from the sweat-soaked bed, all Mira felt was emptiness.

Clearly, this would not do.

Already her parents' guests had fled. The staff, no longer loyal to a house accursed, left as well. The hearths lay cold, the fowl uncooked. Her father had locked himself in his counting room, counting out his money. Her mother had pricked her thumbs with every spindle in the house, but could not sleep.

Mira washed the scent of the man from her body and discovered that a fingertip slid against the pearl hidden inside her soft folds could bring her pleasure so intense it weakened her knees. Was this, then, completion? She stroked again and dipped a finger inside her heat much the way her lover of the night before had used his cock to fill her. She moaned and bit her lip, grasping the edge of the wooden bathtub, as pleasure coursed through her.

And then...nothing.

Frustrated, she stroked harder, pulling on her nipples. Heat rushed through her veins and she sank to the rush-matted floor of the chamber. She pumped her hips upward against her now-grasping touch, and still the sense of something building inside her grew and grew without cease. Without release.

She could not eat, nor sleep, for the fire consuming her took up so much of her attention. Yet instead of turning her ill, this fever only made her all the more beautiful. She saw it in her looking glass. Her hair was like shining silk. Her eyes, each as lovely as a jewel. Her mouth, ripe and plump and ready for kissing.

In the past her father had hoarded his gold, but now he

received an uncommon summons from the king to pay some taxes to which he'd never before been held. He wept as the messenger carried away bag after bag of clinking coins. Her mother sought the solace of the wine barrel. This was but one day after the dark fairy's curse, and Mira knew she had to find her completion soon or everything she'd known her entire life would be lost.

She made it known that she was now entertaining suitors, and as bad news travels fast, so did this. On the fifth day after the fairy's curse, men had begun lining up outside the gate. Most of them, she assumed, had come for a chance to wet their pricks inside her, though a few of the more intelligent would have known that the man who managed to satisfy her would gain more than a willing cunny in which to spill his seed, but a vast portion of her father's rapidly diminishing fortune, as well.

Mira cared little for her father's fortune. She cared more for his happiness, and her mother's, for though they had not bred or borne her, she loved them as dearly as if they had. Truth be told, she loved the line of men waiting to fuck her, too, for the fairy had been right about desire being a gift.

And still, no matter how many men entered Mira's bedchamber and touched her, no matter how many urged her body to writhe and squirm beneath talented tongues and fingers and cocks, not one of them left her with anything other than emptiness when he'd gone.

By the tenth day after the fairy's decree, the line had dwindled as fast as her father's fortune. The men who now waited at the gate were those a little needier, a little less affluent. Men to whom a pretty wife who'd lain with a hundred men and a bit of a fortune were better than a farm-roughened wife and no fortune at all. Mira took them as she'd done the ones in fine leather and velvet, and like their richer predecessors, none left her complete. One by one, the men left her chamber, grumbling that there could be no man who would finish her.

"Daughter, don't kill yourself to find the one," Mira's mother urged, voice slurred, dress askew. "A fortune can be rewon."

"Tell that to my father," Mira said from her place in front of the mirror, where she searched her mismatched eyes for any sign of something different. Something new. "He's the one killing himself, sitting in the counting room enumerating his coins and gnashing his teeth at each one he must relinquish."

She turned to her mother. "Both of you believe you can do nothing to change the dark fairy's curse, but I know I can."

Again, she looked at her face. She'd become a woman, with a woman's secret smile. She touched her bare breasts, the tight pink nipples. The floss between her thighs. The box that would bring her pleasure if only she could find the right key to unlock it.

"And I want to," she said.

Winter eased into spring with little fanfare. Mira's parents had done little to fight the fairy's curse. It pained her to see her beloved mother and father give themselves so quickly to despair, and she was determined not to let them wither away. The line of men waiting to sample her beauty had dwindled to nothing, no more than one or two a sevenday.

Until one day, as Mira sat in the warming garden where the flowers had just begun to show their heads, two men arrived.

One as fair as sunshine, the other dark as shadows. They reached the gate at the same time, one from each direction. From her seat on the stone bench, Mira could see them both, but at first neither looked at her.

"Gerard," said the dark-haired man.

"Alain," greeted the fair-haired man.

Mira got to her feet. Both had put their hands to their belts, one to pull a dagger and the other a short sword. Neither moved after that, each watching the other, until the dark-haired man gave a slight nod and stepped aside just enough to let the one called Gerard pass. Both of them came through the gate, and both stopped when they saw her.

"Madame," said Gerard with a half bow. "We seek the lady Mira."

"Many have sought her," Mira said. "What makes the two of you any different than the hundreds of others?"

Alain stood an inch or so shorter than Gerard but still towered tall over Mira. He held out his hand for hers, and she took it at once. "I've heard she's been gifted by the dark fairy."

"Everyone knows that." Mira tugged away her hand, still tingling from his touch.

"Ah," said Alain with a half bow nearly identical to the one Gerard had already bestowed. "But not everyone else has received the same gift.'

Mira looked at them, from one to the other. "And you have?"

"Lady," answered Gerard. "We both have."

Most of the other men had arrived intent on seducing her at once. Some had been kind, a few considerate, but none of them had wasted their time with conversation. Alain and

Gerard, however, followed Mira into the large dining hall where they set about laying a fire in the long-neglected hearth.

"Wine, lady?" Gerard's question seemed more command than request, and Mira found herself scurrying to the sideboard in search of a bottle.

Alain watched her, his gaze like sapphires. "Where are your servants, lady?"

"Gone," Mira said as she poured three glasses of almost sour wine. "My father can't afford to pay them any longer, and they fear the dark fairy's taint. My good mother has taken to her bed. And my father has gone mad."

She expected the blunt statement to take the men aback, but neither looked surprised. She offered glasses, one to Alain and one to Gerard, and both took them. Gerard drank his at once with a grimace, but Alain waited for Mira to sip before he drank.

Gerard gave a low grunt and put his cup on the long wooden dining table that had hosted so many guests over the years. "Come here."

Mira did at once, though she stopped far enough away from him that he would have to reach to grab her, if that was his intent. Gerard didn't reach for her. He studied her.

"You are beautiful," he said. "The fairy didn't give you that."

Mira shook her head. "No, sir, I don't believe so."

She looked at him. His pale hair fell to his shoulders, loose. He had the sharp features of a hawk and the body of a warrior beneath his simple, solid clothes. She shivered, thinking of his muscular arms around her, of his thick legs pushing hers apart. He would not be gentle, she saw this already, and her pulse beat faster between her legs.

"Would you have me?" he asked her, his voice low and rough.

Mira's mouth parted, and she looked toward Alain, who had not yet put down his glass. "What of your companion, sir?"

Gerard laughed. "What of him?"

"You both arrived at the same time. You both want the same thing. How am I to know which of you can provide me with what I need if I don't sample you both?"

From another woman these words would have made her a doxy, but Mira had long ceased caring. The dark fairy had gifted her with desire, and it built and built inside her every day without cease. Her mother was trying to sleep away her life and her father had gone insane because of it. She would fuck a thousand men if it meant she'd find the one to complete her.

Gerard gave Alain a challenging look. "Would that you had traveled a mile faster, brother of my heart. You might have been the one to fill this lady's bucket."

Alain put a hand over his heart and bowed his head to Gerard. "Would that you had traveled but a mile slower, oh my brother. For then, indeed, I might have been the first to reach her."

Mira looked at them. They had history, of that there was no question. "You are brothers?"

Without looking away from Alain, Gerard said, "We have different parents."

Without looking away from Gerard, Alain replied, "We have fought at each other's side and won. We've shared much, Gerard and I."

They both looked at her, but it was Gerard this time who held out his hand. "Lady, take me to your room, and I will give you what the dark fairy promised would save you and your family."

Mira, having no reason to decline, took his hand and led him to the stairs. Halfway up, she looked back. Alain stared after them, but only she saw him press his lips to the tips of his fingers.

Gerard wasted no time with pretty words. He took Mira in his arms the moment the bedchamber door closed behind them. His breath smelled of wine, a heady aroma more tantalizing than the taste of it had been. His mouth took hers without preamble, nudging open her lips to allow his tongue to slide inside. Mira gasped into his kiss, and his arms tightened around her.

"She truly did gift you with desire," Gerard murmured, tracing the line of her jaw with his mouth. Into her ear, he whispered, "You create it and feel it, both. Do you not?"

"Yes." Mira shivered as his large hands roamed her body and cupped her buttocks through the simple linen dress she wore. Without maidservants to wash her clothes and help her dress, she'd gone without a shift or girdle beneath, and it was almost as if she wore nothing at all. "Yes, sir, I feel it."

"You want me to touch you, as the other men have touched you?"

Mira sighed as his hands squeezed and one began tugging up her dress, inch by inch. "Oh, yes."

"Tell me, lady," Gerard said and bit into her soft flesh with a fierceness that urged a cry from Mira's throat. "Tell me how they fucked you."

She told him of men with hard, hot cocks who had used her mouth, her cunt, the tunnel of her breasts, the sweet back passage of her ass. How they had made her feel like she was meant to burst, how she had exploded with pleasure over and over, only to be left aching for more at once. Aching and empty.

Incomplete.

"And why should you be different," she half sobbed as his roaming hands found her slick crevice and parted her folds to allow one of his thick fingers to slide inside.

"Because I have to be." Gerard, one hand still moving inside her, used the other to tear her gown from throat to hips.

Mira's breasts thrust forward as she arched her back. She rode Gerard's hand harder and harder as he thrust another finger inside her. His mouth found her sweetly aching nipples. When he suckled one, she cried out. Her fingers dug into his shoulder. She rocked her hips, seeking release.

But Gerard would not give it to her. "The others made you come, but none of them finished you." He growled the words and withdrew his hand so swiftly from her body Mira stumbled. "Stand there, still. Don't move."

She did, though, taking a step on trembling legs toward him.

"I said," murmured Gerard in a voice gone low and dangerous, "do not move."

This time, Mira stayed still.

Gerard removed his belt, laid aside his scabbard, pulled his shirt over his head and tossed it unceremoniously to the floor. His body beneath was indeed that of a warrior, scarred and hard, with tight bronzed nipples and golden fleece around them and in a line disappearing into the waist of his breeches.

Watching her, he eased down his breeches and kicked them aside to stand before her naked. His cock, surrounded by its fluff of amber curls, rose straight and proud. Mira's pearl beat with the pounding of her heart and her passage tightened in a brief spasm. She moaned, but stayed still as he had ordered.

"The others. Did any bind you? Beat you?"

"No!" Shock sent heat soaring into her cheeks.

Gerard stroked his cock even more fully erect. "Turn around and put your hands on the post."

His gaze flickered to the foot of her bed. Some of the men had taken her on the floor, or across the table. None had told her to hold onto the bedpost. Mira hesitated, but at the flare of heat in Gerard's eyes, she did.

She waited, trembling. Her hair had fallen from its coils and lay across her breasts. Gerard threaded his fingers through it, twisting the gilt and midnight together. His hand covered her breast.

"Move your legs apart."

She did, her muscles tense with waiting. Gerard slid his other hand between her legs from behind. His thick fingers probed her slick folds, finding the bead of her clit and rolling it. Mira pushed her hips forward, wanting more pressure, but Gerard withdrew almost at once.

When she stilled, he slid his hand between her legs again. His fingers dipped into her wetness and caressed her heat. His cock probed the softness of her buttocks from behind, and Mira pushed herself back against him. Again, Gerard withdrew.

"Please." Mira moaned the single word.

"Please, what?"

"Please, touch me."

"Is that what you asked them?" Gerard bit lightly at her shoulder, and Mira jerked away from him with a gasp.

"I didn't have to!" Her chin lifting, she pushed at him. It was like pushing at rock, but he stepped back. Her chest heaved with each breath, and the surprising sting of tears burned her eyes. "They all just did it! All of them just did it!"

"Perhaps, then, that's your problem." Gerard made no move toward her. His cock rose proud and strong in front of him. It begged for Mira's touch, the heat of her mouth, but she didn't move toward him.

"You want me to beg? Is that it?"

Gerard shrugged and moved to the chair in front of the fire, where he sat without regard to his nakedness. Or hers. This, more than anything, moved Mira to anger.

"Please," she said through gritted jaws. "Please touch me, sir. Please fuck me."

"No."

"Then why did you come here?" she demanded, crossing to him. Fury made her want to strike him, but Mira didn't dare.

Gerard looked her up and down, caressing her so thoroughly with his gaze it weakened her legs and tightened her nipples further. "To make you complete. Isn't that what the dark fairy said you needed?"

"What did she say *you* needed?" The words came out broken, edged with glass, on the verge of cruel.

Quick as the sunshine from which his hair had been woven, Gerard grabbed her wrist. He pulled her forward and put her across his lap like a recalcitrant child. His big hand came down across her buttocks, the smack not hard enough to bruise, though Mira cried out at the sting. Heat spread across her flesh and her hips pushed forward, pushing her cunt against Gerard's thigh.

"She told me I needed to complete someone." His other hand pressed her tight against him so she couldn't move.

"By beating me?" Mira cried, voice hoarse, even as her hips rocked.

"This is not a beating," said Gerard. "This is an appreciation."

Heat covered her buttocks and spread to meet the fire already burning between her thighs. As Gerard's hand caressed her skin, Mira sagged against him. Her legs parted, inviting him to fill her with his fingers again, but he didn't, not even when she wriggled and strove to get free of his grip.

Beneath her, his cock pressed. His breathing had grown harsher, his grip tighter as she struggled. Yet he did nothing but rest his hand upon the heat his spank had left on her skin.

"I am making you appreciate my touch," Gerard said in a low voice. "Feel the heat of my hand. Focus on that, not my cock. Not your cunt. Focus on the sound of our breathing. On the brush of your hair against your face."

Mira closed her eyes with a grimace. Her hips rocked again on Gerard's thigh, but without much result. None of the others had done this. All had taken her, some rougher, some with gentler hands, but all had done it.

Gerard held her until her struggles ceased. Every line of Mira's body had gone hot, as though he'd drawn a stick from the fire along her skin. She moaned into her fist as his hand shifted, the fingertips brushing the underside of her buttocks. He moved them lower, to tease her bottom lips. He felt how wet she was for him, how his touch had already teased her so close.

"Please, Gerard," she whispered. "Please touch me."

When at last he did, once more filling her with a phallus created from his fingers, Mira's cry of relief rang around the room. His thumb rubbed at her pearl while his fingers moved inside her, and the ache that had built inside her, up and up, reached its peak and crashed.

Mira's climax washed over her, no, thundered over her, and she jerked with it. She cried out his name, once. Twice. When the throbbing between her legs eased and she caught her breath, Gerard released her from his lap. Mira stood, her hand on his shoulder to keep herself from falling.

She drew in air scented like Gerard and sighed it out again. She wanted to weep. Her body had succumbed to his ministrations, she had reached her pleasure...and still...

"I am empty," she said in a dull voice. She turned from him. She waited for the door to open and close behind him, for her body to cease its trembling. For her breath to fill again with air that smelled of smoke and stale bed linens.

"Lady," said Gerard. "Did you think it would take but once?"

Alain listened for the sound of the lady's cries as Gerard took her to orgasm. He knew too well the taste and touch of the man upstairs, and his cock rose in his trousers at the knowledge of what he would be doing to the woman. Once, they had shared everything, even women.

It had been a woman who drove them apart.

The dark fairy, who had no name any mortal knew, had stalked Alain through the forest and seduced him not once, but twice. She had used his cock for her personal joy, writhing on him and milking him of his seed even as he fought to remember where he was. Who he was. The dark fairy had cared little for Alain's mind. All she wanted was his penis and mouth. His hands. She'd have continued sucking him dry had Gerard not come looking for him. She'd seduced Gerard, as well, and Alain could still recall the sound of their cries as she'd taunted Gerard into fucking her harder and harder.

Then, for fun or spite, she had caused them to quarrel. Not with swords, for at that they'd have been too well matched. It would have ended in death for the pair of them. No, she'd urged them to battle with their words. Accusations, old hurts, imagined slights and falsehoods had torn them apart.

Alain and Gerard had not known each other as children, though that had ceased to matter a mere three days into their acquaintance. They'd both been assigned places in the King's Guard, an elite division of the Royal Army.

The first thing Alain had noticed about Gerard was his hands. Big, strong hands, scarred from work and battle. Gerard had been demonstrating his skill with his broadsword, using the flat of the blade to smack at his opponent. The sun had come out from behind a cloud, highlighting Gerard's hair into shimmering gold and Alain had, quite literally, lost his breath.

"You there," Gerard had said with a crook of his finger. "Get your ass over here and let me beat it."

Even now, recalling Gerard's surprise at not winning that first fight, Alain smiled. Arrogant from never losing, Gerard hadn't paid enough attention to the newcomer and had ended up on his back with Alain's blade at his throat.

It was the last time he didn't pay enough attention to Alain.

They'd forged the deepest of bonds, the pair of them matched so well physically there were none who could stand against them. They fought hard for the king, and they made merry with equal fierceness...for themselves.

Alain had long known his cock rose without hesitation at both the curved softness of women and the hard, muscled planes of men. Physical love between men wasn't forbidden in the King's Guard, where it might be weeks before a man could find a woman, but it wasn't exactly encouraged, either. Alain, who felt no shame at his proclivities, also felt no need to fight to defend them. He'd surely kill anyone who came up against him, and while his blade had tasted the blood of many of the king's enemies, he had no desire to spill that of his comrades.

Gerard had never shown signs of liking cock, and Alain had never made a move to push their friendship into that place. They fought, they wrestled, they shared a room and a bath. They often visited the brothels together or sampled some of the same tavern wenches. Gerard had a heavier hand with his women than Alain, who had no desire to bind or beat his bedmates. When Alain sought the company of men, he did it discreetly, and without Gerard. It was the one thing they didn't share.

Until the night Alain came home from an encounter with one of his favorite male partners to find Gerard waiting for him.

"Where do you go?" Gerard had asked in a deceptively gentle voice that didn't fool Alain.

"I didn't know I owed you an accounting of my time," Alain had replied mildly.

Gerard had drawn his brows. "You stink of fucking."

"I'll wash."

Gerard's hand had flown out to grab Alain's wrist as he'd passed. "I don't smell a woman's sweetness on you, Alain."

Alain had looked down at Gerard's fingers gripping his wrist but made no move to pull away. "No."

They had trained together so often Gerard's move shouldn't

have surprised him, but then perhaps Alain had chosen to be surprised. Gerard had turned him and pressed him forward, both
hands tight on his wrists, in the time it took to draw a breath.
Alain hadn't struggled. Against his back, he'd felt the familiar
breadth and width of Gerard's body.

Gerard had pushed Alain toward the room's rough-hewn
table and pinned his hands to the splintered wood. He'd kicked
his legs apart and pressed harder against his back. Alain had
closed his eyes, breathing hard, making no offer.

"You like it this way?" Gerard had breathed in Alain's ear. The
touch of Gerard's hot breath had sent a shudder down Alain's
spine and still he said nothing, made no move to get away,
though he easily could have.

Gerard's hand had let go of one of Alain's and moved around
to cup Alain's hardening cock. "Your prick is hard, my friend."

Gerard hadn't fumbled with the ties of Alain's trousers, nor
had his touch hesitated when he took Alain's hard length into
his palm. He'd stroked, hard, in the way only men knew how
to do, until at last Alain had pumped his hips forward with a
cry.

"Yes," he'd said. "Yes, Gerard, I like that."

He'd groaned when the bluntness of Gerard's thick cock
nudged at the passage of his ass, and cried aloud when Gerard
had eased his way inside. Gerard had fucked him fast and hard,
jerking Alain's prick at the same time, until they'd both
exploded into pleasure.

"You can share everything with me," Gerard had said then,
and until the dark fairy came along, they had.

Alain's cock had risen at the memories and now pressed un-
comfortably against the front of his breeches. He turned at the

soft noise behind him to see Mira, her lovely skin flushed and that marvelous hair hanging in tangled curls around her face.

"He sent me to fetch him some ale." Her voice was scratchy, hoarse.

"My lady," Alain said kindly, for he knew well enough how Gerard's touch could leave one shaken. "Would you sit?"

He pulled out a chair for her, and she sank into it as though her legs had been about to collapse. He brought her mulled wine and a hunk of bread from the sideboard, but she neither drank nor ate.

"My lady," said Alain gently and waited until she looked at his face. "What do you need?"

"I don't need wine and bread," she snapped suddenly, her intriguingly mismatched eyes flashing. "I need fulfillment!"

He'd been certain she'd find it with Gerard, and yet the moment she said the words Alain knew she spoke the truth. A smile tugged at his lips. Now it was his turn to try.

Mira's buttocks still held the heat left behind by Gerard's hand, but she refused to squirm on the hard seat of her chair. The humiliation of what he'd done—and without lifting the curse!—brought heat to her face equal to that in her bottom. She scowled at the dark-haired man in front of her.

"Bring me a dipper of cold water from the well," she demanded and pointed out the window to the garden. "That's what I want."

She felt certain he'd balk at her imperious tone, perhaps even take her in hand the way Gerard had, but Alain only ducked his head and strode to the doorway on his long, long legs. The well of which she spoke hadn't been used for a long time because the winch used to lift the bucket from its depths had rusted. Even so, the water drawn from it was the sweetest she'd ever tasted, and she wanted it now.

More than that, she thought as she watched him disappear through the door, she wanted to make someone suffer, even the tiniest bit, to make up for the way she had suffered upstairs.

But she hadn't suffered, really, had she? Even now, thinking of the way Gerard had ordered her to hold tight to the bedpost while he plundered her body from behind caused Mira's nipples to tighten and her pulse to throb harder between her legs.

As the beloved only child of doting parents, Mira had never been spanked in her life. No one had ever even raised their voice to her. Yet, she mused, her thighs slipping apart enough to dimple the fabric of her gown between them, there had been nothing parental about Gerard's treatment of her.

The other men had fucked her in all manner of ways, but none had commanded her so. Thinking of it now sent a shiver through her. Her sex, still wet with her own slickness, clenched hard enough to force a small moan from her lips.

"My lady."

At the sound of Alain's reverent voice, Mira's eyes flew open. She'd arched back in the chair, her hips lifting at the memory of Gerard's touch, but having Alain witness her reaction to those thoughts didn't quench her arousal. She studied him, the pail from the well brimming with water.

"I brought your water."

She didn't know what made her do it, except that all at once she lost all grasp of the difference between memory and reality. Gerard had commanded her but now she would command

Alain; all of it seemed to make sense the way light will suddenly shine through the one clean spot in an otherwise filthy window.

She kicked the bucket of water from his hands. It hit the floor with a thump and split into several pieces. The cold, clear water, sweet as honey, splattered Alain's boots and breeches. Frigid droplets hit her bare toes and calves, but her gasp wasn't from their small sting. It came when Alain went at once to his knees, his head bowed.

"My lady, I have displeased you."

Mira had been protected and indulged her entire life, but just as Gerard's treatment of her didn't echo anything parental, neither did this new desire sweeping her have anything to do with her previous experiences. She had always taken her clean clothes and prepared food as a fact of her existence and considered the servants who'd provided them a part of her family, like her parents. She'd never demanded anything from them.

The sight of Alain on his knees sent waves of pleasure through her so strong her head spun. Her legs parted further and she inched her skirt to her knees. Her fingers fisted in the fabric and she imagined how it would feel to bury them in the thickness of his dark hair.

"Tell me how I might serve you, lady," Alain murmured, "and I shall do my utmost to please you."

"I would have your face between my legs." The words rose to her lips as haughtily as any queen might have said them, and emboldened by her own tone, she added, "Pleasure my cunt with your tongue."

The dark fairy's gift had stolen any shyness from Mira, but even so it was the first time she'd ever said such a thing aloud.

Her heart pounded. She'd begged Gerard to touch her a mere hour before and now she ordered his comrade to do the same. Opposite ends of experience, yet both had made her heart trip faster in her breast.

"If it would please my lady to do so," Alain said without hesitation, "then it will be my pleasure to serve her."

His strong hands, only slightly smaller than Gerard's but with the same delightful calluses, slid up her thighs and pushed her skirt to her hips. She was bare beneath. She'd washed upstairs, but her sex glistened anew with her arousal. The smooth bead of her clitoris protruded sweetly from its hood of flesh and her soft curls.

Alain used his thumbs to stroke along her folds and brought them together, one on each side of her clitoris. Mira hissed out a gasp and her hips rocked forward again.

"Your mouth," she ordered.

He obeyed at once, dipping his head to press his lips to her flesh. His tongue, hot and wet, stroked her folds and anchored itself on her clitoris. He worked her flesh with his lips and tongue, and her desire coursed through her like flames consuming paper.

She fisted her hands in his hair and held him tight as his mouth moved. His tongue flickered, fast, then moved in slow, deliberate circles that had her writhing.

"Fuck me with your fingers," Mira gasped when Alain's tongue alone wasn't enough to send her over the edge.

Alain did as she ordered. His fingers were longer but not so thick as Gerard's, and in her ecstatic delirium Mira wondered if their cocks would be as disparate. He pushed two fingers deep inside her, curving them slightly upward as his tongue kept its steady pace. Bright sparks of fresh pleasure shot through her, and again when he pressed deeper and his knuckles provided additional pressure on her back passage.

She moaned his name, and again, louder. She closed her eyes and threw back her head to allow the ecstasy to take her over entirely.

"I want you to fuck me," she gasped. "Fuck me, Alain!"

Her climax shook her, the pleasure so intense she went briefly blind. Her toes pointed, her thighs fell open, her hands clutched at nothing. The words spewed from her mouth, yet she knew what she said and meant it.

"Be careful, lady," said a familiar male voice, dipping low with amusement. "For if you command it, Alain will feel compelled to obey."

Mira opened her eyes as the vestiges of ecstasy seeped out of her. Alain still knelt before her, his mouth glistening and his eyes hot with desire, but it was to Gerard she gave her full attention. Her heart still pounded from her climax but now the pitter-pat stepped up at the sight of the man who'd so recently mastered her. What would he do to her? To both of them?

Gerard spoke in a voice that could never have been called kind but was at least not cruel. He put his hand on Alain's head the way a man will touch his hound to prove his ownership and its loyalty to him. "It's in his nature, you see."

Mira swallowed hard, though her mouth had gone dry at the flare of lust in Gerard's blue eyes. In front of her, Alain remained on his knees, his head slightly bowed beneath the weight of Gerard's hand. He didn't look frightened. She watched as he licked his mouth of her sweetness.

"How does she taste, Alain?"

"Like sweet honey, Gerard."

Gerard's smile sent a frisson from the base of Mira's spine all the way to the sensitive flesh of the back of her neck. The curve of his lips affected another part of her as well, the soft and slick center between her thighs.

"Alain made you come, lady?"

She lifted her chin, almost defiant. "Yes."

Gerard's hand stroked down Alain's hair. "His tongue is most talented, is it not? And yet you screamed for his cock, too?"

Even now, her body twitched and shivered at the thought. The dark fairy had blessed her with desire, and it had grown tenfold since Gerard and Alain had walked through her garden gate. She covered herself with her hand.

"Yes," she said.

"You are not yet complete," said Alain.

She shook her head. Alain got to his feet, shrugging off Gerard's hand. "I can complete you, lady. Allow me to serve you."

"The lady seeks to serve," Gerard said in a deceptively kind tone. "She is natural at it, Alain."

Alain turned to face the other man. "You didn't complete her, Gerard. The weight of desire hangs heavy on her shoulders. Her burden has not yet been lifted, and nor has ours."

Gerard stared at Mira. "I haven't yet had my full way with her, Alain. Once I have——"

"Once I have," Alain interrupted, "the curse will be lifted."

"You?" Gerard turned his face to Alain and laughed. "I know well how your mouth can service, Alain, but you're not the one for this lady. I can feel it."

"I feel it," Alain said in a low, dangerous voice, and while in the past he might have served Gerard the way he'd served

Mira, it was clear to her that whatever rift had been torn between them had not yet healed.

"Will you ask the lady to choose?" Gerard asked in a frightening voice.

"I will not choose!" Mira cried so loudly the china in the cupboard rang. She got up from the chair, her skirts falling around her bare feet. "It is not for me to choose! It is for you to complete me!"

She pointed at each of them. "It is not a contest of who is the manlier!"

Alain ducked his head at her words and put his hand over his heart. "My lady—"

Gerard, however, had drawn his sword with a growl. "It is a contest, lady, for just as you seek completion and the breaking of the fairy's curse, so I seek it. Alain!"

Alain had drawn no weapon but Mira, heart thudding again, had no illusions he was not as ready to wage battle as Gerard. "Yes, brother of my heart."

"Outside."

"Yes, Gerard."

Again, Alain inclined his head, but though it gave the appearance of him following Gerard's command, Mira was not fooled. Alain was his own man. Her breath hitched faster in her chest when Alain followed Gerard out into the garden.

When they fought over her.

The room was not the best he'd ever been given, but it was clean and bright, and the bed was softer than any had ever been in the barracks of the King's Guard. The basins, one filled with hot water and one with cold, were of finer porcelain, too, as were the cloths Gerard now used to wash the worst of his wounds. Alain's blade had some time ago become nicked, and the cuts it gave were ragged. He hissed as he smoothed the water over his bleeding flesh.

It gave him no small pleasure to hear the same pained noises coming from the room Alain had been given. Though the rooms were separated by a door, it hung open. Gerard could hear Alain's measured pacing as he bathed and dressed his own wounds. He might have taken more pride had he known his comrade's injuries to be worse than his own, but Gerard was no fonder of lies told to himself than he was of untruths told to him by another.

Neither had held back in their fight to prove who was better suited to bring the lady Mira her completion, but, as in all else, they were so even in skill neither had been able to win. They were not a pair of matched ponies to draw a carriage, he mused as he watched Alain's shadow lengthen and shorten in the doorway. Rather they were as firmly opposite as the sun and moon. Like a lock and a key, Alain and Gerard were fair to useless without one another.

"Alain!"

The shadow paused and in the next moment, Alain's familiar form appeared in the open doorway. "Yes, Gerard."

"Come here."

Alain did at once, and though he refused to show any sign of it upon his face, Gerard ached inside for the days before the dark fairy had come between them. No woman ever had, not even the prettiest. No man had, either. Yet the dark fairy, on a whim they'd never understood, had taken the core of their friendship and used it to tear them asunder.

"I have missed you," Alain said simply, and Gerard hated and admired him for his ability to put voice to his emotions. "It's been overlong since we were able to practice together."

It was just like Alain, Gerard mused, to make it as though they'd been exercising rather than trying to kill one another. He wanted to keep from smiling but felt his mouth curve anyway. "Aye, brother of my heart, I have long regretted our distance as well."

Only Alain knew him well enough to know there was more to what he felt than what he said. Of all the lovers Gerard had ever taken, only Alain had also been his friend. He reached to grab Alain's wrist and tug him forward, and Alain stepped toward him without resistance.

"We have never let a woman come between us before," Gerard said. "Only that bitch of a fairy has ever separated us. Let us not allow this like-cursed lady to widen the gap."

"Mayhap," Alain said as he ran his hand through Gerard's hair, "she can help us bridge it, Gerard."

Alain had ever been the one of them to think more thoroughly, and Gerard had always been the one to take action. Together it had made them formidable foes to any who opposed them. Now Gerard would listen to his friend, to his brother of the heart, and they would take their action together.

"The fairy cursed us all three with desire," Gerard said. "All the same curse. Might we all have the same cure?"

"I think we might."

Alain's fingers tightened in Gerard's hair briefly as Gerard's hand on his wrist pulled him yet closer. It was not often that Gerard was the one looking up, but he did so now. Alain's gaze held a hotness he recognized. His cock had become thick and pushed the front of his breeches.

Alain gasped aloud when Gerard tugged open the laces of his breeches and drew forth his erect cock, and louder when Gerard slid the hot flesh between his lips, for it was not often Gerard's pleasure to provide this service. Gerard opened himself to take in Alain's length, sucking hard. Alain's hips bumped forward as Gerard's hands found his ass and gripped. The muscles of Alain's thighs jumped and twitched as Gerard sucked and licked all the way down to the root and up again, paying special attention to the crown. One hand left Alain's ass to grip the smooth foreskin and slide it back and forth as his mouth worked.

It might not have been Gerard's habit to suck Alain's cock, but he did it well nonetheless, for he knew just what Alain liked. In moments Alain's guttural growls were becoming the slow, deep moans that signaled his release, and now it was Gerard's turn to seek his own pleasure.

Without preamble he removed his mouth from Alain's erection and stood so suddenly Alain had no time to react. With his fist gripping Alain's prick, Gerard captured Alain's mouth in a harsh, demanding kiss. It would leave them both bruised, but the small pains were as nothing compared to the damage they'd already caused each other, and Alain's moan and the throb in his cock told Gerard he didn't mind.

"You think you deserve to spill?" Gerard growled into Alain's ear, his own cock as hard and thick as granite at the thought of what was to come. "Do you really think I'd take your seed down the back of *my* throat?"

Alain had his triggers and Gerard knew them all as well as he knew how to make him come. "No, Gerard."

Gerard let his hand drift along Alain's cock before letting go of it. "How long has it been since anyone's taken a strap to your ass, Alain?"

"Too long." Alain's voice pushed from gritted jaws, and Gerard heard the truth in it. "Not since you, Gerard. That last time."

That had been a long time then, for the dark fairy had cursed them more than three moons before. Until this morning with Mira, it had been just as long since Gerard had beaten anyone, though he'd taken countless women to his bed while seeking to break the curse.

Gerard gripped Alain's chin in his hand and looked hard into the other man's eyes. "It's been too long then."

He ordered Alain to take his position against the plastered wall, his hands at shoulder height and fingers spread. They had no safe word. They didn't need one. The position of Alain's fingers would tell Gerard how much pain he was able to take— today, with his previous injuries, it might be very little. The wider apart his fingers, the more he could take. If he closed them together, Gerard would know to ease off.

Just as using his mouth to service Alain was not his habit, neither was undressing him, but Gerard knew Alain was so close to coming, his cock already so hard, that bending to remove his breeches would only give him additional pleasure. Gerard intended to keep Alain balanced on the knife's edge for a sufficient time, so he was the one who pulled off Alain's breeches until Alain stood naked.

Gerard admired the lines of Alain's back and ass as he pulled the sturdy leather strap from his bag. The leather was supple and oiled and fit his fist exactly. He tugged it between his two hands to snap it, and his cock twitched at the way Alain's muscles jumped, though he showed no other sign he'd heard.

"By the time I'm done," Gerard said, "your back and ass are going to be on fire, Alain."

"Please," Alain murmured.

Gerard laid the strap in even lines along Alain's skin. His cock stiffened further at the red stripes and the low, strangled grunts of Alain's ecstasy.

Alain's head hung and his entire body quivered with exhaustion and still he did not push his fingers together, but it was Gerard's duty to know when Alain could take no more even if Alain himself could no longer tell, and he put aside the strap. He ran his hand over the heated flesh of Alain's back and delighted in his hiss. He slid a hand over Alain's ass and felt the muscles twitch and jump. He pulled a bottle of soothing oil from his bag and poured a palmful and repeated the motion. Alain's body tensed at the contact of the smooth oil on his flesh, and his hips pumped forward recklessly as he moaned.

He was so close Gerard knew it would take very little to send him over the edge, and for a moment he thought of allowing his friend that final release, but his own nature made him grin slyly instead. He ran his fingers, slick with oil, down the crease of Alain's buttocks and teased the hot, tight circle of his anus with one finger. Alain bucked and cried out, but his hands never left their places on the wall.

"Such a good soldier," Gerard murmured as his finger probed slightly deeper. "So good at following orders."

Alain's low, gasping chuckle sounded tortured, but he said nothing. He pushed back a bit against Gerard's hand. From a true slave Gerard would have not tolerated the insubordination, but Alain was not his slave even though they sometimes played at that game.

"You want this?" Gerard eased his finger into Alain's hot passage. "Or would you like my cock there, instead? Fucking you? How long has it been since anyone's been inside you, Alain?"

"As long as it's been since anyone's strapped me," Alain managed to say, though his voice shook with effort. "Please, Gerard, for the sake of our friendship...."

Gerard could be cruel, but this was not about cruelty, and he reached to stroke Alain's cock with his oil-filled palm. Once, twice, and Alain was crying out and pumping into Gerard's fist. Once more and his seed spilled, hot and fragrant, into Gerard's hand.

"Now," Gerard said when Alain had ceased his jerking and moaning, "use your mouth on me the way you did for her."

Alain turned and fell at once to his knees. He took Gerard's prick deep down his throat and sucked. He used his hand in tandem, stroking and caressing Gerard's balls in the way that made his mind go blank of any thought but the supreme pleasure between his legs.

It took only moments for Gerard to explode into ecstasy, and when he did he shouted Alain's name. As Alain got up from his knees, Gerard put a hand on his arm to keep him from turning immediately away.

"I have missed you, as well," Gerard said.

Whatever had happened between the two men, the last to come through the gate for a fortnight, they had somehow repaired their bond. Mira had expected them to leave when both realized they were unable to bring about the end to the dark fairy's gift, but as the days passed and Gerard and Alain ingratiated themselves into the household, Mira realized they intended to stay. More than that, they were wooing her, each in his own way, and neither was competing with the other for her affections.

In the past, of course, guests of the house had sought to court her in proper fashion as befit her status as the daughter of a very wealthy man. No suitor would have dared do more than walk with her in the garden, much less have been so bold as to kiss her, and anything more intimate than that was strictly forbidden.

The fairy's curse had changed all that. The first men who'd come seeking her had been satisfied to fuck her and move on when they failed to break the curse, but Alain and Gerard were not like any other men she'd ever met in her life.

Gerard set her to tasks such as polishing his boots and serving him his food, and his hand could be heavy when she didn't serve to his pleasure. The first time he'd tied her hands and feet to the posts at the foot of his bed and strapped her, she'd wept tears of pain and anger even as her cunt wept with arousal, yet she hadn't sent him from the house. Her body had grown to crave Gerard's discipline, as harsh as it could be, and he brought her to climax over and over with the flat of his hand or the leather strap he wielded with such proficiency. He fucked her thoroughly as well, when she pleased him, and denied her that ecstasy when she did not.

With Alain, however, Mira played the mistress without a second thought. He was as eager to serve her as she was to submit to Gerard. Alain took whatever abuse she offered him, whether it be her refusal to allow him to achieve orgasm when he used his mouth to satisfy her, or the performance of countless meaningless tasks meant only to prove she controlled him. He made love to her with worshipful hands, when she allowed it, and Mira found his touch as satisfying as Gerard's even if it was in a totally different way.

Both men pursued and pleased her over and over, yet no matter how many times her body sang with desire, something was still missing. She waited for one of them to finish her completely, to break the dark fairy's curse, but no matter how many times she submitted to Gerard or governed Alain, nothing seemed to change.

Her father's fortune continued to slip away in summonses from the king, extra taxes, small disasters to the house. Her parents sought their comfort in elderberry wine and madness, leaving Mira to run the much-diminished household with no advice.

Summer had passed and turned to autumn, and still a space in her soul remained empty and bleak. She began to despair of ever saving her parents or ridding herself of the fairy's cursed gift. Her two lovers might fulfill her body, but it wasn't enough.

"It's not enough," she said aloud to the last nodding flowers in their beds.

The flowers didn't reply, though the wind tossed their heads and ruffled their petals as prettily as if they were the dresses of innocent maidens. Mira hadn't been innocent for the passing of several moons, and she wept now for that lost innocence and the life she should have had. She sank onto her knees in the browning grass and fragrant earth and buried her face in her hands.

"My lady, what ails you?"

Mira lifted her head at Alain's low voice. She wiped her face as he crouched beside her to cradle her. He took a fine linen handkerchief from his pocket and dried her tears, and not for the first time, Mira realized Alain was no common soldier. He had wealth of his own, and status. Under other circumstances he might even have been of a high enough class to court her properly.

"If not for the curse," she bit out through a fresh veil of tears.

Alain didn't ask her to elaborate. Instead he bent his mouth to hers and kissed her through the salty wetness. His tongue slipped between her lips until she opened her mouth.

As always, that gentle touch set her body aflame with desire, but Mira struggled this time against the pleasure coursing through her. It would be fleeting, that ecstasy, and leave her with naught in the end.

"What can I do to please you?" Alain asked and cupped her face in his hands. "Only tell me and I'll do it."

Mira shook her head. "If you could do it, Alain, you'd have done so already."

All he could do was kiss her, which he did, and touch her, which he did as well. His hands slid up beneath her skirts and found her bare and ready for him, as she always was. Mira muttered a curse under her breath when his fingers stroked her pearl and the first spasms of climax began building inside her. It was so easy to give in to her body's longings. Nearly impossible, in fact, to refuse them. Alain brought her to the edge of orgasm with only a few practiced strokes, and when he slid a finger inside her to stroke from the inside as well, Mira shuddered and tossed her head back with a sigh.

"Well, well. What a pretty sight."

Mira bit down on the strangled cry seeking escape from her throat and looked up. Gerard stood watching them, an unreadable expression on his handsome face. His lips tilted, finally, when Alain's stroking hand tipped Mira into a helpless rush of orgasm that jerked her entire body. She didn't look away from Gerard's eyes the entire time.

Though she had made no secret of the fact both men shared her bed and her body, none of them had ever mentioned it aloud. She'd wondered privately if Gerard and Alain had worked out some sort of system so each could have their turn with her, for they'd never overlapped or intruded upon the other until now.

"Alain," Gerard said in the voice that made Mira shudder anew with fresh longing. "Have you pleased our lady?"

Alain withdrew his fingers from Mira's center and slid them along his lips. "I think so, Gerard. But only just once, so far."

Gerard's lips skinned back from his teeth in a grin so feral and frightening Mira let out a startled squeak. "We'll have to remedy that, won't we?"

They meant to take her at the same time, she saw, and her heart threatened to fly entirely out of her chest, so fiercely did it pound. She'd experienced every intimacy a woman and man could share with both men in front of her, but the thought of them both taking her, both touching her…both fucking her! She shook at the thought.

"What do you suggest?" Alain asked and pinned her with his gaze.

Gerard came up behind him and cupped the back of Alain's neck in a gesture so intimate Mira's breath lodged in her throat.

She'd known the men were close, and had oft wondered at their friendship, but the way Gerard touched Alain gave proof to what had only been a thought. They were lovers, too.

She'd heard of men who preferred the company of their own sex, yet she knew both of these men to be fervent and skilled lovers. Gerard's smile grew broader at what must have been a puzzled look upon her face. Alain reached to stroke her cheek, perhaps in reassurance.

"We only want to please you," Alain said.

Gerard nodded and crooked his finger to her. So accustomed to obeying him had she become, Mira stepped at once toward him. Gerard kissed her as skillfully but with less tenderness than Alain. When he probed without warning between her thighs, she cried out. Her knees sagged a little, but Alain caught her.

"We will take care of you, my lady," he said. "Don't fear."

"I'm not afraid." Mira wet her lips. Something kindled deep within her. "I've been waiting for this."

"Take off your gown," Gerard ordered.

Mira didn't hesitate, though the garden was bright with sunshine and would provide no shadow to hide her nakedness from the eyes of anyone passing. Gerard had commanded it, and so she did it, her nipples already peaked and throbbing and her sex dewed. She tugged open the laces of her gown and dropped the material to the ground, then stepped out of it.

"She is so beautiful, Gerard."

"She is, indeed, brother of my heart. She is indeed. I want you to get on your knees for her and pleasure her with your tongue."

Alain ducked his head in acquiescence and Mira parted her legs to allow him access. His tongue, hot and sleek, dove straight to her center and licked and swirled on her until her hips began to rock. She kept her balance with one hand on Alain's shoulder, but the other drifted from breast to breast, pinching her nipples as Gerard watched, his eyes gleaming.

The front of his breeches tented and he pulled the laces free to push them down over his strong, muscled thighs. His shirt came off over his head until he stood as naked as she. The sun was kind to him, casting him in glittering rays of gold, as if he'd been covered in gilt.

Alain still knelt between her legs, his midnight-black hair streaming over his shoulders. Mira climaxed under his tongue as Gerard watched. Alain kissed her and drew back as Gerard came forward to claim her mouth. When he pulled away, Alain had stripped as well.

Side by side, their differences only proved how well-matched they were. Dark and light.

"Key and lock," Mira said aloud. "Both of you."

"And you the door that makes us worth our function," Alain said as though teasing, but the instant he spoke the words Mira knew them as truth.

"Get on that bench," Gerard told her. "Alain is going to make love to you now."

"Oh, yes," she breathed and settled herself at once onto the carved wooden bench overlooking her favorite flowerbed. Far from being too hard or uncomfortable against her bare skin, the smooth, sun-warmed wood caressed her as she lay back and opened her legs for Alain.

He slid inside her with ease, both of them groaning when he sank to the hilt. He paused before thrusting, but when he began his motions were slow and steady. The bench was high enough off the ground that he could stand, knees slightly bent, to press into her. His hands gripped her hips as he thrust, and when Mira cried out one of them left her curves to stroke her clitoris in time to his thrusts.

The pleasure swept over her in waves so strong they brought tears to her eyes. Alain moved inside her as Mira blinked away the blur and murmured words of encouragement...and love.

It was love, she realized with a wonder even the mind-fuzzing pleasure couldn't conceal. She loved Alain for his tenderness and gallantry, and her orgasm swept over her as she cried the words over and over.

Alain shouted out his reply as his hips rocked inside her and slowed. They stared into each other's eyes, smiling, and Mira only looked away when she saw Gerard appear over Alain's shoulder.

"I love you, too, Gerard," she said and gave a low cry as Alain's thrust began another surge of climax building inside her. She loved Gerard for his command and discipline of her.

Each of them gave her something different, something she'd craved without knowing it. She loved them both, and at last understood how to break the curse.

Gerard and Alain seemed to have come to the same realization as Mira, for Gerard again cupped the back of Alain's neck with one large hand. Watching the men kiss sent a thrill through Mira unlike any other she'd experienced. It would have been easy to fear their fondness for each other, to worry she'd have no place with them, but Alain had said she was the door and now, more than ever, Mira felt it.

Gerard kissed Alain but briefly, for Alain still thrust ever so slowly in and out of Mira. Gerard moved behind Alain. His hands gripped Alain's hips, and in a moment Mira felt the added pressure of Gerard's thrust inside Alain. The two men moved in perfect tandem, in and out. Alain cried out, his fingers on Mira's clit pausing their circling, and it was the hesitation in the stimulation that sent her over the edge once more.

Together, the three of them fucked. Together, they made love. And when Gerard cried out first her name and then Alain's, and Alain shuddered and grunted with his climax, Mira tipped once again into a spiral of ecstasy so great all she could do was let it sweep her away nearly to oblivion.

When they had untangled themselves from her and from each other, Mira kissed and embraced the two men who'd come through her garden gate and changed her life forever. One fair, the other dark. Gilt and midnight, her own dual nature split into two lovers, each providing the final piece of what she needed to love.

More than that.

Each what she needed to be complete.

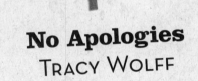

No Apologies

TRACY WOLFF

CHAPTER ONE

HE WAS STARING AT HER. THOUGH SHE DIDN'T look—why ruin the game so soon—she felt the heat of his dark chocolate gaze cruising down her neck to her partially bare breasts and beyond, taking in every detail of her new dress and the body that lay beneath it. She'd thought of him when she'd chosen the red silk. Imagined his expression the first time he saw her in it and the unbelievable pleasure she would feel as he slowly peeled her out of it.

He shifted in his seat and a shiver of pure liquid lust shot through her at the simple movement, though she caught it only out of the corner of her eye. She shouldn't be this attuned to him—it just wasn't normal, no matter what wicked, wonderful things she'd let him do to her body for the last three months. And, she admitted, she'd let him do a lot. She'd given him everything he asked for and more; so much more that it disturbed her sometimes.

She didn't know how to deal with this…obsession. Annalise cringed at the word, but could think of nothing else to describe the craving she had for Gabe every moment of every day. No one else could satisfy it, no matter how hard she'd tried to find someone who could. And God, how she tried—every chance she got. Nearly every night he wasn't with her she made sure she was flat on her back beneath someone else. A momentary diversion, a last-ditch effort to stop the need he built so explosively, and effortlessly, within her.

She refused to turn out like her mother—her beautiful, youthful, completely insane mother. Living with one man while chasing after another, changing marriages like underwear—until her life was nothing but one long nervous breakdown. No thank you. Been there, seen that.

Yet her feelings for Gabe remained more powerful than she liked. Obsession. Need. The words whispered through her until all she could think about, all she could feel, was Gabe.

The distance between their tables was negligible in the sleepy little restaurant. He sat halfway across the room, immersed in a business discussion of stocks and commodities and so many other things she couldn't care less about, but Annalise felt each of his glances like a caress.

Though she refused to look up from the menu she was oh so carelessly perusing, his pull battered her defenses. Enveloped her until she was wet and aching and ready to let him fuck her right there in the middle of Emilio's exclusive dining room. Yet, when she'd risked a glance at him earlier, he'd looked completely unruffled. How could he turn her into a raving, sex-crazed lunatic and still manage to stay so untouched?

Fuck it. She reached for her wine, took a healthy sip. Two could play his game. After all, she'd been doing it for more years and with more men than she could count. She had to remember that Gabe was just one more.

Deliberately she uncrossed her silk-clad legs, one slow inch at a time. Leaning back in her chair slightly, she let her knees fall open—nothing too graphic in dear Emilio's little restaurant—just enough to reveal a smooth expanse of leg and a hint of the shadow near the apex of her thighs.

She used one slender finger to toy with her water glass—a careless slide around the rim, a little dip into the cool water, an absentminded skim across red lips. She studied her menu—though she knew it by heart and he knew she did.

But it gave her an excuse to ignore him as his eyes forged a blazing path up the long legs he loved to kiss. Legs made even longer by the Jimmy Choos with the five-inch heels she had just spent way too much of her last paycheck on. But the second she'd seen them it had been love at first sight.

Annalise couldn't help grinning. What did it say about her that she had a more emotional and lasting relationship with her shoes than she did with any man? Even Gabe.

Smart, she decided as she glanced down at the sparkly crimson miracles, admiring the sheer beauty and craftsmanship that had gone into her most recent purchase. Investing in her shoes instead of a man definitely made her smarter than so many of the women she competed with on the dating scene.

She glanced up as her waiter approached. "Can I get you another chardonnay, Annalise?" Angelo asked, laying a familiar hand on her shoulder and leaning down to speak quietly in her ear.

Taking the last sip, she handed him her glass with a flourish. "You bet, sugar. But just one more—I'm driving."

He glanced across the restaurant. "Gabe's busy tonight, huh?"

"Oh yeah. You know Gabe and his one-track mind." Though

she was doing her best to distract him. Leaning into Angelo, she gave a breathy laugh and laid a well-manicured hand on his forearm.

He nodded, his blue eyes darkening as she stroked him through the thin fabric of his suit. "If he's busy for the rest of the night, I get off at ten-thirty." His hand slid from her shoulder to the small of her back.

Annalise grinned up at him——she couldn't help it, he was just so irrepressible. And one of her favorite fuck buddies for just that reason. "It's been a while, hasn't it?" she murmured, turning in to him so that her breasts brushed against his arm.

"Too long," he answered, his voice deepening as her nipple hardened against his muscular bicep. Gabe and his hot stare had her in such a state of arousal that just that one quick brush against Angelo had her nipples standing at attention.

But she had bigger plans and, with a sigh of regret, she eased back from him. "I've got something going tonight, sugar. But if you're free on Monday…"

His grin was frankly sensual. "I'll call you."

"You do that." She gave him a slow smile and a wink before letting her hand drop, oh so leisurely, from his arm. "And I'll take the pasta primavera whenever you get a chance."

"You got it." After an intimate shoulder squeeze, he headed toward the kitchen, a noticeable spring in his step.

Annalise grinned before she could help herself. Men were just too easy. Or at least, most men were. She spent a minute watching Angelo walk away, giving both Gabe and herself a chance to process the interaction.

Not that Gabe really needed much time to process, she mused. His fury was a living entity, crossing the space between them and skewering her without a word. She was playing with fire and she knew it—but the pleasurable pain that came with the burn made the game impossible to resist.

Besides, Gabe's possessive nature was beginning to grate. She'd made it abundantly clear before they'd gotten together—and in the months since—that they weren't exclusive. They weren't serious. And they certainly weren't emotionally involved. She didn't do emotions and hadn't for eight long years. And Gabe had agreed when she'd laid out the rules.

Agreed, hell, he'd been right there with her—looking for a good time with no strings attached. It's what had made them so perfect for each other. He knew she had guys on the side—she let things slip every once in a while, sometimes refused to see him because she already had a date, occasionally answered calls from other men when she was out with him. Just little clues, enough to make sure he knew that she wasn't harboring any happily-ever-after fantasies like so many of the other women in his life. And he definitely had other women—she wasn't naive enough to think that he didn't. Nor did it bother her—why should it when he always had more than enough left to give her what she wanted?

Refusing to be a coward—she'd done nothing wrong, after all—Annalise slowly lifted her head and let her blue eyes meet his nearly black ones across the dining room. Sparks leapt between them, as they had every day since they'd first laid eyes on each other three months before.

She'd been having dinner with some friends at a trendy La Jolla restaurant and he'd been involved in yet another business meeting. She'd brushed past his table on her way to the ladies' room and had fallen instantly in lust. Not that any sane woman could blame her. The man was yummy—with a capital *Y*. Beautiful mocha skin covering incredible muscles. Dark, sexy eyes that promised more pleasure than it should be possible to feel. And those strong, work-roughened hands that had delivered on all the promises his eyes had made and many more to boot.

They'd spent the first two days of their acquaintance in his bed, and she'd come so many times in the first twenty-four hours that she'd lost count some time after number twelve. Much of their subsequent acquaintance had been spent in bed as well—at his place and hers.

Taking a long, cool drink of water, she smiled sassily at him. Tried to appear unaffected by the rage sizzling—hot and dangerous—in his eyes. It was setting fire to the very air around them until she felt like she could barely breathe, the oxygen trembling in her suddenly shaky lungs. Anger, possession, lust—and other emotions she couldn't begin to name—shot across the room from him to her. Her nipples—already pressed against the thin silk of her dress—tightened to the point of pain. She knew he could see them, but she was too far gone to care. It took all her control not to spread her legs and beg for it.

But she refused to back down—even if the prize was the hot and satisfying sex he was the absolute best at providing. Besides, they'd get there eventually. The attraction between them wouldn't allow anything less.

Leaning back in her chair, Annalise let her head drop back and ran her hands through her long black hair. The action thrust her full breasts forward, making her erect nipples even more obvious. She stretched, a long, feline movement that inched her dress farther up her thighs and revealed the lace tops of her thigh highs and the smooth, pale skin above them.

Angelo let out a long, low whistle as he dropped off her second glass of wine. "You'll have him whimpering in a second, babe," he whispered in her ear. But a searing look from Gabe had him hightailing it back into the kitchen before she could answer.

Need shivered through her—hot, aching, alive—and she pushed away from the table before she lost it completely. Grabbing her skinny purse with one hand, she ran the thumb from her other hand over an aroused nipple. Once, twice, in plain view of anyone who cared to look. She didn't care who else saw as long as Gabe was watching.

As she turned toward the bathroom, the heat skating up her spine assured her that he was indeed watching her instead of concentrating on whatever his clients were saying. She wasn't the least bit sorry.

CHAPTER TWO

AS ANNALISE CLOSED THE RESTROOM DOOR BEHIND her—Emilio's had one of those big private bathrooms—she was thankful it was at the end of a hallway. It saved them from looking too obvious if Gabe chose to follow her. She laughed before she could stop herself. Like he had a choice.

Killing time, she reached into her clutch for her favorite lipstick. Fuck Me Red, she reflected as she slicked the sassy gold tube over her lips. The makers had labeled it Valentine Red, but Annalise liked her name better.

She had no use for valentines. A good fuck, on the other hand, was just about her favorite thing.

After dropping the lipstick into her purse, she stepped back to get a good look in the full-length mirror to the side of the sink. Red dress, red shoes, red lips. Maybe she should make red her signature color, she mused, her mind shooting back to the heroine's red gown in the drippy movie Kate and Iris had talked her into watching the night before. She sneered, refusing to remember the sympathetic tears that had sprung to her eyes before she could stop them. She'd batted them away before her best friends could see them——she never would have lived down the chink in the harder-than-diamonds aura she'd spent the last eight years of her life cultivating.

But the red dress did look hot, she admitted. It brought out the spark in her blue eyes, showed off the natural shine of her long dark hair. And it looked great against her pale skin. Flashy without being slutty; eye-catching without bringing down the house. Or the beasts, she admitted as she turned left and right, checking out her look from every angle. She'd run into her share of animals on the San Diego dating scene in the last few years and while she was a good-time girl, she drew the line at partying with swine. What smart girl didn't?

She glanced down and the sequins on her Jimmy Choos winked up at her. God, she loved these shoes. She'd bought them for Gabe——he loved the way she looked naked except for a pair of stilettos. He loved even more the way she wrapped her legs around him and dug the heels into his ass. Just enough to pinch——a little pain to sharpen the pleasure. Her favorite kind.

Plus, he towered over her very respectable five-foot-seven-inch frame——the heels made it just a little easier for him to fuck her in unusual places. Like restaurant bathrooms, she smirked to herself.

Suddenly the door crashed open, hitting the wall with a loud bang she refused to react to. Instead, she let her slightly mocking gaze meet Gabe's infuriated one in the bathroom mirror.

"What the fuck are you playing at?" Gabe demanded. He was enraged——she glanced downward——and hard enough to pound nails through concrete. Certainly hard enough to pound on her for a while. She grinned despite the menace fairly dripping off him, fighting the urge to lick her lips in anticipation.

"Hey, lover. What happened to your clients?" She kept her voice low and sassy, just the way he liked it best.

"Discussing my proposal." His eyes narrowed dangerously as he studied her. "I decided to give them a few minutes alone."

She nodded sagely, her reflection mocking him. "Smart move."

"Now answer my question," he all but snarled, grabbing her arm and spinning her to face him.

Annalise shrugged, giving him a look brimming with mischievous innocence. "No game. Just a simple pasta dinner." And an overwhelming need to see him, not that she'd ever admit it.

It absolutely killed her that she'd wanted to see him so badly that she'd crashed his business dinner to do it. When had he stopped being just a guy she liked to screw and become a guy she couldn't get through a week without?

"Bullshit," he sneered as he slammed her back against the mirror. She could feel his cock—long and thick and hard—pressed against her mons and she fought the urge to spread her legs and ride him. It wasn't time yet. "You've been playing with fire since the moment you walked in."

She shrugged. "Well, I do like the burn."

With a sound that was part angry and part turned-on, he leaned into her until every inch of him was touching her from shoulder to thigh. He spread her legs with one careless push of her knee and settled between her thighs. Where she'd wanted him all along.

And then his mouth found hers. Hot, hard, shockingly possessive. Reckless where he was normally careful. Violent where he was normally tender. But tenderness wasn't what she wanted or needed tonight. Right now, she needed to feel the burn.

Wrapping her arms around Gabe's neck, she pulled him closer even as she lifted herself toward him. The mirror was cold against her partially-bare back, but Gabe was scorching hot—the combination of two such different sensations excited her to a fever pitch before they'd even started.

Opening her mouth under his onslaught, she let him devour her with his lips, his tongue, his teeth. Let him feed on her as if he would never get enough. She wanted to surrender everything she had to that mouth, everything she was.

He pressed deeper and deeper, demanded more and more. Her head whirled, her knees trembled—and Annalise realized suddenly, as his tongue raided every corner of her mouth, that it would never be enough. This would never be enough. She would die wanting this man inside of her. The realization was as unexpected as it was devastating.

"Don't do it again," he growled, his hands cupping her breasts while he squeezed her nipples between his thumbs and index fingers. Hard.

She wanted to whimper but pride wouldn't allow it. Even so, she had to bite the inside of her lip to keep from crying out when he began to move, his hot cock thrusting between her legs.

"Do what?" Her voice was shakier than she liked.

His fingers tightened on her nipple, bringing her to the very edge of madness. "Play me against another guy like that."

She arched her back, pressing her nipple more firmly into

his hand. "Is that what I was doing?" She sounded breathless but was too far gone to care.

"You knew exactly what you were doing." His fingers tightened punishingly, giving her the pleasure-pain she so desperately craved. And then she was melting, burning, so wet and creamy she didn't know how long she'd last.

Letting her head fall back, Annalise took as much of the insidious pleasure as she could handle without coming. Then she pushed him away, using every ounce of strength she possessed to get the job done. Gabe was a brick wall, hard and heavily muscled, but he let her shove him back.

He stood there, chest heaving, cock twitching, eyes blazing with a fury and lust that were intertwined and suddenly she knew. The game wasn't over. It would never be over.

She took a deep, steadying breath. Maybe she was caught by these riotous emotions, this incredible, overwhelming lust for him that dominated every moment of her every day. But two could play by the rules Gabe was so brutally establishing.

Reaching down, she pressed a hand firmly against Gabe's beautifully aroused cock. He thrust himself into her fingers over and over again, and she grinned. Oh, yeah—he needed this as much as she did. Maybe more. She continued stroking him through the fine silk of his trousers. She loved how big he was, how long and thick and desperate he was for her. Before she was done, he would be begging to be inside of her.

Turning, he pulled her into his arms as he lowered his mouth to her ear. "Let's go find the car," he murmured.

"The car?" she asked, pretending ignorance as she reached between his legs and cupped his balls in her hands, her fingers slowly massaging him. She knew her eyes were almost as glazed as his, but she couldn't help it. Having this big, strong man at her mercy was the biggest turn-on she'd ever had.

"I've got to be inside you, Annalise. Soon."

She licked her lips even as she wrapped her arms around his neck and pressed against him. "Here. Now."

"Right now?" His cock jumped against her stomach, growing harder and thicker——though she would never have imagined it possible.

She could tell he wanted to protest, to tell her all the reasons why sex in this bathroom with a restaurant full of people outside was a very bad idea. But her words had put a picture in his brain——just as she had intended——and his unruly cock was more than willing to accommodate her. Thank God.

She kept her triumph to herself as she nodded and pulled him back against her. "Right now." She opened his belt and unbuttoned his pants. She gasped when his cock sprang free of the confining clothes——he was always ready to go, but tonight he seemed larger than usual.

Annalise grinned as she dropped to her knees. Her own personal plaything——huge and hot and dying to be inside any part of her body it could reach. She shivered as her own arousal quickly spiraled out of control. What else could a girl ask for?

Leaning forward, she delivered one long, leisurely lick—— from the base of his cock to the very tip. He shuddered and stiffened against her, his hands suddenly fisting in her hair. Curling her tongue in, she used the underside to stroke him on the torturously slow return journey.

"Annalise." His voice was hoarse, strangled, the hands in her hair tightening almost to the point of pain. But she didn't stop, couldn't stop. She wanted him to come, to flood every part of her until she no longer felt so alone.

Before he could protest, she took him in her mouth. He was so huge that she struggled for a moment until, with a sigh, she let her throat relax and his cock slid deep—all the way to the base.

"Fuck, Annalise." The words were whispered, urgent, and sent a shot of pure molten heat directly through her cunt. She was already wet, her thighs slippery with desire, and her muscles were clenching rhythmically—desperate for Gabe's cock to slide inside and put out the fire that was rapidly burning out of control.

His hands in her hair tightened even more and the almost pleasurable sting turned her on as nothing ever had. Or maybe it was the situation—fury mixed with passion. One hell of a potent aphrodisiac.

She was barely aware of her own hand creeping between her thighs in a desperate attempt to stem the ache. She pressed her fingers against her clit—just to get a little relief as she didn't want to come yet—but her hips moved of their own volition, arching and twisting against her hand as blinding pleasure shot through her.

Her other hand slid around to cup his ass, pressing his throbbing cock even more deeply down her throat. She sucked firmly and rhythmically while her tongue stroked every inch of him it could reach. She loved how his breath hitched, how his ass tightened, how curses slipped, softly but unchecked, from his lips as he thrust against her again and again. He was usually such a gentleman that seeing him with the civilized veneer ripped away was a total turn-on. Even more so was knowing that she was the one who had made him lose it so completely.

Suddenly, he stopped, tried desperately to pull away. "Annalise, stop. I'm going to—"

She grabbed him with both hands, pulling him deeper as she hummed low in her throat. No way was she giving up her prize this close to the finish line.

"Fuck!" He came, flooding her, his cum shooting in spurts into her mouth, down her throat. And still she didn't stop, intent on sucking him dry and into firm arousal again. After all, she wasn't close to finished with him yet and they still had a few minutes before his clients missed him. The way she was feeling, thirty seconds was about all she'd need.

"Baby, stop," he groaned softly until she pressed her fingers on a spot just behind his balls. God bless the Internet and all the information a girl could find on it—he hardened instantly, thrusting helplessly against her. "Goddamn, how'd you do that?"

She licked her lips and shot him a sultry look. "A girl's got to have her secrets."

He eyed her grimly. "And you certainly have yours."

Grinning, she released him slowly and let him pull her to her feet. "My turn."

The look he shot her was wicked, as were the fingers he slid slowly over her incredibly tight nipples. He squeezed, hard, and she gasped, her back arching to give him better access.

"Touch me." Annalise guided his hand under her skirt and up to her hot, wet folds.

His fingers found her, stroked her clit. "You're not wearing any—"

"Nope. Just a pair of thigh highs and a spritz of Paradise." She grinned despite her growing arousal. "No pun intended."

His black-magic eyes darkened even more. "You sat there and

let that idiot touch you, knowing you had nothing beneath this dress?"

She raised an eyebrow. "Is that a problem?" She strove to sound normal when what she really wanted to do was beg him to fuck her, to fill her, to give her what no one else had been able to.

"Damn right it is," he growled as he thrust one long, thick finger into her. Followed it with a second. "You belong to me."

She moaned low in her throat, arched her hips and pulled him deeper inside of her. "I belong to myself. Now fuck me before I explode."

His answering laugh was low, aroused, and more than a little bit threatening as her words speared through him and brought his excitement back up to fever pitch. "I don't think so. You're done calling the shots." He thrust another finger into her, roughly, and she saw stars. The walls of her vagina clenched tightly around him and a series of small explosions started deep inside her. He ground the heel of his hand against her clit while his fingers moved in her.

She moaned, her head falling back even as her legs opened to give him better access. She knew he was watching her, assessing every expression flitting across her face. But as his other hand squeezed her nipple just to the point of pain, she didn't care.

One more quick press of his hand against her clit and she was coming, biting desperately on her bottom lip to keep from screaming as wave after wave of mind-numbing, bone-jarring pleasure swept through her.

He groaned as she clenched around him and he used those talented fingers of his to take her higher and higher. The pleasure went on and on—a liquid pull from her tits to her cunt that electrified everything in its path.

When the contractions finally began to subside, he pulled out of her with a groan. She whimpered, her hips moving desperately against him until he slipped his hands under her ass and lifted her against the wall. His cock pressed urgently against her, wetness already leaking from its head.

"Wait," she cried breathlessly, reaching into the very top of her stocking and pulling out a condom. "You need this."

He lifted an eyebrow. "Always prepared," he murmured.

"Always," she answered, her hips moving urgently against him.

"But was it for me?" He pulled back, moving his cock away from her though his strong hands kept her suspended against the wall. "Did you put that condom there for me, Annalise?" He traced a finger over her overstimulated nipples. "Or would any guy do? As long as he had a dick?"

She met his eyes, suddenly as furious as she was aroused. "Get over yourself, Gabe."

He lifted an imperious eyebrow. "I am over myself. The question is, are you?" He bent down and roughly took her nipple in his mouth. His teeth closed around her and she screamed, arching wildly off the wall, desperate for him.

"Don't do this," she whimpered as he held himself away from her, their only points of contact the hand holding her against the wall and his teeth nipping sharply at her breast.

"You started it, baby. I'm only finishing it." His tongue soothed the little hurts his teeth had inflicted.

"Then finish it!" she shrieked, grabbing his tightly shorn curls with both hands and trying desperately to pull his mouth to hers. He avoided her, refusing to give her what she wanted.

"Tell me," he demanded as he shoved two long fingers into her.

"No." She moved against his hand. She was so close——

He pulled out abruptly. "No!" she wailed, too far gone to care that she was practically begging.

"Tell me." His voice was hoarse with restraint, but she could see the resolve in his dark chocolate eyes. She would get nothing from him without the truth.

"It was for you." She pushed her hips out from the wall, blindly, desperately seeking him. "I put it there for you. I came to Emilio's looking for you." She glared at him, more furious and aroused than she'd ever been in her life. "Are you satisfied?"

"Not yet," he grunted, yanking the condom from her non-resistant fingers and making short work of rolling it on. Then, with one hard thrust, he buried himself to the hilt. She went off like a firecracker, would have screamed the place down if he hadn't found her lips with his own.

"Fuck, Annalise. You're wicked." Again and again he pounded into her willing body.

"I know." She pushed against him. "Harder, Gabe. Please. Harder."

He glanced in the mirror and she turned her head to do the same, loving the picture they made. Her long, pale legs were locked around his waist. Her head was thrown back, her nipple in his mouth. His dark head and mocha-colored skin made a beautiful contrast to the fair skin of her breasts. One of her hands was wrapped around his shoulders while the other slipped between them to stroke her clit as she pleaded with him for more. He gave her what she wanted, thrusting harder and deeper than he ever had before and her eyes closed, the visual stimulation suddenly too much along with everything else.

As Gabe filled her completely, as he pounded into her as hard and as fast as possible. it came to her. She could love this man—if she wasn't careful, if she didn't take a few steps back, if she didn't watch herself, she could fall for him. Hard. She, Annalise Gallagher, queen of the love 'em and leave 'em crowd, was on the verge of falling head over heels.

The shock of the realization, the utter horror of it, nearly cooled the fire raging inside of her. But Gabe sensed her sudden withdrawal and, with a stroke of his finger and a shift of his hips, brought her right back to crisis point.

Deliberately she clenched her muscles around him, massaging him even as he pounded into her. "Annalise," he gasped, his teeth sinking into her shoulder, holding her in place like an animal claiming its mate. "I can't last much—"

The pleasure-pain of the bite was all it took to send her over the edge. With a low keening cry she shattered, her muscles milking him until he too let go of his control and came apart in her arms.

CHAPTER THREE

WHEN THE LAST SHUDDERS PASSED, ANNALISE RESTED her forehead against Gabe's. Mission accomplished. She'd set out to remind him of what he was missing without admitting how much she'd missed him, and she'd done one hell of a job if she did say so herself. Not that it had been exactly difficult. He was the most passionate, responsive man she'd ever known. What she hadn't expected was the strong emotional response he pulled from her more and more often lately. But she could handle her feelings—would handle them—like she always had. By ignoring them until they went away.

He slid her slowly down his body until her Jimmy Choos hit the tile floor. With a cocky grin he stepped back and disposed of the condom before fixing his pants. Ignoring him, she pulled her dress down and turned toward the mirror to study her reflection. She felt branded, exposed, her emotions completely bare for his scrutiny. What was it about this man that tore her open? How did he touch a heart she'd spent years forgetting she even had?

Her own vulnerability hit her and suddenly she wanted to be anywhere but where she was.

Gabe straightened the back of her dress. "This shouldn't take much longer." He glanced at his watch. "I'll meet you at your place in about an hour."

She shrugged carelessly, refusing to let him see how confused she felt. "If something better doesn't come along." There was no one better than Gabe, but she'd burn in hell before she let him know it. It never paid to let a guy get too cocky—pun totally intended—and right now, Gabe looked about as cocky as a man could get.

His eyes darkened at her words, anger still sizzling right below the surface. But she ignored the warning sign—something reckless had grabbed ahold of her, making her push at him harder than usual, making her flex her claws. Demanding that she prove she was still a badass, despite the emotions tying her stomach in knots.

Maybe it was that damn movie and the chink it had put in her normally impenetrable armor or maybe it was this strange tenderness for Gabe that wouldn't go away. Whatever it was, it wouldn't let her back down—even as Gabe's hands tightened threateningly on her upper arms.

"I'll be at your place in ninety minutes—tops. Be there."

"Oooh. I just love a man who beats his chest," she murmured, brushing a careless hand over his nipple. "Or anything else for that matter."

"You don't want to push me on this, Annalise."

Their eyes met and locked, the power struggle that had been in evidence from their very first meeting rearing its ugly head again. Part of her wanted to back down, to give just a little. But she had no give in her—Michael, the lying, cheating, scumsucking bastard—had ripped it out of her eight long years before.

"And you don't want to push me."

His grin was mocking. "Try me."

He turned and left before she could think of a comeback. Goddammit.

Furious, frustrated, and completely unsure of what to do next, Annalise headed back to her table. Once there, she asked Angelo to box up the meal that had arrived in her absence. Tossing a couple of twenties on the table, she gathered up her wrap and doggie bag and headed for the car, making sure not to glance in Gabe's direction even once. But she felt his eyes on her anyway.

Outside, she took a few deep breaths and leaned a steadying hand against the old brick building that housed Emilio's. What had she gotten herself into? Falling for another highly sexual, dominant guy? One who drew women's eyes wherever he went? How could she have done this when she'd sworn after Michael that she'd never give another man that kind of power over her? How could she have not learned from her mistakes?

"Hey, Annalise, you okay?"

She glanced over to see a couple of the valet-parking attendants looking at her with concern. She must be in worse shape than she thought. Fishing in her bag for her valet ticket, she answered, "Just fine, boys." She handed her ticket to the tall, blond one. "You guys look swamped." She nodded toward the full parking lot.

"Never too busy for you," he answered with a grin as he took the ticket, letting his hand linger on her own just a little longer than necessary. She returned his smile and added a wink. Mickey was a cutie and she remembered fondly a couple of hours she'd spent on top of him late last spring. He'd been a young, but enthusiastic lover.

Though she was still sticky from Gabe, for a split second she thought of taking Mickey up on his unspoken offer. Just to prove to Gabe that he didn't have any power over what or who she did. Just to prove the same thing to herself.

But she wasn't in the habit of fucking men to make a point— even to herself. She fucked them for a good time. Sometimes just for a few moments of blessed oblivion. But she'd never been the kind to cut her nose off to spite her face.

So it was with a sigh of regret that she climbed into her two-seater, electric-blue BMW. She waved to the boys and slowly pulled Fancy Pants into traffic.

The girls laughed at her for naming her car, something they thought she should have outgrown by the ripe old age of thirty-four. But for years, her only salvation had been whatever car she was driving. When things got too tough, she could grab the keys and simply fly away for a while.

Fancy Pants was a far cry from the rusty old Chevy she used to drive, but no less a friend for all her dressed-up parts. She had come a long way from the one-bedroom walk-up she used to share with Michael. She shied away from the memories— eight years wasn't long enough to forget how it had felt to walk in on him and her perennially youthful, pathetically dependent mother getting it on. Annalise snarled despite herself. Could her life have been any more Jerry Springer?

She'd pulled out of the restaurant parking lot with every in-tention of going to the Gaslamp Quarter and partying until two, so it was a surprise when she found herself turning right onto Harbor Drive and heading toward Coronado. But, she supposed, it shouldn't have been. She loved driving along the bay, watching all the tourists with their kids and cameras. She wanted nothing to do with that life, but it was interesting to observe on occasion. Besides, nothing beat the smell of the ocean.

And, she admitted with some difficulty as she took the left onto Harbor Island, she was too wound up to hit the clubs just yet anyway. In the mood she was in, she might end up doing something stupid just to prove a point.

So she drove—for hours—before she ended up at her favorite spot along the ocean, watching waves that had originated thousands of miles away roll in over and over again. Reminding herself how inconsequential her little problems were in the grand scheme of things and that she should be grateful for every day, and everything, that she had. Eight years wasn't so long that she had forgotten what it was like to wake up so emotionally devastated that she couldn't get out of bed until she'd worked out a suicide plan.

Dawn was slowly streaking the sky when she finally made it home. Carrying her precious Jimmy Choos in one hand—the beach had left her feet wet and sandy—she limped up the staircase to her apartment. All she wanted was a long shower and some sleep. She'd call Gabe later, much later, as she wasn't in the mood to have the argument she knew they were due for after she'd deliberately stood him up.

Lost in thought and drooping from exhaustion, she flipped on her apartment light and let out a startled scream. Gabe was stretched out on her sunny yellow sofa, his shoes off and his eyes blazing with anger and something else that looked a lot like disgust.

"What are you doing here?" she demanded. "How did you get in?"

"Iris took pity on me and let me in, after watching me sit in the hall for two hours waiting for you." His eyes were dark and dangerous, his full lips compressed into a thin, grim line. "Where the hell have you been?"

Closing her eyes, Annalise nearly swayed with exhaustion. She didn't have the energy for this, didn't have the strength right now to keep up the party-girl facade she'd spent so damn long cultivating. But when she opened her eyes again, none of the misery she'd combated on the beach showed.

"Out."

"Yeah, I got that impression." He stalked toward her, a gorgeous tiger of a man—all long limbs and careless grace. Intense eyes and bared teeth. A low growl rumbled from his chest, making her eyes widen and her heart beat faster.

Standing her ground in the face of his aggressiveness was one of the hardest things she'd ever done. But Annalise planted her bare feet and refused to budge, even when he got so close that she could feel his breath on her forehead.

"Where have you been, Annalise?" He repeated the question, his voice lower than she'd ever heard it, and a shiver of unease—and God help her, arousal—shot up her spine before she could stop it.

Angry with him, furious with herself, she ignored his unspoken warning. "That's really none of your business. I went out, had some fun and now I'm home and ready to sleep." She gave him her most disdainful look and started past him. She'd almost made it to her bedroom door when he grabbed her wrist and spun her around, pressing her against the living room wall.

His pelvis pushed insistently against hers and his hand rested at the base of her throat. Neither was anywhere close to painful, but the inherent threat was enough to stiffen her spine and harden her voice. "Let me go."

"Did you fuck him?" Those sorcerer's eyes blazed angrily, even while his lips hovered just a hair's breadth above her own.

"What do you care?" she tossed back. "As long as I fuck you too?"

The hand near her throat tightened warningly, though his grip remained painless. "Did you let that fucking waiter touch you? Put his hands on you? Put his cock in you?" His breath was coming in short pants. "Or was it someone else?"

She shoved against him, but it was like trying to push a mountain—his muscles were like granite under her hands. "Let me go!" she demanded loudly, her voice rising despite her best efforts to keep it even.

"Not until you tell me, damn it. Who was it?"

"Gabe—"

He shook her then, not hard enough to do any damage, just enough to get her attention. "Tell me." He was wild, out-of-control, his possessive instincts dangerously aroused.

She wanted to lie because it was easier. Wanted to tell the truth, though he would never believe her. But when she opened her mouth to speak, nothing came out. She shook her head, shrugged, looked down at the thick, cream-colored carpet beneath her feet.

"Damn it, Lissy, just tell me." The rage was gone and in its place was a sad acceptance she'd never seen from him before.

Her resolve broke at the sadness in his voice and at the sound of her nickname on those beloved lips—he was the only man to ever care enough to give her a nickname. Unless "Oh yeah, baby, do it again" counted.

"I was driving, Gabe. Just driving. Sorting some stuff out in my head." She gestured to her sand-covered feet. "I ended up at that spot in Coronado we found a couple of months ago."

He let out a long, shaky breath, his dark skin paling considerably. But those watchful eyes continued to study her for a moment before closing as he sagged in relief. He bent his head, rested it in the curve between her neck and her shoulder, and she was shocked to realize he was trembling.

"Gabe?" Her arms came up and wrapped around him before she could stop herself. "What's wrong, sugar?" Her lips grazed his ear. "Why are you acting like this?"

He shook his head, took a couple of deep, steadying breaths before stepping away from her. "I'm sorry. I shouldn't have…" He gestured at the wall before shoving his hands in his pockets and turning away.

"Shouldn't have what?" she asked. Suddenly the tables were turned and it was she following him around the apartment.

He whirled to face her, somehow even paler than before. "I didn't mean to hurt you. I—" His voice trailed off.

"You didn't." Her voice was clear. "If you had, you wouldn't still be standing here."

Those black-magic eyes studied her for a moment, looking for the woman behind the mask, searching for the soul she didn't know she still had. And then he said, simply, "I love you, Annalise."

SHE STARED AT HIM WIDE-EYED, FEELING LIKE SHE'D just been run over by an eighteen-wheeler. "Gabe—"

"I know." He nodded at her skeptical look. "I really do. I didn't mean to, I did everything I could to avoid it, but it's true. Somehow, despite my worst intentions, I fell in love with you."

Annalise shook her head, backed away. She didn't do love. Not now, not anymore. "I—"

His smile was sad. "I know. I shouldn't have said anything. I never meant to tell you."

"Gabe—" She was beginning to sound like a broken record, but she had no idea what to say. He'd completely blindsided her.

He grabbed his keys off her coffee table before leaning down and brushing a kiss against her cheek. "Get some sleep. I'll call you in a couple of days."

A couple of days? He was going to drop a bombshell like that on her and then leave—for a couple of days? Was he insane?

"Don't go." It was ripped from her just as he turned the doorknob.

Gabe stiffened, then turned to face her. "I don't want or need your pity, Annalise."

"I know." She stared him directly in the eye, her gaze rock-steady though her stomach pitched sickly. "I want you to stay." She reached for him. "Please stay."

He studied her from across the room, his eyes hopeful but his mouth grim. "I don't think that's a good idea until you figure out what you want."

"I don't know what I want. I don't know how I feel." She swallowed. "All I know is that I don't want you to go tonight." She glanced outside at the blossoming daylight. "This morning. Whatever."

"That's more than I expected," he murmured, striding across the room and yanking her into his arms. Then his mouth was devouring hers, his tongue teasing and tasting, thrusting and stroking, until her eyes crossed and her knees turned to jelly. He tasted like he always did—like rain and the ocean and a raging inferno that burned her alive. But he tasted sweet, too. The mixture of the familiar and the new nearly drove her over the edge.

Her hands reached up and tangled in the thin silk of his dress shirt. She needed him inside of her, needed the long moments of oblivion he always provided. Just a little while where she wouldn't have to think.

Her hands slid down his arms to cup his ass as she pressed firmly against him. Gabe moaned low in his throat, his hands pulling her even closer into the shelter of his body.

She loved the feel of him, the hardness of his muscles, the roughness of his hands, the surprising softness of his skin everywhere else. Breaking away from his kiss, her fingers scrambled frantically at the buttons of his shirt.

But he stilled her, his hands finding hers, his thumb stroking the urgency from her fingers. "Let me take care of you this time," he murmured, guiding her slowly backward toward her bedroom.

Tears stung her eyes, but she batted them determinedly away. This was no different than all the other times, she told herself. It was just sex. Just scratching an itch.

But as he lowered her to the bed, she knew better. This was everything she'd run from for eight long years, everything she'd hidden from in the arms of friends and strangers alike. She knew she should protest, that she should push him away. But she simply didn't have the energy to do so. Or the heart. For once, she wanted to let a man make love to her. To love her. Only her.

Gabe stretched out beside her, elbow bent, head resting on his upturned palm as he studied her. Those wonderful eyes had gone completely black, an intense heat burning deep inside of them. His desire was palpable and a shiver of excitement skittered up her spine. She licked her lips, and even she didn't know if she did it to be provocative or because it was suddenly necessary.

"I need you." His voice was soft, seductive. A silken whisper stroking along her skin. A velvet caress igniting every nerve ending in her body. "I need all of you."

"Yes." It was a whisper, as confusion and excitement surged through her with every breath. His face was serious, focused exclusively on her. His body was hard, completely unyielding against the softness of her own. But it was his eyes, so full of hunger and desire and need for her—and her alone— that made her pulse quicken and her inner thighs grow wet. It was that hunger that also began the slow, inexorable task of melting the first of the many layers of ice she'd built around her heart.

He reached out, cupped her breast in his strong hands. Let his thumb run in light, seductive circles over the already aroused nipple. Annalise arched against his hand, increasing the pressure, and she could have sworn she heard electricity crackle around them. That one simple touch seared through her, through veins and muscles and organs until she began to fear spontaneous combustion.

She moaned low in her throat and reached for Gabe, pulling him over her, onto her, wanting to feel every inch of his body pressed against every inch of hers. He stared at her out of eyes burning with need, studied her, watched her, waited for her.

Cupping his face in her hands, she looked deep into his eyes. "Please." She arched her back, spread her legs, tugged at him until his cock was pressed against her. "I need you. Please."

She saw the moment he slipped the restraints he'd placed on himself, saw lust, raw and needy, explode within him at her words. Grasping the front of her dress in his strong hands, he shredded it from neckline to hem with one downward tug. She gasped as the cool air hit her hot body, arching her back, and he took one of her ripe, raspberry-colored nipples in his mouth.

She screamed then, her hips moving restlessly against his, the muscles of her vagina contracting again and again. She wanted more, needed more, but he held her there, pinned by his weight and suckled while her body caught fire. Each swipe of his tongue made her moan, each graze of his teeth took her higher and higher until she could think of nothing but him, desire nothing but his hot possession. Forever.

She was wet and slick, her thighs drenched and her clit aching for his touch. He ground his cock against her, once, twice, and she came—her body going off like a firecracker on the Fourth of July.

He reached a hand to her other breast and squeezed the nipple tightly. The painful pleasure took her higher and she convulsed again, her orgasm going on and on.

And still he wasn't done tormenting her, tasting her, driving her completely mad. His hands tugged at her hair until her mouth met his for one long, passion-drenched kiss. And then he was moving, his lips grazing across her cheek, stopping momentarily to blow on the sensitive spot behind her ear. He turned her onto her back, and stripped the ruined dress from her. Roughly. Deliberately. Then he leaned forward and bit the nape of her neck. And lit her up all over again.

She screamed again, her hands fisting in the bloodred sheets beneath her. "Do it," she begged. "Please, just do it!"

"Do what?" he answered, pressing his cock against her ass as his wicked, wonderful mouth worked its way over her shoulder and down her arm.

She cried out, unable to stop the sound or the sobs of desire that then wracked her body, one after another. She arched against him, helped him settle more firmly between her thighs. He rewarded her with a sharp nibble along her spine while his hand crept around to her clit and began to stroke her firmly.

Every muscle in her body stretched tight and she rode his hand, too far gone to care that she was begging him with every movement she made, every sound she uttered. "Fuck me," she demanded, burying her face in the sheets to stop herself from screaming. "Fuck me, fuck me, fuck me." It was a litany, her new mantra, and she didn't care how desperate she sounded. She *was* desperate. He was going to kill her if he kept this up.

"Where do you want me?" He turned to her side, ran his tongue over her suddenly dry lips. "In your mouth?" he asked, before licking his way to her breasts. "Between your tits?"

She whimpered and bucked against him as her need shot out of control. "Yes," she gasped. "Yes!"

He straddled her, his eyes gleaming. "But I haven't finished listing your choices." He drew first one nipple and then the other into his mouth as his talented fingers rubbed teasingly over her breasts.

He rolled her over, worked his way down her spine one teasing lick at a time. Without warning, his teeth sank into her ass, nipping her before his tongue soothed away the sting. Straddling her, he grabbed a wrist in each hand, spread-eagling her before she knew what was happening, holding her in place while he explored every inch of her back.

"Is this what you want?" His voice was darker, more seductive than usual as he traced the line of her ass teasingly. "Do you want it here?"

He followed the line around until he found her, hotter and wetter than she'd ever been. He pulled her onto her knees and slid his hand under her to get better access to the slick, hidden folds, his fingers running back and forth against her slit over and over again. Dipping inside just enough to make her crazy, rubbing her inner lips just hard enough to have her gasping for breath and pressing back against him.

"This is what you want, isn't it, baby? You want me right here, between your thighs." He thrust one finger inside of her hard, followed it with another, and another. Her inner muscles clutched at the fingers greedily and Annalise screamed at the pleasure he brought her.

"That feels so good," she gasped, moving her hips in rhythm with his questing fingers. "You feel so good."

She looked over her shoulder at Gabe, saw a dark intensity shining in his eyes that she'd never seen before. For a minute he looked wicked, wild and she knew that she should be afraid. But she was too far gone to worry, too aroused to do anything but ride out the unbelievable sensations he drew from her body without any effort at all.

"It's about to feel better," he murmured, shifting so he lay beneath her, her legs on either side of his head.

His tongue—his wicked, wonderful tongue—darted out, caressing her inner folds again and again. Annalise spread her legs wider, seeking something more, something deeper. With a groan, he clutched her ass and spread her legs as wide as possible, thrusting his tongue deep inside her.

She came instantly, screaming and bucking wildly against his mouth. He held her in place, his iron grip unbreakable as he continued to lick and suck her through the first climax and into a second before he relented.

Settling next to him with a low, satisfied moan, she was focused inward as aftershocks of incredible ecstasy continued to rack her body. Sweat gleamed on her brow as she sucked air into her oxygen-deprived lungs and her hips moved restlessly against the bedspread, searching for Gabe.

He was right next to her, smiling, as he reached a hand out to stroke her hair. To toy with the pearl necklace she still wore.

"You didn't give me a chance to take it off when you ripped my dress off me." Her smile was lazy, her voice content even as she reached for him. "Your turn."

"Not yet." He shook his head, his eyes as turbulent and mysterious as the ocean she could see from the balcony of her apartment.

Her hand found his erection and she pumped gently as she ran her thumb back and forth over the tip. "Now." She leaned forward and took him in her mouth, savoring his low groan as much as the feel of him against her lips, in her mouth.

His hands fisted in her hair, anchoring her in place as she slid her tongue up and down the length of him. She glanced up and found him watching her, his hot eyes following her every movement as she slid her lips up and down his cock. She swirled her tongue around him before pausing, deliberately, to flick at the drop of moisture he couldn't hold back.

She tried not to react as he ran a finger lightly down her cheek, treating her as if she was fragile, as if he feared breaking her. Those damn tears sprang to her eyes again and she lowered her lids, refusing to let Gabe see her at her most vulnerable.

Determined to beat back this rising tenderness for him, Annalise took his entire cock in her mouth and encouraged the involuntary thrusting of his hips against her. Reaching beneath him, she grabbed his ass and held him to her as her teeth lightly scraped the underside of his cock.

He nearly shot off the bed, and she relished her ability to turn this strong man on. To turn him inside out and make him forget everything but how much he wanted her. Needed her.

But those were dangerous thoughts, so when he sat up abruptly and flipped her onto her back, she didn't fight him.

Instead she looked into his passion-glazed eyes and licked her lips, savoring the sweet and salty taste of him on her tongue. Sweat was trickling down his forehead and over his chest as he fought for control of his raging body. She loved knowing that she had pushed him right to the limits of his self-control. But she had to know—

"Why did you stop me?" she asked, eyeing the rampant proof of his desire for her.

"When I come, it'll be inside you." His voice was harsh, rusty with need.

"Sounds good to me," she purred, turning behind her to the nightstand and the condoms that rested there.

He took advantage of her turned back, reaching up and unhooking her necklace before she realized it. She turned back, eyebrows raised. "What are you doing?"

His grin was wicked. "I have a better use for these."

"Better use?" As his words sank in, she knew her eyes widened in surprise. "Really? That's not just a myth?"

"Definitely not. Now lay down."

She followed his directions, her eyes both wary and excited as he began arousing her all over again. His lips were everywhere at once—her face, her breasts, the back of her knees, her shoulders, her ankles. Every place he touched caught fire and soon she was thrashing against him, as desperate for him as he seemed to be for her.

Gabe reached a finger between her thighs, tested her readiness. When it came away soaked, he grinned before toying with her for a little longer. "Are you ready?" he asked, rolling the pearls slowly over her breasts and stomach.

Her eyes met his, clung, and she knew he saw the beginnings

of trust there. Taking a deep breath, she tried to relax, to ignore the sudden nervous flutterings in her tummy. She was out of her element, out of control. Uncomfortable doing something she'd never done before with this man who was pushing for everything.

Before Gabe she had thought she'd tried everything once—why then did it surprise her that Gabe was the one showing her something new? It shouldn't, not when he'd already shown her more about who she really was than she'd ever wanted to know.

Taking a deep breath she reached for him, running a hand over the short, tight curls on his scalp. "Yes."

Her eyes met his and clung. As if he sensed her sudden uneasiness, he stopped for a moment and lightly kissed her cheek and the corner of her mouth. "I love you, Annalise."

And then he began slipping the necklace, pearl by pearl, inside of her, murmuring encouragement until only a few remained outside. "How's that feel?" he asked, brushing soft kisses over her abdomen and upper thighs.

Annalise wiggled her hips experimentally, more nervous and more turned on than she'd ever been in her life. The pearls shifted inside of her as she moved and she gasped, awed by the pleasure the simple movement sent shooting through her. "Wow," she answered, looking into Gabe's bold, beautiful eyes.

His grin flashed, dark and dangerous. "Good." And he then thrust a finger inside of her without warning, manipulating the pearls against the walls of her vagina as he did so.

She gasped, arching off the bed as a wave of ecstasy more intense then anything she'd ever felt before rocketed through her. The pearls were everywhere, touching every single spot inside of her. Gabe found her G-spot with his finger and rolled pearl after pearl against it until she screamed with frustrated abandon.

"I can't take it, Gabe. I swear I can't."

His grin was dangerous. "You want me to stop?" His voice was low and teasing, his eyes glazed and sexy.

"Yes." Her hips arched against his hand. "No. Oh God, I don't know. Do something. Do something!" Her hips jerked with each word, her voice growing louder and louder as he continued to torment her.

"How about this?" Gabe leaned down, blew against her clit and Annalise jolted, her hips coming completely off the bed.

"Finish it," she begged. "Please. Don't leave me like this. I can't take it. I can't—" Her hips jerked against him, again and again, as her head thrashed back and forth on the pillows. "Gabe!"

He grinned, watching as she undulated against the sheets, desperate for release. Then he closed his mouth over her clit, sucking until she was at fever pitch. Her hands grasped the sheet greedily, her legs moved restlessly against him, and tears poured, unnoticed, down her cheeks.

She'd never felt anything this intense before, never imagined that pleasure could be like this. Insidious, never-ending, taking her higher with every breath she drew. Orgasm beckoned, the ecstasy so intense that nothing else mattered. She couldn't think, couldn't worry, couldn't control herself at all and she didn't care. All that mattered was the pleasure, and the man giving it to her with every move he made.

Suddenly Gabe reached between her legs and slowly, slowly, began to pull the string of pearls out. One bead at a time, letting each slip against her clit as he did so. She began coming with the third pearl, clutching his hair and screaming his name loud enough to wake half the apartment complex. But he didn't stop—he continued to draw the necklace out slowly, steadily, making sure each bead rubbed both her G-spot and her clit as it came out.

When the last pearl was removed she was still coming, still screaming. He rolled her onto her stomach and pushed into her from behind. Thrusting into her again and again, harder and harder, he rode her through the contractions rhythmically milking his cock. She felt his orgasm approaching and the tension magically built within her again. He twisted his hips, slammed into her at a new and different angle and she shot unexpectedly over the edge again. Then, and only then, did Gabe finally let himself go. He poured every ounce of himself inside her and she couldn't help hoping, praying, that she could give him just a little of herself back.

GABE WAS ASLEEP. HE'D GIVEN HER THE MOST moving sexual experience of her life and now he was sprawled across her bed, snoring. Annalise snorted softly before gently untangling herself from the arm and leg he had draped over her in an effort to keep her in place. Like she'd ever give a man even that much control.

After slipping into a short, leopard-print robe, she headed toward the kitchen to mainline some caffeine. It was ten on a Sunday morning and she should have been sound asleep—particularly after the sexual marathon of the night before.

But her mind refused to quiet—every time she closed her eyes she saw herself sinking deeper and deeper into a nightmare she couldn't escape from.

After filling the tank of the coffeemaker with water and switching it on, she sank onto one of her kitchen chairs to wait. Gabe wasn't like Michael. She knew that, absolutely. She could never have been with him, even once, if he was.

But just because he wasn't an amoral alley cat didn't mean he wouldn't eventually betray her. Already he'd gotten a foothold in her heart and mind, something no man had been able to do for eight long years. Not since she'd thrown whatever she could grab into a tattered duffel bag and climbed into her Chevy with no other plan than to get as far away from her fucked-up family life as she possibly could.

How could she ever face herself if she let a man rip her hard-won confidence to shreds? Again?

Annalise heard a sound behind her and whirled around, her body tensed for a battle she hadn't had to fight in almost a decade. Thoughts of Michael invariably brought back the pain and anger, leaving a metallic taste in her mouth and a chill on her skin that she could normally escape.

"What are you doing up?" Gabe's voice was husky with sleep, his eyes half-closed as he settled himself across the table from her.

Even dressed in boxer shorts and more than half asleep, he was attuned enough to her to miss her. She had to fight the urge to take a bite out of all that inviting skin. It was the same color as her favorite treat—hot chocolate—and the desire to taste him, to drink him in, was almost overwhelming.

What was wrong with her? She was usually done with a lover the second he so much as intimated the *L* word—in her experience it brought nothing but pain. But with Gabe, something was different. Everything was different.

"Nothing." She shrugged. "I couldn't sleep."

He raised one sardonic eyebrow. "I guess I didn't do as good a job of tiring you out as I thought I did." He reached a hand across the table and stroked her arm with one gentle finger. "We could head back for round two."

She snorted. "More like round fifteen. And even if I was up to it, I can't see how you could be."

His smile was almost mischievous. "You'd be surprised."

She glanced down and was, indeed, surprised. How could he still have a partial erection? He'd come at least six times in the last six hours, not nearly as many as she had, but still. He was a guy in his late thirties—didn't he know his body wasn't supposed to be able to do that? "Holy shit," she commented, reaching a hand out to touch, shocked by how hard he was. Again. "Didn't anyone ever tell you, guys can't do that?"

His shrug was self-deprecating. "Yeah, well, you bring out the beast in me."

She twisted her hand around until her thumb rested on top of him. Then she began the slow, firm stroking she knew he liked. "Is that what I do?" she asked almost breathlessly as he arched into her hand once, twice, a third time.

"Annalise, stop." His hand covered hers, tugged it away from his suddenly raging hard-on. "Come here."

He pulled her up from her chair in one smooth motion. Before she knew it she was curled on his lap, her knees drawn up to her chin and his arms wrapped around her while he rocked her slowly. His chin rested on the top of her head and his hands, his gentle, wonderful hands, stroked her back through the thin fabric of her robe.

"You think too much," he said quietly.

She glanced up at him in surprise. "Moi? I think you have me confused with someone else, sugar. I'm the original good-time girl. If it feels good, do it—that's my motto."

It was his turn to snort. "You wish."

"What's that supposed to mean?" She drew just far enough away to look up at him through her lashes.

"It means I've never known a thirty-four-year-old woman who knew so little about herself."

She shoved him away—a knee-jerk reaction she couldn't stop. "Don't do this," she said, her voice surprisingly small as she got up and reached for a coffee cup. "Don't ruin it."

"I'm not ruining anything," he commented as he reached for her. "Why can't you see that?"

She shook her head as she thrust a cup of coffee—black, one sugar—into his hands.

Since when did she care enough about a guy to remember how he took his coffee? The realization shook her up so much that she bobbled the coffeepot as she was pouring herself a cup. The outrageously hot brew streamed across her hand and the pain was so unexpected that she couldn't move for a few, long seconds. Couldn't stop pouring the coffee. Couldn't stop the burn.

"Shit." Gabe sprung to his feet and grabbed the mug and coffeepot away from her, even as he used his hips to guide her to the sink. "What are you doing to yourself?"

She looked at him, dazed, so lost in her own torturous thoughts that she barely registered the pain or the blisters quickly forming on her thumb and the top of her hand. "It's nothing."

He growled low in his throat, turning on the tap and thrusting her hand under the streaming cold water in one smooth movement. "What's the matter with you?" he demanded as he held her hand under the water. "Do you really like suffering so much?"

"It's all I know." The words slipped out before she could censor them and hung there, between them, for long moments.

She prayed for the floor to open up and swallow her—but it wasn't to be. He was pressed firmly against her back, his arms around her while he kept her hand trapped under the running water. How was she ever going to turn and face him after that stupid admission?

She let out a halfhearted laugh. Followed it with a careless toss of her jet-black hair. "I didn't mean that the way it came out. I'm just being my melodramatic self."

"I think you knew exactly what you were saying." His answer was grim as he reached into the cabinet above the sink for some Neosporin and a bandage. "When are you going to stop hurting yourself?"

They weren't talking about her stupid little burn anymore. But she couldn't admit—to him or herself—how close he'd come to the truth. "It's not like that."

"It's exactly like that." He covered her blisters with the Band-Aid and then headed to the bedroom without a backward glance.

"Where are you going?" she asked, ignoring the panic skating up her spine.

"To work."

She entered her bedroom right behind him. "It's Sunday."

"Then I'm going home." He pulled on the dress trousers he'd been wearing the night before. "Don't ask me to sit around and watch you self-destruct. I can't do that."

"Now who's being melodramatic?" she demanded, blocking the door when he would have barreled through it.

One look from those burning eyes seared her, and strangely, froze her in place. "This isn't melodrama. It's pain. I'm surprised you don't recognize it—and my need to get as far away as possible."

"I don't run away" She was insulted and it showed in her voice.

He snorted. "Well, you sure as hell don't stick around."

"This is my apartment. You're the one running."

He shook his head in disgust. "You were running even before you got out of bed this morning. You know it and so do I."

The truth knocked the air from her lungs. "You don't understand."

"I understand plenty. I've been involved with you for three months, Annalise. You think I haven't gotten to know you, the real you, despite your best intentions?" He snorted again. "Give me a break. I know you better than you know yourself."

"That's bullshit." She was suddenly, inexplicably furious. How could he be saying these things to her? How could he mean them?

"You don't believe that for a minute. If you did, you wouldn't look so scared. When are you going to grow up and stop playing at being a badass?"

"I am a badass. You're just too besotted to realize it."

"You've got the most tender heart I've ever seen—you just hide it behind layers of protection so you can't ever be hurt. Explain to me how that's living, Annalise, because I just don't get it."

"It's better than the alternative."

Their eyes met for the first time since the argument began and all the fight seemed to drain out of Gabe. He looked... defeated, something she'd never seen from him before. "I guess it is." He sank onto the bed and slipped his shoes on without bothering with socks. Then he stood and headed for the apartment door. "I'll call you."

"I'll hold my breath." There she was, the sarcastic inner bitch she'd spent so many years cultivating. Why had it taken her so long to show up this morning?

"Annalise." For one moment his eyes softened and he reached for her. But she shrugged him off.

"Go home, Gabe. We're done here."

He turned on his heel and walked out without looking back once. He didn't even have the courtesy to slam the door on his way out.

Her knees trembled and she slid slowly down the wall she'd been using to prop herself up ever since he'd said he was leaving. Well, she'd done it. She'd driven him away.

Good riddance, she decided, right before she rested her face on her knees and sobbed like a baby.

CHAPTER SIX

IT WAS A DREARY MONDAY EVENING, FOLLOWING AN equally dreary day. Rain pounded the pavement—a rarity for San Diego at this time of year—and everyone on the street was scrambling for some kind of cover. Except for her. Since Gabe had walked out of her apartment eight days before, she'd had a hard time getting excited about anything.

Annalise meandered along the downtown sidewalks, lost in thought, barely noticing where she was going or how wet she was getting. She hadn't seen or heard from Gabe since he'd walked out of her apartment less than eight hours after telling her he loved her. She snorted. So much for love.

But it wasn't Gabe she was angry at. No, she was mad at herself for believing him. For starting to trust him. For ignoring all the hard-learned lessons and warning signs that she'd gathered through the years.

No, it wasn't Gabe's fault that she'd put aside everything she knew and had started to fall for him. Had almost started to fall for him, she corrected herself, stepping off the curb to cross the street and narrowly missing a huge puddle as she did so.

Seconds later, a car making a right hand turn hit the puddle and sprayed it all over her anyway.

Annalise ground her teeth in irritation. What had possessed her to walk to work this morning? She never walked to work. Never. So why today, of all days, had she chosen to start her campaign to get into shape with a mile-and-a-half walk to work?

Because she'd thought the walk would take her mind off Gabe, she admitted ruefully. Normally she loved downtown— all the people on the streets, all the cars honking and driving by in such a hurry. It was hard to concentrate on feeling sorry for herself when she was surrounded by so many other people doing so many different things.

But it hadn't worked. Gabe was still front and center in her mind and it was driving her nuts. She'd worked too hard to bury her vulnerabilities in the last few years to backslide because some guy told her he loved her and then walked away. Could she be more of an idiot?

As she waited for the light to change so that she could cross yet another puddle-ridden street, a car pulled over right in front of her. Her heart sank to her knees when she realized it was a dark-blue Acura.

"Need a ride?" Gabe asked as he rolled the window down. "You're getting soaked."

Getting soaked? She was soaked—all the way through to her bra and panties. Didn't it figure that she'd see Gabe again when she looked as bad as it was humanly possible to look? What the hell had she done in a past life to deserve this kind of crappy karma?

She wanted to refuse, scared of what she might let slip on the ride home. But at the same time, she didn't want him to think she was afraid of him. Didn't want to let him know that he'd managed to hurt her, despite her best intentions to the contrary.

So she tossed her rain-soaked hair behind her shoulder and shrugged. "Sure." He leaned over and opened the passenger door for her—always the gentleman—and she slid into the car. "I'm going to ruin your leather," she commented as she closed the door.

"I doubt it," he answered with a grin. "Cows get wet all the time."

"Thanks for the ride. I decided today was as good a day as any to start getting into shape, so I walked to work." She grimaced. "I should have checked the weather first."

"It's San Diego. Who actually checks the weather?"

Annalise grinned at him before she could stop herself. "Exactly."

He looked her over, his eyes dark and approving despite her impersonation of a drowned rat. "Besides, you look great to me."

She laughed. "Well, what woman doesn't look great with mascara running down her face?"

See, this wasn't too bad. She just needed to engage in a little harmless conversation until he got to her building and then she never had to see him again. Never had to wonder how he was doing.

What was left of her heart cracked wide open at the prospect. Damn it, when had she turned into such a girl? And how did she make it stop?

"I've missed you." The words slipped out before she had a clue she'd been thinking them.

"What did you say?" Gabe glanced at her abruptly, those black-magic eyes of his dark with confusion.

She shrugged again, cursing herself. Then looked him straight in the eye and lied. "Nothing. Just rambling."

He stopped at a light and silence stretched between them for a minute. "I missed you, too."

"I could tell." Shit, shit, shit. What was happening? Someone had hijacked her mouth and nothing was coming out the way she wanted it to. She was supposed to say something about how busy she'd been, about how she'd barely noticed he hadn't called. What she wasn't supposed to do was sound like a miserable, whiny little girl who wasn't getting her way.

"Annalise."

"Look, just forget it," she said. She gestured to her building, less than a block ahead on the right. "Drop me here and you can make the turn for your place. Thanks for the ride." She gathered up her briefcase and reached for the door handle.

But Gabe didn't stop, not at the corner before his turn or even in front of her building. Instead he cruised down to the next street and made a left, heading out of downtown and away from where they both lived.

"What are you doing?"

"Taking you somewhere we can talk."

"We are talking!" She knew she sounded panicked, but she couldn't help it. Her defenses were too low for her to stand up to him for long. "I want to go home."

"Tough." He kept his eyes on the road and drove for about ten minutes before she realized where he was taking her.

"No, Gabe. I don't want to go there."

"Why not?"

"I just don't." He couldn't take her to Coronado, to the small, secluded spot she had begun to think of as theirs. He just couldn't.

But he ignored her protests, and didn't say another word to her until he'd parked the car next to the private little cove they'd found two months previously. Before he could say anything, she asked, "So do you want to fuck me one last time? For old times' sake?" She unfastened the first button on her sheer pink blouse, just to let him know how little she cared. "I don't have much time, so we should probably get right to it."

"Stop it!" He knocked her hand away. "I'm sick of games, Annalise. I'm sick of pretending that nothing that happens between us matters."

"I'm just being honest, Gabe. Isn't sex what you brought me here for?"

"You don't know the first thing about honesty. You're too busy proving how tough and unfeeling you are to let anyone see the real you."

She pushed her wet hair out of her eyes, went nose to nose with him before she could think better of it. "This is the real me, Gabe. I'm sorry I don't live up to your stupid expectations."

He studied her for a minute, shook his head. "I don't believe you."

"Well, that's your problem then. I never promised you a damn thing."

"You're right, you didn't. I was just too stupid to realize it." His mouth turned grim. "But things change. We've been playing this stupid one-upmanship game since the day we met. And it was fun for a while. But I want more from you now. I need more."

"I've given you more than I've given anybody else. Why can't that be enough?"

"Because it isn't."

His eyes held hers, and she realized that she was trapped, unable to look away. Unable to walk away. "I don't have anything else to give," she whispered.

"That's bullshit. What you mean is there's nothing else you will give."

"Do you have to push?" She looked at him imploringly. "Can't we just do this for a while?"

"What exactly do you want to do?" His eyes snapped fire at her as the tight leash he was keeping on his temper slipped.

"You know," she shrugged, gesturing with her hands. "Do—"

"What?" Gabe demanded, before slamming out of the car.

"Do what?" he asked again as he came around to the passenger side and yanked her out of the car and into his arms.

"Do this?" He let her slide down his body, then turned her so that she was facing the car, her hands planted firmly on the hood. He pushed her pants and underwear down to her ankles with his right hand while he thrust the fingers of his left as far into her as he could go. As he found her G-spot and began to stroke he asked, in a voice made husky with desire, "Is this what you want to do for a while?"

She struggled against him, furious that he could make her want him with one stroke of a finger. But each movement she made brought him deeper, pressed him harder, made her wetter.

"Gabe, stop!" she demanded, her voice high and panicked as she moved restlessly against his hand. How could he turn her on so completely that she would fuck him right here, out in the open, while cold rain lashed at them from every direction? Where was her self-control? Where was her pride?

Leaning forward, he grazed her long, elegant neck with his lips while he used his free hand to fumble his belt and zipper out of the way. She felt his cock against her bare ass and couldn't prevent her whimper any more than she could prevent the blind instinct that had her pressing back against him. Searching for completion and to hell with pride and everything else that was keeping them apart. She loved him and if this was all they could ever have, then so be it. Annalise cried out as he bent her over the hood of the car and surged inside of her with one powerful thrust of his hips.

She moaned deep in her throat and spread her legs, desperate to have him as deep inside of her as he could go. It had been a long few days without him, without anyone, and the relief of having Gabe inside her was totally overwhelming. She tried to speak, but couldn't form words around the high, hungry sounds clawing their way out of her throat with each surge of his cock inside of her.

Reaching behind her, she raked her nails down his bare ass as she tried to pull him even closer. "Harder," she finally managed to gasp. "Please. Harder."

He heard her strangled gasps and responded with even more pressure, even harder thrusts until she feared he would rip her apart. But he felt so good and she'd missed him so much. She needed everything he could give her and more.

His left hand moved between her legs while his right one remained on the small of her back, keeping her bent forward for the best access. He spread her open, stroked the spot where they were joined as she pressed against him, desperate for release.

"Come on, *Lissy*. Come for me. Let me feel you, baby." He reached for her clit, stroked his thumb over it once, twice, a third time. She shattered, screaming his name as he rode her through her orgasm. Wave after wave of sensation crashed through her, weakening her knees and sending slivers of electricity to every part of her body.

Her muscles clenched rhythmically, milking him with every contraction of her strong body. She felt him pull back, felt him as he fought his fast-approaching orgasm with everything he had. He wasn't done yet, and she understood. She wasn't ready for this one, perfect moment in time to end either.

Taking a couple of deep breaths through his mouth, he reached under her shirt to rub her nipples through her bra. "I can't," she gasped, pushing weakly against him. "No more, Gabe."

"More," he said, squeezing her nipple between his thumb and index finger, feeling her muscles clench around his cock in response. "There's always more. I can't get enough of you, Lissy. More and more and more."

He moved his hand down and with his index finger gently tapped a pattern on her clit. She moaned his name, her head lolling forward even as her questing body arched into his caresses.

"That's it, baby. That's it." He continued the pattern, watching as her hips moved more and more urgently against his hand. "I love it when you come. I love watching you and feeling you. I love being inside of you when your muscles clench around me again and again."

He bent his head to her neck, licked the line of sweat dotting her nape. "I love your hard nipples and your hot little clit." He brushed his lips over her lobe, his tongue sweeping against the sensitive spot behind her ear as he whispered to her.

Annalise moaned deep in her throat, her body moving feverishly against his even as tears of need streamed down her face. His words were enflaming her, taking her closer and closer to another climax, something she would have sworn was impossible only minutes before.

"I love that you're always hot for me, always wet and willing. I love to fuck you, to thrust inside you and feel you clench around me." He pulled out slowly then slammed back into her. "I love how you take all of me, how you always want more." His mouth fastened on the juncture between her neck and her shoulder, sucking ravenously.

"I love how you seduce me, with your wild ideas and your open responses. I love how you let me fuck you anywhere. I love thinking of new places and new ways to fuck you." He pinched her clit with his thumb and middle finger, leaving his index finger free to stroke the sweet bundle of nerves again and again. "I love you."

"Gabe, stop!" she sobbed, her entire body shuddering. "I can't take it. I can't."

He squeezed her clit a little harder and was rewarded by a high-pitched scream as she thrust her ass even harder against him. "You can take it. And more. Can't you, baby?" His hips moved harder and faster against her as his control slipped another notch. "Can't you?" He moved his right hand from her back to her nipple, flicking his thumb over the hard peak again and again. "Because you love fucking me as much as I love you."

"Yes! Yes! Gabe, please!" She was screaming, sobbing, wilder than she'd ever been before. He thrust into her again and again, and she knew he was claiming her, branding her as his so that no matter how far she ran she would always remember that she belonged with him. As he pounded into her, she knew he took a part of her with him. Knew that she'd never forget the feel of him inside of her while his voice and hands took her someplace she'd never been.

He shifted so that he hit her G-spot with each thrust of his hips and she screamed. She was completely his at that moment, completely at his mercy, and she knew he realized it. She should be frightened of the control he had over her, but she was too aroused to care about anything but her next orgasm. She was going to die if he didn't give in, if he didn't come soon and stop this totally incredible, absolutely amazing torture. Desperate, she closed her legs, trapping Gabe between them, and then clenched her vaginal muscles as tightly as she could.

She was rewarded when he groaned deep in his throat and thrust against her one final time before spilling himself inside of her. His orgasm triggered her own and she screamed his name, again and again, completely caught up in the physical and emotional storm ripping her body apart.

When it was over, when they finally came back to themselves, Annalise tried to pull away from him. But he wouldn't let her go, his body keeping hers pinned against the car while his fingers toyed endlessly with her nipples.

"I'm not letting you go, Annalise." He thrust against her, more to make his point than for any sexual gratification. "You're going to have to get used to that."

She turned her head, met his steady gaze with one of her own. "You can't keep me if I choose to go."

He pressed more deeply into her, as if he could lock them together for all time. "So choose to stay," he said, putting his hands on her hips and pulling her ass backward as he thrust forward as hard as he could. She gasped and he did it again. And again. "Stay with me, Lissy. Choose me."

She swallowed, her eyes still locked to his. "I'm scared."

He snorted. "So am I. Do you think you're easy, Annalise?"

Her smile, when it came, was self-deprecating. "I'm pretty much the definition of easy."

"Not anymore you're not." He pulled her up so that her back rested against his chest and he could wrap her securely in his strong arms. "I love you and I need you to stay with me. Please."

His eyes were dark and vulnerable, his love for her right there for her to see. She stared at him for a moment, soaking up all the emotions pouring out of him and into her. And then she nodded, because there really was no other choice she'd rather make.

Anything You Want

JENESI ASH

I HAVE THREE LOVERS.

Jealous?

You shouldn't be. Sure, they have money (otherwise, why would I be with them?) and the sex is nonstop. The men treat me right and shower me with gifts, but, you know what? It's damn hard keeping them happy.

It's even more difficult keeping them a secret from each other.

I have the system down pat. For the past year, Monday nights are for Calvin. At twenty-eight, he's younger than me (although he doesn't know it!) Tall, athletic, and very energetic. He has more money and more kinks than anyone I know. One would automatically think he's a keeper. Ha. Ever try to fuck a hyperactive guy? You should see the skid marks on my back.

Wednesdays are for Dennis, and they have been for about eighteen months. He's not so hot, and he's not so rich. He has a receding hairline and the beginnings of a beer belly. I have a strong feeling he's married—he has that henpecked look about him—but I follow the "don't ask, don't tell" rule.

Normally I wouldn't give Dennis the time of day, but there's something to be said about being the highlight of his week. Hell, who are we kidding? I'm the luckiest thing that's happened to him in his life.

But that's not why I hook up with him every Wednesday. The guy comes in handy. He can call in a favor for anything at any time. I would think he was part of the Mafia or something, but he's just not that interesting.

And then there is George. George is the oldest of the lot. He reeks of sophistication and success. I would love for some of that to rub off on me, but after seeing him every Friday for two years, I can safely say if it hasn't happened yet, it's not going to.

George was my first provider. He bought the condo for me in downtown Seattle, and on special occasions he gives me some kick-ass jewelry. Not that I would know this at first sight, but I had the baubles appraised by a guy Dennis knows. Calvin pays for my utilities and food as well as my "incidentals."

Yeah, you got that right. I fool around for food. I figure it's no different than going out on a date because the fridge is empty. Only with this setup our expectations are clear and up-front. No confusion. No hurt feelings. I'm a sure thing and so is my dinner. I like this kind of deal and I've long decided dating is for amateurs.

Wait. Was that the doorbell? Uh-oh... What day is it?

Shit! I have no clue. My gut twists sharply. I wrap my arms around my stomach and stare at the door. I hate when this happens. That's the downside of being a moonlighting mistress.

Is it Wednesday? I frown as I try to recall. No, I think I've already seen Dennis this week. It's so hard to remember. We do the same thing every freaking time.

Dennis isn't the only reason I have bouts of déjà vu. Not having to work outside my condo makes the days bleed together. Not that I'm complaining! These moments of panic are still better than all those years in dead-end, minimum wage jobs.

I hurry toward the entrance, fix an inviting smile on my face and grab the doorknob. My heart is pounding against my chest. Sometimes I have weird dreams of all three guys showing up at the same time. Not that it would happen; I made sure of it. But the possibility, no matter how remote, still gets my blood pumping.

Swinging the door open, my first thought is that there is only one man in front of me. *Whew*. I pause, connecting the name with the lover.

I'm very proud that I have never called out the wrong name. Okay, I admit that I use the same endearment for each of them. It's safer that way, especially when my mind wanders during sex.

"Hello, love!" My smile grows and it's probably wobbling with relief when I see George. I lean forward, letting my high and full breasts brush against the sleeve of his fine cashmere coat. I place a gentle kiss on his lips and slyly dart my tongue in his mouth, tasting a hint of cigar. I usher him inside. "I've missed you."

Okay, not entirely true. So what? It's what they all want to hear and my job is to create a fantasy. And it's not like I can't stand being around George. I like him. I like having sex with him. I like getting paid to have sex.

I probably shouldn't admit to any of that, especially the last part, but it's true. Would I spend my Friday nights with him if money wasn't involved? I don't know.

"I know I'm late," George says in his usual brisk tone. He steps inside and takes off his coat.

"Would you like something to drink?" I ask as I close the door behind him. He's into red wine, but do I have an open bottle ready? No. I'll have to improvise.

"No, thanks, baby. I can't stay the night."

I pout and look at him through my long eyelashes.

I'm really good at pouting. It's one of my most effective weapons. You wouldn't believe the stuff I can get out of men just by protruding my lower lip.

"I know, I know." George cups my cheek with his hand, cold from the winter night. "You hardly get to see me as it is. It can't be helped. I'm a busy man."

I quickly lower my eyes, hoping I'm the picture of disappointment, but my mind is whirring. Does George truly believe I wait all week for him with bated breath? That I live for these precious hours? Is he for real or is this part of the fantasy?

Men are so gullible, I think as I watch George heading straight for the bedroom. Hmm...he's not stopping for a chat or cuddle. He really is in a rush.

Sometimes I suspect George has me on the side simply because he can. I'm like the fire-engine-red Ferrari parked in his garage. Expensive, high-maintenance, and designed to make people envy him.

And, like all status symbols, successful men don't have time to maintain and enjoy them. That Ferrari is rarely taken out for a spin, and George can only fit me in his schedule once a week.

I don't have a problem with that. Really, I don't, but I know I better make these visits worth every penny. If I'm not raring to go at a moment's notice, I bet he'll trade me in for a cheaper model. Or worse, someone with all the bells and whistles.

It can happen. I might get paid to have sex, but that doesn't mean I'm the most knowledgeable person about the subject. Being a kept woman isn't about knowing ancient sexual secrets, I remind myself as I stroll into the bedroom. It's all about attitude. I am to act as if I exist solely for his pleasure.

I step into the bedroom and see George loosening his necktie. "Sit on the bed," he tells me.

Maneuvering around him, I'm about to perch on the edge of the mattress when he stops me. "Wait," he says. "Your hair. It's wrong."

I instinctively reach up and touch my hair. It's loose and skimming my shoulders. Oops. George prefers my hair up. Not like a bun or twist. He wants to see ponytails or braids, the higher the better.

"Hold that thought!" I rush into my bathroom and sort through my barrettes and rubber bands. I hurriedly gather my hair in high, messy pigtails using plastic holders. They are bubble gum pink and tacky. I can't believe someone as elegant as George likes them.

I try not to glance in the mirror because I know I look ridiculous. I quickly return to the bedroom and I see George standing by the bed, his hands on his hips. He's frowning. I'm in trouble.

Lowering my head, I place my hands behind my back and shuffle toward him. "Sorry," I whisper, but I don't really feel that way.

"Sit on the bed."

I gingerly sit on the corner of the bed. George stands in front of me. "Spread your legs," he says gruffly.

I follow his order, but I take my own sweet time doing it. After being with George for this long, I can read his moods. He wants me to act shy instead of naughty today. It's my goal to give him anything he wants.

George steps between my legs. He reaches out and places the palm of his hand on the top of my head. His touch is tender as he strokes my hair. I glance up at him, but he's not looking at me. He's watching our reflection from the mirror above my bed.

"Undo my belt," he says hoarsely.

I slowly unbuckle his belt, my fingers fumbling. It's not easy pretending that this is the first man's belt I've encountered, but I have my routine. Once I pull the leather from George's belt loops, I reach for his zipper.

By this time, George is reverently fondling the plastic ponytail holders in my hair. "Take off my pants," he whispers roughly.

I drag the zipper down and peel away the expensive fabric. I cup his stirring penis that is concealed in his silk boxers. He's hot to the touch.

"Come on, baby. You know what I want." George grips my ponytails in his fists. I wince, but the bite of pain adds to my arousal.

I slip my fingers under the waistband of his underwear and push it down his hips. His penis is right in front of my face. I lick my lips with anticipation as I inhale his hot, musky scent.

Stroking his penis with my fingertips, I know the sensation is too light and teasing for him. He thrusts his hips closer. "Suck me," he says, his voice almost a growl. "I want you to take every inch."

I grasp the root of his penis with one hand and squeeze him. The way he flinches gives me a perverse sense of satisfaction. I show no expression as he twists my pigtails around his fingers and yanks my head back.

"Do I need to feed you myself?" he asks. His low, commanding voice makes me wet.

"No," I tell him and wrap my lips around the tip of his penis. I love the taste of George. Salty, warm and male. I swirl my tongue and suckle while I pump the base of his erection.

George keeps playing with my hair and murmurs encouragingly as I slowly make my way down his penis. It doesn't take long before his length is deep in my throat and my nose is firmly pressed against his wiry pubic hair.

I now have my hands on George's testicles. I fondle the sacs, enjoying how he twitches beneath my touch. He's panting and vibrating with need. I can feel his muscles bunching and shaking.

George yanks my pigtails hard, maneuvering my head just the way he wants it as he begins fucking my mouth. I groan as his tempo increases. His thrusts grow choppy and uncontrolled.

He grunts and suddenly pulls out. I squeeze my eyes shut as he bellows, his hot semen splattering on my face. I remain still, my mouth still open, as the sticky come drips from my nose and chin.

George's hand trembles as he pats me on the head. His praise tumbles over me as my body pulses for completion.

"Go and clean up," he suggests. "And then you can see me off."

It looks like I'm in charge of my own satisfaction for tonight. I stumble into the bathroom and strip off my clothes. My shower takes longer than necessary as I grab the handheld showerhead and turn the speed onto massage. Aiming it close to my swollen clit, it doesn't take long to go over the edge.

I clench my teeth and swallow back the moans. Black spots dance before my eyes as my legs wobble. I want to sink to my knees and continue, but I know George is outside, waiting.

With great reluctance, I finish washing and turn off the shower. I grab my bathrobe and pull it on, loosely tying the sash. The gap offers glimpses of my firm breasts and my Brazilian cut. Just enough skin that will make George do a double-take. It doesn't matter if he just sampled me; I'm a firm believer in advertising.

When I get out of the bathroom, I see that George is waiting for me in the condo's entry. All traces of my lust-driven, out-of-control lover are gone and replaced by the sophisticated gentleman in a hurry.

"I'll see you next week," he promises as he leans down for a swift kiss and a possessive grope of my breast. Before I can say a word, he's gone.

I close the door behind him and lock it. I turn off the lights and check the windows, deciding I'm ready to call it a night. I wander into my room and notice how everything is quiet and undisturbed. That doesn't stop me from stripping the clean sheets off the bed.

The champagne silk is beautiful, but I see them more as a prop to set the mood. I toss them in the hamper and grab my favorite sheets from the linen closet.

The bright red poppies design is too feminine for my lovers, so I save this bedding just for me. It's a private ritual I have. The sheets signify the start of my weekend. I remake the bed, take off my robe, and dive under the warm covers. The next two days are strictly for *my* pleasure.

Before I know it, my alarm clock wakes me up. I reach out and slap it into silence. I have a lot of plans for today and I should hop out of bed and hit the ground running. Instead I stretch slowly, opening my eyes as the morning sun filters past the drapes and into my room.

I look up at the ceiling and see my reflection. I'm sprawled on my bed, taking up every inch. For a brief second, I see why these guys are willing to pay for an invitation to my bed. My dark hair fans out on the pillow. The sheets are down around my waist, revealing my breasts.

I watch as I leisurely slide my fingers along my collarbone. My hand drifts down to cup my breast. The nipple is rosy and puckered. I pinch it, watching it redden. I pinch harder and gasp as the intense pleasure zips through my veins.

My breasts feel full and heavy. I fondle them, plucking at my nipples until they sting. I stare at my reflection. I'm not the prettiest woman, or the sexiest, but I work with what I have.

I drag my fingers down my stomach. I look good, but that's because I spend a lot of time taking care of myself. I pamper my body. It's all a part of the package, for the men and for me.

Even now, as I've been doing this for years, I'm not sure what made me place a price on my body. What made me think men would pay top dollar for me? Flattery? Curiosity? Or did I like how powerful it made me feel to be paid when they could go elsewhere to get the same thing for free?

I dip my hand underneath the covers and cup my sex. Parting my legs, I watch the sheet move as I rub my fingers along my wet slit.

All I know is that once I had set an outrageous price for sex and George agreed to it, there was no looking back. I can stop at any time, but I don't want to. I want to enjoy every minute of this agreement while I can.

I kick the sheet away and watch my reflection. My vulva is slick and puffy. I massage my clit, circling my hips as I enjoy the sensations.

Reaching for the bedside table, I pull open the drawer as I furiously rub my clit with my other hand. I don't want to stop as the pleasure builds inside me. My hand curls around the vibrator and I switch it on. The intense pulsing makes me moan in anticipation.

I place the juddering tip against my clit. I grit my teeth. The feeling is so pure, so white-hot, that I cry out as the wave of pleasure scorches through my body.

Spreading my legs wider, I dig my heels into the mattress. I watch the mirror in a haze as I guide the vibrator into my pink and juicy vagina. The toy barely penetrates me and I'm rocking my hips.

The headboard butts against the wall as the sheet pulls away from the corners. I watch my breasts jiggle and bounce as my hips rise off the bed. I can't help but be fascinated at how my body responds.

A flush spreads from my chest and creeps up my neck. My reflection suddenly wobbles. I squint at the mirror. My image lurches. It's closer. Too close!

I tuck my knees and roll off the bed. I hit the carpet and I'm still rolling, hearing the mirror fall from the ceiling and shatter.

For a second or two, I just lie there on the floor, my face turned toward the wall. What the hell just happened? The sound of broken glass still echoes in my ears. I gulp for air. My throat, raw and hot, clamps shut.

I slowly get on my feet, brushing my arms and legs to see if I got hit. So far I'm lucky. Kicking the vibrator out of my way, I feel an aching twinge in my leg thanks to the fall.

I turn and stare at the jagged shards scattered across the bed. They grab the sunlight making me wince. The giant poppies suddenly look like pools of blood. *My favorite sheets,* I want to wail, *they're ruined.*

Okay, so I'm not sounding very reasonable. Who cares? I was almost killed! I could have been cut into ribbons! I stare at the ceiling, wondering how this could have happened.

The ceiling looks smooth and innocent. I don't see any cracks or signs of trouble. Warning skitters down my spine. Something isn't right. I need a closer look.

I grab my robe and give it a good shake in case it has bits of mirror clinging on it. I put the robe on, my hands shaking as I tie the belt tightly. I find my slippers. The men love the way I walk in the impractical mules, but right now the ridiculous heels protect me from any sliver of glass. I slide them on and carefully step onto my bed.

Pressing my fingertips on the ceiling, I look for what caused the mirror to fall. There is nothing wrong as far as I can see. I look at where the mirror used to be fastened. How could all of the bolts fail at the same time? What are the chances of that?

Maybe someone didn't leave it to chance.

I shiver at the thought and immediately discard the possibility. No one is trying to kill me. I'm being paranoid. Unreasonable. There is a simple explanation, and I need to find it.

I study the spots where the mirror used to be fastened.

There is no sign of stress or fatigue. Rubbing my fingertips against the bolt holes, I feel the freshly disturbed grains of plaster.

Someone had loosened these bolts.

I pull my hand away and scurry off the bed. I back away until my spine hits the wall. Wrapping my arms tightly across my chest, I can't stop looking at the broken mirror. My skin suddenly feels too tight as I stare at the pointed tips that could have sliced right through my flesh.

Someone tried to hurt me.

No, it's worse than that. Only three men had the opportunity to do this. That means one of my lovers—one of my *protectors*—tried to kill me.

Ungrateful scum. Sick bastard. I oughta—

But which one did it? And why? I try to consider the possibilities, but it's like a metal door slams shut in my brain. It's almost as if I'm too scared to dig deeper.

Police. I need to call the police. I hurry out into the living room to get the phone. I stumble at the threshold as reality hits me.

Am I crazy? Call the police? And say what? *Excuse me, officer, but one of the guys is obviously not happy with my sexual services. Can you tell me which one?* I can't tell them the truth! They'll arrest me for sure.

I sink onto the couch and hold my head in my hands. I can't turn to anyone. I'm on my own with this. What am I going to do?

Dump them. The answer is instant and comes from the gut. Dump all the men. Right now. If I can't trust any of them, then it's time to retire.

I look at my condo, absently wondering what I can take with

me. Tears prick my eyes. It isn't fair. I invested my time and energy and now I have to walk away with nothing to show for it. All because of one man.

Frustration and anger bloom inside my chest. I don't want to quit. For once in my life I'm calling the shots. I'm in charge of my destiny and I can't go back to letting someone else dictate my actions and choices. If only I could figure out which one would do this to me.

There is one way I could find out. I rise from the couch and slowly make my way back to the bed, surveying the mess. I can clean up the broken glass and replace the mirror this weekend. Act as if nothing happened.

And then when Calvin shows up, I'll lure him into the bedroom and watch his reaction. I'll do the same with Dennis and George. The guy responsible will give himself away the moment he tries to save his hide.

That is, if I don't mess up. I have to have sex with these guys, knowing one is trying to hurt me. Kill me.

I lean against the door frame, imagining myself naked and vulnerable as the killer hovers above me. Stretched out on the bed before him as he makes his move. My stomach rolls, but I remain still until the nausea subsides. I'm not going to run. I can't hide. I need to face him down.

This isn't one of my better plans.

Too bad it's the only one I have.

It's Monday night and I'm a nervous wreck. I watch Calvin over our intimate dinner. He's charming and attentive. Well, as charming as a computer nerd with no social graces can be.

He's getting better. I allow him that. I can get him to sit

through a meal before he pounces on me. He can now carry on a conversation that doesn't have to do with sex. It helps that Calvin wants me to be a sophisticated, glamorous creature, but that doesn't stop him from claiming me with the crudeness of a barbarian.

As I watch him toss the napkin onto the table, I realize that one day he is going to restrain his insatiable sex drive and become a legendary lover. All that he needs right now is practice and a patient teacher.

That would be me.

I should be proud of this moment, feel a sense of accomplishment for polishing this diamond in the rough, yet all I can do is keep track of the silverware. I'm counting forks and knives while knowing where his hands are at all times. This hyperawareness isn't going to save me. Calvin is clever enough that he could gut me with a spoon.

I should have planned a menu filled with finger foods. I should have fed him myself. I want to thwack my hand on my forehead. Why didn't I think of that sooner?

"Are you listening?" Calvin asks.

My gaze collides and locks with his. "Yes, love," I say with a smile. "I...just realized I didn't have your favorite dessert."

His eyes take on an unholy gleam. "I know how you can make it up to me."

My smile stays put but I feel my stomach free-falling. Oh, boy. Here we go. I can do this.

Well, I thought I could. After all, I went through the checklist and left nothing to chance. My bedroom is spotless and I paid triple for a new mirror to be installed on the ceiling in record time. I planned countless scenarios in my head on how to get my lovers into bed and watch my back at the same time. I think I have it all figured out, but when it comes right down to it, I'm a basket case.

Calvin scoots back from the table and hooks one arm over the chair. His T-shirt pulls against his lean and wiry body. I stand up and my legs are shaking.

"You know," he says as he musses his spiky short hair with his fingers. "I think you're overdressed."

Damn. Okay, sure, my halter dress isn't a suit of armor. It's not going to protect me, but I want to hide behind *something*. I want to refuse his unspoken request, but that's not going to lull him. I need him cooperative and in a good mood as I guide him to my bed.

I look at him in the eye and reach for the knot at the base of my neck. I tug it free and the black dress slides off my shoulders and breasts. I can feel Calvin's gaze focusing on my pointed nipples.

Pushing the dress over my hips and dispensing with my skimpy underwear, I stand before him wearing nothing but a pair of high heels. "Is this better?" I ask. My voice comes out in a rasp. I want to clear my throat, but that isn't going to get rid of my nervousness.

"Come closer," he tells me.

I force myself to comply. I want to believe that Calvin isn't the one who wants to hurt me. I want them all to be innocent.

It's quite possible that I'm wrong. It could be that the mirror was a freak accident, despite what the installers said as they replaced it. Calvin wouldn't have tampered with the mirror, I argue to myself. He's a software guy, not hardware.

And Dennis? The man doesn't like to exert himself. George

might have had the opportunity to do it—hell, they all did—but he's not the type who uses power tools.

I jump when I feel Calvin's hand cup my ass. I look down, startled, just as he places his other hand on my breast. His chest rises and falls as he strokes my skin.

"Closer," he says, his eyes never leaving my breasts.

I'm tempted to tell him that my eyes are up here, but I don't trust myself enough to tease. I straddle his lap. His hard dick creates a tent in his jeans. I wiggle my slit against the denim. Pleasure sparkles under my skin.

Calvin squeezes and kneads my ass. His touch is almost too much, but as long as both hands are on me and not on the cutlery, I won't complain.

He's showering kisses on my face and neck. Wet, fierce kisses that make my sex swell. His good manners are slipping fast as he sloppily licks my ear and stabs the tip of his tongue in the canal. He's breathing hard and I can hear the satisfied growls deep in his chest.

I know I need to get him to the bed now if I want to entrap him. "Love," I say as I get on my knees, slowly rising off of the chair, "take me to bed."

"No." He shakes his head vigorously and his fingers dig into my ass to stop me.

My heart trips a beat. Why is he so adamantly opposed to the idea? The hot fear congeals into ice and slams into my chest. Goose bumps dot my flesh.

"I got you right where I want." His tone is low and flat, as if the words were dragged from the recesses of his mind. I stop breathing as my muscles tense. I'm paralyzed with fear.

He plunges his face between my breasts.

"Perfect," he says in a muffled groan, nuzzling deeper.

I want to sag and fall down as my pulse skips and stumbles. I should have known. He was talking about *sex*.

The stubble from his chin scrapes my skin, but I don't flinch. I don't move. I feel like I've dodged a bullet and don't know where to run for cover.

Calvin opens his mouth and stuffs one crest as far as it will go. His teeth nip my flesh. He closes his eyes and I can see the pure bliss etched in his face. He lets go and I know he's going to make a lunge for my other breast. I turn slightly.

"It's too uncomfortable here," I tell Calvin, lowering my voice as if I'm confiding something naughty. "The bed is better." I tug at his shirt, silently indicating that he should follow me.

"Table's closer." He suddenly leans forward, ready to clear the table with one sweep of his hand. I barely stop him in time.

"The table is not big enough," I say in a rush.

"Not big enough?" he repeats dully. He looks at my breasts and licks his lips. His eyes are glazed with lust.

My window of opportunity is closing fast. I can see the signs. Calvin is right where I can guide him. But once the level of needs rises, there's no stopping him.

"What do you have in mind?" He captures one of my nipples between his teeth and sucks hard.

The violent pull goes straight to my clit. I arch my back and let out a guttural groan as my sex creams. I'm ready to ride his dick hard and fast. It's a struggle to remember the plan. "Anything you want," I tell him shakily.

He stops sucking, but his hands grip my ass tighter than ever. Calvin lifts his head and looks straight in my eye. "Anything?"

I swallow roughly. I know what I'm agreeing to, and I usually hold back on this because Calvin is so rough. "Anything," I promise in a whisper.

Calvin shoots out of his seat with such speed that the chair crashes to the floor. I know I should take his enthusiasm as a compliment, but I'm too busy holding on for dear life. One of his arms is across my thighs while the other holds me tight against his chest. My high heels clatter to the ground as he carries me to the bedroom before throwing me on to the bed.

I bounce on the mattress and grab for a corner before I fall off. As the world rights itself, I roll onto my back and stare up at the mirror.

Well, I thought, that answers that. He's not too concerned about shaking the walls and letting the mirror come crashing down. But he's not on the bed, either. Call me suspicious, but he might try to do me without getting in the hot zone. Men have a tendency to be greedy that way.

"Where's the lube?" Calvin asks as he strips off his clothes. I'm surprised he doesn't tear them into shreds at the rate he's going. I sit up and reach for the bottle in my bedside table.

"Lube me up," he says. He stands by the bed with his legs braced apart, his dick hard and curving upward.

I have to get him on the bed. I squirt the lubricant in my hand and curl my fingers in what I hope is a seductive manner. "Come here, love."

He eagerly crawls onto the bed and groans appreciatively as I liberally coat his dick. I hand him the bottle so he can apply it to me.

I reluctantly turn around and get on my hands and knees.

My stomach tightens as my heart pounds in my ears. I instinctively tense as he rubs the lube in my anus.

My hesitation isn't because of the anal sex. I like it, and can reach an orgasm unlike anything I've ever achieved, as long as the guy doesn't shove his dick in me and starts rutting.

No, my reluctance is placing myself in this submissive position for someone who might want to kill me. I can't see what Calvin's doing. I shiver at the thought. At least I know he's naked and not concealing a weapon.

I can also tell that he's enjoying his duty a little too much. I squirm as he teases my tiny rosebud with his fingers. He spreads my cheeks and I force myself to relax.

"Careful, love," I say. "Nice and easy." But does he listen?

I feel the crown of his dick pressing against me. I take a deep breath just as the thick, mushroom head eases in. Already he's stretching me. It's uncomfortable and stinging, and my body is determined to reject him.

Arching and dipping my spine, I push against Calvin. Bad move. He slides deeper and I can't remember to breathe. My entire body is tingling. Burning. I want to pull away, but my ass is clamping snugly around his dick.

"Slower," I say through clenched teeth, but I know my instructions are useless as he holds my hips tightly. He draws back, his dick retreating, only for him to pause and plunge deeper.

I bite back a scream. My body is shuddering as the pain and pleasure mix into a potent combination. Calvin retreats and advances with choppy, wild thrusts. Faster and faster. I bunch the sheets under my fists, but I can't find anything to hold onto.

The bed shakes under my knees as the mattress slides more

to one side. My breasts swing wildly as Calvin humps me with ferocious speed. I'm dizzy, I can't catch my breath, but my entire world is centered on his dick.

I close my eyes and the sensations sharpen. My clit is pulsing heavily, and my sex is so drenched I can smell it. Moisture drips on my thighs. If Calvin would pinch my clit or sink his fingers in my vagina, I would shatter and disintegrate.

He does neither. Instead he gives a mighty shove into my ass and I collapse onto the mattress. He falls on top of me, his dick driving deeply inside me.

Our groans mingle as his hips thrust against me, his balls slapping against my ass. Calvin brackets his arms at my side and sets a demonic pace. My breath sputters out of my lungs as he sinks his teeth into my shoulder.

I rear back and the last resistance inside me snaps. I'm about to come. I can feel it swirling, building power. It's going to be dark and brutal, and I can't wait.

As Calvin's flesh slapped against mine, I realize that he's not the one trying to kill me.

At least, not with the mirror.

His stamina, however, will be the death of me.

If it's Wednesday, then I'm with Dennis. I lean my head on his shoulder and let his body heat envelop me. His dress shirt is soft under my cheek and I inhale the faint scent of his cologne.

He lowers his head and brushes his lips along my forehead. I hum with contentment, knowing that by the end of the night I will have been kissed and petted all over. Dennis can't get enough touching and affection, and, I confess, I find it addicting, as well.

We're slow dancing to the music on the CD player, our hips gently swaying to the beat. His hands glide over my spine and I shiver. I made sure to wear a backless dress tonight so he could caress my bare skin.

I can feel the changes in his body as he gets aroused. Dennis likes to take things gradually, which is a nice change of pace from Calvin. I'm still walking gingerly and not my usually graceful self.

As much as I appreciate Dennis's slow and steady pace, it's not always the easiest approach. It can take all night before he finds satisfaction. I have to be on the top of my game and lavish so much attention that I'm exhausted afterward. He's lucky I don't charge by the hour.

I tilt my hips against his and feel his cock. It's time to take him to the bedroom. It's been hard not to hurry him along tonight. Dennis can't be rushed. If I try—and I know this from experience—then we are back to square one and have to start all over again.

I step back and capture his hand in mine. "Come to bed," I say with a smile. I walk toward the bedroom and I feel the resistance in him.

Looking over my shoulder, I see the indecision flittering across his face. I wonder if I still rushed it. Should I have given him another couple of minutes?

"Let's do something different tonight," he suggests.

I try to hide my surprise as a curl of warning slithers coldly down my spine. Dennis who wants to do the same thing every time we meet now wants to veer from routine? If that isn't suspicious!

I do my best not to follow my instincts, which consists of

pointing my finger at him and accusing him of murder in his cold, black, devious heart. Instead, I gently drop my hold on his wrist. "Are you sure?" I ask as sweetly as possible while I take another step back. "What do you have in mind?"

Dennis looks at his feet and rubs the back of his neck with his hand. "I dunno."

"I'll do anything you want," I remind him softly. Except for roll over and die, but he'll find that out soon enough.

He doesn't respond. Most guys would have instantly come up with the dirtiest, nastiest, in-your-dreams suggestion. Dennis, on the other hand, gives a furtive look over my shoulder.

Guilty! The man is guilty! Time to call in the cops.

I try to stop this train of thought. I could be jumping to conclusions. It's been known to happen. It might be a coincidence that he wants to shake things up on the very day I need it to be business as usual.

But I doubt it.

My feet step on the threshold to my bedroom. I picture the bed behind me. What would be the one thing I can do that would make him launch for the bed like a heat-seeking missile?

It has to be something good. I need to be sure. If he doesn't jump for the offer, then I know he's the one who tampered with the mirror.

"Hey, I have an idea," I say as my blood pumps hard through my veins. "Would you like to tie me up?" I walk to the bed and flop on it. I'm spread-eagled on the bedspread, my legs going as far wide as my dress will let me.

Dennis hangs back. I notice he's stepping into the room. I need to sell this harder.

"My hands will be tied to the bed and I won't be able to move," I continue cheerfully. "Sounds like fun, huh?"

He shakes his head and I see his gaze dart to the ceiling.

"Just imagine. I'll be tossing and turning—" I act it out, exaggerating my moves so the headboard butts against the wall "—and I will be at your mercy."

"No, I don't think so. Why don't you get off the bed and—"

I rise on my elbows and tilt my head. "Did you hear something?"

Dennis freezes and looks up. "No."

"It's a strange noise. Was it the bedsprings?" I rock my body hard from side to side. "No, that wasn't it."

"Sweetheart, get off the bed." He steps into the room and then takes another step back. His attention doesn't leave the mirror.

"Maybe it was when the bed frame knocks against the wall." I jut my hips up and down, moving the bed as hard as I can. "There's that sound again," I lie. "Do you hear it?"

"Get off the bed now!"

I swing my legs over the mattress corner and sit up. "Don't worry, Dennis," I say coldly. "This isn't the mirror you tampered with."

The tension in the room suddenly arcs and quivers. Dennis drags his stunned gaze onto me.

"That one came crashing down a couple of days ago. As you can see—" I rise from the bed and motion at my body like a game show hostess "—I got out in time."

"And...George?"

I stop in my tracks. How does he know about George? Panic

claws in my chest and I try to hide my true thoughts. "George?" I ask idly.

"Did he get hurt, too?" Dennis persists.

Is that what this is about? He knows that I have another lover? He knows George's name? Should I act dumb or play it straight? I don't know. I'm flying blind and I don't like it.

I also don't know if he's aware of Calvin. That might send him over the edge. "George wasn't here when it happened," I answer carefully.

He looks up at the mirror and frowns. "Then how did..." His voice trails off as he wrestles with the laws of physics.

I shrug and fold my arms across my chest. "I don't know. I was lying on the bed minding my own business. But that's not the point. Why would you do something like this to me? We were good to each other." I thought he worshipped the ground I walk on, but if I say that out loud it's going to sound conceited.

Dennis tilts his head back and wearily closes his eyes. "You don't understand."

I scoff at that and put my hands on my hips. "I understand plenty. You're consumed with jealousy. Did you ever think of confronting me? No. Instead you went off the deep end."

Dennis slowly opens his eyes and I get a sense he didn't hear a word I said. "What does George know?"

I roll my eyes. I want to scream out my frustrations. For the first time since we've been together, I'm telling Dennis how I feel, and all he cares about is George's opinion. Men! They're the lowest. They're—

Wait a second. It's like something clicked in my brain. I gasp as the truth hits me like a slap in the face. This isn't about me. It's about *George!*

I don't realize I'm talking out loud until Dennis nods. "It's true," he confesses. "I wanted to hurt George."

"What about me?" I stare at him incredulously. "Didn't you think I would have gotten hurt, too?"

Dennis casts a questioning look in my direction. "You thought the mirror was planned for you? Why would you think that?"

I storm over to where he stands. "When someone tries to kill me, I take it personally."

He holds his hands out as if to ward me off. "You aren't my target."

"I know, I know." In Dennis's eyes, I was the not-so-innocent bystander. I know I should ask why he wants to hurt George, but you know what? At this moment I am too pissed off to care.

Don't my feelings or my life matter? After eighteen months, don't *I* matter? My stomach clenches. If I have to ask it, I already know the answer.

Dennis approached me because of George. He had sex with me to get into my condo. Every time we were in bed, he hadn't been watching our reflection. Dennis had been coming up with a plan of action. I shudder with revulsion.

I can't believe it. This is the guy who adored me. He couldn't get enough of me. I thought I was the highlight of his week and instead I was...in the way. No, not even that. I was simply there.

How could I have read Dennis so wrong? What else am I wrong about? Am I less than George's status symbol? Do I even rank in his mind when he's not here?

And what about Calvin? Does he see me as a teacher, or is that a whimsical thought of mine? Does Calvin even see me, or does he only look at the tits and ass.

Why did I think I was the center of attention and that their lives rotated around me? I thought that I held the reins, dictating the schedule and the price. The truth is that they could have cared less.

All this time I laugh over my lovers' misconceptions, but the laugh is on me. I've been living in a fantasy world. I saw things the way I wanted to see.

I rearranged my life to be with these men and risked everything, but they are never inconvenienced. I put my pleasure secondary to theirs, believing that by doing so, I'm in control. I thought I was someone special, but it's all a lie. I'm a plaything. Someone easily discarded, easily dismissed.

I slowly walk out of the bedroom. My legs feel like lead. My head is in a fog.

"Where are you going?" His voice sharpens, piercing my troubled thoughts.

"I'm calling the police." I say it as if I'm in a trance.

"What?" He is suddenly at my side. "No, you can't."

"And then I'm calling George." He has to be warned. He's going to dump me, but at this moment, I feel like saying good riddance to him.

"No, sweetheart." Dennis pulls at my arm. "You can't do this."

I have the phone in my hand. "Watch me." I don't look at him. I feel so used and insignificant.

"We can come to an agreement."

I stare at him. Is he for real? Does he think I can be bribed for my silence? My body has a price tag, so he thinks my life does, too?

"I'll give you anything you want." Desperation blurs his voice.

I turn on the phone. "I've heard that before." I should; I say it all the time.

"No, really." He falls to his knees, pulling at my arms. "I mean it. Anything. Name your price."

He's pleading. Begging. It's a new look for him. For any of my lovers, now that I think about it.

And I realize that *this* is what's missing in my life.

I like sex. I like getting paid for sex, but what I want more than anything is what I thought the sex gave me. Power. I had assumed the money represented my power. The higher the price, the more control I had.

Boy, was I wrong. I don't want Dennis's money. Well, I do, but not at this moment.

I want him to see me as a dangerous, don't-mess-with-me woman. I want him to know that I have him by the balls and I won't hesitate to squeeze them off.

It's an odd feeling. For once, my lover's main concern is pleasing *me*. He will do anything I want at the risk of his own pleasure and convenience. He will strip his pride and ignore everything else to make sure I'm satisfied.

Right now, I am the most important person in his life. The absolute power heating my blood is sweeter than any aphrodisiac I know.

The tables are turning and I'm liking it. I shouldn't. What he's suggesting is breaking a few laws. Probably some morals, too, but I'm just guessing.

Possibilities and options cram into my brain. I should tell the authorities, but where's my proof? I should warn George, but would he do the same if he were in my position?

Oh, who the hell am I kidding? I'm not thinking seriously

in these terms. What I really want to know is how long can I enjoy this before it becomes too risky? How far can I go before I lose the power I hold over Dennis?

"Sweetheart?"

I remember feeling like this when I first named my price to George. Wild and strong. Important. Whatever I say, my answer will rock his world.

I hang up the phone with a decisive push of the button. "Before we discuss anything," I say in a firm, no-nonsense tone, "I want to make one thing clear. I'm *not* your sweetheart."

Dennis swallows hard. His nerves are shredding and he's holding his breath. He knows I'm not going to let him off easily.

I study his upturned face. I like the view from up here and it's going to take a hell of a lot to take me down.

I arch my eyebrow. "My name is Anna."

The Queen's Tale

GRACE D'OTARE

"SHALL WE HAVE A STORY?" DEVLIN SUGGESTED, AS ANOTHER enormous clap of thunder rattled the rooftop. He traced the curve of his wife's bare shoulder with the tip of his finger. "A bedtime story. Something distracting. Something to keep us warm on a wicked night."

"What sort of a story?" Maeve turned her head, hiding her eyes but not her smile. His wife knew exactly what he had in mind.

"Oh, an erotic story, to be certain." Dev's finger traced her collarbone to the hollow in her throat. And then down. A thousand and one times he'd touched her, and still he felt the heat. "Those are the ones that warm and distract me best."

It was a challenge. It was a game—a game he and his lovely Maeve had played before. Never quite the same, but always exciting.

Maeve plumped the pillow behind her and sat up. The candlelight caught the twinkle of her glass, half-full of sherry. Dev watched her take a long swallow and lick her lips. The storm whistled outside. She made a point of snuggling deeper under the bedclothes, tucking the sheet around her.

"Tonight I'm Scheherazade?"

"And I'm your king."He tugged at the sheet, until it spilled around her waist."Entertain me, madam, or suffer the consequences."

"Well, let me think..."

Queen Philomena waited.

Not patiently, and not without anxiety. As she came to the end of the rug, she turned on her heel, flipped her skirts behind her, and began to pace the opposite direction. She had chosen to wear a simple gown so that once the time came, it would not be necessary to summon an abigail for assistance.

"A who?"Dev whispered, his hand creeping under the sheet.

"A maid," she explained. "Stop that."

"Stop that, Your Highness."

"Oh!"She caught her breath."Your Highness, that sort of thing will make it very hard to concentrate."

"'Very hard' seems fair to me. Go on then."

Queen Philomena waited...and wondered.

Perhaps the gentleman would consider it an insult? He might think she did not value his...service, if she did not wear something appropriate to her status.

She would have to address the situation directly. Frank discussion and a thoroughly negotiated agreement was her best hope of resolving any delicate issues that might arise.

Or so the king, may he rest in peace, always said. Philomena touched her wedding band as she thought of him. It slipped easily around her finger; nerves always left her hands cold and dry.

"Your Majesty," her handmaid called. "They are here."

"Show him—them—in." Philomena smoothed the front of her gown and assumed the face of the queen.

Three soldiers entered the room.

She suffered a moment of panic. What was she to do with *three* of them? Was she supposed to choose?

One of the men seemed familiar—a freckled young man who'd served on the court guard the last year or two. The second man was very large, tanned and weathered, the sort whose military career had been served in the rough. His face was plain, but his eyes were kind and full of good humor.

The third man was a shock.

He was fair, in all manner of the word. Sunny hair and sky-blue eyes. Almost pretty, Philomena thought, except there was too much intelligence in the candor of his gaze. He was scant inches taller than she. Not quite as large in height or frame as either of the other two men, but somehow Philomena felt his presence more forcefully. He was certainly the soldier in charge.

"Good evening, gentlemen," she said, as the queen ought.

All of them bowed respectfully.

"Thank you for…attending me," Philomena began. "Has my lord chamberlain spoken with you?"

The third man answered. "Yes, Your Highness. May I introduce Joseph, my sergeant major." He waved a hand at the rough-hewn man. "And you may already know Thomas, of your own house guard? The lord chamberlain suggested a small, personal guard might be best this evening. All others have been dismissed."

There was no smile on his lips, but Philomena saw it in his eyes and heard it in the tone of his voice. She turned to hide the coloring of her cheeks, and fiddled with the contents of her open lap desk.

This would not do. She must be committed. She must hold to her resolve, or she would begin her next life with regrets.

"Yes. That seems wise." Closing the portfolio of documents she had vacantly reviewed for the last hour, she called, "Thank you all, gentlemen, for your discretion in this matter. That will be all."

She heard heels click, boots crossing the marble floor, and the thunk of the heavy oak door as it closed.

Philomena peeked over her shoulder.

This time, the smile teased the corner of his mouth. "Did you expect me to take my leave also? Wouldn't that have been counterproductive to Your Majesty's desires?"

Desires.

The word slipped like steel from a scabbard. Philomena's heart raced; her throat tightened.

"Indeed." Philomena inclined her head. "Your name, sir?"

"I am Dante."

"Dante. Welcome. Before we begin…our business, I would like to come to an understanding on certain things." She smoothed her gown and sat, very upright, on the chaise near the fire. The door between the sitting room and the boudoir was partway open and the sight of the bed made it hard to think. Waving him to a slipper chair across the rug, she managed, "Please. Be comfortable."

He sketched a bow, recognizing the honor of being asked to sit in the queen's presence, and settled himself on the silk chair, legs wide, black boots gleaming all the way to the knee. Normally, she kept her gaze firmly fixed at eye level. What was normal about this situation? She stared. His thigh flexed. Her hands burned to feel that muscle flex and tighten again.

In a soft voice, Dante repeated her words. "An understanding?"

"Yes, yes. Forgive me. What was I saying?" She folded her hands in her lap. "I believe my lord chamberlain has explained the requirements of the situation?"

"Your Majesty is to be married tomorrow and—"he paused to remove a speck of lint from his trousers "—seeks amusement before her vows are spoken."

Philomena coughed. "Amusement? Is that how he...no. No. That is not the message I asked to be relayed. I...well, let me see if I can...explain."

She rose and began to pace the length of the carpet, yellow silk slippers peeking out as she kicked her hem. This was no time for words. It was time for action. Reaching into her hair, she removed first one pin and then a second. A curl of dark hair fell over her shoulder.

"I am to be married tomorrow, that much is true. For my country's good, I will be married to King—" She wiggled her fingertips and tried to recall the man's name.

"Benvenuto?"

"Yes! That's him." Philomena shook her head, her hair loosening. It felt...good. Free. Normally, she braided it again for sleep and went directly to bed. Tonight would be different. Tonight, she would remove every restraint.

"How ridiculous of me. I ought to remember the man's name. I am marrying him tomorrow after all." Repressing her giggles felt like being tickled on the inside.

Philomena shivered. Squaring her shoulders, she toed off her slippers. Lifting her skirt to the knee, she set her foot on a little crewel-covered footstool. She unclipped her stockings, one by one, and rolled them down her legs.

Dante did not answer. He watched her carefully, but his expression was somewhat colder than before.

Philomena tried to explain. "There were several men in contention for the job, you see? The treaty was the important thing. The lord chamberlain and I always referred to them by their...advantages. King Trade Agreement. King Fishing Rights. Benvenuto was King Western Border."

"If you would permit a question," her soldier asked, in a rather choked tone. "Why him? Why not one of the others?"

"For the good of the country, of course. My marriage will cement an alliance protecting our most vulnerable border." One, two, her stockings floated to the floor beside her slippers.

Oh, my. She'd never walked barefoot on the sitting room rug. Her toes wiggled into the darkest reds of the pattern. So soft...for the first time that evening, she spoke without tightness in her throat. "It will give the mountain folk access to the sea and trade opportunities. This marriage will create a great good for my people."

"You care so much for your people, you'd marry a man whose name you barely recall?"

She offered him a sympathetic smile. "You are a soldier, sir. You offer your body and your life every day. Could I do less?"

Philomena sat down on the rug, crossing her legs like a girl. She removed the golden bracelets from her wrists, her ear bobs and the necklace at her throat, dropping each into a pile in her lap. Her rings were the last to go. She hesitated at her wedding band.

"You are too young for such sacrifice," he said.

She tried not to laugh. "I am more than twenty, sir. And joined in holy matrimony to His Majesty, the king, God rest his soul, at the age of thirteen."

"Good lord." The man paused and she could almost hear the clicking of his mental calculations. "The man was close to ninety when he died."

With a clank, she dropped her wedding ring into the pile. Tomorrow, she would wear another. Tonight, she would wear none.

"And well past seventy when he consummated our marriage."

"Thirteen," Dante mumbled under his breath, his eyes on the pile of jewelry in her lap.

"Do not think ill of the king. He was a good man—he waited until I was of an age to carry a child without danger before he…initiated marital activity. Then he became ill and such activities were no longer of great interest." Philomena took hold of the lace at the front of her dress and pulled. There. Another tie undone.

"We found other joys, other comforts."

"But, if you have no interest in—"

"I did not say, *I* had no interest," she interrupted, slightly flustered. "But tomorrow such choices will be taken from my hands. I will make vows and I will honor them, sir, make no mistake."

He studied her with those blue, blue eyes. "I believe you will."

Philomena took a deep breath. Something in her eased. "His Majesty, God rest his soul, taught me much. How to understand my people. To be a good ruler. But there is one thing he was unable to teach me...."

"Yes?"

She stared down at the gap in her bodice. Without lacing, her breasts shifted freely. The brush of silk brought a nearly painful tightening of her nipples.

In a voice too breathless for a queen she answered, "The ways of love. Physical love."

"How long?" Dante asked gruffly. He leaned forward, shifting as if his seat were suddenly uncomfortable. "How long since you enjoyed the marriage bed?"

"Six years."

How could eyes so blue hold so much heat? "Forgive my casualness earlier, madam. You have every right to a night of...enjoyment, before you commit yourself again."

"I wish more than enjoyment, sir." The longing in her voice pinched her pride. "I wish understanding. I wish to know what my people feel when they marry in the flush of youth." With shaking hands she slipped her arms out of her dress and let it puddle around her on the floor. "When they choose a lover freely, when they enjoy all the pleasures of the body...for one night I would like to be a woman. No more. No less."

Was it her words or the sight of the queen in her shift that pushed him back against his seat?

"And are you certain you do not wish to wait for your new husband to show you these pleasures?"

She hid her face in both hands and laughed. "Oh, Dante, when you have attended as many state dinners as I... Kings are old men who have battled long and hard. Most are stooped with woes. This is the way of the world. I hope to respect and, perhaps someday, care for my husband, but physical love is not a luxury a queen can expect."

"I see."

"You are a soldier. My lord chamberlain has asked you to... perform a duty for queen and country." Philomena cleared her throat. "If it is a duty that seems distasteful to you—"

"Distasteful?" It was his turn to laugh. "Not at all, madam. Not at all. We shall find our way tonight, together." His whole body seemed to relax with his laugh. In a simple, fluid motion, he removed his jacket and hung it on the chair's back and popped the studs of his starched collar and cuffs. He grabbed his shirt behind his neck and pulled it up and over his head, tousling his hair. "Consider me entirely at your disposal."

The man was bare to the waist and smiling. An unnerving sort of smile. The type of smile a queen rarely saw.

Another swoop and tickle rolled up her spine.

"Come here, Your Majesty."

Philomena rose from the carpet, leaving her gown and jewels where they lay. "Turn around," he asked.

"I beg your pardon?"

"Turn around. I need to get these boots off."

Confused, but pleased by his respect for her modesty, Philomena did as he requested. From behind, he took hold of her hips. With a firm yank, he pulled her rear backward at the same time as he lifted a large booted foot between her legs, hiking her shift nearly to her knees in the process.

"What are you doing?!"

"Grab that heel and pull," he ordered, good-naturedly.

"Good God, woman, have you never helped a man off with his boots, either?"

"The king—God rest his soul," she muttered, gingerly grasping his ankle, "did not wear boots."

She tugged once to no effect. Wanting this awkwardness finished, she grabbed him tightly and felt the long, hard muscle of his calf flex inside its leather casing. Her breath caught in her throat. "Sir, your boots are too tight."

"The fit is meant to be tight."

His hands splayed across the curve of her hips. Philomena felt the pressure of each fingertip distinct from his wide palm. There was a teasing quality to his voice that roused her nerves.

"A tight fit feels best on a long ride." With that, he set his second, still-booted foot against her backside. "Pull!" he ordered, and slapped her haunch with a loud smack.

She jerked upright, the heel caught in her shocked grip.

"That's the way!" Dante congratulated with a hearty pinch to the same tingling spot. His empty boot thunked to the floor.

Philomena tumbled forward, whirling around to face him. She clenched her hands, too embarrassed to actually rub the spot that stung.

"I beg your pardon!"

"My lady." Dante's head tipped forward, but there was no meekness to his bow. "You wished to know how a woman experiences 'the pleasures of the body.' A woman is meant to be...touched."

Philomena stared. What had he meant to say before he'd settled on the diplomatic use of the word "touched"?

"I am your queen, sir. First. Last. And always." She had never found the words so difficult to say. Without her dressings and jewels and coiffed hair, she felt oddly vulnerable——but a queen was more than clothes and jewels. "I will not be pawed like a common bar wench."

He looked straight into her eyes as few men ever did.

Again, she felt that disconcerting ripple.

With the voice that opened Parliament and welcomed enemies of the state to her dinner table, she added, "Make no mistake, Dante. I expect to surrender to a king tomorrow, but tonight, I shall rule here. Do you accept my terms?"

He took her hand and bowed low to meet it. His breath warmed her knuckles His thumb stroked the skin on the edge of her hand. Turning her palm, he licked the plump curve at the base of her thumb.

"What——"

Before she could speak another word, he sucked that tender morsel between his teeth. Wet warmth melted into a sharp ache, which was suddenly soothed by the press of his lips. Once. Twice.

"What was that?"

"A kiss," he whispered, hovering over her hand. "Only a kiss."

"That was not a kiss," she argued in a girlish voice. "The old king kissed me many times."

That blue-eyed smile chased after her again. Warmth drizzled down her spine.

"There are many kinds of kisses, Your Highness," Dante said. "This is a kiss."

Courtly and charming, he bussed the back of her hand lightly.

"And this is a kiss."

Cool and formal, he slid his hand up to clasp her elbow, then pulled her closer for a continental touch of cheeks.

"And this."

Cupping her head with a gentle hand, he slowly, sweetly, pressed his lips to the center of her forehead.

Philomena's eyes drifted shut.

"This is also a kiss."

His lips parted, barely brushing hers. Licking became tasting, tasting became toothy nibbles and a hungry growl for more. His fingers massaged restlessly though her hair.

Philomena felt as though her nerves existed in an exaggerated state where he touched her, hand to head, lips to lips, breasts pressed against his chest. She could not pull back.

"Enough," she whispered. "Enough."

"More." He opened wider, breathing his desire right into her, a warm liquid over her crystalline interior. His enormous, burning hand gripped the curve of her behind and hauled her closer.

No petticoats, no corset, nothing but a thin silk chemise—she felt everything. Every seam, every button, every edge of his flesh.

"Good heavens." Her heart fluttered. "What is that?"

"Your Highness?" he answered with a very unsubtle rock of his hips.

Philomena pulled back. She waved in the general vicinity of his trouser buttons. *"That."*

He winked. "Evidence."

"Evidence?" She glanced down, then quickly up again. She took another step back. "Of what?"

"My willingness to serve, of course." His face was flushed, his breathing obvious. He looked like someone ill with fever.

"Are you certain you're quite well?"

"Not…quite." He took a step toward her.

"There does seem to be an excessive amount of swelling." She kept the words formal, polite, as if she were commenting on a horse to one of the groomsmen, while she moved to the far edge of the carpet. The old king's weapon had never achieved quite the same amount of upright vigor, as far as she could recall. "Does it pain you much?"

"'It?'" he smirked. "Is that any way for a grown—queen—to talk? Understanding begins with words, Your Majesty. That is not an 'it.'" His voice dropped, husky and dark. "That is my cock, also sometimes dick, or willie, roger, john thomas—"

"Yes, yes. We've met—Richard, William, et cetera." She waved a hand, stuttering. "Does he, I mean, your—"

"Cock?" he inserted carefully.

"—hurt?"

"You've no idea." He took another purposeful step forward.

What next? Philomena scrambled behind a chair. "Stop!" She held up a firm hand. She needed to regain control. "Wait. Don't move."

"Don't be ridiculous." Dante stalked forward.

"Guard!" she called out, instinctively.

The door swung open almost instantly. Joseph and Thomas appeared a second later, swords drawn.

"Get out, you idiots," Dante said. "We're fine."

"Restrain him," Philomena ordered. She pointed to Dante's shocked face.

Joseph glanced back and forth between them, seemed to struggle with a grin and then turned to his partner. "You heard your queen. Rope or chains, ma'am? Or you want us to each take an arm and let you have at him? He can be a right pain in the arse sometimes. I don't wonder you've lost patience already."

"Joseph," Dante warned.

"No, thank you," Philomena stuttered. "Use whatever you think best."

"Queen Philomena," Dante interrupted. "You don't want to do this."

Everyone in the room felt the threat. Joseph broke the tension with a booming laugh.

"Well, she might not, but I know I do. Story to tell the grandkids, you know." He winked at Philomena. "I've just the thing, your ladyship." He reached behind the flap of his great coat and pulled out a pair of shiny silver bracelets, linked by a short length of chain. "Hands out, Captain. Are you going to snap to or are we going to have to tell the lord chamberlain that he should send another man for this job?"

"Philomena," Dante said.

Embarrassed to the core, she fell back on old habits. "I did not give you permission to use my name."

"We'd better gag him for you too," Joseph suggested. "It's his mouth that always gets him into trouble."

Philomena touched her lips, thinking of the kisses Dante's mouth had demonstrated. When she realized he was watching, her face began to burn.

Joseph took advantage of the distraction and locked one side of the wrist manacles in place while quick-stepping the man into a headlock.

"That's my boy!" he laughed, as Dante swung his head back and narrowly missed slamming the bridge of Joseph's nose.

"Grab his other hand, Thomas! If you're not too busy just standing there?"

Thomas jumped into the fray.

"Behind the back is better—oomph—ow! Blasted—never mind. That'll do."

The handcuffs were snapped into place. Grunts, fleshy smacks and thudding violence had Philomena cringing. A length of sturdy rope appeared from inside one of Joseph's bottomless jacket pockets.

"Rope his hands up. No! Top of the bed frame. Watch his knees," Joseph grumbled. "Little bugger's faster than he used to be."

"Perhaps we should reconsider—" Philomena started.

"Not at all! Only another—oof!—moment, Your Majesty. We'll be out of your way."

"Don't hurt—"

"Nonsense. Just a bit of roughhouse."

Joseph and Thomas both stepped back, slightly out of breath. "There you are."

Dante's arms were loosely suspended over his head, his manacled wrists roped to the top rail of her bed. The frame was ancient mahogany; the canopy pole thicker than Philomena's arm. They all watched as Dante wrapped his hands around the rope and swung his weight against it.

The rail held.

"When I get out of here—" Dante lunged toward Joseph "—you'd better hope—"

"The pubs are still open?" Joseph winked at Philomena. "No worries. We'll all still be celebrating the queen's special day. Won't we?" He tipped his head toward the exit, and wrapped an arm around Thomas's shoulder to lead him out. As he closed the bedroom door, he bowed deeply.

"I don't like this," Dante began immediately.

"Nevertheless—"

"Untie me."

"I think not."

"You can't do this to me!"

Philomena blinked.

She was the queen. Of course she could. Point of fact, she could do much worse, if she were that sort.

"You never answered my question," she realized. "Did you?"

"Question?" he snapped in frustration. "What question?"

"Tonight, it's queen's rules." She walked to the door and picked up the key that Joseph had left on the small table. "That is the question you must ask yourself, sir. If you cannot accept that, I will release you. And you will leave this chamber and never return. Answer me now, Captain Dante. Queen's rules. Do you accept?"

He hesitated. His eyes narrowed. Philomena was certain she heard his breath hiss as he exhaled. But he answered clearly.

"I do."

A long sigh of relief slipped out. She felt lighter. The queen gave way to the girl inside. She didn't resist the sudden need to smile.

This beautiful man was hers to play with, feast on, enjoy for the entire night.

All of him was pleasing to her, from the cut and curve of the arching muscles across his shoulders, to the shadowed hollow at the center of his chest, down to his navel, and even there, in the deep vee of his thighs. She squeaked with her next sigh.

"Do your worst, Majesty. Anything you like."

"My worst?" she repeated.

"As you can see, I'm helpless to resist." His words pleaded weakness, but his stance shifted as if he were readying for a fight.

"I would like——" Philomena cleared her throat "——to stand closer. And to kiss you. Again."

He didn't answer at first. His arms flexed, pulling against the rope and relaxing. "Come then."

She took one step. Another. Watching him carefully. She'd seen how he'd used his legs when he was fighting the other men.

"A little closer, Your Highness." He nodded toward the small padded footstool near her chaise. "Bring that——if you like."

Arms raised and tied, he could not bend to meet her kiss. The stool's height lifted her to meet him eye to eye, lip to lip.

The heat of his skin went right through her shift, with a shocking stillness.

"What now?" he asked.

"Now…I touch you." Philomena replied before gently placing her hands low on his waist. She flexed her fingertips, testing the muscle over hipbone. Everything in her that had been stiff and dry with nerves suddenly softened, dripping with desire.

"And now, I will kiss——"

"*We* will kiss," he contradicted her softly.

She brought her mouth to his and tried to recreate the moment before she'd panicked, that rich swirl of lust and play and wonder and…

The chains clinked as he moved to reach for her.

"Remove the rope at least, my lady. Please. I only want to touch you."

When he spoke, Philomena felt him strain to remain still, forced to wait for her. Her heart beat faster.

"Very prettily said, but no. I think…not."

Philomena skimmed her fingers down his chest. Young man's skin…so different from the old king. Dante resembled the marble statues in the castle loggia, expect for the fine, pale hair that softened the curves of muscle.

"You're blushing."

"Am I?" She continued touching him, one fingertip, then another, curving down and around, watching his skin react to her touch. A perfume seemed to rise off his skin, a scent unlike anything she'd known. Spicy yet delicate. Her mouth watered, inspired by an unfamiliar appetite. "Have you seen the statue in the loggia, the one titled 'Hero'?"

Dante did not answer. His eyes had drifted shut; his weight thrust forward. Even his bare toes arched against the floor, his partially nude body strung into one long line of tension.

Philomena's fingers meandered down past his navel to the buckle of his leather belt.

"It's a lovely work of art," she chattered away, distracting herself from the scandalous task of loosening his belt, then unbuttoning the top of his trousers. "Confidentially, the lord chamberlain has caught me observing that particular statue more than once."

"I've seen it. A statue to celebrate the human form, as I recall." He sounded very calm for a man whose body was a bowstring of tension.

Releasing the final button, his pants dropped with a thud. He'd certainly dressed for the occasion—he wore absolutely nothing under his uniform. Philomena celebrated his form with a gasp of appreciation.

"Nude," he went on gruffly and jerked against the rope. "Free of all restraints."

"Free of clothing alone, in your case," she teased. "You bear a—I mean, you *resemble* the statue," she stammered. "Rather disconcerting, to think how well the lord chamberlain knows me. The man's old enough to be my grandpapa." At hearing herself babble, her voice crept higher. "Perhaps you've not had the experience of being so continually, thoroughly observed… how very alarming it can be."

"Alarming?" Dante's voice, by contrast, seemed even deeper. He shifted his legs, stepping free of his pants with obvious relief. His wider stance hollowed the muscle from buttock to thigh that she'd admired earlier. "Do you find it alarming?"

"What?" She tried to focus on the conversation. "Well, when it's the lord chamberlain and my privates—" she choked on the word "—my private *thoughts.*"

"Tell me more," the handsome stranger tied before her whispered. "Tell me your private thoughts, Philomena." He jerked his arms downward, reaching for her. The silver cuffs jangled against the rope.

The sound startled her. She stepped back, down off the stool.

A growl rolled in Dante's throat. He tipped his head and narrowed his eyes as if assessing a target.

"Where are you going? I'm chained. Helpless. Come back, Your Highness. Touch me again."

"Touch you?" She concentrated on his blue eyes. "Where?"

"Wherever you like. I can't stop you, can I? It's all up to you."

Heat whipped up her spine, flushing her face. So many tiresome things were all up to her. For once, it was wonderful to be the one deciding. She glanced down. Swollen and flushed, the tip of him was a deep royal red. She had never seen anything like it.

"I wish to touch your...cock," she whispered. Moving back onto her stool, she tenderly laid her hand, wrist to fingertip, against the long, hard rise of his penis, pressing as if it were a wound to soothe.

Dante's answer was a slice of indrawn breath.

"Still hurts?"

"Mmm," he answered, closing his eyes.

"Poor thing," she murmured.

He rocked his pelvis into her palm, a sound vibrating from deep inside his chest. He pushed at her so strongly, Philomena had to reach up and grip his shoulder with her other hand, steadying herself as she might with a demanding waltz partner.

The movement brought them chest to chest. Dante strained forward, nuzzling her ear with a whispered kiss.

Philomena began to curl her fingers one by one around his thickness. He made a handful, all of it warmer than she'd expected. She tested firmness and length with a long, slow, heart-stopping tug.

Dante strained as far as the rope would allow to press his lips to her throat. Philomena recognized the sharp nip, immediately swallowed by the same hot pulling comfort she'd felt on her palm. She released him immediately and stumbled backward off the stool again, twisting herself in a circle of confusion, once, twice.

His chains clanked with frustrated restraint. "Your nipples. They're darker now...and so tight." Dante's voice dripped honey over her thoughts. "Do they ache? I can help with that, if you'll come back. Come to me."

How did he know? Her hands twitched with the need to press and soothe her aching breasts, to bind them tightly into her corset, anything to end that burning distraction.

Her expression seemed to amuse him. He shook his head, half laughing. A shock of blond hair dropped across his brow. "I know what would help." Disheveled, he was even more appealing, more approachable. "Let me suck them, Philomena. It's good for the ache. It makes it so much—" he stretched the rope to its limit, looming over her "—worse."

She almost jumped. Embarrassed, she pushed hard at his chest, setting him back on his feet. "Behave, or I'll call the guards and have you gagged."

"You wouldn't," he said, assessing her with a narrow look.

"Oh, I think I would." Throwing her shoulders back, she asked, "But now you have me wondering, would sucking ease your ache or make it worse?"

She'd heard of such things, hints and jokes and whispers. That men liked a woman's mouth as much as other parts.

His eyes glittered. He seemed to be struggling with the urge to laugh or lunge for her.

The air prickled with possibilities. Philomena sank down onto the stool. His penis bobbed right under her nose, a thick, rosy flower. Taking him in hand, she inhaled the scent of the dewdrop at the tip. Sugar musk. Sweet spice.

"Just a taste," she whispered. Her tongue slipped out and ever so lightly touched the tip of him. The skin was smoother, softer than the rest of him, closer to the feel of his mouth when they had opened to each other. She licked again. Again.

"Perhaps a little more."

It felt odd to open so wide; a very unladylike amount to put inside her mouth. She wasn't quite sure what to do with all of it. She wiggled her tongue around the fullness, surprised that there was no taste, really, only smoothness, slicked by the wetness of her own saliva.

Somewhere above her, she recognized the hurried twist and tug of his arms. There was a swish of rope falling, but she was too busy to care. The heat of his open hands suddenly hovered over her head in benediction, then dropped with a faint metallic jingle as his fingers slipped behind her neck into her hair, gripping hard.

"Mehnnaaaa…" He exhaled the last of her name with longing.

No one had called her Mena in years. It was a sweet name, a pet name, far too undignified for a queen. Philomena smiled, accidentally popping him free of her lips.

He groaned and shivered in her hands.

"You like that?" She tried it again, tightening her lips as she pressed the head of his cock in and out. His hips began to shift, almost imperceptibly, then more forcefully, the chuff of his breath marking the motion.

The sound and motion made her giddy as she realized what he sought to mimic. He liked it; he liked it very much. One hand awkwardly cupped her head, encouraging her. *Don't stop. Don't go. Once more…*

She released him, pressed her tongue to trace a wide path from the stiff root to the smooth tip.

Dante's hands dropped heavily to her shoulders. He swayed, his breath cutting the silence with short, sharp pants.

Nuzzling the smooth muscled cradle of his pelvis, Philomena

wrapped one steadying arm around his thighs. Her other hand slid up the back of his leg to cup the weighted muscle of his bottom cheek. She inhaled deeply, holding him tight, feeling everything low inside her twist with the luscious scent and feel of this man's skin. She could not sit still.

"Did that make it better or worse, Dante?" she murmured.

Her eyes were closed but she recognized the jingle-clink of his chains, right before he caught her under the arms and pulled her up in a motion so sure and sudden she could not resist.

He opened his arms, resting the weight on her shoulders, encircling her. Startled, she gasped. Dante pulled her close, capturing the sound that might have summoned the guards in a kiss.

Philomena tensed her neck, resisting. She jerked her bottom backward, rocking the footstool off balance. One second they were together, the next they were tipping.

His reflexes were better trained than hers, thank heavens. Slipping free of his linked arms, Philomena plopped butt-first onto the carpet. Dante followed, his grim expression floating over her before he flipped to land with an undignified thud alongside her.

"So help me, Mena—" He sounded winded. "When I get..."

Philomena covered her face with her hands...and laughed. "I don't believe I've given you permission to speak to me so familiarly, sir. However, under the circumstances—"

"Under the circumstances?"

"—I shall make an exception." She wiped tears from her eyes. When was the last time she'd laughed so hard? Ages. *Years.*

"You honor me, Your Highness." Dante rolled onto his back, studying her painted ceiling as if it held the secrets of the night sky. His hands were cupped casually over his belly, his erection resting lightly on top of them. He turned his head and grinned. "Care to honor me again?"

"Perhaps."

Philomena marveled at his aplomb. What would that be like? To be so aroused, and still calm. To enjoy the sensation for minutes at a time, even with another person watching. Her own body was creating a panic of awareness: the piercing tight- ness in her breasts, the slippery moisture between her legs, the throb that made it hard not to flex her private muscles and squirm...

"What next?" She forced the whisper through her tight throat.

"Next?" He rolled close, kissed her mouth softly, pushed up on one elbow and slung his leg over her. "Reach me the keys, so I can show you."

"Keys?"

"I need my hands free, Mena, to do what comes next."

This kiss opened her. His tongue erased the boundaries between them; thick and wet, it reminded her of having his cock in her mouth and she couldn't hold back the sound of the hungry yearning she felt.

"Oh God, Mena. My hands. Now."

"No." She shifted out from under him and sat up. "*No.*"

Even handcuffed, he held so much power over her. Shaking, she pushed him flat on his back. She shifted to her knees, looked down into his wide blue eyes. "Twelve years I was married. I've never been the one to say how, when or where. I don't need your hands. I need your cooperation."

She crawled over him, one knee to either side of his hips,

one hand flat over his heart, his wrists chained, hands open, reaching… She took his cock firmly in her other hand, and stopped breathing as she notched him into her wet folds. She meant to go slowly, to give herself time; it felt so different than she remembered, so full, warm, harder, stiffer…

But Dante had other ideas. He thrust quickly upward, crying out as if he were the invaded party, catching her wrists in his shackled hands.

Trapping her. Trapping himself.

"Oh, oh my." Philomena tipped and rolled, locked in place above him.

"Again," he groaned.

Panting, she tried to feel one thing separate from the rest, to repeat what he needed, to understand the sensations lighting her body on fire. She pushed back, sitting up straight, sending his cock higher inside.

Dante's head tipped back, exposing his throat and releasing a gasping, guttural "Oh, fuuuuck."

Philomena nearly laughed aloud—again. Happiness bubbled through her, making her lighter and lighter inside. She lifted her hips off her heels and slid down hard and fast, hoping she might be able to make him do it again.

It worked. Three times in a row, in fact.

Then all at once, they began to gasp together. Lift to meet each other. Separate with intent. It was the sweetest feeling she'd ever experienced. Her palms pressed solidly over the bones and flesh of his hips, she lifted and fell…"Dante," she whispered. "Shouldn't we move to the bed?"

"Beds are for old, married people. Lovers prefer the carpet."

"They do?"

"Or the wall, the closet, the carriage…"

His words filled her mind with images as his body filled her with sensations. "But why?"

"Lovers…need…quick…fierce." Each of his words punctuated a thrust. "I'll…teach you…Mena. Every…single…way."

"How?"

His answer was startlingly swift. The muscles of his stomach tightened, his thighs flexed. He pushed forward with his chest, cradling her in the vee of his lifted torso and raised knees. The moment she'd adjusted her limbs for comfort, he pressed his advantage and carried her backward, flat onto the floor, rising on his splayed knees. Frustrated by his restraints, he pulled her into him, one side then the other, locking her tight to his body, her bottom wedged against the slant of his thighs, her knees wide on either side of his hips.

Here again, the sensation of him changed. How many different ways could it feel? Now there was more than his thickness and heat. She felt the stroke of some sweet, sharp nerve inside. She felt the pinch of tears.

"More, more. Oh, please…"

"More like this? How beautiful you are, my Mena, my queen." Talking while tilting his hips the smallest amount, just enough, Dante pressed inside. He opened her with his body and his words. "Look at me here, on my knees for you. Still wearing your chains. You're safe with me, yes you are, my queen…." His words wove a spell. "Let go."

He bent forward and, with his teeth, caught the tiny blue ribbons that held her silk chemise closed. Tugging, tearing at her last covering, and always tilting, tipping, rocking her inside.

She hadn't wanted to be naked in front of him. She'd chosen to keep that thin garment, mindful as a queen of every layer of meaning. A warning flared through her over-sensitized body.

"Stop. Wait." She squirmed and her own motions shrugged the fabric from her shoulders, exposing her. "Oh no, don't. I'm too…"

"You're beautiful. Let me see. Please."

He locked her wrists in the circle of his fingers—held them tight as any handcuffs He never stopped moving, stroking her, asking for something she didn't know how to give.

"Mena, look at me, on my knees. Begging. Do you feel me begging?" He straightened his thighs, pulling her up into him. His shoulders relaxed, his eyes closed and he thrust, hard.

And did not stop.

She answered with a sound that mingled exclamation and warning. It was different again—the sweet and sharp punctuated by crashing violence. She arched her feet, digging her toes into the soft carpet, and still was rocked with each powerful thrust.

"Let go." His voice was deep, clear, his words a command. "Let go. Now."

No one could resist. No one.

She went in all directions, with a heart-stopping disintegration, disappearing inside and suddenly beginning again, all at once, all together.

"Yes!" he shouted, chest thrust forward, head back, fingers sprung open releasing her, snapping the chain between his cuffed hands.

The next moments were disorderly.

* * *

Philomena heard his footsteps, then the jingle and clink of keys and metal falling on the nearby chest of drawers. A rustle of linens preceded the soft warmth of a blanket falling around her, a pillow being tucked beneath her head.

He slipped in behind her, pulling her bottom into the warm nest of his body.

"Can we try the wall or the closet next?" she whispered, fighting to hear his answer before sleep.

"Another time, my queen. Rest."

"Promise me."

"Yes?"

"I know we have never encountered one another before in the palace." She covered his hand where it lay against her belly. "But should you ever by chance come upon me, at court perhaps or even in some state procession, will you turn away? Quickly. Don't speak to me. Don't even look."

She felt him pull back, cold air slipping between them. "Why?"

"I'm afraid."

"Of what?"

"I will be another man's queen. I'm afraid I will not remember my duty, should I ever see you again."

With a sigh, the distance between them closed. "Fear not, my queen. Fear not."

Philomena melted into his warmth and let herself go again...this time into deep, restful sleep.

"Poor queen," Dev murmured.

The rain pattered softly now, on the roof. He pulled Maeve in close, rocking his hips steadily against the pillow of her ass, nestling his cock along the damp warmth of her cleft. He could come like this, spooning, her voice creating pictures in his mind. The longer the story, the harder it was to resist.

"Only if we end it there," she answered breathily.

"There's more then?" He flicked a finger casually, and grinned when she squeaked.

"Would you like more?"

He thrust and withdrew, slowly. Letting them both enjoy the wait. "Always."

The next day was diabolically beautiful. The sun shone. The birds sang.

The queen wept.

Discipline supported her. She bathed, dressed and sat for her hair exactly as always. Exactly as if it did not matter.

The moment she swept into the church, in a sigh of lacy silk, the organist stopped. The audience rustled to its feet. Philomena's eyes filled with tears and blurred the particulars of the faces around her. Her people.

One foot in front of the next.

Duty.

As she stepped up onto the dais, the king she would marry took her elbow. She nearly resisted.

And then she nearly fainted.

His smile dripped wicked satisfaction. His voice was pitched for her alone. "It is *quite* frightening how well your lord chamberlain knows you."

"Dante?"

"King Western Border to you, my dear." He pulled her closer

to whisper in her ear. "Tonight, we use the bed. And you wear the handcuffs."

Thank heavens her veil disguised the shocking, meltingly hot blush that kissed her body.

But he felt it. She knew he did.

"Your Highness."

"Absolutely, *Your* Highness," she agreed.

"Happy after all," he cooed in her ear.

"I like a happy ending, don't you?"

He rolled over her, crushing her flat beneath him and reaching over the side of the bed until he found the slippery silk of a discarded stocking. Her giggle was hard to hear around the mouthful of pillow. "Very. Allow me to demonstrate my appreciation for your creativity."

Dev grabbed one of her hands and knotted the material around her wrist. He flipped her onto her back, wrapping the stocking around the spindle of the bed frame in one smooth motion. Her arm stretched over her head. He grabbed her other wrist and looped the loose end of her stocking around it.

She cocked an eyebrow as she watched him go about the business of tying her to the bed. "That stocking is Donna Karan."

"Oh?"

"Silk."

"Never looked better on you," he said, letting his eyes feast on the sight of her. "Handy, too."

"You're cheating. In my story, the king was the helpless one."

"The king never cheats." He nipped the tip of her breast, and sucked it hard, exactly the way Dante had kissed his queen. "The king makes the rules. Tonight, we pick up where your story left off."

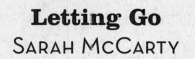

Letting Go

Sarah McCarty

THE CAR PULLED UP IN FRONT OF THE DARK CABIN. The white glow of the moon reflecting off newly fallen snow highlighted the isolation of the log home set at the foot of the mountain. It was perfect. Remote. Comfortable. And it was theirs for the weekend. No work. No pets. Nothing to distract them from each other.

The uncharacteristic shyness that had been plaguing her the entire four-hour trip came back in spades as Marc switched off the car's engine. Which was absolutely ridiculous. They'd planned this weekend for a month. Nothing was going to happen here that either of them hadn't eagerly anticipated, but now that it was time for the planning to give birth to fantasy, she was shy to the point of blushing. She, the woman who never blushed, never embarrassed. Never lost control.

Becky pretended an interest in the scenery as the driver's side door opened. Marc's gaze slid over her like a touch, poking at her insecurities, asking silent questions she didn't want to answer. Anticipation and nerves fluttered in her stomach in a queasy combination. She made her expression blank to hide her discomfort.

Marc sighed. The door creaked open. "We don't have to do this, you know."

She kept her voice just as balanced as her expression. "Yes, we do." Because she was so sick of not being who she wanted to be with him.

"Then why the cold shoulder?"

That got her looking at him. He thought she was brushing him off? She took a subtle steadying breath, inhaling the scent of the outdoors…and Marc. Both were clean, crisp and intangibly tied together in her mind, maybe because they'd met on a weekend kayak excursion, but more than likely because the man was as elemental as the forest around them.

She unclenched fists she didn't know she'd been clenching. Good grief! No wonder he was asking questions. She looked more ready to go into battle than indulge in a romantic weekend. Becky shook her head at her own idiocy, her hair swishing around her shoulders with the movement. She brushed a strand away from her mouth. "Believe it or not, I'm nervous."

"Why?"

He didn't try to make eye contact again, which was good. If she'd looked at him, pride would have demanded she lie. "Because I'm afraid I might not live up to your expectations."

The back of his fingers brushed down the side of her cheek. His low chuckle still sent a shiver down her spine the way it had the first time she'd heard it. Not for the first time she wondered what attracted him to her. He was as sexy and as uninhibited as a man could get, and she had more inhibitions than…well, than anyone needed.

"Baby, we've been married for two years—do you really think I don't know what you're capable of?"

She looked at him then, taking in the amusement and understanding in his gaze. He was so sure this wasn't going to be a disaster. "Neither of us knows that."

His smile was a slow, sexy stretch of the lips she'd seen many times before. Masculine. Knowing. And confident. He was always so confident. "I know."

She clung to that confidence as his hand skimmed her neck, her shoulder, then her thigh. A pat on her knee followed by a quick squeeze and then he was out of the car, leaving her alone with her hopes, fears and that borrowed bravado. Crisp night air swept in on his exit and she jumped as the door thudded shut.

She shook her head at her own cowardice. They'd devoted this weekend to obliterating the inhibitions between them. Inhibitions neither wanted. Becky slung her purse over her shoulder, watching in the rearview mirror as Marc walked around the back, a tall muscular silhouette cast in moonlight. Cowering in the car wasn't an impressive start on her side.

She yanked the latch and shoved the door open. Snow crunched beneath her feet as she stood and stretched. The night sky expanded before her, a satiny carpet of black speckled with shining stars and dotted with glowing planets. She took a deep breath of the frigid air, shivering as it bit into her lungs.

A cloud wafted across the moonlit sky. She released her breath, watching the frozen vapor rise until it seemed to meld with that wispy traveler, becoming more than what it was, and yet still less than it would be. For a minute more, she watched the cloud skate along, free and unfettered, and then smiled as, with absolute certainty she knew everything was going to be all right. There was nothing she and he couldn't do. Nothing they couldn't accomplish. Not together. Together, they were like that cloud. More than what they had been before, yet ever growing with boundless potential. She just had to stop being afraid to let go.

Anticipation skittered through her veins as she walked around the back of the car. The view here was as interesting as the night sky, seeing as Marc was stretched forward, retrieving a suitcase. The man had the body of a runner, roped with lean, hard muscle. She slid her hands up the side of his thighs, smiling as taut muscle flexed under her touch, gliding them up over his narrow hips, under his jacket, around his waist.

He jumped at the chill of her hands and then relaxed into her hug, settling his palms over hers, pressing them into his abdomen. As always, he communicated so much with a touch, his thoughts as clear as if he'd spoken. She pressed her cheek against the smooth leather of his jacket.

"I love you, too," she whispered. And because she couldn't resist, added, "And I swear, I'm not going to be like this all weekend."

"Sweetheart, a few nerves aren't going to send me running scared."

"Even if I babble occasionally?"

He turned in her arms, his hands dropping to the hollow of her spine. "I've never seen you babble. Might be cute to witness."

She tilted her head. With a foot difference in their heights, she had to lean back a bit before she could see his expression. "Trust me, it's not a pretty picture."

That half amused, half indulgent smile was still on his face. His head bent. Just before his mouth met hers, he whispered, "I'll chance it."

If there was ever proof that the man got her, it was right there in his kiss. He didn't just take what he wanted like she expected, but rather he seduced, his mouth rubbing against hers in a subtle coaxing that sapped the anxiety right out of her and replaced it with a warm willingness. Willingness to trust him, to do what he wanted, to be what he wanted. What she wanted.

She opened her mouth and stretched up on her toes, accepting the thrust of his tongue, the natural dominance in his hold, tilting her head to give him more, letting him lead her past the point where caution said stop. Spreading her legs for the insertion of his thigh between, she checked her impulse to control the need to rub against him, following her instinct and his lead rather than her head. With her next breath she inhaled his groan of satisfaction.

"That's it. Just let it happen."

His grip moved to her hips, lifting her up against the thrust of his cock, pressing down as she worked her hips in an effort to get closer, to his heat, his cock, to him....

Too soon he was sliding her down his body, setting her feet on the ground, separating their lips.

"Hold that thought."

She didn't want to hold anything but him. The press of his thumb at the corner of her mouth sent a shock wave of need through her. Everything she ever dreaded seeing in a man's eyes was there in Marc's: amusement, satisfaction and, worst of all, a complacent grin that said he knew exactly how weak she was when it came to him. But her inward flinch never got a running start because there was no malice in that grin, just a bone deep satisfaction that was as arousing as it was comforting because it said more than anything else that at least one of them knew what they were doing. And it was completely natural that it was him.

His jacket whispered a protest as she slid her arms free. His hand cupped her cheek in one of those easy touches that reached all the way to her soul, catching her before she could step away. His hazel eyes were dark in the moonlight. She leaned her cheek into his gloved palm and sighed. "I'm an idiot."

His answer was immediate. "Yes, you are, but you're mine, and I kind of like you this way."

She raised her eyebrows. "A neurotic mess?"

His thumb brushed her mouth and a chuckle quirked his lips before his hand dropped away. "Vulnerable."

She held out her hand for her suitcase. "Uh-huh. Well, don't get used to it."

He paused before dragging the cooler out and putting it on the snow-encrusted ground. "I'll try to keep my appreciation limited to the weekend."

She averted her eyes as he settled a brown box on the cooler's white top. "Thank you."

He closed the trunk and hefted the cooler and box. "My pleasure."

Becky followed as Marc led the way down the hill to the cabin, admiring the way his jeans clung to his thighs with each step delineating the strength beneath. She wondered if he was thinking the same things she was. She wondered if his cock was hardening as quickly as her pussy was moistening. God! She wanted him. Wanted this. And she shifted the suitcase as she hurried to keep up, she was not going to allow anything to stop her from obtaining her goal. She might have more than her fair share of inhibitions, but she also had more than her fair share of determination, and of the two qualities, the second was stronger than the first.

The cabin was cold, the vaulted ceilings and log walls harboring the chill of the outside. She turned up the thermostat on the furnace and set to work on the fire as Marc made the bed and unpacked the food.

From the corner of her eye, she could see the brown box on the coffee table, looking lost in the vastness of the room. The innocent-looking brown box that held all the sex toys they'd selected together. Anything and everything they'd seen that they thought they might use. It had been tough to ignore the expense, but as it seemed the height of ridiculousness to be prudent when pursuing decadence, she'd conquered her caution to the point of maybe going overboard. She battled an unreasonable urge to toss the throw from the couch over it.

As if there was anyone here to see. As if Marc was going to have a problem with anything contained in it. The man had adventure in his bones. She was the one with all the good-girls-don't hang-ups. Heck, judging from his comments as she'd pointed out a few things she'd been interested in and from the confidence with which he'd made his selections, there probably wasn't anything in the box of which he didn't have firsthand knowledge. Just not with her.

And that fast, she added another emotion to the turbulence of the evening. Jealousy that her husband's past lovers had been more adventurous than she.

He came up behind her as she stood by the fire. She shivered as he moved her hair aside, baring her neck. The heat of his breath touched her first, moist and tantalizing, brushing across her sensitive nerve endings in an evocative arc.

"Ready?"

The question whispered against her neck. Goose bumps sprang up in a silent "Hell, yes," she couldn't get past her throat. She tilted her head, inviting a kiss instead, shuddering when he gave it to her. His cock pressed against her buttocks, rock-hard and eager while his hands slid down her sleeves until his fingers intertwined with hers.

She gripped his hands in hers. "As I'll ever be."

He laughed into the curve of her shoulder, sending new goose bumps chasing after the last set, the flick of his tongue encouraging their tingling spread to her breast and nipples. His big hands whispered across the front of her coat, taunting both breasts with the promise of a touch she couldn't feel, making her strain for any ghost of sensation. The tension in her limbs gathered in her pussy, throbbing with an eagerness that faintly embarrassed her. As if a woman should consider her attraction to her husband a weakness.

"Having second thoughts?"

"I'm a little stuck in my ways."

He turned her in his arms. "At the risk of repeating myself yet again, I like your ways."

No, he didn't; he couldn't. She didn't even like them. "And that's why you always hold back with me."

"Is that a complaint?"

She wanted to stamp her foot in frustration. "I'm not the one who should be complaining."

Two fingers under her chin brought her gaze up. "The reason you haven't heard me complain is because I don't have any complaints."

"You want a woman who lets go, who can let you be in charge."

His gaze never wavered from hers. "The only woman I want is you."

She dropped her forehead into his chest. The down of his coat cushioned her landing. "I know."

His arms came around her shoulders. "So what's the problem?"

"I want to be that woman, too!"

There, her not-so-secret secret was out.

His coat rustled as his lips touched her temple. "Have I ever told you I think you're a nut?"

She shook her head.

His smile spread against her temple. "I'm fairly sure I have."

"Not today."

"My mistake." This time it was his thumb that propped her chin up. "You know I'll give you anything you want, in or out of the bedroom."

She knew that. He was a very generous lover. She turned her head and cleared her throat. To her dismay, her voice still held a betraying husk of uncertainty. "I know."

"And you want this?"

She wrapped her fingers around his wrist and held on. "The one place I never wanted to be in charge was the bedroom."

And it was the one place where she couldn't seem to let go. His hand stroked her hair, pulling her cheek to his chest, holding her tight. "Ah, baby."

"I know." She closed her eyes. "I'm a nut."

His thumb pressed against her lower lip, bringing her eyes back open. "No, you're my wife."

She angled her head back and wrinkled her nose. "Who's a nut."

"Who's everything I want." His gaze didn't leave hers. "Just the way she is."

That wasn't good enough anymore. At least not for her. "But what if I don't want to be this way?"

"Then we change."

She had so many hang-ups, so many reasons for how she was, none of them worth holding onto. "What if I can't?"

"Then we keep trying."

She took a breath and released his wrist, clutching his coat sleeve instead. She sighed. "You make it sound so easy."

"All you've got to do is whatever I tell you. No right, no wrong. No need to think." He arched his eyebrow at her. "How hard can it be?"

Not that hard. At least in theory. "Marc?"

He reached around her and closed the door to the wood-stove. "Right here."

"Have I mentioned how much I love you?"

"I'm open to hearing it again."

The familiar response given with that familiar smile took away more of her nervousness. This was Marc. She trusted him with her life. She could certainly trust him with her sexuality. She linked her hands around his neck and snuggled her hips into his, giving him a smile back of her own. "Make it worth my while and I will."

His brow arched. "Is that a challenge?"

She did her best to look demure. "Maybe."

"That sounded like a challenge."

"I would never challenge you."

His smile spread. "Like hell."

"Well," she amended, "not without reason."

His hands cupped her hips, his fingers stretching to the sensitive inside of her thighs. With an easy flex of muscle he lifted her up. Becky wrapped her legs around his hips as he turned. This close she could see the desire darkening the green of his eyes, feel the tension humming under his skin, feel that side of his personality she'd always fought surge. His gaze held hers, the blue more prominent than the green as it always was when he was aroused. "It's risky business challenging a man with my nature."

She feathered her fingers in the hair at the base of his neck. "Maybe I've just decided it's time to see how much bite there is to your bark."

"Uh-huh. Know what happens to women who play with fire?"

Her hips jostled against his as he walked to the bedroom, the soft cotton of her sweatpants doing nothing to protect her from the pressure against her clit. Desire sparkled through her blood. Excitement shortened her breath. She loved it when he went all macho on her. "Nope."

Marc stopped just inside the bedroom door, his gaze holding hers as he let her slide down his body, the hot length of his cock caressing the inside of her thighs until her toes touched the floor. Her held her there, suspended in his embrace, his cock notched between her legs, pressing against her through his jeans and her pants as he drawled, "Their husbands get to see how hot they can make them burn."

He let her go. She stumbled, caught between the king-size bed behind her and her husband in front, daring and dread rising with equal fervor.

Of course, he saw. He touched her cheek. "What?"

"Don't let me ruin this."

He shook his head, the firm line of his mouth softening. "There's no way you can ruin anything."

But she could fail. She grabbed his hand. "Promise me you'll just do it like we talked about."

He frowned. "I can't promise that. Not if you're not enjoying yourself."

"I might be uncomfortable at first, but I swear I'll enjoy it."

"Let's see."

He took her hand in his, pulling it behind his back, pulling her into his arms. The touch of his lips on hers was firm when she'd expected soft, commanding when she'd expected reassurance, throwing her off balance. While she struggled to find the rhythm in the kiss, he caught both of her hands and moved them behind her back, anchoring them in one of his, keeping her helpless as his mouth took charge of hers. Fire streaked from her breasts, her thighs, her lips, leaping along her nerve endings, the feeling of helplessness feeding the flames.

The zipper of her coat rasped louder than her heartbeat as he slid it down. His palm swallowed the small mound of her breast, bare beneath her shirt because he'd requested it, pressing and massaging, stoking the burning ache, sending it deeper, and all she could do was stand there and take the pleasure he was giving her. The way he wanted. Oh God. Her knees buckled. It was so good.

He caught her easily, holding her still for more of his touch, his desire. The pinch of his thumb and forefinger on her nipple made her jump, except she couldn't go anywhere, do anything. He was in charge. In complete control. Her lids fluttered open.

He was staring down at her, the desire burning so brightly in her mirrored in the tight set of his expression. Along with that realization came another. He liked her like this. The knowledge settled deep, giving her the courage to lower her lids, lick her lips, and ask, "Is that all you've got?"

His laugh was more sensual than amused; the answer he gave short and to the point. "Hardly."

The pressure on her nipple increased to the point of pain. His gaze never left hers as she waited, breath suspended in her chest, womb clenched expectantly, whether in hope or dread, she didn't know. With a small smile, he released her nipple and turned her around. Becky stood there, breath shuddering, adrenaline flowing for three uncomprehending seconds until he said, "Bend over."

And the conflagration started again, her mind racing ahead of her actions, picturing how she'd look to him, her hands braced on the bed, her rear thrust back in a purely submissive pose.

When she would have shrugged off her coat, Marc caught her shoulders.

"No."

Subtle pressure bent her over. She caught her weight on her hands, feeling awkward and vulnerable and as turned on as she'd ever been as his hand grazed up the inside of her thigh, pressing her leg to the left in a smooth demand before repeating the same caress with the other leg.

His fingertips pressed lightly against her pussy. "I've been thinking about this since morning."

It was a struggle to find her voice. "What exactly is 'this'?"

His shadow fell over her as he stood, making her vividly aware of his size, the need to dominate he'd always kept in check for her. The need she'd asked him to let loose. His hands on the waistband of her sweatpants were cold. She jumped. Her pants and underwear followed the shiver as it snaked down to her toes. "Your ass."

Which told her nothing and suggested everything.

The snap of his fingers against her right cheek had her jumping again. "Push back."

She did.

Another tiny slap, this one so soft it seemed to absorb the sting of the other. In the aftermath, his palm lingered. "You liked that?"

There was no way she could deny it, even if every liberated bone in her body demanded that she do so. Those betraying goose bumps were at it again, telegraphing her delight. The zipper of his jeans rasped loudly in the silence. She swallowed hard; the image of him taking her fully clothed played like a siren's lure in her mind. Hard, deep, his focus on his pleasure. Oh yes. She wanted him to take her like that. To use her for his satisfaction, to let her be nothing more than what he needed this once. Not having to think, to worry, just being there to satisfy him would be so good.

His fingers slipped between her thighs, callused and rough, sliding easily across her shaved labia. His laugh, when he found her open and wet, held the smile she'd missed earlier.

"Looks like you've been thinking, too."

"Yes." She always thought about him.

"Did you prepare yourself like I ordered?"

He could feel that she had, so he must just want to hear her say it. "Yes." Admitting that sent another quiver of delight through her. Took her another step deeper into her fantasy where her submissive side got free rein.

"Good."

He eased his cock up the crack of her ass. It slid smoothly on the lubricated skin, making her shudder and push back. His thumbs rubbed the inside of her cheeks, holding her open for the next stroke.

The fat head of his cock caught on the edge of her anus. Hunger, hot and dark, shot inward. Her cry was involuntary. He didn't move, didn't even seem to breathe for a second—and then he snuggled the broad head against the tight opening, teasing her with the promise of the forbidden.

"Step out of your pants," he ordered darkly, then stood still, letting her efforts to follow his order work him up and down the crease.

As soon as she was free, she resumed her position. He pushed her ankle with his foot. "Wider."

She complied immediately, feeling completely exposed. It only increased her excitement. His cock throbbed against her. The touch of his fingers changed from caressing to possessive as he moved her around, letting the head of his cock probe first her ass and then lower; not entering, just stroking like one might with a finger.

It was pure torment to stand so, bent over, exposed, wondering where he would take her. When? Would he be fast or slow? Would he let her come, or would he leave her hanging, deliciously full of his semen, pulsing with anticipation?

He rubbed his cock over her buttocks. Despite her efforts to stay quiet, a whimper escaped. It felt too good to tolerate in silence. He rubbed some more. She gave up the effort to control her breathing. It came out ragged and loud.

He pulled back and his cock tapped at her anus. "Are you ready for me?"

He had to know she was. He'd told her to keep herself always ready for him and she did though he'd never taken her that way. Mainly because she always froze up. Her "Yes" was a soft moan of expectancy.

He slid a finger in her ass. The tight ring spasmed, clutching him hard.

"Oh God," she moaned, trying to steady her knees beneath the surge of pleasure.

"I guess you are," he murmured at the smoothness of his entry, probing gently. She moaned again and pushed back, trying to establish a rhythm. He stretched her wider and introduced another finger. For a moment, she balked, tightening against the invasion. He paid her no mind, pulling his fingers out, dragging against her sensitive flesh as he withdrew.

"Relax and push back," he coaxed, easing them back in, spreading her as he did. "You know you love this."

She did. She loved it when he played with her ass, no matter how he took it. Gentle or rough, it turned her on until she could scream just thinking about him eventually claiming it. She took a breath, waited for the next withdrawal and then pushed back.

"That's it," he murmured. "Show me how much you like it."

She didn't have much choice. Her nerves were on fire. Her entire being focused on his fingers and the pace he was setting, slow and easy when she wanted hard and fast, every twist, every scissor of his fingers divine torture. When she was almost screaming with frustration, he pulled free.

His cock tapped her frantically throbbing opening. She jerked up, hips hungrily rearing back, wanting the consummation. Only to be denied again when he stepped back. She dropped her head to the mattress, her pussy aching, ass clenching, feeling so empty she thought she'd die from it.

Marc nudged her foot with his again. She widened her stance. It took two more nudges before she was at the level he wanted, legs wide, tight muscles straining, every sense attuned to him, wanting him. "Perfect."

It was the only warning she had before he pushed his thick cock into her pussy. She bucked and would have collapsed if he hadn't anchored her hips with his hands, holding her steady for the solid penetration.

It wasn't easy taking him like this—he was a big man and her inner muscles struggled to accept his width as he pressed inexorably inward—but it was also arousing as hell. Feeling his cock drive deep, having him pull her hips back into his on the grinding descent; hearing his orders to take him, to fuck him, moaned hoarsely in her ear as his fingers dug into her thighs, giving her no choice but to do as he ordered, to pleasure him as he needed. It was her wildest fantasy, having him use her like she was there for his pleasure only. And it was now coming true.

She pushed back, taking another inch, his curse flowing above her just so much sweet music because she knew she'd drawn it from him against his will. Just as she knew the next thrust wasn't as controlled as the first. Yes, yes, yes! With every hard thrust she opened wider, took him deeper.

She braced her arms on the bed, pushing back further. It wasn't enough. She wanted more. She wanted him to pound that thick cock into her, ride her until he couldn't hold it anymore. She wanted him to claim her, to make her his in a totally primitive way that went far deeper than any woman would consider politically correct. She wanted him to fuck her without finesse, without control. Just him and her and the need she inspired in him. She wiggled her hips. A smart sting on her right cheek halted the movement. "Stay still and take it."

Oh God! She bit her lip as the sting melded with the heat burning her from the inside out, feeding it. How had he known? In her dreams he said things like that to her, did things like this to her, but she'd never told him, never written it down. How had he known this part of her fantasy she'd never dared to confess?

His cock continued to plunder her pussy, pushing solidly in, catching on sensitive nerve endings as her muscles parted to accommodate his width, dragging and stretching her flesh as he withdrew, every stroke, every heated inch destroying the control she prided herself on. The control she didn't want in bed. Her clit ached and pulsed, needing his touch, her touch, anything. All it would take was the barest stimulation there and she'd go hurtling over the precipice she could sense him approaching.

He didn't give it to her. Just kept filling her with his cock, feeding her need, her desire, building it until she wanted it to go on forever yet she didn't think she could bear it if it did. Continuing until she couldn't think of anything beyond the fact that she was his, and she loved him so.

With a thrust so deep it pierced her soul Marc came, grinding his hips so deeply into hers, his zipper cut into the flesh of her buttocks. She pushed back, begging for more. Becky could feel his cock pulse that brief second before it jerked, tapping against her G-spot, filling her with his hot come, giving her some of what she wanted but not enough. Not enough to come. She clawed at the comforter and clenched again. His dark laugh let her know he knew what she was doing. What he was doing to her.

"You want more?"

She shuddered and admitted the glorious truth. "Yes."

His big hand worked between them, cupping her pussy. "Greedy thing."

She had no defense. She was greedy. She wanted more. Everything he could give her.

His cock jerked within her, touching that spot. His fingers snapped against the pad of her pussy, sharp and hard. She stiffened in shock as wild sensation burned up into her womb. Before she could sort it out, he was doing it again, harder, stronger. Delight cut through shock, a mixture of sweet pain and searing pleasure, too strong to deny, too overwhelming to sort out. Too fucking fantastic to resist.

"Come for me."

Low, deep and intent, the order didn't leave her any choice. On the next slap she did, bucking and arching her hips for more of whatever he wanted to give her, open to the pleasure, the pain or a combination of the two. Just open...

He was holding her, his arms wrapped around her while his big body covered her. With every breath she took, she absorbed his scent, hers, theirs.

His cock flexed within her. They were still joined. Becky opened her hands on the mattress, bracing herself—for what, she didn't know, just whatever was going to happen to destroy this moment.

His lips skimmed her temple, her cheek, soft gentle caresses that melted into her soul.

"Can you feel my seed in you?" he asked, pulling his still-hard cock almost all the way out before sliding back in, his voice as quiet and as deep as the night around them.

"Yes."

"It makes you hot, doesn't it?"

"Yes."

"Tell me."

The order wasn't unexpected. The surge of lust at hearing it, at contemplating obeying it, was. She dug her nails into the sheet, holding on as the quiver shook her from head to toe. Her voice, when she found it, was husky and raw, as if all the screams she'd suppressed over the years had left their mark. "When you fill me with your seed, it makes me crazy."

He stroked her again, slow and lazy. "How crazy?"

"I can't get enough of it," she admitted breathlessly. "Of you."

She surged back, almost there, but he stepped away.

She was suddenly, devastatingly empty. She groaned a protest.

A brush of flesh on flesh, and then there was only the lingering warmth of his seed inside her, keeping her achingly aroused. She knew she'd stay that way until she could no longer feel his essence.

"Take off your clothes," he instructed quietly. "And then climb into bed and close your eyes."

A light slap on her rear had her hurrying to comply. The sheets were chilly. She lay there on her back, shivering with cold and anticipation until the heat from the fire seeped through and then it was just anticipation shaking her from head to toe.

It took her a minute to realize Marc had left the room. With her eyes closed, every other sense seemed to magnify, especially her sense of hearing. She could hear him in the bathroom washing up, track his move to the living room, and then back. He stopped just inside the bedroom door.

She pushed the covers down, the smooth cotton gliding sensuously across her stomach and thighs. The catch of his breath was audible. She smiled, drew up her knee and arched her back, giving him a view of everything that was his.

"Still playing with fire, sweetheart?"

"Mmm." She spread her legs wide, imagining how she looked to him, wanton and eager. His shirt dropped to the floor in a soft rustle. His wallet hit the bureau with a heavy thud. The change in the pocket of his jeans jingled as they slid down his legs. The mattress dipped under his weight.

It dipped again as he moved closer. His arm brushed her shoulder. The heat of his body covered her as light as a touch. His scent enveloped her in a familiar hug.

She sensed his lips before she felt them pressing against hers. His whispered, "I love you," wove around her in a protective spell. She whispered it back, letting the vow follow her breath into his mouth, envisioning it blending with his until the two were hopelessly intertwined. His hand curved around her head in a gentle vise, holding her still for his kiss. Her arms wrapped around his shoulders, keeping him still for hers.

Marc separated his mouth a scant inch from hers. "Don't open your eyes."

"Okay."

His finger traced her lip. "No matter what."

Anticipation nudged her pulse up a notch. "No matter what."

His fingers fanned over the side of her face. He eased her

lower lip away from her teeth with his thumb. "I like your mouth."

She didn't know what to say to that, so she settled for a "Thank you."

"I want it on me."

She touched the fleshy pad of his thumb with her tongue. "Now?"

"Yeah. Now."

When she would have slid down his body, he tightened his grip on her head. "Turn around first."

The covers wrapped around her as she shifted, then were tugged away, leaving her with only smooth cotton and smooth skin to guide her. She fumbled a little without the use of sight, relying on his hand for guidance. The tendons in her inner thighs strained as she straddled his chest. He was a big man all over. Built strong, inside and out. Solid. Someone she could depend on always. She kissed her way down his stomach, going with the rise and fall of his abs, counting the ridges. One, two, three.

Her lips dipped into the well of his navel, explored and then moved below, following the thin line of hair beneath. His hand tangled in her hair. Ignoring the silent demand she worked lower, not stopping until she found the soft sac of his balls. It came as naturally as breathing to kiss them. His breath hissed in only to be released immediately, sighing, "That's good."

Marc widened his thighs. She nuzzled them gently, sucking softly on the delicate flesh, before kissing them again. Against her cheek, his cock stirred. Because she loved to feel him quicken with life, she snuggled his semisoft penis against her tongue, cherishing this brief time when she could hold him in his entirety.

With a tug on her thigh, he drew her across his torso until she was covering him like a living blanket. That was fine with her. Having him like this, relaxed beneath her while the echoes of their previous pleasure wrapped them in an intimate cocoon was a pleasure unto itself. She scooted back as his cock grew too big to hold in her mouth, letting her lips slide up his length until only the mushroom-shaped head rested inside the taut circle. She twirled her tongue around the firm tip, compressing with her lips before sucking lightly, the spike of his hips a hot incentive to do it again.

He moaned and shoved the blankets clear. The hand on her head pushed down even as he pushed his hips up. Becky took what she could, giving him as much as she could, wanting to please him this way, too. A bead of pre-come spilled into her mouth, salty, spiced with that flavor that was uniquely Marc, seeping into her desire in a lazy intoxicating wave that gathered momentum as another deep, masculine moan flowed into the darkness around her.

God! She loved the taste of him. The feel. She grasped the base of his shaft in her hand, angling him back. She kept up a lazy rhythm, her senses focusing on the moment and everything surrounding it: the heat of his cock, the throb of his pulse, the stretch in her thighs, the ache in her core, the weight of his palm. In her pussy, she still felt the hot weight of his seed like a loving promise yet to be fulfilled.

Beneath her, Marc shifted. His chest muscles rippled along the inside of her thighs as he reached for something. In her hypersensitive state, she could feel every ridge of muscle, every expansion of breath.

"Are your eyes closed?"

His voice was husky. Deep. Intent. On nothing more than the nuances contained in the question, her womb clenched. She slid her mouth free of his cock. "Yes."

"Keep them that way."

The order didn't require a response. She gave it to him anyway in a slow breath that wafted across the head of his cock in a whispery tease. The hard shaft jerked in her grip. She followed the airy caress with her tongue, flattening it across the broad head, holding it there, holding him there for a heartbeat before wiggling her tongue in the tiny slit at the center, then doing it again when his big body jerked in response, fucking it in tiny pulses that had his breath hissing in between his teeth. Oh yes, she liked him like this.

She laughed, taking him deep, letting him share in the re-verberations of her pleasure. He pushed high with his hips, getting her to take a fraction more, reestablishing the power between them, reinforcing who would give and who would take. While she struggled to accept his cock, something cool and smooth pressed against her anus.

"Umph?"

The answer to her incoherent question was an increase in pressure against the tight ring of her ass. She froze. He had been in the toy box. Her ass twitched in apprehension while her pussy wept with need. She pushed up on her arms. The move pressed her harder against the would-be intruder. "Stay still."

It was a no-nonsense order followed by a no-nonsense push against her butt. Whatever he had chosen felt huge. She re-membered some of the toys they had selected. They *were* huge. Her muscles tensed in an agony of indecision. He pushed the fake penis against her butt again. She moved forward to his balls to postpone the inevitable penetration. She made an involuntary move to close her legs, but only succeeded in clamping her thighs around his ribs. His chest hair abraded her clit, making her gasp and twist.

He laughed, a low, husky, distracted sound. His palm cupped her rear holding her to the pleasurable friction while with unrelenting pressure against her anus he forced her body's acceptance. "Relax, Becky."

She tried, but it wasn't easy. He didn't desist.

"You can take this. Just relax and push back."

He didn't give her any choice. Untried muscles gave up on the unequal battle. She panted through the foreign sensation, a combination of pleasure and pain.

More pressure, this time at the back of her head, keeping her mouth full of his cock as he slowly breached her ass with the thick toy.

She breathed through her nose, struggling to relax, torn between wanting him to stop and needing the dark consummation to continue. The slow penetration finally stopped. The rough calluses of his fingers grazed the hypersensitive skin of her rear as he asked, "Okay?"

She took a breath, stilling the panic to try to find an answer. The dildo stretched her past comfortable but not fully into pain, creating contrary signals that her desire absorbed and translated into something darker, something deeper, something intriguingly different. She nodded yes.

"Good. Now, I want you to use your mouth and show me how you want to be loved."

He was allowing her some control, letting her set the pace for her seduction. She was intrigued. Tempted and intrigued.

Indecision held her immobile for a timeless, breathless second. She felt too...stretched for anything vigorous.

With the slightest of hesitations, she took just the tip of his penis into her mouth. He throbbed against the inside of her lips. She eased her head gently up and down. The dildo moved with the same shallow motion, forcing her tight muscles wider and the burn higher, the joy higher still.

She could handle that, she decided, repeating the move. It still wasn't exactly pleasurable. There were too many conflicting emotions inside for her to sort out the pleasure from the other, newer sensations, but she could sense it waiting, just beyond her grasp. She forgot to caress his cock, and he stopped.

Darn. She squeezed her eyes tighter and resumed her movements.

"You want it like that for a while?" he asked.

Feeling vulnerable and exposed, she nodded her head.

"Okay. Rest your cheek on my hip and we'll try this for a while."

At first, she couldn't relax, but the steady massage of the penetration soon eased the tension from her muscles. The motion became smoother and easier as she relaxed into the play. She loved the feeling of being penetrated almost more than she loved to come, and the sensation was even more intense, more satisfying this way. And now, with Marc's permission, she was able to fully focus on the stroke of the toy over her most sensitive nerves, to wallow for as long as she wanted in the pure bliss. She lifted her hips facilitating the easy rhythm.

Her ass began to throb and twitch, and the easy screwing became more irritating than satisfying. Rooting with her lips, she found his cock and engulfed him in one deep swallow. The dildo echoed her efficiency.

Her satisfied groan danced down his shaft.

It felt good. So damn good.

She took him again, deeply. Her ass relished the same treatment. Marc caught the rhythm, slow and deep, hovering on the retreat before plunging back in to linger on the push. Unlike a cock, the dildo didn't get too excited and put an end to the sensation. She was free to enjoy it as long as she could, letting the burn become an ache that sharpened to a high-pitched need that spread outward, building in a wave. She yanked her mouth off his cock, sinking her teeth into his thigh, biting down as she took more, her ass clenching down hard, holding tight....

She felt his laugh more than heard it. "Feels that good, huh?"

Again, all she could do was nod.

"Imagine how good it's going to feel when it's my cock instead of a toy."

She closed her eyes, imagining it, wanting it. "Oh yes."

She shifted up and caught the tip of his penis in her mouth. Just the tip. She closed her lips tightly around it and slid it in and out, flirting with the idea of penetration, making him relive over and over the thrill of possession.

"Oh God," she moaned as he forced her ass open again and again with the same piercing motion. "Don't stop. Please."

"I wasn't planning on it." Desire roughened his voice to a hoarse parody of his low drawl and any doubt she had that he was enjoying this as much as her died a quick death. "But I think it's time to change things up."

His cock slid impossibly deep, hitting the back of her throat, holding there while she struggled not to gag. The dildo plumbed her ass with the same erotic efficiency over and over again, taking her higher but not giving her that extra something she needed to relieve the screaming demand ripping along her nerve endings. The hot, burning need to come. She twisted in his grip, sucking his cock harder, taking it deeper, faster, needing him to come so she could.

"Son of a bitch." Hard hands fastened on her shoulders, pulling her up with the same wildness beating inside her. "Come up here."

She did, kissing her way frantically up his chest, nibbling on his flat brown nipples, savoring the jerk of his chest until he pulled her away.

"Tease," Marc murmured without heat, flipping her onto her back.

She rested her palms on his shoulders, sinking her nails into the thick pad of muscle, anchoring the wildness inside. "Can I open my eyes now?"

"Yes."

His big hands slid down the back of her thighs. He lifted first one and then the other over his arms with deliberate slowness, walking his hands up the side of her torso with that same determination until he had her wide open and exposed.

She didn't understand when Marc reached between them, holding her gaze with his until, with a twist, her ass came alive with powerful pulsing throbs. Her eyes flew wide. The dildo was also a vibrator.

"I always wanted to know what one of those vibrating beds felt like," he murmured.

"Oh God!" She dug her nails into his shoulder, her teeth into her lip as he nudged her with his cock. He tucked it into the small slit, forcing her tight pussy open with the same inexorable pressure with which he'd opened her ass. It was too much. The overstretching, the throbbing…Becky closed her eyes and struggled to adjust.

Marc didn't give her time, just threw them both into the chaotic well of need with a slow, steady push. And she took him, all of him—muscles straining, quivering, parting, struggling with the near painful tightness caused by the dildo, nerve endings singing as his groin pressed into hers. And still he pushed, as if as close as they were, it wasn't close enough. She closed her eyes, savoring the feeling. It would never be enough.

She had to move, needed to move, but there was no give in his hold, no leeway in his possession. All she could do was clench around him and beg. "Please, please, please!"

The words filled her head, the room. She was begging aloud and she didn't care. She needed him, needed this.

"I've got you, baby."

And he did, in every way that mattered. She opened her eyes, loving the passion in his face, the lust, the pleasure, knowing that she was giving this to him even as he was giving it to her. Ten more strokes and he came violently, slamming hard against her, holding himself high inside her pussy, his cock jerking with spurt after spurt of hot come.

The power of his release triggered her own, sending her surging up against his chest, twisting violently in his arms as overcharged nerves screamed for a reprieve. He gave her none, forcing her to ride every wave, holding her still when she would have ripped free, nipping her breasts when she swore she couldn't take anymore, sending her into another orgasm as if to prove her wrong.

In the aftermath, when everything had subsided to a quivering ache, he lowered her legs back to her sides, and suckled her breasts more gently as he whispered over and over, "I love you."

Inside her, she felt his softening penis and the hot warmth of his seed. Her pussy clung to both, the pulsing arousal inspired by the latter rivaling the toy. With a soft sigh, he eased out of her, still loving her breasts.

As always, she protested the loss. He'd come in her not once, but twice. She'd be achingly aroused all night unless she cleansed away his seed. She was reluctant to do so, especially when he patted her affectionately between the legs on the way down to turn off the vibrator.

"That was so good," she sighed.

His smile was a tightening of his lips against her nipple. "Glad you enjoyed it."

Her nipple sprang into the cold air with a soft pop as he released it and said, "Why don't you turn over? You know you can't sleep on your back."

She turned over onto her stomach, facing him. Resting her cheek on her forearm, she asked, "Aren't you forgetting something?"

His big hand smoothed down her back. His fingers flirted with the crease of her buttocks before dipping between. With a delicate push, he re-seated the toy. Her oversensitive body made more of the movement than she'd expected, quivering and tightening. His fingers lingered almost contemplatively.

"Nope."

She cracked an eyelid and noted his speculative expression as he played with the dildo. "Is there a problem?"

"Not a one." He eased down beside her, patting her rear in

a sweet caress before encompassing the curve. "I was just thinking——"

"What?"

His lips brushed her shoulder. The sheets rustled as his chest half shifted over her back, covering her with his heat and strength. His cock thrust against her hip as he drawled in her ear, "There are a lot more toys in that box...."

Come Back to Me

KIMBERLY KAYE TERRY

"ARE YOU WEARING THE PANTIES I SENT YOU?" A deep voice I had come to know so well, whispered huskily.

My breath quickened and my pussy clenched in automatic response to his deep, chocolate-smooth baritone.

Oh God, it was him again. I swallowed nervously.

We'd been communicating for less than a week and each time I had the same reaction when he'd call me after my radio talk show ended. Right off the bat, he'd asked me such intimate questions I'd wanted to hang up in his face. Yet, I hadn't.

He'd called every night over the last week, and to my shame, I'd come to need his nightly calls. Normally, he called when my show had ended, and I'd sent my engineer home and was all alone.

I glanced at the clock mounted on my desk, surprised to hear from him so early in the night. Tonight was a rerun of a previous show, and for all intents and purposes neither I, nor my engineer, needed to be in the studio.

Yet, there was no way I was going to stay away whether I needed to be here or not. I couldn't even if I wanted to.

From the first time I heard his voice he'd captivated me and I hadn't been able to deny him anything. He'd started out talking dirty to me. Asking me if I had a man, if I needed one, and telling me he wanted to be the one to give me what I needed. The way he'd laid it down so smooth, so hot, I tried my best to hang up. Damn, I did. I wanted to tell him to go straight to hell. But I couldn't.

From the first night, well, things had progressed. And after what he had me doing to myself last night...I swore I wouldn't take any more of his kinky calls. Particularly, when I came into work and found his "gift" on my desk, wrapped in a pretty pink box with a pearl-beaded bow.

"Did you hear me?"

My heartbeat slammed against my breastbone, and my treacherous nipples beaded in response to the low-toned voice pouring from the small speakers mounted in my desk.

I quickly glanced up to see if my engineer, Trina, had overheard.

I released a heartfelt sigh of relief when she wasn't looking my way. Thank God, she didn't seem to be paying me any attention behind her soundproofed glassed-in booth, gathering her things as she prepared to leave for the night.

Nevertheless, I quickly snatched up the phone and sat back down in my chair.

"Please...I told you, no more calls. If you want advice on love, call during the show's regular time, and currently we're doing a *Best of* show, so that's not going to happen tonight. I suggest you find somewhere else to get your kicks," I ordered, trying my best to infuse as much attitude as I could in my tone, but even to my own ears it came out sounding pitiful and weak.

His answering, deep-throated chuckle confirmed it for me.

"Keep saying that, Dr. Adams, and maybe you'll convince yourself. Damn sure not convincing me," he arrogantly replied.

"Look, Mr.——"

I waited for him to fill in the name, knowing full well he wouldn't.

"Dr. A, I'm going to be leaving for the night, to meet my mon…aw no, woman! Is that another caller? I thought I'd put the answering machine on." Trina came hustling out of her control room and groaned. She flipped one of her long dreads over her shoulder and came to a halt near my desk, her large hemp bag thrown over her shoulder.

"No, Trina, it's okay. You get out of here and go and meet your man. This isn't anything I can't handle." I smiled reassuringly at her and held the phone away from my ear as I spoke, purposely allowing *him* to hear what I said.

Some of my nervousness must have come through. Trina gave me a *look*. "Dr. A, Jerrod can wait, if you need me to stay…" she said in her deep Jamaican accent, allowing the sentence to trail off questioningly. Despite the nervous feeling in the pit of my stomach, I laughed.

"Go! You aren't going to get that man of yours mad at me because I kept his honey, knowing full well you two have plans," I said, laughing, reminding her of their plans to get away for the weekend. "Honestly, this is nothing. I'll wrap up in a minute and do some odds and ends. I plan on heading out of here within the next hour or so myself," I reassured her.

"Are you sure, then?"

"Yes, I am. I'll have one of the sound guys make sure the tapes run smoothly. There's no need for me to be here." I reminded her that I wasn't needed at the station, either. "I'm going to head home early. In fact, could you close the blinds for me?" I asked.

"And I'll be believing that when I see it, Doctor A! I don't tink you'd know what to do with yourself if you weren't here." Trina laughed.

I took a mock swipe at her. "I'm fine...now go before I change my mind and keep you here with me all night!"

"I'm going, I'm going!" she said, laughing, and quickly closed the blinds before she scurried to the door.

Right before she opened it, she turned back to me and gave me a small half grin, a look of concern crossing her pretty cocoa-brown face. "Seriously, Dr. A, you give all the great advice on love, and you know I be admiring you...but maybe it's time for you to take your own advice, woman!" she said, stretching out the word *woman*. "Let go and have some fun." She blew me a kiss before closing the door behind her.

I smiled and almost forgot the one waiting for me on the phone. As if he'd allow that to happen.

"She's right," he said before I'd had time to gather my thoughts, and pull myself together. "You give all that great advice on love, life and having fun. When's the last time you had any fun? When was the time you let go and enjoyed a man?"

"What makes you think you know anything about me?" I asked around my pounding heart. I rushed on, filling in the answer before he could speak. "You don't know *anything* about me. Not one damn thing."

"I know enough. Enough to know you're tired of talking about sex and ready to do it. But not just any sex. You need hot, raw, dirty sex."

Oh God, please make him stop. My eyes drifted closed and the walls of my pussy clenched at the way he dragged out the word *raw*.

I released a shaky breath. "You don't know anything—"

"Enough to know you're wearing the special panties I sent you. How long did it take you to convince yourself to put them on when you received the package today?"

"I am *not* wearing—"

"Shh," he interrupted me. "Close your eyes. Slide your fingertips along the inside of your thigh. Pretend they're mine."

I bit my lower lip and did as he demanded.

"Push up your skirt and spread your legs. What do you feel?"

Why was he doing this to me, forcing me to do things I shouldn't, feel things I didn't want to feel?

"Exposed, vulnerable," I admitted, my voice barely above a throaty whisper.

"Are you wet?"

Unable to hold back, a whimper escaped.

"That's okay, baby, you don't have to answer. I already know. Good, because I want that pussy drenched, bared and ready for what I want to do next."

"I'm not doing this with you, again," I choked out, determined not to give in to him.

Despite my denial, I found myself obeying every single one of his edicts. It was late, no one was around the nearly deserted radio station, but even had they been, I knew it wouldn't have made a bit of difference. I would have still given in to his every demand.

"How does it feel to have those beads scraping, rubbing against those plump, juicy pussy lips?" He didn't even have the decency to wait for me to respond. "Spread your legs, rock back and forth, and ride those beads, baby. Pretend it's my fingers, my tongue licking, stroking you, and tell me how good it feels."

Oh God, it felt *so* good.

My body was humming; what he was doing to me—forcing me to do to myself—was the most incredibly erotic experience I'd ever had.

Yet I was ashamed of myself, even as I slid my creaming pussy against the beads attached to the panties, not caring that anyone could walk in the studio and catch me in the act of pleasuring myself.

"This is so wrong," I sobbed, the words escaping of their own volition.

"No, it's okay, it's okay, baby. You're doing fine, there's nothing to be ashamed of. It's just you and me, and this is good," he murmured.

It made no sense to me, but his words soothed me. *He* soothed me.

The shame of what I was doing washed away.

"Put me on speaker and hang up the phone. You're going to need your hands, now." His voice had grown increasingly rough, and I wondered if he would come with me this time. With shaky hands, I did as he instructed and pressed the speaker button and cradled the receiver.

"Are you still there?"

"Yes," I answered, reluctantly.

"Good. You're doing real good, baby. Unbutton your blouse and undo your bra for me, can you do that?"

"Yes," I croaked, my trembling hands smoothing over my straining breasts. My fingers trailed along the silk-covered buttons and slipped them open. I then unsnapped the front closure of my lacy demi-bra and my breasts tumbled free.

"We can't leave those pretty little tits of yours unattended, can we?"

"No," I groaned.

I already knew the drill. He would draw this out, wring out every bit of emotion every hot sinful sensation that he could from me, not relenting, until I came all over myself. And there wasn't a damn thing I could do about it.

"Cup them."

"What?" I asked, my mind spinning, body taut, ready.

"Cup those pretty tits while you ride the beads."

I gingerly cupped my breast as I continued to undulate my body, grinding against the beads now deeply centered between my slit.

"No, that's not good enough."

"Wha—what do you mean?" I groaned. The sensation of the beads rocking against my clit was unbearable in its pleasure as I lightly toyed with my breasts.

"Harder. Pinch them, roll those long nipples and pinch them. It'll feel good, baby. Trust me." His lava-hot voice issued the demand.

I pinched my nipples, and the slight pain caused a direct zing to my clit that forced me to buck harder, my body now writhing mindlessly. The room was filled with my low moans and the creaking sound of my chair as I bounced my butt and clit against the hard beads and desperately reached for the pinnacle just out of reach.

"God, I can *smell* you." he groaned and the hot words sent

me that much closer to the edge. "Keep playing with those pretty nipples, pull them, tug on them."

"Oh God, I need to come, I need to come so badly," I cried harshly, no longer caring if anyone came by the booth and witnessed what I was doing to myself, what I was allowing someone else to do to me.

"Shh, baby, it's okay. I'm going to take care of you." Again his voice calmed my spirit, soothed me. "Slip one of your fingers inside the edge of your panties, and rub your clit. Play with it, roll your fingers around it."

Immediately I did as he said. I tugged on the blood-filled turgid tip of my clit, pinching it, and rolled it between my fingers until a sob tore from me. Dear God, it wasn't enough. I needed something, *something* to quell this fire raging inside of me.

"You belong to me, your body is mine to pleasure. Say it." His harsh demand pierced my brain, despite the fire raging inside. I refused to give him that and it hurt so badly not to, to force myself not to give over completely.

"No." I denied him, refusing to give him that last bit of control over me even as I played with my clitoris and tugged on my nipples, all because he told me to, all because it felt so sinfully good.

"Say it! If you want relief, say it!"

"No!" I cried out, the truth of his words raining down on my head like a warm shower.

But my body belonged to him. I knew it and so did he.

It belonged to him this night. It belonged to him this week... and heaven help me, it had belonged to him for most of my life. *I belonged to him.*

I felt tears slip down my face, as I continued to thrust my hips and grind against my fingers.

Unable to hold back any longer, I felt the orgasm slam into me. My body bowed down, overwhelmed as sensation upon sensation flooded me. My head ached and I was no longer in control as I screamed my release.

When the trembles left my body and a semblance of normalcy returned, I glanced up, and weakly leaned back against the cool leather seat.

Naked and exposed, my skirt hiked up, blouse draped open, and fingers buried deep inside my vagina, I met the familiar blue-eyed gaze of the one man I thought I'd never see again.

My husband.

"Come back to me."

PART II

MACK CLOSED THE DOOR AND LOCKED IT BEHIND him, the sound of the bolt turning unnaturally loud to my overly piqued senses as I waited, my heart caught in my throat, for him to reach me. I closed my legs and tugged my blouse shut, suddenly embarrassed to be found half-naked, even though he was the cause.

My hungry gaze roamed his body. I hadn't seen him in over ten years, yet it was as though not one day had passed.

He was dressed elegantly, his loosely fitted trousers and casual shirt draping his long, hard frame to perfection, his large feet encased in dark, Italian-styled loafers. So well turned out, so different than what I last remembered.

But it was him.

No finely tailored clothes or handmade shoes could disguise his raw masculinity.

I nestled my flushed and heated back further against the cool leather seat and desperately kept my face blank to keep the wild emotions crashing over me from showing in my expression, trying to keep it all together.

I wanted to either run to his arms or go screaming and crying in the other direction as far away from him as possible, to put as much distance between us as I possibly could.

My gaze returned to his face and I recognized the determined expression in his hauntingly familiar gaze. Dark slashing eyebrows were set above bright blue, deep-set eyes that were surrounded by lashes so thick they seemed unreal.

His aquiline nose was saved from model perfection with the addition of a small bump in the middle, one he'd gotten in high school playing football. Chiseled cheeks, a well-defined, determined squared chin, and a hard yet sensual wide mouth completed the picture of utter masculine beauty.

As I had been hungrily checking him out, he had been doing the same. "God, you're beautiful, Sheena," he groaned.

I knew what he saw; not much had changed with the exception of my hairstyle in ten years. Outwardly at least. I was still average height, with the same dark brown eyes, slightly rounded nose and full cheeks. And a body that still had a tendency toward curves.

I wanted to do what most women did and instantly refute his compliment, but the look in his heated eyes told me he meant every word of what he said.

I ran a self-conscious hand over my short, curly hair and laughed nervously.

"My hair is different, I imagine, than what you expected," I answered. The last time we'd seen one another, I'd worn my hair long and relaxed, having chemically straightened my natural curls.

"After you…left, I changed. Matured, made my own decisions, even about my hair," I said, hinting at those long-ago days when I allowed others to make decisions for me.

"I love it," he said and the sincerity of the compliment eased the nervous swell in my belly. "Make love with me," he boldly asked, his deep voice hoarse, his beautiful eyes pleading.

His hand rested at the top of his pants, waiting for me to give my assent.

I didn't say a word. I couldn't speak; emotions were crowding in on me, memories...

"Say something, baby." No longer the forceful stranger who'd made love to me over the phone, no longer the arrogant stranger who forced me to surrender to his demands, he was a man asking a woman to allow him into her arms.

And damned if I could say no. I opened my arms, inviting him to come to me.

With my silent acquiescence, a change immediately came over him. Within moments he'd crossed the short distance separating us, lifted me from the chair and plopped me onto my desk and covered my body.

We clutched and grabbed at one another, buttons popping, shoes kicked off and clothes flying everywhere in our haste to bare our bodies, wanting nothing between us but hot sliding skin.

With a feral growl of need and arousal he pushed between my legs, shoving them high, forcing them wide apart and planted my feet on the desk. I felt the hot knob of his shaft press against the entry to my vagina, waiting for approval before entering. My gaze flew to his, measuring his heavy regard.

"Take me inside of you, baby."

I expected him to forge ahead, he was so hot with the need to fuck me. I was surprised at his hesitancy.

I held his gaze and reached one hand down and lightly toyed

with his twin, silky-skinned spheres, teasing them, rolling them around my hand in delight.

"Oh God, baby," he laughingly groaned. "This is going to be hard enough without you playing with my balls."

"Turnabout is fair play, Mack," I said, reminding him of the way he'd been playing with me over the last week. With one final caress, I allowed his heavy sac to gently fall back against his thighs. I circled the base of his penis and wrapped my hand around its thick circumference. My pussy tightened in response and my heart ached at how much I anticipated feeling all that delicious dick imbedded deep inside me.

"Just take me, baby…ah, yes…just like that," he said as I guided his rock-hard shaft inside my body, the cream from my pussy soaking him even as he pressed inside of me. We both groaned in delight when my pussy instantly latched on and gripped him. I bit my lip to keep myself from crying out when he began to feed me his dick in delicious increments.

He gripped my hips and forced my body to still in order to take all of him in. I was unable to hold back the cry as he fed me the rest of his shaft, the feeling so exquisite, so hard…

"Oh God, Mack…oh God, oh God…" I chanted over and over, my voice shaky.

He stopped, a crease of worry knotting his brow. "Are you okay? Am I hurting you, baby?"

I squirmed around his massive shaft. Yes, there was some pain, but there was no way I was going to allow him to stop.

"It's been a while for me," I admitted. "But it's good, Mack, it's good, baby. Now, do me."

He didn't wait for me to change my mind. He drove his

shaft home, so far inside of me I felt the tip brush against my womb.

"Wrap your legs around me," he directed.

I clasped my legs around his narrow waist and grabbed onto his thick forearms with my fingers, digging into his flesh as he stretched me wide, and began to move.

And oh God, when the man moved…he moved.

He held on to my hips and leaned down on top of me, pinning me beneath his powerful body and he fucked me hard. He jostled my body, the hardness of his flesh competing with the unyielding wood of my desk.

"I missed this tight cunt, so hot and juicy, fitting my dick just right." He breathed the scorching, coarse words against my neck.

"God, Mack, I missed this, too!" I whimpered, loving the hot nasty words, loving the way he made me feel as he drove inside my creaming heat, working me in a way that only he could, in a way I'd not had in over ten years.

He leveled himself away from me, lifted my leg and dug into me again, knifing me in hot easy glides, moving my body the way he wanted, positioning us to achieve mutual satisfaction. On and on he thrust inside of me, hammering into me; nothing was heard but our heavy breathing and the wet sound of bodies slapping, harsh groans and sighs of pleasure.

When he ran one hand down my trembling thighs and captured my clit between his thumb and forefinger, pinching the turgid tip, I blew out a harsh strangled breath. My head tossed back and forth on the desk. I slid myself closer to him and gasped when he rotated his hips, corkscrewing his dick inside of me, and jammed into my body.

I began to move, I had to, with all that hard, pounding, overwhelming dick rutting inside of me; if I didn't, I would have lost my mind.

"No…don't move yet…you feel so good on my dick. If you move, this will be over with, before we both want it to be," he laughed huskily.

"Please, Mack, I need to move, I can't take it——"

"You can," he said and covered my mouth with his, shoving his tongue deep into the recesses of my mouth, effectively shutting me up.

His strokes were slow, deliberate and forced me to take all of him, not sacrificing one scorching inch as he fucked me.

"You feel so good wrapped around me like this, so wet and good," he murmured, releasing my mouth. "Do you like the way I feel, Sheena? Did you miss this from me, baby?"

"Yesss!" I panted. "Yes, Mack, yes I missed this." I cried out harshly when he reached a hand between us and spread the lips of my vagina wide, around his straining dick, and spread my own lubricant up and over my clit.

The hot strokes of his rod, the sweet massage of his hand, sent me over the edge in minutes, and I cried out as he continued to plunge into my body, loving me in a way I hadn't been loved in years.

My orgasm triggered his and within minutes he was joining me in the release. He shouted hoarsely, reared his big body away from mine, and pulled out at the last minute.

I felt the hot stream of his seed jet free and land in a scorching river on my belly, before he collapsed on top of me.

"Come back to me," he repeated in a hoarse whisper against the side of my neck. "I should have never let you go."

PART III

MY ORGASM LEFT ME SO SPENT, SO *FILLED* I WAS BARELY able to lift my head from the desk, but his words sent a rush of adrenaline coursing through me.

"God, Mack, I can't go through this again...not again," I whispered, my voice strangled even to my own ears. I swallowed deep and felt him take a deep breath in response.

I pushed against Mack's chest, silently asking him to move. The instant the cool air from the overhead vent hit my bared body, I wrapped my arms around myself and shivered.

"Come here, you're cold," he murmured. He gathered my resistant body into the shelter of his arms and lifted me, carrying me to my leather chair and sat down. I laid my head back down on his chest, listening to the reassuring, steady thump of his heartbeat against my ear.

"Sheena, baby...you're not going to have to go through anything else with me. I'm a changed man—I'm not the same guy you married ten years ago. We were so young, damn baby, we were kids! I didn't know anything about being a man, much less a husband...or father," he said, forcing my body closer into the warm hard muscles of his chest.

The admission tore into me. I wished we could have avoided all mention of the baby, and for him to bring it up now, after the extreme eroticism of our lovemaking had left me shaken, my body not yet recovered from what he'd done to me...my emotions were all over the place.

I felt like raw meat, exposed and completely *undone*.

"Don't—please don't go there. I can't—" I wrenched myself away from the warmth of his embrace, knowing that if I stayed there much longer, I wouldn't be able to do what I needed to do. And what I needed to do was end this now, before it went any further.

"Fuck, *yes!* Yes, we are *going there*. Not going there is part of the reason we couldn't make it in the first damn place, Sheena. Not going there is the reason you left me, didn't help me..."

I spun around so hard, my head almost separated from my shoulders. "Shit, I didn't help you, Mack? Are you serious? God! Please don't tell me you're serious!" With angry precise movements, I picked up my blouse and shoved my arms through the sleeves, tears blinding my eyes.

He leapt up from where he was sitting and grabbed me, pulling my face close to his, forcing my head to snap up and look him in the eyes. "Yes, I know, I was scum, I wasn't there for you. You've told me that a million times, and if you weren't telling me, it was either your mama or your grandmother letting me know what a complete failure I was. That you would be better off without me."

"Wha...what are you talking about? What do my mother and grandmother have to do with this? Mack? Mack!" He turned and walked away, leaving my arms to dangle at my sides.

He glanced back over at me.

"Yeah, sex has always been a good thing between us, Sheena. But it wasn't the only good thing. No matter what your family thought, I have always loved you. I probably always will." My heart wept at his words.

There was a wealth of silence before I spoke, and my heart ached at emotion crossing his suddenly gaunt-looking face.

"Mack...I didn't know. What happened?"

He turned away from me and walked toward the window, staring out at the sound booth.

"After we lost the baby—" His voice cracked. He stopped and cleared his throat before he continued. "After we lost the baby, I was lost, Sheena...just like you. But I knew I had to be strong for you, for us. You completely withdrew from me, you couldn't even look at me," he said, and he was right.

I remembered how hard it was for me to look at him, seeing his bright blue eyes, wondering if the baby would have inherited them or my brown eyes, if he or she would have had his stubborn chin, his loving nature...

"You couldn't stand to even look at me," he repeated, turning to face me and I knew he saw the truth of what he said reflected in my face.

"I couldn't. I was in such a dark place that I—"

"I know."

He slowly walked toward me and I reached for him. We clutched one another, no words needed.

"You know your family never did like me, always thought I was bad news for you, didn't like us together. Your grand-mother never wanted you with that 'poor white boy.'" He laughed with no real humor.

"Grandma is old-school, Mack. Her generation saw things differently. Besides, she never thought anyone was good enough for me. It wouldn't have mattered if you'd been the darkest brother on the planet, nobody would have been good enough," I said and Mack snorted.

I felt his hand caress the top of my hair, smoothing over my short curls.

"A month after you miscarried, your grandmother came to visit me at the shop one afternoon," he began, referring to the garage he'd worked at full-time at night as he'd attended college during the day.

"Yes..." I encouraged him to continue when he hesitated.

He sighed and guided me back to the chair and sat down, before pulling me down to sit on him. After he'd comfortably arranged us he wrapped his arms around me and inhaled a deep breath.

"She told me you were miserable, that without the baby there was no need for us to stay together, that our marriage had nothing to keep it together," he continued. "When she made the suggestion for me to leave you alone, that a life as a mechanic's wife wasn't something your family wanted for you, that you had too much potential for that, I knew she was right. But you were my wife and I loved you. Yes, we married young because you were pregnant, but that wasn't the only reason I wanted to marry you, Sheena. I thought we could make it. I thought you felt the same way I did."

"I did. That's why it devastated me when you left," I cried out, the cry wrenched from that place inside of me I kept buried. The pain of him leaving was still raw, unhealed. But if

I didn't tell him now how I felt, we...I...could never heal. I could never move ahead with my life.

"I kept the pain of you leaving me layered deep with self-avowals and mantras I'd learned in graduate school, refusing to give you or anyone else control over my life, my feelings, my emotions ever again." I took a deep, steadying breath and forged ahead.

"When you left it took me a long time to get it together, but I did. I took a *long* hard look at what I wanted in life. I decided it was time for me to take control, and that I wouldn't allow you, or anyone else, to make me doubt myself or who I was. I wouldn't get so caught up in someone else that I lost sight of who I was."

"Sheena—"

"No, I need to say this, Mack. None of those mantras did a bit of good. When your heart is wounded and the one person you need to help you heal doesn't care enough to stick around when you need them the most, it's a painful lesson."

"I didn't want to leave you. I did it because I thought it was what you wanted—"

"Did you bother to ask me? Or did you just go along with what my family wanted, go by what they were telling you?" I demanded and struggled against his hold, pulling away from him and sitting up in his lap.

"No, damn it, I didn't! And even had I, what would you have done? What would have been your response? Could you have gotten past the pain of the miscarriage to accept me, to fight for me?" Mack was just as affected as I was, his chest heaving, the look in his eyes angry and accusing.

"I—" I stopped.

What would I have done? Would I have accepted him, reached out for him, when he needed me, too? Or had I been so young, filled with so much pain that I wouldn't have been able to give him the reassuring words he'd needed at the time.

I laid my head back down on his chest. When I felt his fingers stroke my hair I relaxed.

"I don't know," I whispered.

For long moments we stayed in that position, my arms loosely holding him, his hands playing in my hair.

"As angry as I was, and as badly as I wanted to keep us together, I think I understand what your grandmother was trying to tell me. I didn't want to hear it, thought I could give you everything you needed, but what you needed was time. Time to heal without me there, a constant reminder of what might have been with the baby, and time to come into your own."

"And what about you?"

He laid his head against the top of my hair and I felt him smile. "I needed time too. You're not the only one who's grown."

"Yeah, I noticed," I quipped, feeling his thick, hard shaft nestled firmly beneath my bottom.

"You always were a smart-ass."

He laughed, and I giggled along with him, breaking up some of the tension.

When our laughter subsided Mack spoke.

"I left town, knew I had to or I wouldn't be able to resist saying to hell with it, and forcing you to come back around."

"That wouldn't have been so bad," I murmured.

"No, it wouldn't have," he agreed huskily, before continuing.

"I finished school and went on to graduate school for a degree in computer engineering. I started a small computer company and recently sold it."

"I always knew you would be successful," I said and meant it. "Why did you sell? Wasn't it doing as well as you wanted?"

"Hmm, I think it was going all right, you might have heard of it, Amara technologies?" he asked and I felt him hold his breath.

Tears filled my eyes. I had not only heard of the firm, but had been receiving quarterly stockholders' reports for the last five years, along with a hefty-sized check. The money had helped me finish school and buy my home. But that wasn't the only reason for my tears.

"Amara..."

"Yeah, I named it after our baby,"

"Oh God, Mack!" I turned around in his lap and clutched at him frantically, tears streaming down my face. "But, my grandmother said——"

"I didn't want you to know it came from me, that it was my company. I told her to tell you she'd invested in a new company and had put shares in your name."

That explained so much to me. Not only had he given me stock in the company, taken care of me all this time, but dear God, he'd taken care of my family as well.

"I miss you, us. I've never stopped loving you, Sheena, never. And I never will."

His deep blue eyes seemed to darken and I felt my nipples rasp against his hard muscled chest. The soft head of his dew-covered shaft brushed against my stomach.

"I missed you too, Mack. Baby, I've never stopped loving

you. The pain of losing you was so much harder than the pain of us being together after we lost the baby. I realized that once I came out of the depression. I want you, Mack…I need you," I whispered and wrapped my hand around his shaft as I bent my head to meet his kiss.

"Please, baby, don't say that if you don't mean it, please," he pleaded against my lips, his hands roaming over my face, my neck and down my body, frantic.

"I do mean it. I'm not a little girl anymore. I know who I am, I know what I want. And I want my man back." I slid my hand down and grasped his heavy balls in my fingers. I toyed with them before easing my hand around the base of his rod and with featherlike touches, stroked up the long hard length of him. "What about you, do you want me? For better or for worse?"

"God, Sheena, do you even have to ask?" he groaned and pulled me down to meet his kiss.

Our lips met in a clash of heat, desire, passion and remembered pain. For long moments we feasted on one another until Mack pulled away from me, both of us breathing hard.

"I need to feel your sweetness wrapped around me, baby. I need to make you mine, forever this time."

I moaned, a contented sigh of pleasure, when he captured one of my nipples in his mouth, greedily lapped, licked and rolled the hard bud around his tongue, before he trailed a hot wet path between the valley of my breasts and captured its twin.

I arched my body fully into his as renewed desire and moist heat aroused the hard shaft nestled between us. "I need you now, Mack! Now!"

His jaw tightened, tensed as he stared into my eyes. "Are you sure? There's no going back this time." He gave me one last time to walk away from this, from us.

No way in hell.

"Yes…now love me, baby, love me!"

He lifted me, positioning my streaming portal in line with his dick and with a smooth jerk of muscle and hips, in one powerful thrust he embedded himself deep inside me. Once I was seated fully on him, his dick rammed tight in my pussy, he began to flex.

He moved one of his hands to cup my bottom and scooted me closer, impossibly closer, until our bodies were flush against each other, nearly one.

"Are you ready?" he asked.

At this angle I could feel every long hard inch of him; it was pure heaven and after a few adjustments I nodded my head and answered, "Yes, yes…"

"Ride me, baby, and take your time."

Keeping his hands steady on me, biting into the flesh of my bottom, he slowly began to move, his intent gaze locked with mine.

I reached for his hands and laced our fingers. Not looking away I began to ride him.

I glided my pussy up and down his thick, corded shaft, riding him nice and slow, remembering the way my man loved to be fucked, and determined to give as much pleasure as I was receiving. His rigid jaw and tightening fingers told me how much he enjoyed what I was doing to him, what we were doing to each other.

"Hmm, these perfect little breasts of yours. So smooth and

creamy, so chocolaty in their perfection." He cupped my breasts, molding and shaping them in his big hands as I bounced and glided along his erection.

He rutted into me, working me as I worked him, fucking me just the way I liked, and I felt out of control with need and love for this man and the smooth feel of his creamed dick sliding in and out of my drenched pussy.

He released my hands and reached between our bodies and found my clit. While he continued to work my cunt, he simultaneously rubbed the blood-filled tip, hard, until I felt my orgasm break.

I screamed, crying and bucking against him, frantically clutching his wide shoulders and...released.

"Yes! Yes, yes, yes! Just like that, baby, come for me, with me. Let it go and come for me!" He encouraged me and that was all the encouragement I needed.

At the moment I cried out my release, Mack shouted in unison, loud and long. His grip on me was painful, yet welcome.

"God, I love you, Sheena, I love you so much, baby, and I'm never letting you go, never!" He cried out and I felt the long hard jet of his semen splash against my womb.

In that perfect moment of joining a vision slammed down on me, nearly as intense as the orgasm; a vision of me, Mack and a little brown-eyed baby with a determined chin, lying between us.

I held on tightly, crying, releasing control, but not ashamed. "I love you, too, baby, and I'm yours, forever this time."

Forever Yours

CHARLOTTE FEATHERSTONE

CHAPTER ONE

HER BODY WAS WEEPING FOR HIS TOUCH.

He knew it, understood it, the need growing inside her. She sensed his desire as well; heard it in the way his breath caught then rasped against her cheek in hurried, uneven caresses.

Hands, sliding beneath the cool bedcovers, searched until they found each other. Fingers laced, his long ones slipping between her delicate ones, gripping, clutching, holding...

Look up at me.

He didn't. Instead he climbed atop her, straddling her thighs with his hard ones as he slid his palms beneath the hem of her nightrail, the pads of his thumbs brushing her thighs in feathery strokes, a silent command to open to him.

Yes, touch me...stroke every inch of me with those beautiful hands.

God, how she adored his hands—all hot, hard palms and long elegant fingers. Fingers with just the right amount of smooth skin and callused edges. How those hands could bring such pleasure, such exquisite delight.

Slowly, teasingly, his expert fingers trailed up and over her inner thigh. Holding her breath, Elizabeth waited to feel him part her sex with one long, tapered finger, before sinking inside her wet and willing body. A body that had been ready— waiting—for him all night.

As the passion built and the ache in her womb intensified, her mind drifted, fantasizing all the things she wanted him to do to her. Mentally, she saw his hand roaming every inch of her body then filling her with two fingers, then three...then his tongue.

She moaned, allowing her lashes to flutter closed. How long it had been since he'd made love to her with his mouth. She wanted to put her hands on his shoulders and guide him down her body. To hold his mouth against her and demand that he take his time licking and stroking, leaving no inch of her undiscovered.

Knowing what she needed, he stroked her with the tip of his finger, petting her until she could stand the wait no longer, until she had fisted the sheet between her fingers and allowed the image of his dark head between her legs to take over. She could come like this, with her fantasy and his light, teasing touches. Yet she did not want to have an orgasm by simply remembering what she had dreamt he did to her. She wanted the real thing. His mouth against her, the feel of his lips, the scrape of his stubble, the hot stabs of his tongue and breath against her as she arched and shook.

She was weary of fantasizing. Tired of dreaming of sex acts she craved, yet were never performed.

Kiss me, she pleaded in her mind, terrified to give voice to her yearnings, to let him know how unsatisfied she had been these past months. *It has been so long since we have kissed like lovers.*

Thunder rumbled across the heavens and a flash of lightning lit the sky. Outside her bedroom window, Elizabeth saw the tops of the trees blowing in the wind, which was growing violent. Another roll of thunder...another bolt of lightning.

No, not yet...not yet...please... She moaned, tossing her head on the pillow as his hands cupped her bottom. He raised her hips to meet his hard arousal.

Not yet...

Even she did not understand the truth behind that silent plea. Was the entreaty skipping through her thoughts because she felt it too soon for him to take her, now, when her body was just beginning to heat, or was she praying that Mother Nature could hold off the storm for just a bit longer...just a few minutes longer...

Fuck! He needed to get inside her—*now.* Goddamn her, why did she insist on wearing a nightgown to bed? All these layers of ruffles and lace were impeding him from finding her quim and sinking his cock deep inside her. And his damned fingers, they were shaking like those of an untried youth, preventing him from doing anything but fumbling like a novice as he drowned in ruffles.

She writhed beneath him, her thighs moving languidly along his. Her soft belly brushed against his cock as she twisted and squirmed. He pressed it against her softness, needing to sink into something until he could once again find the blasted hem of her gown and shove it to her hips.

He should just tear the damn thing from her, ripping it to shreds and exposing her so that he could feel every inch of her against him. All that warm soft flesh...

Thunder cracked, rattling the windowpane. He felt her stiffen beneath him. Heard her stop breathing as she listened to the sounds of the night and the storm that raged outside. *No, not yet.* He cursed, ruthlessly shoving the hem of her nightrail to her belly.

It was dark in the room. He could see none of her, but he smelt her. Feminine arousal and floral soap. He couldn't wait. He was on fire for her, for her wet body and the feel of her legs wrapped around him. How long had it been? A month? Yes. A whole damned month he'd been without his wife—even though she had not been away, had been right here at Sutcliffe Hall—their home. But she *had* been away from him. In fact, she'd been gone from him in one way or another for the past three years.

Sinking himself inside her with one swift thrust, he moaned, feeling her pulsing around him. He nearly came right there. It had been so damn long and she was tight, gripping him greedily with her sheath. Yet he managed to grit his teeth and distract himself long enough to thrust again, filling her fully.

She arched, bringing her knees back to her chest, sucking all his length inside her. He took her in slow, deep stabs that made her moan and sigh. Christ, when was the last time he had heard that sweet sound? So long...

Another clap of thunder was followed by the brilliant flash of lightning. His lips sought her ear and he traced the shell of it with the tip of his tongue. She was panting, scratching her nails down his back, arousing the primitive male in him. For the first time in a long while, he felt like a man with her. Not a duke or a husband. Not a father. Just a man.

Catching her hands in his, he brought her arms above her head so that her breasts escaped the bodice of her gown. Instinctively her hips arched, driving him deeper. He heard her breathing quicken as his chest brushed her breasts. He saw her face in the moonlight, awash in pleasure, and knew she wanted to be taken like this, with her arms held high and his cock pounding into her.

"You like it like this, Elizabeth?" he whispered in her ear. "Or should I flip you over and take you from behind? Do you want me to fu—"

"Mama! Mama!"

"No," he groaned, pressing his face into her neck. *Jesus, not now!*

Her hands stilled against his, her body went rigid beneath his. He knew she'd heard the frightened little noise from down the hall. He knew everything they had just done, everything he wanted to do, was now over.

Capturing her mouth with his, he tried to kiss her as he thrust his cock deep inside her, demanding she shut out the sounds and feel—hear—only him. But she pushed him away. Instantly he lost his erection and pulled out of her.

"Mama! Mama! We're scared. Papa!"

Groaning, Christian rolled off his wife and allowed her to straighten her gown before their children exploded into the room carrying their blankets and bears and Lord knew what else.

"It will only take a minute to settle them," she tried to assure him, "and I'll send them back to Nanny."

"If Nanny had any brains, she would have kept them in their room to begin with," he snarled.

"Christian!"

He saw Elizabeth's horrified expression in the moonlight, but he didn't care. He was tired of this. This marriage. This wife. He wanted more. Something more than what his life had become.

"You know the children are frightened of thunderstorms."

"And everything else that goes bump in the night," he said with disdain. "And we mustn't overlook Richard's nightmares and John's bed-wetting. And let us not forget how arduous a task it was to get Jamie weaned from your breast."

Her eyes narrowed to angry slits. "They're only children."

"Richard is eight. He shouldn't need to come to his mama's bed because of a little thunder."

She shot him a disapproving glare. "They are just children, Christian. You are a grown man."

"Well, I have needs, too. What about mine? What about yours, or do you not need me inside you anymore? Are you just a shell of a woman now that you've borne children? Is that it, Elizabeth, you can't fuck anymore because you're a mother?"

He looked away from her and wiped his hands along his face as he fought for some measure of control. This was his wife, he reminded himself, whom he had once loved more than anything—whom he still loved. These were his children, his own flesh and blood—yet he swore he almost felt hatred for them as they flung the door open and ran into the room crying and sniffling.

"Darlings," Elizabeth cooed, opening her arms and allowing their dark-haired "darlings" to crawl into their bed. Their youngest, Jamie, who was not yet two, struggled to climb up the tall bed. Christian hefted him up and watched as Jamie scrambled out of his hold in order to cuddle up to his mother. His four children were now nestled against Elizabeth's generous breasts, their faces pressed into the starched linen of her gown, which concealed the sweet scent of her flesh.

His children were exactly where he longed to be. A place he hadn't really been since the birth of Rachel, their third child. Christ, had it really been three years since Rachel had been born? Three years since their marriage and sex life had begun to dwindle, then all but grind to a halt? Three years of living with someone he no longer knew or felt close to.

"Papa, your knee is against my back and it's hurting."

That was John, their second child. He was only six, but tonight, for Christian, he was much too old to be running to his mama because of a little thunder and lightning.

As John grunted and shoved him away, Christian swore beneath his breath. Snatching the sheet covering his waist he tore it from the bed. Elizabeth glared at him.

"I'm sick to death of this," he blurted. He saw the blue gaze of his oldest son peeking out at him from the protection of his mother's arm. Unable to help it, he glared angrily at him——a frightened eight-year-old boy——then turned his back, hating himself for what he had just done to his son.

"Christian," Elizabeth sighed, the sound so full of confusion and disapproval. "What is it you want?"

A fucking wife! But he could hardly say that in front of his children. So instead he said nothing, only sighed, knowing she would understand exactly what was wrong. Their marriage was over. It had been for some time now. It was well past time they admitted it to themselves——there was nothing left. Nothing except resentment, distance and emptiness.

"Where are you going?" she asked as he stalked to the connecting door to his chamber.

"I'm leaving."

Silence followed him. There was no plea for him to stay, no tears and whispered words of love. Nothing that showed him she cared a thing for him.

Did she give a damn? Did she care that there was nothing left of their marriage, or was it merely a relief for her to know she no longer had to put up with him?

CHAPTER TWO

"YOUR EYES DO NOT HAVE THAT SPARKLE, ELIZABETH."

Tilting her head, Elizabeth tried to smile. She doubted anything could make her eyes sparkle. Not now, not after it was so apparent that her marriage was over. But she could hardly explain that to her friend. He was a man and a bachelor. He would not understand the complexities of a woman in her sexual prime, nor the intricacies of marriage.

"No, no," Adrian muttered, rising from behind his easel. "Your head is tilted all wrong. You will want the sun to shine on your face. You have such lovely features and the sunlight will only enhance them."

"You'll see the lines around my eyes," she grumbled. "Sunlight is so very unforgiving on a thirty-five-year-old woman's face."

"Nonsense. You've nothing to be concerned about, Elizabeth. You're beautiful. Lovely." Kneeling before her, Adrian fussed with her skirt, fluffing it and spreading it out at her feet. Next he gripped her shoulders and posed her so that her bosom was more pronounced and her waist turned, making it appear slimmer. When their gazes collided, she could not hide the wetness in her eyes. "What's this, Elizabeth?" he asked, wiping away a crystal drop.

"Nothing," she sniffed. Tilting her chin away, she broke the contact of his fingers. Avoiding his concerned expression, Elizabeth stared out the window of the conservatory that overlooked the long gravel drive of the Sutcliffe estate.

"I don't believe I've ever seen you cry before."

"The sun is bright."

Clasping his hands on her cheeks, he turned her so that she was looking at him. "You haven't been yourself for months, Eliza. Tell me. You do know there is nothing you cannot tell me."

They were the very best of friends, had been since childhood when they had lived down a lane from each other. She had known Adrian longer than her husband, and Elizabeth had the sinking feeling she knew him much better than she knew Christian.

Christian...her husband. Where was he? What was he doing? He hadn't been home in a sennight, not since...she swallowed hard. Not since that night when they had been making love...no, not love, they no longer made love...they had been having sex, and the children had disturbed them. How furious he had been with them, and her. He had left and not come back, leaving her to wonder what would become of them.

Had he found another? Was he visiting the brothels of London? Had he secured himself a mistress? She had never thought him capable of betraying her, but much had changed in the past few years and now she wasn't so sure of him, or herself. She hardly knew him anymore. He certainly was not the man she had married.

It made her retch, thinking of him in bed with another woman, his beautiful hands stroking her breasts and thighs. She thought of all the endearments, all the love words he had once whispered in her ear, then imagined him saying them to another and she broke out into a sob.

"What is it?" Adrian asked again. His voice was so soft, so concerned. Adrian would understand. He always seemed to understand her, where Christian hadn't sought to understand her needs for the past three years.

"Is it Sutcliffe?" he asked. When she nodded, he blew out a breath and brushed his thumbs along her cheeks, wiping away her tears. "He no longer satisfies you," Adrian stated flatly.

Nodding, Elizabeth balled up a linen square and dabbed at her eyes. "Yes," she whispered, ashamed to confess something like that in front of Adrian. She was shocked by how much it hurt to finally admit the truth. "He does not make me happy. I…I haven't been since before…well, after Jamie's birth. It's as if we are distant acquaintances passing one another from time to time. We no longer talk, touch…kiss," she hiccupped. "I hardly know him anymore. We've become strangers to one another."

"How can that be?"

Tears fell in earnest from her eyes, and Elizabeth did nothing to stop them. "He does not want me as a woman, Adrian. He no longer desires me. It's as if he is only doing a duty when he comes to my bed. He hurries on with the business and it leaves me frustrated and yearning. It is obvious that he no longer wants me, or our children. It is obvious he is no longer happy with me. Even now he is in London, doing God knows what—probably bedding every woman under the age of twenty-five.

I can't compete with those young women anymore, Adrian. I can't give him what he needs."

"Come here." Adrian held out his arms to her. Silently, she pressed forward and allowed him to hold her. There were no words, no admonishment for crying or command that she cease sobbing, no statements about what to do to fix things. Christian always tried to talk her fears away. He always wanted to fix whatever it was that troubled her, but never once had he mentioned trying to repair their marriage. The simple fact was, he didn't care that it was ending.

"I am here for you," Adrian murmured, holding her tighter to him as she sobbed. "I am here, Eliza, in whatever way you may need."

Raising her head, Elizabeth looked at him through watery eyes. He comprehended her—completely. Why couldn't Christian understand her like Adrian?

As they looked into each other's eyes, Elizabeth saw a dark curtain suddenly draw across Adrian's green eyes. Despite her openness with him, she knew he hid much from her. There was so much about Adrian that she did not know, that he would not speak of.

What was he thinking now? Did he fear she might accept his offer? Did he know that she yearned not for a husband, but a lover? A man to worship her body and fulfill the sexual urges she felt? Was he hoping to be that man, or did he secretly fear her asking him?

"Elizabeth." He pulled away from her. "I can hardly believe I am going to say something so contrived, so trite," he rasped, pressing his lips to her brow and kissing her gently. "But a marriage is like a garden. It needs to be tended year after year.

To be cultivated and fed. And when the weeds begin to sprout, as they always do, they need to be plucked—immediately. Sometimes love just isn't enough to keep two people together. Do you understand, Eliza, what I mean?"

She did understand him. She had neglected their marriage, and now it was being choked, stifled by stagnation and complacency. By routine and fatigue. She had taken Christian for granted. She had expected him to know what she wanted, what she desired—in and out of bed. She hadn't thought to ask for it; she had thought he should simply know.

"Your thinking is all wrong, you know. You're a beautiful woman, Elizabeth, and very desirable. Any man would give his soul to have you in his bed."

Smiling, Elizabeth dabbed at her eyes. "I wish," she murmured into her linen kerchief, "that my husband agreed with your assessment of my desirability. I fear ten years and four children later that desirability is severely in question."

"Do you want to know what the allure of a thirty-five-year-old woman is for a man?" Adrian asked. "It's confidence. Maturity. Acceptance. The confidence to pursue what she desires and know what she wants. There are no coy games, no crying and stomping and pouting like there is with young, silly girls. Older women have the maturity to ask for it—demand it, whatever they want, be it in life or the bedroom. They accept the fact that they can be both mother and wife as well as a sexual creature with the same needs as their husbands. Those young women you worry about," he whispered in her ear, "are no threat to you. Learn to ask for what you want. Demand you be allowed to do whatever you want to him, and I guarantee you, he will be yours. Never doubt, Elizabeth, that Sutcliffe is still yours. How could he leave someone as lovely, as desirable, as sexual as you?"

Desirable...sexual...

Christian stood in the doorway of the conservatory watching his wife in the arms of Adrian Wallace. Goddamn bastard! He had always known that Adrian coveted his wife. Had always feared that one day, Adrian might replace him in Elizabeth's affection.

And why not? Adrian was a rogue. A dark and romantic artist with a hint of danger about him. What woman wouldn't fall for him with his black tousled hair and green eyes that always seemed to flash a sensual invitation. Why wouldn't Elizabeth desire someone like Adrian? Hell, half the women of London practically threw themselves at his feet. But by God, his wife—Elizabeth— would not be one of them! Over his dead body would he allow her to toss away their marriage for a romp in the artist's bed.

So what if he wasn't as romantic as Adrian? So what if he couldn't shoot Elizabeth smoldering looks from beneath black lashes. Christ, he'd made her a duchess on their wedding day. He'd given her wealth and land and estates beyond her imaginings. He'd given her four beautiful, healthy children, and the creation of those children had been passionate and loving. He had given Elizabeth everything of himself, which, he was willing to bet, was more than Adrian Wallace would give Elizabeth, or indeed, any woman.

By God, he wasn't just going to stand here and allow his wife to slip through his hands. Nor was he going to let her forget what had brought them together—love, and an incredible passion for each other.

This marriage was *not* over. He had realized that this past week. He'd spent the past days away from her, dying for her. He would have sold his soul for just a glimpse of her and her smile, some sign that she still wanted him, that he still held a place in her heart, no matter how small.

He'd reached the conclusion that although he hadn't been happy for a while, it was not because of Elizabeth. It was not because he was tired of her, or because he desired someone else. He wasn't happy because his marriage was dying, and it was all because he'd let it go to rot.

He was no idiot. He knew the source of her unhappiness. It was the same as his. They were no longer passionate. They no longer laughed and kissed for hours on end. He no longer stole illicit touches, or stroked her breasts when no one was watching. They didn't make love, they mated. Once a week maybe, if the children weren't ill, or there weren't any thunderstorms, or if he wasn't exhausted from a day of riding and looking over his estate, or if he hadn't drunk too much after dinner, drowning his thoughts with port. If Elizabeth wasn't worn down by a day of constantly chasing the children and seeing to her charities and her duties as his duchess…sometimes then, if none of those things intruded, they might come together for five minutes of perfunctory sex.

How had it come to this—Elizabeth wearing herself out with their children and him drinking so much? How had they managed to become complete strangers after ten years of marriage and four children? How could he not feel close to the woman who had borne his children, who had shared his life for nearly a decade?

Christ, they had become like automatons, living life in a

haze. Day in and day out, the routine was the same, predictable, boring, *stifling*. He didn't want to live this way. He didn't want Elizabeth to live this way. And he didn't want to lose her, nor did he want his children to despise him because he was a miserable sod whenever they were around.

He needed to find the magic of those years when they had made love on the grass, or while their guests mingled in the next room. He needed to seduce her and he, in turn, needed to be seduced. They needed time alone, to get to know one another again, to reconnect as friends and as lovers.

Christian stepped back into the shadows, shielding his presence from his wife as she rose from her chair and smoothed her hands down her midriff, brushing the wrinkles from her muslin skirt. His heart leapt in his chest as he studied her. When was the last time he really looked at her? Truly saw her as a woman, as his lover? He couldn't remember.

These past years she had been his wife—his duchess. The mother of his children. He wanted more from her than that. He wanted the woman. The lover she had once been to him.

He would find a way back to that woman. He had to. Because he could not stand the thought of losing Elizabeth. He could not bear to think of her being any man's lover but his. Especially not Adrian's. He'd cut his heart out before he let her go to Adrian.

CHAPTER THREE

ELIZABETH SANK DOWN ON HER BED AS THE
children washed for luncheon. Sighing, she closed her eyes and
immediately felt tired and lonely. Their butler had informed
her that her husband had arrived home two hours earlier, yet
he had not sought her out. Had he even missed her? Had he
found someone else? Someone younger? Someone thinner,
whose body was firm and not soft from bearing children?
Someone who could fawn over him and devote hours and hours
to lovemaking? Someone who could fulfill his every wish,
without interruption?

Lying back, she nestled her head against the soft pillow. They
had once been able to make love for hours. To escape to a
private corner of the house and shut themselves away, tearing
their clothes in their haste to feel each other's body. In those
days, they had actually made love in the daylight or on a settee
or in the carriage on their way home from a dinner or a ball.
Now, they came together in the dark, the standard woman-on-
bottom position their only method of coupling. The foreplay
and seduction which Christian had excelled at had been gone

for a time now, leaving only a hasty and automatic penetration. The intimacy of lying in his arms after climaxing, just kissing and touching and whispering words of love, had been lost. More often than not, Christian left the bed, forced out either by their children, or his dissatisfaction with what she assumed was her and their coupling.

He never whispered anymore, while in the heat of lovemaking, how much he desired her. How much she pleased him. How much he needed her in his life. *But neither have you . . . you've done nothing to assure him that you still desire him. Need him,* a venomous little voice whispered to her. And she accepted it for the truth. Was she not also to blame for the distance between them? Had she not had a hand in creating that distance?

Why could she not let him take her into an empty room and raise her skirts for a quick, hard loving? He had tried often enough, and each time she had slapped his hands away and sent him an impatient glare. Tonight, she had always said. But tonight never came, and he no longer tried to tempt and tease her into an indiscretion.

She missed that: the temptation, the seduction, the thrill of spontaneous passion and the risk of getting caught. Did Christian long for those moments like she did?

Smoothing her fingers along the starched pillowcase, needing to feel his imprint, despite the fact his head had not rested on the pillow for a week, Elizabeth turned her face to his pillow and tried to remember the scent of his skin—lemon soap and leather. Tried to recall how it felt to run her fingertips through the silk of his chest hair and the feel of it rubbing against her nipples, hardening them to little pebbles before he took them into his mouth.

Something crinkled beneath her hand and her eyes flew open. Raising her head, she saw the folded piece of parchment and opened it.

I have been wrong in my dealings with you, Elizabeth. I have wronged our children, and I am sorry for it. I have thought of nothing but you and our marriage while I have been away. I know you are not happy and I want to fix that. Believe me when I say that I want to bring you happiness and pleasure.

Pleasure...it has been a while since I have brought that to you, hasn't it? It has been forever since I have spoken of such things to you. I hardly know where to start, or what to say. I am not a romantic, as you well know. Yet I do have feelings, thoughts—of you and me, and us together.

Her heart raced, pounding hard against her ribs. It had been ages since Christian had written her a letter. But this was unlike any love letter he had ever penned. This was something entirely different. It was something in his words, in the tone. It was very provocative, and it made her stomach tighten and her womb clench.

I dream of you, Elizabeth. I fantasize about all the things I want to do to you and the things I have yet to try. I want the passion back. I want you back as my lover.

"Mama! Mama!" the children cried as they ran down the hall. "It's time for luncheon."

Putting the letter in her bedside-table drawer, Elizabeth contemplated what she was going to do. This was the olive branch.

Christian felt it too, this distance, both emotional and physical. He wanted to make things right between them, and Lord knew she wanted the same thing.

She hadn't known where to begin healing the breach between them, but his letter gave her an idea.

Reaching for a quill and the ink pot, Elizabeth jotted a few lines on a sheet of paper. Blotting it, she folded it in thirds and shoved it beneath her bodice, making certain her breasts cradled it.

With a smile, she left the room.

His oldest sons ran into the dining room, shouting and jumping. They stopped dead in their tracks when they saw their father seated in his chair at the head of the table.

"Papa," Richard said, sobering immediately as he took his chair. "It is nice to have you home."

"Sir," John nodded, taking his place opposite his brother.

"Richard, Johnnie," Christian said, smiling at both boys. "I think you might have grown while I was away." The boys' eyes lit up and they both straightened in their chairs.

"Nanny says we're growing like bad weeds," Richard announced proudly.

"But surely you're not too big now for a kiss?" he asked as he rose from his chair. "I missed you both, very much," he murmured, kissing the tops of their dark heads. When he opened his eyes after kissing Johnnie his gaze caught Elizabeth's as she stood in the doorway. Jamie was on her hip, fast asleep with his cherubic face pressed against her neck and his chubby hand gripping the lace of her bodice.

"Let me." He walked over to Elizabeth and reached for his sleeping son whose cheeks were crimson and chafed.

"Molars," Elizabeth stated, pointing to Jamie's cheeks. "He's been up the past two nights crying."

Fitting Jamie against his chest, Christian bent toward his wife. He caught himself reaching for her cheek, and stopped himself. It had become a bad habit, a little peck on her cheek. Sometimes his lips barely connected before he was taken away by business, or Elizabeth's attention was drawn away by the children.

How complacent they had become.

Lowering his gaze he sought her lips. Plump, pink. Sinful lips that aroused him, pleasured him. Lips he had not properly kissed in ages. Lips he had once watched do very wicked things to his body. He grew hard remembering those days, and his heart hurt, wondering if they would ever return.

"I missed you." He lowered his mouth to hers and sensed her surprise as he pressed his lips against hers.

"Eww," Richard and John both groaned, covering their eyes.

Christian found himself grinning until the shadow of Adrian appeared in the doorway. He was carrying Rachel, and something inside Christian snapped when he saw his daughter in the arms of another man. He didn't want any other man holding his children. He didn't want any other man in his children's lives, or Elizabeth's.

"Your Grace," Adrian muttered as Rachel squirmed out of his hold and scampered over to Christian. She hugged his leg and pressed her cheek against his knee. With a smile, he raked his fingers through her black curls. So much like himself, he thought. Looking down at her lovely crystal blue eyes he ran his finger along her rosy cheek. So much like Elizabeth.

"Papa, you're home. I missed you, Papa."

"And I missed you too, sweetheart." It was the truth. He'd

missed them all so much. As he lay alone in his big bed in his town house in Mayfair, he had ached for those nights when his children climbed into their bed and took up all the space and the blankets. He had never realized how much he enjoyed seeing their children lying asleep between them. He missed lying in the darkness, silently watching them as babies at Elizabeth's breast. Missed kissing their chubby little hands as they nursed. Missed kissing Elizabeth and thanking her for all she had brought to his life.

He could not help but let his gaze wander over Elizabeth's face, then down to her bodice. He had the mad urge to clasp her to him and bare her to him. To possess her. To take from her and have her give to him.

"I think I'll take my leave now," he heard Adrian murmur next to Elizabeth. Their gazes collided over the top of Elizabeth's blond head, and Christian knew that Adrian had seen and correctly interpreted the expression in his eyes.

"What of your riding, sweetheart?" he asked Rachel. "Have you been out on your pony?" She shook her head as she looked up at him. "Well then, we shall have to go riding after luncheon, won't we? And we'll bring your brothers, too."

Christian turned to look at Elizabeth, and saw that Adrian had left them. The front door closed, and he felt an immense relief that his rival was gone. He wanted to be alone with Elizabeth. To heal the wounds that were festering between them. He did not want Adrian with his brooding romantic aura to be present while he tried to get his wife back.

He searched Elizabeth's face, looking for any regret he might see at Adrian's absence. And it was then that he finally admitted the truth. He was afraid that when compared to Adrian in Elizabeth's eyes, he might come in a poor second. He was only a duke, no match for the brooding artist who seemed to know how to bring a woman to her knees with his sensuality and silky tongue.

"Why don't you rest," he said to Elizabeth, taking her hand in his. "You look tired."

She ran a self-conscious hand over her hair and he wanted to kick himself for saying such a thing. So much for romance and courting. *Fuck*. Why was he so inconsiderate to Elizabeth's needs? Why couldn't he remember that she was a woman, and that women did not want to hear they appeared tired and worn. Adrian would not have said something like that. He would have made such an observation into a sexual invitation, not a criticism.

When was the last time he told her she was beautiful? Or how damn arousing her body was? Or how erotic he thought it was when she dragged her tongue along her bottom lip.

"Elizabeth?" He bent his head and captured her gaze, hoping he could muster some grace and skilled conversation. "I will stay with the children while you rest. Perhaps I will come and look in on you later, hmm?"

Her eyes instantly flared to a brilliant shade of blue. He saw the invitation shining in them. Yes, she wanted that, him coming to her in the daylight when the children were outside running around and Jamie was fast asleep in his crib. And God, how he wanted it, too.

She reached for his hand and pulled him through the door, away from the children and the servants' curious gazes. Jamie was asleep against his chest, oblivious to what was happening, and they were alone in the empty hallway.

"Christian, I missed you," she said, her gaze warm and inviting. She reached up and ran her fingers through his short hair as she brought his mouth down to hers. With a groan, he kissed her, slipping his tongue inside her mouth and moaning as she reached for his free hand and brought it to her breasts. Hungrily, greedily he cupped her, squeezing her, feeling her flesh spilling over his palm. God, he wanted her, just like this, against the wall, her breasts freed from her bodice. He wanted to raise her skirts and palm her full bottom. Wanted to take her legs and wrap them around his waist. Wanted to fit his cock inside her and whisper heated words in her ear. He wanted to tell her of his dreams, of every secret fantasy he had ever had of her.

On and on they kissed, and he mimicked with his tongue what he wanted to do with his cock. She moaned and pressed against him, rubbing her belly against his prick, which was bursting behind his trousers. Over and over she tantalized him, until he wanted to say *Get me off* and shove her hand down his waistband so that she could stroke him till he came.

She controlled him with that kiss, and when he finally opened his eyes, he found his fingers down her bodice, resting against the cleft of her breasts. He felt the paper there, nestled tightly, and smiled as he slowly pulled it out from between her breasts. He brought it to his face, indulging in the warmth of the paper, heated by her flesh. He inhaled it and closed his eyes. It smelt of floral soap and honey, of talcum from his children's morning baths, and Elizabeth's own womanly scent. It smelt of his wife.

She kissed him once more then left him standing alone with their sleeping child against the wall, his heart still beating madly in his chest, his fingers shaking so much he could barely open the letter.

Tell me these fantas.es you've had of me.

What an erotic game this could be.

Looking up, he watched her round the corner to the upstairs apartments. Her gaze found his, and he saw her lashes lower. Was it shyness? Sensual invitation?

Yes, they could have a lot of fun with this little amusement. In fact, it might be exactly what they needed to find their way back to one another.

He was definitely game for writing Elizabeth some very wicked letters. And, he mused, he looked forward to receiving some of hers, too.

THE FIRST LETTER APPEARED ON THE PILLOW NEXT to her when she awoke from her nap. Breaking the wax seal, Elizabeth tore it open and devoured his words.

Fantasies? There's so many. Where would you like me to begin? In my dreams I've had you so many ways. Of course, they are most shocking, not at all appropriate for a lady of your station... yet I'm aroused by just thinking of sharing them with you. Are you aroused, Elizabeth, thinking of what I might write, what illicit dreams I've had of you?

What would you think of performing for me, Elizabeth? I always thought you'd look stunning dressed in tawdry silks and lace. There is something so very erotic, so forbidden about a lady of breeding acting like a fallen woman.

In my fantasy you make me a lovely, skillful whore, with your full pink lips and gorgeous breasts. And your soft thighs... what I would want to do with them.

That is my first fantasy: I'd love to pay you for a night of service. I would command you to do so many things with those lovely full lips and glorious...tits. I'd want to sit in a chair and watch you undress for me, watching your lush thighs being revealed through layers of cheap, flashy petticoats and satin. I'd want to take you standing up against a wall, wearing only your silk stockings and garters...I'd like to tie you up, and have you all to myself so that I could explore every inch of you with my hands, my tongue, my cock. .

Looking up from the letter, Elizabeth fanned herself with it. Reading his words aroused her in a way she never had been before. Her thighs were damp. Her womb was clenched tight in anticipation.

This was a side of Christian she had never seen. He had been passionate, yes. Skilled, most assuredly. But this...she never would have dreamed that he desired her to play the part of a common whore. It titillated her to know he wanted to play games. It made her want to haul out the laciest thing she owned and parade before him bringing his fantasy to life. But she wanted to know more. She craved more of these letters and the naughty intimacy they created.

The sun was shining on the grass as Christian walked in a large circle, the leather reins in his hands. Slowly he guided Rachel's pony and laughed as she giggled in delight.

"Mama! Mama!" she squealed. "Look, I'm riding."

"I see, darling," Elizabeth said as she fell into step beside them.

"Have you come out to ride with me, Mama?"

"No, I have not, sweetheart. I have come out to tell Papa that I am taking the carriage into the village."

"Now?" he asked. Narrowing his eyes against the sun, Christian studied his wife. Elizabeth's color was high and her fingers were fidgeting with something. Had she found his letter? What did she think? Did she think him perverse to have written such a thing, confessing his long-hidden fantasy to her? Was she shocked and offended that he dreamed of her, a lady of breeding, a *duchess,* acting the part of a harlot?

"I won't be long," she whispered before reaching up on tiptoe and brushing his cheek with her lips. He felt her fingers engulf his, felt the sharp point of a folded piece of paper being shoved into his palm. "I'll be leaving in three quarters of an hour."

She left him then, and he watched the way her hips swayed beneath her muslin gown, the sun illuminating the contours of her rounded thighs through her shift as she retreated from them. When his daughter's attention was diverted by the pony's mane flapping in the breeze, he opened the missive.

How I would love to play the wanton for you. But what does a harlot do? Tell me what a man wants when he goes to a courtesan.

With a smile, he looked up and saw that she was glancing back at him over her shoulder. Tell her...indeed he would.

The carriage door opened. Elizabeth accepted the hand of the footman as she stepped up into it. She half expected to find Christian inside, waiting for her. He was not.

With a little pang of disappointment, she took the bench and settled her skirts around her. He was much too busy with estate affairs, she told herself. He'd been gone a week and had things to see to. He did not have time to accompany her to the village for an hour of shopping, even though she had purposely orchestrated the whole affair so that they might be alone in the carriage. He had once ravished her in a carriage and she had never forgotten the feeling of it, of the hurried loving and the threat of discovery by the coachman.

The carriage rocked as the footman jumped onto the back. The horses whinnied and jostled in their harnesses, making the carriage sway from left to right. As she waited for the coachman to crack his whip and give the command to begin trotting down the lane, Elizabeth looked out the window and saw that Christian was standing at the window of his study, watching her with an intent stare that seemed to go all the way to her soul.

She broke it by looking away. Something white caught the corner of her eye. It was then that she saw the letter awaiting her on the opposite bench, its red seal bearing the mark of the Duke of Sutcliffe. Snatching it off the velvet squabs, Elizabeth tore open the seal.

Tell you what I want? In graphic detail, Elizabeth?

I could show you, I suppose, by tearing out an explicit drawing from a book. But I think what you are asking for is something altogether different. You want the rush that comes with reading something naughty. You want the excitement of reading my words and imagining them being uttered by me in your ear... You want to become aroused—wet—by reading something vulgar and forbidden.

She swallowed hard, trying not to give in to the urge to nod her head in agreement. Yes, this is exactly what she wanted, to see this other side of her husband. Not the elegant and poised duke who was everything proper and honorable. Not the dutiful husband or father, but the man. The primitive male inside him that he had never allowed her to glimpse.

You want to know what sort of things I would do to you. You want to know how I would ask you for what I want, is that it? You want me to talk commonly...to write something dirty to you...

Her heart was near to bursting, it was beating so hard. How had he known? How had he guessed that secretly she longed to hear him say something so very improper? Something the duke would never say, but that the man longed to.

Admit to me that you long for that, and I will tell you every-thing I want you to do. In base words I will tell everything I think, everything I feel. I will tell you everything I've ever whispered to you in my mind while I have been loving you.

She looked up, just as the carriage began to rock forward. She found him, still standing at the window, watching her. She nodded, telling him that yes, she wanted that, to know what he thought when he was making love to her, to hear his fanta-sies. She wanted nothing more than to connect with him like this, to connect in a way they never had before.

His eyes, so dark, almost black, seemed to darken even more as he watched her nod, silently admitting the truth to him. His gaze, so intense upon her, made her shiver. There was a promise in those eyes. A promise of the sinful, carnal delight that awaited her when she returned to him.

Elizabeth almost ordered the coach to stop, yet she didn't. It wouldn't do to fall too easily into his hands. A common whore might do such a thing but a grand courtesan would not. An elite member of the demimonde would know that she must keep her prey hungry, keep him yearning if she was to successfully snare him.

"So, you've finally returned."

Elizabeth whirled around at the sound of Christian's voice. He emerged from the shadows as he strode toward her. "I didn't think I was gone all that long."

He stood before her and caught her face in his hands. "It felt like forever." He kissed her then, a slow, seductive kiss that made her heart pound. He couldn't know what that simple admission had done to her.

They kissed, slowly at first, before giving in to the hunger of deeper, more passionate kisses. Breaking away to regain her breath, Elizabeth gasped as Christian proceeded to rain openmouthed kisses along her jaw and down her throat to the mounds of her breasts.

"I want you to touch me," he murmured, reaching for her hand and bringing it to the tented folds of his trousers. "I want you to look at it. I want you to tell me how much you want to feel me inside you. I want to see how much you want it."

Elizabeth ran the tip of her finger along his erection that was pressing against his trousers. He was long and thick, and harder than she could ever remember him being. "Oh yes, Your Grace," she whispered as she wrapped her fingers around him, "I want *all* this inside me." Elizabeth felt him swell even further.

"Then why did you leave this afternoon?" he rasped as he

inhaled the fragrance of her hair. "I could have throttled you. I was achingly aroused."

"Were you?" Elizabeth closed her eyes as his lips found the pulse in her throat. "Tell me."

He inhaled sharply, his body tensing as he fitted his palms against her hips. His fingers bit into her before they skated over the shape of her curves. "My cock was so damn hard I had to palm it to relieve the ache. I haven't tossed off like that since I was a schoolboy, so frenzied and hard and fast. But I needed to get off, I couldn't wait for you."

She leaned back against the wall as his hands slipped around her waist and coasted downward, to the apex of her thighs. She imagined Christian pleasuring himself while thinking of her and she grew wet. "I would have liked to have watched."

"What, me with my cock in my hand?" he asked, clearly surprised. "Does it excite you to know that you forced me to masturbate?"

Nodding, she brought her mouth to his and kissed him, dragging her lips against his. She let her hand brush the front of his trousers again, then whispered into his mouth, "It's not like I've never touched myself while thinking of you."

He made a choking sound. "That is something I'd give my entire estate to watch. I'd want you on a lounge, fully open to me so I can see everything."

"What else would you want me to do?"

"To fondle your breasts. As I watched, I'd imagine tonguing them." Elizabeth placed her hand atop her breast and brushed her fingers along her nipple. He watched her, his tongue wetting his lip. "Show me."

He didn't wait for her to lower her bodice; instead, he did

it himself, hurriedly pulling at the lace and exposing a large portion of her breast. Lowering his head, he brushed his lips along her, seeking her nipple. When he found it, he sucked it into his mouth. The sucking and tugging aroused her until she had more than dampened her linen drawers. Reaching down between their bodies, she stroked the front of his trousers.

"I want your cock."

"I want to see it in your hand," he hissed, bringing her hard against him. "I want to see it in your mouth."

"Your Grace—*oh!*"

Shreeves, their butler, came to a grinding halt before them, his normally placid features a riot of red embarrassment. "Y-y-your, my pardon," he exclaimed in a choked whisper as he turned his back to them.

"What is it?" Christian barked, making the servant flinch as if he had been whipped.

"Your land steward, Your Grace, he's arrived with some papers you need to sign. Shall I have him return later?"

"I shall be there directly," Christian stated, then looked down into her face with his black, intense eyes. "Touch me, Elizabeth," he groaned. "Brush your hand along my cock. It's so hard, so hungry. So wet," he whispered, pressing his forehead to hers.

One glance over Christian's shoulder told her that Shreeves had taken his leave. They were now completely alone in the hall outside her little salon. She was half tempted to pull him inside, but instead, she did something she had never done before—she unfastened the top buttons of his trousers and wrapped her fingers around him. Never had she felt him hotter or thicker in her hand.

"Oh, Christ, yes," he moaned, as his hand came up to cup

her cheek. Stroking him, she caressed him with her palm and fingertips until he was shoving himself into her hand and panting against her mouth. "Christ, Elizabeth, yes. Faster. God, I wish we were someplace where I could push you to your knees."

Her blood racing with excitement, Elizabeth stroked him faster and watched the emotions play across his face. He was so close…so close. And she wanted to do this, to please him. And there was no one about, and it would only take a second…

Sliding down the wall she came to rest on her knees. Looking up into his astonished face, she held his gaze as her hand engulfed his rigid cock.

"What are you thinking?" she asked, feeling her cheeks flush with excitement and with the fear of possible discovery.

"How very much I would love for you to take my cock in your mouth, and pleasure me right here, where anyone might happen to come across you sucking me."

Closing her eyes, she took him between her lips. He was so hard and thick that she could only get a bit of him into her mouth. But it was enough for him, if his moans of pleasure were any indication. Wrapping one hand around her nape and flattening his other hand against the wall, he thrust into her mouth.

"*Fuck.*" It was a ragged half whisper in the quiet of the hall. His fingers pressed into her neck as he rocked his hips, withdrawing then pressing forward once more. "Looks so good, filling your mouth."

She looked up as she curled her tongue around him and their gazes met. His jaw clenched and she felt his cock throb and lift in her hand. He was close.

"Take more of me," he commanded, as his fingers pressed

against her neck, angling her mouth to better take his length. "Yes, like that, Elizabeth. Christ, you're going to suck it right out of me, aren't you?"

And then he was coming, pulsing hot for what seemed like forever before he was able to draw her up and enfold her in his arms. He held her tightly, kissing her cheek, the shell of her ear, the corner of her eye.

"I'm not going to be able to concentrate on a bloody thing my steward is saying. Not after this."

"What will you be thinking?" she asked, pressing her face into his shoulder and feeling safe within his arms.

He lifted her face and smiled wickedly at her. "Reach into my pocket." She did and found the note nestled there. "My thoughts are there, Elizabeth. Everything I was thinking this afternoon. Read it if you want to know what I was thinking while my cock was in my hand."

She watched him walk away, his shoulders so broad in the sunlight that bathed the hall through the transom windows. When he reached his study, he turned and looked at her.

"I will send a servant for you when I am finished. Come to me here, Elizabeth, in my study. It's where I want you to live out that." He nodded, indicating the letter in her hands.

Elizabeth waited till he closed the door behind him before opening the letter. She bit her lip on a smile as her eyes greedily ate his words.

I'm watching you through the window, sitting in the coach. I'm wondering what you're wearing beneath your pelisse and gown, imagining your breasts pushed up by your corset. I'm envisioning my hands all over you, undressing you. I'm dreaming of the way you sound, moaning and panting, silently begging me to touch you, to fill you with my cock.

I'm thinking of you, with your legs spread, your quim glistening for me. I want you wearing nothing but your silk beaded slippers and demure lace stockings. And the image of that, Christ, it makes me so hot, so hard, that I know when I'm done writing this, I'm going to stroke my cock, imagining it's you . . . your hand, your mouth, your tight sex.

And when I finally have you all to myself, I'm going to press against you and not ask you, but command you to fuck me. And what will you say then, Elizabeth? Will you let me fuck you?

CHAPTER FIVE

"YOUR GRACE?"

"What is it?" Christian demanded as a footman peered around the door of his study.

"Her Grace asked that I give you this. She said it was most important."

Waving the footman in, Christian sat back in his chair and smiled to himself. Lord, he was erect again, just thinking of what was going to lie within that little pink folded paper lying in the footman's white-gloved palm.

"Thank you, Jenkins. That will be all." Ignoring his steward, who was politely flipping through his folio of documents, Christian flicked opened Elizabeth's note.

I wouldn't say anything, because I want to be taken. Taken by you, however you want me. Hard, animalistic, like strangers who have just met and who burn for the feel of each other. Like lovers who have been denied too long.

He stifled a groan. Another one of his fantasies, just taking her as if she was his possession. As if he had total rights to her body.

I am wet. Aching for you, for your cock deep inside me. I still have the taste of you in my mouth. I can still feel you inside me, thick, hard...filling me so full with your beautiful length...

I want to watch as you fill me. I want to see the slow slide of your cock in and out of my body. I have never confessed this to you before, but I have always wished to make love before a mirror. To see your body and mine together.

He swallowed—hard. "Where is Her Grace, Jenkins?" he asked without looking up from her elegant handwriting.

"I believe the duchess is in the garden, Your Grace. I saw her with her bonnet and rose clippers."

"Excuse me."

His steward gaped at him, but nodded, clearly bewildered by his actions. Eagerly, his long steps ate up the distance from his study to the back terrace which led to the gardens. He didn't stop until he had rounded the corner of the mansion and found her humming while snipping pink roses from a bush and dropping them into the basket that rested at her feet.

He came up behind her and wrapped his arms around her waist, dragging her against him.

"What!" she gasped then turned around. Her bonnet fell off, and he raked his hands through her hair, dispelling pins and combs and watching as the blond tresses fell down her back.

"Lift your skirts," he demanded as he pushed her back against the brick wall of the house.

She did, eagerly, and his blood raced at the sight. He grasped her hands in his and held them above her head with one hand. With his free hand, he undid his trousers then lifted her skirts until he felt her sex, which was wet, swollen.

"Fuck me," he ordered, whispering the command into her ear. He pushed up inside her and listened to her keening cry. "You like that, don't you?" he asked her as he thrust harder into her, watching her long lashes cover her eyes. "You like being taken like this."

"Yes," she whispered. "Like this. I want this from you. I never thought you wanted me in such a way."

"You think I haven't thought of having you like this?" he asked, unable to conceal his surprise. "You think I've never wanted you this way, wanton and wicked and craving me. That I've never dreamt of fingering your quim while seated at a dinner party, watching your face, knowing my fingers are deep inside you while you try to act the part of a duchess? Do you think I haven't wanted to pull you into my study and lay you across the desk and pleasure your sex with my mouth?"

Elizabeth could barely concentrate on what he was saying. She was shattering inside, aware of nothing but the feel of his hand around her wrists and his cock inside her. Between them there were clothes and the whispering caress of the wind, but inside her was Christian—hot and hard.

"Do you think I haven't wanted to fuck you up against a wall? Christ, Elizabeth, I've thought it more than I'd care to admit, and doing it now is better than any fevered imagining I've ever had."

She was excited by this, being taken by him in such a way—up against a wall, still clothed. He was panting in her ear, his fingers were biting into her wrists as he increased the rhythm of his strokes, and then she was crying out and shaking around him.

He didn't cover her mouth, concealing her sounds of

pleasure. Instead, he watched her, encouraged her, before splashing his seed deep inside her.

"You've more than lived up to my fantasies," he murmured as he nuzzled the patch of skin beneath her ear. "I want to make you happy. Tonight, Elizabeth, I swear I will. I want you to come back to me, Lizzy. Please come back."

"I have never left you, Christian, I swear it."

He looked up at her and she saw his love for her in his eyes. "I am forever yours, Lizzy, never forget it."

"Your Grace?"

"Damn, that will be Jenkins," Christian muttered, letting her go from his hold before the footman came upon them. "I am here," he called, buttoning his trousers.

"Mr. Struthers would like to know if you wish him to remain in your study or if he should return another day."

He cast her an apologetic look and raked a hand through his hair. "Go back to your work, Christian," she said. "I am always here."

"That is what got us into trouble in the first place, Elizabeth. I always thought you would be, and then when it became apparent you might not, I realized how terrified I was of losing you."

"That is all I wanted to hear," she cried, flinging her arms around his neck and kissing him. "I only wanted to know that I still mean something to you."

"You are my life, Elizabeth," he whispered, sounding choked with emotion. "Our children are my life. Being a duke is a duty, my occupation, but it is not what I live for. I live for you."

"Your Grace?"

"He is already on his way, Jenkins," she answered for her husband.

Christian's eyes seemed to turn blacker as he looked down at her. "I couldn't have let you go to him, you know."

"Who?"

He reached out and placed his hand along the side of her face. "Adrian. I saw you together in the conservatory this morning. I wanted to kill him and drag you to our room, never allowing you to leave it, or me. I can bear anything, Elizabeth, except the loss of you. You're mine. You have been since the minute I saw you sitting on the terrace at Lady Ashton's garden party. You don't know how much I love you. How much I want to make you happy. How sorry I am for not being what you have needed in a husband—a man—these past months."

"You're everything I want and need. Right now, Christian, this is it—all I ever needed from you."

He kissed her, slowly, more lovingly than ever before. "It is just the beginning, Elizabeth. I swear it."

CHAPTER SIX

IT WAS LATE AFTERNOON WHEN THE SERVANT
Christian sent for her knocked on her chamber door.

"Your Grace?" a maid asked. "His Grace has requested you join him in his study."

Putting the last pin into her hair, Elizabeth took a step back and examined herself in the looking glass. On the outside she looked like herself, the Duchess of Sutcliffe, but beneath her elegant gown was someone new.

"Your Grace?"

"I will be there directly," she called, slipping her feet into her cream-colored, high-heeled shoes. They were beaded with seed pearls and pink bows and cream lace. Made in Paris, they were all that was fashionable and decidedly feminine. Hopefully Christian would slaver at the sight of them, not to mention her matching stockings and lacy unmentionables.

Poised and refined, she strolled to the door and walked down the long carpeted hall that led to the stairs. With an air of nonchalance, she proceeded to her husband's study. She was surprised to see that a footman was not standing sentry outside the door, waiting to open it for her. Smiling to herself, she wondered if Christian had dismissed them in order to allow them some privacy.

"You called for me?"

He was standing at the window sipping a glass of brandy as he gazed out over his land. He turned his head and allowed his gaze to flicker along her body. That gaze, that look, heated her blood. There was blatant lust in his eyes.

"I thought perhaps you might want to play a game of chess with me."

"Chess?" she asked, suddenly deflated.

"Yes, chess," he said, smiling as he stretched his hand out to her. "It is a pleasant afternoon and the breeze is blowing in just the right direction through this window. I thought it would be an enjoyable interlude. Come, one game, Elizabeth, that is all I ask."

Confused, she arched her brow. "Game?" she asked, unable to comprehend what exactly he was asking.

"Why, a game of chess, of course," he said, smiling like a panther stalking its prey. "What other sort of game did you have in mind?"

"Nothing," she murmured, shaking her head. "One game of chess it is."

"Excellent." His teeth flashed behind a devilish smile as he sat her on a settee and pulled the chess table before her, centering it so that the white pieces faced her. Then, reaching for a chair, he turned it so that he straddled it, his muscular legs evocatively outlined in his trousers while he removed his jacket and waistcoat. Elizabeth had never seen him in such a state of undress. He was either immaculately turned out, or naked.

Both states were arousing, but this, this half-undressed look did something to her insides that was utterly scandalous.

"You may make the first move."

Tearing her gaze away from his thighs, she advanced a pawn and within four moves had Christian's knight in her sight. "This is almost too easy." She clapped with unconcealed glee as Christian moved his bishop, leaving the knight vulnerable. "Really, Christian, allowing your knight to be captured by a pawn. What were you thinking?"

"My attention does seem to be waning," he murmured, looking up through his long dark lashes. His gaze burned into her face before lowering and searing the mounds of her breasts. "Perhaps we should play for more, shall we say, interesting stakes."

"Gamble?" she asked, pretending outrage at such a thing.

"Not as such," he grinned, his long tapered fingers resting on the piece he intended to move. "More like a boon. I will request something of you if I take one of your pieces. Likewise, you may do the same if you manage to capture any more of mine."

"If I manage?" she sputtered. "How arrogant of you to think you can best me. You have captured only one of my pieces. I, on the other hand, have your knight, a rook, and numerous pawns in my keeping. In fact, your queen is even now in jeopardy of my bishop."

"Hmm," he mused, studying the board. "You appear to be correct in that assumption. Perhaps with those odds, and your obvious superiority at the game, you feel more interesting stakes might be worth the risk?"

Something about the way his eyes gleamed made Elizabeth wet. This was all part of some grand strategy of his and she was thoroughly enjoying it. The children were upstairs napping and the servants all occupied with their duties. The study door was locked and the key to the door was lying beside Christian's hand. They were utterly alone and secluded in his study. No one dared to disturb the great Duke of Sutcliffe while he was in his study.

Playing along, she smiled seductively. "Very well, Your Grace. I will grant you whatever boon you request if you succeed in taking one of my pieces."

"Excellent," he drawled.

In two astute moves, Christian had captured her knight, and was seriously bearing down upon her bishop.

"You seem to have improved."

"Hmm," he agreed. "I've always been one to find high stakes vastly motivating. Now then," he said, after his last remaining knight took her bishop. "I believe you owe me a boon, madam. Well, two boons, but I shall settle for one large one."

"Yes?" Elizabeth asked, striving for an air of boredom, when all she really felt was a keen sense of anticipation. "What is it you want?"

He smiled then, a grin so superior, so blatantly sensual, that Elizabeth blinked several times to make sure she had interpreted it correctly.

"Take off your gown."

"Here?" she asked, unnerved by the thought. It was broad daylight. Anyone might wander outside and look in through the window. The children…

"Elizabeth," he said, drawing out her name, "I want you out of that gown. And I want to watch as you disrobe for me."

"Rogue," she muttered, while her trembling fingers fumbled

with the fastenings at the back of her gown. Only when she started to slide one sleeve over her shoulder did she dare to look at him.

He sat before her on his chair, his chin resting on his folded arms, watching her every move. His gaze, unblinking, followed the printed muslin as it slid down her arms and over her breasts. When the bodice rested against her waist, she hesitated, looking up to gauge his reaction.

"Take it off," he commanded. "All the way."

Elizabeth stood up, allowing the fabric to skim over her hips and down her thighs until it was just a puddle around her ankles. With as much grace as she could muster, she stepped out of the gown and stood before him. She had removed her corset after her nap, and had not bothered to put it back on. Her large breasts were now straining against the pink and cream chemise. The French silk hugged her body like a glove, the lace fringing the neckline and hem skimming her breasts and thighs in what she hoped was a provocative invitation to explore her body.

She saw his gaze slide up the front of her till their gazes met. He reminded her of a pasha as he sat staring up at her, his eyes boldly raking over her as if she was a slave he was considering buying.

"You're stunning, every inch of you," he whispered as his gaze once more caressed her breasts, her belly and the apex of her thighs. "I'd pay a pretty pence to have you for a night, Elizabeth."

"Would you?"

"What man wouldn't, with breasts and hips such as yours? You are every man's dream, Elizabeth. Every man's sexual ideal."

"But am I yours, Your Grace?" she asked boldly. "Am I your dream?"

His lashes flickered revealing his black eyes. "You've been the leading role in every wet dream I've had since I met you. And believe me, I've had many of those these past years."

"Oh?"

"Indeed. I believe I'm living one out now, right here."

"Playing chess?" she asked coyly.

"Playing games. Acting out fantasies." He straightened in his chair and Elizabeth could not help but lower her gaze to see how magnificently aroused he was. "You see, in my mind, I'm going to win this game, Elizabeth, and in winning you, I'm purchasing you for the rest of the day. And in purchasing you, you are mine to command."

"And what will you have me do?"

"All in good time," he whispered. His lashes lowered and she saw that his gaze was fixated on her breasts and the nipples that jutted out against her chemise.

"Very well," she murmured, sitting back on the settee and reclining so that her chemise inched up to give him a glimpse of the lace tops of her stockings. "I believe it is my turn, is it not?"

Elizabeth tried to ignore the way her chemise tightened and pulled over her breasts as she leaned forward to move her rook. The movement caused a strap to slide down her shoulder, baring the swell of her breast. She felt Christian's black gaze fixated there, on the white flesh. She went to hook her finger around it and slide it up her arm when Christian said rather thickly, "Don't." She met his eyes and saw desire burning in them. "I want to see you like this. I want to be teased by that flash of your breast. It makes me want to work so much harder to capture your king. Perhaps, though, after hearing that confession, you may wish to grant me a favor, and show me your breast."

Her belly tightened and wetness coated her thighs. Slowly, seductively, she lowered one side of her bodice and revealed what he wanted to see. Instantly her nipple hardened, jutting out towards him. Pressing forward, he ran his fingertip over it.

"Fabulous," he murmured. He looked up at her through a veil of dark lashes. "Perhaps you will allow me to take it into my mouth?"

Pulling the bodice up, she concealed her breast. "Not yet," she replied, and watched as he scowled. Satisfied with his reaction, she picked up her knight and moved it. Content with her maneuver, she settled back against the curved arm of the settee. Her smile melted away as Christian proceeded to overtake her rook with his queen. Their gazes met instantly over the board, and Elizabeth swore her heart stopped beating.

"What a pretty picture you make, Elizabeth. I hardly know where to begin. Are you wearing drawers, or a pair of French panties?"

"Why do you wish to know?"

"This is a game of strategy, my dear. For I may only ask for one thing, and I do not wish to waste it. If you're wearing panties, while I am sure they are lovely, they will cover the area that I most want to see—your darling cunny," he clarified. "On the other hand, that glimpse you gave me of your breast induced many ideas in my mind."

"I am naked beneath this chemise."

"Are you?" he asked, raising his brows. "How lovely. Well, then, your charming chemise—lift it so that I can see the top of your stockings."

She waited, drawing out the seconds as her fingers leisurely skimmed down her thighs to rest against the lace hem of her shift.

"Do it," he commanded, his eyes never wavering from hers as he set the rook with her other captured pieces.

With a deep breath, she inched her chemise up. Her breasts were spilling from the bodice, the straps wrapped around her arms as they slid off her shoulders. She watched Christian swallow hard as she assumed a more seductive pose for him.

"Higher."

She smiled at him before sliding the hem up along her legs until it rested beneath her garters. The pink lace of her stockings was exposed, as well as the feminine pink bows that attached her garters to the silk.

"More," he said thickly, wetting his lips. "Until I tell you you may stop."

She sat frozen, her eyes wide, her head feeling almost dizzy. How commanding he was like this. Her body seemed to respond to his voice and his instructions. A thrilling tension swam in her blood as she wondered just how high he would have her pull her chemise up, and just how much she was willing to accommodate him. This was a game after all, and a game required two players.

With shaking hands, she did as he asked, raising the chemise until the pale flesh of her thighs was revealed above her garters. She watched with what could only be described as feminine satisfaction as Christian straightened in his chair, taking his time looking at her.

"You'll be worth it, every damn second of waiting," he said, his gaze hungrily roving over her thighs and hips. "It'll be worth it just to feel my thumbs pressing into that soft flesh, right there, above your garters. Can you feel it," he asked, "my thumbs pressing against your thighs as I spread your legs? Can you imagine what I will want when I do that?"

"You are not there yet, Your Grace," she purred, schooling her expression into one of polite boredom. "I believe it is my turn."

His gaze flashed to her as her queen overtook his bishop. His face bore an expression of admiration. "Your boon, I believe."

It really wasn't much of a dilemma. Elizabeth knew exactly what part of Christian she wanted to see naked. His chest. She had always been fascinated by the amount of firm muscle and the contours of his belly. And seeing him in nothing but a pair of black trousers, straddling his chair, would be highly arousing.

"Well?"

"You may remove your shirt."

He raised his brows as he unknotted his cravat. She felt his eyes on her even though she refused to meet his gaze. Instead, she concentrated on watching his tanned fingers working to untie the linen. Sliding it from his neck, he let the starched fabric dangle from his fingers before finally dropping it to the floor. Elizabeth couldn't help but follow it with her eyes as it floated to the ground. His shirt landed unceremoniously atop the cravat before she could look away.

Raising her eyes from the floor, Elizabeth looked her fill, taking her time studying the way his tanned skin glowed, the way the waning sunlight flickered along his chest, outlining his broad shoulders. The muscles feathering out beneath his ribs fascinated her, making her wish to run her fingers along every inch of him. Her eyes lowered to the flat planes of his belly, to the dark line of hair that stole beneath the waistband of his trousers. With a flick of his thumb, he undid the first button, allowing her to see more of him, and the spectacular erection he was sporting.

"Will I do, Elizabeth?" he asked, his eyes glittering wickedly. "Can this body please you?"

"Indeed," she averred, running her fingers down her thigh. She allowed her fingers to sneak beneath the hem of her shift. She watched as Christian's eyes darkened.

"Yes," he rasped, his gaze focused on where her hand was hidden beneath the lace hem of her chemise. "Touch yourself. I want to watch you. I want to see you part your thighs and see your hand between them."

"Not yet, Your Grace. For you have not yet managed to steal another piece of mine."

He growled. Actually snarled like an animal, and Elizabeth laughed. Laughed like she hadn't in a very long time. She stopped laughing as he stole her rook. He slammed the piece down atop the table with the others then turned his attention on her.

"I want to watch you touch yourself, and I want you to look at me and say my name when you do it."

Elizabeth parted her legs and showed him her sex. Stroking her finger down the length of her labia, she parted them and swirled the pad of her fingertip against her clitoris. Closing her eyes she moaned, knowing he was watching her.

"No, Elizabeth, open your eyes and look at me."

She opened them and saw how he watched her. She felt

beautiful, wanton. "Christian," she whispered as she slowly brought herself to the crest of an orgasm.

"What are you thinking, Elizabeth?" he asked as he stood up from his chair.

She arched her hips and bit her lip to keep from crying out. She was so close, so wet.

"Tell me, Elizabeth, what thoughts are running through your mind?"

"How I want your mouth on me, pleasuring me. How I want to watch you do it."

Christian walked to the settee and dropped to his knees. He watched her fingers in the pink silk of her sex, working the little nub of flesh until her body was arched, drawn like a bow, and her thighs began to tremble.

"How I want to be there," he murmured out loud, no longer hiding his thoughts behind stony silence.

"Where?" she asked, gazing at him with her heated eyes. Her cheeks were kissed with red, and her breasts rose and fell heavily against her chemise. He gazed up at her and brushed his fingers down her sex.

"Here, in your body, feeling your pretty cunt squeezing my cock."

She came then and he watched it all, how her body twisted and grew taut. How her breasts seemed to swell and her nipples curled even tighter as they brushed against the silk. How beautiful and erotic it was to watch her, and he had done nothing but look at her and say heated things to her.

Christ, how he wanted to hear her say the same things to him.

"Let me taste." Reaching for her hand, he sucked first one,

then another finger into his mouth. Closing his eyes, he savored her, enjoying the memory of her pleasuring herself and the taste of her sex on her own fingertips. Her hands raked through his hair, and he looked up at her, just as his tongue stroked the length of her finger.

"You said you would tell me what you wanted," she whispered, her cheeks growing crimson.

Letting go of her hand, he moved toward her and reached for her chemise. He pulled it up, over her belly, her breasts, and then up over her head. She was now completely naked with the exception of her tempting stocking and garters, and hell, what an erotic sight it was to see his wife like this, a seductive temptress.

Reaching out, he circled his fingertip around the rose-hued areola of her breast. "Do you really want to know?" he asked, unable to look away from the sight of his fingers caressing her puckered nipple.

"Tell me," she begged. The way her voice sounded in the charged quiet of the room made him nearly explode. Grabbing her, he wrapped his hands around her waist and brought her to him so that her breasts were against his chest and he was reclining back against the pillows of the settee.

"I want you, with your lovely mouth around my cock and my words in the quiet instructing you. I want your wet body open for me, your willingness to let me pleasure you in all the ways I desire."

The stark need Elizabeth saw in his eyes made her smile. It was a wanton, womanly smile she knew, as she made a show of sliding her body sensually along his. She reached his waist and tore at the opening of his trousers, freeing him. She clutched him in her palm and stroked him, watching his lips part as his gaze fixated on her hand. "Such an eager little thing, are you not?"

When she saw he was watching her every movement, she strove to make her hips move in a painfully slow and erotic rhythm, teasing him as he had teased her.

"God, but you act like the most skilled courtesan, and yet you look like an angel. I vow you could make a saint sin, Elizabeth."

"You're no saint," she whispered wickedly before flicking her tongue along the tip of him, enjoying the power she wielded and embracing the sexual freedom he encouraged in her.

His hand fisted in her hair, dispelling the pins. As her hair cascaded over her shoulders, his breath came in increasingly harder and shorter pants. "Sweet Jesus, Elizabeth, that looks so damn good, too good," he moaned, thrusting upward with his rigid length. "Good God," he growled as he grasped his erection in his hand and traced her lips with the tip. Her tongue came out and circled the head of his phallus and he groaned at the sensation as well as at the visual of it. He pumped himself and demanded she do it all over again, just so he could have the pleasure of seeing her pink tongue glide along him.

Leaning back, he spread his thighs, allowing Elizabeth to kneel between them. Like an Eastern despot with a houri, he ran his fingers through her hair and watched her work his cock with a mouth that was far from angelic. She tormented him with sultry looks, peeking up at him as she trailed her tongue down his shaft, teasing him mercilessly until, in a state of suffering, he reached for the back of her head and brought her mouth down to his straining flesh. "Deeper, Elizabeth. I have to feel all of your mouth around me."

Reaching for her breasts, he brought them together and pinched her nipples so that she moaned, the sound vibrating along him, making him shudder. Close to finding his release, he reached for her and positioned her so that she sat astride him. Her sex was wet as she lowered her bottom onto his lap, and the discovery thrilled him.

Reaching out, he trailed his fingers along the indentation of her waist and up and over her hip, then down her thigh and over the tops of her stockings. She still wore her shoes and the sight enflamed him. "Christ, I want you. You in these stockings and shoes is everything I've ever dreamed of. I can hardly wait to get inside you. I can hardly wait for you to watch me loving you." Gooseflesh sprung to life beneath his fingers and he felt, as well as saw, Elizabeth sway into him. His hand at last found her bottom and he squeezed it.

"I forget everything when you're touching me like this," she said on a sigh. "I love the sight of your dark hands covering me, possessing me."

"God, but I want to possess you, Elizabeth," he groaned. "I want to mark you as mine so you will never forget that you belong to me." Her body trembled and he ran his thumbs over her nipples, eliciting another ripple of tremors through her limbs. Then, fitting his hands around her waist, he lifted her up until his mouth found her sex and he was pleasuring her with his lips and tongue.

Elizabeth couldn't say a word. She was lost in the sensation of being above him, his mouth on her sex. His hands no longer supported her but were skimming along her back and buttocks, his fingers caressing her cleft and sinking into her aching quim.

She was shaking, trembling, and reaching for his head, she

raked her fingers through his hair and held him there, his tongue pulsing against her clitoris until she cried out and climaxed. He did not give her a chance to float back down but lifted her and placed her on the settee, her legs spread wide, her sex, wet with her arousal and his mouth, exposed. Running his hands along her thighs, he pressed his thumbs into the flesh above her garters and spread her more, so that one foot rested on the back and the other was arched delicately on the seat of the settee.

She was flagrantly posed and she loved it. Adored the way her husband was hungrily examining her, loved the way his body responded to the sight of hers.

"Put me inside you," he asked, and she did, watching as he entered her.

Resting back on her hands, Elizabeth watched as he entered and retreated, loving the way his body disappeared inside hers. Slowly he made love to her, and together they watched—something they had never done before.

There was a closeness in that, watching themselves making love, seeing the way her body took him in. On impulse she reached down between her legs and ran her finger along his cock. "How beautiful you are, Christian."

He looked up at her and cupped her face. He said nothing, but closed his eyes and Elizabeth felt the hot rush of him inside her.

A long while later, Elizabeth stood at the French doors, looking out at the patchwork of farms. Christian was sprawled gloriously naked, soundlessly sleeping on the settee behind her.

Elizabeth brought her arms tight about her waist. She'd

donned Christian's shirt when she had risen from the lounge. His scent still lingered and she swore she could feel remnants of his body heat clinging to the linen.

Suddenly she was aware of Christian's heat enveloping her. Caging her with raised arms, his fingers curved around the molding of the door frame while he proceeded to nuzzle her hair.

"Sorry to fall asleep on you, love. You should have woken me instead of standing here all alone. Although," he murmured wickedly, "I enjoyed waking up to the view. You look rather fetching in my shirt. It's very alluring you know, what you look like in white linen. Just as fetching as cream silk and pink lace. Though I'm likely never to forget how damn gorgeous your legs looked in those stockings." He traced the outline of her bottom that peeked out from beneath his shirt while his mouth roamed her neck. "The sight of this perfect bottom will not soon be forgotten, either."

"You cannot possibly be hard again," she admonished as she felt his erection pressing into her back. "My God, you're insatiable."

"I've missed you, Elizabeth. God, I've missed this—us—for so long. Is it too much, sweetheart?"

Closing her eyes, she rested her head back against his shoulder. "It is never too much. I will never grow weary of making love with you."

His fingers cupped her thigh and he hooked her leg over his. "I need you again. Can I take you like this?"

Immediate desire flared to life within her and she writhed against his hand as he stroked her, swirling his fingers along her clitoris until she was trembling and teetering on the edge of orgasm.

She sighed as he slipped inside, stroking her deeply. He moaned and thrust deeper into her, his fingers biting into her waist with the force of his desire.

"I want you hard, Elizabeth, so that you never forget that it's me inside you." He reached for her breasts beneath his shirt, fondling and cupping them in his hands. "I have to feel all of you. I have to see you." And then he pulled out and turned her around so that her back was against the wall. He tore at the fastenings of his shirt and roughly shoved the material aside, baring her. Greedily he mouthed her breasts before slipping her nipple into his mouth. When she was moaning and tugging at his hair, he grasped her legs and wrapped them around his waist. His arms were above her head, resting against the wall as he thrust hard into her waiting body. Their eyes were locked and their breaths mingled together with each pant, each sigh, each erotic whisper.

"Tell me you want me, Elizabeth. That it is only me and our children in your life," he rasped as he filled her once more and allowed his seed to empty into her.

"I want you. I always have. It has ever only been you. I love you, Christian."

He held her close, rocking her slowly before he turned her so that she was once again facing the window and the green pastures of their estate.

"Do you see where the fields taper off on the horizon?" he asked. "I own the land as far as your eye can see and even farther. It has flourished under six generations of Sutcliffes. This land has been the pride and sustenance of every duke, including myself. I think it the most beautiful place on earth and yet for a long time whenever I would look out this window, I would be filled with an empty, hollow feeling I didn't completely understand till this past week." His grip tightened and he pulled her closer to him and entwined his fingers with hers. "I want to share this with you—all of it. I want the estate to bear the fruits of our labor. Whenever I look out this window I want it to be with you, Elizabeth," he whispered, holding her gaze. "I don't want to lose you, or the children. I don't want to lose us. Everything I have is yours. And my love, Elizabeth, is forever yours."

A fluttering feeling, as if a hundred butterflies had been let loose in her stomach, quivered to life inside her. She pressed her fingers against his, melting in the emotion she saw in his eyes. "Someone very close to me said that marriage is like a garden. It must be tended to year after year. And I now believe it. I allowed other things to intrude in our lives. I've learned now that I must not take even a day with you for granted."

"A new beginning then, my love?"

"Yes." She nodded, hugging him. "A new beginning. From this day forward."

"I look forward to your future visits to my study, if this is what I may expect of your behavior."

"And what of future letters, Your Grace?"

"You may be assured of that. Now then, let us go upstairs and find our children. Then, later, we will repeat this performance in front of a mirror."

Psychic Sex
CATHLEEN ROSS

I HAD A STUD PUT THROUGH MY TONGUE TODAY. I love the anticipation of getting a piercing and it didn't hurt the way people think it does. If anything, I get a thrill out of it by thinking about on whom I would like to use my stud. I want to see if the combination of hot flesh and metal heightens sexual sensation when used on a man.

I work in a gym at Bondi Beach, in sunny Sydney, which has lots of hot guys, except as a personal trainer, I'm not supposed to have sex with my clients.

As if I'm going to let a few rules get in my way!

I have to be subtle though. I've already had one warning from my supervisor, a stuck-up bitch who looks like she never gets laid.

Everyone in the gym commented on my new stud piercing, except ironically, the stranger—my chosen stud—who signed up to do a one-on-one session. My stranger's name is Tom. I didn't ask him his surname. I don't want to know. It spoils the fantasy for me.

Now, a one-on-one with me is pretty intense because I like

to put a man through his paces. I want to see him sweat. And while my client is training, I get to admire the lines of his body and the way his muscles bulge, not to mention the size of the bulge in his shorts. Best of all, I imagine what he would look like when I'm having sex with him and he's working hard to please me.

So, I started our session with running on the treadmill and stood back a little to admire Tom. I'm supposed to talk to my clients to put them at ease, but quite frankly, I don't bother. I'm not interested in men for their conversation. I have my girl-friends for that.

Although I don't encourage them, my wealthy male clients talk about their investments in Sydney's expensive real estate market, cars and football. My poor clients talk about how they can't afford to buy real estate and you guessed it, cars and football. Boring!

Quite frankly, unless the car is something shiny and fast like a Porsche or a Ferrari, I don't get why a man thinks a car is interesting at all.

What catches my interest is if a man talks about sex and all the delicious things he'd like to do to me in bed, which they tend to do once I've bedded them, but I don't usually go back for seconds, you see—I like sex with strangers.

Right now, Tom is walking on the treadmill and he's trying to start a conversation with me, something about the new car he's bought. Oh please, no! I increase the speed to make him run and to shut him up. So I don't have to listen to any car talk.

I love having power over a man. He's mine for an hour and I intend to have him sweating and submissive by the time I've finished with him because I have plans for him.

My nipples tighten as I admire Tom's physique.

I felt an exciting tingle between my legs the moment I met him at the front desk. When I feel that tingle I know exactly what I want to do to my client.

Tom has cropped dark hair, blue eyes and a nose with a slight hook that heightens his masculinity. His skin is invitingly creamy and smooth for a man who lives near the beach. Most of my clients are tanned. I'd like to stroke him all over and enjoy the sensation of his skin over tight muscles.

What I especially like about Tom is his mouth. He has full sensual lips, the type that make for great kissing, not to mention sucking on my clit. Not that Tom knows that I intend him to do that, he's too busy running, keeping up the high pace I've set for him.

Guys have no idea when they get me what a ride I'm going to take them on.

I look sweet.

I'm not!

When I picked Tom up at reception, he greeted me with a great smile, and his eyes took on that special "I'm interested" look.

And why shouldn't he be?

I have long blond hair which I keep in a plait down my back, unless I'm in bed, and then I let my hair out so that it flows in wild rivulets. This combined with large green eyes, a neat nose and mouth means I look like Jennifer Aniston.

I spend my mornings sunning myself wearing only a G-string, on Bondi Beach. I work out with my clients every afternoon, so that I'm toned all over. I don't have huge breasts and I certainly wouldn't go plastic, but I'm confident with how I look. That's why I'm so good at seducing men.

I narrow my eyes and size Tom up as he runs. He's beginning to build a sweat. I can see beads of it on his broad chest. I'd like to lick Tom just to see what he'd taste like. I enjoy the taste of exertion on a man. By the time I've finished with him, he'll be dripping. And no, I don't intend to lick off all his sweat. That's gross. I want to get him so hot that he goes and has a shower in the gym. That way I'll find out if he has a big cock.

I won't bother with him if he doesn't.

Tom has a promise-of-orgasms-for-me body. He's over six feet tall with an athletic build, but more long distance runner than a footballer's build. I can imagine stroking him between his legs, cupping his soft sac in my hands before I take him in my mouth.

Tom looks at me unsuspectingly as he runs. I smile back. Sometimes I think I'm like a vampire, except I don't want blood; I want sex. "Keep up the pace." I cross my arms to emphasize my cleavage which is tight against my spray-on tank top.

Tom breaks into a grin as he eyes my breasts. Good. I want him submissive and horny.

"You're doing well," I say.

It's important to give small compliments to a man because then he will do anything for me.

I smile back. I'm sure he's noticed that my nipples are hard and that I haven't worn a bra today. I can't wait to get him into my bed.

While Tom is doing twenty minutes on the treadmill on high, I set the inclinator on six to make it harder for him. I want to see what his face looks like when he grimaces. That's the look on a man's face when he orgasms. I enjoy watching the combination of pain and pleasure.

But Tom doesn't break, which shows he has a good fitness level. He doesn't stop and complain that I'm too hard on him. Pity. Sometimes, it amuses me when a man begs for leniency.

I never give an inch.

"You get one minute to rest and then you're moving to the rower," I say.

Tom nods. He's panting.

"Need a drink?" I ask him.

He shakes his head.

Good. The man's got stamina. My stomach muscles tighten with anticipation.

I reach over and take Tom's pulse to see if he has a good recovery time. It's a legitimate way to touch a client. I'm not interested in his pulse though. I'm interested in the way his skin feels against mine. Under my fingers, he feels warm and clean. His skin has a smooth feel to it and I can quickly conjure up what his naked body would feel like next to mine. The thought makes me horny.

I can smell him too. He has a terrific scent like fresh soap and male pheromones. This is what he would smell like in the heat of sex.

I'm aroused enough to have him now. Pity the gym is crowded. I've done it before when the gym was quiet, lying back with my legs spread open in the thigh extension machine.

While Tom continues his workout, I savor the way his muscles flex and bulge with every row. He really is magnificent. In gym talk, we say he has good "guns." This means big arm muscles. Some guys concentrate on their chest areas only, which leaves them with chicken legs, but Tom is well proportioned.

He'd better have a good-sized cock or all this anticipation will have been for nothing.

"Keep your stomach muscles switched on," I order as Tom works out on the rower. "Remember to breathe evenly. Pull. Pull. Pull."

Fuck. Fuck. Fuck. Is what I'm really thinking.

I can feel my nipples tighten as I give Tom orders. The more I tell him what to do, the more used to my orders he will be when I seduce him, which suits me as I like to dominate in bed. I expect a man to do what I want, when I want and how I want.

While I'm training Tom, I see that the pump class has just finished and out comes Pinky. Everyone in the gym knows our gay masseuse, who is my best friend. You can't miss him. He's fifteen stone and as round as he is tall. He's been trying to lose weight all his life and despite all the classes he does, doesn't lose a pound. I commiserate with Pinky about his weight and Pinky in turn colludes with me on my client seductions. He doesn't get much sex, so he's more than happy to live vicariously through my experiences.

I point to Tom behind his back, to signal to Pinky that Tom is my chosen stud. Pinky looks at Tom and raises his eyebrows. He gives me a nod.

Good. Pinky can stay back. I need him to do a job for me.

Tom, of course, is oblivious to all of this. He's so busy rowing, he has no idea.

For the next half an hour, Tom pushes and pulls for all he's worth and then we move to my favorite part—stretching. I like it because I get to put my hands on a man and really feel what his body is like.

While we're stretching, I tell him about the great new bar down on the beach, which I'm hoping to go to tonight. I smile and flirt a little. Normally my chosen stud offers to take me, and from there, I take over.

Tom frowns at me and says nothing, which was fine when I didn't want him to talk, but now I'm expecting some sort of response from him. What's wrong with the man?

I bend his leg at the knee and push it across his torso to stretch him out. I like the way his skin feels silky, but his leg hairs are crisp. I have my other hand inappropriately on his butt, which is tight and hard. Just how I like it.

Bet Pinky would too. I can see him hovering near the shower block waiting for my signal.

Tom is flexible for a man, which makes my imagination run wild. I want to run my hands over his taut body.

"So, have you been to Coco's Bar before?" I prompt.

"No," Tom responds.

I pause. Come on Ask me. Do something! Men like to think they're doing the chasing.

"It's fun there. Why don't you come down tonight?" So much for the chasing. I guess I'm the impatient type.

I walk behind Tom, take him by the arms and pull his guns back at the elbow to stretch out his shoulders. He feels incredibly firm and sexy. My nipples are so hard I want to pinch them myself and think about sex with Tom. I can't see his face and I can't believe he's so slow to answer me.

I thought he'd be a sure thing.

I'm leaning so close now that I could kiss his neck. I really want to. I'm sure he can feel my breath on the back of his neck.

I drop his arms and Tom climbs to his feet. "Thanks, Gabby.

That was great. I'll book another session with you tomorrow," he says and walks toward the showers.

I glance at Pinky who raises his plucked eyebrows in expectation.

I frown.

I can't believe it. Tom didn't take the bait. He didn't even bother to answer my question. I never miss my mark. It's unheard of. I'm so mad, I feel like going into the shower block and sticking a dog collar on him and leading him home, but I don't think my supervisor would appreciate it.

I signal to Pinky to follow Tom into the shower. That's the best way I can find out whether Tom has a big cock. Five minutes later, Pinky comes out and spans his hands to give me an idea.

Tom is big.

Now I am really pissed off.

I'm an earthy kind of girl. I don't believe in psychic phenomena, but my crazy, psychic sister gave me this book—*How to Astral Travel.* I am bored and horny that night, after Tom didn't take up my offer, so I decide to flick through it. What catches my eye is that the book claims that through meditation, the spirit can leave the body and do whatever it wants.

Wouldn't that be fun?

Hmmm. I think about Tom, my escapee-love-slave. I turn back to my book.

What if I could meditate, leave my body, visit Tom and bonk him senseless in the middle of the night? I could do everything I wanted to him while he thought he was dreaming. What an interesting idea. It would be worth a try because I certainly wasn't getting anywhere with him in daylight.

Even my darling Pinky was amazed Tom had brushed me off. "Perhaps he's gay," he'd said hopefully.

"No way." I jabbed my index finger into Pinky's butterball chest. "Don't even think about making a move on him. He's straight and he's mine."

So tonight after my shower, I rub rose-scented moisturizer all over my body paying special attention to my breasts. My nipples harden. I am so ripe for sex I am almost aching.

According to the book, all I have to do is to focus on what I want. That's easy. Sex! I breathe deeply in through the nose so that my whole torso fills with air and then expel the air out through my mouth I do this in a repetitive motion so that there is no break in the rhythm.

I visualize Tom naked, not to mention his "long dong," which Pinky assures me he has.

Damn it. I want that man. I keep breathing deeply until I'm almost hyperventilating. I can feel a tingling sensation on my fingertips and the cynical side of me wonders if I'm overoxygenating my body. I'm certainly not going anywhere. Not rising out of my body, not hovering over an unsuspecting Tom, like I should be doing.

In frustration, I get up, fling the book against the wall and decide to try and get some sleep. My tongue has swollen from the piercing and seems to be filling my mouth. Perhaps sex wouldn't have been so great tonight after all, unless Tom did everything to me. Now there's a thought.

I drift off to sleep with the thought of Tom kissing my breasts before trailing a pathway down past my navel and ending up between my legs.

I stretch and sigh as I imagine what his tongue would feel like as it lapped at me. I can imagine him folding my inner lips apart as he starts to lick slowly up and down my slit like it is a juicy peach.

I'm in that drifting, half wake, half sleep mode and thoroughly enjoying my fantasy. I feel like I'm floating, and I'm a little chilly. My bed feels hard under my back. It would normally bother me, except my imagination is so good, that I can feel Tom circling my clitoris with his tongue.

I moan softly and thrust upwards. I can't believe how good it feels to have Tom eating me. I've noticed that men with generous mouths are made to do this, that's why I liked the look of Tom's full mouth from the moment I saw him.

My sexual imagination has always been good, but something really strange is happening. I can feel a man's hands on my thighs and his tongue, which is sliding up and down, becomes faster so that my stomach muscles clench with pleasure.

My eyes snap open. What the hell is going on? I look around and discover that instead of lying on my bed, I am lying on the sloping bonnet of a car. And not just any car. It's a shiny red Porsche. Weirder still, between my legs, lapping my sex like it's a melting ice cream, is Tom. I'm so surprised that I attempt to close my legs, which means I nearly jam Tom's head between my thighs.

He looks up. "Aren't I doing it the way you like it?" he asks. "You seemed into it."

Hello? Is this for real?

"Um…er…you're doing okay." Well, more than okay, actually, once I get over my shock. Am I really here in what looks to be a spacious garage? Am I asleep? I must be here, I decide, because I'd never be stupid enough to want to have sex on a car when I have a nice comfy bed. Trust a man to want to involve a car with sex. Still, lucky for Tom, it's not just any car.

I'm still tense. Still in a state of disbelief, but given that nothing has changed in the past surreal seconds, and that Tom is still hovering above my clit, I decide to lie back and signal Tom with a flick of my index finger to keep going.

I mean, someone has to test out this astral fucking gig, so it might as well be me.

Tom runs his hands over my thighs as he eats me. The skin of his hands is smooth and it sends tingles up my spine. I pinch my nipples and I rock back and forward enjoying what he is doing to me. I can feel an orgasm building and I strain to meet his tongue. I want him to go harder and faster.

I can't stand it if a guy licks me like I'm a delicate flower about to break. I might be slender, but I work in a gym all day heaving weights.

I'm just about to come when Tom pulls back. Talk about lack of good timing. He has "born to perform" looks but he sure needs some training. I look downwards over the hood of the shiny Porsche and my own sleek body.

What is wrong with this man?

He's holding his cock in his hand. Now I have to say, orgasm-ready as I am, it looks very tempting. The head of his cock is taut and bulging. The shaft is long and thick. Pinky knew his stuff when he'd done his hand measurement back at the gym. I'd have a lot of fun sliding that into me, but I'm not quite ready.

"Don't stop," I say.

"I'm dying for you," Tom says. "The moment I saw you at the gym, I wanted you. That's why I booked another session with you tomorrow. I wanted to take you out in my new car."

He looks longingly towards my sex. "I just want to know how good you'd feel. Just for a moment."

His handsome face is strained with desire. He is desperate for me. I have to admit that it's flattering that he wants me so much, but I torture men all day at the gym for a living so I see no reason to change my style now.

I raise my long index finger and point to my sex. "I didn't tell you to stop. You'll know when I've had enough."

I stare at him and I swear I can feel his will. He's desperate to ride me. He's standing at the base of the bonnet of the car, leaning over me on one hand, with his cock in his other hand, determined to defy me. His whole body is trembling with lust and I can see veins standing out in his neck from the strain of my denial.

Judging from the three other sports cars that are lined up in his garage, he's a wealthy, spoilt kind of guy, used to getting what he wants. Tough luck. He kept me waiting because he was too busy with his new car, now it's my turn to keep him waiting. I can sense I have power over him and I want to test it out. Already, I can see the dewy end of pre-cum forming at the end of his cock. He's stroking it up and down, getting it ready for me.

"Climb up here," I order. "Put your knees either side of me."

Tom does so eagerly. My gaze roves over his body, as he moves with grace and athleticism. He is pumped to perfection. I don't know who trained him before he came to me, but they've done a good job.

One drop of sweat leaves Tom's brow and drips between my breasts. Lazily, I scoop it up with my fingertip and taste it. It's salty and warm.

"Nice," I say.

Tom is balanced over me, his weight mainly on one hand and knee. He wants to ram himself in me, lose himself in the desire that is fomenting in his brain, but I have other plans for him. I open my legs wide. My pelvis is heavy and hot as I strain with anticipation. "Take the head of your cock and rub it over my clitoris."

Poor Tom is so desperate, his face is suffused with sexual frustration, but I enjoy torturing him. Like in his workout at the gym, he doesn't bitch or moan that I am too hard on him, which is just as well, because whining only makes me tougher.

I watch as he takes the head of his cock in his hand and rubs it all over me, to lubricate the head. He stops at the entrance of my sex and looks me in the eye.

"Don't even think about it."

Tom bites his bottom lip in frustration and slides his cock over my clitoris.

I sigh. Now, he's doing it right. I know because my clitoris is swollen and burning and every time his cock rubs on it, I think I'm going to come. I straighten my legs and arch my back, reaching down to expose my clit to Tom's delicious rubbing. The steel of the Porsche is warm under my back. I'm enjoying this.

The head of Tom's cock feels hard and warm. I soon match his pulsating rhythm until I can't take it any more. My whole body is shuddering and I scream out loud. This is the moment I love when I'm at the peak of an orgasm. I want Tom's cock inside me, and I'm sure he wants that too.

I can see the veins of desperation standing out on his neck, his face is flushed with exertion. I don't have to say anything because I suspect the expression on my face matches Tom's.

He moves upwards between my legs and pushes his way inside me. I savor the sensation of his initial entry, enjoying the size and feel of him. Every nerve ending is alive and open. I rise to meet his first thrust.

"All right?" Tom asks.

Of course it is. How could it not be, but I like it that he asks.

I wrap my legs around his hips in assent, wiggling my hips so that I can get the point of contact right. I can feel an orgasm building again in the base of my spine. I dig my fingernails into Tom's back. If this is real and it certainly feels like it is, then Tom will have my imprint on him tomorrow.

I love the way he is big, hard and fills me. Every thrust, every movement is sending me close to what I need. I unravel my legs and arch when Tom hits the spot deep inside of me that feels so good. My orgasm climbs on the back of the first, more powerful and exciting than before. I'm gasping for breath as I come. Straining. Thrusting. Every nerve point tingling.

Tom must be close with me writhing under him. I realize at this point that I actually really like this guy.

I hold him tight to keep the moment, to keep the high, but he melts through my fingers like a phantasm. I can see disappointment on his face, which I'm sure is matched by my own.

"Hey!" I yell. This wasn't quite the time I planned to make an exit, but it's not like I had a say in it. Sure I was having my share of orgasms, but I was enjoying Tom enough to care whether he was getting his end off too.

I find myself falling. I wave my hands to catch onto something but there is nothing there but air. Thump! I land on my bed. I'm breathing hard and looking wildly around me, but it is hard to see in the darkness. With trembling fingers, I reach over and turn on my bedside lamp and sit.

I'm in my room. Everything is just as it was. My head is still swimming from my breathtaking orgasm. I flop back onto my pillows and try to make sense of what just happened. I reach between my legs and feel my throbbing sex. This was more than a dream. It just had to be.

The next day at the gym, I go to reception to collect Tom for his training session. He greets me with a big smile. "Hi, Gabby. Good to see you."

"Hi. How were you feeling after yesterday?" I stop and stare at him for a moment, trying to work out if he's thinking about last night. I want to know if he experienced anything or if it was just some wacky dream. I certainly haven't got over the experience myself. If anything, it really makes me want him in the flesh, but I've never been interested in permanent relationships.

"Bit stiff," Tom says. "I'm sure you'll iron that out." He gives me a grin, but doesn't meet my eyes.

Is he shy? Is that his problem?

I start Tom with some lunges today. I hand him his weights and show him what I want him to do. I'm waiting for him to say something, but he doesn't.

"How was your night, last night?" I ask.

"I picked up my Porsche," he says as he continues lunging. I keep my hand on the small of his back so he knows how low to go.

"And?" I ask.

"Sensational," he answers.

I give him a sharp look. Is he teasing me?

For once, I'm interested in talking, but Tom isn't saying much other than the occasional grunt of exertion.

I see Pinky standing outside the massage room. Pinky is beside himself with desperation after I told him my story. He's raising his waxed eyebrows and fluttering his fingers at Tom. Pinky thinks I've found a new portal into having irresponsible sex, which excites him tremendously, seeing as he never gets any. He's already asked to borrow my book, which is a scary thought.

I ignore Pinky and give my attention to Tom. We move from station to station, and Tom focuses on his exercise. For once, I want a client to talk to me and he doesn't, but he does perform every exercise to perfection. I enjoy watching him move like a well-oiled machine. It's rare for me to get a perfectly built man.

Was last night a dream? If it was for real, did I really have the power to make Tom do what I wanted? Was it the power of that last orgasm that shook me back to my bedroom? If I held off my orgasm, would I be able to astral travel for longer?

I have too many unanswered questions. I bite my lip in frustration. My nipples are tight and I feel like rubbing them.

I look at my watch. "Time to stretch," I say. "Lie flat on the mat."

Tom looks up at me. "Like your tongue stud," he says.

I grimace. "My tongue is swollen. I'm out of action."

I take Tom's leg in my hands, bend it at the knee and push it across his body to give his cute butt a stretch. His T-shirt rides up a little on his back as I push his knee further towards the floor.

He has fingernail marks on his back.

I run my finger over the mark. It's an intimate gesture. In

the background, I see Pinky shiver with anticipation. "Big night, last night?" I ask.

Tom sits up, twists around and stares at the fingernail marks as if he's never seen them before. He colors and can barely look at me.

"I had the weirdest dream. I was polishing my car..." His voice trails off. He stares at the fingernail marks as if he can't believe what he is seeing.

My grin spreads across my face. "Until you got distracted," I can't help adding. This has opened up a world of possibilities for me.

I see my next client turn up at reception. He's powerfully built, dark and brooding looking. I bite my bottom lip.

"Gabby?"

My attention turns back to Tom. "Would you like to go to that bar you mentioned tonight?"

"Thanks, Tom, but I'm busy tonight," I say eyeing my next client, too distracted by the possibilities opening up for me. "We'll have to go another time."

The new client is over six foot five, and spectacular. I can't wait to get home tonight and try this astral traveling gig again. No way am I passing on my book to Pinky yet.

I love sex with strangers.

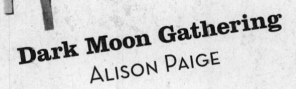

Dark Moon Gathering

ALISON PAIGE

I SMELLED THE STALE BEER AND CHOCOLATE CAKE long before the park pavilion emerged in dark relief from the blue-green shadows that surrounded it. I raised my muzzle, scenting the air.

Humans; hours ago, their perfumes, their body secretions, still lingered on the air, like the first tinge of meat going bad. They'd left their scent everywhere, like fingerprints. Not that I minded. I'm human too, most of the time.

It was late. The park was empty. I padded onward, eager to finish the game, my paws silent through the short, manicured grass. The pavilion's floor was concrete and my claws tick-tacked as I crossed. My nose led the way to the cake, following the chocolate-scented footprints to the garbage can at the far end. There it was, a big slice, icing-side down, tread marks squishing the corner flat, the whole of it covered with ants. *Gross.*

I backed away, running my long tongue around my muzzle, over my nose, fighting the creepy-crawly feeling tickling under my fur. A hard snort shook my whole head and finally blasted my senses clean.

Damn, Mattie Banebridge, you are good. Nearly giddy with the win I gave a sharp yip of a bark, turned and took a running leap onto the wooden picnic table. I raised my head, filled my lungs with night air and sent a high, clear yowl up and out through my throat. The sound pierced the night, echoing off the wood rafters of the pavilion, filtering through the surrounding trees, traveling long and wide. The howl died as my lungs emptied.

God, it felt good, primal, natural. A heavy thud on the picnic table turned me around.

The large honey-blond wolf was double my weight and several inches taller. He moved in near silence. Scary for something so big and potentially deadly. But he was beautiful. A soft thick coat smelled of fresh air, forest and earth, with the faint hint of men's cologne underneath. His eyes were an amazing shade of blue that looked almost violet in the moonlight. And even in wolf form his lean muscled body made a girl go warm and wet in all her special girl places.

He closed the small distance between us and licked the side of my face behind my eye to my ear, his tongue barely rough enough to feel through my fur. I leaned into him, nuzzling my head under his chin, running my body along his. As solid as a mountain, he didn't budge, taking the full press of my weight so my fur stroked against him. When I reached his tail my nose tickled with a familiar scent. Arousal.

I dropped my snout; a quick peek between his back legs and my suspicions were confirmed. There, nestled among all that lush fur, wagged his stiff, glistening, pink penis. I wasn't surprised. A late-night run always made me horny as hell, too. But when I felt the cool wet nudge under my tail and then the sudden stroke of his tongue over my pussy and anus, I nearly jumped out of my fur.

Instinct spun me around, teeth bared, a hard snap clenching my mouth. Anthony yipped and jerked backward to avoid my bite. Not fast enough. I was spitting fur from my tongue as he tumbled off the table and landed with a clumsy grunt on the cement floor. His whole body twisted and spun to get his feet under him again. And when he stood I could've sworn he was laughing.

I shifted forms, fast and painless. I can shift at a run now, sensing the second before my hands and feet become paws so my stride remains unbroken. It had taken practice, and a lot of tripping ass over head.

Thirty seconds, maybe a minute later, I was sitting on my hip, my legs curled, my arms locked, bracing me. Anthony waited until I finished before he shifted and I couldn't help watching that pink little penis grow and thicken into a fully erect human cock. It made my thighs cream. No matter how large a guy is, he's bigger, much bigger, in human form. And Anthony was scary big as a wolf.

Fur receded as though pulled beneath tan, taut flesh until all that remained was a wavy butterscotch mop on his head that brushed his shoulders and the darker thatch that encircled his cock. The body of an athlete, long and lean, broad-shouldered and powerful.

"Not into the fur-on-fur scene, love?" he said the second he was able.

Anthony Ricci wasn't British; he was Italian. But sometimes he slipped into this weird British accent. I don't know why— I never asked. Besides, I thought it was kind of cute, sexy even. Most of the time.

"I don't screw dogs," I said, rolling onto my butt, shifting my hands to brace behind me on either side. Anthony moved toward me, using the picnic table bench to climb on.

He positioned his long, hard body over top of me, kneeling between my open legs, his hands next to mine, his bearded, scruffy face inches away. "But pet, you were a dog."

I narrowed my eyes, forced a scowl I didn't feel. "Do you want to fuck me or poke fun at my hang-ups?"

"Not hang-ups, sweet Mattie. Endearing quirks that make you even more irresistible." His gaze dropped to my mouth and he leaned close like he'd kiss me. But he didn't. His warm lips hovered a hairsbreadth from mine, waiting. Waiting for me to kiss him. It was one of those unspoken games we played. Who wanted whom more?

Anticipation tightened my nipples, pulling a light tingle through my breasts. Muscles in my sex flexed and a hot rush of liquid flooded between my thighs.

Screw that. I found the cake first. I already won.

"Right." I sounded almost unaffected. Pretty good, considering. "Stop trying to charm me and start putting that thing to good use before you pass out from lack of blood flow."

He glanced down his chest to his cock and I snuck a look. Lord, he was even thicker than he'd been when he'd shifted. Ropy veins twisted beneath the darker flesh, the fat head glistening with a small bead of come at the tip. I licked my lips on reflex, wanting to be filled by him in any way.

When he looked back he must've seen the need in my eyes and his expression heated to match. His lids sank low over those violet eyes, and his voice came deeper, resonating through my body like the strike of the lowest key on a piano, echoing forever inside me. "Winner's choice. How do you want me?"

My breath shuddered. I couldn't help it. Every muscle in my body tightened, heat thrumming through my veins and pooling wet and wanting between my thighs. "I wanna ride you."

One brow lifted, a crooked smile slanting his mouth. "And so you shall, love."

He shifted backward and sat, swinging his feet to the bench below, knees spread, cock thick and stiff like the pole of a carousel horse between his muscled thighs. He held out a hand to me. "All aboard."

My hand in his, I found the bench with my feet and stood. My legs trembled as I shifted around him and placed a foot on the outside of his. He was watching me, our gazes locked, as I straddled him, my hands on his shoulders, fingers squeezing those hard round muscles beneath hot flesh.

His grip tightened on my hips, tugged lightly at my body, encouraging me to lower myself onto his shaft. I resisted. Winner's choice. His face was chest level—perfect—and I arched my back, offering my breast to his mouth. He dropped his gaze and seemed only then to realize the treat at his lips. His mouth opened, eyes fluttering closed as though the taste and feel of me on his tongue was something to savor.

Hands slipped from my hips to the rounds of my ass; fingers squeezed, pulling me toward him until the damp hairs at my sex crushed against his chest. I knew he must feel my wetness on his skin. With my knees spread wide to accommodate his large lap, my pussy was open against him.

The low moan that vibrated through his chest rumbled into my groin, humming over my clit, and sent a quick shiver of delight racing through my veins. He suckled harder, tongue flicking over the sensitive nipple, teeth nipping and tugging, making my breath catch and my sex ache for the same attention. He released me and shifted to my other breast, lavishing it with the heat and suction of his mouth.

I couldn't breathe, muscles squeezing throughout my body, tensing, wanting more. I sank my hand into his thick wealth of hair, fisted, letting the beast in me rise, rough and ready. A gentle tug and my breast fell from his lips, the night air tingling an erotic chill over the tight, moistened flesh. His gaze slid up to mine and I pulled harder on his hair, not to hurt—much—but to bend his neck back so his lips rose to mine.

What he'd done to my breast he now did to my mouth, suckling my tongue, my lips, exploring my mouth with his. My body lowered, and somewhere in the far recesses of my mind I knew my brain must've given permission, though I couldn't think past the feel of him. The taut skin of his chest smoothed along the folds of my pussy, warm and hard. His hands wrapped around the back of my thighs, cupping my ass and guiding my body onto his.

Fat and round, velvet flesh over marble, his cock pressed into me, stretching me so I had to close my eyes, relax, to take him in. He was too big and just right all at once. The muscles inside me cleaved to him, fluttered as he pressed in, deeper and deeper. Pressure built as he filled me, tingling, electric sensation dancing through my body, humming over my skin. I had to hold my breath to withstand the barrage on my senses. I opened my legs wider, lowered my body, sent him deeper— and there was still more of him to come.

Even before my thighs pressed flat against his and his cock seemed to fill me up through to my chest, I knew he'd ruined me for lesser men. I didn't care; my flesh hugged around him, milking his cock, coaxing it to harden and swell further. This wasn't our first time, but his size made each encounter a delicious mix of pain and pleasure.

"You good?" he asked, breathless.

I swallowed and gave a weak nod. Then he lifted me, using my body to stroke his shaft and his shaft to send pleasure rippling through my body. Muscles snapped tight, tensing my legs, wanting more, wanting speed, needing friction. My fingers clenched on his shoulders, skin catching under my nails. I raised myself to the very tip of his cock then slammed down, impaling myself to his hilt.

Air whooshed out of me and I gasped for more, rising up to do it all again, and again. A fast rhythm set in, my hips rocking, his fingers gripping tight on the back of my thighs. Sensation swirled through me like a glittering river behind my eyes, tingling through my veins, sizzling over every nerve ending. Faster, deeper, harder—the pressure swelled, pushing up from my belly, squeezing through my chest, thick and tempting in my throat. *Right there. Almost.* A promise of ecstasy I couldn't resist a moment longer.

Like a swollen river overflowing its banks, sensation crested then gushed, liquid hot, from my head, down my neck and chest, shuddering through my belly and legs and out my toes. My release quaked through every muscle, my sex pulsating around his cock until the stimulation grew too much for him to deny.

"Fuck…Mattie…yessss…" A burst of frantic thrusts sent my body cascading over into another release with Anthony trailing close behind.

I collapsed boneless against him, satiated. My breathing

slowed, found a natural rhythm with the galloping beat of my heart. I rested my cheek on his shoulder and sighed. "Ready to go again?"

I wasn't; I just liked freakin' him out. Imagine my surprise when he tensed beneath me and his cock stirred between my walls.

"Gimme a minute," he said low and breathy.

When I lifted my head to look at him, a set of bright, blinding lights glared in my eyes then traveled the edge of the pavilion and stopped. *Headlights.*

Public nudity. Lewd and lascivious behavior. Trespassing. And those were just the charges I could think of off the top of my head.

"Park security." I didn't bother to wait to see if I was right about the car idling in the parking lot above the pavilion. Adrenaline surged through my tired, aching limbs and I jumped to my feet. Two strides had me across the picnic table. I jumped, shifting before my feet hit concrete.

"Hey! Hold it! What is that?" Flashlights swept over me before I swerved and they lost me to the shadows.

"All's I'm sayin' is, if you don't choose a mate by the end of the Gathering this weekend, they'll choose one for you," my mom said while she screwed the metal lid back on the sugar dispenser. I could see her slide it across the counter to the herd of filled jars from the corner of my eye. She reached for one of the empty containers and started the process all over again.

Two-thirty at the Banebridge Pop & Pup Diner was always slow. I loved the place, but after my dad was shot and killed three years ago by a farmer for poaching his sheep—he wasn't—so much about the diner had changed. Nothing you could see though.

"They can choose all they want. Doesn't mean I'll take some wolf I hardly know as my mate. No matter what those animals think, we're not living in the dark ages." I shoved a stack of paper napkins into the spring-loaded dispenser and got my finger pinched in it—again.

"Mattie, honey, you're in for a rude awakening. Most werewolf males aren't like your father." She loaded the filled sugar dispensers onto a plastic tray and walked around the counter to grab it from the other side. "Sometimes I think it was a mistake raising you the way we did, treating you the same as we did Donny."

My brother Donny, the pup in "Pop & Pup," firstborn and only male, apple of my parents' eyes and dead at twenty-seven. T-boned by a driver who tried to make a yellow light. Stupid.

"Too late now," I said. "I love ya, Mom, but I am who I am. I won't be some cocky alpha's subservient female. I can't. I don't care what they think. That's why I stopped going to the Gatherings. It's also why I'm not going this year."

Mom's whole body froze midstretch across a table, sugar dispenser in hand. "What do you mean you're not going?" She straightened with a leashed hellfire look. "The Gathering's the only time of year we're all together. Packs are coming from all over. There'll be food and games. You'll be able to visit with friends and family you haven't seen in years."

"It's a meat market, Mom." I scooped the metal napkin holders into my arms and walked through the tables depositing them. "And this year will be worse than ever since I'm the meat *du jour*. Everyone knows I have to choose a mate or risk the pack being split by lesser males."

She smiled, all caring and momlike. "Well, honey, you're a beautiful girl. Any man would feel lucky to have you. And you're the highest-ranking member of a fairly large pack. A pack, thanks to Daddy, that's financially secure."

"Rich, you mean."

"Yes. The point is we've got no males old enough or strong enough to take over as alpha and none of the females outrank you."

"They've never tried." Being the daughter of the strongest male and female made challenges for my position rare. But like any healthy wolf I was always up for a good fight.

"That's beside the point. Since Donny passed away the pack falls to you and, as much as you might like to wish otherwise, a woman cannot hold a pack on her own. You must take a mate or one will take you, and the rest of us with you. Heaven help us if a Purist sets his sights on you."

My stomach knotted at the thought. My dad was a modern werewolf, believing in women's rights, partnership with his mate and a kind of democracy within the pack. Purists believed wolves like my dad would destroy our species by allowing women too free a hand and slowing down birth rates by giving them a choice in the matter. To call them chauvinists would be an insult to chauvinists.

"I won't let that happen, Mom," I said, looking her in the eye. "Promise."

She smiled, but her lips trembled trying to hold it. She was scared and that scared me. I turned away, pretending that placing napkin dispensers required my full attention.

Mom had good reason to be scared. Wolves mate for life. But Purists chose to forgo the pesky limitations of a life mate and enforced pack polygamy. One of the first things a Purist would do, after fucking me, was stake his claim on every female in the pack, married or not—including my mother. To a Purist every pack member belonged to him and should carry his scent. He'd screw all the females and banish any males he saw as a threat.

Some women chose that lifestyle—at least that's what they'd say if you asked. But usually they were seduced into it. They actually believed the guy when he told them they were special. Never mind that the Purist male says that to all the females in his pack. By the time they figure out the lie, it's too late.

"I'm nobody's possession and I'm certainly not gullible enough to believe a Purist's line of bull," I said. "No guy's that good-looking or charming."

The cowbell over the front door rang and Mom and I both looked. But I could already smell it was Anthony. The scent of fresh air, forest and wild hay swirled through the diner before him like an outstretched hand. My heart skipped, my body warmed with memories of last night and so many other nights we'd spent together over the past six months.

"Hello, Mattie." His voice vibrated through my chest and straight on down to lower regions that went all warm and moist at the sound.

Okay. Problem. I'd accidentally on purpose forgotten to mention to Mom that I'd been seeing Anthony since the day after Donny's funeral. Why? Two reasons. One, I was worried she'd remember him, go ape-shit, and forbid me to see him. And two, I was afraid he'd charm her into not remembering him, go ape-shit, and nag me to marry him. You see? A no-win situation. Trust me.

So I played dumb. "Hi. Welcome to Banebridge Pop & Pup Diner. Have a seat anywhere and I'll be right with you."

He opened his mouth like he'd say something, but read my narrow-eyed expression and changed his mind. Good boy. He went to the side wall lined with tall windows and red cushioned booths without a word and slid into the fourth booth from the front.

I put the last napkin holder on the counter and noticed Mom waving at me like she was landing a plane. I went the long way around so I could pass near to her. "What?"

"You know him? Smells familiar."

I glanced at Anthony sitting with his back to us and shook my head. But it was hard lying to the woman who taught me how to sneak tampons into the bathroom so the sixth grade boys wouldn't know. "I, ah, I don't know. Maybe."

"I think he's alpha. Cute, too." Her brows sprang up to her hairline and her voice slid higher at the end like she was asking a question.

I flicked my gaze back to him. "Cute's the last thing on my list for potential mates," I said and turned the bend at the end of the counter. Okay, maybe not the last thing, but when it came to Anthony Ricci, cute was about the only thing on my list he matched.

I couldn't help a quick glance in the mirror that covered the top half of the back wall. I was a woman after all and checking hair and makeup before speaking to a good-looking man was like breathing.

I'd forgotten I'd pulled my hair into a ponytail and cringed when I saw the look of an athletic twelve-year-old staring back at me. For half a heartbeat I considered yanking the elastic band out and letting my hair fall loose past my shoulders. But health codes and the fact he'd already seen me this way changed my mind. Instead, I pulled a few more of the lighter blond strands loose from my ponytail of caramel hair, and smoothed them in thin lines to frame my face. At least this way it looked like a style rather than the result of a bad scare.

Makeup? Wasn't wearing any. One less thing to worry about. Besides, Mom always said I had a soap-and-water beauty that didn't need makeup to enhance my brown eyes and thick lashes. I loved my mom.

I tugged my apron smooth over my pink T-shirt and blue jeans, turned from the mirror and walked quickly behind the counter to the other end. I grabbed the order pad I'd left next to the register and crossed the diner to our one and only customer.

"Hi," I said, resting my weight on one hip, pad and pen at the ready. "What can I get for ya?"

"Uh…" He laughed, confused, his brows knitting over his eyes. He glanced at my mom, then back to me. "Well, I dunno. What've you got for a bruised ego?"

"Tea?" I said. But with my eyes I was screaming, *Keep your mouth shut ya big dope. My mom will have you kicked to the curb or married to me in three seconds flat if she finds out we're sleeping together. Run away, run away!*

I don't think he caught all of it though.

His shoulders shook with another laugh, his smile crinkling the corners of his eyes and pulling sexy little dimples in both his cheeks. "What's going on, Mattie? You look like someone's got a gun to your head. I wanted to ask you something last night but—"

"What's that? The specials?" I said to stop him. "Ah, yeah. Tomato soup and grilled cheese. Can I get you a plate?" My face was so tense from the huge fake grin the muscles were already aching.

"Uh, no." He shifted in his seat, angling his body to rest his elbow on the cushioned bench back. "Jeezus, Mattie, relax. I haven't seen you this uptight since we were kids and I sat on your back, pulling your ponytail until you promised to be one of my females."

"Anthony Ricci?" Mom asked. She used that motherly voice that said *I know you're bad news, but saying so will only make my daughter want to date you,* and closed the distance from the back of the diner to his booth. "Anthony. That is you. Haven't seen you since the funeral. I can't remember if I thanked you and your parents for coming. Are they well?"

Crap. All the tense effort I'd been using to communicate with Anthony telepathically drained from my body and made me feel like a deflated balloon. The jig was up. Mom remembered him. Worse, she remembered his family. Anthony was her biggest fear realized. Eldest son of Richard Ricci, alpha of the Ricci pack, Anthony stood to take over. If he hadn't already; I'd never bothered to ask.

One of my brother's friends, he'd been an arrogant little jerk when we were kids. He was four years older than me, and had strutted around with a gaggle of hormone-crazed girls following behind ready to mount him if the mood struck.

Not that he didn't get my juices churning too—obviously. He was handsome, sexy in a way I found weirdly hard to ignore. Power swirled around him, clung to him like armor, and he carried it well, like a second skin.

"Hello, Mrs. Banebridge. Yes, ma'am," he replied in that guy voice that said *I'm too charming for you to be wise to my guy ways.* Nobody was fooling anybody. "My parents will be at the Gathering. I, ah, stopped by to see if you and Mattie will be there this year."

I'd sooner chew off my foot than marry Anthony. Richard Ricci was a Purist and last I'd heard or seen, Anthony was his father's son.

Mom sniffed, loading volumes of mistrust and disapproval into the small sound. Still, she smiled. Totally fake. "Well, of course. Mattie has…responsibilities there this year."

Anthony blinked, all signs of his good humor vanishing. "It's been six months since Donny was killed. Mattie's time of mourning has passed. She needs to choose a mate or someone's bound to challenge her hold on your pack soon."

"I'm well aware of our customs, Anthony—"

"No one's going to challenge my hold," I said before my mother blurted something she'd worry over for the next week. "I'll choose a mate by the lunar eclipse, on the last night of the Gathering."

Anthony's smile made a grand return. "I was hoping you'd say that. Have dinner with me. Tonight."

I almost laughed, but that would've been rude. "Why?"

"Because I want you to choose me to be your mate."

Aw, hell. I laughed. Loud. Couldn't help it.

"IF YOU'RE NOT EVEN CONSIDERING ME AS YOUR mate, why'd you come on this date?" He actually sounded upset.

"What date? This is eating together. Wait. You were serious?" Anthony and I were screwing, not dating. There was a difference.

"*Yes,* I'm serious." He dropped his fork so it clanked against the porcelain plate and yanked the cloth napkin from his lap. A quick swipe across his mouth and he balled it into his fist. "Dammit, Mattie. We'd be perfect together."

I didn't laugh this time. But it wasn't easy. "Ya think? Why's that?"

"You mean aside from the last six months we've spent in sexual bliss?"

"*Sex* being the operative word. Sex is sex. Don't read more into it than there is," I said around the wad of spaghetti in my mouth. What more proof did he need that this wasn't a date? I was actually eating.

"Sex is never just sex. We're compatible. We fit."

I set my fork on the edge of my plate and daintily wiped the corners of my mouth. "Anthony, is your pack still Purists?"

"Yeah."

"We don't fit."

"This isn't about my father's pack. This is about us. What we can build together.' He reached across the table and took my hand. My belly fluttered at his touch, warm and strong. *Damn.* "I want to start fresh with you, Mattie. I want to take care of you and your pack."

I took my hand back. "I don't need to be taken care of. And my pack's fine the way it is."

"That's the dumbest thing I've heard you say since we were kids." His voice held that same twang of condescension that used to make my fur bristle.

"Well, hey, with sweet talk like that how can a girl refuse?"

"I didn't say *you* were dumb, I just meant... *Hell.* Never mind. Listen, I'm asking here, but we both know it's just pretense. If I really wanted..." He let the sentence die unfinished.

Smart boy. "I know our laws. I don't need you to tell me that as a woman I don't count for crap in our world. One of the most important things my dad wanted to accomplish was establishing more rights for women. And his biggest detractor was your father."

"Leadership of a pack requires strength. Physical strength. That's a fact." He gripped both sides of the table. His knuckles whitened and his jaw looked stiff.

"It takes strength because so many of you men behave like animals." I lowered my voice and leaned in. "We're only half beast. Forcing a woman into a marriage she doesn't want is barbaric."

"It's your position, your rank in your pack, that's forcing the issue. Otherwise you could marry who and when you like."

"Not according to your father," I said, my tone growing more heated by the second. "If I was in his pack I'd already be able to answer the boxers or briefs question. Hell, I'd have my own set of sheets in his closet. A man like your father would dominate me and all the women of my pack. We'd be his possessions, with no rights, no voice. I couldn't live like that. I won't."

"Right. Which is exactly why I'm here. You think I'd go through all of this if I was anything like my father? There'd be no debates—I'd just tell you whatever I had to to get what I wanted. You wouldn't know what hit you. Jeezus, Mattie, you're like a dog with a bone."

A half beat of silence passed while his last statement sunk in.

"Cute." I had to fight the sudden smile tugging the corners of my mouth.

"Sorry. Bad choice of words." His cheeks twitched as though he was fighting the same urge, but he kept control.

I sat back in my chair and crossed my arms over my belly. "So, what, you're not a Purist anymore?"

"Never was," he said, mirroring my pose.

"Bull. You think I don't remember 'your girls' when we were kids? There were what, around five of them you were sleeping with at once? Like father like son."

"Jealous?"

"No." *Yes.* But that wasn't the point.

"C'mon, Mattie. I was a teenage boy and they all wanted to be an alpha's mate. Your brother wasn't exactly monogamous either, but you know he believed in your father's views. Donny was a big influence on me. So was your dad. He was more of a father to me than my own."

"Yeah, my dad liked a lot of people. Didn't mean he wanted them marrying his daughter. Besides, you never had my mom fooled. She's always hated you." It was too hard not to smile when I said that.

"The only reason your mom never liked me was——"

"She still doesn't, ya know. Just sayin'."

"Was because she knew, despite all the girls I had to choose from, the only one I wanted was you. And just like you, she couldn't trust that I wasn't my father's son."

"Oh." It took me a second to process that. "Me? You never——"

Anthony leaned forward and caught my gaze. His voice came smooth and rich like thick, melted chocolate. "I'm not a kid anymore, Mattie. I don't want to play games. I know what I want. Give me a chance."

My heart skipped a beat, and a warm tingle raced down my spine. Every instinct inside me told me he was speaking the truth, or he thought he was. But I'd never considered Anthony as a possible mate. His Purist upbringing had kept him firmly in the *no friggin' way* category. But now...?

"Excuse me." I pushed to my feet, tossed my napkin on the table and grabbed my tiny clutch purse.

Anthony blinked, brows tight above violet eyes. "Wha— where're you going?"

"To the ladies' room," I said as though I wasn't really just escaping an uncomfortable situation. "Do you mind?"

"Oh." He glanced toward the restrooms and back. "But you haven't answered my question."

"I'll be right back, Anthony. Sheesh." I shook my head and made a beeline for the restroom.

Thank goodness the long, narrow room was empty. I tossed my clutch purse on the sink counter and paced. "Shoot, shoot, shoot." My voiced echoed off the tile walls. Bad enough I was reduced to talking to myself but now I was doing it in stereo.

"Okay, pros—He's an alpha. Check. He's sexy as hell. That's always nice. He's amazing in bed. A must—naturally. He makes me laugh and listens to me, asks my opinions and takes my advice...sometimes."

I stopped and closed my eyes, resting my head against the cool tiled wall. He had a lot of great attributes for a mate. But he was raised Purist and could a person really turn their back on their upbringing? In a moment of crisis how could I ever be sure he wouldn't fall back on old habits?

"Wow, this place is huge."

I think I screamed. Anthony's very male, very loud voice startled the breath out of me. "What're you doing in here?"

He strode past me to the far end of the restroom, checking out the stalls and then pausing at the tampon dispenser on his way back.

"Hel-loo?" I said when he seemed to be enjoying the tour a little too much.

"What do you need a room this big for?"

"Anthony."

His gaze snapped to mine, suddenly serious. "I figured you were in here doing one of your pros and cons lists. I'm looking to sway the tally."

"It doesn't work that way."

He grabbed my hand and turned, leading me back to the last stall with the handicapped plaque on the door. He twisted the little silver lock behind us and backed me to the wall.

"If anyone comes in... We'll get thrown out if they catch us," I said even as he unbuttoned my blouse and slipped his hand in to caress my breast. My breath shuddered with the delicious warmth and pressure.

"Then you'd better not scream this time." His free hand brushed the long strands of my hair from my neck and he leaned in to press his lips to my collarbone.

"I don't scream." But I did moan at the featherlight kiss and the sharp nip that followed.

I bent my knee between his legs and he rocked his hips forward, stroking the hard line of his sex against my thigh. My hand slipped between us; I couldn't help it. I wanted that thick, long shaft in my palm. I wanted to wrap my fingers around it, feel its length, its hardness. But his dark slacks allowed only a muted experience.

He had my blouse unbuttoned to my skirt in seconds and pushed the collar off my shoulders. It caught at my elbows but he'd already moved on, scooping my breasts from the cups of my bra. The cool air-conditioning chilled my skin, pulled my nipples tighter. His thumb brushed over one and then the other, sending quick jolts of pleasure through my body. He pinched and rolled the hard nubs between his fingers, and my breath caught; a sweet pinch of pain in a wake of tingling pleasure that filled my breasts.

Heat swelled inside, blossoming out from the center of my being, flooding my veins, sizzling through my sex, making me wet and ready. His head dropped to suckle me, his strong mouth drawing on my breast, teeth nipping, tongue teasing over the tight puckered flesh. My back arched, offering more of myself as I worked his belt and zipper.

Were we really going to do this? The thrill of possible discovery raced through my blood, made my heart beat faster, my skin tingle. Lord, I hoped no one came in...and I wished someone would.

With his cock free, thick and heavy in my hand, I stroked the length of him, a bead of pre-come wetting my palm. His breaths were quick and shallow and his body a solid mass of tense muscle, his kisses near frantic with need. The risks of our erotic tryst vibrated through every inch of his body, charged the air between us.

He hiked my skirt to my waist and took my small panties in both hands. A quick tug and I felt them loosen, another and they dropped to the floor. I opened my legs as wide as I could and he lifted me, using the wall behind me as leverage. The smooth hot tip of his cock pressed between the slick lips of my sex and—

"Umm, are you okay in there?" someone asked outside the stall.

We froze, his cock stretching the entrance to my body, making the muscles of my sex flex, trying to pull him deeper. "Uh...uh-huh," I said.

I bit my bottom lip to stop a moan when Anthony suddenly let gravity impale my body with his. He filled me fast, too fast, shooting a searing mix of pain and pleasure through my body. My lungs squeezed, my breath caught. He froze again, buried balls deep inside me.

"I'm sorry," he whispered, breathless, trying not to move, his lips brushing my ear. He held his body so still and tense my fingers couldn't dent the flesh across his shoulders. "I'm sorry, sweetheart. I had to be inside you. I'm so sorry."

I squirmed on his cock, my pussy adjusting, flooding with cream, muscles flexing. I couldn't take it. I turned my head and bit his ear. "Fuck me, already."

And he did.

He rocked his hips, pounding sensation through my sex, electrifying my skin so every part of me hummed with the feel of him driving in and out of my body. Sweet friction built the pressure, coiling my muscles, tightening through my chest. My fingers fisted his hair, his face buried in the crook of my neck.

Someone turned on the water and someone else flushed a toilet. The room roared with sound but nothing could drown out our howling cries of release.

Seconds later when our passion was spent and blood flow returned to our brains, a palpable silence filled the restroom. Then someone crumpled a paper towel and a woman's heels clicked-clacked across the tile floor. The door out to the restaurant opened and swung slowly closed.

"Let's pay the check then get out of here," I said. "And, ya know, never come back."

"Right." He put me on my feet and we dressed like frantic teenagers whose parents had just pulled into the driveway.

I grabbed my ruined panties and opened the stall door. A quick peek to make sure the coast was clear and I tiptoed over to the sink to where I'd left my purse.

"Mattie?"

I turned in time to see him tuck in the last of his shirt. "Yeah?"

"How's that pros and cons tally going?"

I sighed. He looked so hopeful, his shirt wrinkled, hair

mussed. He'd tried so hard and well, hell, I liked him. I winked and let my smile have its way. "Heavy on the pros side, love. Definitely heavy on the pros."

"SO YOU AND ANTHONY A THING NOW?" BRAD asked, his arm loose around Amy's shoulders. Friends of both my brother and Anthony, they were part of the older crowd I'd shadowed as a kid. I had to admit, I got a stupid kind of thrill being part of their group now.

"We're, uh, exploring our options," I said, feeling like the new girl on a date with the star quarterback.

The group dynamics had changed over the past ten years since I'd last seen them. Brad and Amy were mates; I could see it in the way they touched each other, always some part of their body in contact with the other whenever possible. But more than that, I could smell it. A melding of individual scents to create something new and unique to the couple by the simple act of accepting the other as mate. Werewolves didn't need a formal ceremony or even a verbal declaration. It just happened. Life mates.

Brad chuckled and tipped his chin toward the other side of the clearing. "Yeah. Looks like Anthony's exploring a few options on his own."

I looked over my shoulder. The Gathering took place every year in a thousand-acre animal reserve in rural southwestern Pennsylvania owned by the werewolf council. After more than fifty years of Gatherings the forest had succumbed to our needs and now trees refused to grow in the football-sized field we used to set up fire circles, food tents and run carnival type games for the kids.

My eyes found Anthony after a quick scan through the three hundred or so faces dotting the field. My stomach rolled then twisted tight.

"I don't know how you girls do it," Amy said. "I couldn't share Brad with anyone. It seems so, I dunno…unnatural. Oh. Not that I'm prejudiced or anything. I mean, if that's what makes you happy. Some people are just…different. Right?"

I nodded, still watching the three nymphets clustered around Anthony. They were pretty, all of them—long-haired with bright eyes and tight, shapely bodies. They laughed when he spoke, pressing against him, touching him. Though Anthony's hands stayed firmly in the front pockets of his jeans.

"The way your dad felt about giving everyone a voice— women same as men—never pegged you for a future Purist when we were kids," Brad said.

"I'm not." I was mad, upset, and when I'm upset I get blunt. "Anthony and I are fucking. That's it. Obviously, our lifestyle choices make anything more than that impossible."

"That's a relief." Amy sighed. "I love Anthony to death, but for years his father's been pushing him to seduce females who have either money or power, or both."

"He's damn good at it too," Brad said. "The guy's either a wild man in the sack or he's hung like a friggin' donkey." I knew the answer to that. I kept it to myself.

Brad traced a finger down the arm Amy had nestled against his side. I don't think he realized he was doing it. I looked away. I hated being jealous, but I was.

"Actually, I'm a little disappointed in Anthony. I thought he'd stand up to his father. But those women all think he'll choose one as his life mate and he has yet to do it." Amy pointed to the brunette on Anthony's left. "Candice was so sure he'd choose her, her body started producing mating pheromones. Now her offer's kind of…out there, waiting for him to make a decision. Bet it's the same for the others. Once their body starts the process they can't turn it off until he commits to someone."

"And if he doesn't commit he gets them all for as long as he wants," I said, glancing back at Anthony.

"I'll admit," Brad said, "if I didn't know better I'd say he finally caved to his dad and started collecting women for a new Purist pack."

"You sure he hasn't?" I said. A chill iced down my spine. Was I supposed to be the newest member? A sixteen-member pack had a lot of power and it'd go to whoever I chose as my mate. Even if Anthony never committed to me he'd still have the benefits that came with my choosing him.

Brad scoffed and shook his head. "I don't buy it. He's never been into the Purist scene the way his dad and the others are. You ask me, I think he's been holding out for someone special his whole life."

Amy turned soft, romantic eyes to her mate. "Aww, that's so sweet."

"Yeah. Whatever." Their sappy lovey-dovey crap made me ill. My foul mood might've had something to do with it, too. Hard to say.

"It's not fair these stupid mating pheromones don't work the other way." I could feel my scowl narrowing my eyes. "A man's mating pheromones can overpower a woman's. He can force her to be his mate, but not the other way around. Unfair!"

"Yeah," Amy said. "That, periods, bloating and PMS, totally unfair. What else is new?"

At least he couldn't force me into a Purist pack. Committing to me would free the other women to rescind their offers. Bye-bye harem. But how close had I come to choosing him? I would've been trapped just like those girls fawning over him must be. My stomach roiled. I couldn't keep thinking about it.

"You're Mattie, right?" I turned at the sound of a masculine voice behind me and almost strained my neck.

"Yeah. I'm sorry, do I know you?" The guy was seven feet if he was an inch, lanky but toned. He was cute though, with long sun-bleached hair, spiky ends brushing the tops of his shoulders, and skin bronzed so perfectly he looked like he'd been dipped. He reminded me of an ad for sunless tanner.

"Awe-some," he said, very surfer dude. "Name's Brodi. This here's my bud, Samson. Word is you're lookin' for a mate. Like fast, right? Well, uh, me and Samson might be able to help you out." He shrugged. "You know, if you're willin' to make a couple...allowances. Right?"

I shifted my gaze to Samson. The anti-Brodi. He couldn't have been more than an inch taller than me. The top of his neat, dirt-brown hair barely reached Brodi's shoulder. With paler skin, a heavier build and a freckled face, Samson's dark brown eyes said timid, beta, whereas Brodi oozed alpha male.

Samson slipped his hand into Bodi's larger, long-fingered grip and dropped his gaze under my more dominant stare. He tucked his free hand under his arm, hugging himself and shifted his weight to lean into Brodi. Suddenly Samson's body language wasn't saying beta as much as it was screaming *I bat for the home team*.

They weren't the first today to throw their hats into my ring, so to speak, but they were definitely the most interesting. I struggled not to let my smile grow too wide, not to let the crazy laughter tickling up my throat color my voice. "Thanks for the offer, but—"

"She's taken."

The group of us turned to see Anthony striding toward us, butterscotch hair waving over his shoulders, thick arms pumping at his sides. His blue silk shirt gave his eyes an unearthly luster that I noticed even at a distance and clung to his chest and arms so every roll of muscle made my heart race. The crazy desperation I'd felt swamping me a moment ago vanished. Lord, what he did to me.

"Am not," I said. Yeah. Clever. That's me.

Anthony's hypnotic violet eyes shifted to Brad and Amy. "Guys. Thanks for entertaining my future wife. You won't mind if I steal her away."

Reaching out he snagged my hand as he passed, not even breaking his stride. Like a boat on water my body turned and followed, my brain too stunned to protest. We needed to talk anyway, to end what was going on between us before it went too far and I stupidly found myself joining his stable of women. But the power that swirled around him, the warmth and strength of his hand, the confidence in his stride, it was all too intoxicating. Damn, I was sunk.

Twenty feet beyond the tree line into the forest Anthony spun me around, pinning me against the fat trunk of an oak. His face nestled against my neck, warm breath and hot kisses snaking ribbons of heat along my skin that pooled fast between my thighs. "Drives me crazy to see all these other guys sniffing around you."

He pressed his body against mine, sealing us from chest to groin so I knew exactly how happy he was to be alone with me. "And yet you managed to contain your mental distress long enough to tighten the leashes you've got on your current pussy supply."

He raised his head, the upper part of his body separating from mine, and looked me straight in the eye. "I didn't ask those girls to offer to be my mate. I don't even know why they did. I'm not gonna be mean, though. What am I supposed to do, commit just because they offered? Doesn't it matter what I want?"

"What *you* want?"

"Yeah. Don't I get a say in who I spend the rest of my life with?"

Wow, that sounded familiar. "You didn't seduce them, make them think you were interested in life mates?"

His brows lifted, a dimpled smile tugging his cheeks. He chuckled, looked away and back again, a bad-boy glint in his violet eyes. "Yeah, I seduced them. I like to fuck. But I never offered to be life mate to any of them."

"Right." God, I wanted to believe him, but everything I knew about Purists told me he was lying. He had to be. It was what they did.

The lines across his forehead deepened, tightening his brows and turning his smile serious. "You're the only one, Mattie.

Ever. If they sensed I wanted a life mate then they sensed my feelings for you."

He pinched my chin between his thumb and forefinger and brought my mouth to his. I let him. Even as our lips touched and he coaxed mine to part, somewhere in the back of my brain I knew dictionaries were quickly switching the picture next to the word *chump* with mine. But I couldn't care.

He just smelled so damn good, like fields of sweet hay after a spring rain and musky human male. I was swamped by the scent of him; every breath took him deep inside me, flavored my tongue, made it hard to think. My heart raced, hot blood flooding my nerves, tingling through my senses. He rocked his hips, reminding me his hard cock was thick and ready, pressing against my belly. It'd take zero convincing to have him naked inside me. And I wanted him inside me, filling me, making my body melt and my sex muscles spasm. The very thought of it made me wet.

Crap! I turned my head, breaking the kiss and gulping air while I could. "Anthony, stop. I have to think of my pack. It's over. You're not right for me. I have to choose someone else."

His hand slipped between my legs, stroked the curve of my pussy through my shorts. "Bullshit. No one else gets you this hot, Mattie. Admit it."

"You don't know that." Never mind that it was true. Something about him seemed to trigger instincts in me I had to fight hard to ignore. Saying no had never been so hard.

"It's the same for me," he said. "We're meant for each other. Our bodies recognize it." His hand stroked between my legs. I wanted to push it away. Or at least I wanted to want to push his hand away.

"Anthony, I——"A low growl and then a rustle of leaves off to my right drew our attention.

A flash of fur, a flicker of flesh, it was hard to see clearly through the bushes and leaves. A tail swooshed, hindquarters pumping fast, a woman moaned and an instant before my mind puzzled out the pieces, the image changed. Fur vanished, replaced by the taut, hard ass of a man thrusting deep behind the plump bottom of a woman on all fours. A heartbeat later the rhythmic, frantic sounds of flesh smacking flesh left no doubt.

"Oh." I wanted to look away, but I couldn't. Anthony's fingers rubbed along the lips of my pussy through my shorts, his scent filled me, his body pressed warm and hard against mine. It was too much to refuse. I let my legs relax, allowing the caress. It felt too good.

"She's going to come any minute. So is he. Do you smell it?" Anthony turned his face into my neck again and mumbled, "I can feel you want it too, Mattie. Let me make you come with them."

I didn't answer—not a yes, but not a no either. My belly tightened, my sex flooding with cream watching the man's body tense, glisten with sweat as he pounded his cock into her pussy. Her body shuddered with each hard thrust, rocking back and forth on her knees to drive him deeper, harder.

Anthony's kisses heated down my neck, his teeth nipping my skin, sending jolts of pain and pleasure tingling through my veins. His hands slipped behind the elastic band of my shorts, pushing them down, snagging my underwear as they went, shoving both past my knees.

I looked to see him kneeling before me, pushing my bottoms

further down my legs then coaxing me to slip one sandaled foot free. He straightened, running his hands up my thighs, an expression of rapt desire filling his face. His mouth was belly level and he slipped his hands around to my butt, pulling me to him, and pressed a kiss there. I felt it…everywhere.

"Anthony." It was barely a whisper.

"Let me," he said, his lips tickling my belly, his voice vibrating through my sex.

I was going to stop him. I'd pretty much decided…almost. But then he kissed lower on my belly, his fingers squeezing the cheeks of my ass. And then he kissed lower still. I leaned my head back against the tree, dug my hands into that thick wavy hair and caught my breath when his next kiss teased right above my clit.

His palms seemed to burn across my skin as he smoothed them over my hips to between my thighs. He nudged my legs wider, his thumbs spreading the lips of my sex, holding me open to him. I rocked forward, couldn't help it—the heat of his breath tickled like wicked feathers over the sensitive flesh.

The noise he made sounded more like a growl, but when I looked I don't think he'd even realized he'd made the sound. He lunged forward, like a wolf devouring a kill, pressing his face into my pussy, his tongue finding the sensitive flesh of my clit. With firm, teasing licks, he brought me into his mouth, suckled, drawing a rush of sensation from every part of my body straight through to my sex.

I bit my lip, fought not to cry out and glanced at the couple fucking on the other side of the brush. I gasped, surprise stealing my voice.

He was watching me, watching us, even as he pounded into

his lover's pussy. His gaze traveled over me, watched Anthony eating me out, watched me holding him to me. My body tightened, a quick thrill zinging through my veins. Our eyes met, and for a second I don't think he realized I was seeing him. And then it clicked. His eyes focused, his blank lustful expression warmed.

A crooked smile tugged across his face and a kind of intimate heat flashed in his eyes. He looked to the woman's ass, and my gaze followed. He shifted, bringing one hand to his hip so I could see his ruddy cock, wet with her cream, driving in and out of her swollen pussy.

As though he knew what I was seeing, Anthony slipped a finger inside me, filled me like the man's cock filled the woman. I couldn't keep the moan in my throat.

"Oh, God…" My breaths came in pants, my hips moving with the ever-quickening rhythm he set. My pussy tensed, clamped around his finger even as moisture gushed, slicking the way for him to add another.

The man's cock pumped in and out, keeping pace with Anthony's fingers fucking me. My hands fisted in his hair, held his face against my pussy. Sensation swirled through me, excitement swelling so fast I couldn't breathe, couldn't think.

Like the undeniable pull of the ocean, a delicious tide pushed me closer and closer toward that blissful edge. I tried to hold back, tried to ignore the muscles tingling and coiling inside me, the knot tightening low in my body. But it was too much, the feel of his mouth suckling me, my sex milking his fat fingers, the sight of the couple fucking, the man's big cock rosy and wet, pounding into her. Too much.

The man's cheeks flushed, ropy veins pressing along his neck and forehead, his thrusts frantic, both hands gripping her waist. Sensation crested inside me. Muscles flexed on his ass, his thighs and arms, his jaw tight. The woman cried out, throwing her head back and the hot wash of release flooded through me. Orgasms rocked her, him and me all at once and filled the forest with our lascivious cries.

My knees buckled and only Anthony's fast reflexes, snaking his arms around my waist, kept me on my feet. I closed my eyes and let my head tilt back against the tree trunk, struggling for breath, for clear thinking.

"Jeezus, Mattie, I almost came listening to you," he said, nuzzling my belly. 'You drive me crazy, woman. I told you we're perfect together."

I flicked my gaze to the couple. They were gone. I sighed, glad for small favors, and looked down at Anthony. Most men couldn't do to me with their whole body and several toys what he'd done with just his mouth and fingers. My heart slowly found a steady beat but I knew the ache pressing at my chest had nothing to do with exertion.

"I'm sorry, Anthony," I said. "It's not going to work. I can't do this. Tomorrow night, I'm choosing someone else as my mate."

"WHAT DO YOU MEAN YOU DIDN'T ASK? YOU'RE an alpha, boy. Lead the damn pack," Richard Ricci said. "They'll follow if you're even half the man I raised you to be."

Twenty feet across the clearing I could hear him as clearly as if he stood next to me. Richard's deep baritone voice, like his son's, carried as though he spoke through a megaphone.

I looked at Anthony standing in front of the big man, arms folded tight across his chest, feet planted wide, chin high, firm. "Don't worry about it, Pop. I'll work it out."

Richard snorted, his hard barrel belly shaking up through his chest with a laugh. Even at this distance I could tell there was no humor in it. "The rabbits are loose, boy. The hunt's about to start. You've got no time left to work it out. If you can't lead them tonight, you won't pull them in line tomorrow night when it really counts."

"It's just a stupid game, Pop," Anthony said. "Some things are more important."

"The hell you say, boy. Nuthin's ever just a game." He stood four inches taller than Anthony and looked like he outweighed him by forty pounds easy. He wore his pure white hair cut short enough to see the pink hue of his skin underneath. He had a round face and arms as thick as my thigh. Even happy the man could intimidate a rattlesnake. And Richard Ricci was not happy.

Anthony shook his head and turned to leave, but Richard reached out his long arm and snagged him by the scruff of the neck. It was really the back of his shirt collar, but the effect was the same. The big man jerked Anthony backward so fast he nearly fell. Good balance and an athletic build was all that saved him.

"Don't you walk away from me, boy," he said, trying his best to lift Anthony off his feet. He was about fifteen years past that ability.

Anthony jerked free easily and turned on his father, face tight with leashed anger. "I said, I can handle it, Pop. My way."

"Your way? You mean your mother's way," Richard said. "Women ask permission, boy. Men, true alphas, take what they want and fight to keep it."

"Right. Like you know anything about my mother." Anthony turned and disappeared into the crowd surrounding them.

"I know she's mine," Richard said, obviously confident Anthony could still hear him. "Can you say the same for the Banebridge female?"

My whole body flinched. I blinked while my brain struggled to accept he was talking about me the same as he would his car or his shoes. Heat rose in my cheeks as those nearest to me turned to see my reaction. I felt two inches tall.

Richard's voice grew louder, carrying over the murmuring crowd of nearly three hundred werewolves who'd gathered in the clearing for the evening sport. "Maybe one of your brothers can seduce the bitch. You're my first son, Anthony. Not my only son."

An uncomfortable quiet settled over the clearing, anticipation thick on the air, but Anthony didn't answer. After several pregnant seconds the soft murmur of conversation began again.

"We gonna have to be part of the Ricci pack?" my ten-year-old cousin, Claudia, asked.

I tucked a few strawberry strands behind her ear then ruffled the top of her head. "No, sweet pea. No matter what he says we don't have to do anything we don't want to."

She folded her arms across her chest and tightened her brows. "Good. 'Cause I don't like that man. He's too loud and bossy."

"Like father, like sons," Mom said beside me. "You heard him, Mattie. Those Ricci boys will be jockeying for position around us all night. What are we supposed to do with no one to fend them off?"

Richard Ricci had four sons, including Anthony, each to a different mother. Competition among males in a Purist pack could be lethal. If Richard wanted me under the family wing, the pressure on his sons to be the one to deliver could force them to desperate measures. And my pack would be at the center of it. I had to do what I could to protect them.

"You follow me. That's what we do." I turned to face my pack. "Until I take a mate, *I'm* leading this pack. Understood? I don't want anyone trying to be a hero. I can handle their advances if I know my pack trusts me. If I know you'll follow my lead, no matter what, I can take care of the males."

A few of my cousins nodded and some mumbled agreement. No one refused. That's all I needed.

"We still hunting our rabbit?" Claudia asked.

"Absolutely," I said. "They set free twenty rabbits last week. One for each pack. Ours was scented with jasmine. Do you know that smell?"

She shook her head.

"Well, then we'll get you a sniff. I'm pretty sure the perfumes belong to one of the councilmen's wives." When your mate is on the international werewolf council you can afford to scent game rabbits with twenty different kinds of expensive perfumes.

Tonight was sort of a practice run for the big hunt tomorrow night, more an exhibition, a show of pack teamwork and tracking ability than an all-out hunt.

"This is supposed to be fun. That's what this Gathering is all about. Right? So let's have some fun." God, I hoped that sounded more genuine than it felt. Tonight the rabbits stood a better chance of coming out unscathed than me.

The forest was nearly as bright as it could be on a cloudless night, with the moon waxing one day till full. At a glance, David and Brian Ricci looked just like their older brother, Anthony. Both big-boned, larger than a normal timber wolf, with thick, butter-blond fur and bright eyes. Markus Ricci, Richard's youngest son, had fur the color of strawberries and cream, so identifying him was a snap. But I didn't need to rely on my eyesight to know the difference between the brothers. I could smell them. All around me.

Only my mother and I raised our muzzles to the wind, scenting them. The rest of my pack remained oblivious, their noses to the forest floor tracking our rabbit. I caught David's scent off to my left, still hidden behind trees and underbrush, but growing closer. Brian was on the right, watching me from beneath a thick pine. Markus stood a few feet back from Brian, too young to make a play for me on his own.

The moment our eyes met, Brian started toward me, head low, stride slow and steady, muscles rolling smooth and fluid beneath his thick fur. Markus followed but several paces back. I knew by his body language he'd only watch.

Good, one less challenger I'd have to worry about.

My pack was spread out behind me, some as far as thirty feet back. My mother was the closest and she closed the distance the instant she saw Brian advance. I snapped at her to keep her back, keep her safe. There was nothing she could do. This was about strength and dominance, about proving a point.

There were a lot of ways for a potential mate to prove he was strong enough to lead me and my pack. When both parties agreed most of them were symbolic. But the hairs bristling at my hackles told me the Ricci brothers really weren't into symbolism. Wolf instinct—it was a good thing.

I crouched, keeping my center of balance low and my eyes glued on Brian. He circled me, his lips trembling back to bare sharp, white teeth, his low growl rumbling between us. I flicked my ears, pivoting them to locate David. I could survive a challenge from one scary, big male, but two at once just wouldn't be fair.

I found him, pacing the ridge of a small hill about twenty yards to our left. His big paws crunched leaves, twigs and other forest debris with each step. He was waiting his turn. *Thank goodness.*

I focused my attention back on Brian an instant before he lunged. A flash of icy blue eyes and white teeth, a blur of yellow fur and then——*bam!* He slammed into me so hard it took a second to believe I hadn't been run over by a bus. I hit the ground hard. Someone yelped. I'm pretty sure it was me.

Shards of pain tore through my side and down my back leg. The air punched out of my lungs and my vision starred. If it weren't for the fee of razor-sharp teeth pressing against my neck, I might've lain there for several minutes trying to suck a single good breath. But I didn't have that kind of time.

I writhed underneath Brian, his body heavy, almost suffocating, on top of me, pinning me at the shoulder. I wasn't ready to give up.

I used my tail to pinwheel my lower body, twisting enough to get my back legs under me. My wild thrashing edged his weight to the side, but his jaw tightened its grip on my neck. I dug the long nails of my back feet into the soft forest floor, then pulled back.

Brian's teeth pierced my skin trying to hold me under him. My mind screamed, but it came out as a yelping kind of wail. I didn't stop. I wiggled and twisted and pulled, feeling his big, heavy body lose its leverage. Suddenly he slipped off and all he had was his mouth on my neck.

Warm blood trickled down my skin under my fur. I blocked it from my brain and slammed back against him, driving us both up onto our hind feet. I snapped my head over his, twisting his neck. His teeth tore my flesh. Pain burned through my body, squeezing my lungs so I couldn't breathe, couldn't see for the blinding shock of it.

The speed and twist made him lose his grip, and we both tumbled to the ground from the force of the quick maneuver. I was free, but with only an instant to turn the tide.

Our fall had landed Brian beneath me on his back, soft underbelly—and other things—exposed. I did the only thing I could think of to end the battle; I fought like a girl.

I lunged toward the soft fleshy pocket of his testicles and clamped my razor-sharp teeth down.

Brain suddenly went very, *very* still.

I growled, low and menacing, then closed my teeth a hairsbreadth more. Brian whimpered, his tail stiff. I growled again and pulled on the tender flesh, just enough to force a mental image of his balls snipped off. It worked.

His whole body went pliant. His whimpers became sounds of submission, soft snorts, quick breaths, cajoling me however he could. He twisted, struggling to reach my face, licking my fur at my shoulder, my neck, stroking me, assuring his surrender. I let him go.

He swung his feet under him in an instant, met my gaze and then backed away. I'd done it. I'd held my ground and proved my dominance. Never mind that it was dumb luck he'd lost his balance and exposed his Achilles' heel, so to speak. It counted.

I turned to face David, my body going low, centering my balance. The bite on my neck stung like the constant press of a hot poker and the muscle around the wound ached. But it was the sharp pain in my hindquarter that worried me. I must've landed on a rock or a hard root; the pain forced me to favor the leg and that could be lethal. Unfortunately, there were no time-outs in battles for dominance. That was kinda the point.

Anthony's scent tickled my nose before I saw him. A blur of fur, a flash of teeth and two yellow wolves came tumbling down the hillside toward me. They landed in a heap four feet away, a twisting knot of snarls and snaps, bone-chilling growls and sharp, gnashing teeth.

They got to their feet, circled. David's ear was torn, bleeding. Their growls rumbled like the roll of a kettle drum through the forest, the sound vibrating through my chest. There was nothing I could do but wait to see who won.

Muzzle to muzzle Anthony was the taller, heavier wolf, but size didn't always mean victory. Dominance was as much mental as physical. But I knew in my gut David didn't have what it took to go toe-to-toe with Anthony. He was weaker in every way and his weakness fragranced his skin, his fur, like something half ripe, half ready. He couldn't escape the fact. Unless fate intervened and his luck turned, it was only a matter of time before he accepted it or died trying.

David stopped, and Anthony mirrored him——then took a step forward. As though instinct took hold when good sense was lacking, David moved back quickly keeping the distance. Just like that the battle's outcome was sealed.

If wolves had facial expressions I imagined David's was a mix of confusion and indecision. He hadn't meant to concede, I was sure of it. But that single reflexive step backward had given victory to Anthony. Of course, he could ignore his accidental retreat but the mental edge it'd given his brother and the damage it'd done to him was usually irrecoverable.

Anthony straightened, his thick furry ears perking as though waiting for David to make it official. With a hard snort and a shake of his head, David turned and jogged over the hill, disappearing deeper into the forest. Markus hurried after his brothers.

Anthony turned to face me and my body fought itself for the

correct response. My legs bent, lowering my center of balance, ready to fight, even as my belly fluttered and my sex pulsed. Instinct, primal, powerful, pounded through my veins, craving the strongest, victorious suitor like it craved air. Instincts be damned; I wasn't about to become a Purist no matter how much of an animal turn-on it was to see him battle for me.

He was riding a triumphant high as he jogged toward me. I could smell his thick musk billowing before him like an intoxicating cloud. The scent surrounded me, spiked my wolf lust to mate with the proven superior. I fought it. He didn't.

Anthony was acting like a wolf not a man, so when I launched myself at his neck he was taken by complete surprise. I managed to graze his flesh, felt the thin scrape of his skin curl up the inside of my teeth before he dodged and shook me off.

I'd landed on my side and pain shot through my hind leg tearing a line straight up my spine like fire on a fuse. I barked, high and sharp, half from pain and half a result of air forced out of my lungs.

He narrowed his eyes on me, his stance suddenly more aggressive, more determined. I had to get up, had to fight. I knew this time it wasn't about proving a point. This time it was about taking what he wanted, taking because he could. This time it was about sex. But each twist of my body to get my feet under me sent new shards of agony through my leg.

I wasn't fast enough. Anthony closed the distance he'd thrown me in a heartbeat. He leapt around to my tail end, his powerful front legs clamping around my sides, his claws digging through my fur to my flesh. I'd only caught a glimpse of his little pink penis wagging out from its pouch. His hips were already pumping against me, though he missed my pussy with every thrust. Eventually, he'd find the mark.

No. I squirmed, tried to swing my hind end out from under him, but he held on, dancing along behind me. His sharp teeth nipped at my shoulders, the back of my neck, trying to hold me still. I couldn't get free. Somewhere in the back of my mind I heard my mom barking at him. I knew she was biting his ass, tugging on his tail with her teeth. He didn't seem to notice.

Panic sunk through my veins like ice, freezing my brain, making me stupid. Then it hit me. There was nothing I could do to get through to him. He was a Purist at heart, just as I feared. My wants and needs meant nothing to him. I was female. He'd won me. I was going to be raped.

White-hot pain sliced along my side and ripped through my brain with such force that for one terrifying moment I couldn't breathe, couldn't think what had happened. A screaming yowl exploded out of me, the sound so close to human I thought for a second I'd shifted. I wrenched my head around to see blood soaking my side, turning my caramel fur brown as rust, wet and clumping.

His claw had cut through to the meat. I fell, not even realizing he'd let me go until I felt the soft grass under my hip. Anthony shifted fast, faster than I'd ever seen anyone shift. One second he was wolf, I blinked, and he was human, naked, panting, his violet eyes wide with worry.

"Mattie, oh God, I'm sorry. I'm so sorry." He drove his fingers through his mop of hair. "Damn it, this challenge bullshit is making me crazy. I thought I felt you offer and then you refused me. Hell, maybe I just wanted you to offer so badly I imagined it. I dunno. Why the fuck won't you just choose me? Please. You're killing me. You know I love you. I never would've—"

I spun around and bit the hand he held out to me—hard. When he jerked back I took off and my pack followed. They'd been watching helpless for some time, I realized, but now I needed them, their protection, while I shifted to heal the wounds on my hip, neck and side.

I ran through the moonlit forest, trees and brush raking through my fur, my heart thundering in my ears. Anthony's words rolled through my brain. I hadn't offered to him; I was sure of it. But I'd wanted to. I realized now, when I saw him drive David off I'd wanted him, then, always and forever.

Could he be so attuned to me that he understood my thoughts better than I understood myself? Or had desperation driven him to revert to his Purist upbringing for answers? Was he a heartless, self-centered Purist, or my perfect life mate? And how the hell was I supposed to know the difference?

"HE'S A LONE WOLF NOW. EVERYONE'S TALKING about it," Mom said. "Apparently, after we left him last night he went straight to Big Richard and broke his ties with the pack."

There are three surefire ways to get information out: telephone, e-mail and tele-my-mom. "So what, that somehow makes him a better mate for me?"

Mom snorted. "Well, yes. It proves he's been telling the truth. Purists never break rank. Never really leave their core packs. Anthony did.'

I shook my head, not wanting to believe and wishing I could at the same time. "It's not just Big Richard. Anthony will never be a lone wolf with all the women he's got offering to him. And after what he almost did last night—"

"I know the definition of the word lone, dear," she said, indignant. *Oops.* "He's ended things with those other girls. Flatly refused each of their offers. I hear one of them, the one with the big nose and god-awful taste in clothes, I heard she threw an absolute fit when he turned her down."

Sheila Tully, a model who enjoyed the perks of wearing designer clothes every day, but alas would never hold a candle to me in my mother's eyes. I loved my mom.

"And last night…well, honey, I love you, but if you hadn't suddenly tried to bite his head off, we'd have snuck off to give you two some privacy."

My jaw dropped. "Seriously? Mom, he jumped me."

"I know, sweetheart, but to be fair you'd invited him to enjoy your…feminine delights before."

My cheeks warmed. *Crap.* I was twenty-three, a werewolf and a liberated woman. Of course I wasn't a virgin and my mom's not stupid. Still. She's my mom and hearing her refer to my feminine delights is just…*shudder.*

"I think he just got a little caught up in the excitement of fighting off other suitors," she said. "If it'd been any other time, say a few nights ago, would you have fought so hard to stop him?"

If he'd tried to screw me in wolf form? Uh, yeah. But only long enough for us both to shift and then… Go figure, my mom was right. But was she right about everything? Was Anthony my true life mate?

"It doesn't matter. He was raised a Purist," I said. "Even if he turns his back on that now, he'll never be like Dad. I want what the two of you had. A partnership. Can someone raised as a Purist ever see a woman as an equal?"

Mom shook her head, and made a tsk-tsk sound with her tongue. "Your father was a rare find. I don't think there'll ever be anyone quite like him. But then, you're not exactly like me. And maybe, just maybe, Anthony can be for you what your father was for me. There's only one way to find out."

Yeah, stick my neck out and hope no one bites it off. Won't that be fun?

* * *

"Ladies and gentlemen," Councilman Lynwood said from the metal ladder they'd erected at the far end of the clearing. "In exactly—" he checked his watch "—eight minutes the lunar eclipse will begin. As is tradition, the hunt lasts the duration of the eclipse while our abilities are uniquely heightened. This year we've got a full two hours."

The crowd cheered around the group of us who were naked and ready for the hunt. More than three hundred wolves running through the woods after a lone deer just isn't practical. So each pack chose their best five, which typically equated with the top five ranking members.

There were only four of us from my pack: me, Mom, and my cousins, Glenna and Oliver. Glenna was my blood cousin; Oliver was her mate. A fluke of members being injured, pregnant or underage coincided to make us short one. We weren't the only pack participating in the hunt with fewer hunters though.

Plus, we were good. Real good.

"You still pissed at me?"

I turned from Councilman Lynwood's speech about how an alpha member of each pack had scented the deer that morning before they'd set it loose and said, "Anthony."

"Wanted to stop by and wish you luck tonight," he said, hands stuffed aw-shucks style in the front pockets of his jeans. His gaze traveled down my body and left a trail of heat in its wake. My breath shuddered but I covered with a deeper breath, waiting for his eyes to come back to mine. Nudity wasn't normally an issue with werewolves, unless you wanted to have sex with the person and then we're men and women like everyone else.

"Thanks. Putting my name on the Gathering cup this year's gonna be sweet," I said, skillfully hiding the quiver in my voice.

Damn, those jeans hugged his muscled legs like indigo skin. Then again the tight T-shirt didn't leave much to the imagination either. And I had an excellent imagination. My belly fluttered, thoughts of shredding the black fabric off those hard pecs flashing through my brain.

"Oh, right. The alpha of the pack to take down the deer gets the honor. You'd be the first woman." His smile dimpled his cheeks. If I didn't know better I'd think he actually looked… proud.

"That's the plan." I swallowed, tasting his sweet-hay-and-all-male scent on the back of my tongue. The flavor sparked so many memories: my lips on his skin, his arms around me, his body deep inside mine. "You going out with your dad's pack?"

He shook his head then looked away, brows tight. "No. I, uh, I won't hunt with a pack I can't respect. I'm not a Purist and my dad can't accept it. So…"

Hope clogged my throat, made my stomach churn and flooded my sex with liquid heat. "That right?" I kept it cool.

He looked me in the eye, his voice smooth, sincere. "I told you that already. I'm not a Purist. Never have been. Last night, Mattie, that was me being crazy-out-of-my-mind in love with you. Nothing else. I didn't mean to hurt you and I sure as hell wouldn't have forced you. I swear it."

It was my turn to look away, to hide the blush I felt warm my face. "So you really cut bonds with your dad and his pack? You're a loner now?"

I glanced back and caught his nod. "Yep. Not all it's cracked up to be, though."

My smile flashed on reflex. "That right?"

"Yeah." He hiked his shoulders, hands still in his pockets. "Think I could hook up with you guys tonight?"

Muscles across my back tensed. "Why not just take my pack, if that's what you want? You could force me. If you're not a Purist you've got nothing to lose." *Except my respect.*

"Yeah, I could force your pack to follow me. I could force you to be my mate." He closed the distance between us, cupped my face. "But I'm asking. The decision is yours. Can I join your pack, Mattie? Will you have me?"

My stomach flopped and fluttered. It felt like I was riding a roller coaster. "You can't just join another pack. You—you have to be born in or mate in."

His hands slipped to the tops of my arms, fingers squeezing, pulling me close so my naked breasts brushed his chest. "Think you could help me out with that?"

Tingles raced over my skin, from the top of my head to the bottoms of my feet, anticipation, hope, and blind lust making me light-headed. God, it was such a risk. What if he was lying? If I just had some kind of proof, some way to know for sure.

"You can run with us, but I'm lead. If you take down the deer it's yours. I—I mean—the pack won't want the credit."

His gaze stayed fixed on my mouth, watching me speak, his lids low, making those sultry violet eyes all the more sexy. *Damn.* "Got it. So I'll follow. Act as your fifth."

"You'd follow me in a hunt? A woman?"

"I'd follow you anywhere, Mattie. *Because* you're a woman, the woman I love."

Someone sighed. "Aww…" It was my mom.

* * *

I led my pack to win the hunt, but not alone. In wolf form, under the strange power of a dark full moon, instinct took over and everything snapped into place. Like the teeth on a gear, Anthony and I, the members of my pack, all meshed together, worked as one. Like it was meant to be.

But the evening wasn't over. I had a decision to make. After all, no matter how much I wished it, a woman couldn't hold a pack on her own. Funny thing. I didn't really want to hold it on my own anymore.

We weren't the only ones to take a dip in the lake after the hunt. Anthony and I had swum out near a small island for privacy. He pulled me to him, coaxing my legs around his waist under the water, kissing my neck. His hot breath sent a shiver down my spine, a delicious contrast to the cool water hugging my body, lapping at my breasts.

His muscles tensed, his cock a hard line pressing against my ass, he rocked his hips to stroke himself against me. "I'm going out of my head here, Mattie. The Gathering's almost over. I want you. I want you now, and forever. Tell me I'm the one or put me out of my misery."

I turned my lips to his ear. "I want you…inside me."

Anthony's whole body shuddered around me as though my words had touch and weight. A blast of his exhaled breath bathed my neck and back. His arms tightened and he shifted, lifting me so his cock pressed against the sensitive lips of my sex. I floated down, my pussy opening over him, taking the thick round head of his cock inside my body.

My chest tightened, trapping my breath. Sex muscles fluttered, pulsed, tried to pull him deeper. I caught my bottom lip between my teeth to muffle a moan.

"I can't refuse you," he said, his hands slipping down to my ass, squeezing. "But is this all you want from me?"

His hands pressed as he rocked into me, driving his thick shaft through the tightness of my pussy. I cried out from the suddenness of it, from the thrust of sensation that exploded through me.

Yes. I wanted this, him, his body, his soul. I wanted Anthony as my mate. I knew it then; I'd known it since he'd asked to join us on the hunt. But I'd worried for so long, I'd allowed my fear to wall up my heart, to become a solid obstacle inside me. It weighed down on me, trapped the words in my throat like debris in a stream. I couldn't break through. I couldn't let go.

"Just...just fuck me." My voice came soft, breathy. I clung to him, my arms wrapped around his neck, my heart racing, need screaming through me to move, to ride him, to feel him slipping in and out of me.

"Damn it, Mattie, you're pushing me to the ragged edge," he said, his jaw clenching as he pulled out then rammed his cock deep.

The force of his thrust shook through my body, electric sparks flashing behind my eyes. Water splashed around us, wetting my shoulders, my face, sending waves rippling out in a fast-growing circle. Again and again his body stroked inside me, fit me perfectly, filled me up. Sweet friction sizzled along my skin, hummed through my veins, coiled low and tight in my belly. My sex muscles squeezed, milking his cock, begging for more. I held my breath, felt the climax rise, closer, closer.

And then he stopped.

"Is this all you want?" he asked again, his lips brushing my ear, his cock pulsing inside me.

"I'm so—I'm so close. Please…"

"First tell me. Is this all you want from me? A fuck? Or do you want more? Do you want what I want?" He nipped my ear and sent a quick jolt through my system that nearly undid me.

I gasped, my senses teetering at the edge of bliss. His sweet scent filled my nose, my lungs, his warm breath and hot body drowning me, penetrating deep inside me. My mind scrambled to understand.

I couldn't think. I could only feel. "I want…I want… Anthony!"

Suddenly I didn't have to think. The dam broke. Nature roared inside me, reached out from my soul like an invisible hand stretching to him. An offering. He took it, and with it went my body, tumbling over the edge. Sweet, sweet release.

I knew the moment, the instant, his soul linked with mine and our union was sealed. Life mates. One for the other, together as one. Forever and always.

Hot For It

JODI LYNN COPELAND

Carinna

VEGAS. THE CITY OF LIGHTS, LAUGHTER AND ILLICIT sex.

Tonight, when I craved each of those things almost more than my next breath, not a damned one of them was to be found.

The lights in the off-strip funeral home couldn't have been further from the clichéd glittering lights of Sin City. Already dimmed throughout my father's afternoon showing, with night fast falling and every other visitor gone, I'd had the funeral home director take the lights even lower, as if that somehow would make it easier to accept that my father was dead. That the heart-clogging meals he'd been ingesting for fifty-plus years had finally gotten the better of him.

Christ, how long had I been after his ass to give healthy eating a try?

Not long or hard enough, judging by the sickening pallor of his skin and that his final breath had been drawn two days ago. Approximately one hour after I could recall laughing for the last time. Laughter I'd shared with Jack Dempsey, my best friend. The bosom buddy who'd been by my side for over two decades.

The man who wrapped his arms around my waist now, pressing his strength against my back and reminding me that I wasn't alone but with a guy who knew exactly what I needed tonight.

"There's a bottle of Bombay Sapphire waiting for you in the passenger's seat of my truck." The words left his mouth as a whisper.

But the deep timbre of his voice could never be mistaken for a true whisper—Jack's voice was as solid as the rest of his big body. Perhaps from ten years of yelling to be heard over the chaos that ensued while fighting fires. Perhaps just because he was one damned fine-looking man—with thick, wavy black hair that matched his mustache and predatory blue-green eyes—and God had seen fit to gift him with a sexy-as-hell voice to match.

Whatever the case, he was offering what I wanted. A chance to drown the tension and sorrows I had amassed over the last two hellishly long days.

I turned in his arms, burying my face against the crook of his neck and inhaling his familiar masculine scent. Normally I had a serious loathing for letting my emotions show, even around Jack. Tonight, now, I just had to say "fuck it" to appearances and sniffle.

I went with the need for a few minutes, blubbering into his neck, probably ruining his best dress shirt. Then I sucked back my grief, accepted the shitty hand fate had dealt me—first my mother walking out years ago and now my father gone as well. At least I still had my grandmother, irrational as her aging mind could be at times.

At least I still had Jack.

I stepped back from his embrace to offer up an appreciative smile. "What would I do without you?"

His own smile flashed; a touch of the cockiness coming through which—along with our mutual take on relationships being for others—made us such compatible friends. "Get shit-faced drunk, hook up with an asshole, then wake up tomorrow wondering who the hell the guy in bed with you is and where the hell are you anyway?"

Yeah, it was a damned good thing I had Jack. Just like that he refilled my laughter well with his spot-on observation of my character. Not with bust-a-gut laughter, but laughter all the same; it rolled from my lips and felt like everything I needed right then.

Well, that, alcohol and an old friend to share it with.

Turning to my father's casket, my momentary amusement vanished with the roiling of my insides. I said a final goodbye, laying the last kiss I ever would upon his pasty cheek and shedding a few more of those unavoidable damned tears.

Then I turned back to Jack and nodded. "Take me home and get me smashed."

Jack

I'd been to Carinna's apartment thousands of times—hell, I even had my own key. But something about tonight was different. From the moment I stepped inside her small but cozily decorated living room, something had my gut tightening and every nerve in my body going on full alert the way only an all-alarm fire could typically accomplish.

I knew that something had to do with the weakness she'd let show back at the funeral home; those brief minutes when she'd cried and let me hold her. I knew that letting her more tender emotions show meant she was down and out in a way I'd never seen her before today, and for good reason. I also knew the last thing I should do was sit on the couch beside her and get hammered the way she was asking me to do.

We shared a healthy love of sex, and experience had taught me that mixing sorrow, alcohol and a member of the opposite gender generally led to precisely that. I valued our friendship way too much to risk ruining it over a hasty screw.

"C'mon, Jack," Carinna goaded me from the couch.

The bottle of gin I'd picked up on the way to the funeral home dangled from her fingertips, open now and several drinks shy of full. Those drinks seemed to be working their magic on her mood—all trace of vulnerability was gone from her gray eyes, the self-assured arrogance I knew and respected shining through.

A teasingly sultry smile lifted her lips. "Be a man and drink up."

Precisely the problem here was that I *was* a man. One who had long ago noted she was more than an average woman. With her centerfold curves and Latin coloring, she was stunning, gorgeous. Thoughts of her body, nude and sweaty and on the verge of orgasm, had been my masturbation material for years.

Those X-rated thoughts attempted to enter my mind and harden my body. I quashed them by grabbing the transparent blue bottle from her hand and crossing to the open kitchen. "Tonight's a martini night."

Much as she might prefer to get sloshed fast, I knew she wouldn't say no to martinis. They would still get her drunk, and possibly me as well, but with luck we would pass out before she forgot I was her best friend and I forgot I was a gentleman.

I almost laughed over the irony of that thought—I liked my

loving fast, hard and dirty, and for the time being, with no strings attached. I probably *would* have laughed if Carinna hadn't chosen that moment to start undressing.

First, the black slacks came down her long, toned, naturally golden brown legs and were kicked aside.

Then the black, short-sleeved silk shirt was unbuttoned and shaken off her shoulders and down her arms.

As a cocktail waitress for a tequila bar on the strip, she was required to wear a risqué uniform that exposed more of her stunning body than it covered. Still, that uniform concealed more than her miniscule black panties and matching bra.

Or not panties, I realized on an indrawn breath as she turned and bent to grab her slacks from the floor. A thong that disappeared between her firm butt cheeks, and had my heart pounding like a jackhammer and my cock rock solid in the space of a heartbeat.

Before I could disengage my brain from the vicinity of my balls and question her motive, she had her clothes in hand and was moving past me, down the short hallway that led to her bedroom. "I just want to relax and forget for a while," she tossed over a slim, bare shoulder. "That isn't going to happen dressed in this crap."

I grunted with the closing of Carinna's bedroom door, the sound sharp enough to make my erection jump. Then I considered beating my head against the overhead cupboard in the hopes of knocking some sense into it.

Shit, I was an idict. Make that an ass. She wanted to relax with an old friend, and all I could think about was plowing into her from behind and fucking her stupid.

While her emotions might be in turmoil, despite the confident, even teasing face she currently wore, I was damned glad her head was on straight. Much as I wanted to think I would be a good friend and turn down an offer of sex dealt at the hands of grief and gin, I honestly wasn't sure I could be that strong.

Carinna

With my bedroom door firmly closed, I sank down on the edge of the bed, pushed my hands through my tangle of curls, and accepted the throbbing ache in my core for what it was: the raw desire to fuck Jack.

The want came as no surprise, or was anything I could pin on alcohol—though the handful of drinks I'd downed before he'd confiscated the gin bottle did have my tension lessening and my belly buzzing with warmth. The truth was I'd had dreams of sleeping with Jack since I was old enough to appreciate the concept of fitting tab A into slot B.

Tonight was no dream, and I'd long since moved past giving juvenile names to body parts. What I wanted was to strip him naked, put my hands and mouth all over his work-hardened body, and take his cock into my dripping pussy again and again. I wanted to forget the events of the last two days completely. Forget how weak my father's death had left me, how emotionally drained and wrung out.

I wanted to feel whole, and I knew Jack could give that to me.

But would he?

Parading around in my underwear had definitely roused his interest—I'd seen the flicker of male awareness in his eyes. Had it roused the rest of him, as well?

Any other night and with any other man, I wouldn't be sitting on this bed wasting my time by wondering. I would be out in that kitchen, pushing him up against the table, taking his cock inside me and riding him hard. But tonight was no typical night and Jack was no ordinary man. With him I had to consider the repercussions. All those many reasons that had stopped me from giving voice to my desire for him in the past.

All those many reasons, and yet now I couldn't think of a single one.

Maybe the gin had gotten to me more than I realized, beyond relieving my tension and warming me through. Maybe it had stolen away my logic.

Whatever the case, I couldn't see the disadvantages of sleeping with Jack. I could only see the pleasure to be found in his strong arms. The relief, the release…

Everything I needed right now. And yes, I assured myself as the conceit I normally laid claim to slid mercifully back into place, everything I would give him.

Confidence and a dirty-girl smile as my guide, I tossed my pants and shirt into the hamper and headed back to the kitchen, hot for it and ready to let Jack know.

Jack

My body and mind coming under control with the knowledge Carinna didn't want anything more from me than a shoulder to lean on and a friend to reminisce about her father's life with, I focused on making the martinis. After adding too much gin and too damned little vermouth—had I honestly thought we would consume less alcohol this way?—I dropped a green olive in each glass. Reclining against the kitchen counter, I sipped at my drink and waited for her return.

She reappeared as the second swallow of martini hit the back of my mouth. Between her wickedly carnal smile and the discovery that she'd neither removed her sinfully tempting bra and skimpy thong, nor covered them, I nearly choked to death.

Liquid fire scorching its way down my throat, I eyed her over the rim of the glass.

First, her head full of untamable, rich brown curls that my fingers itched to bury in. Next, her toenails, painted the same shade of siren red as the Ladder 19 fire trucks. Then I sucked up my courage, told myself I could handle looking without touching, and sent my gaze upward to check out the parts of her I'd intentionally glossed over the first time around.

I counted my blessings that the cut of her thong wasn't as obviously erotic from this angle. The bra was a little harder to ignore.

Her ample breasts strained hard against the black lace cups, the top edge of her large, dusky areolas spilling out. The scent of her excitement on the air was just as damning to my state of mind and body. A feminine musk coupled with her light vanilla perfume had my tongue anxious as hell to find out exactly how wet she was by pushing aside the crotch of her thong and licking deep inside her folds.

With a seductive sway to her hips, Carinna joined me at the kitchen counter, her barely clothed body inches from mine. Heat emanated between us, animalistic, intense. Returning my cock to its stiff-as-stone condition and making me wonder how it had taken her father's death to bring us to this fated moment.

Were we fated to sleep together? And would it ruin our friendship or were we adult enough to share in a night of ecstasy and then return to the everyday?

Lifting her martini from the counter, she stopped short of placing the glass to her lips. She looked over at me. Desire smoldered in her eyes, turning them the color of smoke. "Jack?"

My shaft throbbed from the throatiness of her voice. Half fearing, half praying I knew what was coming next, I asked, "Yeah?"

"I'll race you to the bottom of the glass."

My laugh was rough, raspy, edged with the lust threatening to consume me. We'd been challenging each other in one way or another our whole lives. This should have been familiar terrain, easy to take on. But this challenge came spring-loaded with potentially shitty side effects.

Still, I accepted. "You're on."

I guzzled my drink, barely noticing the slow burn of gin this time as I watched Carinna down her own martini. Her throat worked in much the same way I could imagine it working as she took my cock between her lips and sucked me dry.

After a handful of seconds, she slammed her emptied glass onto the counter. Parting her lips, she revealed the olive between her teeth. Carinna edged her finger and thumb into her mouth, sensuously sucking off the olive as she pulled it free and dropped it back into her glass.

Her heated gaze fell to my lips and then far south, to the bulge of my groin pressing painfully against the zipper of my dress pants. "Can I suck off yours?"

Though I knew damned well it wasn't my olive she was after and she could undoubtedly tell that I knew it from my heightened breathing, I chose the path of feigned ignorance. Setting my drained glass on the counter next to hers, I nodded at the olive lying in its center. "Help yourself."

Or maybe it *was* my olive she was after. At least as a prop.

Lifting the martini-coated olive from my glass, she sucked it for a second or two. Then, holding it in her fingers, she trailed it downward, from her chin to her throat, to let it slip from her grasp and disappear into the hollow of her cleavage.

With the fringe of her long dark lashes half masking her eyes, her gaze met mine. Challenge simmered there. "Why don't you get it out?" she taunted huskily.

I swallowed hard as my blood sizzled and my cock pulsed. I'd never wanted anything more in my life. Still, that same question ate at my conscience.

Could we handle this? Then there was the alcohol to consider—was it skewing her judgment? "Carinna—"

"Jesus, Jack!" The challenging look gone, she devoured the inches between us, pressing the softness of her breasts against my chest as her fingernails curled into the front of my shirt. Her eyes pleaded with me to give in. "I need this. Can't you see that? Can't you see what this fucking day has done to me? It's wrecked me."

Knowing how much both the silent pleading and those words cost her, how could I say no? Knowing how many years I'd spent wishing for this very moment, how could I refrain from touching her a second longer? Even so, I had to lay voice to my concerns. "Doing this—sleeping together—will wreck our friendship."

Stubbornness narrowed her eyes. Her chin jutted out. "It won't. You know I'm not looking for love—ever—and you're too focused on your job to want a serious relationship anytime soon."

Solid points, logical even, which made it seem that liquor wasn't clouding her judgment and driving her need for me. Solid though they may be, those points weren't what swayed my decision. It was her stubborn, pointy chin. That haughty look I'd been a sucker for the better part of my life. That look, and the intimate push of her pelvis against mine

Through my dress pants and boxers, I shouldn't have been able to feel her heat and wetness. But my cock seemed to think it felt both and jerked hard in response. My mind was right there with my body, never wanting anything worse in its life. Never more ready to live out my fantasy of loving Carinna all night long.

Pulse pounding in my ears, I lifted my hands to her back. The smoothness of her skin was in complete contrast to my work-callused palms, a fact that I pleasured in as I ran my fingers down the sweep of her spine to cup her supple ass.

Aware that I'd crossed the point of no return, I shut out the last of my concerns and concentrated solely on ecstasy. On crashing my mouth down hard over hers, slipping my tongue past her lips, and tasting sweet, heady nirvana.

Sultry air puffed into my mouth with her muffled growl. A sound I mimicked as her tongue went wild, twining with mine, sliding feverishly along my teeth, not leaving a single part of my mouth untouched. Her hands moved just as urgently, jerking from between our bodies to yank my shirt from my pants and then travel beneath.

Shivers racked my body with the divine scrape of her fingernails along my back. Those shivers magnified as she pulled her mouth from mine and parted her kiss-swollen lips to demand, "The olive, Jack! Get the olive."

Carinna and I had been recounting our sex tales for years, and I knew exactly what her expectations were. She wanted to come at least twice before I found my own release. First, fast and hard, then slow and easy. My cock was too far gone with thoughts of finally surrendering to my hunger for her to deliver multiple orgasms all on its own. Fortunately, I also knew about her kinky side.

Using my grip on her ass, I lifted her up my body. The rub of her pubis against my solid staff pushed a needful groan from the back of my throat. Swallowing it down, I set her on the edge of the counter, with her bare inner thighs cradling my lower hips. I would have loved to have taken the time to bare all of her and then look my fill of her succulent body, but she wanted fast this first time and she was damned well going to get it.

I flicked my gaze to hers, saying what I didn't have the time to say with words—how unbelievably hot she was, how excruciatingly hard I was. Then I shoved my face against her breasts and used my tongue and teeth to fish the olive from her bra.

Biting down on the tender yet tart meat, I took the olive in my mouth while I used one hand to unclasp her bra and the other to find the gin bottle. The bra clasp gave way, the straps slipping partway down her arms and freeing her beautiful breasts from the cups. The olive left my mouth. Greedily, I brought my lips to one big nipple and sucked.

Carinna cried out as first I sucked her nipple tight and then retreated just a bit to roll the hard crown with my teeth. I nipped at the hypersensitive point, then bit down.

Her hips canted forward. Grasping the edge of the counter, she sighed out, "Oh God, Jack."

Oh God was right. The desperate throbbing of my shaft epitomized how long I'd wanted to hear those words, to hold her this way.

To take her over the edge.

Her thighs squeezed around my hips. Her hands moved into my hair, urging me to go faster, to deliver her to thought-fogging orgasm. Eagerly I obeyed, using my free hand to gather the sodden scrap of black material at her crotch and tug it aside to reveal her juicy opening. I dragged the damp silk back across her slit, burying it inside her folds a fraction, eliciting creamy juice from her pussy and a sexy-as-hell pant from her lips. Then, once more, I pulled the cotton aside and, bringing my other hand to her juncture, pressed the cool mouth of the gin bottle against her sex.

She gasped at the contact, her hips bucking hard. Her fingers tugged from my hair to claw at my shoulders. "Holy shit, yes! Fuck me with the bottle!"

The dirty words and the nip of her nails stoked through me, increasing the fireball of tension mounting in my lower back and drawing my balls painfully snug.

Holding firm to my control, I teased the bottle's head inside her folds a half inch. She spread her thighs wider and her labia parted, so open, so pink, so wet for me.

"Now!" she ordered. "Give it to me now!"

"Christ, I want to." The words sailed out of me like a curse. So damned badly I wanted to fill her pretty pussy up with my aching cock. Wanted to bring my mouth back tight to hers and never let up.

Instead I gave her the bottle, filling her engorged sex with gin while I pumped the short head inside her and ground the beveled edge against her clit.

Carinna's breathing turned ragged. Cream and liquor trickled in rivulets along her inner thighs. Her hips went from thrusting to slowly gyrating, and then she was gripping my shoulders hard and letting out a rapturous scream of release that I felt all the way to my balls.

My breathing coming in erratic fits and starts, I set the bottle aside, fitted my mouth to her opening, and gave in to my urge to sink my tongue deep inside.

My heart skipped a beat. My cock leapt.

Hell, yes. Like the woman herself, Carinna's taste was sweet, sexy and sinful all at once.

Savoring her salty juices underlain with the flavor of gin, I brushed my mustache across the pearl of her clit, while I used my tongue to take her ever higher.

Almost before the shock waves of her first orgasm were finished, a second climax began coursing through her. Her thighs tightened around my head, her nails sank into my shoulders, and her pussy delivered the sweetest of juices onto my tongue.

I licked at her come for long lazy seconds, relishing her taste and giving both our hearts a chance to slow. Then I grinned against her sex with the knowledge that the fast, hasty screwing was done and it was time for the slow, thorough loving of my fantasies to begin.

Carinna

How had we put off sleeping together for so long? And how would I ever move past Jack's mind-bending style of screwing come tomorrow?

They were the only thoughts I could manage in my post-orgasmic state.

Then I managed one more, as he lifted me off the counter,

wrapped my legs around his waist, and started down the hallway to my bedroom.

He wasn't done.

My pussy swelled with fresh excitement. My heart started back into a thunderous tempo. Each step he took was bitter-sweet torture as my sex rubbed against the hard ridge of his cock through his clothing. Finally he reached my bedroom, my bed.

Jack was many things, including graceful. But the way he lifted me off his body and tossed me back onto the bed was pure caveman.

I scuttled back against the headboard and faked a glare. "Big oaf."

His grin was pure arrogance. "You liked it."

"Loved it," I admitted, returning his grin.

He stepped back from the bed a foot and his fingers started in on the buttons of his dress shirt. With each new inch of skin that came into view, I remembered how much I loved Jack's body as well. I'd never seen him completely naked, but I'd seen him shirtless plenty and the developed muscles of his chest, arms and abs were the makings of every woman's fantasy. They were the reason those firefighter calendars sold so well. The reason my so recently satisfied clit was again tingling for relief.

The shirt came down his arms and then off. He didn't go right to work on his pants, and that was just wrong.

"Take it off!" I chanted strip-show style. "Take it off! Take it off!"

He laughed out loud. "Whatever happened to slow and easy the second time?"

"You can do me slow and easy—just get to the merchandise fast."

"Merchandise coming up." His arrogant smile fell into place, growing a little with each new piece of clothing he removed—probably because I was eyeing him like he was a human Popsicle and I wanted to lick, suck and nibble him from head to toe.

Then it was my turn for arrogance, as I latched onto the sight of his thick shaft bobbing toward me, pre-cum oozing generously from the plump head. "And you thought this was a bad idea," I said smugly.

His smile lost some of its confidence, but he only said, "Just call me dumb-ass."

"Dumb-ass. Speaking of asses, get yours over here, so I can smack it."

He moved, but not toward the bed. Rather, he took his cock in hand and slowly pumped. Veins corded in his hand and shaft in succession. His blue-green eyes turned predatory and knowing as they met mine. "You want to suck it, don't you?"

"That's the understatement of the century."

Laughter rumbled from his lips as I crawled to the end of the bed and rocked back on my haunches. I reached out an impatient hand and he came forward, just far enough to allow my fingers to join his.

Much as I ached with the need, I didn't touch his hard, steely flesh. I brought my fingers to his stomach instead, trailing them reverently along his lusciously defined abs, down the long, lean lines of his hips and around to his ass. I gave one taut cheek a swat. His breath drew in sharply and his stomach muscles tightened reflexively.

The rhythm of his fingers along his shaft slowed to near stopping. A drop of cum pearled at the tip of his cock. Another joined almost immediately. A glance up at his face revealed his features tight, his neck corded with delicious muscle. He was close to losing it. I was just as primed to come. I could take him into my mouth and bring him to a fast finish, knowing I would climax as well from that act of pleasure alone.

But I didn't believe in giving second-rate head, particularly to my best friend. And I was too far gone with anticipation to do the job any better.

I brought my hand back around and threaded my fingers through his black pubic hair, fondling the base of his cock and his scrotum before finally joining my hand with his. Together, we glided our fingers along his hard sex, gazes locked and our breathing steadily increasing with each pump, until a moan slipped from his lips.

I couldn't sit back and not taste a second longer.

Bringing my mouth to the tip of his cock, I intended to take a single lick of salty fluid. But his pre-cum tasted too damned good to not want more. I took more, a dozen more greedy licks that turned to ravenous sucks.

"Fuck, Carinna!" Jack's fingers pushed into my hair with his savage growl. "Keep that up and you won't need to worry about slow and easy."

From what I'd seen so far and had heard the many times we'd shared sex tales, I had faith he could get hard again fast if he came now. That made it damned tempting to forget about giving my best blow job ever and settle for my best one tonight. Only his hold on my mass of unmanageable curls stopped me from doing so.

His look was pure shock as I released his cock and sank back on my heels, so I explained, "My hair's the equivalent of a

Venus flytrap for fingers. Get them in too deep and you'll never see them again."

Back to grinning, he sank his fingers in even deeper and squatted far enough to brush my mouth with a far too gentle kiss. "I love your hair."

His tone, normally so deep and rough, was also too damned gentle. Anxiety attempted to rear its head over his tenderness, and I risked the pain of jerking my curls from his hands and scooted back up the bed.

With my back to the headboard, I wriggled out of my thong and spread my legs, centering all of his attention where it should be——on the need throbbing in my core and leaking out as cream from my pussy. "I love your body——"

"Race you to the first orgasm." His words cut me off as he dove onto the end of the bed and crawled up and over my body.

The wet tip of his shaft nudged my inner thigh, inches from my weeping sex, and I whimpered before pointing out, "You're a little late for that. And I thought we were going slow and easy?"

"I meant the first orgasm we give each other."

"Mmm…my kind of challenge." Licking my lips, I glanced down and took his erection in hand. "My kind of cock. Before I stick it in me, contracted syphilis lately?"

"You know I'm clean."

"Me, too. And protected. So let's get to the fucking."

Between the rearing of his hips and wickedly wolfish smile, I expected him to pull his shaft from my hand and thrust it inside me. I was partially right. He pulled it out of my hand. Then he brought his own hands to my waist and jerked me down the bed, until I fell back onto the mattress.

"You have a great ass." His voice was back to rough, raspy as he reverted to caveman. Jerking me over onto my hands and knees, he stroked his rough palm across my butt cheeks. "I owe you a swat."

"You wouldn't dare," I gasped, even as I waggled my butt and panted for that very thing.

"I would." He lifted his hand away. "And you'd love it."

I didn't bother to respond, just tightened my cheeks and waited to feel his swat. Waited while my sex throbbed, then leaked juices down my thighs in expectation of his touch.

It never came.

"What the hell are you doing, Jack?"

"Making you come," he said, sounding equally smug and amused.

"It's not working"

"Sure it is. Or is your pussy not aching for me to fill it up? Is your ass not tingling to feel my hand against it? Is your clit not on fire for release?"

Okay, so maybe it was working. Maybe he knew me too damned well that he could voice my body's desires with such clarity. Maybe taking this thing slow and easy was a damned bad idea. "Fuck me. I lose the race—just make me come already."

"Always so greedy." But he came over me, pressed the virile hardness of his chest to my back and brought his arms around mine.

Supporting his weight with his palms against the mattress, he surged his hips back and, in the next instant, shoved his cock gloriously deep inside me. I panted out a hard breath with the intensity of the rapid entry, and heard Jack do the same. Then his breathing became harsh in my ears as he set a reckless pace.

Speed and angle worked in tandem to bring my body screaming to the edge of orgasm in seconds. So fast. I'd always wanted
to come so fast with Jack.

I didn't think about what that meant—didn't even want to
consider it—just concentrated on making him climax equally
as fast with the pump of my ass against his balls and the squeeze
of my feminine muscles around his shaft.

"Slow down," he warned, his voice strung tight.

"No. You come first." I'd already thrown in the towel on our
challenge, but still I didn't want to come again before he did. I was
a greedy lover, but I didn't have to be *that* greedy, not with Jack.

"Not going to happen."

A husky laugh slipped from my lips at his cockiness. "How
do you plan to stop it from happening, Einstein?"

"Like this." One of his hands left the bed to move between
my legs and capture my clit between thumb and forefinger.

I knew with the first tug that he was right. I was going to
come first. When he altered from tugging to squeezing, I was
a goner. And then I was wrong once again. I didn't come first.

He came with me, impaling me as far as I could take him,
emptying his hot seed into my sheath. Shouting his climax as
loudly as I shouted my own while I erupted around his cock.

My orgasm was stronger than I'd ever experienced, string-
ing my body tight, flooding it with heat. Stealing all trace of
strength from my muscles. Leaving me feeling stripped raw,
open. Needy for Jack to support us both.

He did.

Like the best friend he'd been for over two decades, he was
my staying point, not letting me fall as I grappled to breathe
normally again. Even when I found my breath and my strength,

he stayed with me. Even as I attempted to get away from him by rolling to the other side of the bed, he followed me, burying his nose in my hair as he dragged my back tight up against his front and whispered so goddamned compassionately, "I wish I could bring your father back. I hate to see you hurting."

Already I was feeling so vulnerable, so raw, and he had to go and say *that?*

My tears from the funeral home resurfaced, stinging my eyes with salty water. I fought off the urge to sniffle, wanting to call him a thousand kinds of bastard for making me cry again. Instead, I managed a terse "You just helped me forget about his being gone. Don't be a jerk and ruin that."

Obviously, I didn't speak tersely enough to dissuade him. One of his hands came up to my cheek, urging me to look at him, to reveal what I'd tried to hide. I did so out of defiance, glaring past my blurred vision.

He didn't say a word. Didn't offer further sympathies. Just ran his mouth along my cheek, caressing with his lips. His tongue joined in, sliding out to capture my tears, licking them away. Licking his way to the corner of my mouth. Licking his way inside.

I shifted in his arms, and he turned me to face him fully. His kiss softened and his body hardened, and he gave me the slow and easy sex I'd always expected from my lovers in the past, and yet tonight, with Jack, I feared it.

I feared the way his tender handling tore at my emotions. I feared how much I loved the comfort of his big body. And I feared just how much this felt like honest-to-God lovemaking.

Shutting out my fears, I closed my eyes and allowed myself only to experience the pleasure. The feel of my best friend bringing me to climax for the fourth time tonight. The feel of him helping me to forget the pain of the last days. And the feel of his hot fluid coming into me as we surrendered to ecstasy.

Long after the sex ended, he held onto me, his softening shaft inside of me, his mouth nuzzling my ear. "Carinna—"

The emotion in that one word was as raw as my own, and I stopped him from saying more with the press of my lips against his. I rolled from him then, from his warmth and solidarity and comfort, to curl up beneath the sheet on the far side of the bed.

I willed him not to say anything more. Not to follow me across the bed and pull me back into his arms. He remained silent, still. I rewarded him for that, looking over and smiling appreciatively.

After a few seconds he smiled back, enough of the cocky edge in place to grant me hope that everything would be okay. That the tenderness of the last loving was truly nothing more than his trying to help me to move past thoughts of my father, to make me feel whole again. "Thanks for making tonight bearable, Jack."

His lips twitched a little, like his smile might falter, like that wasn't what his intention had been. But then he just said, "G'night, Carinna."

Jack

"Fuck." Sitting on the edge of Carinna's bed in the predawn hours, I buried my head in my hands and grunted the word a second time.

I'd seriously screwed up last night. Let her talk me into becoming her one-night lover with little more than a handful of words, a lone martini, and a scanty bra and silk thong.

Worse, though, far worse, I'd let myself sink into the fantasy of making love to her. I'd let my mind become as involved as my body. I'd let myself stop loving her as a lifelong friend and start loving her as the woman I wanted to wake up to for the rest of my life.

Hating myself for that weakness—not being strong enough to keep from giving my heart away when I knew damned well Carinna wanted nothing to do with relationships, and I wouldn't enter into one until my days of laying my life on the line for the sake of my job were over—I stood from the bed. Quickly I gathered my discarded clothes, refusing to remember the pleasure I had taken in removing them while she ravenously eyed my body. Refusing to think about the carnal bliss I had found first in her arms and then while sinking into her warm, wet, welcoming body.

Refusing to even look back at her, curled up and sound asleep on the far side of the bed, as I left her room.

I *had* screwed up, but I'd get over it. I'd get over this ache to take her back into my arms and never let go. I would forget that I loved her beyond friendship.

At least until I found another line of work. And then I would do everything in my power to convince her that she *was* the relationship kind, and it was me she wanted, forever.

Carinna

As if sleeping with him had somehow merged our thoughts, I knew the instant Jack rolled from the bed. I woke up in that moment, but I chose to keep my eyes closed. I could hear him moving almost soundlessly around my apartment—no doubt he'd taken his clothes into the living room and was dressing en route to the front door.

Don't go.

I wanted to shout the words. But I couldn't. Not just because there was a very good chance it was his pager that had pulled him from bed, notifying him he was needed at the firehouse, even though it was his day off. And not just because I was damned tired of acting so emotional and needy.

I kept my eyes closed and my mouth shut because both my mind and the repercussions of sleeping with Jack were suddenly crystal clear. It seemed we'd skated around those consequences. It seemed by his smile last night that, despite his warning a night of sex would ruin our friendship, I still had Jack as my friend.

If I asked him to stay, to crawl back into my bed and love me again in a way that tore at my every emotion, my every desire, it would be at the risk of him thinking I was after more than just one night.

I didn't want more. Couldn't want more. Not after all the two-timing sleazebags I'd encountered on a daily basis while cocktailing at the tequila bar. And not after hearing my father's firsthand accounts of the way commitment had ruined every one of his relationships and ultimately made my mother leave us.

I had just wanted this one night as lovers. And every day after this as friends.

I clung to those thoughts, and the smell of Jack on my sheets and skin, as I listened to my front door shut and the lock snick into place. And then I drifted back to sleep, for one night my mind free of sorrow and my body free of ache.

Tokyo Rendezvous

Jina Bacarr

I LAY ON MY BACK, MY HEAD RESTING ON A BLACK satin pillow shaped like an oversized boxing glove. Comfy, cozy. And naked. I took a deep breath and let it out slowly, spreading my legs and exposing the tender lips of my pussy, hot and moist.

"Let's get ready to rrrrrumble..." I said, twirling my *R*s like a professional ring announcer.

The nude man watching me grinned, then joined me on the bed, which was square-shaped like a boxing ring with ropes and stanchions. I reached back and grabbed onto the golden ropes surrounding the bed, parting my lips in anticipation and surrendering myself to the expertise of his bare hands.

They were everywhere at once, caressing and stroking me, sliding over my thighs, then gently untying the thin silk belt holding together my short red kimono. I tightened my stomach, taut muscles straining while I pulled on the golden cords. Tingling, gripped with a hunger for his touch, I pulled harder. He sensed my need and rubbed his palms against my hard nipples, sending me into a dizzying spiral, somewhere, everywhere. I loved the feeling. I wanted more.

"Ready for the next round?" he whispered, never letting up with his hands.

"Yes...*yes!*" I cried out.

Kissing, fondling, massaging all over my body, this was only the beginning of the game. A game that rocked my world and sent me to new heights of sights, sounds and smells, not to mention great sex.

It was called the *love hotel*.

I learned about the intimacy and excitement of the love hotel on an extended business trip to Japan. It was a typical can-the-Nikkei-go-any-higher day Americans working in the Land of the Rising Sun know all too well. After a long morning of "yen highs and dollar lows," Steve, a tall, ruggedly handsome American co-worker I'd met on my first day in Tokyo, suggested we go out to lunch.

Why not? I needed a break. Working for a big advertising company handling talent for Japanese commercials wasn't all glam. Did you see *Lost in Translation?* Then you know what I mean. I was the liaison between the actor who wouldn't-be-caught-dead-in-his-skivvies-on-American-TV-but-in-Japan-anything-goes and the Japanese director with the hard-on for every blond ingenue I sent his way.

Speaking of hard-ons...

I noticed Steve eyeing my rear when he thought I wasn't looking. I returned the favor. The man had a set of buns that made my sex-o-meter soar up higher than the Nikkei. Here was a man who knew women admired him, and understood all too well the raw lust in my eyes. I welcomed him being the object of my imaginings, and by the time he brushed up against my breasts and promptly uttered, "Excuse me," my body was yearning with the most delicious hunger, my pussy wet and ready, begging for satisfaction.

Arm in arm, we headed out to lunch, leaving the office behind. It had been a difficult morning; the Japanese director was upset because he hadn't been advised of a change in the shooting schedule to accommodate the lead actor's request to go deep-sea fishing in Thailand. His long, straight black hair flying around his face, his eyes blazing behind his dark glasses, he had ranted on for an hour, frightening the young OL or Office Lady who worked for me.

Enter Steve, calming him down and giving me pointers on how to deal with him. Standing close to me, his hot breath on my neck making me shiver with a pleasant tremor that extended down to my pink-polished toes, he had explained the director was behaving in a manner expected of him to save face, similar to the way Japanese workers scurried around the office, always in a hurry even if they weren't. Giving the appearance of urgency, he said, was an important tradition in a Japanese office.

Steve was a veteran adman, having lived in Japan for several years, and he knew how to handle the difficulties of the job. But what impressed me more was that he took the time to help me. I'd always considered what I did in my job an art—coordinating the production, being on location during the shoot, then following through with postproduction. Steve helped me take it one step further by showing me how to break down the barriers I'd faced since coming to Japan. I respected him, but I was also wildly attracted to him. Did he feel the same way about me? Although he was *gaijin,* foreigner, as I was, he followed the ways of the Japanese. Taking his time, not acting on impulse, conferring with the team before making a decision. Did he also follow their ways in the art of love?

Was he unattainable?

I was determined to find out.

Light perspiration dampened my white, sheer silk blouse and a sweet smell wafted up from between my legs. I took a sniff and a scent of another kind made my heart beat faster. A pleasant musky smell, the scent of a man, so unlike the rose menthol odor all the rage among the men in my Tokyo office. It came from a gum that made them smell like roses after they chewed it. Seemed Japanese women preferred men who smelled like an indoor flower garden. I, on the other hand, favored raw male pheromones to rev up my libido. And Steve's did the job to the max.

He sensed my hunger and smiled. "You smell good," he said, taking a whiff of my hair.

"So do you."

He grinned, then gave a playful tug on my long strands. "We'll continue this discussion at lunch, if you're game."

"I am. By the way," I said, baiting him with a verbal hook, "I've noticed the Japanese are great game players." I referred to their obsession with video games and *pachinko,* a noisy pinball game. I pushed out my breasts, then wet my lips with my tongue. "I'm curious to find out what kind of player you are."

"Don't worry," he teased. "You will."

I smiled, aware that the mere suggestion of becoming intimate with him ignited a flicker of pleasure low in my belly.

Once outside in the cool air, I tried to quell the slow fire building within me, but the closeness of Steve's body pressed up against mine made my temperature rise. We stood huddled together under my umbrella to keep out of the rain. A soft, steady, dewy rain that rolled off my umbrella and fell at my feet like silky, liquid petals.

The rain didn't stop the Japanese from crowding the streets, I noticed, though it wasn't all salarymen and OLs rushing out for a quick lunch. I saw Goth girls in their black garb vamping through rain puddles with their huge black and white polka-dotted umbrellas, as well as tough-looking guys with auburn-dyed hair wearing square-toed boots and long black jackets that extended down over their hips. I drew in my breath when I observed a beautiful woman in a mauve kimono with delicate white blossoms embroidered on her *obi* or sash, text messaging on her cell phone as she got into a limo. *A geisha?* I wondered. Her presence reminded me I was living in a land of make-believe, where nothing was what it seemed.

Though I found Tokyo intoxicating, it made my head spin as I tried to traverse my way through a world so foreign, a world where anything goes: from pulsing neon lights everywhere to heated toilet seats to the vivid colors of Kabuki and men playing women's roles.

I also had to deal with Japanese co-workers who nodded their heads and said, "*Hai,* yes," when what they really meant was, "I understand." A polite way of saying "no." Showing what they called *tatemae,* face, instead of *honne,* their real feelings. The Japanese have a saying, "Face is more powerful than money." To the Japanese, yes. For me, trying to live and work in a culture I didn't understand was making me lonely.

Very lonely.

And Steve was just the magic pill I needed. I could already

taste him on my tongue. Hot and salty. I imagined my lips and tongue working along his shaft, sucking on him, around the head, my tongue diving into the little hole on top, before bringing him to a climax as pleasure overtook him. My daydream made me hot and wet, but it wasn't enough. I wanted more. I wanted Steve.

I hungered for his strong body and firm touch, his arms holding me, his cock driving again and again into my tight pussy. I'd been too long without sex, busy with twelve-hour days casting actors, consulting with legal regarding the contracts, getting the proper filming permits, checking with post to make sure they'd have the spot sweetened with music in time to give to the client on the pre-arranged date. Hectic, exhausting work with no time for play. A lunch date was exactly what I needed to rev up my energy.

Tired and wet, we sat down on stools in a tiny shop and ordered a typical Japanese lunch of soba noodles. While we ate the noodles with chopsticks, I made every attempt to keep my mind on business as we discussed tomorrow's shooting schedule for a *genki,* energy drink, commercial. When I asked Steve his opinion about the location of the shoot, he smiled.

"The Tsukiji fish market is my favorite place in Tokyo," he said, slurping his soup, his tongue darting in and out of his mouth. "Slick, wet, and it smells of the sea."

Smiling, I nodded. The sexual innuendo of his answer wasn't lost on me. Open at 5:00 a.m., the famous fish market was abuzz with flatbed carts zooming from one end to the other with their wayward drivers shouting everyone out of the way as they skidded across floors slippery with chunks of ice. Meanwhile, sharp-eyed restaurateurs elbowed each other through the narrow walkways lined with fresh seafood, vying for the best pick. A colorful place to showcase the product.

"Ever find a mermaid among the bluefin tuna?" I asked, referring to the local fish used in sashimi.

He grinned. I loved his smile. "Not yet. But there's always a first time." Then he was all business, sketching the layout of the market on his napkin and showing me how his Japanese crew would set up the shot. "We'll sit the pretty model in a rickshaw carting a three-hundred-pound tuna, then shoot the actor sipping the energy drink as he pulls the two-wheeled conveyance."

"Sitting on *top* of the tuna?" I asked, studying Steve's drawing showing the rickshaw hooked up to a truck off camera to give the illusion the actor pumped with caffeine and vitamins was pulling it.

"You'd rather be on the bottom?" he asked.

"No, I mean, I…she…" I said, stuttering. A flush of heat came over me, a sensation that made me feel awkward, knowing he could probably read my sexy thoughts. He knew we'd hired a popular Asian actress to do the spot with the American actor, but I didn't mind him teasing me. In fact, I rather liked it. Recovering my composure, I said, "That sounds perfect."

"Yes, perfect." I looked up at his absent tone. His eyes were riveted on the pointy outline of my nipples molded against the transparency of my rain-soaked, white blouse. The look on his face made me shake with excitement. His comment restored my confidence and made me daring.

So, he wanted to play.

With a naughty twinkle in my eye, I picked up a noodle with

my chopsticks and dropped it between my breasts. His eyes never leaving mine, Steve picked up the noodle with the tip of his chopsticks and ate it. I wiped the perspiration from my bottom lip. The soup was hot, but I was hotter.

"Do you always take what you want?" I asked.

"Always. Though I also enjoy following the customs of Yoshiwara when I want to impress a woman."

"Yoshiwara?" I repeated, trying to grab another noodle with my chopsticks. "What's that?"

"The old pleasure quarters." Steve explained that prostitution had been legal in Japan until the 1950s. "The ladies who inhabited the brothel had a hierarchy, a caste system," he continued, "where the most expensive courtesan had the luxury of choosing whether or not she wished to entertain a customer."

"Even if he was paying?" I splashed my chopsticks around in my soup. Damn, all the noodles were too short for an encore performance.

"Yes," Steve said, noting my flailing chopsticks splattering broth down my cleavage. Was that a twinkle in his eye I saw, as if he enjoyed my frustration? "A man had to impress her with his style. He made many visits to the brothel, and even then he couldn't be sure he would make love to her."

"What did they do during these visits?" I had to ask.

"He'd drink with her or give her poems. If he was successful in his quest, he'd share a pipe with her."

From the corner of my eye I saw him squeeze his wooden chopsticks so hard he broke them in two. I lowered my eyes and chewed on the end of my thumb before asking in a low voice I hoped was dark and husky, "What kind of pipe?"

"Long and hard," he said without missing a beat.

"Mmm..." I licked my lips. My eyes never leaving his, I imprinted my pink lipstick on my napkin then set it down beside him. Grinning, he poked his chopstick through my paper lips then simulated pushing it in and out of my mouth.

I choked, anticipation making me breathe harder. "What happened next?"

"The courtesan disrobed behind a screen, removing her kimono, her numerous undergarments, and her sash—cords snapping, silk rustling—driving the man crazy with erotic sounds as her garments came off, one at a time."

"Sounds intriguing," I said, choosing my next words with care. "Like the sound of a zipper going down in the dark."

He smiled, but not before scanning my blouse and skirt.

Looking for zippers? my eyes asked him.

He matched my stare, his dark eyes challenging me. I lowered my gaze. I wasn't ready to let him know how much I wanted him. Not yet.

I slurped up the last of the juicy noodle soup as I'd seen my co-workers do, then I was careful to arrange the chopsticks across the bowl in the proper manner to avoid offending the shop owner. Smiling, Steve complimented me on my ability to pick up Japanese traditions so quickly.

"I love Japan," I said, "and everything about it. The cherry blossoms, the temples, the geisha—"

"Did you know geisha don't wear panties?" he asked.

I stared at him, but said nothing. I wasn't about to ask him how *he* knew what geisha wore under their kimonos, but that didn't stop him from slipping his hand under the counter and running his fingers up and down the inside of my thigh. Was he wondering if *I* wore panties? I'd heard about the *no-pan kissa,* bottomless coffee shops, popular in Japan but I hadn't seen them. I let out a soft moan as he stroked my skin, then tugged on my panties as I hoped he would, though he didn't push his fingers underneath my cotton crotch. I sighed, wishing I had gone commando.

I stared glumly at the empty soup bowl. What was I going to do? Have sex with him under the table? Yet it wasn't just sex I wanted, but something more. He exuded competence and trustworthiness, something I'd noticed was also characteristic of Japanese workers, something I admired. I felt such a closeness to him. Maybe it was the romance of the rain, the pleasant odors of steaming soup, the fatigue of overwork, even that feeling of camaraderie that overtakes you when you're far away from home and you meet a fellow countryman. Whatever it was, his touch was magic. And I wanted him.

But it wasn't possible. Not when we had such an important shoot tomorrow morning. No doubt I'd be working in the office until at least midnight, then I had an early morning call. No time for a date, even if he asked me. Or as I'd heard the Japanese say many times during a meeting when they didn't want to agree with you, "That would be difficult...."

Yearning to let go, my whole body screaming for him, I was grateful when Steve removed his hand from under my skirt and changed the subject. We discussed the shoot tomorrow and how he had talked the energy drink client into going beyond pairing up the Japander, what we called well-known foreign actors who did commercials in Japan, with cartoon characters. The beautiful Chinese actress would be a welcome change, compared to the talking ham the actor had shared a bed with in the last spot.

"Speaking of bed," Steve said, again turning on that twinkle in his eye I was beginning to know so well. "We could move our afternoon meeting from the boardroom into the bedroom," he suggested, squeezing my leg.

"What did you say?" I asked, squirming in my seat, aching for him to slide his hand back up my thigh and push his fingers under my panties. He didn't, frustrating me more.

"We could go to a hotel." Straight face, no snickering, though I noticed his dark eyes crawling slowly over me.

I couldn't stop looking at him, though my emotions, *no, dammit,* my raging libido made me too unsettled to speak. Was he crazy? We couldn't go to my hotel—I shared a room with another girl from the office—and he bunked in the company-paid bachelors' dormitory. No women allowed past the welcome mat.

"The only cheap hotels in Tokyo are capsule hotels," I said, casting him a questioning glance. Overnight plastic cubicles stacked on top of each other. Men only, as a rule, *sans* tattoos to dissuade the local *yakuza,* mobsters, from using their facilities.

What about tattooed Westerners? I wondered, rocking my buttocks back and forth on the hard wooden bench as if to rub off the *fleur-de-lis* tattoo on my left buttock. I'd taken the plunge on my last trip to Hong Kong and visited a tattoo parlor. I giggled, curious how Steve would react if he saw it. The capsule hotels were completely private, but so small you could only lie on your back. Interesting, but too confining for what I had in mind. I'd been eyeing the brown-ribbed cowhide belt Steve wore around his trim waist, and couldn't stop imagining the kiss of leather on my bare ass. I wasn't into S and M, but too many late nights watching Japanese game shows featuring playful bondage and half-naked men wielding black latex whips had made me curious. If not horny.

Seeing my turned-on expression, he laughed. "C'mon, I'm going to show you the Japan most tourists never see." He grabbed my hand, pulled me out of the noodle shop and across the street to his parked car, talking as we went. "We're going up the hill to a *rabuho.*"

"Did you say rabbit hole?" I asked. "As in Alice peering through the looking glass?" I bounced that off my list of well-known Tokyo watering holes and came up empty. What manga fantasy was he into? The only rabbit I was on a first-name basis with had a rotating shaft with plastic pearls inside that made a snap-crackle-and-pop sound when I used it. Attached to the shaft was a little bunny, whose ears flicked and vibrated my clit with orgiastic delight.

"No, that's Japanese for love hotel."

"Love hotel?"

"Yes, though they're often called boutique or fashion hotels. Back in the days of old Japan, they were called *deai chaya,* tea houses, where lovers went for a tryst."

Steve explained how short-term hotels for privacy and sexual pleasure were later known as *tsurekomi yado,* rendezvous hotels. The love hotels so popular today developed out of the curfew rule back in the 1960s, he told me, which barred women in men's hotel rooms after 9:00 p.m. It was a common practice for a business-man to meet a bar hostess and take her to a Western-style hotel.

"What happened at nine o'clock?" I asked, envisioning a quickie, Japanese style.

"The businessman became embarrassed when he was subjected to the gaze and smirks of the desk clerks and other couples who knew why they were there. So he had to find an alternative to satisfy his sexual urges—*and* keep his secret." He grinned, his sexy smile promising an equally sexy answer. "And the love hotel was born."

No reservation needed, Steve explained. Popular with singles as well as married couples, love hotels were open twenty-four hours a day: lunchtime, after work, before a late movie, anytime you and your partner were in the mood for a few hours of fantasy and sexual thrills.

I jumped into his car, fascinated by his knowledge of this unique Japanese phenomenon. I'd heard Japan was a sexual supermarket, but I never thought I'd have the opportunity to explore it firsthand.

We drove to the other side of town near the railroad station, cruising into a seedier part of the city, a neighborhood of small wooden houses and closed backyard gardens. I wondered why he'd brought me here until I saw the word *Hotel* lit up in blue neon with blinking red and green stars. Perched like a beacon atop a high-walled cement building, it looked more like a prison cell block than a pleasure palace. An uncomfortable wetness made me rub my thighs together. What had I gotten myself into?

"Most love hotels are identified only by a simple sign," he said, reading my mind as our car sped down into the underground parking garage. "Although some love hotels, like the famous one in Yokohama shaped like the Queen Mary, boast outlandish landmarks."

"Don't people object to having a love hotel in their neighborhood?" I noted the number of cars in the garage. More than

I would have guessed for a rainy afternoon. On closer inspection, I was surprised to see the license plates had been covered up to protect the owners and their guests from prying eyes.

"Love hotels outside the city are often shaped like castles or spaceships," Steve said, "but in the city exteriors are understated to fit in with the surrounding shops and houses."

With a resounding echo the steel door slammed shut behind us. I shivered. The anticipation of spending the afternoon with Steve made me flush with excitement, though I was torn between guilt, apprehension and curiosity.

"What now, James Bond?" I asked, getting out of the car and looking around. I half expected to see Japanese co-workers racing from their cars into the hotel to avoid being seen. Instead, I saw no one. We were alone. I didn't find out until later we were being watched on video cameras and no one else would be admitted through the gate until we were inside the hotel and out of sight.

"Your elevator awaits you," Steve said.

I grinned. "Then what are we waiting for?"

My attention was on the handsome man standing beside me in the tiny elevator pulsing with flashing lights, but I was having difficulty treating this like a regular afternoon meeting. The warmth of Steve's body next to mine created a giddiness I hadn't felt since I mislaid my bikini panties in the back of a limo at the senior prom. I struggled not to become lost in my anticipation of what lay ahead.

"I've heard Tokyo boasts more than four thousand love hotels," Steve said, bringing my mind, but not my hormones, back down to earth. "They're so popular on Saturday nights and weekday afternoons they're called *gokiburi hoihoi*."

No translation needed. I knew what that meant: cockroaches in a box, something *gaijin* learn quickly about in a land infested with the ubiquitous creatures.

Then where is everybody? I wondered, my eyes darting left and right, my mind working overtime as we walked through the bright pink hotel lobby. If you could call it a lobby. No doorman, unless you counted a gilt copy of the Venus de Milo winking at us. Not even a front desk. Just a closed cubicle with a mail slot in it.

We stopped in front of a large display board with checkerboard squares showcasing backlit photos, each depicting a Disneyesque fantasy, with the dark squares denoting rooms already occupied. Mickey does Minnie any way you like it, I imagined. Old West, Hello Kitty playroom, French bordello, hot-air balloon, boxing ring, spaceship, medieval torture chamber, harem, race car, jungle, even a room with a heated swimming pool.

And the beds. Revolving, vibrating, massaging, tanning, water. Filled with Evan, I hoped. Shaped like hearts, pineapples, jet planes, spaceships, even a 1959 Cadillac, complete with chrome fins and taillights.

Two prices were listed under each room. The cost for the average length of stay, half a day, was around $200. Double for overnight. Unlike hotels back in the States, we weren't asked for a credit card on check-in, but I found out later some love hotels have yen meters to keep you informed of how much all this pleasure is costing you.

"What's your fantasy?" Steve asked, squeezing my hand.

"You mean like the image clubs?" I'd read about the upscale clubs where Japanese businessmen engaged in sexual fantasy role-playing.

"No, this is better," he said. I detected a challenge in his voice. "Here you know your fantasy will come true."

Our eyes met and he attempted a smile, allowing me to choose the room, but he didn't fool me. His jaw was clenched, his eyes dark and serious, like storm clouds rumbling, eager to shake free their heaviness. He was counting the minutes—or was it the seconds?—until I made my choice. I knew without a doubt it didn't matter what my fantasy was, he intended to make sure we had a good time. Unlike most men I'd met on business trips, Steve recognized my feeling of isolation and had gone out of his way to help me, translating documents and encouraging me not to be hesitant in dealing with Japanese clients.

Breathing hard on the back of my neck, Steve again reached down and slid his hand up and down my thigh. I didn't resist. Why should I? We were alone. No one could see us. His hand slipped under my skirt, but I didn't move away as he tugged at my panties, this time inserting his fingers inside me. I pretended not to notice, though I was aroused and couldn't help but let out a soft groan when he found my hard bud and stroked it back and forth in a slow but steady rhythm.

I didn't speak. Instead I moved my hips in time to the silent beat we both heard in our heads. I enjoyed the pleasure he gave me with his fingers and I didn't want him to stop, but I had to choose a room. Fast, before I lost control here in the lobby.

I tapped my finger against my lips, thinking. I always wanted to play Annie Oakley, and popping off Steve's hot pistol sounded interesting, but since he was an avid boxing fan I opted for the knockout.

"Put on your gloves," I challenged him, pointing to the boxing ring photo, "and we'll spar a few rounds."

"You got it, babe."

Removing his fingers wet with my juices, he didn't wipe them off but let the sweet smell drift between us like magic mist. Breathing in my own scent with Steve watching me was a total turn-on. I couldn't stand still, shifting my weight from one foot to the other while he pushed the button under the photo and a key popped out into the tray below. I expected a bag of potato chips and a chocolate bar to follow.

Giggling like two teenagers ditching school, we followed the miniature lights on the floor that lit up to guide us like a yellow brick road through the darkened hallway to our room. I asked Steve if they checked IDs.

"If you're old enough to pay," he quoted a local saying, "you're old enough to play."

Play was an understatement. I was astounded at the room, furnished with every conceivable toy and designed solely for sexual pleasure. Besides the lavish bed decorated in red, black, and white satin like a boxing ring, I counted mirrors everywhere, a forty-two-inch plasma TV stocked with porn DVDs, a camera and equipment to make your own videos for instant replay, a karaoke machine, and a refrigerator stocked with coffee, green tea, beer, and Bang cola. Erotic pictures of naked women with their genital areas covered hung on the wall. Nearby stood a vending machine stocked with condoms in neon rainbow colors, dildos, French ticklers, and a string of pearls known as anal love beads.

And an open bathroom.

No door.

I was surprised to discover the love hotel steeped in privacy everywhere except in the room itself. I thought this strange, since the whole concept of the love hotel grew out of the lack of privacy in the typical Japanese house. Imagine, only thin *shoji* or paper walls separating you from your in-laws in the next room.

I turned and looked at Steve, his breath fast and shallow, perspiration beading his brow, and his teeth clamped together with the effort of waiting for me to undress. I smiled at him. My spirits were too high and the bulge in his pants too big to spend time contemplating Japanese architecture.

I kicked off my shoes and started to unbutton my blouse.

Steve shook his head. "Uh-uh."

"You want to watch a DVD first?" I asked, disappointed. I was hot and didn't need any prelims to get me started.

"A Japanese girl waits for the boy to undress her," Steve said, unbuttoning my blouse and sliding my slim skirt down over my thighs. I stood there, mesmerized. What was wrong with the lighting? It changed colors every time we spoke, from blue to orange to yellow to purple. Before I could adjust my eyes to the sound-sensitive lighting, dimming and changing color at the command of his raw, sexy voice, he unhooked my bra, then pulled down my panties. He grinned when he noticed the tattoo on my left cheek. He slapped my butt and I moaned, enjoying the pleasant sting of his palm on my hot flesh. He said, "I like the way it wiggles."

"My butt or the tattoo?"

"Both."

I looked straight into his eyes and asked, "Now that you've shown me what the boy does, what does the girl do?"

"She lets him know what she wants by her actions."

"Like this?"

I sashayed over to the black marble Jacuzzi, tossing my hair over my shoulder and letting it ripple down my naked back. I knew Steve was watching me as I turned on the jets. I wiggled my big toe in the gurgling water, then sat down on the edge of the tub. He joined me and was soon busy soaping up a sweet, redolent lather. He rubbed the green foamy stuff all over my body, around my breasts, down to my stomach, and between my thighs.

Waves of pleasure rushed over me, his touch arousing me. I groaned. The smell of the exotic soap was almost overpowering, along with his hands sliding all over my body. My skin tingled, my muscles relaxed, my pussy throbbed. I began to writhe under his expert touch then shivered when his fingers slid in and out of me, exploring the depths of my body, making me groan louder when I let myself go and my pussy tightened around his fingers, drawing him deeper into me.

"Think of this as your own private soapland," he said, removing his fingers, then, using his muscular chest as a washcloth, rubbing, sliding, and stimulating my nipples with his rhythmic up-and-down movements.

"Isn't that just for men?" I asked, trying to regain my composure. The Turkish-style baths included young women using their bodies as a sponge to help the customer reach orgasm.

"Not anymore," he said. "I've heard the soapland service for women includes biting their toes."

"Lucky you," I said, lifting up my pink-polished toes and resting my feet against his chest. "I just had a pedicure."

He laughed, then sucked on my toes, licking all around them and tickling more than my fancy. So titillating was his tongue, I couldn't fight the tingling sensation rushing up my ankles, my calves, my thighs, all the way up to my pussy. Laughing, I begged him to stop, then before he could grab me, I eased my body into the tub. He followed.

We splashed each other, laughing, then sank down into the hot, steamy water with only our chins showing, and soaked. I closed my eyes and the fragrance of ginger and sandalwood filled my head. Sitting in the hot water, my mind drifting, I felt the probing touch of Steve's hands pushing my legs apart and sliding his fingers into me again. Twisting, stroking, he took me on a sensation-filled journey. The pleasure was so intense, I cried out with joy.

Before I could catch my breath, I felt my whole body being lifted up out of the water. Steve held me in his powerful arms in midair, then sat me down gently on top of soft, fluffy white towels. Water dripped from my heaving breasts and the inside of my thighs were slippery. He dried me off with a towel, taking his time and chafing my nipples with the looped cotton until they peaked hard and brown. Then he rubbed me all over with the towel, his hands massaging and stroking my shoulders, my hips, the insides of my thighs. His touch made me shiver and I didn't protest when he wrapped me up in a short, red silk kimono. The slippery fabric hugged my curves and its soft touch radiated over my body like a thousand fingertips in constant motion.

Eyes closed, my body warm and comfy, I relaxed. His hot skin brushed against my bare legs when he lay down beside me, his hard chest smashing my breasts as he turned my face toward him and kissed me. I could feel his teeth through his lips, then his mouth opened and his tongue darted inside mine, tasting, exploring, depriving me of air with his passion until I couldn't breathe. I opened my eyes and seeing me gasping, he slowed down, his lips touching mine with a gentle kiss, whispering to me that the Japanese considered kissing to be foreplay to sex.

I wasn't fooled. Steve was telling me in that indirect way I was beginning to know so well what was coming next.

After slipping on a neon blue condom, he parted my legs and slid into me, pumping his cock into my pussy. The hot steam surrounding us blurred our images, but I could feel his long, hard thrusts sending me into an orgasmic spiral that felt never-ending. Deeper and deeper he pushed into me until I thought I couldn't take it any longer; I was so close to crashing in a shuddering orgasm, my cries mingling with his loud grunts. Then he pulled out and it was more than I could bear. Desperate for him, I arched my back, pushing my hips upward and gyrating like a tigress clawing at a fiery dragon.

"Steve…" I whispered, reaching out to pull him into my arms. "Is something wrong?"

"I have a surprise for you," he said, moving our lovemaking to the bed where I discovered the real erotic Far East. He produced two metal balls, shiny and heavy. *Where did he get them?* I wondered, but I didn't ask. I was more curious about what he was going to do with them.

"Japanese women have been using *rin no tama* for hundreds of years," he said, inserting the two metal balls into me. I swayed my body back and forth, the balls producing gentle and persistent vibrations as they knocked together, sending a range of sensations throughout my body every time I moved. It was a pleasurable feeling, and I giggled every time the balls clicked together.

Then he entered me again. Gently rocking back and forth,

he gyrated his lower body with interesting twists and turns in perfect timing with the clicking sound of the ben-wa balls inside me. I could see his eyes light up with excitement when the tip of his penis touched the metal balls. But he was holding back, waiting for me.

He didn't have long to wait. I cried out with such passion the voice-sensitive room lighting glowed a fiery red. I shuddered over and over again, still the force of Steve's impending climax threatened to overtake mine, so powerful he was, snorting and bucking like a wild man. He filled me up, pushing into me, hips shaking. My sugar walls vibrated with pleasure, both from his thrusting cock and the metal balls hitting each other. I thrashed about, my body trembling, my legs shaking, as the spasms peaked again and again, his thrusts driving me mad until his body jolted and he let go with a final shudder before he went limp.

Our passion spent, we muttered a few subdued moans and the room lighting mellowed to a soft blue. Showering me with kisses on my cheeks, my nose, my lips, my breasts, Steve collapsed next to me, his breathing ragged, but with a smile on his face. He reached over and cradled me in his arms. I squeezed his hand and sighed. Time to go back to the office.

We slipped the money through the slot in the cubicle in the lobby but we never saw anyone, although I heard the soft shuffle of feet as we left. Probably the maid preparing the room for the next customers.

It was still raining when we left the love hotel, our car streaking out onto the sleek, wet streets. The blue neon sign blinked at us as if to say, "Come back again."

We did. Many times. So many we won a trip to a famous

Tokyo theme park by staying in all the rooms of the hotel within a six-month period. It wasn't difficult. Steve and I worked together many hours in the love hotel, coming up with ideas for goofy ad campaigns in spite of the shrinking budgets of Japanese advertising agencies. Snuggled up in our vibrating pineapple bed or our bondage dungeon or our rocket ship with smoke that came out of one end when we rocked the bed hard during lovemaking, we orchestrated some of the best commercials on Japanese television.

I'll never forget my time in Tokyo. And I'll never forget Steve. My samurai in the bedroom.

When I returned to the States, I brought back several souvenirs, but the ones everyone asks me about are the intriguing paperweights sitting on my desk: two metal balls the size of quail eggs.

I don't have to say a word.

I just smile.

Postscript: *I just got a call on my cell. Guess who landed at LAX ten minutes ago? Steve. He's here in L.A. to do a job for the agency.*

I grab the metal balls off my desk and rush out to the parking lot. I'm leaving the office early to pick him up and take him back to my place. My bed doesn't vibrate or revolve or have smoke coming out of it, but I don't think he'll mind.

Do you?

The Well-Tutored Lover

ALICE GAINES

CHAPTER ONE

EVERY WOMAN REMEMBERS EXACTLY WHEN SHE lost her maidenhead, but how many can recall the moment when they first lost their heart? For me, it happened on a sunny afternoon in June of 1886. The man appeared at the doorway of my private conservatory as though the earth had conjured him out of the same riot of fertility that produced the swelling fruits on my squashes.

Although the cut and fabric of his clothing spoke of wealth, his features had a coarseness one usually associated with the working classes. The line of his jaw——rather too square to be considered aristocratic——seemed especially out of place against the stiffness of his collar.

His size alone would have made him stand out in any gathering. With his broad shoulders, powerful chest and long legs, he nearly filled the doorway. And yet, tousled blond hair and brown eyes that held a hint of laughter softened him. Indeed, he made an impressive display with the late spring sun beating down on him.

He nodded his head in greeting. "Your Grace."

I set aside the cattleya I'd been repotting. "If you want to see me, please call at the front door and provide your card to my butler."

"The usual way to do things." He smiled. "Would that get your interest?"

"Most likely not." In fact, I often ignored overtures like that. Most people who sought me out did so out of curiosity or in search of fuel for the gossip about the notorious dowager duchess. Life in the country could get dreadfully dull, even with the usual round of house parties. A few tidbits about that strumpet—what had possessed the Duke of Millford to marry such a woman, anyway?—could help to pass the long evenings.

"I'm right then?" he asked.

"I'm sorry?"

"You wouldn't have seen me if I'd sent in my card."

"I don't think I'll see you now," I said. "You can find your way out, I trust."

He didn't leave but instead reached into his coat and produced a calling card. Holding it out to me, he stepped inside the conservatory and approached the bench where I worked. I reached out and took the card, my fingers leaving smudges of compost on the vellum.

"Mr. Arthur Chatman," I read out loud.

"At your service, madam."

"What sort of service did you have in mind?" Dear heaven, would I never learn to curb my tongue? It was exactly that sort of thing that had earned me my reputation. Not that I gave a fig for what any of polite society thought, but the buzzing and the sideways glances did become annoying after a bit.

Arthur Chatman didn't look the least alarmed, despite his

youth and, one would have to assume, relative innocence. He appeared just shy of full manhood, probably a dozen or more years younger than my own thirty-five. He didn't stammer or avert his gaze but looked at me evenly, as if considering my question.

"I was hoping to ask a favor of you," he said.

"There's nothing I can do for you," I said. "After my husband's death, the queen doesn't even have to pretend to tolerate me any longer."

He laughed. "I don't want to go to court. We can do what I'd like right here."

I raised an eyebrow in a manner that would normally make the timid turn tail and run. Chatman didn't.

"I think you'll be intrigued," he said.

"Really." I set his card on the potting bench and wiped my hands on my apron. "Let's walk then, and you can do your best to intrigue me."

He offered his arm, but I walked past him and led him outside. Our footsteps crunched along the gravel path as we went through the vegetable garden toward the lawn. He placed his hands behind his back and kept up with me, but made no move to touch me.

"So what is your favor, Mr. Chatman?" I asked.

"You have an…um…interesting reputation, Lady Millford."

I stopped walking. "Shall I slap you now and send you on your way?"

"I hope not. At least let me do something to earn getting slapped."

He was a cheeky pup, I had to give him that. "Go on, then. I haven't managed a decent umbrage in at least a week."

"From what I understand, you haven't done anything that a man wouldn't do after his wife's death, but society doesn't see it that way."

"Hang society."

He smiled. "Exactly."

I turned and resumed walking. "So, you want to teach society a lesson?"

"I want you to teach me a lesson," he said. "I want you to teach me how to fuck."

I didn't just stop walking at that one. I tripped over my own feet, nearly falling over. He caught my elbow in his large hand and steadied me. The contact felt at once reassuring and disconcerting. A combination of gentleness and strength that couldn't help but remind me he was so much bigger than I. And yet, with a shout I could call any number of servants to subdue him if I felt at risk of assault. Teaching him to fuck could prove much more dangerous.

"I've shocked you," he said.

"*Fuck* isn't a word that comes up in most polite conversation."

"I could have said I want you to teach me how to make love," he said. "But that isn't the same thing, is it?"

"Let's stick to fucking, shall we?" Good Lord, I must have taken leave of my senses. Here I was, standing in my own garden talking to a perfect stranger about fucking. A very appealing stranger, granted. He grew more appealing by the minute. A cheeky pup with an innocent smile and a strong, young body. Although my husband had been an accomplished lover, I'd never experienced lust with a stud like this one. None of the lovers I'd taken since Millford's death had a physique anywhere nearly as well built as his. He had intrigued me after all.

Still, I had to chuckle. "It's my experience that most men are born knowing how to fuck. It's instinctual with them."

"That's true, but I want to know how to do it well."

"And you think I can instruct you."

"It's a bit complicated." He blushed. The curse of fair skin. The color on his cheeks was endearing, really, and emphasized his youth.

I began walking again, now across the more formal part of the garden where shrubs and flower beds lay in orderly geometric patterns.

"I've had some experience with women," he said. "At my age, most men have."

"You didn't find it satisfactory?"

He shrugged. "I don't have much to compare it to."

"Did the women seem to enjoy it?"

"Not because of anything I did. They seemed happy with…" He cleared his throat. "…my size."

"Ah." I cast a quick glance at the front of his trousers, but his jacket hid anything interesting.

"All the women I've known were quite experienced. That'll change soon," he said.

"You're going to start ravishing innocents, are you?"

"I'm not a cad, Lady Millford."

"I'm sorry," I said. "Of course, you're not."

"My family will want me to marry," he said. "I'll probably have a choice of several young women, all of them virgins."

"You want to seduce your wife?"

"Mostly, I don't want to frighten her."

"With your size," I said.

He didn't answer. Instead, he cleared his throat again and blushed even deeper.

I blushed myself, I'll admit. He did have a problem. If his cock was in proportion to the rest of him, he couldn't help but cause a virgin pain. Only arousing her to the point of desperation could make her beg to take something so big into her body.

I, on the other hand, had only dreamt of taking a lover so well-endowed. Millford, bless his heart, had given me everything he could but not that. I'd given up on filling that erotic dream. Now Chatman was offering me the opportunity.

"I know what marriage is," he said. "I don't expect my wife to love me but I don't want her to cringe when I slip into her bedroom."

And there it was. The exact moment when I first fell in love. I just didn't realize it at the time. It felt like a surge of lust so powerful it made my knees weak.

Millford had cultivated my lascivious nature for both our pleasure. I'd always known that his body had been aging and imperfect, but I'd counted myself so lucky to have a husband who cared about my satisfaction, I'd never thought to indulge myself with a large and eager young cock. I'd searched for what I'd missed after Millford's death, but none of the men I'd had offered the combination of kindness, beauty and sexual prowess I'd desired. Chatman did, and I could have him. The possibilities set my mind to racing.

"You're thinking of helping me, aren't you?" he said.

"I could hardly think of anything else."

He smiled. "Then you won't slap me."

"Not unless you ask me to."

He stopped walking, turned, and took my hand in both of his. He stood there, looking down at where his fingers held my own. "I'd like your help."

"Are you sure you'd find me attractive? I'm quite a bit older than you."

His head snapped up and his eyes widened in surprise. "You're a handsome woman, Lady Millford."

I blushed again, the heat creeping over my cheeks. Nothing made me blush anymore. Nothing except for this man. My heart tripped in my chest. For a moment, I might have been a young girl with her first suitor.

I looked back up at him. "Come back tomorrow. We'll begin your lessons then."

I spent the next day berating myself for not telling Chatman what time to come. After spending most of the night dreaming of huge cocks and strong fingers teasing my pearl, I had awoken in a state of anticipation that stole my breath and left my skin tingling. I might have slipped my fingers between my thighs and given myself some relief. But that would have taken the urgency from my need without fully satisfying it. In the end, I decided to enjoy my arousal as it grew over the hours.

I tried reading, but the words swam past my eyes without penetrating my brain. I picked strawberries and ate them still warm from the sun. Their succulence and sweetness only heightened my sensual awareness, and I imagined licking their juice from the swollen flesh of my new lover's cock. I tried taking walks to clear my head but—as I hadn't worn drawers in order to be ready for my young lover—I only became more and more aware of the friction between my legs.

Finally, I lay quietly on my fainting couch—closer than I'd ever come in my life to actually swooning—and counted the hours every time the clock chimed.

In midafternoon, Woodson appeared at the sitting room door with a silver salver in his hand. "A visitor, my lady."

I sat up on the couch and extended my hand. Woodson approached and held the salver out to me. For a moment, I hardly could bring myself to look at the printing on the card for fear it was someone besides Chatman. If it was, I'd have to send them away and hope they didn't cross paths with my young swain on his way in.

I took a deep breath and read. Thank heaven. I looked up at Woodson. "Send him in."

I arranged my skirts around me but stopped when the trembling of my fingers became pronounced. An observer might have thought me a green girl for all my fluttering.

He appeared in the doorway wearing riding clothes and carrying his hat in his hand. If he'd tried, he couldn't have found clothing to outline his physique better. The britches stretched taut along his thighs and the jacket barely contained his shoulders. His hair was pleasantly mussed as though the wind still rustled through it.

He gave me a tentative smile. "Thank you for seeing me."

"Please close the door and come in."

He did as I asked and then stood in the middle of the room as if waiting for my next command. My heart pounding, I patted the surface of the couch beside me. He sat and fidgeted with his hat until I took it from him and set it onto the floor nearby.

"We don't have to do this if you don't want to," I said.

Although, heaven only knew how I'd manage my lust if he decided to back away.

"I want to," he answered. "I just don't know what I'm about."

"That's why you're here. So I can teach you."

He took a breath. "Right."

"Let's pretend that I'm an innocent. We've met several times, and I've been showing interest in you. We've sneaked away, and we can't know when someone will find us."

"Miss…" He stopped. "It would help if I knew your name."

"Lily Sandridge." My last name hadn't been Sandridge for years, and only Millford had called me Lily during our marriage.

Chatman took my hands and gazed into my eyes. "Miss Sandridge."

"Very good. Start slowly, and if the woman shows any reticence, retreat. She must feel safe."

He cleared his throat. "Thank you."

I studied him for a moment. "Have I made you uncomfortable?"

He looked me straight in the face. "What makes you say that?"

"You seem…I don't know…hesitant."

"I can manage hand-holding on my own. I'd like to move past what would be appropriate between us if we might be discovered."

"Certainly." I wanted that, too, of course. I'd spent the entire day waiting for his hands on my body and mine on his. I might not have his rod inside me during this lesson, but I'd get a good idea of its dimensions. That would fuel more erotic dreams and a heightened tension for more days yet. With a bit of skill, I might stretch out the titillation until it had reached unparalleled levels. And to think, if Chatman hadn't appeared out of the blue the day before, I might never have thought of such delicious play on my own.

"Good, then," I said. "Let's move on."

"Yes, let's." He gave me a wicked smile then, so unlike his earlier shyness. It made his eyes sparkle and formed his lips into sensual curves too delicious for any mortal woman to resist. Yes, we'd start with kissing.

"We'll assume you've already touched the young lady several times—all innocently and by accident."

His smile broadened. "Of course."

"Now, the two of you find yourselves alone. Her chaperone has nodded off or some such."

He leaned toward me, his eyes bright with excitement. My own most likely looked the same.

"It's time for your first real kiss," I said.

"Oh, yes." His voice came out husky and full of promise.

"You still should move slowly. Signal your intent and let the lady come to you."

He leaned closer to me, his lips nearing mine.

"That's it," I said. "Hesitate, looking into her eyes. Show her you want her but that you'll wait until she's ready."

He stopped there, his mouth only inches from my own. I'd never had a more tempting invitation and I paused to savor it. The world slipped away as we sat there, each waiting for the contact that would begin our ascent to heaven.

Finally, weak human flesh that I am, I surrendered. I closed my eyes and sampled his lips.

And, oh, what lips they were. Soft and full, yet firm. Sweeter than my strawberries and headier than brandy. He held himself still while I explored every inch of his mouth from the corner to the fullness of his bottom lip and to the other corner.

After a moment, he began to tremble, so I ran my arms around his neck to encourage him. He took the message and groaned as he pulled me against him. Then his lips moved, brushing mine and sucking. Soon a fog of arousal filled my brain. This was no lesson but an assault on my senses. One I happily surrendered to. I offered him my tongue, and he grazed it with the tip of his own.

A shock raced through me, and I gasped. Immediately he pulled away.

"I'm sorry." He took a shaky breath and then another. "I was carried away."

I pressed a palm to my chest, as if that would help me get air. "My fault. I moved too quickly."

"I'm not complaining."

"Nor I. That was quite remarkable."

He smiled. "You liked it?"

"My dear Mr. Chatman, when you know women better you'll realize that you seduced me thoroughly with a kiss."

"Please call me Arthur." He looked quite pleased with himself. A true rake in the making. Only the flush to his own skin gave him away. He'd become as aroused as I was.

"Well, Arthur, you've done a very good job of kissing an experienced woman. A virgin will take a bit more work."

"That's what I'm here to learn."

With another man, it might have worried me to give a fellow such power over women. An unscrupulous rake could cause misery for large numbers of young girls. Though I preferred adventurous men myself, I found the predatory sort beneath contempt. Taking someone's innocence for one's own enjoyment with no thought of the consequences was a selfish act of the worst sort. Selfishness had no place in good sex, as I'd learned from my late husband. But Chatman seemed to honestly want to please his wife-to-be. In that regard, he was much like Millford. In fact, if I'd believed in the supernatural, I might have thought Millford had sent him to me so I could have the joy of mutual pleasure with a strapping young specimen.

"What are you thinking?" he asked.

I brought myself back to the present and found him studying me. Rather than the timidity he normally displayed, he gave me a frank appraisal, as if he could see inside my mind. For just a moment, I got a glimpse of the man he'd become in the prime of his power and worldly accomplishments. A glimpse of a stunning man, indeed.

"Hmm?" He leaned toward me and pressed his lips to my temple. His hot breath slipped into my ear, and I couldn't help but tremble.

I put my hand on his chest and pushed him back. "I think you're getting much too good at this."

"Let's go on."

"Now then, after you've shared several of those kisses with your young lady, you'll find she makes more and more opportunities to get you alone."

"I do hope so."

I raised a finger in true instructor fashion. "Always pretend to be surprised. Pleased, but surprised. It'll make her feel very clever."

"That's dishonest, isn't it?" he asked.

"An innocent deception. You want to encourage her."

"So, what should I do once she has me to herself?"

"More body contact." I rose from the couch. "Here, let me show you."

He stood, too, and stretched out his arms. I walked into his embrace and held myself against him, my head on his shoulder. I'd never had such a large man before. Size like that could intimidate, or it could feel like a shelter. He held me so gently— as if he feared I'd break—that my heart melted. Truly, I could have rested against his chest forever, except for one thing. The fire still burned inside me. I needed far more than such innocent contact could give.

I looked up at him. "Kissing's more intimate in this position."

"Yes." He'd gone breathless again. No doubt the press of my body against his had aroused him as it had me. In fact, a definite hardness pressed against my belly. With a more experienced man, I would have pressed against his britches to stroke his cock through the fabric. Before he left today, I would feel the thickness of him between my fingers, and naked, too. For now, I'd find some patience.

"If you've kissed the lady before and she's come willingly into your embrace, you can do it now with more authority," I said.

He didn't wait for more instruction but bent to take my mouth. Again, his kiss sent heat spiraling through me. Strong and yet soft, his lips moved over mine with just the right pressure. Not pushing or demanding, but drawing me to him. I clung to his shoulders as my knees grew weak. Since my marriage, I'd led a voluptuous life—first with Millford and then with other lovers. Nothing had ever made me hotter than the feel of this man's lips on my own.

I whimpered and opened my mouth under his, begging without words for more. More of his heat, his strength, his sweetness. He held me, his hands roaming my back. When they went lower to cup my buttocks, I pressed myself against him until my belly rubbed against the bulge of his cock.

A roar rumbled through his chest, and he pushed me away. His strong hands gripped my arms though, holding me up. If not for that, I would have fallen.

"Mercy, Lady Millford," he said. "I'm only human."

"You wanted me to teach you how to fuck." The disappointment, the hunger, the desperation rang in my voice. Normally I kept tight control of my emotions and only surrendered to my own orgasm. In another moment, this man would reduce me to begging.

"I want to fuck you, too," he said. "But we must go slowly, or I'll spend in my britches."

Again, my heart soared. The fact that I could capture his body as completely as he'd captured mine promised pleasure beyond anything I'd known. Patience. I only needed patience.

I nodded my understanding and rested my hands on his arms, leaning into his strength while I gathered what I could of my wits.

Finally I was able to stand on my own, and I smiled at him. "All right. Slowly."

He rubbed his hands over his face for a moment and took deep, even breaths. Then he dropped his arms to his sides and straightened. "Will an innocent respond like that to a kiss?"

Honestly, his questions about how another woman might feel about his touch were growing tiresome. Especially his emphasis on innocence. I'd never cared about that sort of judgment, but now, for some reason, it mattered.

"An unpracticed girl won't respond as well," I said. A bit petty, perhaps, but true. If he thought a prissy young thing would be as passionate as I was, he'd be sorely disappointed. "But, if she seems agreeable, you can press on."

"How would I do that?"

"Nibble at her earlobe. Press kisses along the length of her throat."

"If you don't mind...." He swallowed. "Can we keep that for another day? I feel...well...overwhelmed."

As did I, but I had no intention of stopping here. "Touch her breast and see what she does."

His eyes widened and he stared at me. I'd confounded him. Good.

"Through her clothing," I said. "Pretend it's an accident."

"Her breast." His gaze fixed on my bosom. Slowly, his hand came up as if acting on its own. He watched its progress as it approached the swell of flesh under my bodice.

When the backs of his fingers grazed my waiting nipple, I couldn't hold back a little cry of pleasure. Again his gentleness threatened to undo me.

"Soft," he whispered. He moved his hand back and forth, teasing the nipple until it ached, and then cupped my breast. The flesh felt hot and heavy as he stroked it. I could have melted right then, and indeed, my pussy grew wet. How I burned for him.

"What else should I do?" he asked. His voice was none too steady and his breathing had grown ragged.

"Before she's agreed to marry you, probably nothing more."

He dropped his hand. "Nothing?"

"Anything more could ruin her."

His brows furrowed. "But, surely there are other things I could do without taking her virginity."

"But they'd ruin her, nevertheless."

"I don't understand."

I sat on the couch again and gestured for him to join me. "If you awaken her lust but don't marry her, she'd most likely search for satisfaction with another man who might not have your scruples."

"Now I really don't understand."

"A woman's sexual needs are every bit as strong as a man's. Perhaps stronger," I said.

He looked clearly surprised at that. "Can that be possible?"

"You must have pleasured yourself, haven't you?" I asked.

His cheeks grew bright red. "Every man has."

"Then you know you can spend without penetration."

He didn't even try to answer that but only nodded.

"For every climax a man has, a woman can have two or more."

"The tension, the inevitability and then the explosion?" he said. "More than once?"

"You could make a woman spend without taking her virginity."

"I'd like to see that," he said.

"I could show you right now."

He smiled, but his cheeks turned a flaming red. "Lady Millford!"

"Lily."

"Lily, I…" His voice trailed off. "You want me to watch your orgasm?"

"I want you to give me one."

"Now? Today?"

"Your kisses have aroused me beyond what I can endure. I imagine you feel the same," I said.

He took my hand and brought it to his lips. "You have no idea."

To the contrary, I had a very good idea. Both of us needed more. If he left now, he'd no doubt take his sex in hand and finish matters. I know I would. How much sweeter to do it for each other.

"A gentleman wouldn't leave me in such misery," I said.

"I would never hurt you, dear Lily."

"Then touch me. Reach beneath my skirts and share heaven with me."

I leaned back against the cushions and brought one foot up to rest on the sofa. With my legs parted in invitation, he could have no doubt what I wanted. Immediately, he reached to my ankle and moved his hand upward to where the garter held my stocking. From there, his fingers traveled over the naked skin of my inner thigh, headed toward my aching cunny. I sighed, closed my eyes, and waited for the touch I'd craved since awaking that morning.

"When you find my lips, you will have reached your goal," I whispered, scarcely able to talk because of the anticipation.

"Ah, yes." He touched my sex, stroking the swollen flesh. "Lovely."

A jolt of pleasure raced through me and my back arched, pressing my flesh harder against his hand.

"Did I hurt you?" he asked.

"Don't stop!" I cried. "Whatever you do, don't stop!"

"It's very wet. My fingers are covered with moisture."

"My cunny's readying itself for your cock." As much as I'd love to tear off his clothes and mount him, I'd save that for another day. No need to rush, especially when today's pleasure had grown so intense.

"This is where you'll take my rod." He slid a finger inside my depths. "It's so hot."

"Dear heaven," I gasped. "Don't stop."

He slid another finger inside me and pumped until all reason fled and I was utterly at his mercy.

"Hot, sweet and wet," he murmured, his own voice strained.

"Where the lips meet…above…" I had to fight to form words. "There's a nubbin. Hard. Rub that."

His thumb flicked over my pearl. "Here it is."

"Yes. Yes. Oh, yes…"

His fingers still probing my cunny, he kept stroking my clitoris with his thumb. All the lust I'd endured during the day, all the passion of his kisses, the burning of my pussy—all of it built to impossible heights. I hovered on the edge of bliss for a long moment, and then the storm burst over me. Unable to endure further, my sex clenched and then erupted into spasms as I spent with a force that stole my consciousness.

After it finished, I lay back, boneless with pleasure as my sex continued to flutter around his fingers.

"My dearest Lily." He removed his hand from under my clothing and leaned to press a kiss to my lips. "What an honor. I'll never forget this moment."

I held him to me as I drifted back to reality. "You did that very well."

"I had no idea such a thing was possible."

"There's much more possible than that. In a moment, I'll show you."

We sat that way for a bit while I returned to full reality.

Finally I couldn't wait to continue our explorations. He'd touched me in the most intimate places and reduced me to pure lust. I'd do the same to him—and delight in making him the slave of his own passion.

I raised his face and looked into his eyes. "Now, dear Arthur, don't be shy. I must see your cock. I must feel its weight in my hand and pet its length."

Instead of a blush, he gave me a smile as warm as sunshine. Still innocent, but lusty and open to whatever I'd planned. I'd planned a great deal, and now I'd drive him to the same ecstasy he'd given me.

He straightened and opened his riding jacket. Finally I had a view of the outline of his rod where it pressed against the tight fabric of his britches. He hadn't exaggerated its size. A broad ridge extended from the space between his thighs to the waist of his pants. I pressed a palm to it and marveled at how thick and hard it was.

He closed his eyes in bliss and pressed his pelvis against my hand. "Take care. You'll make me wild."

"My intent exactly." I unbuttoned his britches, my fingers fumbling in my haste I would have this treasure in my hands. I would stroke and caress it until I could watch it let loose his seed. Only I needed to work quickly, as he'd spend soon.

When I finally had the fastenings open, his cock nearly sprang free, it was so eager to be petted. I'd seen a few pricks in my day, and this one put the term to shame. The thorn of a rose could prick, as could a needle or knife. This resembled a mast, so thick at the base I couldn't close my fingers around it. The tip was a wonder—as large and purple as a ripe fig. My poor lover had pushed himself to the breaking point while bringing me pleasure. He'd put off his own completion to satisfy me. Now I'd take care to give him the reward he deserved.

I stroked the length of him, all along the shaft to the balls beneath. Then I bent to kiss the head and lick the ridge that circled it.

He jumped and his eyes flew open. "What are you doing?"

"He's such a fine, lusty fellow. Let me love him. Let me suck him deep into my mouth."

"You'd want to do that?" he asked.

"Can you doubt it?"

"Other men have told me no lady wants to take a man's member between her lips."

"Then I'm no lady," I said. "Because I want to savor every inch of you."

If only that were possible. Nothing this large would fit into my mouth. But I'd take as much as I could and stroke the rest. With some effort, I could massage his sac at the same time. I bent to my work—sucking at the head of his marvelous tool while my fingers were busy with the rest of him.

He took a shuddering breath. "Oh, Lily. By God, I never imagined. Ah, my love."

He seemed to swell even further, and I strained to take more and more of him. Oh so gently, I slid my teeth along the underside of his shaft. In response, his pelvis moved, imitating the thrusts of a man about to spend. Indeed, a slight tang of salt told me he'd released that first droplet that preceded the rush of his lust. He wouldn't last much longer.

No longer speaking in words, his sounds told me of his mounting arousal. Murmurs and soft grunts—the song of the male in full rut. I didn't slow, but worked him for every second of madness I could give him. Truly, a cock had never been more thoroughly loved.

Finally, he snapped. "Stop!" he shouted. "Oh, now…I can't… Stop!"

I removed my mouth from his rod and stroked him hard and fast. He roared as his body went rigid. Semen shot out the tip of his cock in hot waves. It sprayed on him and on my hand. So hot and sweet.

I kept up the pressure until he'd finished and then gently released him to float on the same cloud of bliss I'd just occupied. Disturbing him as little as possible, I reached into my bodice to find my handkerchief and then blotted up his love juices. It seemed as if they'd gone everywhere.

After a moment, he sighed and slipped his fingers into my hair. "You've undone me. I'll never be the same again."

"Any lusty woman would do the same for you."

"No, Lily. Only you."

My heart shouldn't have warmed at that. A man would say anything for fellatio. He'd just had his first taste and was understandably moved. He'd come to me for an education, no more. I'd enjoy the considerable pleasures of his body, and he'd go away again. The two of us would make some young girl happy in their marriage. A boon for all around, and yet…if I had foolish notions about men and love…

He sat up and pulled me to him, taking my lips in a kiss so sweet it brought tears to my eyes. He was such a mixture of innocence, passion and tenderness, only someone heartless could fail to respond. I'd best rein in my own heart before it came to hope for more than it could have.

I straightened and gathered my skirts around me. "That's enough for today, I think."

He tucked his limp but still impressive cock into his britches and did up the buttons. "May I come again tomorrow?"

"Oh, yes. Please do."

THE NEXT DAY, I SENT WOODSON INTO TOWN ON AN errand that would put him right in the path of the butcher's widow——a lady he admired for her generous disposition and even more generous bosom. If I had to rid myself of him so that I might enjoy an afternoon in my lover's arms, he might as well enjoy himself, too. I told my maid that I had a wicked headache and would snap at anyone who showed her face, so she disappeared as well. In this way, I was able to pace the length of the drawing room in nothing more than a shift and dressing gown in complete privacy. I left the door open so that I could hear a knock at the front.

Heaven help me if anyone else were to drop by, but then, everyone for miles around knew my reputation. If they found me *déshabillé,* they had only themselves to blame.

My darling boy was punctual, and his knock came at exactly the same time it had at our last meeting. I greeted him at the front door, put my finger against my lips to command his silence, and then took him by the hand to my bedroom. The moment I'd locked the rest of the world out, he took me in his arms and gave me a kiss that set my senses reeling. After several moments of breathless sparring of our lips and tongues, he broke off and rested his forehead against mine.

"I can't believe I'll finally have you," he said. "We will fuck today, won't we?"

"I swear, I'll perish if we don't."

He laughed and kissed the tip of my nose. "I wouldn't want you to die on my account."

"Oh, but we will die. Both of us."

"I was awake half the night thinking of this. I had to use my hand to get some relief."

"I wish I could have done that for you," I said.

"When I remembered your mouth on my cock, it made me mad with lust."

"Today you'll feel my cunny around it."

I could have taken him right then—I'd grown that wet and hot. But I'd agreed to teach him how to pleasure a virgin. The lesson would be long and slow, and we'd both approach the boiling point before I could have his huge tool inside me. What a glorious coupling that would be.

"Now then, we'll pretend that I'm your virgin bride," I said. "You'll have to work to win your reward."

"How should I start?"

"Undress me, and as you go, praise my body. A woman glows when she believes she's pretty."

He opened the top button of my dressing gown and slowly moved to the second. "You're far more than pretty, my dearest Lily."

"Do you really think so?"

He opened a few more buttons and stroked my skin. "It feels like rose petals. I must kiss it."

Playing my part, I pulled the dressing gown closed and pretended shyness.

"You like my kisses, don't you?" he asked.

I bit my lip and nodded.

"Then, let me kiss you everywhere. It won't hurt, I promise."

He undressed me further, bent, and placed his lips in the hollow at the base of my throat.

I'd had furious couplings—clothes flying, hands groping, bellies slamming together. I'd had the expert touches of my husband, as he'd taught me my own body's responses. I'd never had anything like Arthur's tenderness and reverence as he lowered his lips to the top of my shift. My breath caught and my skin grew extra sensitive. My breasts, especially, felt heavy and full. As if reading my need, he slipped a hand inside my dressing gown and cupped one peak through the fabric of my shift. The nipple hardened instantly, and I couldn't hold back a gasp of surprise and pleasure.

"I must see you naked," he whispered. "I must have all of you."

"It isn't right." Although my voice came out strained with desire, it might have sounded like fear. Playing my part again.

He looked down into my face. "Lily, I'm your husband. Nothing is wrong between us."

My husband. This mythical Lily he spoke to had better be worthy of him. If not, I'd find her and steal him from her. But then, who could be worthy of such a man?

I moved my hands and allowed him to finish unbuttoning my dressing gown. Once he'd done that, he pushed the garment over my shoulders and let it drop to the floor. My shift went next, as he bunched it up in his hands and pulled it upward. I lifted my arms to help, and in a moment I stood before him without a stitch on my body. Not acting this time, I covered myself as best I could with my hands. Thirty-five isn't old for a woman, and I'd kept my figure well. But I didn't have the bloom of youth he'd expect on his real wedding night.

He took my hands and moved them away from my body and stared at me until I trembled.

Finally I couldn't bear his scrutiny another second. "Do you find me pleasing?"

He looked up at me as if he didn't know the meaning of the word. "Pleasing?"

"I'm not young."

"You're magnificent." He stroked my shoulder and then lowered his hand over my chest and cupped my breast. "I've never seen anything so beautiful."

Something broke free inside me and my spirit took flight. He thought I was beautiful. His face showed no guile, no act for the benefit of another woman's pleasure. He wanted me as much as I wanted him. I could give in to passion, knowing that he shared it.

"You may take me to the bed now," I said.

He lifted me up into his arms and whirled me around as if I weighed nothing at all. I'd only meant for him to lead me to the bed, but floating in his embrace was so much more exciting. I could have him now. I could touch him anywhere and order him to do the same for me. My hours of waiting had come to an end. Satisfaction was within my reach.

He walked to the bed and laid me on the comforter. I lay

there, gazing up at him, and oddly, this did feel like a first time. Certainly, he looked at me out of fresh, young eyes. What did he see? A woman past the blush of innocence that so many men valued above all else?

"Tell me again that I'm beautiful," I said. Pitiful, and yet I couldn't stop myself.

"You're the most beautiful woman on Earth," he said. "Your limbs are graceful, your breasts lush and full. And your cunny...ah, your cunny. It looks like heaven."

"You can see it?"

"The lips are pouting beneath their curls. Luscious. I want to devour them."

I did my best imitation of a girlish giggle. "You mustn't. It's wicked."

"I want to kiss every inch of you," he said. "That spot especially."

He took off his jacket and dropped it to the floor. His collar and cravat went next, and then he unbuttoned his shirt, showing the smooth muscles of his chest. Even in trousers looser than his riding britches, his cock made a definite impression against his front.

Staring at it, I put my hand to my throat in mock alarm. He sat on the bed and took my hand. "I'll be gentle, Lily. The pleasure will make up for any pain. Do you trust me?"

I nodded, and he bent to press a chaste kiss to my lips. Then he removed his shoes and socks and stretched out next to me.

"Our life together begins now, Lily, and you mustn't be afraid of me." With that, he kissed me in earnest, and the warmth of his body enveloped mine. I dropped all pretense and welcomed him, running my arms around his shoulders and answering his lips with my own.

The caress stole my breath as I opened my mouth to accept his tongue. He groaned and took us deeper, running his lips over mine and taking the lower one between his teeth to nibble gently. Heat rose between us, and I pressed myself upward against him so that I could savor the fabric of his shirt against my nipples.

He trembled, leashing in the power of his body. "I want you so much. It's killing me to go slowly, but I will."

I stroked the side of his face. "Kiss my breasts."

"Ah, God, yes." Moving lower, he let his lips trail over my chest until he reached one nipple. Teasing that with his tongue, he circled it until it hardened, peaking upward. Finally, he took it into his mouth and sucked—and I nearly flew off the bed, the feeling was so intense.

He assaulted all my senses—the pressure of his mouth against my breast, the sounds of his ragged breathing, the sweetness of his kiss. My entire body screamed for him, silently begging for more. I needed his hard rod inside me, and yet I needed to hold off the ultimate pleasure to make it more intense.

After loving that breast, he moved to the other one and continued his magic. His hands moved over my ribs, massaging me and pulling me to him.

He released my nipple and looked up at me. "Am I doing this right?"

I stroked his face. "Wonderfully right."

"You make it easy."

"You make me wild with lust."

He grinned. "I plan to have my revenge on you for yesterday."

A thrill rushed through me. "By kissing my cunny?"

"That intimate spot you told me about," he said. "I want to make you spend again."

"Oh, my." A pointless thing to say, but all other words flew from my mind. He'd aroused me already, but now my poor sex throbbed with wanting him. In my mind's eye, I saw his cock as it hardened to an impossible size, grew crimson and then released the hot stream of semen. I couldn't take the sperm, of course, for fear of getting with child. But I would take his bulk inside me and ride it to my own release.

He moved lower, sliding his heat over me as he ran his tongue down the center of my body. Then, past my belly and to my pelvis. My heart hammered in my chest as he neared the seat of my desire.

After long moments, he blew hot breath on my thatch. "Open for me, Lily."

Helpless to resist, I let my thighs part and waited.

"So beautiful." He pressed his hand against my sex. "You're wet for me again."

"Arthur...I need...oh, please."

"This?" Something hot and moist touched my nether lips. His tongue. It stroked upward and then grazed my pearl. I gasped at the contact as hot currents of need spiraled from my cunny to every part of me. He'd set a fire in me that would soon overcome me completely, and I had no choice but to surrender to it.

He slid his arms under my thighs and pulled my cunny against his face. His tongue continued taking me apart. He rubbed, he pressed, he traced circles over my clitoris until I could scarcely draw air into my lungs. When he sucked that sensitive flesh into his mouth, my hips jerked upward so hard that he had to clutch me to keep up the friction.

And—oh!—did he. Over and over. Now harder, now softer. The world became a red haze of lust as he pushed my body to unbearable levels. I needed to spend, wanted to make the pleasure last but needed to release my lust before I went mad with it.

In the end, I had no choice. My body took over as he worked my pearl. The universe condensed into that one spot between my legs, and the wildness took me. I coiled, shuddered and screamed as the spasms shook me. It went on so long I almost lost consciousness. No one could survive pleasure that intense without losing touch with reality.

When it ended, I lay back, limp and gasping for breath.

He slid up beside me and took me into his arms. "My treasure. You make me so proud."

I burrowed my nose into his neck and breathed in his scent, which was now mixed with my own where his lips had touched my sex. In a moment, I'd open my eyes and ask him to proceed. Right now, I didn't have the strength.

We lay that way in silence as consciousness returned. Sunlight slanted in the window and heated the skin of my back. He shifted and removed his arms from around me. I opened my eyes to see he'd risen from the bed to remove his unbuttoned shirt. I stretched my arms over my head and watched him undress. Heaven forbid I miss this display.

His chest was an expanse of smooth flesh stretched over sleek muscles. It went from broad shoulders to a narrow waist. Once he had his shirt fully off, his hands moved to the buckle of his belt and then to the buttons of his trousers. Under the fabric lay a considerable bulge. I'd seen his cock before, and now I'd take it inside me. My cunny heated up again, waiting for him to enter it and make it whole.

When he had the pants open, he pushed them and his drawers over his hips and to the floor. After stepping out of them, he stood there and let me worship his body with my gaze.

He took his erect rod in his hand. "This will frighten my wife, won't it?"

"It would terrify any virgin."

"What should I do?"

"Tell her the truth," I answered. "Tell her it will hurt the first time but will give her great pleasure once she's used to it."

"Will it hurt you?"

"It'll stretch me." I smiled to reassure him. "I'll love it."

"I'll go slowly."

"Delicious. Sink into me one inch at a time."

He joined me on the bed and stroked my face. "You really are a wanton, aren't you?"

"I hope so. Only, why are we talking?"

He circled his fingers over one of my breasts. "You're to teach me how to satisfy my wife."

"Ah, yes." That aspect of the encounter had grown decidedly tedious. Why should I have to tutor him in making another woman happy when I wanted nothing more than for him to frig me with all the power of his body? I wanted him blind with lust and pounding his tool into my wetness. Oh, well…this was my part of the bargain and I'd live up to it.

"Now that you've shown her how good a cunny can feel, stimulate it again. Eventually she'll beg you for more."

He slipped his hand between my thighs and stroked my

nether lips. I stretched the way a cat does when petted and let him work his magic on my body.

"So soft and sweet," he murmured. "I can't wait to feel its heat around my rod."

"Oh, yes," I sighed.

He slid two fingers into me and probed, stretching me. I gasped as the heat of his loving claimed me again. Teasing me even further, he removed his fingers, drew them over my pearl, and then slid them into my depths again. I'd spend this way if he continued, but how much sweeter it would be to grasp at his huge cock when I did.

"Do you want me?" he asked.

"More than my next breath."

He gritted his teeth. "Good Lord, you inflame me."

I parted my legs and gazed into his face. "Take me now. Please."

"I can deny you nothing." He positioned himself between my legs. "Take my cock in your hand and guide me to you."

I reached down and grasped his hardness, then brought it to my waiting cunny. He pressed forward until the head entered me. It was indeed enormous, and he waited until I'd accepted that before going deeper.

I gasped in surprise and delight. "Oh, my. That…feels…so…good."

"Another inch?"

"More. Please more."

He pushed more of his cock into me and my eager sex devoured it.

"I want it all!" I cried. "Please."

He held himself above me, the muscles of his arms trembling. "I'm trying to go slowly."

"Never mind, just fuck me."

Yet more of him went into my wetness, and I strained upward to take it. "I'm dying!"

"We'll both die. You said so." He pushed forward, now almost filling me. "Right now I like hearing you beg."

I struck at his shoulder. "Cad."

"Is this what you want?" A bigger thrust this time, and his thickness stretched me even wider and sent me near to heaven.

Finally—finally!—he pushed his hips forward, fully embedding himself inside me. Such a feeling—pleasure so intense it tore a cry from my chest.

"I hurt you," he said.

"No," I answered. "Oh, no, my love. You feel glorious inside me."

"Truly?"

I moved upward, stroking his cock with my wet pussy. "See how I want you."

"Then may God help me, because I can't hold back."

He began moving. Strong, slow strokes. Deep inside me, then sliding back and thrusting forward again. I'd never felt the like, and my breaths turned to gasps, rising in time with his movements. He filled me perfectly, and the root of him made contact against my pearl. I'd spend again, and soon. No one could withstand this assault and not die of pleasure.

He moved faster and deeper as his own need grew more urgent. Holding onto his shoulders as an anchor in this storm, I urged him on with my own answering movements. I'd need to stop him soon, ask him to withdraw before he shot his sperm inside me. But how could I live without him inside me at the ultimate moment? Perfect bliss. I needed more and more.

I'd stop him later. For now, I had to have him inside me.

He grunted and strained as his movements became more frantic. Harder, deeper, pushing us both to the limit. My lust tore me from the real world, leaving nothing but the friction of his body against mine, the pressure of his cock inside me, and the fire building in my belly.

Stop him! my brain shrieked. But my body drowned it out. A few more seconds and I'd spend as I'd never done before. I couldn't stop him without having that.

Too late. I reached the crest and soared past. Every inch of me burst into flames as it hit, starting deep within me and then rushing along the length of my cunny. Everywhere. I grasped his cock as the explosions wracked me. Heaven.

He pounded into me, wild with his own need. He growled and then roared as he stiffened. Another massive thrust and then another, and he went rigid in my arms. He'd spent, sending his semen in waves inside me.

I should have been angry, aghast at what we'd done, but all I could do was hold him while he reached his own heaven and then floated back to earth. After several heartbeats, he went limp, moaning into my ear, "Oh, Lily. Lily, Lily. I never dreamt…"

I stroked his face and placed kisses against his lips. "My darling Arthur. No one ever dreamt it could be like that."

"I love you. I swear it."

My sweet lad. He'd had his first real taste of good sex. Of course he'd say he loved me. At this moment, he did. That would fade. For now I'd take his words and hold them in my heart.

After several shuddering breaths, he opened his eyes and

looked down into my face. "I meant to pull out, but I'm glad now I didn't."

"My silly boy."

"I'm not a boy. I know what I've done. I'll marry you, of course."

"That isn't necessary."

He looked down at me, his brow knitted with puzzlement. "We may have made a child. Of course it's necessary that we marry."

"How sweet of you." I stroked his face. "I have the means to take care of things on my own."

"It's not a thing. It's my son or daughter." He pulled out of me and sat up. "I can't believe you'd take this so lightly."

I sat up next to him and put a hand on his shoulder. "There's no need for this conversation. We don't know that I'll conceive."

"If you do, we *will* become man and wife. I insist."

"Arthur, that isn't really what you want."

He turned and glared at me. "I want you as my wife, and I want to raise our child together."

Oh dear. The man was a romantic. I should have guessed as much, given his tender concern for a virgin wife he hadn't even met yet. Now, out of misplaced obligation, he planned to tie himself to an older woman with a ghastly reputation.

"You're a dear man," I said. "But you're very young. You'll change your mind."

"You're wrong about that."

"We had a wonderful fucking." *Wonderful* didn't do it justice, actually. *Glorious, spectacular, transcendent* were better. In my whole adventurous life, I'd never had its equal. "Once we've been apart, you'll see things more rationally."

"Stop telling me my own mind."

"If you feel so sure of yourself, stay away for a month. We'll know by then if I'm with child. We can deal with each other reasonably."

"Reasonably." He huffed. "I don't see anything reasonable about it."

"Then stay away because I ask it."

"All right." He got up, found his drawers and pants and shoved his feet into them. "One month. Not a day longer."

"Thank you."

He slipped on his shirt and scooped up the rest of his things, then went to the door and let himself out. As the latch sprang closed again, I lay back against the bed.

That was that. He'd come to his senses in the next weeks. If he did come back, he'd most likely agree that we didn't belong together. A polite conversation between two acquaintances. Damn. It would hurt less if he didn't come back at all.

WEEKS LATER, ARTHUR CAME TO ME IN A DREAM. Actually, I had dreamt of him almost every night, but this particular nightly visit was the most erotic of any of them. The two of us floated in a warm pond with a waterfall at one end. Fields surrounded us, filled with wildflowers. Brightly colored insects flitted from blossom to blossom. The natural beauty around us fairly demanded nakedness, and the water lapped at my breasts. As my excitement grew, Arthur's cock slipped inside my cunny, filling me and stroking my inner depths.

If only it were real.

I clung to the image. Savored the feeling of his bulk inside me. Strained for completion before the dream faded. Faster and harder he moved as I got closer and closer to orgasm.

Just seconds from spending, I awakened. *Damn.* My breath was coming hard and I needed more. I reached to the lips of my sex to stroke myself and found fingers already there.

I gasped and jumped.

"It is only I," a male voice said from behind me. *Arthur.* "Go back to sleep."

"How did you get in here?"

"A determined lover finds a way." He slid two fingers inside me.

"Arthur…"

"Shh." He lifted my leg over his hip and inserted the head of his cock into my cunny. "Now be a good girl and let me fuck you."

As if I had a choice. He pushed forward, embedding more of his thick tool inside me. Shameless, I pressed my hips toward him until I'd taken all of him.

"Ah, God, you feel good," he gasped.

"You said you'd stay away for a month."

"And so I did." He started moving, even thrusts in and out.

"It isn't a month until tomorrow."

"It's after midnight, so it is tomorrow. You didn't specify what time I was to come."

He kept thrusting and I matched his movements with my own hips. Reality was more erotic than my dream, and soon I'd grown so aroused that my sex made wet noises as he glided in and out of it.

"You sneaked in here when I was defenseless," I said hoarsely.

He chuckled, but the sound was strained. "Is it working?"

"Not fair," I gasped.

With his cock still moving inside me, he reached to my pearl and stroked it. "Shall I go away again?"

"No! Please, don't stop."

"Don't worry. I doubt I *could* stop."

Thank heaven. How I needed this. Weeks of wanting him, dreaming of having all of his hardness inside me and his fingers driving me until my soul shattered in bliss. Tomorrow I'd puzzle out how to deal with him again. Right now, I'd take the pleasure he offered.

"How I missed this," he said. "All I had was my hand and my fantasies of you."

Another image to play through my mind as my body caught fire. His cock, rigid and crimson, spraying hot semen in powerful waves. It would do that inside me in a moment, and I'd take it all.

"Now, my love," he crooned. "You're so close."

"Yes."

He moved faster—great, frantic thrusts that went right to my core. His fingers burned as they teased my pearl.

"Now!" I cried. "Please, now!"

Finally I exploded, overcome with lust. Tremors wracked my cunny, grasping at his hardness. I sobbed as I spent.

Behind me, his cries joined mine. We strained against each other, together flying into white-hot heaven. His hips jerked as he emptied his essence into me. My cunny soaked it up eagerly, taking every drop of him as my juices mingled with his.

When it was over, we lay together, his cock still buried in me, and floated off, enshrouded in each other's warmth.

"That's settled, then," he said after a bit. "We'll be married as soon as we can make the arrangements."

"Nothing's settled," I answered. "Nothing's changed."

"We'll have to wait again to see if I've gotten you with child."

I rolled over and looked him in the face. In the dim moonlight from the window, I could just make out the smile on his face. He looked inordinately proud of himself. In fact, he looked outright smug. "You didn't get me with child last time."

"Then I'll keep trying until I do."

I slapped his chest. "You're incorrigible."

"Determined," he corrected. "Face the truth, Lily. You can't resist me."

I huffed my disapproval. In much the same way a prude would, I'm ashamed to say. I could hardly contradict him, as it was true—I couldn't resist him. If he came back to my bed, I would surrender. And he showed no inclination to stay away.

"I'm too old for you," I said. "Too much of a pariah."

"While we were apart, I tried taking an interest in innocent young things. They bored me into a stupor."

"I'll grow old before you do."

He kissed me briefly. "You'll still be the most beautiful woman in the world."

"You're a fool."

"I'm in love," he said. "I think you love me, too."

"What does love have to do with marriage?"

"I can see it in your eyes," he said. "You may as well admit it."

I huffed again.

He chuckled. "I can make your body tell me you love me. It's on my side, you know."

"Don't be ridiculous."

He reached between my legs but I pushed his hand away. He could make my body do whatever he wanted, and I needed my wits about me if I was going to talk sense with him.

He laughed again. "Come on now. Admit it."

"Very well. I love you, you insufferable man."

"Then you'll marry me."

"Oh, for heaven's sake." If I'd known he was not only foolish but obstinate, I'd never have let him in my bed. No, that was a lie. The moment he'd blushed and mentioned the size of his cock, I'd been lost.

"What would your family think of me as your bride?"

"My mother will take to her bed, no doubt. My father will question my sanity. My sister will love you. She's a bit of a hellion herself."

"Well, you see then. Both your parents would hate me, and I'd be a bad influence on your sister."

"They'll accept you after a while. They only want me to be happy."

"I wish I could marry you, Arthur." The moment the words left my mouth, I recognized the truth. I did wish I could marry him. I wished I could spend every day basking in his smile and every night in his bed.

"You might as well relent," he said, "because I'm not going to give up, no matter what you say."

"See reason, my darling…"

"It's you who needs to see reason." He stared at me, a stubborn set to his jaw. "I'll either marry you or no one."

"But, you can't do that." Why had I never noticed his obstinacy before? He'd seemed so shy and agreeable. When had he turned mulish? "You'll disappoint your family."

"Then they'll be disappointed. If I can't marry you, I'll play the paramour. I'll slip into your bed every night, no matter what obstacles you throw up."

"That would ruin your sister."

Even that didn't penetrate his skull; the determination remained in his face. "She won't care. She'd gladly ruin her own reputation if it would win her freedom."

"Then you must care for her."

"You're hardly one to lecture about decency," he said. Damn him.

"So, neither of you will marry."

"And it'll be all your fault." He paused to let his words hit their mark. "Now, if you married me, we could all be very respectable."

"I've never heard anything so ridiculous."

"All right, then. We can all be very happy."

The man was insane. Worse, I was catching his madness. Why in heaven's name *shouldn't* I marry him? He loved me and wanted me, and I felt the same about him. I had never given a fig for what anyone else thought—why shouldn't I take this chance at happiness and thank heaven for it?

"Very well," I said finally. "If you're a fool, I suppose I am, too."

His eyes went wide as he stared into my face. "Then you will marry me?"

"It seems I must."

"Oh, my darling." He gave me a quick kiss. "I'll make you happy, I swear it."

I looked into his dear face, although my vision had blurred with tears. "You already have."

He cupped my breast and then ran his hand over my abdomen, headed for my sex. "I can always strive to make you even happier."

And he spent the rest of the night doing exactly that.

An erotic novel by

CHARLOTTE FEATHERSTONE

HE IS RULED BY TWIN CRAVINGS: OBLIVION AND PASSION…

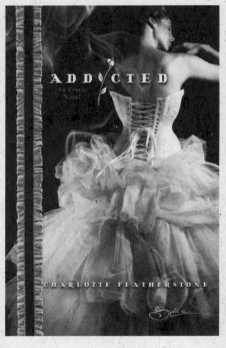

Friends since childhood, Anais Darnby and Lindsay Markham have long harbored a secret passion for one another. When they finally confess their love, their future together seems assured, sealed with their searing embrace.

But when a debauched Lindsay is seduced by a scheming socialite, a devastated Anais seeks refuge in another man's bed, while Lindsay retreats to the exotic East. There, he is seduced again—this time by the alluring red smoke and sinister beauty of opium.

Tortured by two obsessions—opium and Anais—Lindsay must ultimately decide which is the one he truly cannot live without.

ADDICTED

Available wherever books are sold!

Spice

FROM THE BESTSELLING AUTHOR OF
DIRTY, BROKEN AND *TEMPTED*
MEGAN HART

I pay strangers to sleep with me.
I have my reasons…but they're
not the ones you'd expect.
Looking at me you wouldn't
have a clue I carry this little
secret so close it creases up like
the folds of a fan. Tight. Personal.
Ready to unravel in the heat of
the moment.

Then one day I signed on to "pick
up" a stranger at a bar, but took
Sam home instead. And now that
I've felt his heat, his sweat and
everything else, can I really go
back to impersonal?

www.Spice-Books.com

SMH527TR

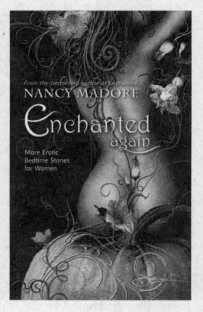

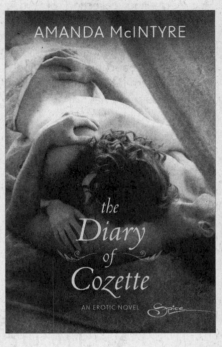

USA TODAY bestselling author

kayla perrin

After Sophie Gibson's husband confesses to a racy but ultimately unfulfilling affair, her rage leaves her raw, unable to process his attempt to repair the damage by suggesting she have her own tryst. Soon, though, the idea of sex as retaliation begins to intrigue her. Hooking up with Peter, a dark and dangerous artist willing to push the limits of Sophie's lustful, quivering need, fits the bill perfectly.

Soon the affair runs its course and now it's time for her to focus on her future... with Andrew. Except, Peter is convinced he can't live without her. Then come the cards, the presents, the calls...the hint of a threat. One way or another he will *have* Sophie. Even if that means exacting revenge of his own.

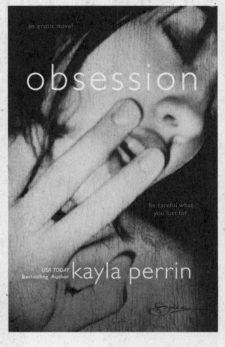

obsession

Available the first week of September 2008!

Spice

www.Spice-Books.com

SKP60520TR

Praise for The Commuter Marriage

"Tina Tessina's *The Commuter Marriage* is *the* guidebook for which so many couples have been longing. Always practical, logical, and extremely sympathetic, Dr. Tessina lays it all out—the points to consider, the do's and don'ts, the potential pitfalls, and, yes, even the advantages of this very modern phenomenon. No one should even think about making arrangements for a long-distance relationship without her book in hand."

—Isadora Alman, MFT, board-certified sex therapist and author of *Doing It: Real People Having Really Good Sex*

"If you're in a commuter relationship, or considering one, you and your partner should read this book cover to cover. Dr. Tessina anticipates every challenge you're likely to face, and gives a solid perspective and self-help exercises for dealing with each one. Learn how to keep your marriage close when you're apart and reunite when you're together. *The Commuter Marriage* stands out because it is up to date—for example, using current technology to share thoughts and photos—and because Dr. Tessina is a world-class expert on making relationships work."

—Joan Price, *www.joanprice.com*, author of *Better Than I Ever Expected: Straight Talk about Sex After Sixty*

"As a public safety psychologist, I work with police and firefighter families as they struggle with shift work and emergency deployments. Help is on the way. Dr. Tessina's easy-to-read new book, *The Commuter Marriage*, is full of sage advice, tips, and skill-building exercises for a range of topics from the practicalities of managing time, money, and childcare to the emotional challenges of intimacy, communication, and jealousy. Along the way, she shows the reader how real couples cope with a variety of long- and short-term separations."

—Ellen Kirschman, Ph.D., author of *I Love a Cop: What Police Families Need to Know* and *I Love a Fire Fighter: What the Family Needs to Know*

Praise for The Commuter Marriage

"As a licensed marriage counselor, I appreciate the practical and effective advice in Dr. Tessina's book. These are the major issues for commuting couples, and the exercises and information in these pages will help any couple navigate them."

—Riley K. Smith, M.A., MFT, author of *How to Be A Couple and Still Be Free and True Partners*

"In today's economy, we sometimes need to go where the jobs are—even if that means temporarily living far from home. Tessina helps couples keep their marriage, kids, and sanity together with solid tips for staying close to your children, and parenting as a couple, while you're apart."

—Kathy Sena, Parent Talk Today, *www.parenttalktoday.com*

"With so many couples living apart at least some of the time, Tina has written an enlightening book with lots of tips and insights into keeping a commuter relationship healthy."

—Daylle Deanna Schwartz, self-empowerment counselor and author of nine books, including *All Men Are Jerks Until Proven Otherwise*

"An inspiring, insightful book for husbands and wives who desire a fuller, more satisfying, and healthier relationship. It offers a variety of practical solutions to assist and empower married couples in creating a productive, gratifying, and meaningful lifestyle that works best for their family. Every married couple should read it!"

—Hogan Hilling, author of *The Modern Mom's Guide to Dads*

"In an age when most of us are separated by long distance and time or are apart because of demanding schedules, this book hits a chord. Simple, straightforward, practical, and compassionate, this book offers just-in-time wonderful advice for our crazy-busy lives. I need it!"

—Eileen McDargh, international speaker and author of *Gifts from the Mountain: Simple Truths for Life's Complexities* and *Work for a Living & Still be Free to Live*

Praise for The Commuter Marriage

"Tina Tessina's advice to commuting couples is thoughtful, direct, and smart. She provides a straight-talking but sympathetic roadmap through a situation that can be full of stress."
—Maryn McKenna, author, *Beating Back the Devil: On the Front Lines with the Disease Detectives of the Epidemic Intelligence Service*

"As a specialist in modern women, I often refer my readers to Tina Tessina and her books. Tina writes in a way that is relevant and interesting and her unique style resonates particularly well with women and the challenges they face in modern relationships."
—Kylie Welsh, journalist and author of *Impertinent Women? Women in Pursuit of the Extraordinary!*

"As Dr. Tessina says, commuter marriages are not new. I was married for over 40 years to the late Rudy Bond, an actor who spent much of his time in Hollywood or on the road in plays. Our marriage worked very well, perhaps better than a more conventional one, as we both were people who needed our space. Each coming together was a honeymoon. This intelligent book will help other commuting couples achieve success."
—Dr. Alma H. Bond, psychoanalyst and author of several books, including of *Who Killed Virginia Woolf? A Psychobiography*

"She's done it again. Like her many other helpful books, this one is just loaded with practical doable suggestions. Sometimes you just want to say, 'Why didn't I/we think of that?' but in the midst of the issues, one doesn't. [For those] suggestions you may have thought of, but decided [they might not work], and Dr. Tessina gives you courage to try. I plan to give this to several friends immediately."
—Rev. Dr. Mary Ellen Kilsby, pastor emeritus, First Congregational Church, Long Beach, CA

"Being far apart doesn't mean you can't be close. . . . A good guide for couples who want to stop arguing about finances."
—Stacie Z. Berg, award-winning journalist and author of several books, including *Consumer Reports Money Book*

Other Books by the Author

Money, Sex, and Kids: Stop Fighting about the Three Things That Can Ruin Your Marriage (Adams Media, 2007)

It Ends with You: Grow Up and Out of Dysfunction (2003)

The Real Thirteenth Step: Achieving Autonomy, Confidence and Self-reliance Beyond the Twelve-Step Programs, Revised 2nd Edition (2001)

The Ten Smartest Decisions a Woman Can Make After Forty (2001), also on audiotape and in three languages

The Unofficial Guide to Dating Again (1999)

Gay Relationships: How to Find Them, How to Improve Them, How to Make Them Last (1989)

Lovestyles: How to Celebrate Your Differences (1987)

With Riley K. Smith

How to Be a Couple and Still Be Free (1987; 3rd edition, 2002)

True Partners (1992)

Equal Partners (1994)

With Elizabeth Friar Williams

The 10 Smartest Decisions a Woman Can Make Before 40 (1998), also in seventeen languages

Keep Your Relationship *Close*
While You're Far *Apart*

The
commuter
Marriage

Tina B. Tessina, Ph.D.

A adamsmedia
avon, massachusetts

Published by
Adams Media, an F+W Publications Company
57 Littlefield Street, Avon, MA 02322. U.S.A.
www.adamsmedia.com

ISBN-10: 1-59869-432-4
ISBN-13: 978-1-59869-432-1

Printed in the United States of America.

J I H G F E D C B A

Library of Congress Cataloging-in-Publication Data
is available from the publisher.

This publication is designed to provide accurate and authoritative information with
regard to the subject matter covered. It is sold with the understanding that the publisher is not engaged in rendering legal, accounting, or other professional advice.
If legal advice or other expert assistance is required, the services of a competent
professional person should be sought.
—From a *Declaration of Principles* jointly adopted by a Committee of the
American Bar Association and a Committee of Publishers and Associations

Many of the designations used by manufacturers and sellers to distinguish their
product are claimed as trademarks. Where those designations appear in this book
and Adams Media was aware of a trademark claim, the designations have been
printed with initial capital letters.

*This book is available at quantity discounts for bulk purchases.
For information, please call 1-800-289-0963.*

*To the clients who teach me
and the friends who support me.*

contents

acknowledgments

It's not easy to be the supportive spouse when all you see of your partner is the back of her head backlit by the computer screen, but my wonderful husband of twenty-five years, Richard Sharrard, does an amazing job. He supports me through all the stress of writing, and he is one of the kindest, most caring men on the planet: generous to neighbors, friends, family, and to me. Anyone in Richard's life is blessed by his kind and caring nature. Thank you, Sweetheart, for your love and support, and especially for making me laugh!

Thanks also to my guardian agent Laurie Harper, who has been my sole literary agent since 1995. Without her, this book would not exist. She is what every writer needs: a champion to help reshape proposals into successful sellers, present me to new publishers, and support me through the writing process. I have been blessed to work with her for twelve years, and I'm looking forward to many more. It is incredibly valuable that Laurie can tell the hard truth when it's necessary yet be kind about it. She has guided and goaded me into giving my best.

I'm grateful, also, for tech support: Charles Fleishman, of *www.booksandauthors.com*, is my Webmaster of many years, and always there when I need him. Irving Sanchez seems to know everything there is about computers and has fixed mine on an emergency basis to rescue me several times.

I couldn't write much without the support of my chosen family, in (more or less) alphabetical order: Isadora Alman, Maggie and Ed Bialack, Victoria Bryan and Carrie Williams, Sylvia and Glen McWilliams, and Riley K. Smith. All of you are great friends, and I am surrounded by love, laughter, and caring because of you. Also to Beverly Terfloth, for tea and sympathy at the Vintage Tea Leaf, and Cindy Cyr Atkinson and the staff at The Coffee Cup.

Thanks also to my editors at Adams, Jennifer Kushnier and Katrina Schroeder; publicity director Beth Gissinger; and to the staff at Adams Media, for their expertise and support.

while we are absent,

one from the other

Your marriage vows may have said "till death do us part," but no one said anything about what happens when career, circumstances, or a child or family member with a problem makes it necessary for you to part and you want to maintain the closeness in your relationship. Being married at a distance is not as unusual as you may think. More and more couples are being separated by work, money, and family considerations. In fact, most long-term relationships encounter a period of living separately for one reason or another. As a counselor, I've seen more and more couples who must deal with the special circumstances of a commuter marriage. As our society becomes more mobile, jobs become scarce, and both spouses routinely have careers, commuter marriages have increased.

You can find the help you need in these pages if you and your spouse are either in or contemplating a situation where you are:

- Temporarily living apart due to job or other reasons
- Living at a distance you hadn't planned on
- Working such different hours it feels as though you are living apart
- Away from home for days or weeks at time due to a job or other necessity

- Trying to decide if a new job or opportunity is worth the separation you'll have to endure
- Dealing with the difference between your image of commuter marriage and the reality

Living separately really wasn't what you had in mind when you got married. You probably dreamed of quiet evenings sitting cozily on the couch, fun-filled weekends bicycling, hiking, or trekking the swap meet together, joint expeditions to the grocery store or the home improvement warehouse, working together on renovating the bathroom, or even just hanging out with friends or family. To your surprise, that's not what you've got. Instead, you're spending most of your time apart due to shift changes, job relocations, or too much work travel. Chances are it's so far from your dream that you don't really know how to handle it. You may be squabbling about being stuck with all the household chores while your partner pines away in a distant location, or you're the one who's all by yourself every night away from home. You both may be feeling all the intimacy and partnership gradually draining out of your relationship, leaving you with an empty shell where your marriage used to be.

Spouses left at home have to deal with all the household problems: plumbing that doesn't work, financial decisions to make, all the child rearing and discipline, and all the chores usually shared by two. Spouses not at home are lonely, isolated, and feel out of touch with family.

Commuter Relationships Are Different

You've heard a lot from various experts on TV, radio, and in magazine articles and books about how important communication and intimacy are to the health and survival of your relationship. But they don't talk about how to stay in touch when you can't touch. Phone calls, e-mails, photos, and instant messages help, but it's hard to feel as close when you don't see each other. It's also difficult to make joint decisions when one of you is far removed from the problems your partner is facing.

Commuter marriages and long-distance relationships are increasing as people become more mobile. While there have always been reasons couples had to be apart, many now experience it routinely, and there are many more tools, gadgets, and solutions than for previous generations. For example, when sailors went to sea a hundred years ago, their wives often knew nothing of how they were, or they received letters that were months old. Even twenty years ago, a salesman or truck driver who was on the road would have to wait until he could find a telephone to call home or the office and check in. Today, the sailor, soldier, or salesperson might as frequently be a "she," and you can carry your telephone, e-mail, IM, video, digital pictures, and text messaging around in your pocket. Whether you or your spouse is the modern commuter, you have a choice of methods for instant communication around the world. What would that previous-generation salesman think of the ability you have today to surreptitiously snap a picture of an obnoxious speaker at a boring meeting and phone it home or text-message beneath the edge of the conference table?

As people become more mobile, more and more couples must deal with making their relationships work long distance. Your relationship configuration might be a short-term but regular separation, as when your partner makes a lot of business trips, is a firefighter or in the merchant marine, or drives a truck. It might be temporary if your partner gets a job or promotion that requires a move and you stay behind because of work, family obligations, or to sell a house or keep the kids in school. Perhaps your separation is much longer term, for example, if one of you is in the military or working overseas; perhaps you still live together, but you're on opposite schedules and see each other so infrequently that it feels like you are commuting.

A Guidebook for Commuter Marriage

If you and your spouse are in a long-distance or commuter marriage, you probably have been wishing for an instruction book, something to tell you what to do with the problems you're facing that just aren't part of a living-together marriage. This book is just what you've been looking for. *The Commuter Marriage* will answer your questions, such as:

- How can we still feel close while we're both geographically challenged?
- What can we do about mistrust and jealousy during the times that we're apart?
- What are other couples doing in commuter marriages?
- What are the special problems of commuter marriages?
- How can we communicate effectively when we don't see each other often?
- Why is it so difficult to reconnect when we do get together, and how can we fix it?
- What can we do to relieve the stress of being apart?
- How can we learn to make decisions together from a distance, without fighting?
- Are there any benefits of commuter marriage?
- How do we decide what to do when each of us wants something different?
- What can we do to make things fair for both of us?

No matter what kind of commute you're making, the information and guidelines in these pages will help you keep your relationship connected when you're disconnected. *The Commuter Marriage* is designed to help you manage a long-distance or commuter relationship:

- Whether your separation is temporary, forced, or by choice, long-term or brief
- Whether you're newly married or long married

- When your job keeps you away from home a lot
- If one of you was recently promoted to a different city
- If you live a bicoastal lifestyle
- If you work such different schedules you hardly see each other.
- If your spouse is overseas due to military service

In these pages, you'll find case histories of couples who face the same issues that exist in your marriage—being separated and struggling to maintain your partnership mutuality and equality. You'll meet them in Chapter 1, and we'll follow each couple throughout the book to see what problems their commuter marriages presented and how they solved them.

For each problem you face, you'll find specific solutions as well as the examples of how other couples use the exercises and guidelines to solve the problems created by their long-distance situations.

You'll also find step-by-step guidelines, how-tos, and exercises to teach you the skills you need to manage your unique and challenging situation, and to maximize the advantages of your situation, as well as case histories that illustrate both the problems and the solutions. These couples' case histories illustrate the possibilities and difficulties of loving over a distance and how and why both positive and negative dynamics arise. The case histories also show how couples have effectively used the tools, guidelines, exercises, and solutions presented in this book.

Each subsequent chapter begins with a list of the questions answered in that chapter. You'll find you want to keep *The Commuter Marriage* handy as a reference book for when long-distance relationship problems arise.

what is commuter marriage
and who's doing it?

Commuter marriage is as old as legend and history. From Antony and Cleopatra, who ruled different countries, to Odysseus and his patient wife Penelope, who waited for twenty years for him to return from his odyssey, to modern day businessmen and career women, spending time apart while being married is not a new idea.

In recent years, however, new types of distance relating have emerged that don't always involve long distances or even living apart. In my counseling practice, I work with many couples who are struggling to stay in touch and trying to keep their marriages on an even keel while they are separated by work-related travel, jobs that require staying on-site for days at a time, and conflicting schedules that allow them to raise their children while both parents are working.

I also work with involuntary commuter marriages in which the partners live apart because one of them has been transferred at work, they have a family need such as the care of aging parents or a seriously ill child, or a military deployment has separated them.

Some couples experience temporary long-distance situations. This could be because one of them one has been promoted to a new job in a different city, and the other parent and the children stay behind to sell the house or finish the school year. Actors and others in the movie, TV, and theater industries are often separated because the job (movie, TV series, or play) requires being at a location far from their primary residence. Even couples who live together but work opposite shifts (one works days, the other nights) can feel that they're in a long-distance relationship.

No matter what the circumstances are that create the commute, all these couples face remarkably similar problems and issues, which are probably similar to the problems and issues that caused you to pick up this book.

Either you're already in a commuter marriage, you're contemplating one, or you know someone who is and want to help, so let's begin by defining commuter marriage, taking a look at who's doing it, and exploring the various arrangements that can be called commuter marriages.

About Long-Distance Marriages

Commuter marriage, or long-distance marriage, is a noticeable trend that is apparently getting bigger. According to the U.S. Census Bureau, the number of married Americans who said their spouses lived elsewhere—not including those who were separated—increased 21 percent from 1994 to 1998, and today 3.2 million married Americans, including military families, live separately, a 26 percent increase since 1999. The Center for the Study of Long-Distance Relationships Web site (*www.longdistance relationships.net*) states there are "3,569,000 married persons in the United States who live apart for reasons other than marital discord in 2005 (the latest data available). This is 2.9 percent of all US marriages." Not only does the war take husbands away from their wives, but the greater involvement of women in the military means that more husbands are also left behind during wartime deployment.

Most of the literature on commuter marriage maintains that many more wives follow their husbands to new locations because of career than husbands who follow wives, which is also what my counseling practice reflects. But because women are becoming more career oriented, they are often less willing to just pick up from a job they love and move because hubby had a great offer somewhere else. Statistics show that 80 percent of the work force is now made up of two-career couples, and 60 percent of all workers are women. Two-career couples are more likely to find themselves spending time living apart than couples with one stay-at-home partner, and the great ease of transportation today means there are many more jobs that require extensive travel. When both partners work, the likelihood is that they'll face commuting at some point during their marriage.

Your Personal Style of Commuter Marriage

For you and your partner, commuter marriage may mean:

- You're living apart, temporarily or for a long time.
- You spend days or weeks apart sporadically or on a regular schedule.
- You both live full-time in the same house but rarely see each other because of work schedules.
- You may have chosen this lifestyle by preference or been forced into it by circumstance.
- One or both of you may be traveling, frequently or occasionally, but not together.
- One of you is forced to travel far away for long periods of time, either because you work in the military or some other traveling occupation.

Any of these situations can be called a commuter marriage. Perhaps you're not married, or you're contemplating marrying. Perhaps you're in this situation because you met while living far apart and your relationship has progressed to commitment or marriage, but you're still not living together. Many commuter marriages begin as Internet dating, because the partners met while traveling for work or other reasons, or with partners who met at college and whose careers took them to different places.

Some Possible Scenarios

Of course, there are many possibilities and varieties of how couples can live apart, for long or short periods of time, and still keep their relationships vital. Let's look at each of these scenarios and see what the dynamics and possibilities are.

One of You Commutes

There are many reasons why one of you might commute while the other stays at home. You or your partner may have a career that requires travel or training away from home. This travel can be frequent or occasional, regularly scheduled or sporadic, but when it happens one partner is left at home. When only one of you is traveling and the other is stationary, there are both positive and negative effects on your relationship.

For example, getting a brief break from each other and your routine can be helpful. If you're at home, you can catch up on chores, go out with solo friends, and use the time as a gift. On the other hand, you can feel lonely, burdened by all the responsibility, and neglected.

As the traveling partner, you might feel excited about travel, energized about the job, and spend downtime in hotels and on the road working out, catching up on portable or Internet projects and hobbies, and enjoying some alone time. You might also feel isolated; guilty for neglecting home, spouse, and children; unhappy in hotels and airports; stressed by the travel; and overworked.

Each time you come back together, you can be excited to see each other and make the most of your time together, or you can immediately continue the squabbles you were having on the phone. Sometimes a commuter marriage that begins great becomes harder as circumstances change, as with Lucy and Josh:

lucy & josh

Lucy, forty-five, and Josh, forty-six, have been married twenty years and have two children, fifteen-year-old Ben and seventeen-year-old Josh Junior. Josh makes a good living as a long-haul truck driver and enjoys his job, but his work leaves Lucy at home alone with the children for a week or two at a time. Lucy says, "In the early years, before the babies came, it was fun to have Josh gone. I always knew where he was and when he'd be home, and I was working as a movie extra then, so I got to go out when I wasn't working, see my friends, and visit my parents on the weekends. I even took some short trips with my sister. Every time Josh came home we had a great reunion, and he had several days to spend with me until the next job. I wouldn't accept any extra work while he was home, and we had fun. Then Josh Jr. arrived, and everything changed. Staying home with one baby and then two, while Josh was driving, was a lot harder, and he'd often come home to find me irritable and complaining. All the responsibility fell on me while he was gone."

Josh agrees: "My job is hard, physical labor, and it's pretty grueling to be on the road for days at a time, but I always looked forward to getting home to Lucy. We had great reunions in those early days. But when the kids were little, and Lucy did most of the child care, she couldn't wait for me to get home and take over caring for the kids so she could have some time to herself. That made it very hard for us to feel close."

Lucy and Josh made it through that difficult time. In later chapters, you'll learn the techniques they used to change their struggle and make the relationship work.

Both of You Commute

It's not unusual these days to find situations where each of you leaves home at different times because:

- Both of you have careers that require travel.
- One of you travels for work, and the other travels for a different reason.
- You have a job (such as fire fighter, military, or merchant marine) that requires you to leave periodically and stay for a few days or longer at a time.
- You have a circumstance such as an ailing relative or child that requires you to travel to be a caretaker or receive medical care.
- One of you works a graveyard shift or rotating shift job that limits your time together, so both of you feel as if you're separated for extended periods.

Schedule juggling can present an enormous problem in this situation, because you are not always in control of when you're required to be away from home. When both of you are gone at the same time, you must solve problems about how the household chores will be handled, bills will be paid, and children and pets will be cared for. The other major problem with two different commuting schedules is finding time to be at home together. It is also possible to have so much to catch up on when you're home that there is little time for the two of you to reconnect. When your schedules mesh well, it means that one of you can take care of things while the other is gone, and you get enough time together to enjoy each other and feel like a family. When it works well, this type of alternate commuting can make it possible to have two incomes and still care for children, family members, and household responsibilities.

judy & nick

Nick, thirty-one, is a fireman, and Judy, thirty, works as a flight attendant. They have two children ages five and seven. Nick has a regular schedule of three twenty-four-hour days on shift, where he lives at the firehouse, and five days at home. Judy flew more hours when they were first married, but now she has enough seniority to fly only once a month, usually for a full weekend. She sticks to this limit most of the time to keep her seniority, her benefits (such as low-cost travel for her family), and to supplement the family income. "I enjoy flying," says Judy, "and I know Nick loves being a firefighter. Neither one of us likes being away from each other or the kids for nights at a time, but the benefits are worth the separation. Nick is great at taking care of things when I'm not home, and when I'm home he's not actually far away, so if something goes wrong while he's working I can usually contact him. The biggest problem we have is when I have trouble scheduling my flight week or weekend during the time he's at home."

Nick says, "I do love my career, and I love my family. Firefighting pays pretty well, has good benefits, but the best part is that I get several days and nights at home with Judy and the kids. Judy loves her job too, and it's amazing how well it pays and how few days a month she has to work now that she has seniority. Actually, I enjoy most of the time when she flies, because I get to hang out with the kids. It was a lot harder taking care of them when they were little, but now we can do things together. I used to run with the baby in a stroller, but now the kids ride their bikes along side me when I run to keep in shape. It's always great to see Judy when she comes home—we have a reunion. The only time we struggle with it is when our schedules aren't working well together."

Your Traveling Is Sporadic

Sporadic and infrequent travel seems as though it would be easier to handle, but the unpredictable nature of it can create problems. If your job or a family responsibility requires being away from home on occasion, but you can't schedule it very far in advance, it becomes more difficult to plan your time at home and to care for responsibilities while you're away. Couples with sporadic traveling challenges usually have more time at home together than couples with more predictable travel, but because the travel is often unexpected and perhaps rushed, it can be much more disruptive to your lifestyle and family schedule. In order to be successful with this commuting style, you and your partner need to learn to be flexible, solve problems well, and enjoy your occasional breaks from each other and your routine.

jane & edward

Edward says, "I like the travel part of my job, and I like being so busy. The stress sometimes gets to me, though, and I wish Jane and I had more time together. Sometimes, when she has day shifts, we get to hang out together, but other times she has to schedule intern shifts for school. We're lucky when she can manage to use some of her nursing work as her practicum for some school courses and save some hours, but it doesn't always work that way. We're hanging out together when we can and trying to keep in mind that it won't be forever."

Your Traveling Is Scheduled

One of the good points about regularly scheduled commuting is that it's predictable, and if you are organized and orderly about it, you can build a routine around it that serves both of you well. It's important for the traveling partner to be willing to pitch in at home when there, and it's equally necessary for the stay-at-home partner to give the traveler credit for working and to understand the stresses of travel. Of course, the more frequently the traveler travels, and the longer the trips (even though they are planned), the more stress they can create.

Gail & Charles

Charles, thirty-four, is an officer in the merchant marine and onboard a ship for weeks or months at a time. His wife, Gail, twenty-four, is pregnant with their first child. In five more years, Charles will have put twenty years into his career and he can retire. Gail was working as a schoolteacher, but now she's at home, preparing to have their first child. "It was easier dealing with Charles being away when I was teaching and busy," says Gail, "My days were full, and I spent time with my family and friends. Now that I'm so housebound and uncomfortable, it's much harder. Thank God he's coming home soon, and I can look forward to having time here at home with him for two months. We're hoping the baby will be born on schedule during that time so he can be home with me and our daughter during her first few weeks. I've stayed close to my parents because Charles is gone so often, but when he retires, we will probably move somewhere else where he can start a business." Charles looks forward to his retirement too. "I loved my career for the first ten years, but I've done enough traveling, and I've learned about all I can learn here since I don't want to stay aboard ship. I'm looking forward to retirement when I can be home with my family and start my own specialty freight business. I think I've learned what I need to know to be successful. I spend the long days onboard ship studying business and longing to be home with my wife. When I was single, I wanted a girl in every port, but now the only girls I want are Gail and my daughter."

Living Apart Was Imposed by Circumstance

Perhaps your situation is not really a commute but a necessity imposed by a job in a different city or state, one of you must live with an ailing parent for a time, one is in the military or on assignment in another country, or education that takes you away from home for an extended, possibly indefinite, period of time.

Several extra dynamics may be present in this situation. For example, the circumstances that make it necessary for you or your partner to commute could involve stress, difficulty, grief, or another strong emotion. When there isn't time to plan the move and the separation, everyone involved feels upset, scattered, and in turmoil. Stress levels can rise when your circumstances involve a lot of unknowns because you can't try them out in advance, and there are other unstable dynamics. When you don't know the timetable or outcome and a lot depends on the future, it's normal to speculate or fantasize about what will happen, which can be scary or set you up for disappointment.

Strictly speaking, your situation probably involved many choices. You might be the sibling who decided to go live with mom, or maybe you're the partner who took the job away from home because it was better than the offers you got that were closer to home. What makes it involuntary is that the choices you make to live apart are necessitated by external circumstances, and you'd have done something different if you had the opportunity.

Sara & Paul

Paul, twenty-four, and Sara, twenty-five, have been married for five years and have a daughter, Lacey, three, and a baby on the way. Paul was an insurance adjuster who had joined the National Guard after high school. His guard unit was called up to Iraq, he left two months ago, and neither of them knows when he will be back. Sara has gone back to work as a legal secretary, which makes it harder for her to care for Lacey. Sara's mother lives and works in another state and comes to help when she can. Paul's mother is also still working, although she can watch her grandchild some evenings to give Sara a break. Both grandmas do what they can to help out with the cost of child care. Paul says, "My income fell way down when I had to quit my job to come over here. This is a big struggle for us. When I joined the National Guard, I thought I might have to help with a disaster for a few weeks at a time, but I never thought I'd be sent overseas. It didn't occur to me or to Sara until the war started. We got married and had the kids partly in case I was sent. I'm glad we began a family, and I'm excited about the baby, but I feel terrible being over here away from them."

"This is so hard," says Sara, "I didn't mind Paul being gone for one weekend a month and one week in the year, but this was way more than we ever anticipated. Thank God for our mothers and my sister Susan. Susan has a couple of kids of her own, and she can take mine when I'm ready to scream, or if the baby sitter lets me down."

Living Apart Is Voluntary

When you decide you'll live apart for specific reasons and you both agree to do it, the situation is a little easier than for involuntary separations. When you're making a voluntary decision, you and your partner usually have a chance to plan and investigate the circumstances. While the reality may be different than you expected, and there are always some surprises, this kind of situation is usually much more manageable.

Jill, forty-six, and James, fifty-one, have been married ten years and have no children, but James has two grown sons from a previous marriage. Jill is a writer/editor, and after struggling with the idea, she decided to accept a very tempting magazine editor position several hundred miles away. James is a lawyer with a partnership in a firm and is staying home. They commute most weekends, taking turns to see each other, but when magazine deadlines or a big court case intervenes they can't always make the trip. "I am so excited about this job—it's a magazine I've always wanted to work for, and they like me, and I love the work. If it hadn't been for my marriage, I'd have snapped up this job without a backward glance. I used to move for big job opportunities regularly when I was single. It's normal in the magazine business. But being married to James makes a big difference. I had an awful time learning how to sleep alone again, I miss having those easy little chats you can have when you live together, and I feel guilty about making it difficult for him. It's not the money, he makes plenty, and I was making a good salary before. This is my career, I love magazine writing and editing, and I want to do it for a long time. I was established before I met James, and I think I'd wither away if I didn't challenge myself. Hopefully, I'll find another great job closer to home soon. But it takes a toll on the marriage to be so far apart and see each other so sporadically. The traveling is tiring—it's not like getting to rest on the weekends." James understands Jill's decision, but "I'm not nearly as happy in this marriage as I was when we were both living in our home. It does give me free time to see my sons, but I'm visiting Jill a lot of weekends, when my sons have time off from work. I can get some briefs done commuting on the train, but it's not as comfortable as working in my home office, and Jill and I are often too tired to really enjoy our time together."

Sometimes only one spouse feels it's voluntary, and the other feels forced and resentful.

Colette, thirty-one, and Harry, forty-two, have been married for twelve years. Colette is on tenure track at a local university after six years of teaching. Harry, who is a marketing executive, has just been offered a very lucrative and powerful position as a CEO in another state. Colette says, "I have worked so hard to gain tenure here, I've almost achieved it, and now Harry wants to move? I love teaching

colette & harry

biology, and these obs are not easy to find. I've been conducting experiments and publishing, and I have years invested in it, and years to go before I'm finished. I always thought I'd retire at this job. I like where we live, and I don't really want to move to the city, where Harry would have to go. He has a great job here, I don't know why he needs more."

Harry says, "This CEO job is my fondest dream come true. It will set us up for the rest of our lives, and I'll be earning enough that Colette won't have to work at all. If we ever get around to having the children we want, they'll be well taken care of. I know Colette loves her teaching job, but she can find a new one where my new job is. If she insists on staying at her job. we'll be separated for years before we get to move together."

Your Situation Is Short Term

Some commutes are significant but temporary, such as when you're waiting for the children's school year to end, trying to sell your old home before you can buy a new one in the new location, or the reason for one partner to travel won't last more than a few months or a year. It's usually easier to be patient with such a situation, but patience can be a trap. You tell yourself, "It's OK, it's only for a short time and I can handle all the household chores, being alone, and the disruption for that long," but if you're not careful, your frustration and resentment can build until you and your partner are squabbling about things you originally thought were fine. Even when the long-distance situation is temporary, it's important to pay attention to how you feel and handle your dissatisfaction or problems when they arise rather than letting frustration build.

Michael, fifty-four, was downsized from his executive job at fifty-two and had trouble finding a new one, so he finally took a position in another state while his wife, Rachel, fifty-one, stayed in their original home, close to her aging mother and their grown children and grandchild. "My mother is seventy-seven and she needs me," says Rachel. "She's getting more and more frail. She had a small stroke and lost the use of one arm, and even though she has a caregiver every day to help, I don't want to leave her at the mercy of strangers. I understand why Michael had to take this job—he wasn't ready to retire, and it's difficult to find an executive position at his age. I have to admit, I'm much more comfortable here on the East Coast then out West, where he is. We're fortunate that his company provides a condo he can live in while he's there and covers his travel. But he's got a responsible position and can't just hop back and forth whenever he wants to. He comes home for all the holidays and his vacation, but the rest of the year I'm the one who travels. I go visit him a weekend at a time. It's not great for our marriage, but we've been married thirty-two years, and we've survived worse." Michael says, "It's lonely here. I'm beginning to make friends, I golf with the guys, and sometimes one of the other execs will invite me home for a nice dinner, but most of the time I eat out or bring takeout food in. One bright spot is that my children love to visit me in this vacation paradise, and my condo has a guest room, so I get to see each of my kids for a week or two at a time. Sometimes my daughters even cook for me, which is super. I love it when I get home or Rachel visits, but I can see she's worried about her mom, and I worry about her. I've got to put in at least two years here, and then I'm hoping I can either be transferred back home or find another job there. "

Your Situation Is Long Term

Interestingly enough, in my experience of counseling clients in long-distance relationships, most couples seem to handle long-term situations much better than short-term ones because they take them much more seriously, plan better for them, and understand that it will be a tough situation. Even so, there are many problems that arise as the situation drags on, especially if it's very long-standing. You and your partner will be drawn closer together at first, looking forward eagerly to the time when you can be together, but gradually you each build a daily living pattern in your separate locations and it's easy to grow apart. A long-term separation needs special care to keep your relationship fresh and close.

cindy & bill

Cindy, thirty-five, got her nursing training by joining the Navy and worked at a naval base hospital close to home for the first ten years of her career. Her base was closed, and now she's commuting 120 miles for the next five years, until retirement, which she did not expect to have to do. Her husband Bill, forty, is a self-employed building contractor in the city where the original naval base was located, and they have a seven-year-old daughter, Chloe. Cindy feels the stress: "I love my Navy career, and I'm grateful for the wonderful education, training, and experience I've gotten by working at the base. But I never considered the possibility of having to complete my tour of duty by commuting."

"She's got that right," says Bill. "Neither of us anticipated the base closing and throwing our lives into turmoil. Cindy used to be here every evening to help Chloe with her homework, make dinner, and put her to bed. Now she's only home on the weekends. It's good that the hospital changed her shifts so she can work four ten-hour days. She gets to go in on Mondays and leave Thursday night for home, but it's a lot different. Now the homework and dinner chores fall on me. I've gained a lot more respect for the hard work Cindy does at home."

You Both Live at Home but Don't See Each Other

No one is technically commuting in this style of marriage, but it feels like it because you see each other so seldom. Couples often find themselves in this situation because they're trying to find a way to make sure one is home with the children all the time, yet they need two salaries to make ends meet. Or a partner will work plus go to school at night to get ahead. Other couples choose to work in fields that have alternating schedules that limit their time together.

Susan & Bob

Susan, thirty-two, and Bob, thirty-five, have been married nine years and have three children, ages eight, six, and five. When Bob lost his aerospace project management job, Susan went back to work. She works days as a teacher's aide, and Bob has taken a daytime computer programming job and is taking classes at night to begin a new IT career. Bob says, "This job pays a lot less than the job I lost, but at least it pays the bills and provides health insurance for the family. Susan's job doesn't pay much either, but it allows her to be at school where the children are, and to have the same hours, and the money she does bring in helps. It's hard going to school at night and working days, and Susan and I only see each other on the weekends, so we feel as though we're living apart during the week. Plus, I have to travel for training classes that take me away some weekends. We're making sacrifices so I can get into a better-paying career, so we're willing to do this for our future."

"I'm actually enjoying working as a teacher's aide," says Susan. "I'm surprised, because I really didn't want to have to go back to work. But when Bob lost his job, it was necessary, and now I like it. What I don't like is that Bob and I hardly see each other, except on weekends. We sleep in the same bed, which is a comfort, but other than that, he might as well be out of town. I really miss him at meals during the week, and to go to the kids' games and recitals. The kids miss him too. We all understand that it's worth it and the future will be better, but it's not easy right now."

Your Commuter Marriage Situation

From the following choices, select the ones that most describe your current commuter marriage situation. If your partner is also reading this book, compare notes after each of you makes your choices. You may be surprised to find that your partner has chosen some different options.

What kind of couple commute do you have? Check off the situations on this list that apply to you and your partner:

- ○ One of you commutes
- ○ Each of you commutes
- ○ Your traveling is sporadic
- ○ Your traveling is scheduled
- ○ Living apart was imposed by circumstance
- ○ Living apart is voluntary
- ○ Your situation is short term
- ○ Your situation is long term
- ○ You have children
- ○ You have no children
- ○ You're commuting for financial reasons
- ○ You're commuting for other reasons
- ○ You envision living together again soon
- ○ You don't see yourselves living together soon
- ○ You enjoy your current commuting situation

Compare lists with your partner. (If your partner isn't available to do the checklist, do it yourself from your partner's point of view. For example, perhaps your spouse commutes for financial reasons but you don't—you're taking care of an ailing family member.) Use this list as a point of discussion to begin the mutual evaluation of your circumstances and open the dialogue between you.

Tools for Your Commuter Relationship

Each of the couples described in this chapter is in a unique situation. Your own commuting arrangement may contain some of the components of theirs, but because every couple is different, your circumstances will most likely not be identical to any of our case history couples. Their stories are presented to illustrate the problems and solutions discussed, to help you understand the problems other couples face in situations similar to yours, and to illustrate how they handle them. In the next chapter, you'll see some of the specific problems that arise for each couple prompted by the dynamics of their situation, and you'll learn specific communicating and problem-solving techniques you can use in your own, unique situation.

commuter marriage problems,
questions, and answers

Like everyone else who spends time apart during their marriage, you and your partner probably hoped everything would work itself out and you'd find a way to deal with the stress and problems of being away from each other. And you probably discovered it's not that simple. Every marriage encounters stress and problems in the ordinary course of events, but in a commuter marriage you face additional dynamics to the usual problems. For example, take Jane, the nurse who is also in college, and her husband Edward, who sells medical equipment. Every marriage has to manage money and financial problems, but Jane and Edward must deal with many extra expenses such as Edward's travel costs and Jane's school expenses, including:

- Occasional airfare
- Housing costs when he's staying away from home
- Extra charges for telephones and other equipment
- Car rental fees
- Tuition, books, and lab costs for Jane's college courses
- How to handle finances from a distance

Edward says: "It was difficult in the beginning to anticipate the extra costs and financial decisions we'd have to make. My company reimburses me for some expenses, but not all, and we really didn't know how to even think about the financial issues we'd face."

This chapter will help you think clearly, anticipate, and solve problems about money and other issues you might face within your commuter marriage.

Questions about Commuter Marriage

No matter what kind of commuting situation you have or are contemplating within your own marriage, you are likely to encounter many of the same problems and questions that many of my clients have experienced. Here are some frequently asked questions I encounter from couples who are contemplating or actually involved in a commuter marriage:

- How do we decide whether to commute or to move or change jobs so we can stay together?
- How can I manage the family alone?
- How do we handle all the changes in our lifestyle?
- How can we keep our intimate connection strong?
- What happens when one becomes jealous or suspicious?
- Is it OK to develop friends and activities away from home?
- How do we keep the workload fair when the stay-at-home person is stuck with chores, household maintenance, and child rearing?
- Is it OK to fight long-distance, or what do we do instead?
- What about fighting when we're home?
- How do we discuss and balance the workload?
- What if we don't agree about parenting decisions while apart?
- What if my partner undermines my parenting?
- How can we manage finances when we have all these extra expenses?
- How do we decide whether or not we should set up two separate homes?

- What kinds of stress are involved, and how can we handle it better?
- How do we manage the limited time we have, the different time zones we're in, and having enough time for each other and the family?

If you find yourself asking questions like these, or hearing them from your partner, or even lying awake in the middle of the night worrying, you'll find the answers you're looking for here. You'll get some basic answers to these specific questions, and in the following chapters you'll learn more specific skills and techniques for handling the basic issues behind these problems. First, we'll see how these specific questions came up in the lives of the couples in the case histories and discuss some solutions.

Planning

Several of the guidelines in this chapter, such as the exercise for balancing the workload and the guidelines for discussing parenting, are really about planning because it is so central to making your situation work well. Planning is an important tool for any partners who are commuting or anticipating it. There will be a lot you can't plan for, but having a good plan, with flexibility built in, will help minimize unpleasant surprises.

You can plan for:

- Whether the commute is a good idea
- How long it may last
- Extra costs and financial problems
- How to share responsibilities
- How to communicate effectively when you're apart

But, of course, the biggest planning issue is planning to live apart in the first place.

How Do We Decide Whether or Not to Commute?

Many spouses who commute have a choice and many don't. Either way, planning becomes necessary. When you have a choice, such as with a job offer, planning helps you figure out whether it's a good choice or not. If you don't have a choice, such as with a military deployment or tending a family member who's ill, planning will still help you make the best of the situation. If you know in advance that you'll be living apart, you can plan ahead, but if the situation comes up suddenly, planning even after the fact will still help you handle the situation more easily. The following exercise will help you plan effectively.

EXERCISE: PLANNING FOR YOUR NEW SITUATION

1. *Get the facts.* Gather as many facts as you can about your anticipated move (or the move you've already had to make) and write them down.
   - How long will it last?
   - What is your main reason for going?
   - What are the benefits of commuting?
   - What are the biggest challenges?
   - Will you need to pay for housing?
   - What other costs (transportation, phone/computer/ PDA costs, taxes, clothing) are involved?
   - How will it affect your financial situation? (Is there income, and does it offset expenses?)
   - What will you miss?
   - How will you compensate for what's missing?
2. *Research.* If there are any questions in step one that you can't answer, or if the answers aren't clear enough to understand, do some research and see how much you can find out. By searching on the Internet, asking people you know who have done what you're doing (other people at work who have lived separately or traveled a lot), or researching rent and food costs in the place you'll be staying, you can find out a surprising amount, and your plan will be more realistic and effective.

3. *List positives and negatives.* Make a list of the positives, such as:
    - It will be great for your career.
    - Your mother needs you and you'll feel good about helping.
    - You'll earn good money.
    - Being apart might help you appreciate each other more.

    List the negatives, such as:
    - You'll be away from each other.
    - There are extra expenses.
    - You'll miss out on your kids' activities.
    - Travel can be exhausting.
4. *Anticipate problems.* Analyze your situation for the problems that may come up, such as:
    - Too much responsibility placed on one of you
    - Taking care of the kids when one of you is gone
    - Keeping your intimate connection alive while you're apart
    - Extra expenses or changes in income
5. *Create solutions.* Brainstorm to create solutions for each of the problems on your list. Some of your solutions may be speculative, and different problems may arise, but if you've thought about the problems beforehand, you'll have an idea what might work for both of you.
6. *Make your plan.* Using the information from the previous five steps, write out a plan, on paper or the computer, with steps to follow. As you complete the steps, mark them off, and if new ideas come up, add them in. You'll find this plan will become a guideline to follow and a touchstone to get you back on track when you become confused or discouraged.

How Do We Handle the Changes in Our Lifestyle?

All of us are hard-wired to seek out patterns and operate according to them. Every waking moment bombards each of us with overwhelming floods of data, infinite numbers of choices, and confusing and conflicting information. Sheer survival depends upon your brain being able to sort through all of this every minute. The ingenious solution, built right in to your brain and nervous system, is the ability to operate according to patterns.

Visual patterns make it possible for you to identify the chair from the table, the dining room from the bedroom, and whether you see them in their three-dimensional form or see a photograph, or even see the drawing created by your six-year-old. A table on a canvas by van Gogh or Picasso is recognizable even though the perspective is skewed and the colors are strange. It still fits the pattern of table.

Kinesthetic patterns mean you can reach for a utensil, pot, or dish in the kitchen without even looking where you reach, or stumble into the bathroom and grab your toothbrush before you're really awake. A combination of kinesthetic and visual patterns means you can drive the familiar route to work without even thinking about it until it becomes so automatic that when you get a new job or home, you find yourself taking the old route if you don't pay attention.

Auditory patterns are what make it possible to recognize a favorite song from the others, to know if a small sound from your child or your partner's tone of voice indicates distress, or to finish your spouse's sentences.

Patterns are helpful because they enable you to recognize familiar things so you do not have to pay attention to each detail. The stress of paying attention is one of the major reasons why change is difficult, and patterns are helpful. Research shows that moving to a new home is one of the most stressful experiences you can have, almost as stressful as the death of a loved one. This doesn't appear to make sense (because moving to a new home is usually a desirable change) until you think about patterns. All those kinesthetic, visual patterns have suddenly changed—the pots, dishes, and your toothbrush (not to mention the bathroom) are all in different places. So is the furniture. You're tripping over chairs that seem to be in the wrong places. You have to think every minute of the drive to work because the route is unfamiliar. Each of these changed patterns represents a lot of stress. When you're operating within old, familiar patterns, you don't need to think about what you're doing. Your body is wired to do familiar things without having to think about them. This leaves your mind free to wander and to destress. When you're dealing with new situations you don't have that luxury, so a larger percentage of your time is stressful, and everything new is a little harder.

Making Change Easier

To make all the changes you're facing easier, use the plan you previously made and list every detail you know about how your new situation will work to picture yourself in the your new setting and arrangement. For example, if you're going to be sleeping by yourself for the first time in a long time, go through your bedtime routine in your imagination to see how it will feel and what changes you want to make. Once you visualize it a number of times, it will become ingrained enough to feel more comfortable and you won't feel so stressed about doing it. Having something different to focus on will make the psychological changes easier.

jane & edward

"On nights when Edward is gone," says Jane, "I sleep better if I leave the radio on playing soft music and lay Edward's pillows end to end in his place next to me. The music masks little noises and the background noise is soothing, and when I roll over, there's a feeling of something there where Edward should be, which keeps me from waking up in the middle of the night. Of course, it's no replacement for my husband in the flesh, but it does help me get a better night's sleep."

Programming Your Attention

All of us have a brain mechanism psychologists call *preparatory set*. It's one of the inspired tools the mind uses to sort through and manage the enormous amounts of data that flow in daily. By writing down the things you want to accomplish and visualizing them to make them clear, you can program that mechanism. Once programmed, it directs your attention to certain events and occurrences. This amazing selective tool of the mind controls most of what you notice and remember from your experiences, and this selection process explains why two people will have a totally different memory of the same event. Once you program your expectations to conform to your new goals (by writing them down and picturing yourself achieving them), you will automatically be more aware of certain events, opportunities, and people who can be helpful. You'll also be clearer about what you want, and this will sneak into your conversation and your general attitude where others can pick up on it. It's so effective it can feel like magic, but it's really a normal brain function. To make mental pictures of how your commuter marriage will work:

- Picture yourself being successful in your new situation.
- Imagine reconnecting seamlessly.
- Visualize yourselves enjoying the time you do have together.

When you create a mental picture of how your relationship will look, you'll feel more comfortable with your changes. Change will still take work, but using this mental trick will help you reach your goals easier and faster. You will also find several of the exercises in Chapter 4 useful for negotiating change.

What Kinds of Stress Are Involved?

All the newness and change you're facing is very stressful, and various kinds of tense situations can arise. Here are some of the most prevalent sources of stress.

Anger. When you're stressed it can be easier to be angry. But being easily angered or irritated raises your blood pressure and can create unnecessary problems with your partner. Anger interferes with clear thinking, and being irritable makes it unpleasant and difficult for others to interact with you. To reduce the negative effects of anger:

- Learn to slow down and relax your high expectations.
- Counting to ten works wonders.
- Take three deep breaths when you are upset, to reduce the charge of the hormone adrenaline in your body.
- Strenuous physical activity is great way to burn off anger.
- When you're angry, express it calmly ("I'm angry about ..."). There's no need for drama; it won't get you what you want.
- Remember your anger is a normal emotion and is satisfied by being acknowledged.
- Use your creativity to change what's not working.
- Handle your excess emotion or energy by being active (run, walk, hit golf balls or a pillow) writing, or talking to someone who is not part of the problem.
- Don't direct it personally at anyone. You can't vent and solve problems at the same time.

Insecurity. When you're faced with change, it's common to feel insecure because so many things are new. Insecurity and feelings of incompetence are definitely stressful, but they may also be useful because they can show you where you feel unprepared for the task ahead. Take these steps if you're feeling insecure:

- Don't be afraid to ask questions or ask for help.
- Remember that it's OK to be a beginner, even if you're an expert in other things.
- Don't try to pretend you're more in control than you feel and you will get more help from others.
- Take each new situation slowly, and allow yourself to learn as you go.
- Be supportive to yourself, and don't subject yourself to harsh self-criticism.
- Reduce your expectations of what you can accomplish, and allow others to help you when they offer.
- In the long run, being a team player is usually more efficient than trying to do it all alone and becoming overwhelmed.

No time for yourself. This may be a sign that you think of yourself last and tend to neglect your own well-being. Try these steps if you're feeling like you have no time for yourself:

- Learn to schedule time to relax and to play. If you write "personal time" on your schedule the same way you do appointments with others, you'll be more likely to actually do it.
- Join a class or group that meets regularly for a relaxing activity such as yoga, dancing, or tai chi, or schedule a regular massage, manicure, or facial so you'll have a guaranteed place to relax.
- Ask friends to call you and invite you out to play, and when they do, say yes as often as you can.

Anxiety. If you frequently feel anxious, you are probably running nonstop negative self-talk, which keeps you anxious about everything. Try these steps if you're feeling anxious:

- Use positive statements, affirmations, and/or prayer to counteract the running negative commentary in your mind.
- Learn to breathe deeply from your diaphragm when you feel anxious—it slows your heartbeat and calms you down.
- Make a list of everything that is going well to balance your focus on problems.

Pessimism. If your idea of the future is to focus on bad outcomes, it may mean you learned to think badly of yourself and your abilities in childhood. Techniques such as noticing the positive and counting your blessings help you have a more positive focus. Try these steps:

- Talk to your minister, priest, imam, rabbi, or other spiritual advisor about having more faith. Ask for a blessing you can use when you feel down.

- Set small goals every day, and check them off the list. You'll feel a lot more encouraged that you can turn this around.
- Find a book of affirmations or prayers and commit to saying one every day.
- Ask an upbeat friend to help you learn to expect good things and not sweat the small stuff.

Exhaustion. Most of us can deal with small amounts of frustration or feeling overwhelmed, but if it goes on too long, we lose all our motivation and become burned out. Motivation comes from celebration and appreciation, so try to learn to celebrate each little accomplishment. Try these tips if you're feeling exhausted:

- Seek appreciation when you need it.
- If you're really feeling burnt out and overwhelmed, get some help. Perhaps it's time to make a career change or to change some other aspect of your life.

Loneliness. When you're apart from your partner for long periods of time, you may feel very lonely. Don't isolate yourself; spend time with your friends and family. Keep these things in mind if you're feeling lonely:

- Be wary of spending too much time browsing on your computer or in chat rooms. These activities absorb time but do little to dispel loneliness.
- Make sure you schedule some time with a friend at least once a week.
- If you don't have friends where you are, take a class or join a group (for example, a book club or sports group) that will give you a chance to make new friends who live close by.

If you take care of these signs of stress as they arise, they won't take over and make your situation even more difficult.

Time, Time Zones, and Time Enough

When you're living apart, your time together is at a premium. Different time zones can also make it more difficult to connect. You may be asking yourself how you can manage the limited time you have and the different time zones that you're in and still have enough time for each other and the family. The following are guidelines for stretching your time together.

Choose Your Priorities

Are you spending the most time on what is most important? Sit down together and decide what activities are really worth doing, what each of you can do separately or while you're traveling, and what must be done at home.

lucy & josh

Truck driver Josh and his wife Lucy are both in their mid-forties and the parents of teenagers. He drives all week and comes home on the weekend. They have decided to get more organized about their responsibilities, so each of them made a list of the major tasks that had to be accomplished, including going to their sons' sports events, getting chores done, and doing some work on their house. Then they went through the list and decided what could be eliminated. They also decided to ask their boys to pitch in more to create more time for the family to go to games and have friends over for barbeques.

Divide and Conquer

For couples who live together all the time, sometimes running errands or working on a project is a pleasant way to pass time together. But when you're living apart, it can save time if you do chores separately and get them done in half the time. One of you can buy groceries while the other picks up batteries, light bulbs, and computer or office supplies. You're giving up spending time together doing chores but gaining time when you can focus on each other. Get as many chores, maintenance, decision-making, bill paying, and other tasks done while you're apart to save your together time for the important stuff—each other!

Josh has a laptop he can use at night when he is parked at a truck-stop with a wireless hotspot, so he decided to take on all the bill paying and finances and do it online. His company pays him via direct deposit, so it was easy to convert to paying all bills online, and Lucy let him know via e-mail when she took cash from the ATM for groceries or wrote a check. He took on all the home bookkeeping chores, which freed up some of Lucy's time. He also decided to help the boys with their homework by e-mail, since each of them has computer access at school, and Josh can even carry out teacher conferences by e-mail. He also has kept in touch with their team coaches and set up a schedule to help the team a bit on weekends when he was home. Lucy says: "It's a big burden off me to not have to worry about the guys' homework and to know Josh is communicating with them. He takes care of some of the 'guy stuff,' which helps him and the boys feel closer."

Choose to Save Time

When you have a choice, such as whether to eat out or make a simple meal quickly at home, choose whichever uses less time to save time to be together. Keep in mind that traveling from place to place eats up time, and minimize driving time whenever possible.

When Josh, Lucy, and the boys began to focus on saving time (and the boys understood they were saving time to do more of what they wanted), they were all surprised at how easy it was. They also found ways to combine errands and chores so they took up less time. They found, too, that communicating about what everyone was doing saved time. Lucy says: "Once the boys got the idea that saving time was a way to get more of what they wanted, they turned into the 'time police.' Most of the time now, instead of my having to badger them about hurrying up or being on time, they're more on my case about getting things done during the week so our weekends are free."

Think in terms of saving time with every choice or plan you make. You'll be surprised how much time you can save by just being aware.

Use E-Mail

You can spend some of your time apart discussing plans and decisions by phone or e-mail. Consider doing more of the problem solving and planning by e-mail, especially if you're in different time zones or on different schedules. You may both be too tied up for phone calls and IM, and text messaging doesn't permit enough words. But you can compose and send e-mail at different times, from different time zones, or when you're awake at odd hours and your partner is asleep. With e-mail, you also have time to compose your thoughts and consider what your partner said before responding.

Josh says: "I feel so much more in touch with my kids now, because we e-mail about other things besides homework. I didn't realize how comfortable my kids are with the e-mail, and how much more they open up. We've also taken to playing an online game together when the homework is done. And I get to do all this on my downtime from work, when I'd just be filling time anyway." Lucy says "I actually prefer discussing important decisions (like big purchases or where we're going on vacation) and resolving arguments by e-mail because I can get all the facts and really understand what Josh is saying. It's easier to keep the facts straight, and we don't get so emotional. Plus, it doesn't cut into our precious time together, as partners and as a family."

Plan Your Schedule Together

Work together to create as much free time as possible, and discuss how effectively you're using your time, both while apart and while together. Ask for help from each other that you can do while you're apart and while you're together. Knowing what each other is doing every day will help you work more as a team.

"Ever since we made a point to keep in touch," says Lucy, "life apart has been much easier. I really feel that Josh is involved in our everyday life, and knowing where he is and what he's doing makes it easier for us to work smoothly together."

Go on a Time Diet

Identify and avoid time wasters such as nonessential e-mail, watching TV you don't care about or enjoy, or allowing people to soak up your time with useless meetings or boring phone calls. Instead, choose to spend your time on the things you really want or need to do. For example, if you're traveling and all alone in a hotel or apartment, why not use the time to do family chores? You could pay the household bills, do the computer research on buying a new family car or house, or make phone calls to find out how your children are doing in school. If you play solitaire on your computer to reward yourself for work that you've done, limit yourself to one or two games, and don't play endlessly. If you're gaming online, set a timer and limit your game time. The idea is to eliminate activities that absorb a lot of time but are not worth it and replace them with something productive you can do that will save time when you're together. Or use the time for something that is truly more fun. Become time aware and you can free up time you can use to spend with each other.

> "At Dr. Tina's suggestion," says Lucy, "we made a game out of timing ourselves on the phone, the computer, and waiting for each other, using the minutes as 'points.' We were astounded when we saw how many points we racked up—they represented wasted time. The boys began a contest, adding up points they 'saved' by not wasting time, and not letting senseless things take up their time. Now I notice that we all zone out on the computer a lot less, and we magically have more time for truly fun things."

Create a Child-Care Network

If you have children, there's a surprisingly effective way to get time off that's good for the children and for your marriage. The options it gives your commuter marriage for more time alone together are so valuable that I will recommend it several times in this book. Because you rarely see each other, you can maximize your time alone together by having others who will gladly watch your kids some of the time. Cooperating with other families means you can share driving, trade baby-sitting, host each others' children overnight, and expand the amount of time off that each family enjoys. This allows both sets of parents a chance to be alone, to go out, or to have a break. Usually, watching someone else's children along with yours is not that much more difficult, and when the other parent takes your children, you get free time together.

Lucy used to go along on Josh's route once in a while before they had children, and they both really wanted to do that again. Now that their kids were teens and still needed supervision but not constant care, Josh and Lucy were willing to ask some of the parents of their sons' teammates, whom they knew to be responsible, if the boys could stay over for a weekend so Lucy could go with Josh. Lucy says, "I was really delighted when Tommy's friend Joey said that his family was going camping and wanted to take our boys with them for a week over Easter break. So Josh and I got on the road and had lots of fun running his route together. It was like old times, and we felt like a couple of kids ourselves. When Joey's mom and dad need a break, I'm going to take the kids for a week. It's actually easier than having just my two, because they generally behave better when their friends are here."

Mistrust and Jealousy

"O, beware . . . of jealousy; it is the green-eyed monster" wrote William Shakespeare in the early seventeenth century. In four hundred years, we don't seem to have gotten much better at taming or conquering this monster. Jealousy still rears its ugly head often in relationships, and when you are not together, your imagination can run wild and exaggerate it into even more of a problem. When you are lonely and apart, it's tempting to worry about what your partner is doing and even to convince yourself that a problem exists when there is no real evidence. Nothing will harm your relationship more than jealousy, suspicion, or mistrust. Especially when you are apart, you need to find a way to trust each other.

What Happens When One of You Becomes Jealous?

Most jealousy is not based on any real betrayal. Usually, it is a fearful fantasy of what might happen. Jealousy involves various combinations of fear, suspicion, envy, rage, competitive failure, humiliation, grief, self-contempt, betrayal, and abandonment. Sigmund Freud thought jealousy was a delusion rising from excessive dependence and lack of self-esteem. Jealousy is often based on insecure feelings of wanting to "own" the other person and not allow him or her to fill different needs with different people. Because we can't be everything to each other, most jealousy is illogical and unrealistic. Most people consider jealousy normal, and it is common to experience the feeling, but I don't believe it should be accepted as OK in a relationship because it's a corrosive emotion that comes from a feeling of inferiority. It's insulting to yourself and to your partner, because when you're jealous, you're thinking that someone else is more attractive to your partner than you are and that your partner is not loyal. While you may envy someone of any age or gender who gets to spend more time with your spouse than you do, the intense feeling we call jealousy is usually about fears of losing your spouse to someone else. Jealousy is usually less about your partner's behavior than it is about what you're afraid the behavior means.

Jealousy can often lead to upsetting arguments, tears, resentment, and accusations, even when no actual infidelity exists. You can be fearful, self-protective, and jealous as a result of being hurt in a previous relationship—acting as if you believe your partner will hurt you the same way you were hurt by someone else.

Overcoming the Monster

Most jealousy arises when someone feels insecure or threatened—either you're afraid of losing your relationship or that someone else out there will get the attention (love, affection) you want. The most important thing you can do is to remember that when you handle jealousy properly, it will be a passing emotion you discuss with each other, not a disaster.

Gail & Charles

Gail, whose husband Charles is an officer in the merchant marine and away for weeks or months at a time, says, "I used to get very jealous, but then I realized I had a choice: I could choose to feel scared, angry, or even to feel generous and loving instead of jealous, if I thought about it. I don't regard jealousy as a desirable emotion, and when it comes up, I work to overcome it.

"I found that when I had more of a sense of humor about my jealousy, I could talk to Charles about it, and he was happy to reassure me. When I saw a model in a bikini on TV, and then looked at my pregnant belly and got worried that he'd find a hot babe who looked better than I do, and I told him, he said 'Hon, your belly is very beautiful to me, and I can't wait to be there beside you and to hold our new baby daughter after she's born. Nothing is more attractive to me than that.' And I felt much better."

Here are some steps you can use to overcome jealousy in your commuter relationship:

Step 1. Discuss your jealous feelings, if you have them. Ask yourself and your partner these questions:

- Where do they come from?
- Have you been betrayed or abandoned before?
- Did something trigger your jealous thoughts this time?
- Does your partner sometimes have jealous feelings too?

Be willing to open up about how you feel and to hear how your partner feels. You can't reach a mutually satisfactory result if you don't tell the truth or listen to your partner.

Step 2. Make some rules about behavior when you're apart. To do this, ask yourself and your partner these questions:

- Is it OK to either of us to go to lunch with a member of the opposite sex?
- What about dinner?
- Can you work out together, or work on projects at night?
- What if the other person is married?

Make sure you and your partner feel comfortable with your agreements. Once you have a list you can live with, promise to abide by it as long as you're willing to keep your promise. Later, when you both feel more secure, you may be able to relax the limits. Don't push too hard, demand the impossible, or risk too much, because you'll frighten each other. Keep in mind that jealousy breaks down trust. If you begin to be upset, talk about it and encourage your partner to do the same.

Step 3. Make changes together. If you want to change your agreements, talk about any changes before you act on them and keep each other up to date. Lying to your partner about whether you broke the rules is far more damaging than whatever you did. If you make a mistake, confess it and offer some kind of plan to fix the problem. If it's your partner who goofed, hear what he or she has to say before blaming or getting upset. Be willing to talk about it, and give yourselves a chance to solve the problem. If either of you cannot behave within your agreements, or cannot keep your jealousy within bounds, then get professional counseling to avoid creating a marital disaster.

Step 4. Cultivate patience. If you take your time and keep your communication open, the trust between you will grow. You'll eventually figure out that both of you are doing your best to stay within the bounds. As you learn and grow together, your trust will gradually build, and as it grows stronger, you can begin to relax the rules and allow yourselves more flexibility and freedom. Read more about patience in Chapter 7.

Step 5. Be gentle with each other. Do your best not to get angry at each other for being jealous. Resist punishing or controlling your partner, especially if he or she hasn't really broken any mutual agreements. If one of you misunderstood and is jealous for no reason, be willing to apologize and reassure each other of your love and faithfulness. You'll have much better luck if you remain calm, remember that jealousy is a normal, human problem, and work it out together.

Creating Separate Lives

If you're spending considerable time apart, you'll be developing relationships, routines, and pastimes that don't involve your partner. If your separation lasts for more than a few weeks, or covers extended periods away at frequent intervals, you'll need some separate interests. What's important in doing this is to make sure your separate activities are helpful rather than harmful to yourself and your relationship and to make sure there are no secrets or surprises for your spouse. You'll learn more about this in Chapter 7.

Is It OK to Develop Friendships Away from Home?

It's not only OK, but it's frequently necessary and often inevitable to develop a separate life, including connections with people and satisfying activities, when you're away from home or when you're home and your spouse is away for long periods of time. Even if you're the spouse at home where your current friends are, you may need to make some changes, because changing the structure and schedule of your marriage often means that familiar friends may only want to relate to you as a couple or may not be able to mesh with your new schedule.

Developing a separate life is necessary if you're spending considerable time apart, because if you don't you'll wind up feeling empty, resentful, and bored. A properly constructed separateness will enhance and not threaten your marriage. For example, whenever you're apart is a good time to take up those healthful or useful activities you've been putting off. You can begin power walking, bicycling, going to the gym, dancing, studying a language, or refinishing furniture. Also, if you make some new friends, eventually your spouse can enjoy the new friendships too. Because you may not have needed to make new friends in a while, it can be valuable to update your definition of friendship and your skills at meeting people.

GUIDELINES FOR DEVELOPING YOUR SEPARATE LIFE

1. **What do you need friends for?** Evaluate what your needs are for new friends and activities in the light of your changed marital situation. Maybe you need a weekday friend, either while you or your spouse is away from home. Perhaps you need a workout buddy, someone to discuss work projects with, another parent to join you at your kids' games or recitals, a friend to go golfing or to the movies or shopping, or a companion for your work commute.

2. **Consider what being a friend means to you.** Who are your best friends, and what qualities do they have? How do you like to spend time with them? Once you have a clear idea of the kinds of friendships you would enjoy, you can decide to create some new ones in your life. This can be done in two ways:

   Make changes in your current relationships: Ask your friends to participate in activities you enjoy, and spend more time with the friends whose style of friendship best complements your own. This is especially good for the person who's at home and who may have work friends or other acquaintances to draw on.

   Create new friendships: Reach out to coworkers, your neighbors, or church members and invite them to accompany you in a favorite activity or for coffee. Join a discussion group focused on literature, film, art, or politics; join a basketball, volleyball, hiking, or running group; or take a class in yoga, tennis, or cooking. When you spend time with people who have similar interests, you will soon create new friends.

3. **Get a life.** To meet people easily, do things on a regular basis that involve others. Activities can range from taking classes, joining hobby clubs, volunteering, playing a sport or game, hiking, or any pursuit that meets regularly. The people you meet will share your interest, and you'll have something in common to talk about and enjoy together.

4. **Find interesting, fun people.** When you get involved in an ongoing activity and meet with the same people on a regular basis, friendships emerge naturally from the interaction. If you travel frequently, join a national group, such as an alumni group or fraternity, computer user group, Mensa, or a political party so you can join in meetings wherever you happen to be. If you travel to the same places frequently, you'll begin to recognize people and will be remembered in return. When you find someone you think is particularly pleasant, spend a little time talking with him or her during or after your activity. Ask questions about the project you are working on, or share experiences and advice. If the conversation goes well, you can offer to meet before or after the session for coffee. From there, you can begin do more things together until you've established a pattern of friendship.

5. **Don't overlook people you know.** While you're making new friends, don't forget the people you already know. Is there a favorite family member you'd like to see more often? Call him or her and suggest going for a walk or to lunch. Are there acquaintances at work, at church, in your neighborhood, involved in your child's (or your own) school, or elsewhere with whom you could develop a friendship? Consider reaching out to them. Let these people know that

you'd like to share events and activities. Spending quality time with friends is beneficial to your emotional, mental, and physical health. If you follow these steps, you'll find that it isn't as difficult as you think to make friends.

Jill & James

Jill, who moved away from the city she lives in with her husband, James, to take a magazine editor job, commutes to her job during the week and goes home on weekends. Away from home, Jill works long hours, but she still has a lot of alone time. She says, "I needed someone I could go to a movie with, go shopping for a new power suit, go walking, or have lunch with. The magazine staffers were my employees, so that was off limits. I love to read, of course, so I went to the local bookstore and joined a 'sack lunch' book discussion group that was aimed at working women on their lunch hour. In a short time, some of the women and I began to connect, and I found someone to walk with in the morning. Then, a little while later, someone else invited me over for dinner, and we began going to an occasional movie or watching a video at each other's apartments. It really made my week-days a lot more fun, and kept me from being so lonely."

Work Distribution, Fairness, and Mutuality

If you were married for a while before embarking on a commuter marriage, you probably had the workload divided in a more or less satisfactory fashion. Perhaps one of you did the inside chores, one the outside work; maybe you both worked together to keep things tidy, create meals, do repairs and maintenance, see that the bills are paid, and care for pets, plants, cars, and kids. But when your situation changes and one of you is not home as much, the work balance is disrupted. A partner who is not at home is obviously not going to be able to keep up on housekeeping chores. If you're newly married, then workload distribution needs to be set up from the beginning to take your commuter marriage into account.

How Do We Keep the Workload Fair?

To avoid frustration, resentment, and other corrosive feelings, you must both understand what the workload is for each of you and figure out how to divide it up more fairly or other ways to compensate. Your ability to work things out as partners is vital in this situation. If one of you is away from home for a long time, such as on military duty or working far away, the bulk of the at-home chores will fall on the other partner. It will help minimize resentment if you acknowledge that this is unfair and express gratitude for the extra work being done. On the other hand, the partner who is away may be under difficult or dangerous conditions and is separated from all the good things about being close to family and friends: No hugs, no play, and no day-to-day interaction. These problems must be acknowledged too. There are benefits and problems on both sides. Couples who are not as dramatically separated have a better chance of working out a more equitable arrangement for taking care of responsibilities, but it still takes more negotiation than it does when you live together full time.

EXERCISE: BALANCING THE WORKLOAD

If you have time in advance to plan for living at a distance, or even if you are already apart, you can use the following exercise to help you figure out how to balance your workload or, if that's not possible, how to make the situation feel better to both of you.

Analyze the workload. On a sheet of paper or a computer spreadsheet, write down all the chores involved in your day-to-day life. (This will be useful even if your spouse has already been relocated somewhere, such as a new job or a military deployment.) Organize them by daily, weekly, and monthly or occasional chores. For example, child care, walking pets, making meals, and bringing in mail and papers would be daily; taking a child to a class or game, doing laundry, grocery shopping, or certain housekeeping chores would be weekly; gardening or paying bills might be monthly; and car maintenance or plumbing problems would be occasionally. You can take a few days to do this, writing things down as you think of them, until you feel the list is pretty comprehensive. This list will help you see everything that needs to be handled in one spouse's absence.

Discuss who's doing what (or did what) when you're together. Using your list, put initials next to each chore to mark which of you has been doing them. This will probably remind you of a few items left off the list, so add them.

Reallocate chores, and make a new work project list. Think creatively and specifically about how the away partner can help. For example, if you pay bills online, that's a chore the away partner can do. Certain things, like needed repairs or taking the car in for service or the kids to ordinary doctor visits, can be saved up or scheduled for when the traveling partner is home to help.

Evaluate the results. You may both find that this new workload is not very even or fair, and that may be just a fact of life in your commuter marriage. However, you can still acknowledge it and see if anything can be done to compensate for the extra work. It's easy to forget all the things your partner does in your absence. Perhaps some chores can be eliminated or made easier. If there's enough money, for example, a maid can be hired to come in once or twice a month and do the heavy housework, or a gardener or neighborhood kid (or even your own teenager) can mow the lawn. You might reorganize your children's extracurricular activities to make them more convenient, or enlist the help of another parent to carpool your children to practices. Perhaps simply giving the partner with the harder load permission to complain on occasion will help.

Ratify this new agreement. Make a new, clean list of chores and responsibilities and who is doing what, and agree to abide by it. If things change, or the new program doesn't work as you planned, follow these steps again to make a new agreement.

Parenting

Parenting is what makes a commuter marriage incredibly difficult, and, paradoxically, it may also be the reason why you're commuting. Even though it's not easy, there are good reasons for living apart when you have children. Perhaps you are planning to move to a new job but did not want to take the children out of school, so one parent stays until the school year is finished. Or maybe you're working different shifts so someone can be with the children all the time. Or you might have a career that involves travel or staying away from home for several nights in a row (like a fireman or flight attendant) and you didn't want it to prevent you from having children. No matter what your reason for commuting while you have children, you still must handle the problems of parenting while you're apart.

How Can I Manage the Family Alone?

When your spouse is away, you are effectively a single parent, and you'll be more effective and less stressed if you take charge of the family's personal and family time. Families need to sit down together and decide what activities are really worth doing.

Sara & Paul

Sara, whose husband Paul was deployed to Iraq with his National Guard unit, is home alone for an indeterminate time with their three-year-old daughter, Lacey, and a baby on the way. She's had to go back to work as a legal secretary, which makes it difficult for her to care for her child. "This is so hard," says Sara. "I don't know how I'm going to make it."

To reduce stress, each child should be allowed one or two activities (such as sports, piano lessons, or scouting) per week, and the rest of the time should be balanced between home-work, family activities, and play. Seriously evaluate any activity that is too demanding. If your child has a real chance at being an Olympic star or a classical virtuoso, hours of practice might be worth it, but for most kids family time is probably more important.

Parents need time off too. This can be achieved through allowing children who are mature enough to spend occasional nights at friends' or family's homes and then reciprocating. This allows both sets of parents a chance to be alone, to go out and have a break. Family networks, in which several families (related or not) share time, driving, or trade off baby-sitting, can really expand the amount of time off that each family enjoys.

> Sara's mother lives and works in another state and comes to help when she can. Paul's mother is also still working, although she can watch the children some evenings to give Sara a break. Sara says, "Thank God for our mothers, and my sister Susan. The grandmas give me a needed break, and I can take Lacey over to Susan's if I'm over-whelmed, exhausted or ill, or just to hang out with Susan. Lacey's happy playing with Susan's daughter Paige, and she can fall asleep there if we watch a late movie. It's a great breather for me, and it's free."

The best way for any commuting family to create more couple time is to network with other young families. If you don't know other parents, meet them via childbirth classes, parenting classes, and school or neighborhood events. You and other parents can share baby-sitting (you take their child for an evening, then they take yours—both couples get a break), socialize together (everyone meets at one family's house with their children, put all the children to bed there, and spend the evening playing cards, board games, watching a video, cooking a meal together or potlucking, or just having a great conversation). If you rotate houses, the burden is shared, and everyone gets to have a relaxing evening. This will work whether your spouse is away or at home.

With these parenting networks, parents of similar-age children work together to share car-pooling, baby-sitting, information, and support. It's especially important for commuting parents, because other commuting couples can help them find daycare and take turns taking the children overnight so the parents who get the evening off are able to get some things done, relax, or have a quiet evening together.

> Sara also enjoys a connection with other families of National Guardsmen. "It's great to get together with them, to visit the base for low-cost shopping, and to spend time together with our kids. These moms really understand what I'm going through, and we can support each other."

What if We Don't Agree about Parenting Decisions?

Establishing child-rearing principles is important for any parents, and even more crucial for parents who are commuting, because it eliminates a major source of conflict. If you're the traveling parent, because you are not around to handle daily problems, you need to give up day-to-day control and adopt the attitude that you are a support system while traveling—there to advise, console, listen, and commiserate. By all means, make your overall parenting decisions together and consult each other about problems that arise, but don't try to manage or control from a distance. If you're the stay-at-home parent, you need to be able to organize the schedule, maintain discipline, and especially to ask for help when necessary.

Sara and Paul had many discussions before his deployment about what they wanted for their children. Paul said: "We set regular times to talk about parenting, among other things, and I was amazed at the ideas that came up for discussion. We talked about things I never would have thought about until they happened, such as how to handle an injury, illness, or school discipline problem. We used stories we had heard about other families having problems and said, 'What would we do if that happened to us?' Now I have peace of mind that Sara knows what I think, and that we agree on the basics. Our discussions made me think, and just in case something should happen, I wound up writing a letter to each of my children about how I love them, and my hopes and dreams for the future."

Use the following guidelines to help you talk about differences in parenting attitudes and principles:

GUIDELINES FOR DISCUSSING PARENTING

1. *Listen to each other.* You may not previously have discussed parenting in the way you need to talk about it now that you're commuting, so it's important you have a "tell me more" attitude when you're talking. Listening does not mean that you agree, but you can't effectively discuss your parenting differences if you don't hear each other. The following questions, organized according to the ages of your children, are just a few of the hundreds you can ask to help you begin the talk, and then you'll go on to bring up more questions that concern you both.

    A. *If you have an infant or toddler:*
    - Who can you agree upon to provide child care?
    - What do you believe is a proper diet and bedtime?
    - How do you want to handle potty training?
    - Does your baby have any special medical needs, and how will you handle them?

B. *If your child is in grade school:*
  - What activities are OK?
  - What might be a problem?
  - What rules do you want to make about chores, bedtime, and so on?
  - At what age can your child stay over at a friends' house?
  - What about computer and Internet use, or video games?
  - Is it OK for your child to have his or her own Web page online?
  - What TV programs are OK to watch?
  - How busy or open should your child's schedule be?
  - What about doing homework and school grades?
  - What if the teacher lets you know there's some sort of problem?

C. *If you have a teenager:*
  - How much do you want to know about where they are and who they are with?
  - What about cell phone, computer, and Internet use?
  - How much are you willing to let them do without monitoring?
  - What about riding in cars, and for older teens, driving or owning a car?
  - What do you want to know about their friends and friends' families?
  - Who is monitoring their homework and grades?

Share what responsibilities you can. A parent who is traveling might be able to help a child or teen with homework if it can be done online, as Josh does, or if the stay-at-home parent can visually check to make sure it's OK. Teacher conferences might be able to be held by phone, or the parent who's at the school can use the speakerphone on a cell phone so both parents are involved. Family meetings, including the kids, can also be held by speakerphone or IM, if possible. Staying connected in these ways can help you feel closer to your kids and can help the stay-at-home parent to feel less burdened.

2. *Seek to understand.* Listen carefully to each other during your conversations about parenting, and try to find out why your partner feels as he or she does. If you disagree about your child's friends or baby sitters, or your partner doesn't want your sister to look after your child, don't just get angry. Ask your partner to explain what he or she is thinking. If your partner can see that you understand what he or she means, then he or she will be more open to understanding you.

Sara says, "Paul had a problem with us spending a lot of time at my sister's because she lets her kids watch so much TV. My first reaction was anger because I thought he was criticizing my sister, but I didn't react, I just listened, and after we talked about it, he realized I'd be there most of the time with the kids, and that I needed the support."

3. *Change your focus from the problem to the solution.* Only focus on the problem long enough for each of you to understand why it's a problem for the other, then switch your attention on what will fix it.

Josh, the truck driver, and Lucy, who worked part time as an extra, had an easy time dealing with separation before they had children, but they had a much bigger problem when the first of their two sons arrived. "After struggling for a couple of years," says Lucy, "and with the arrival of the second child, we finally decided we'd better stop arguing and start talking about parenting. Josh says, "At first, when Lucy would get so upset because I was away and she had to deal with the kids, I didn't want to hear it, and we'd fight about who was doing more for the family, which was stupid. After we started focusing on the solution, we came up with the idea of me helping by e-mail, and that made a big difference. It's not that I spend so much time, but Lucy gets a break, and she doesn't feel so alone. Also, I feel much closer to the boys, and I realize they need me. We're making some plans to take them on the route with me during school vacation."

4. *Stay as calm as possible.* Take the emotion out of the discussion by focusing only on what will work. The time to consider emotion is in step two. It's very possible that one or both of you is fearful about losing touch with your children, or not being able to handle them by yourself. It's common to worry that what bothered you about your own upbringing might be happening for your children, and it's common to want for them what you missed, or what you loved. But your children aren't you, and times have changed. If your children are old enough, you can consult them about what they like and don't like, as long as the final decision rests in the parent's hands. If one or both of you become upset, irrational, or reactive while discussing this, you have stopped communicating. Take a break and try again in a few minutes when both of you have calmed down.

Sara says, "I was so emotional anyway because of the pregnancy and about Paul being deployed that, no matter what we discussed, I started to cry, and I couldn't think. Paul was kind, but he told me I needed to pull myself together; he had no choice, and he felt bad enough without my hysterics making it impossible to talk to me. After that, I got ahold of myself, learned how to keep my feelings out of decision-making discussions, was more able think clearly, and our talks went much better. I learned that I could feel sad or upset without letting it leak out all over the place, and without letting it stop me from thinking and working together."

5. *Get some objective information.* This is where taking a parenting class or reading a book can be very helpful, getting both of you to look at whatever the problem is from a different, neutral perspective. If you're not agreeing on parenting, get an expert's point of view.

> Josh and Lucy began by fighting over who knew more about parenting, and whose parents were best, but after they did some online research and read a couple of books, they found it a lot easier to agree. Josh says, "Once we took a course, our discussions weren't about whose family was right and whose was wrong. We had a neutral system to work with, and it helped a lot."

6. *Include each other and the children.* Have family discussions, by e-mail or phone if necessary, about important decisions involving the family. If the away parent is included in the decision-making process, he or she will feel less distanced and more cooperative. If the kids are included in the discussion, they'll be less resistant to whatever decision the parents make.

> Josh says: "Once we were able to follow these steps and talk about each stage our kids went through, we had a much better idea of what to do, and even how to talk about it with each other. It stopped our arguments, and we had a much easier time."

What if My Partner Undermines My Parenting?

If you have had the initial parenting discussion just outlined and made agreements, and you feel your partner is not honoring your joint decisions, then that's a problem you need to discuss. First, get clear about why you feel your partner is not going by your joint plan, and then explain, calmly, what isn't making sense to you, and listen to your partner's answer. Maybe he or she understood the agreement differently than you did, and it needs to be clarified. Perhaps he or she feels that you broke the agreement too, and you need to hear why. Most of these problems can be solved through discussion, as long as it doesn't deteriorate into a fight.

> "Lucy and I fought a lot about the kids, because every time I'd ask a question about how she was doing something, she thought I was criticizing her. But it really was because I had no idea of what she was thinking, and I had some expectations from the way my parents did it. When we talked about what we both thought should be done, we came to an agreement pretty quickly. I knew she bore the brunt of the parenting, and I was happy to let her call the shots most of the time. I just wanted to understand what was going on," says Josh.

Finances

Living apart can be financially rewarding if you're doing it because of a great job offer, or it can be financially very difficult if you have to leave your job to tend a sick relative or for military service. You may be paying rent on two living places, or spending a lot on phone calls and traveling back and forth.

How Can We Manage All These Extra Expenses?

The best way to handle your new situation is to integrate all your expenses and income into one budget. While you may find you need separate debit and/or credit cards, or separate checkbooks to manage money while you're apart, you'll be much more able to keep track of your budget if you have everything come together in a central location. One great way to do this is with accounting software. You can put "home bookkeeping software" into your search engine or try *www.wealthygeek.com*, which will help you compare various kinds of software, including the most popular systems: Quickbooks, Quicken, and Peachtree. That software will help you create a budget, and you can manage it from home or away, so it allows each of you to monitor how your finances are going. Bills, taxes, and bank reconciliations all can be done online, which allows you more flexibility about who handles the financial chores.

If you have extra expenses without the extra income to cover them (which could easily be true in one of the involuntary situations), it will be necessary to tighten your belts and go on a restricted budget until the situation changes.

Do We Set Up Two Separate Homes?

If one of you is away for an extended period of time, and if housing is not provided, it might be necessary to set up another residence away from home. There are a lot of choices in how to do this, depending on your need and budget. Keep in mind that if you can afford to buy, a second dwelling can become an income property later on or a vacation home, and while one spouse is away from home, the away house, condo, or apartment can also become a getaway or mini-vacation for the whole family.

Jill says, "After I had my editor position for a while, and James had come to visit my tiny single apartment a few times, we adjusted more to the commute and decided we really liked the city as a getaway spot. We researched and found that property values were at a bargain rate, and poised to go up, so we decided to buy a two-bedroom condo. I can live in it while I have this job, and it's big enough to invite friends or James's boys to come play for a weekend. Later, we can rent it out or sell it at a profit. James is much happier with an investment than with just spending rent; the interest is tax deductible, and it's a lot more fun. He also feels less like I'm deserting him when we can have friends or his sons stay for the weekend. I've even started hosting my reading group here sometimes."

Fighting: Whether Long Distance or at Home

Especially in your commuter marriage, fighting is very destructive, whether you're together or apart. Fighting does not solve any problems, it only makes them worse. Fighting while you're apart can be especially destructive, because on the phone or by texting or e-mail, or even Web cam you're missing some of the information and cues you get when you're in each others' physical presence. It's also easier to slam a phone down and cut yourselves off from each other than it is when you're in physical proximity. Anytime you're fighting, you're both struggling to be right, not to solve the problem. Fights at home can use up your scarce time together and sour your good feelings for each other. Much of the information and many of the exercises in this book are intended to give you more effective ways to communicate and negotiate than fighting. As a married couple, you need to have discussions, solve problems, and sometimes disagree, but you don't need to squabble, argue, bicker, or fight. Remember, the point of the fight is to reach a solution, not to win, be right, or make your partner wrong. The following guidelines can help you turn your fighting into constructive negotiation, whether you're apart or together.

GUIDELINES FOR NOT FIGHTING
- Don't try to guess what your partner is thinking.
- Stay focused on the problem you're solving, and don't bring up other issues.

- State the problem, suggest some alternatives, and focus on choosing a solution.
- Make one simple statement at a time; don't get too wordy.
- Give your partner a chance to respond and to suggest options.
- Honor your partner's need to solve a problem; his or her problems are yours also.
- Ask and answer questions directly, and state your problem as a request, not a demand: "What do you think? Or "How do you feel about it?"
- Hold hands, look at each other, and remember you're partners.

Always acknowledge and honor your partner's feelings—don't deflect them, laugh at them, or overreact. They're only feelings, and they subside when respected, heard, and honored. Listen carefully. Paraphrase what your partner says. Check to see if you understand by repeating what is said, "So you are angry because you think I ignored you. Is that right?" Try not to use personal attacks or criticism. Focus instead on solving the problem. Also, it's best not to try to solve a problem if you're impaired: tired, hungry, drunk, or emotionally unstable. If you make a mistake, admit it and apologize. Whatever problems you face in your new situation can be fixed, but not if you fight about them.

Josh says, "I was shocked to be told that fighting wasn't necessary. My parents fought all the time, and Lucy's parents fought less, but they had their spats too. Learning how to disagree without fighting was a revelation. I think I grew up a lot just doing that. It's so much nicer to have a discussion with Lucy because I know we're not going to wind up fighting. If we get close, one of us just calls a 'time-out' and we take a break. It's what my buddies would do if a discussion got too heated. I really like it. I'm sad that my own parents didn't get to find this out before they divorced, because I know they loved each other once, and they were both good people with a bad habit of getting angry at each other. I know my own boys are happier than I was as a kid because their parents aren't fighting."

communication and intimacy
in a commuter marriage

Spending time apart is both a blessing and a problem. Time apart can refresh your relationship and remind you what you miss about each other. On the other hand, if you begin to resent the separations and don't communicate well while you're apart, you'll find it's difficult to feel close to each other. Keeping in touch while apart prevents you from storing up resentments, forgetting important dates and events, and makes sure you both feel cared for and loving toward each other. If you don't keep in touch while traveling, you can set up a backlog of problems to talk about and wind up feeling estranged. In this chapter, you'll find the answers to three common commuter marriage questions:

- How can we communicate effectively when we don't see each other often?
- How can we still feel close when we're geographically challenged?
- Sex: What is that thing we used to do?

Communicating at a Distance

Communication while you're apart is vital, but how you do it depends on what works best for both of you. Because some people are more verbal and others want less communication, frequency of contact is one of the crucial issues you need to work together to solve. If you can't reach an agreement, or if you're not telling your partner the truth about how much contact is enjoyable for you, it does not bode well for the relationship. Finding a mutually satisfactory rhythm of contact is a test of your communication and partnering skills.

How Can We Communicate Effectively?

You may be physically far apart, or perhaps your schedules are just so different that it feels that way, but if you can't see, feel, and sense each other's vibes, you're missing a lot of nonverbal communication clues. In order to compensate for these missing cues, your communication skills need to be better than just OK.

You'll be much easier understood if you compensate for the absent vibes, touch, and visuals with new tools. One advantage you have over long-distance couples from years ago is new technology. Today there are all kinds of amazing communication tools, with more being introduced all the time. Following are several of these options to enhance your communication and how to use them.

E-mail

E-mail is so basic almost everyone uses it today, but if you haven't gotten on the bandwagon yet, you'll find it can really help you keep in touch. Of course, e-mail requires a computer, a cell phone, or a personal digital assistant (Blackberry, Treo, iPhone, and Palm are popular examples.) But if you don't want to invest in any of those things, you can get a free e-mail account and use a computer at the library or a cyber café for very little money. If you're wired already, however, you already know that you can e-mail family and friends at any time, send pictures, attach articles and Web pages, and even (with voice translation software) have the e-mails electronically read out loud.

There are a couple of big advantages to e-mail. You can send it at any time, from any time zone, and not awaken or interrupt your partner. It also gives you a record of what was said. Even for couples who are in the same house, it is sometimes advisable to e-mail each other about a contentious issue, because when you describe the problem, a solution, or even your feelings in writing, you have a chance to fully explain what you mean, edit, rewrite, and even think before you send it. Your partner can choose when to read it, get past his or her first emotions, and then make a more considered response rather than an off-the-cuff reaction.

E-mail also provides clarity, because when info is written down, you can read and re-read it, and it's also there to remind you of what you forgot. It's a great way to save time, because you can work through simple agreements, schedules, and other details on two different time schedules or from different time zones and save your precious face time for more important stuff. You can also easily send e-mails to a number of people at once, which is a lot less time-consuming than contacting each one individually. This is great for scheduling get-togethers, sharing pictures of a family event, or announcing your new promotion.

Instant Messaging (IM)

IM, in case you don't know, is computer software that pops up a window to let you know when certain chosen persons (such as your partner or other family members) are online at the same time so you can have a real-time conversation—that is, you can type comments back and forth instantly.

- IMing gives you a chance to feel in close touch.
- It's a great way to check in at the end of the day or during any time you're both free.
- In some situations, you might be able to IM at work when being on the phone isn't possible.

- IMing is not a good idea if you're struggling or upset, however, because it's too tempting to write something that will work against you.

Keep in mind that an instant message is very similar to a phone call, so it should really only be used in situations when it is not convenient to talk or to supplement phone conversations.

Cell Phones
Cell phones are usually more expensive than landlines, but if you shop around for a good plan with the right combination of free minutes, you'll find it's worth the expense, especially if one of you is often traveling from place to place.

Being able to check in with each other wherever you are can be essential. It's also great when you're coordinating airport pickups and for last-minute reminders: "Honey, before I get home, can you put gas in my car?" or schedule changes "My plane was delayed—I'll be an hour late." It can also save money over long-distance phone rates from a work location or a hotel. Think of your cell phones when you want to connect to each other away from home, briefly hear your partner's voice, or suddenly change plans.

Video Sharing
You can share videos via cell phones, PDAs, or the Internet. Cell phone videos are brief, although the technology is changing rapidly, and you can share digital videos on the Internet through many sites and even e-mail, though it takes a high-speed connection to handle the large file of a video. But if you have the capacity, you can:

- Share a video of a child's game or recital.
- Show color swatches for painting the kitchen.
- Model the new sexy underwear you'll have on when your partner comes home.

- Upload your videos to a video sharing site such as YouTube (*www.youtube.com*) or MySpace (*www.myspace.com*).

Think of video sharing when the moving visuals and sound are important.

Text Messaging

Text messaging is a combination of e-mail and IMing—a typed message sent over your cell phone or PDA. The difference is whether you respond to the message or not. If you don't respond to it, a text message waits to be read, like e-mail. When you do respond, you can text back and forth, much like IMing, but you're thumb typing on the tiny phone or PDA keyboard.

- Kids and teens love texting, and they use a lot of abbreviations, so texting is necessarily brief; adults often get more impatient with it.
- Because kids love it, it can be a great way to connect with your children.
- It's also useful if you're somewhere where silence is necessary, such as a boring meeting or on a train when you don't want your call overheard, and you want to connect.

Think of texting as a quick way to send a message when you're out and about.

Photo Sharing

You can share photos in several ways—via your cell phone or PDA, via e-mail, or via an online Web site like Shutterfly, PhotoSite, or Flickr. The photos must be digital, but if you have pictures taken on a film camera, you can have them digitized at your local photo shop or scan them if you have a scanner.

- Photos taken with your phone can be sent to another cell phone, PDA, or computer.

- Digital photos can be attached to your e-mails.
- You can upload any digital photo from your computer to one of the photo-sharing sites, and then your friends and family can log on and view them. On the sites, captions can be added, and people who log on can comment and buy copies of the photos.
- Photos can help you keep each other up to date on changes, children, pets, or the garden.
- You can share pictures of your office, new outfit, or golf buddies when you're away from home.

Think of photo sharing when you want to show your partner a picture of what you're doing or seeing.

VOIP

Voice over Internet Protocol is a way to make phone calls over the Internet. It works pretty much the same as your home (landline) phone, although the sound quality may not be quite as good. Skype, Vonage, and most landline phone carriers now offer this service, and the options are constantly changing, so do a Web search for VoIP to find current carriers in your area.

- You can talk via a microphone and speakers on your computer, and now VoIP is available to work through that same landline phone using your phone number.
- It can be amazingly cheap, especially for long-distance and overseas calls.

Think of VoIP if you're separated by a long distance and when the savings are substantial.

Chat Rooms

The number and kind of chat rooms are growing and changing too fast to keep up with in this book, but here's a general overview.

- The basic idea of a chat room is that a number of people can have typed discussions at once.
- The discussions can be limited to whatever people you want to choose or open to the general membership of the chat.
- Sometimes the chat comes equipped with an avatar, which is an animated figure you can design to represent yourself, and your chat appears like a cartoon balloon over your head.
- Most chat is simply text, identified by your screen name, which is a name you choose for yourself.

Think of a private chat room when you want to have a discussion with family or friends from a distance and you have ample time.

Internet Games

One way to socialize with friends and family while away is by playing an interactive game via the Web. Many games give you a chance to chat while playing. You can play something as simple as your favorite card game in a closed game that only admits people you choose or as complicated as a fantasy game with complicated graphics and characters, such as Nickelodeon's Nicktropolis or the Web game Karma.

This is only a good idea if you find yourself with a lot of free time and want a format for socializing. Think of Internet games as a way to replace social or family evening entertainments and stay connected.

MySpace

MySpace and YouTube are the most well known of the online video sharing sites today, although the field changes rapidly. MySpace allows you to set up a simple Web site and upload videos, pictures, music, and whatever else you like. Then you invite others to join the site and to be your "friends," which gets them access to your site. It's a more involved and elaborate way to share pictures, videos, music, and articles than simple photo-sharing sites or sending videos by e-mail. Your friends and family can sign on and check out your site any time, from anywhere. Think of it as a simple way to have your own Web site, with a lot of extra features.

Blogs

A blog is a Web log or diary you keep online. Blogs are usually accessible to the general public and are usually comprised of either opinions or an ongoing log of some event or experience. It's a great way to keep friends and family updated on something you're going through when you're far from home. Many blog sites, like *www.technorati.com*, have provisions for readers to comment, which can allow you and your family members to keep in touch. Think of blogging when your experience is unusual and worth sharing.

Talking but Not Communicating

It's much easier to talk than it is to communicate. Like Jane and Edward, you can talk for a long time, about a lot of things, and yet never get to the point or be understood by your partner. This is not so much of a problem if you're just relaxing and having fun, but if there's an issue you need to talk about, or a problem you need to solve, communicating becomes vital.

jane & edward

Jane, the nurse who is also going to college and whose husband travels for his sales job, says: "When Edward and I are together, or on the phone, we talk a lot, we have fun, but we never seem to accomplish anything. I have something I want us to talk about, but we always get distracted, and we don't keep to the point. It's fun while it's happening, but I get frustrated later when I realize we talked but not about anything important."

When you're commuting, your time is at a premium, and you need to know how to communicate effectively and efficiently. The following seven steps for turning talk into communication will help you make sure you are getting your point across and also understanding your partner.

Communicate with Yourself First

Before beginning a significant conversation, take a little time to think about it beforehand. Know what you want to say, what you want your partner to understand, and what you want to accomplish.

If you're upset or anxious about the topic, start by first writing your thoughts down to organize them. When time is scarce, it's actually helpful to begin the conversation with an organized list similar to the agenda in a business meeting.

> Jane decided to identify for herself when a conversation was just for fun and to feel close or when she needed to discuss an important point with Edward. When she had something she wanted to talk about, she opted to make a list of the topics she wanted to cover: household repairs, money discussions, what they wanted in the house for groceries, and so on.

Do You Understand Your Partner?

Even though you are prepared to communicate what you want your partner to know, begin by being willing to listen. If you are receptive and interested, the conversation will go better, and your mate will be more likely to reciprocate and listen to you. While you won't get to say your piece first, you'll be heard a lot faster than if you compete and argue.

"I found that I couldn't just launch into my list," says Jane. "It worked much better if I first asked Edward what he wanted to talk about too. Then I put his topics on the list too. We developed a system of taking one topic from my list and one from his, which made the discussion feel fairer, and we found we could get a lot done this way. Other phone calls were reserved for just chatting, catching up, making plans for our time together, and having fun."

If the Conversation Goes off Track, Bring It Back

Don't let the conversation wander to other topics until you're sure you've finished the first topic. If other topics come up, like past events or other problems, say "I'd like to talk about that too, but let's finish the first problem before we go there." If either of you feels the new topic is important or likely to be forgotten, write it down and come back to it later.

Edward says: "In discussions, I wander all over the place, so Jane's list really helped. When I got off track, she'd say, 'Can we talk about the next item on the list?' Each time we had a 'list talk,' by the end I felt like we had gotten a lot done, and I didn't wind up hanging up and then saying to myself, 'Darn! I forgot to ask about . . .'"

Don't Argue about Who's Right

It's not a relevant question, and it leads to endless arguing, getting nowhere. Instead, grant each other permission to have your own perception, that is, each of you is right for you. Understand that there are unlimited points of view. Switch your focus from right and wrong to what will work. It's not about who's right but what solves the problem.

Edward says: "Our conversations would go off the subject when we got to arguing about details: "No, it wasn't Saturday, it was Sunday." "No, it was Saturday." "No, don't you remember, you had to go out of town on Monday, sc . . ." It could go on forever, and then we'd forget what we were supposed to be talking about. Having the list helped one us say, 'Oops! Off topic. Can we get back to the list?'"

Stay Calm

If either one of you is getting upset, take a break. Do something else to calm down—play some music, cook dinner, take a walk, answer some e-mail, or watch TV. Then come back and pick up the discussion again.

"When we were talking at home," says Jane, "we were more likely to argue. Knowing how to say, 'Wait—we're getting upset, let's take a break,' really helped. We'd take a time-out, then come back and use our 'list' to get back on topic."

Make Constructive Suggestions

For each problem you discuss, offer some possible solutions. This is where you can have a friendly competition to determine who can make the most creative suggestions. When you come up with enough great ideas, it will be easy to choose one for a solution. If you can't agree on a solution, agree to try one temporarily to see how it works.

"Getting creative really worked for us," says Edward. "When we had a little contest over who could come up with the best solution, it turned a problem into a game, and we had an easier time with it. We also found that when we had a lot of possible solutions, choosing one was easy."

Confirm Your Solution

Whatever you've decided you want to do based on your discussion, this is the time to confirm your decision and make sure you both understand your agreement.

> "Whatever we decide goes right onto the list, I read it back to Edward, and we know what we're doing," says Jane.

● ● ●

When your time together or on the phone is at a premium, you'll do a lot better if you concentrate on getting the important stuff out of the way. If you're efficient, you can get it done and still have time to enjoy your conversation.

> "Ever since we've been taking the time to be clear about what I wanted to accomplish when we talk, we've been doing so much better." Jane says. "Now, we get the business done first, then we can relax and just enjoy talking to each other."

Maintaining Intimacy

Maintaining intimacy is an issue in most marriages, and most couples are concerned about how to keep affection, connection, and sexual satisfaction working well over the years of a successful marriage. Living apart or commuting frequently, however, puts extra emphasis on these issues. So it's not unusual for me to be asked, "How can we keep our intimate connection strong?"

> Housewife and mom Lucy and her truck-driving husband Josh found that early in their relationship, before they had children, the separation during his driving trips enhanced their intimacy. Then, when the children were small, the connection between Lucy and Josh nearly disappeared. They still got along, they felt like friends, but their old,

carefree days of spending intimate time when Josh was home, and Lucy's opportunity to be out with friends while he was gone, both disappeared. "I'd get home to find her cranky and desperate to get away," recalls Josh. "She used to be eager to see me, but when the kids were small, the first thing she wanted was time off, and that meant leaving me alone with the kids and going out by herself or with friends. We didn't get time together until after she had her break—and then we still had the kids around—so our time alone together almost disappeared. We'd get a chance to connect after the kids went to bed, and we were both exhausted. My feelings would be hurt, and Lucy would feel pressured and guilty. We really had a rough time then. Our marriage almost didn't survive."

When one partner spends time away from home, whether on a regular or sporadic basis, your time to be together suffers. Whatever time you do have is probably taken up with lots of responsibilities, such as careers and kids. Resentment can build because both of you are more stressed than you were before, and that can make it more difficult to relax and feel close to each other. Because your together time is at a premium, trying to pack in chores, decision-making, child care, and still get in some relaxed time together is not easy.

How Can We Still Feel Close When We're Apart?

In order to preserve time for intimacy and to keep your connection ongoing when you're commuting, you both need to use your time efficiently. Instead of wasting time arguing and bickering about inconsequential matters, it's much more effective to be thoughtful and considerate of each other, and try to understand your partner's point of view. Planning ahead also helps you make the most of your time together. You will be more effective and less stressed if you learn to take charge of your personal and family time. The guidelines for stretching your time in Chapter 2 will help you be efficient and maximize your opportunity for intimacy, and the following guidelines will help you make the most of the time you have. How you spend the time you do have together determines whether your intimacy (affection, connection, and sexual satisfaction) will increase or deteriorate.

Enhance Intimacy While You're Apart

Keep the phone as special as you can. Handle mundane business via e-mail, IM, or text message, and keep the phone for making that intimate connection. As often as possible, schedule a phone call every day, at a quiet time, for some intimate conversation. If you have children, either speak to them first or in a separate call. If you need to make a call to handle problems, business, or decisions, or if you don't have access to e-mail, then find a way to designate a special call for intimate conversation, or at the very least develop a signal to say that the business part of the call is over and your special time is beginning.

Nothing is more intimate than a love note. Mail is one of the advantages living apart has over living together. Sending little gifts, notes, cards, postcards, or pictures to your partner (whether you're the one at home or the one away) takes only a moment and racks up a huge score on the intimacy chart. When you're at a drugstore, grocery store, or card shop, pick up a few affectionate or amusing cards and maybe a little gift or two (it doesn't need to be expensive, a keychain or candle is fine) and then send them at random moments. Send a postcard with a scene of where you are or a cartoon cut from the paper or a magazine. If you have cards, stamps, and envelopes on hand, it's very simple to drop one in the mail.

Before you leave on a trip, plant some Post-it notes—inside the cupboard doors, in the mailbox, under your spouse's pillow. If you're the stay-at-home spouse, tuck a few surprises into your mate's suitcase, briefcase, or between the pages of a book he or she is reading.

Think in terms of making your partner smile as often as you can while you're apart. If you have a nice thought about a time you spent together, write it down so you don't forget to talk about it.

Cindy & Bill

Cindy, the Navy nurse who is also attending grad school and is now forced to commute more than two hours because her base closed, spends four days a week at the distant base, away from her contractor husband Bill and their seven-year-old daughter Chloe. Bill says, "Cindy was so unhappy at having to commute for the next five years until she can retire that Chloe and I decided to do something to make her happier. We made up a kit of her favorite snacks, coupons to eat out at her favorite restaurants, and a bunch of Chloe's artwork to hang on the walls in her room. At the advice of her best friend, Sue, I also put in something called 'aroma sticks' and a card from me. We hid the whole package in her bag before she left, so she'd find it when she got to work. She called us that night, crying because she was so touched. I'm going to send a little something with her every week because it makes her so happy. Sue suggested the next 'care package' should contain Cindy's favorite perfumed soap."

Enhance Intimacy While You're Together

Take time to listen. Time is at a premium when you're together, but talking to each other is still important. So whenever you can manage to do little things together, such as preparing dinner together, hanging out in the living room or bedroom, and just talking about whatever, listen carefully to what your partner has to say and respond thoughtfully. When you live together full time, you can occasionally afford to listen with half an ear or tune your spouse out, but when your time is scarce, listening deeply is the first step toward creating intimacy.

Make eye contact. When you supplement your listening with eye contact, you'll increase the level of intimacy. Seek out each other's eyes while folding the laundry or playing with the kids. Steal glances at each other while driving, walking, or watching TV. Look up from your reading and smile. You will automatically feel closer and warmer toward each other.

Touch each other. Sit near your partner and gently place your hand on his or her shoulder, leg, or arm. If you're in the car, lightly touch your love's shoulder or arm. You'll find your conversation becomes warmer and more caring. After casual touching during the day, cuddling and sexual intimacy are easier to achieve.

Laugh together. The more jokes you can share, the closer you will feel. Cut cartoons out of the paper, play comedy CDs or your favorite funny movies, or watch old *I Love Lucy* reruns or whatever is guaranteed to create a giggle. Remind each other of funny moments in the past or share silly jokes from e-mail.

Express affection in many ways, and don't be stingy with your love. Put a sticky note that says "I love you" inside the medicine cabinet. Leave a chocolate kiss, a rose, a cookie, a plant, a card, or a balloon where your mate will find it; you don't need a reason. Give your sweetheart an impromptu gentle pat on the butt, a little squeeze on the arm, a hug, or a kiss to say: "You're special to me, and I love you." It keeps the affection between you fresh and constantly renewed. Adding a little sweetness to your everyday interaction will enhance your intimacy and draw you closer.

One of the big problems in commuting is that it's easy to lose not only your intimate connection but your sexual connection as well. When you spend time apart, sometimes the separation and reunion enhance your sex life. You get that feeling of missing each other and being happy to be reunited, which leads easily to having sex like you did when you were first in love. On the other hand, the stress and lack of opportunity that comes from being separated can make you feel like strangers and make it difficult to reconnect. Once you establish and renew the closeness between you, it becomes much easier to keep your sexual relationship active.

Better Sex

What's the most fun exercise you can have? Sex, of course! It's a great stress releaser. One of the most effective ways to release physical tension is to clench each muscle as tight as you can, then relax it. An orgasm does that very thing for your entire body at once—no wonder we like them so much.

Sex is also aerobic because it raises your heart rate and your respiration—and you don't even notice you're working hard. Many sexual positions stretch out your muscles and even involve repetitive, weight-bearing push-and-release motions.

All these are just side effects, obviously, and not the reason for having sex in the first place, but they're great extras for something that feels so good. In addition, a good sexual relationship enhances your emotional connection and increases the bonding between you. If sex is that good for you and your relationship, but time is at a premium, how can you get the most out of it?

Sex: What Is That Thing We Used to Do?

Even when you live together and love each other a lot, you can have problems keeping your sexual connection going. If you're living apart much of the time it gets even more challenging. When you do get a chance to have sex, if you're tense and distracted it will be difficult to connect. To enhance your sexual connection, try the following guidelines:

Relax. Nothing enhances sexual experience as much as being relaxed and comfortable. The guidelines for enhancing intimacy mentioned in the previous section will also help both of you relax and be in the mood. Try soothing music, soft lighting, and a quiet talk to set the mood. Being more relaxed will allow you to be more aware of your sexual energy and free you up to respond sexually when you want to. To experience how being relaxed enhances sex, try allowing time for sex in the morning when you are still relaxed from sleep.

Lighten up. For many couples, sex becomes stressful and tense—not fun at all. The sexual images and ideas we are bombarded with daily in advertising, the media, and in self-help articles and books are exaggerated, and if you try to live up to them, you're bound to fail. They've got lights, makeup, scripts, and sets, and all you've got is real life. To have more fun, enjoy every moment you spend with your partner and don't put too much focus on the sexual outcome. Like the rest of life, some sex encounters go well, some don't, and a very few are transporting. By adding a sense of humor to sex, you'll spend more time giggling and talking and being silly together and less time putting pressure on each other. Especially when you're spending time apart and your sexual time is at a premium, keeping a lighter attitude makes sex more fun.

Communicate. Sex is communication, and it reveals a lot about how you really feel to each other. To keep sex enjoyable, keep your communication honest and open. Often the best beginning for a lovely sexual encounter is a good conversation. When a relationship is new, you are eager to talk to one another so you make time and sex happens easily. Use your intimacy enhancers to set the stage for connecting with each other. Allow time to talk, and once you are relaxed and feeling close, it's not such a long distance into the bedroom.

Be flexible. While physical agility can be helpful, emotional flexibility is what really improves your sex life. Try different things, take turns, have quickies, do whatever feels good. Make sex as easy as possible, and have as much fun with it as you can. Don't insist that it has to be your way all the time.

rachel & michael

Michael (who had trouble finding a new executive job at fifty-two and took a position in another state) and his wife Rachel (who stayed at home to be near her aging mother and their grown children and grandchild) thought this was a really bad time in their lives to be apart. They were planning for retirement, and this threatened all their plans. They were afraid it would cause other problems too. Rachel says, "We both thought it would be the end of our sexual relationship. We needed more time, not less, to feel intimate, and sex already wasn't the easy thing it had been when we first met. We were both dealing with self-consciousness about aging, Michael was using Viagra, and the loss of his job did nothing for his self-esteem, either. Add the stress of being apart and of traveling, and I thought it was all over. But I was surprised to find that absence did actually make our hearts grow fonder. Having Michael's compact but lovely condo felt like going to a nice hotel for a weekend, and when he came home, the comfort of being in our familiar surroundings was also conducive to getting close. When we added some new habits, talked about what each of us wanted, and decided to have some fun with it, the whole thing got even better. Yes, we have less time together, but we also are having more and better sex. Go figure."

The Sweetness Factor

Nothing improves communication and intimacy better than enhancing the sweetness in your marriage, whether you're in each other's presence or far apart. We live in a cynical, hard-edged culture, so it's easy to become embarrassed or shy about being sweet to each other. When you see the difference a little sweetness makes in your emotional life, you'll understand why it's worth it. No matter what the bickering couples in the sit-coms say, being kind and tender toward each other creates a much better relationship. If you put more energy into expressing your love and appreciation for each other than you put into arguing and resisting each other, you'll be creating your own happiness. Research shows that a happy, loving marriage will enhance your self-esteem, improve your mental and physical health, and even give you longer life! When your married life is loving and pleasurable, you'll have more energy for success in everything else you do. When you can count on each other to be protective, supportive, kind, and caring, and each of you does your part in the partnership, you have a firm foundation for handling whatever life brings you. The calm assurance you get from knowing you are loved and cared about makes it easier to think clearly and make good decisions. It's a great blessing to be and have a loving and reliable partner with whom to make plans and carry them out.

To increase the sweetness in your relationship, try the following:

Express gratitude. Count your blessings out loud. Remember to say "thank you" to your partner, even for little things. If you're thinking about it, you'll be able to find things to express gratitude for several times a day. If you're religious, give thanks together for everything. My husband and I say "And we thank Thee, for receiving that which we need to know, that which we need, and that whom we need to know, and the courage to act upon it and the energy to follow through" at meals and whenever we want to give thanks.

Be courteous. Nothing ramps up the sweetness more than old-fashioned courtesy. Being familiar with each other is not a reason to drop your pleases and thank-yous. Politeness is like lubricant for your daily interactions; it makes everything go more smoothly.

Look, smile, and touch. There's an actual electrical connection that passes between us when we touch. To demonstrate this in seminars, I use a "magic wand" that contains a battery and is wired so that you have to put one hand on each end of it to light it up. I ask a couple to hold hands and then have each of them hold one end of the wand with the other hand, and it lights. Then I ask them to let go of each other's hand, and the light goes out, even though they're still holding the wand. This even works with a big circle of people when two are holding the wand. When everyone holds hands, the wand lights—if anyone in the circle drops another's hand the wand goes out because the electrical circuit of the connected bodies is disconnected. Also, neurology research shows that your brain "lights up" when you look at someone you love. In my office, I know that when I get a couple to look at each other and hold hands, their arguments become much less angry. You can use that electrical connection to provide juice in your marriage. Look at each other and smile frequently when you're together. Give each other little pats, massages, and gentle touches, and hold hands frequently when you're walking or driving; you'll keep the energy (and the sweetness) flowing between you. Whenever you're apart, your physical body will remember all those little looks, caresses, and smiles.

Give compliments. It costs nothing to say "You look good," or "I like your shirt," or "You did a great job," and it gives back countless rewards. Give each other as many compliments as you can manage, every day. Between compliments and gratitude, you can really pump each other up and both of you will feel great, and look like you do.

Celebrate. Make a fuss, big or small, over every little accomplishment or milestone you achieve. Remember: appreciation + celebration = motivation. If you want to motivate each other to stay together, work toward a good marriage, be a success, or be more loving, celebrate and appreciate every tiny step in a good direction. You'll be surprised how quickly you achieve your goals when you celebrate every step along the way.

Cindy & Bill

Cindy says, "The idea of creating sweetness in our precious time together really meant a lot to me. I feel so lucky to be married to a guy who'd think of sending a 'care package' with me, and who'd actually ask my best girlfriend what I'd like. He deserves all the affection and gratitude I can manage to express. And, it's actually made our time together more joyous. We're celebrating our love for each other in new and better ways. It's even harder to leave on Mondays, but easier in another way, because we're so clear that we love each other. And every time we get back together, the separation adds some extra excitement."

Reassurance

One more way to enhance your communication and intimacy is to learn how to reassure each other. When you and your partner are accustomed to power struggles, your discussions can be blocked by the fear that any conversation will be another power struggle; someone is going to lose, someone will end up feeling bad, or nobody will win. Worse yet, after all the hassle, frustration, and resentment, the problem could still be unsolved. So when you propose to talk, the response is "Why bother?"

If you partner won't talk about a problem, it may be because he or she fears the outcome of the discussion. Determining the source of the fear (is it fear of losing? fear of arguing or fighting? fear it won't work?) gives you an idea about what is needed to reassure your partner. Reluctance or refusal talk is usually the result of one or more specific fears, such as:

- Fear of being manipulated or overpowered: When one of you is more verbal than the other, the less verbal partner can feel overwhelmed and inadequate, and those feelings lead to not wanting to talk at all.

- Fear of being taken advantage of, made a fool of, or conned: If you don't have a history of this within your relationship, this fear may come from elsewhere, such as early childhood. For example, you may have felt that older kids or siblings always took advantage of you. Those feelings persist, and even if you overcame them in business settings, they may come up when you become close enough to your spouse to feel vulnerable.

- Fear of having another fight: When you have a history of fighting with each other, both of you can become reluctant to begin a conversation (or to get into a serious discussion) because you are sure it will become a fight.

- Fear that the process will be a long, complicated hassle (hard work) without a worthwhile result (a waste of time): This fear can come about when you've had a lot of stubborn power struggles, which get nowhere.

- Fear of losing or having to give up something important: You or your partner might be reluctant to discuss an issue because you suspect you might be wrong and don't want to admit it or give up the bad habit.

- Fear that a new approach won't go well or work at all: When you're making changes in how you talk to each other, especially if it doesn't work well when it's brand new, you might be resistant to trying again.

Each of these fears and any others that might come up, can be discovered, communicated, and reassured, and the following guidelines will show you how.

Dos and Don'ts for Reassuring Each Other

- DO: Gently let your partner know that you think he or she is avoiding a conversation by mentioning what you observe: "When I asked if you wanted to talk, you said yes, but then you disappeared. Are you reluctant to talk about this?"

- DON'T: Criticize or accuse your partner. What you observed could be wrong, so ask your partner if your guess is correct and if he or she is reluctant to negotiate.
- DO: Ask for an appointment to talk again.
- DON'T: Accuse your partner of being afraid to talk; just acknowledge your own fears, if you have any. Perhaps your fear is that he or she won't talk to you.
- DON'T: Deny your own behavior. If you argued in the past, acknowledge it and explain what is different now: "You're right, we did get angry and yell before, but we both realize that doesn't work, and we're learning a new way."
- DO: Make some agreements about what to do if your discussion becomes a problem. "If this starts to be difficult, we'll take a break." Knowing that you have a strategy to take care of yourselves if things don't go right will give you the additional confidence to talk.
- DO: Reassure each other. Make an agreement that you will honor each other's opinions, play fair, and seek a mutually satisfactory outcome.
- DO: Agree to do whatever you can to create a pleasant experience with a desirable result.

Knowing how to reassure each other will enhance your communication, your intimacy, and your sexual connection. In Chapter 4, you'll learn how to make transitions, which will further enhance your communication and intimacy.

Gail & Charles

Charles, the merchant marine officer who is away for weeks or months at a time, says, "Gail used to get very jealous, and I'd get angry because I felt she didn't trust me. When I learned that her jealousy was really based on fear, I was able to figure out how to reassure her, and it became a very small problem instead of a big argument. It makes sense to me that she's afraid, she's alone so much at home, and I know the pregnancy hormones make her more emotional. It feels good to reassure her, now that I know how to do it, and we are much closer because of it. We're not fighting about jealousy any more."

Communicating from a Distance with Children

When you're traveling a lot, it helps to have good communication not only with each other but also with your children. If you are a parent who commutes or spends long periods away from home, you're probably concerned about how to maintain contact with your children and remain meaningful and current in their lives. Children grow and change so quickly, and you'll want to keep up to date with their activities and interests.

Keeping in touch with your children while traveling will vary with the ages of the children. Very small children forget quickly, so pictures can help a lot. If you send a picture via cell phone or e-mail when contacting a small child, it helps them understand who is there. Try calling your child while you are at home, for example, calling the house phone from your cell phone so the child can see you while talking to you, and the child will have a better sense of contact with you when you're on the phone but not at home in person. Also, if you're gone for longer periods of time, send cards in the mail with a picture of something that interests your child (dinosaurs for a young boy, for example) and enclose your picture. Have the stay-at-home spouse read the card to your child and show your picture. Send little gifts by mail, too, and be sure to bring some small thing home as a memento of where you were (a miniature Liberty Bell from Philadelphia, a seashell from the coast, a red rock from Arizona), and you can talk with your child about where you were.

For older children, cell phones, IM, and e-mail work great. Be sure to listen when your child talks, and ask interested questions about whatever your teen or grade-schooler talks about.

Connect what you're doing in your travels with your child's experience. ("Remember that boring class you told me about? My meeting today was about the same—the rep from the other business was as stuffy as that teacher." Or: "Remember what you studied in history about the railroad? I took a train today that was a lot like that." Or: "I'm sitting in a room with curtains the same color as your favorite dress.") Connecting your experience with something in your child's experience will bring you closer together.

When behavior or other problems arise at home, talk with your spouse about what the solution or consequences will be, and try to be available by phone to let your children know that both their parents are in agreement about the problem and the solution. You can even attend family meetings (see Chapter 6) via speakerphone!

Bringing home a CD-ROM or DVD about wherever you were, your corporate project, something your children are interested in, or a school project they're working on and looking at it together on your laptop or home computer would be a great way for the family to feel connected with what you're doing while you're away. You could also take digital pictures and send them by e-mail, post them on a picture-sharing Web site, or put them on the computer or TV and talk about them when you get home.

If possible, use one of the online photo-sharing sites (like *www.shutterfly.com*) to post pictures and share comments. Kids and the parent at home can post pix of events, with captions or comments, and the parent who's away can comment on those and post pix of whatever is going on where he or she is. If your kids have pages on MySpace or another Web site, surprise them by posting there.

lucy & josh

Josh the truck driver, his wife Lucy, and their two teenage boys have really become experts at staying connected via the phone and e-mail. The boys love taking pictures of their events and e-mailing them to their dad when he's on his route. They take silly pictures, too, and Josh sends them pix of interesting things and people he sees on the road. When he has a load of something he knows the boys would like, like hundreds of computers, he sends back a picture of it. The whole family also puts up pictures on a sharing site, and that way they keep in touch with extended family, like grandparents, too. "I have used e-mail and my cell phone for a long time for work," says Josh, "but it took me a while to realize I could also use it to stay in touch with my boys. On the way home, I tecse them about what I'm bringing home, 'Guess what I've got for you?' and we can make plans for what to do on the weekend. It really helps us stay in touch. I think it's easier to talk to the boys and they listen better when I send an e-mail or text message."

Staying close to your partner and your family will strengthen your mutual bond, whether you're at home or away.

how to cope with

transition and change

Change is constant in any marriage as it is in life itself, and change is upsetting and difficult for everyone. You and your partner must be flexible to successfully negotiate change, and you need the ability to understand the possibilities and make the best choices. Change always involves loss and gain, so it can be difficult to sort the conflicting emotions. Whether the change is large or small, there is a period of transition in between the "before" and the "after." Creating smooth transitions whenever possible makes it easier for you to deal with the changes. Moving gracefully through the days and years, from work to play and from one stage of life to another, is not always easy. Often when you are struggling with these transitions, you find yourselves in incompatible modes, which lead to conflict and disagreement.

In this chapter, we'll look at transition problems in any marriage and the specific transitions that are peculiar to commuter marriage. You'll see what transition problems our long-distance couples have faced and how they solved them, and you'll find answers to the questions:

- What are the transitions in marriage?
- Why is it so difficult to reconnect when we do get together, and how can we fix it?
- What kinds of transitions are special to commuter couples?

Transitions in Every Relationship

In your marriage, how you manage transitions can make the difference between fighting and enjoying each other. You need to know how to get from paying bills to making love, how to move from an argument to problem solving, and how to cope with all the huge changes life can throw at you: unexpected job changes, illness, natural disasters, growing children, financial problems, and aging relatives. Every marriage faces these changes, and having a commuter marriage doesn't make them any easier. But with the proper information and techniques, you can learn to make smooth transitions and handle change with grace.

What Are the Transitions in Marriage?

As you grow older and gain more experience, your attitudes, expectations, and preferences change. Because your relationship is a reflection of the attitudes and experience of both of you, it must change as you do in order to sustain a mutual sense of freedom. These continuous changes, whether caused by circumstances (a new job means you must move to a new city), personal growth (you become more self-assured and want to make some new friends or develop a talent), or an unexpected event (your spouse gets a serious illness), always create some turmoil and confusion. You and your relationship will continue to grow and change, and you won't always progress neatly from one stage to the next or find an arrangement that is permanently satisfying. Each of you can even be at different stages at the same time!

You can use the exercises and guidelines in this chapter to work out the confusion of new ways of doing things and work together to bridge the differences when they come up. You'll soon learn to see each transition as an exciting new adventure or challenge instead of a frightening change.

Susan & Bob

Bob, who was introduced in Chapter 1, lost his aerospace project management job and had to take a lesser programming job, and he's taking night classes while his wife Susan works as a teacher's aide. With their young three children, life is hectic. Bob says, "We were doing fine with Susan working while the kids were in school, and my job was nine to five, so I was home at night. Losing my job threw everything into confusion. I had to go back to school to get programming certification so I can earn more money, and now I'm not home at night. Sue and I are upset and stressed, and we can fight at the drop of a hat."

GUIDELINES FOR NEGOTIATING CHANGES

- Make sure you're thinking and not just feeling—don't let your emotional reaction overrule your careful consideration of whether you're making the right decisions in the face of the changes you want or have to make.

   Susan says, "It is very helpful to understand the difference between thinking and reacting. When we stay calm and think about what we need to do to solve the problem, we do much better."

- Work together as a team, and discuss what's working and what's not. Pay attention! You're deciding your future happiness, and you have to gather the facts to make the decision.

   Bob says, "I have a tendency to make decisions without discussing them with Susan, and I had to change that."

- Ask questions out loud; don't just guess at your partner's motivation and feelings. The two of you need to be able to discuss your thoughts, feelings, and ideas about the changes and the partnership decisions you'll be making. Each of you must be able to listen to the other and not just react.

Susan says, "I was really guilty of assuming I knew what Bob was thinking, and expecting him to know what I wanted. Then I'd get mad when my expectations didn't happen. Once I began actually telling Bob what I was thinking, and what I thought he was thinking, things became a lot clearer, and we began to feel more like a team."

- Take some time to evaluate how your choices are working. Does it feel like you're creating a good future together?

Susan says, "I admire Bob for getting educated in a whole new field. If what we hear is right, he can make a lot of money with his new degree, and I'm willing to support and encourage him to make it happen. It will be hard for a while, but when we're working together like this, I know we'll be OK."

- Review what has happened, the good and the bad, and don't gloss over problems or discount good times. Remembering clearly and accurately will help you have a balanced idea of how the changes are working.

Bob says, "These changes have been tough, and it felt like we went from having a nice life to struggling. But I'm impressed by how strong and capable Susan is—she's been a trouper through all of it. Once we got over the initial shock and upset, and had a path to follow, we pulled out of our confusion, and we are more of a team than we've ever been. We're learning so much; we're going to be much better off when we come out of this. Talking frankly about the good and bad things that have happened helps us to keep in touch with how we're doing, and gives us the information we need to make the next decision."

- Experiment with problem solving, working through situations where you disagree, and trying new ideas when you don't know what to do.

> Susan says, "We don't always know what to do. Sometimes we get stumped about how to handle our schedules, child care, or finances, but instead of arguing when we don't agree on what to do, we've been just trying one of our ideas. Sometimes we flip a coin to see which idea to try, and the experience of trying it, whether it works or not, gives us more information for making choices. Knowing we're just trying something, and not locked in to it, makes it easier to take the chance."

- Empathize by putting yourself in each other's shoes to really understand what may be going on.

> Bob says, "We make a point of letting each other talk, and hearing what the other person's experience is. Susan needs to know that I understand how hard it is for all the child care to be on her shoulders, and it really helps when she's willing to hear my struggles with going back to school at this point in my life. We can make better choices when we understand more about each other's experience."

When your familiar way of doing things begins to change, it's easy to find yourselves struggling, competing, or fighting you become insecure or frightened. When you have some guidelines to follow and understand the change process, these transitions can become just a series of problems you must solve.

What Transitions Affect Commuter Couples?

For geographically challenged couples, transitions are even more important and more complicated because you're dealing with all the changes life throws at you, plus the challenges of being apart and coming back together again repeatedly. Even the change from living together to commuting has a transition phase, and so does moving back to living together. Here, you'll learn how to handle the kinds of changes that commuter couples face.

Surviving the Change to and from Commuting

Whether your decision was voluntary or made under pressure, changing from living together to any commuting situation isn't easy. It involves making many small decisions and solving problems about financial, emotional, and practical issues. Whether your commute is short term or long term, you're facing big changes, and a substantial adjustment. Even if you're both living in the same house but are adopting schedules that mean you hardly see each other, the change can be overwhelming. The imagining the future exercise that follows will help you cope.

Most couples have problems making good decisions about change because they haven't examined all the options thoroughly enough. The following exercise will help you take a long view of the situation and get some mental distance, so you can see it more objectively, think more clearly about it, and make negotiating the changes easier. No one knows what the future will bring. All we can do is learn to look ahead for possible consequences and outcomes, evaluate the options, and make an informed guess about what results our choices will bring. You can use the following steps to help you make the best possible decisions about your future.

EXERCISE: IMAGINING THE FUTURE

You can do this exercise by yourself and with your partner, and if you have older children, even include them. The more you do this, the easier time your family will have visualizing a different future and adjusting to it.

1. *Picture your future.* Whatever style of commuter marriage you're considering, spend time imagining the future you'd like to happen. Even if this new situation you're facing is not really a choice, it will help to picture it as positively as possible. What will your home life be like? How will it change your work situation? Get as detailed as possible, describing your time apart and your time together. How do you feel? How does your partner feel? Take as much time as you need to visualize your future as completely as possible. You can visit this imaginary future many times, as your information or situation changes.

2. *Explore your options.* Consider what steps you need to take to make this change as positive as possible. You may need to know what things cost, what the facilities are where you'll be living, or where your spouse and family will visit. Perhaps you need to explore:

   - Phone and travel costs
   - Child care
   - Weather
   - Necessary clothing (is it colder, warmer, wetter, or dryer than where you are now?)
   - Insurance costs
   - Communication devices and plans
   - Restaurants, grocery stores, shopping
   - Social venues and opportunities

   Think of as many details as you can about things you'd like to know to help you make the change. You'll need a lot of information about where you're staying away from home, and you may need some new options at home, too.

3. *Do research.* Divide your list into items and choose which ones each of you will research, and decide when to meet again and share what you've learned. Look for realistic

information to help you figure out what choices you actually need to make:

- Find people who are doing what you want to do.
- Read biographies and first-person accounts.
- Ask questions of people who are involved.
- Watch movies or documentaries about the new location.

4. *Revise your picture.* Use your new information to revise your initial visualization of your new situation. This will help you make better choices about how to make the change.

If Commuting Is Sporadic or Temporary

Surprisingly enough, sporadic or temporary commuting can create the worst problems, simply because couples facing them tend to think they can handle it and don't make careful plans or discuss potential problems. If you're commuting sporadically or temporarily, it actually increases the number of reentries you are making and the amount of confusion and change. When you don't know how often or for how long you'll be separated, the disruption becomes more upsetting. Even though you think the commute will be simple or not last long, do the imagining the future exercise to help prepare for the unexpected.

jane & edward

For Jane, the nurse who is getting a postgraduate degree, and Edward, who lives at home but travels frequently for his sales job, things are frequently in flux. Jane's class schedule and nursing schedule change periodically, and Edward travels to different parts of his territory as his customers need him. "It's difficult to establish a routine," says Jane, "Just as we get organized around a schedule, or are expecting a quiet weekend together, one of Ed's customers will call, or I'll get a demanding assignment, or another nurse will need me to take her shift. We learned pretty quickly that we have to be able to shift our expectations and roll with the changes. If we don't talk and keep each other updated, we have lots of confusion and hassles. It's good that we don't have kids yet, because they need more structure than we have."

If Commuting Is Long Term

Long-term commutes offer some benefits and some problems. The benefits are that you have time to establish a routine, support systems, and even develop a reentry system that works. The problems, of course, are that you are spending a lot of time apart, and keeping your connection and intimacy feeling fresh is not easy. Long-term commuting presents transition problems because you need to plan for long-term solutions, such as:

Household maintenance: With one of you gone for an extended period, especially if home visits are few and far between, you may need to change your expectations about how well your house or yard will be maintained in one partner's absence. A stay-at-home partner, especially if he or she is working, may not have enough time or expertise to get it all done alone. If your budget permits, you can pay for some of the maintenance jobs (lawn mowing, basic housekeeping) that you once handled together. If family and friends are helpful, perhaps they can pitch in.

Sara & Paul

Paul, the contractor who was in the National Guard, and his pregnant wife Sara really had to change their expectations of adding on to their home and even just basic yard maintenance when Paul was unexpectedly sent to Iraq. They postponed construction plans and hired a gardener to do minimal yard work, letting the flower beds and fancy shrubbery go because there was no one to care for them.

Ongoing child care: Especially if the stay-at-home partner is working, child care can be problematic when one of you is gone for extended periods. Here is another area that family members and friends might be able to help with.

> Sara counts on her mother and mother-in-law as well as her sister to help her with child care while Paul is deployed to Iraq. She says, "I wouldn't be able to do this without the physical help and the emotional support my family gives me."

Social networks and support: You may be surprised to find that the people you spent time with as a couple aren't as comfortable when you're a single, and the activities you're used to may not work as well. If this turns out to be your situation, you'll need to plan to find different social networks and activities. If your partner is away for an extended time, he or she may also need to find a social network. Changing the people you spend time with and your activities can present some awkward transitions and some concern from your partner.

> Jill, who took the magazine editor job in another city from where her lawyer husband James lived, found she was spending so much alone time in her apartment away from home that she had to make friends there. She joined a book discussion group, which turned out great. "After James and I decided to buy a condo as a home away from home," says Jill, I was able to hold the book club meetings there, and I was also able to invite friends from home to spend a few days with me occasionally. That made the whole thing so much better, and when James came to visit, we had plenty of room to relax in."

New routines for meals, cooking, shopping: If you don't cook and you are alone at home or on the road, eating can present another problem. For the short term, eating takeout or in restaurants can work OK, but in a long-term situation, you'll find you may have to develop new resources of food or abilities to cook. A partner who is used to shopping and cooking for two may find that eating alone becomes a problem. While this is a great time to go on that diet you've wanted to try but haven't because your partner isn't on it, it does require some uncomfortable adjustment and rethinking.

Changing residences: In some instances a place to stay is provided for the away partner, but if not, you need to find lodging that fits your budget since you're paying for home too. A stay-at-home partner may feel like he or she is rattling around in a big house or apartment and if the situation is long-term enough may want to move to smaller quarters.

Colette & harry

Colette, a tenure-track university biology professor, and her husband Harry, a marketing executive, are at odds because Harry has been offered his dream job as a CEO in another state, and Colette doesn't want to leave her hard-won position or her years of research and study for publication. They face many choices:

- Whether they should live apart for a while until they see what happens
- What the changes in their finances would mean
- Whether to stay in their large house or sell it and buy a condominium in each location
- How their marriage might be affected by living apart
- How much they would need to travel to be together part time

By solving each of these problems individually rather than letting themselves see the whole thing as a power struggle, Harry and Colette were able to work out a balance between her career and his opportunity that allowed them both to feel that they could have what they wanted and still spend time together. Harry says, "At first, I just assumed Colette should want to come with me, and I was hurt that she wasn't more supportive. Then, after we discussed it one problem at a time, I realized I wasn't valuing her career and how much it meant to her. So we decided to live in separate places for a while, until we saw how it all worked out.

Colette might find a tenure-track position near where I am and be able to continue her research and publishing, or I might find that, once I get things organized, I can run the company from here and commute back and forth."

Colette says, "I am thrilled for Harry. I know he's always wanted this, but I also know I'd be very resentful if I had to leave my work. So we decided to sell our home, buy a nice condo in each area, and live apart until we have a chance to explore all the options. The house was too big for us anyway, and we can use the condos as investments if we buy another house later. I get a lot of vacation and holiday time, and I can often work from home, so we can have large blocks of time together. We both feel it's important to take advantage of our opportunities."

Ways to communicate about marriage business. We've already discussed many means of communication in Chapter 3, but if you're apart for a long period of time, you may need to find a different way to make decisions about bill paying, hiring help, and budgeting. Especially if the away partner is sometimes incommunicado, the stay-at-home partner needs to have the ability and permission to make unilateral decisions and to know what the parameters are. This can create an uncomfortable change in the power structure of your partnership.

Truck driver Josh and his stay-at-home wife Lucy struggled about the unfair division of chores until they discussed it and came up with the idea for Josh to do the household bookkeeping and bill paying online while he was on the road. He even helped his sons with their homework. Lucy says, "I was exhausted and had too much responsibility for everything while Josh was away. His deciding to do the bills and work with the boys took a lot of pressure off me and kept him closer to the boys. It was a big change, but it really helped."

How to stay emotionally close: When you're separated or the time you have together is scarce for a long period of time, you need to change your routines for keeping in contact and maintaining a strong emotional connection. Commuting for an extended period can be very lonely for both partners, and even if you have close family relationships or strong friendships while apart, it doesn't replace pillow talk, physical affection, and shared experience. We discussed keeping your communication and intimacy strong in Chapter 3, and the changes you'll make to do that are another transition that may be awkward and uncomfortable at first.

Paul and Sara were very worried about remaining close while he was so far away in Iraq. Sara says, "It was a big relief to find that e-mail, digital video and pictures, and letters really help us keep up with each other. Of course, it's not ideal, and I really want him home, but at least we feel able to stay close, and we can talk about our different experiences and how we are learning and growing. That way, the shock won't be as great when he comes home."

Throughout this book, you'll find solutions for all these situations, which you can use whether your commute is sporadic or long term. Making your commuter marriage work begins with getting as realistic a picture of your situation as you can, and then making plans to solve each problem that you envision, as well as learning to solve new issues that arise on the spot.

Reentry—Reconnecting When We Get Together

Like most commuting couples, at first you may be shocked to find yourselves fighting when you get back together. Reentry is a surprisingly touchy time, perhaps because you've both been anticipating it and have developed unconscious expectations of how it will be. When you miss each other, there are many moments when you think, "I wish my partner were here to see this to help me, to talk to, to comfort me, or just to keep me company." So you come back together, full of love and anticipation, and find yourselves inexplicably bickering. If you excitedly launch into describing the great executive lunch you had, your day at Disneyland with the kids, or your new promotion, your partner can feel slighted and undervalued or that you had more fun away than you do with him or her. If you instead talk about everything that went wrong, your partner is likely to feel overwhelmed and responsible for your problems. Either of these sequences leads to bickering. To avoid this problem, use the following guidelines for reentry.

Step One

Prepare in advance by acknowledging that seeing each other after being apart is a tricky time. Accept that it's awkward, and develop a routine to help it go more smoothly. Resist the temptation to impulsively launch into everything you've been waiting to talk about, the latest problem with the kids, or complain about the problems. Instead, begin by saying you missed each other and how good it is to be together again.

Step Two

Together, plan your time for the first few hours or days. Don't plan the other person's time until you talk about it. Each of you has established boundaries as individuals, and you both need to reestablish your bond. This can easily be done if you're intentional about it. Here's a reconnecting sequence you can follow:

- Greet each other warmly, and tell your partner you missed him or her. (This is very important—do not skip this step, and do not assume your partner knows.)

- Ask your partner how the time apart was, and listen to the answer. Then take turns. This is not the time to share all the things that happened but a period of personal sharing about how you feel about being apart and about whether the time apart went well or badly for you. This step begins the renewal of your bond.
- Only after the personal sharing is done, talk about the things that happened while you were away. Then ask for help with problems that may need attention.

Following these guidelines will avoid the pitfall of launching right into the exciting events of the trip, or problems at home, only to have your spouse feel hurt and not valued.

colette & harry

Harry was so excited about his new position that he came home the first week full of stories about everything that happened and about how wonderful it was He says, "I was all excited when I got home, and I never even said 'Hello' to Colette, I just launched in to everything I wanted to tell her. I d dn't say I was glad to see her, or ask her about how it was for her while I was gone. She got very hurt. Since then, I've learned to say hello, tell her I missed her, and ask her how she is. Then she can hear about my new career without a problem, and she's great—she is excited for me and wants to know everything about it."

Mastering Intimate Transition

When you're commuting, in some sense you are replicating the part of your original dating experience, when your focus was on "when will I see you again" rather than the security of living together. This has advantages and problems. The advantages are that you have an opportunity to miss each other and thereby appreciate each other more than couples who are always together and take their closeness for granted. Disadvantages can include feeling lonely and becoming less connected. You've learned how to set up your reentry and reconnect when you get back together. You'll also need to know how to create intimate transitions, which are moments you initiate that help you feel connected during the time you have together. If you and your partner don't realize the importance of transitions or how to develop them, you can begin to feel shy and distant from each other. You may think there's not enough time for intimacy or that your spouse doesn't love you anymore when what has really happened is that you haven't discovered how to move from daily routine to intimacy. Your feelings, bodies, and imaginations don't respond without some preparation.

There are other necessary transitions too. For example, sometimes you need to change from a mental focus to an emotional focus: "I was balancing the checkbook and paying bills, but now I'm relaxed and feeling close to you." Or sometimes you need to change your emotional focus: "I was angry and frustrated at traffic during my commute home, but now I'm happy and ready to have fun with you." You can learn the skills you need to develop transitions.

How to Develop Transitions

Consider all the different activities you each do in a given day when you're home. You work, see friends, play, make love, run errands, solve problems, perhaps even parent children. You can feel tired, exhilarated, defeated, successful, sexy, scared, vulnerable, angry, loving, indifferent, exhausted, and a host of other emotions. Most of the time, you are each reacting to different stimuli, in different situations, bombarded by different ideas. Only on a relaxed day, while doing things together, are you likely to be in compatible moods automatically.

Given that you probably don't have enough relaxed days, how do you get compatible moods going? That's right—transition. Think of transition as a preparation ritual designed to lead you into mutually compatible frames of mind. Don't expect mutuality to just be there or to happen instantly. Refocusing is essential to create the proper atmosphere for quality time together.

GUIDELINES FOR CREATING SMOOTH TRANSITIONS

- *Remember to suggest, or invite, rather than complain or demand.* "I'd love to spend time with you tonight, would you like to . . . ?" works better than "We never have any time together!" When you were dating, invitations were natural. Now, they may feel a little forced, but do it anyway. You'll get more comfortable with it as you do it more and as you see the results!
- *Transitions that are logical work best.* After a demanding workday, a relaxing half hour together before dinner with a backrub, a cool drink, or some light snacks gives you a chance to touch base and tune in to each other. After working in the garden, doing chores, or taking a bicycle ride, showering together (or simply helping your partner towel dry) can become a natural transition to lovemaking.
- *Use your commute for preparation.* When you're driving or flying home, deliberately leave the away problems behind and anticipate the pleasures of arriving home. Talk to each other on your cell phones on your way home to make a connection. If you and your spouse are driving together somewhere, use your time in the car to create your connection with sweet talk, holding hands, and feeling close.
- *Even mental transitions work.* When dressing for an evening out, focus your thinking on each other, on the positive things about your relationship, and on what you appreciate. You'll find the evening is more relaxed. When you've been stressed, frustrated, or annoyed, count the blessings of your relationship and your partner, and your mood will change.
- Whenever possible, reserve a little quiet time—no TV, no chores—to hold hands and be still for a few minutes. Listen to each other breathe. Breathing is connected to your emotional state and has a corresponding rhythm. As you listen,

you'll gradually begin breathing together. Don't rush this or pressure each other, just give it enough time to happen naturally. By the time your breathing synchronizes, you'll be in close enough harmony to know what to do next.

- When doing projects or chores together, take a moment to get in concert about what you are doing. "I'll clean this while you move that" is a simple thing to say, and it adds that feeling of teamwork. Clue your partner in on your plan, listen to your partner's ideas, and you'll be in synch and be able to work together without a hitch. You can even do this when you're apart by suggesting that your partner leave certain things for you to do when you get home.

- When you finish working or doing things together (including making love), make a deliberate transition apart. Congratulate each other on a job well done, thank each other for helping, or simply say: "That was delightful. I love you." Ending your periods of togetherness cleanly allows you to begin fresh with each new time together.

jane & edward

Jane, whose nursing shifts and school schedule change, and Edward, who travels for his sales job, are leaving and reentering over and over. "Learning about reentry, how important it is, and how to do it successfully really helped us. At first we were awkward and tense every time we got back together, but now we've developed some ways to do it, and it's working much better. Taking just a few minutes when we first see each other to be certain we're connected makes everything else easier."

The more limited your time together, the more important it becomes to know how to move easily from one mood or mode to another. You'll be amazed at how many arguments and squabbles can be averted when you simply make a smooth transition. It's pleasant, easy to learn, and magically effective.

Expecting the Unexpected

Because life is always throwing new things at you, and because your situation is unusual enough that you might not be able to anticipate some of the issues that arise, you need to be prepared for dealing with the unexpected. For example, you and your partner may be surprised to realize how the commute changes your relationship with your children.

Handling Commuting Changes with Your Children

As a parent, when you commute, your role changes from being there and being in charge to a more equal position of friend and advisor. Treating your older children as friends will help make this transition smoother. Both parents will usually have less time to spend with the children than before, and other people, such as child-care workers, friends, or extended family, may be taking up the slack. Of course, young children need parents who are not reluctant to take charge and enforce rules and standards, but as a parent you can also treat them with kindness and respect, encouraging them to think for themselves.

When you're dealing from a distance it becomes less possible to enforce rules and even more important to show solidarity with your stay-at-home partner about discipline and parenting. One of the great joys of parenthood is seeing a child grow into a responsible adult, and your commuting situation gives your children an opportunity to take more responsibility and become more autonomous.

GUIDELINES FOR COMMUTER PARENTS' TRANSITIONS

Away parent: Develop a separate relationship with each child. When you go away, it's a big change, especially for your younger children, so make a special effort to contact them and reassure them that they're still important to you and you're still in their lives. You'll be connecting with each child via e-mail, cell phones, IMing, or pictures and videos. Use the suggestions in

Chapter 3 for ways to communicate, but make sure each of your children knows he or she is special to you. Remember from day to day what he or she is doing, and ask about it.

> Truck driver Josh found it easy to keep in touch with his sons by e-mail and phone while he was on the road. "I feel so much more connected with my boys, and I can support their mother when she's trying to get them to do something, so it keeps Lucy and me connected too."

Stay-at-home parent: Keep in mind that your children have probably lost some of your time too. Make sure the time you have with them is quality time, and spend as much as you can, especially while your spouse is away. When your spouse is at home, allow for time your partner can have alone with the children. It will help them reestablish their connection and give you some needed time off.

> Lucy says, "I spend a lot of time running the boys around to practices, school, and other things in the car, so it's a great time to catch up with them. Sometimes they'll tell Josh something I don't know, because they talk so easily on the phone, but I can usually keep up to date by giving them my full attention at the dinner table or in the car."

With small children: Cuddle time is reassuring for any child and really essential with small children. Allow for some cuddle time every day if you're the stay-at-home parent, and whenever possible if you're away frequently. Remember that, with toddlers, out of sight is out of mind, so make sure they see pictures of the away parent regularly and especially any time they're talking to him or her on the phone. While you're away from your child, leaving a tape recording of you reading a favorite bedtime story to be played back in your absence can help your child feel close to you. Don't get upset if your child bonds with a child-care person—regard it as a positive sign that the child-care person is doing a good job. Your child will still recognize that you're the parent where it counts.

Sara, whose husband Paul is in Iraq with his National Guard unit, takes care to give a lot of cuddle time with her three-year-old, Lacey: "I try to play a video with her Daddy, me, and Lacey in it several times a week and cuddle her on the couch while we watch it. I read to her and tuck her in to bed every night. We both miss Paul so much, so I'm trying to give her extra affection and time while he's away."

Older children: Don't limit your conversation strictly to family topics or questions about their personal life. Instead, engage them in discussions of current events and the like to help them feel included. Take a minute to develop topics you'd like to talk about with them. Politics, events, sports, simple finances, facts about your work, political, or local neighborhood issues are all suitable topics at appropriate ages. Explain what they can understand about your commuting situation in a positive manner so they'll feel included in the dynamics.

Josh asks his boys to tell him what's cool on the Internet: "The boys e-mail me links to movies and videos they find on the Internet, I can watch them at night, and we can talk about them in the next phone call. They can send me pictures of the pretty girls at school, or we can talk about a great play in a TV ballgame. It gives us a lot to talk about."

Don't pass your stress on: If you feel stressed, don't pass it to your children. Nagging and constant reminders are ineffective with young children and inappropriate with older children. Of course, you should set limits and make sure that irresponsibility and bad behavior have consequences, but you needn't patronize your children. If they want something from you, don't respond unless they ask you in a polite, adult manner. Include them in your planning discussions and expect that they will take appropriate responsibility for family issues. They'll feel better about your situation if they understand the reasons why they need to pitch in, and they'll feel much more a part of the family if you rely on them to help out in appropriate ways.

Susan & Bob

Susan says: "When Bob lost his job and went back to school nights, our income dropped, and when I began being a teacher's aide there were a lot of big changes. I was very tense, and I heard myself yelling at the kids. I sounded like a crazy person. I realized I needed to calm down, because I was upsetting my children. So I made sure to take a moment before dealing with them to get myself in hand. Things improved immediately. They are sleeping better, they're more cooperative, and I'm doing better too."

Adult children: If you have grown children, don't forget that these changes may affect their time with you too. Don't expect them to just understand what you're doing. Share your reasons with your grown children on an adult-to-adult basis. Let them know how you and they can keep in touch. You have expertise they can benefit from, but be willing to learn from them as well. If they're reading books or taking courses, discuss the information as you would with another adult.

Jill & James

James says: "When Jill first decided to take the editor position in another city, my grown sons were upset because they thought she was leaving me. It caught me by surprise, so all four of us had to sit down and talk about what was happening. When they got to visit us in the condo, they were much more comfortable. Jill is not their mom, but they love her, and they were very worried until we realized we needed to talk directly to them about the move."

Set an example: When you commute, time is at a premium and it's often stressful, but don't let it affect your courtesy to each other. Treat each other, and your young or adult children, as politely as you would a friend. If you're consistent, they'll pick up on your behavior and start being polite back. If they are doing something to annoy you, and you don't react or respond, they will stop. If you expect them to act responsibly and politely, they're more likely to do it, and it will save precious time.

Susan & Bob

"My kids began yelling and fighting with each other when they saw me yelling," says Susan. "When I got myself together and went back to my normal, calm behavior, so did they. It brought home to me that they not only react to my behavior, they also mimic it and learn from it. If I want to raise children who can be calm under stress, I have to learn how to do that myself."

Consult your children: Ask your children for opinions and advice. Even in early childhood, children can be encouraged to develop their own opinions about events and decisions you face as a family; as they get older, you can ask for their ideas about what to do. When your children become adults, you can request advice about work issues, investments, or other concerns. Sharing advice as friends and equals will create the friendly connection you want.

Sara & Paul

"Even asking my kids what we should have for dinner and would they help me get ready for Daddy to come home gets a great response. They would so much rather be asked for help or ideas than to be told what to do," says Sara. "The younger children, especially, see being asked to help as being included; but even the older children like getting credit for being helpful and they all enjoy being thanked and saying 'Look what I did, Daddy!' It works so much better than giving orders, which creates instant resistance."

Think about balance: Pay attention to the balance of your interaction. As a parent, the role of nurturer and caretaker is familiar, and perhaps comfortable, for both you and your children. But you don't want to foster that relationship too much when your children are grown. Don't let your part in the relationship slide into all giving (or all receiving). Remember, the objective is to create a friendship with your children. If your children always seem ready to take from you, make some suggestions of what they can do in return.

"My boys are pretty used to me helping them," says James, "but when I began to commute to visit Jill on the weekends, I asked them to look after the house, mow the lawn, and so on. I was really surprised at how much they enjoyed being asked. I hadn't realized that they'd like a chance to give back. I realized, seeing their pride, that they felt much more grown up, respected and manly. It was a surprise and a pleasure to see what fine young men my sons had grown into."

After following these guidelines for a few months, everyone will get comfortable with the new situation and relax. You'll have more fun with your children when each of them is taking responsibility appropriate for their age level.

Handling the Anxiety of Change

New decisions, especially the major ones, are usually accompanied by some insecurity and anxiety in yourself, and perhaps in the people around you. If you're changing and learning new things, you'll have the added insecurity of feeling incompetent until you've attained the necessary skills and information. For any competent adult, this "beginner" feeling can be very uncomfortable. Once you feel skilled in most things you do, the awkwardness and uncertainty of a new situation are often hard to bear.

For encouragement and assistance during this transitional stage, it's necessary to find support. If you're making a small decision, the support of friends and family (and yourself) is probably sufficient. If you're making significant new choices that involve changing behaviors, learning new things, or confronting a difficult situation, professional support may be valuable. If you're struggling with these changes, don't hesitate to go for counseling or coaching with an expert who can help you through them. If you have colleagues or friends who are commuting, you can share useful information and similar experiences. You may even have the benefit of a family member who has experience. Having such support will help you negotiate the changes and make a smooth transition.

You can also be a support for yourself. You can do the following exercise on your own, with your partner, or even with older children. Focusing like this on a daily basis helps keep problems small, and helps you stay on track with less stress.

EXERCISE: DAILY ANTICIPATION

1. Either in the evening or the morning, sit down with your calendar for fifteen to twenty minutes and think about the day to come. Go over your to-do list, appointments (whatever kind of appointments you have: with a business associate, a customer, your dentist, to take your child to soccer or ballet, or lunch with a friend), and whatever you personally would like to accomplish (for example, gardening, cooking, making a speech, getting a new client, writing your novel, working out, winning at a sport, meditating or praying, creating art or music, or connecting with your spouse and family).

2. If your list is more than you can possibly get done in one day, sort through it now instead of waiting until the end of

the day to find you didn't accomplish the most important things. Prioritize what you have to do, and whatever you're not going to get to today put on your to-do list for tomorrow or next week.

3. Evaluate your schedule as realistically as you can. For example, if you are taking your daughter to ballet class or your son to football practice, consider that it might be important to allow enough time for the two of you to talk. If the client you have to see is long-winded or habitually late, take that into consideration. If you are extra tired, consider not packing your day as full as usual.

3. If you're away from home, your calendar may not be full enough. If you have a tendency to go to work and then come home with no idea of what you'll do for the evening, then give some thought to scheduling some of that unused time. For example, you can:

- Volunteer to help somewhere.
- Invite a friend to dinner.
- Participate in a sport.
- Join the church choir.
- Work out or run.
- Call your partner and ask what you can do to help from where you are.
- Take a class.

You can even decide to get intentional about relaxing rather than letting the TV or the computer absorb time meaninglessly.

In this way you can take charge of your day and make sure that, within the limits of your real situation, you do the things that are most important to you. The few minutes you take at the beginning of your day to organize it can save you hours later. If you focus on planning each day, you will make steady progress toward attaining your future goals and creating a truly great commuter marriage.

change and stress
in a commuter marriage

Whether you entered your commuting arrangement voluntarily or had little choice, you're facing a lot of changes, which is stressful. In this chapter, we'll answer the following questions commuter couples ask about stress and change:

- Why does change create stress?
- Why am I so upset?
- How can we support each other when others criticize what we're doing?
- What can we do to relieve the stress of being apart?
- How can we handle the unexpected?
- How can I stop worrying?
- Where's the partner I thought I had?

Handling the Unexpected

Each time you face a separation, all the routines in your relationship change, and that creates many unexpected events and lots of stress. Whether your separations are regular or sporadic, long or short, the difficulties of going back and forth can make you and your partner anxious and upset. Of course, the nature of the unexpected is that you can't know what it is in advance. Therefore, this chapter contains a number of guidelines and

113

techniques you can use to handle whatever unexpected changes arise and cope with the related stress.

Why Does Change Create Stress?

As you read in Chapter 2, when you are operating according to familiar patterns, you can relax a bit, do things on cruise control, and your mind becomes a little free to wander and destress. When all your familiar routines and patterns change, however, every little thing takes more thought because it hasn't yet become a habit, which is stressful. In addition, changes tend to create anxiety because you're not sure of the outcome, and that, too, is stressful. Stress is not all bad; it can add to your excitement and make life more interesting—but long periods of unrelieved stress can be wearing, and when you and your partner are tense and stressed, it's easy to find yourselves arguing.

Free-Floating Anxiety and Stress

When you're in a time of change, you're experiencing a lot of unknowns, which can bring up fear. If you don't acknowledge your anxiety and work through it, you can find yourself acting out—exhibiting behavior such as drinking too much or creating relationship, work, or money problems as a distraction. This kind of anxiety is not really about specific things, so it's called free-floating anxiety. You don't need the extra tension on top of all the changes you're handling, and you can avoid such problems by following these simple steps for resolving your fear and anxiety:

Steps for Facing and Resolving Anxiety

Free-floating anxiety is the result of not facing your fears and worries directly, which allows them to be vague and therefore unsolvable. These vague worries become a continuous stream of negativity that keeps interrupting your mode of thought and that you find it hard to get away from. It's usually not focused on any one thing but jumps from negative thought to negative thought. These steps will help you pin down your anxiety until it becomes specific enough to resolve.

1. Learn to recognize the signs of your own anxiety:

   - You can't sleep.
   - You worry a lot.
   - You obsess about negative possibilities.
   - You have panic attacks (shortness of breath and hyperventilation).
   - You're unusually irritable or needy.
   - You find yourself eating, drinking, using drugs or medication, or spending too much to soothe yourself.
   - You space out or zone out watching TV, reading, or sleeping too much to avoid your own thoughts.

   When you become aware of any of these signs, it's time to face up to your anxiety and resolve it.

2. Create an opportunity to complain and express your fear. When you're facing the numerous changes that come with a lifestyle change, your tendency may be to pretend you're OK and everything is fine. Instead, allow yourself some moments to complain and be unhappy about the situation. Choose a safe person (other than your spouse) to whom you'll express as many of the negative feelings and thoughts as you can. It's best not to do this step with your spouse, who may feel blamed and not understand you're just releasing anxiety. If no one else is available, try writing about it. Getting your fears down on paper where you can see them will help you understand what you need to counteract them.

Sara & Paul

Sara was very upset when she first learned that Paul was being deployed to Iraq, and after he left, she realized she had most of the signs of anxiety on the above list. She did several things to ease her tension: She began meeting with a group of other wives of guardsmen, she took walks with her three-year-old daughter in a stroller, and she began keeping a diary to share with Paul when he came home. She says, "The other wives were particularly helpful, because I didn't feel I had to pretend to be strong around them. I could talk about what was really worrying me, and they understood. After I began attending the group, I started sleeping better, and I felt much better."

3. Evaluate your fears and complaints. Allow yourself some time to consider the points you made in your complaining session.

Sara thought about what she was complaining about: missing Paul, afraid for him, feeling overloaded with chores at home, being bored and not knowing what to do with her time alone.

- Is there anything that you can do differently? Do you want to?
- Have you made all the choices you can?
- Are you thinking clearly about the problem?
- Are you angry with anyone specifically?
- Are you resisting unnecessarily?
- Are there agreements or situations you want to change?
- If you don't have a choice, can you see some alternatives?
- Do your options look different to you now? (If not, try going through these questions again.)

After Sara considered what she was upset about, she did change some things. She got more exercise, and she went back to church to find a way to ease her fears for Paul. "I grew up in church but got away from it when I was a teenager. Going back there meant I was able to talk to my pastor, share my worries with the congregation, and ask them to pray for Paul, which really helped me cope better. There's daycare for Lacey, which she really likes, and which gives me a break from her, too."

4. **Befriend yourself to build trust.** Discuss the problem with yourself as helpfully as you would with another friend. Brainstorm for ideas, realistic or even silly, about what you could do to make things better. For example:

   - I could move to Timbuktu and avoid the whole thing.
   - I could talk to Pastor Harry and see if he can help me think this through.
   - I could ask Martha to help.
   - I could find a Genie and have him make this all better.
   - I could win the lottery and quit the whole thing.
   - I could go on with my life, doing the best I can, and work on making the best of this situation.
   - I can figure out what I want and talk to my spouse about it.

   Sara says, "This was fun! I solved the war, created world peace, escaped to Costa Rica, laughed and cried, and then I settled down and decided I could make it through until Paul comes home."

5. **Think carefully** about all the circumstances of your commuting situation with an eye toward finding ways to take better care of yourself and your spouse and family.

   Paul says, "Commuting is not something I can do very often, so I need to find a way to take care of myself, to ensure I return, and to stay in touch with my family. I'm fortunate in that my job in the guard is strategic support, so while I'm not exactly safe—no one is here—I have pretty good access to computers and the Internet. So Sara's brother-in-law, Fred, who loves and knows computers, installed voice translation software, speakers, and a video camera. Now I can write e-mail to Lacey, and the voice translator will read it to her. Sara can read Lacey a story in front of the video camera then post it online, and I can see it when I get a chance. I can watch them cuddle and play, and we all feel closer. It's a godsend."

6. Review and decide. Once you've expressed your anger and disappointment, evaluated your feelings, brainstormed ideas, and checked the facts, you will be feeling much more in charge of yourself and this situation. Review what you've discovered and make some decisions.

7. Sell yourself on a positive outcome. Think of all the possible great outcomes of the changes you're making. Consider what you will learn from it. Figure out how you can maximize the benefits of making the change. When you've convinced yourself, make a commitment to your plan.

"At church," says Sara, "I learned some wonderful prayers for Paul's safe homecoming, and for protecting our marriage and family. I shared them with Paul, and we agreed to say them every night before bed. We wouldn't be saying them at exactly the same time, but it really made us feel close and committed to a happy future together."

8. Your partner has probably noticed that you're anxious. Explain that you've been thinking about ways to relieve your anxiety. Then present your ideas to your spouse, listen to your partner's responses, and see what changes you can make to lessen your anxiety.

"I was relieved," says Paul, "that Sara found a place where she could talk and get support, and that she decided to go back to church for reassurance and comfort. It gave me peace of mind to know that she was not too anxious and unhappy. I got our chaplain to say the prayers with me that Sara learned in church, and I also say them every night and morning. It helps me feel closer to home."

How Can I Stop Worrying?

Anticipation is necessary to help you prepare for things to come, and it involves thinking through the possibilities and planning for the unexpected as well as the expected events and circumstances, but if your thoughts turn negative, your anticipation can become worry. If you think about the bad things that could happen, without figuring out what you can do about them, your anxious thoughts will just go around and around in your mind, and you'll feel more and more anxious.

When you listen to your own thinking, you'll hear a lot of specific worries, usually framed as what ifs.

- "What if my car breaks down?"
- "What if I we can't sell the house?"
- "What if Bill and I fall out of love while we're apart?"
- "What if Susan gets mad because I spent this money?"

These questions alone do not create your anxiety, but if you keep ruminating about them and never stop to answer them you'll become worried and upset. To avoid creating anxiety, treat the questions as genuine and answer them:

- "If my car breaks down, I'll use some savings and get it repaired."
- "The market is good, the house should sell, but if it doesn't sell right away, we'll lower the price."

- "Susan's usually reasonable, and this is a sensible purchase. If she doesn't like it, I can take it back or negotiate with her."

colette & harry

"As an experimental biologist," says Colette, "I know that worrying about the outcome of an experiment won't make it go better. Instead, I train my students to use their worries as a way to check their design for flaws. If they're worried something won't work, they should correct the design to make it do what they want. But I realized I wasn't doing that myself. I was letting myself worry about Harry's move, being alone, everything—but I wasn't pinning down the worry and coming up with answers. When I started treating my worries like clues I needed to solve, I felt better."

Negative worrying can be turned into positive anticipation when it leads you to consider alternate possibilities and plan ahead.

Letting Go of Anxiety

When you're commuting, it can seem that there's one new problem after another. Add this to normal life issues, illness, financial stress, and family troubles, and the triggers for anxiety abound. You're in a time of high stress, and changes and commuting problems often bring up fear. Worry is a little more specific than anxiety, because it's usually more focused on a specific thing. Worry drains and wastes your energy and makes you less likely to make good decisions. If you take that same energy you're using to run yourself around in mental circles and do something productive with it instead, it'll serve you better.

Beginner's Mind

To lessen worry, you can adopt the Zen Buddhist concept of beginner's mind in the context of starting over. That is, you learn to approach any new or difficult experience:

- Without expectations
- Willing to learn new things
- Willing to not be an expert
- Willing to feel uncomfortable and incompetent
- Willing to enjoy the experience of being a learner

This attitude reduces stress, takes the limits off your imagination, and leaves you mentally open to better experiences than would be otherwise possible.

GUIDELINES FOR LETTING GO OF WORRY

Learn to accept: Giving up trying to control things makes every situation easier to handle. Another word for this is acceptance. In the long run, you gain more control by letting go. Rather than fight what's going on and try to deny bad things that happen, use your beginner's mind to face it, do what you can, and learn from it.

Take charge of negative thoughts: Letting go in this sense of acceptance is an internal, private process. You don't need to let anyone else know you're doing it. Take charge of your negative thoughts (that's one thing totally in your control) and turn them around—argue with them, fight them off, wrestle with them. Put energy into it. Use affirmations to replace the negative thoughts with positives.

Recognize what you can't control: What you need to let go of are the things outside that you can't control, such as other people, life's events, loss, disappointment. Stop trying to change what won't change, accept what is, let it be, and live life as it is. You may feel it's easier said than done, but once you get a handle on it, everything else is easier. Fretting about what you can't control is an endless, useless waste of energy you can use elsewhere.

Do a reality check: If you're doing a lot of negative thinking, do a reality check. Are the stories in your head about what actually happened or about what you imagine happened? Instead of pretending, worrying, or being in the past or the future, focus on what's real. Don't waste time and energy trying to figure out what someone else is thinking, especially what he or she might be thinking about you. You won't get it right anyway. Ask directly to get the truth.

Remember the positive: Tell the truth to yourself, and make sure you're focused on the whole truth, not just the negative parts. When you're worried, it's common to focus on only the bad news. Remember to include anything that's positive.

Notice what you feel: When you face reality, you must feel your feelings. Denying the truth is a way to avoid your feelings. When you just accept what's happening, your feelings will surface, and you can resolve them.

> Harry says, "I'm a worrier. I always thought it was why I was so successful. But when I learned to let go of worry and grasp on to reality instead, I became much more successful and less anxious about things that weren't even happening. Now when there's a problem I can deal with it and I can also plan ahead, but I don't waste my time fretting about things that might happen. It leaves my mind free to think more productively, and when I'm not wasting energy worrying, I sleep better, I'm more relaxed, and I have an easier time focusing and concentrating. It's made my life so much easier."

Hints for Handling Several Kinds of Worry

Late-night worry: Get out of the habit of using your brain as a memo pad. Keep a pencil and paper by your bed to write down whatever is bugging you. You'll find it's a great sleep aid.

If you're worried about forgetting something, write it down. If you're anxious about something you have to remember to do, organize it with a written plan or checklist.

What-if worry: Fretting about what might happen? Use the guidelines for handling specific worries previously covered to figure out what you would do in case the hypothetical disaster occurs.

Endless replay worry: If you regret something you said or something that happened, figure out how you could handle that situation better next time. Practice it over and over until you feel confident you know what you're doing.

Obsessive worry: If a repetitive thought is interfering with your ability to function, you can replace it with something more positive. If obsessive thinking keeps you from leaving the house or working productively, or if you're sleeping all the time or not sleeping well because of it or it's disrupting your ability to relate, try doing affirmations. Affirmations are brief positive statements you can use when you're worried. Short, memorized prayers are also affirmations, and positive quotes or poems can be used as affirmations too. There are many books of affirmations on the market, as well as prayer books, wisdom quotations, and inspirational quotes. Find one that appeals to you or fits your spiritual or religious beliefs, and select a positive statement to memorize. When you find yourself obsessing on negative things, say your affirmation over and over. Repeating something positive will have a calming effect instead of the anxiety-heightening effect of repeating upsetting or scary thoughts.

When you take the time to examine your worries, you may find some of them are about trying to control small things that are not worth the energy drain. You can stop worrying about small things, let them go, and know you'll be able to deal with them as they happen.

Guidelines for Letting Go of Small Things

1. *Perspective:* Put your worries in perspective. Will it be important two months from now, an hour from now, or even fifteen minutes from now? Most of them won't be.
2. *Self-understanding:* If someone or something upsets you, don't exacerbate the problem by getting on your own case

for reacting. Reactions are normal—it's how we express them or not that counts.

3. *Rise above:* If someone frightened you, say a driver cut you off, then give a little prayer of thanks that you survived, bless the other driver (who probably needs it), and you'll feel better.

4. *Give the benefit of the doubt:* If someone hurt your feelings, acknowledge that your feelings are hurt, then consider that the other person is probably more clumsy than intentionally hurtful. The world is full of emotional klutzes who don't realize the impact of their words and actions, and they create more problems for themselves than for you.

5. *Consider the source:* A neighbor or associate who is truly nasty may repeatedly hurt your feelings. Consider what must be going on inside that person's head, and be grateful that you're not hearing that. Even the meanest people are far nastier to themselves than they are to others. That person is trying to relieve his or her pain by inflicting some on you.

> Harry says, "When I learned to let go of the little things, like what people said about me or to me, I relaxed a lot more and stopped holding grudges. Now I let another person's crabby remark ruin his day, not mine."

The Worrier's Guidelines

Whenever you worry a lot, can't sleep, have anxiety attacks, or obsessively think about future events and problems when you should be concentrating on other things, the following simple steps will help you transform your worry into action:

First, write it down. If you're feeling anxious or worried, or you can't stop thinking about some future event, take a few moments to write down whatever is worrying you, or at least think it through carefully until you can clearly say what you're worrying about. Clarifying your worries will stop the free-floating sensation of anxiety with no basis.

Then, evaluate. Think about the first item on your list. Ask yourself, "Is there anything I can do about it now?" If you're away from home and worrying about your family, or if the problem won't occur until next week or next year, you may not be able to do anything about it right now. If you're worrying about a problem you can do something about, such as call someone, get an estimate of costs, or make a doctor's appointment to check out a worrisome symptom, go to step 3.

Next, do something. If there is something you can do, do it. Sometimes worry is a way to procrastinate. Often, worry is a way to keep a mental list going, as in "I'm worried that I'll forget to bring the slides for the presentation tomorrow."

- If you're worrying about how your presentation will go at work tomorrow, go over your notes and lay out your clothes for the morning.
- If you're worried about a health problem, look up the illness or injury on the Internet, or call your doctor and ask some questions.
- If you're worried about what's going on at home while you're commuting, call and find out, or if it's the middle of the night, send an e-mail. You'll relax knowing someone will get it in the morning and answer your question.
- If you're at home worrying about what your commuting spouse is thinking, call or e-mail to find out.
- If you're at work worrying about cooking dinner when you get home, write down a menu or a list of ingredients.
- If you're worried that you may be fired, update your resume and call some agencies. You don't have to accept a job offer, but if there's a real problem you'll be prepared.

Here's an example: If you're worried that the roof may leak the next time it rains, start making a list about what you can do about it. Your inner dialogue may sound like this:

"The news said it was going to rain next week. I'm worried that the roof might leak, and Paul isn't here to ask."

"Call a roofing company and have them look at it."

"I'm worried that a roofing company will charge me more than they should because I don't know how much it should cost."

"Call my brother-in-law, (or my neighbor, or my friend) who had his roof done, and ask him what it costs and also if he liked the contractor he used."

"OK."

When you reach this "OK," it's time to make the call or, if it's too late at night, make a note to call the next day.

Finally, distract yourself. When you've done what you can, or made your lists or notes, then distract yourself. Get busy doing something else: read, take a walk, or take or a bath. If the worrisome thoughts arise, remind yourself that you've done everything you can do, and bring your focus back to what you're doing now. If it's late at night, distract yourself with calming prayers, affirmations, poetry, or by reading something soothing (not that detective novel that will keep you up all night) until you can get back to sleep.

If you consistently repeat these steps every time you find yourself worrying, you'll train yourself to think more constructively, and over time you'll feel more confident and positive. You can use the energy you save in not worrying to learn the more positive attitudes of anticipation.

Above all, keep in mind what Goethe, the German poet, said:

Some of your ills you have cured
And the sharpest at least you've survived.
But what torments of Hell you've endured
From evils that never arrived.

cindy & bill

Bill (the contractor whose wife Cindy, the Navy nurse, is gone during the week) had a schedule book at work but none at home. He would come home to chaos and confusion, and once his daughter was finally in bed, he sat numbly in front of the TV. When he got himself a planner for his stay-at-home time, he suddenly found it possible to plan ahead, help Chloe get her homework organized, see friends, and even get the laundry done every week. Having a personal schedule that he uses as effectively as the one at work means he can plan for household chores and helping Chloe with homework and activities—and still make sure he gets some relaxation and recreation for himself. Anticipating the day's home chores, as he does the ones at work, means that he uses his time more effectively, gets the most important things done, and actually has extra time for seeing some friends and planning for the weekend when Cindy is home. "I took a chamber of commerce workshop a couple of years ago on organizing the workday with a calendar planner. I knew how effective it was, but it took me a while to catch on that it would be just as helpful at home." laughs Bill. "I can't believe I waited so long to do it. It's a simple thing, but what a difference!"

When you approach life with anticipation instead of worry, your energy rises, you aren't as reactive to small things, and you can think clearly, and that makes everything else easier.

Your Internal Relationship: Why Am I so Upset?

Because most childhoods are not perfect, most of us grew up learning to treat ourselves as we were treated within the family, in school, in church, and by peers. You may still be criticizing or mistreating yourself as you learned from those early experiences. For example, if you were laughed at for your thoughts, habits, or feelings, you may still be afraid of your own feelings today. Or if you were heavily criticized for making mistakes, you may now be overly self-critical. This internal way of relating to yourself can make you feel much more emotionally upset than the real-life mistakes or feelings warrant.

If you have a tendency to get upset at small mistakes, you will benefit from learning to calm yourself down and deal with your mistakes and missteps with kindness and careful thought.

To change the way you relate to yourself you need to become aware of the running dialogue that you carry on with yourself all day, every day. This internal conversation has been going on in your mind since early childhood, and, like many of my clients, you may be so used to it that you aren't even aware that it's there. The operation of your mind is very beautiful, very complex—it's nothing short of a miracle. Your mind and thinking are so intricate that it is possible to have several simultaneous thoughts, each from a different aspect of your mind, a different area of your brain, and each holding different opinions simultaneously! Of course, you don't hear these thoughts aloud, but if you pin them down, you can identify the various "voices" they seem to come from. For example:

- *Your logical self:* You probably have a practical, by-the-book inner voice who considers the logical side of every situation. "This pie has too many calories. I'd better not eat it."

- *Your fantasy/romantic self:* You may have a fanciful voice that comes up with a fairy-tale version of life. "Wouldn't it be nice if the calories didn't count in food I love? I wish I had a fairy godmother to wave a wand over this pie."

- *Voices of others:* Some of your thoughts may be the voices of other people. We all have the sound of other's comments, both loving and critical, in our minds.

jane & edward

Jane, the nurse whose husband travels as a salesman, said: "I was making a candle-lit dinner for Edward's return home, and I laughed out loud as I was adjusting the candles on the dinner table because I just heard my mother's (who wasn't there) voice, saying 'Don't play with the dinner candles!' It was so real, I actually looked around to see if she was there but it was really just a memory from my childhood. As a small girl, I was fascinated by the long candles she'd put on the table before a dinner party, and I heard her say that very thing many times. I guess it's just a recording of her I carry around in my head."

- *Your rebellious self:* This is the voice that expresses your frustration with restrictions. "Screw it. Life is short. I'm having the pie anyway."
- *Your critical self:* This voice gives you a hard time. "You are so greedy! If you eat that pie you'll be sorry."
- *Your nurturing self:* This is your kind-to-you voice, which may need to be strengthened if you're too self-critical. "You're a hard-working, responsible person, you deserve a treat, and I also want you to be healthy."

If you're frequently upset, you may have a virtual battle going on inside between some of these voices. Blaming, defending, making excuses, and resisting—all going on at once within your mind—can be very upsetting and distracting. It's the equivalent of being trapped in a room with a lot of people who are shouting their opinions at you.

To reduce the mental noise and be able to think clearly, use the following steps to learn to sort through each of your varying levels of thought and opinion:

STEPS TO END UPSET AND ACHIEVE CLARITY

1. *Listen to all your opinions and reactions:* When you stop and listen to each "voice" individually, you can find out what the fight is about. Then you can take charge and mediate the conversation so that all your varying opinions of what must be done can be made to work together.
2. *Create a committee:* Your goal is to create a functional committee out of your mental noise. Picture it as a meeting room with a big table and each of your identified voices sitting around the table. Listen to what each voice has to say, and then make your decision. "I know the pie is fattening, and I also know it represents comfort and childhood to me, and I think what I'll do is have three bites and throw the rest away."
3. *Practice and apply:* Practice this process of dealing with your inner turmoil many times on small problems until it becomes easy for you. Then apply the same technique to bigger problems.

When you learn to take charge of all your varied reactions and emotions about a situation, you can then feel upset about something, sympathize with your own upset, and still think calmly about the solution to the problem. You can know you want something, know you think it's bad for you, and decide what to do about it. You'll be amazed at how much easier it is, and how much less exhausting.

Once you've mastered these steps, you'll actually be able to consult yourself about problems and issues you're upset about, as you would consult a friend or your partner. When you and your partner are apart, it's common to wish he or she was here to talk to. When that's not possible, it's a blessing to be able to consult yourself. Just as an experiment, try getting your capacity to listen and support together with your need to be heard and supported. You'll find out it works! Knowing you can and will be there for yourself will raise your healthy self-esteem and reduce your anxiety. Here's how to do it.

Consulting Yourself

If you are often upset and confused, it may mean you may have gone through your life asking everyone else's opinion but never getting clear on your own viewpoint. Like most of us, you may have wished for a consultant to advise you on some of your problems. This exercise will help you learn to consult yourself first. Then if you do get advice from someone else, you'll know whether you agree or not.

1. *Ask your own opinion.* At frequent intervals (about five times a day) during your regular workday, ask yourself:

   - What do I think about this?
   - Do I like it?
   - Does it make sense to me?
   - Do I agree or disagree with the others?
   - If I had unlimited power, what would I do?

   These questions will help you get used to asking your own opinion of ideas and events.

2. *Listen to the answer.* Listen to your opinions as you would to the ideas of a respected friend. Consider them, weigh them, and even discuss them with yourself from time to time. Allow them to influence your daily thought. If you feel, for example, that your work is not satisfying enough, just accept and allow that feeling to be there, and it will eventually create a need to act as well as many exciting ideas for how to act. There is no need to act on your ideas yet, just practice listening to your own opinion for now.

3. *Repeat to make decision-making easier.* After you practice asking your own opinion faithfully for a few weeks, it will
   become automatic to have personal opinions about everything around you. If you don't pressure yourself but let your
   ideas incubate at their own pace, this awareness of your own
   opinion will have a profound effect on what you do and
   how you act. Activating your individual thinking ability
   will gradually increase your options and choices and make
   decision-making faster and easier.

Once you get used to consulting your own opinion on
whatever choices you're facing, you'll feel much more secure in
making decisions.

Stress from Other People

Relatives, friends, coworkers, and even strangers can say the most
upsetting things! Most of the time they're trying to be helpful
or they're worried about you, but even when you realize that,
the critical remarks still hurt. No one likes to be criticized, fairly
or not. It's always upsetting and painful. Whenever you're doing
something different from the norm, like a commuter marriage,
others often feel compelled to criticize, sometimes in a mean
way and frequently without really knowing what they're criticizing. Because we all get criticized from time to time, you may
find the following ideas helpful.

What to Do When Others Criticize Your Situation

Whether criticism is intended to be helpful or harmful, you
can use it positively:

1. Evaluate the critic:
   • Is your critic a good friend, a kind person, a mentor?
     Criticism from any of these people in your life is likely

to be constructive, and you can probably trust it and learn from it.

- Is the criticism from a competitive rival? Then use its mirror image—there's probably something powerful about you that threatens your rival.
- Is it from a family member or intimate friend? Then it can hurt a lot because intimates know where your soft spots are, and they often project their own fears onto you. But this critic loves you and probably thinks he or she is helping you.

2. Whatever the source of the criticism, ignore it for a few hours or a day until the sting has subsided, and then evaluate its usefulness to you. If a trusted mentor is offering constructive criticism, it may be a great gift to you once you have absorbed it. Stretch yourself a bit, look at the comment from an objective viewpoint, and see how much truth you think it holds. Above all, be true to yourself, and know that your own good opinion of yourself is most valuable if it is based on truth.

3. Use some techniques to help the criticism roll off your back:

- First, use a sense of humor. A clever, funny remark that diffuses the criticism is always the most effective way to disarm it, even if it's only in private after the fact.
- Second, give an adult time-out to anyone who is negative and critical: that is, emotionally retreat into politeness. Be very pleasant but distant, and say, "Yes, please," "No, thank you," and respond politely to any request, but don't share any personal information or warmth. This usually causes a negative person to snap out of it.
- Third, ignore any negative thing that is said—don't respond, just treat it as if it didn't happen. The person who said it will realize that you're not answering or defending and start to review what he or she said. In this way, you don't reward it, and the other person will eventually stop.

How Can We Support Each Other When Others Criticize What We're Doing?

Even when others are critical, it's important that you and your partner don't try to motivate yourselves or each other with criticism. It's easier to be self-critical or critical toward an intimate partner because you don't realize the consequences. If you don't realize how self-critical you are, and how much it damages your life, you can continue to harp on yourself. Also, if you were around a parent or sibling who was very critical when you were a child, it will feel normal to you, and you won't realize how it really sounds. Self-criticism damages your quality of life in that it eats away at your self-esteem, which can make you needy in relationships and keeps others from getting close. The only kind of motivation that works in the long run grows out of celebration and appreciation.

Celebration + Appreciation = Motivation

When you find a way to appreciate yourself for what you've already accomplished and celebrate your previous successes, you will find you are naturally motivated to accomplish more. No struggle, no hassle—you accomplish out of the energy and self-confidence created by past success!

To become proficient in appreciation of yourself and each other, try the following suggestions:

- *Make a note:* Write positive comments on your daily calendar to yourself for jobs well done or any achievements you want to celebrate. Write congratulatory notes to each other as you accomplish goals. Frequent positive compliments are a very effective way to reward yourself and remind each other of even small successes.
- *Look to your childhood:* Use activities that felt like a celebration in your childhood. Did your family toast a celebration with champagne or sparkling cider, a gathering of friends, or a thankful prayer? Create a celebration environment: use

balloons, music, flowers, candles, or set your dinner table with the best china.

- *Visible reminders:* Surround yourself with visible evidence of your successes. Plant a commemorative rosebush or get a new houseplant to mark a job well done, or display photos of fun events and sports or hobby trophies. It's a constant reminder that you appreciate each other, and when you see them daily, you'll feel the appreciation.
- *Reward each other:* Little surprises, a single flower, or a loving phone call can be a great reward or celebration when something good happens.

jill & james

James began surprising Jill with little things for her new condo—a plant, a framed photo of the two of them, a shelf to display her writing awards. It was another reason for both of them to look forward to his next visit. Jill reciprocated by bringing a delicacy—fresh bagels and cream cheese, imported wine, or fresh fruit or veggies from a local produce stand—when she came home to visit James. They would make a special dinner together to celebrate their time at home.

- *Party:* Turn any free moments you have together into a party. Have an impromptu lunchtime picnic, breakfast in bed, or dinner out with friends, and toast your success. While I've been writing this book, my best friend supports me. I call her up and tell her how much I've written, and she (a bookkeeper) totes up the percentage done and percentage to go! It's a lot of fun and gives me a quick boost and a brief break in the middle of writing.

Keeping Your Spirits Up

Celebration and appreciation will go a long way toward keeping your spirits up while you're apart, but everyone gets down at times. It's important to be comfortable with your own and each other's emotional ups and downs. Being afraid, ashamed of, or embarrassed by your feelings is like being afraid of the weather, because emotions are the weather conditions of the inner self. Like the weather, most emotional climate conditions are pretty mild, with a few storms here and there.

If you pay the same amount of daily attention to your internal conditions as you probably do to the weather report, and begin to regard and talk about your feelings as naturally as weather, you'll both become much more emotionally comfortable. Your feelings are easier to accept and live with when you manage them, respond to them, and don't try to resist them or deny them. If you understand your feelings as weather, you can have many lovely inner days.

You have five senses: sight, sound, taste, touch, and smell. You can think of your emotions as your true sixth sense. Just like your other five senses, your emotions register data about the external world. With your sight, your eyes take in data about colors, shapes, and relative sizes of the things around you. Touch tells you how things feel, how warm, cold, soft, hard, sharp, or smooth they are. Your emotions tell you what others' feelings are. Before you're told, if you pay attention, you can sense in an almost psychic way how your partner feels; you can tell when your partner is angry, worried, tense, upset, happy, or feeling close to you.

Sight is an external sense—you can only see outside yourself. Touch, however, is both internal and external. You can feel food go down your esophagus, your own heartbeat, and muscle cramps and movement from inside your body. Emotions are also a sense that is simultaneously internal and external. To your emotions, it's as if there's no limit to your body, and your skin is transparent. You feel your feelings on the inside, and yet they reach out and touch your partner too. It is a type of psychic sense, especially when you develop it.

Just as your sight helps you navigate the roads, avoid obstacles, and choose the best route, your emotions help you navigate the paths of your commuter marriage. When you are knowledge-able about your feelings and sensitive to your partner's feelings, you can maximize your love, intimacy, emotional well-being, and happiness. Of course, you must still talk about what you're feeling to be certain you've got it right, but knowing your own feelings and being sensitive to your partner's responses gives you a head start.

You can refine and sensitize yourself to your feelings by tracking what you are feeling on a daily basis. Just stop a few times each day and ask yourself, "What am I feeling right now?" Once you get comfortable with that, you can share what you're feeling with each other.

Into Every Life

Here's a metaphor you can use to develop a shared sense of humor about problems: As a parade went by, one of the horses pulling a float entry left a memento in the middle of the road, right in front of where we were watching from the sidewalk. From that point on, every band or group that came marching down the road marched bravely on, right through the pile of horse manure.

The moment struck a chord in me, one that the band was not intentionally playing. The parade of life does not always go smoothly. Any one of us can be marching along, happily playing our tune, and suddenly be faced with a little mess that is not of our making. Friends can be unkind, intentionally or not, and, as Bobbie Burns wrote, "The best laid schemes o' Mice an' Men, /Gang aft agley." (Often go awry). When you can keep focused on the goal and march right through, you deserve applause.

You don't need to feel guilty for problems in your life, in fact, it's great if you can laugh at them, but it's also important that you deal with them. You're going to encounter unpleas-ant obstacles in your path from time to time. When there's a messy pile in your road, after you get through it, it's valuable to consider how it got there, what to do about it, and how to make sure you don't participate in the creation of new ones. Just because you have to walk through it doesn't mean it's your fault it's there, but it is your responsibility to clean it up as soon as you can and do whatever you can to make sure you don't go through it again. Rather than just dwell on the problem, move your focus to the solution.

Above all, it's important to remember it has an end, it's temporary, and you'll probably survive it. Blaming yourselves or each other won't help you get through it faster; it only makes the slogging more unpleasant. There is nothing to stop you from having fun while you get the job done. On the other hand, ignoring it won't make it go away either. Like it or not, you must take responsibility for turning your experience around by minimizing reaction and maximizing effectiveness. Taking an objective look at how you become part of the problem and how you can be part of the solution makes a critical difference in your outcome.

On the other hand, self-flagellation and blaming won't get you anywhere either. The key really is to respect yourselves and each other. When you love and accept yourselves and each other, you'll naturally do what is necessary to create a positive life.

making smart decisions
and problem solving

Before long, every married couple quickly realizes that knowing how to solve problems and make good decisions together is a key skill for creating a happy marriage. For commuter couples, this is even more important, because it's so easy to get out of touch with each other and what each of you wants. It's not too difficult to make a decision, but making a decision you can trust will be a solid one, that both of you can live up to, and that you're in agreement on requires some know-how. In this chapter, we'll answer the following questions:

- How can we know when we're making good decisions?
- How can we support each other and keep our problems, resentment, and frustration from building to an angry pitch?
- How can we learn to make decisions together from a distance without fighting?
- Once we've solved a problem, and made a good decision, how do we act on it?

Making Good Decisions
When you're in a commuter marriage, making good decisions becomes even more essential for several reasons:

- The time you have to spend in decision-making discussions is limited.
- While you're apart, correcting mistakes and making changes might be difficult.
- Easily making decisions together strengthens your bond and reduces arguing.

Decision-making is a crucial part of all relationships, and when one of you is home and one is away you need to find an equitable way to divide your responsibilities. Knowing how to make agreements you can count on (beforehand whenever possible) will create and maintain a smoothly working partnership within your marriage.

SMART Decisions

To help couples remember the components of good decisions, I use the acronym SMART. The decisions you make determine the quality of your relationship, but you may not be sure which decisions are most important, or how to arrive at the best ones. To get the best outcome, SMART delineates the most important questions you can ask yourselves and tools you'll need to make any decision. In making any decision, jointly or individually, check to make sure you've covered all the bases for a SMART decision:

S = Self-awareness

Knowing yourself, your strengths, weaknesses, and what you are willing and unwilling to do, makes sure your decision is in harmony with your character, which will make your choice much easier to live with. We covered several areas of self-awareness in Chapter 5 in talking about understanding your own feelings and thoughts to help reduce stress. Paying attention to your own personal style will help you make decisions you can easily stick to. Doing the exercise on consulting yourself in Chapter 5 will help you get clear about what you think about the decision you're making.

Intuition or Inner Knowing

Another aspect of self-awareness is intuition. Intuition and empathy are useful tools when you use them properly. When you're talking to someone, or negotiating with your partner, pay attention to get the meta-communication (the things that aren't being communicated verbally) to gather more information about your decision. For example, your partner may be saying "I think this is a good idea," but you get a feeling that he or she is uncomfortable. Try saying that out loud: "I hear you say it's a good idea, but you seem uncomfortable to me, are you sure?" Often you'll find it was just the right thing to ask. If you act on your intuition, balanced by rational thought, it will often lead you to a better idea. Creativity and intuition are closely tied. Intuition is not as magical or mysterious as it sounds. In fact, we discussed a big part of intuition in the last chapter in the section about emotions. Intuition is a mental tool that uses your perception of things that may not be otherwise obvious, such as your partner's facial expressions, pheromones (subliminal scent cues), past behavior, subtle emotional cues, and vibes, to give you an impression you could not get on a rational level. Trusting intuition and giving yourself a chance to check it opens up your receiving process and allows you to notice what's coming your way and be aware of it. In Chapter 2 I explained preparatory set, a tool our brains use to sort through all the overwhelming data coming in every moment and filter out what you don't want to see and highlight what you do want to see. This means that when you are open to getting intuitive info, you'll become aware of it. Both positive and negative opportunities and choices are continuously around you. Your expectations and perception determine which options you notice most readily. With your partner, you can learn to trust your intuition about what he or she is thinking and be aware that you're getting clues or vibes from him or her, which your subconscious is interpreting—and it can be quite accurate. Your partner might be astounded that you seem to know what he or she is thinking, but it's not magic. It's just one more amazing emotional/psychological/mental skill everyone has that you can fine tune and use. The mind, if you relax and trust it, truly has some miraculous abilities.

Intuitive expertise becomes really valuable when you're making a smart decision. Use your intuition to tell if someone else is being honest, feels confident or insecure, or is trying to please you instead of really agreeing. If you become aware that you are uncomfortable at any moment, it's your intuitive early warning system, and if you pay very close attention you can find out what is causing your reaction. Take the time to check out the validity of both positive and negative intuition. Don't just assume your intuition is right, but ask some pertinent questions about why your feelings don't match whatever is on the surface.

When the decision you're making involves other people, you can scan for integrity—make sure the other person walks his or her talk. Anyone can talk big, and some of the most admirable people don't present themselves well. So when choosing people to work with or rely on, don't overlook someone who is not attractive, charming, and glib but has all the honorable, honest, and steady qualities that will make working with him or her easy. Your intuition by itself may not be magic, but when you use it wisely it can help you make wise decisions.

M = Motivation

Motivation is the energy to follow through on something you want to do. If any decision you make is not backed up with the proper motivation, your energy for it will fizzle before you accomplish it. To determine your motivation, ask yourself the following questions:

- Do you want to do this enough to put in the necessary work?
- Will you have the energy to follow through?
- Can you commit to this decision?
- Will you feel good about it when you've accomplished it?

If you can answer yes to these questions, you probably have sufficient motivation. For a long-term decision, motivation can flag anyway, so here are some guidelines about how to keep your motivation level high.

In Chapter 5, you learned why criticism doesn't work as motivation. Motivation grows out of celebration and appreciation: celebration + appreciation = motivation. Your decisions will not work for you if you're not motivated to follow through on them, and motivation begins with self-appreciation.

Self-Appreciation

You probably know how to appreciate others; however, you most likely feel embarrassed and uncomfortable if you are too generous with praise for yourself. Years of being told not to brag or to be stuck up when you were young have taken their toll, and self-appreciation comes awkwardly. However, if motivation is a desirable trait, then self-appreciation becomes necessary and desirable too. The good news is that you can learn it. In order to motivate yourself to follow through on your decisions, you need to manage yourself with a positive attitude; that is, you need to:

- Care about your self and what you want to accomplish.
- Feel proud of your accomplishments,
- Be eager to learn more and accomplish more.
- Treat yourself with kindness and understanding.
- Be very generous with praise and gentle with corrections.

Then you will accomplish your goals with a sense of pride and achievement, and a great deal of pleasure. All of this can be accomplished through the two magic motivators: celebration and appreciation.

A = Appropriateness

In addition to making sure your decisions suit your own personality and your partner's, you want to make sure it is appropriate to your circumstances. You will be much better able to carry it out if it is suitable for your current situation. Ask yourself the following questions:

- Is this decision a good one for you as well as for others around you?
- Do you know who else will be affected?
- Does it fit your budget?
- Does it fit your time schedule?
- Is it respectful of yourself and the others who will be affected?
- Is it realistic given your circumstances?
- Will it be upsetting to anyone?
- If so, are you prepared to deal with the opposition?

If you can answer these questions to your own and each other's satisfaction, your decision is probably appropriate. You can use the following exercise to help you try on a decision for appropriateness:

Visualization Exercise

Daydreaming or visualization is a great way to try on a decision before you actually commit to it, to give you an idea of what it will feel like.

1. Imagine your decision as if you're already implementing it and it's playing out. Describe the action as clearly as possible to each other, making as clear a picture of the scene as possible,

imagining what people are wearing, what the room looks like.

2. Describe the scene as if it's a movie, and see how it develops. Don't worry if it plays out according to your worst fears, just experience it as you would any movie, even a scary one.

3. If it doesn't go as well as you want it to, make adjustments as you go along. Keep retelling the story, making adjustments until it is successful (that is, you handle the situation the way you really want to).

4. Talk through your scenario a few more times, with this successful process and outcome, until you feel confident you can do and say what you are visualizing.

5. If there's time, wait a day and run through your decision again, visualizing your successful outcome.

By creating a mental picture of how your new decision will work, you have just reprogrammed your mind to be comfortable with your new decision and to know what to do when the situation arises. Use this technique any time you're anxious about an upcoming decision or event.

Before James and Jill made the decision to commute so she could take her editor job, they thought James's grown sons might have a problem with the idea. So they ran through the scenario of telling the guys before they actually did it. They went through it several times, and each time one or both of them made some suggestions about improving the presentation and making sure they explained it properly. "At first, my sons thought it was a roundabout way of telling them we were splitting up," said James. "But because we had worked out how to present it, we were prepared and the session went fine. Now the guys enjoy visiting us here, or even using the condo when Jill comes here."

R = Research

If you're not well enough informed before you make your decision, you're making it on a fantasy basis, and you may be setting yourself up for unpleasant surprises if you guess wrong. To make a solid decision, you must research both the current issues and the eventual outcome. Good decisions are the result of a great deal of research. Although a hunch, intuition, or your astrological chart may provide inspiration and creative ideas, those ideas will not become reality until you make sure you get the appropriate facts. Ask yourselves:

- Do we know enough about the problem we want to solve?
- Have we gotten the benefit of others' experience?
- Have we considered our own past experience?
- Do we have the facts?
- Have we experimented enough to have a good feel for the situation?

There is no substitute for solid information to help you decide. There are many sources of information all around you. Talking to others who have more experience in the area, searching the Internet, reading books, and reviewing your own and others' past experiences are all ways you can get more data. If you're feeling indecisive or unsure about your decision, or you're squabbling about it, it may be because you actually don't have enough information to make a good decision. If you feel hesitant about making a decision, perhaps you are trying to make it based on guesswork and intuition instead of solid information.

Sara & paul

Sara and Paul, who were shocked when he was deployed to Iraq, talked with other National Guard families to find out exactly what he was facing and when they might see each other. They talked with friends and family about getting Sara help with the house and baby, especially since she was pregnant. Sara's dad offered to manage

Paul's insurance business while he was gone, making sure Paul's clients were covered and managing the office. Sara says, "It hasn't been easy, but because we checked out all the facts we could before Paul left, and asked for help, it's been working out OK."

If you look in magazines or on the Internet, you can find local classes, books, and articles that will give you plenty of related information on the decision you are researching and any related topic. Don't fall into the trap of thinking what you want to do is impossible before you've thoroughly researched it. You may find that you can have your dream and live it too.

To research a big decision, such as living apart for career reasons, it's worth spending a few months doing informational interviews with or reading books about those who have done it before—anything to get more information and experience before you actually make a decision that will affect you for years to come.

T = Team Support

No matter how carefully you research a significant decision before you make it, there will be plenty of times when you feel discouraged or shaky about succeeding with it. Nothing helps more at those times than having a support network or team. Of course, the principle members of your team are you and your partner, but you need to have others as well. Other commuter couples, if you know any, can be very helpful with: "Oh, when that happened to us, this is how we handled it—it will be OK." Family members and friends can help, too, as well as professional support such as a therapist or coach. It's also essential to not talk about your decision too much to people (no matter how well intentioned they are) who discourage, frighten, or criticize you. To help you think about forming a support team, try answering the following questions:

- Can you support yourselves and each other in making this decision if it doesn't go well or if you are challenged?
- Who do you know you can count on to be encouraging and supportive?
- Do you have a support team in place to help you and encourage you in the hard parts?
- Have you told the people who will be encouraging that you need their support?
- Can you refrain from talking too much to people who will be discouraging or critical?

Sara says, "I don't know how I would have survived this, especially being pregnant, without my Mom and Dad, my sister, and the Guard wives' support group. Someone always has an answer or a resource when I need one. A couple of my former friends were very negative, so I focused on the people who were supportive. I began to spend most of my time with the people who supported and encouraged me, and who were hopeful and positive about the future. I didn't make any big announcements, I just started spending less time with the naysayers."

How Can We Support Each Other?

One way to ensure that you have the support of each other (and your older children) is to have a regular family meeting. For couples, I call this a relationship maintenance meeting. Having this weekly keeps both of you updated and prevents problems from being ignored or unspoken until they become huge.

Relationship Maintenance Meetings

Having a regular weekly meeting date to discuss the state of your situation will help you build support between yourselves, and it's a great opportunity to discuss when you need the support of others. Problems, resentment, and frustration don't get a chance to build when you have a regular opportunity to talk about what's going on in the relationship. Each of you has a right to have your opinion respected. Regular meetings, where you both express your feelings, negative and positive, and then work together to solve problems, can help a lot.

Begin couple meetings as early in your relationship as possible, whether you think you have any issues to discuss or not. If you set a pattern of doing this, it will be easy to expand to include children when you have them. If you are not used to it, it might feel awkward to begin but if you abide by the following steps, everyone will soon experience the value of having an appropriate time and place to talk about issues and plans. Once you become familiar with the process, the formality of the meeting will relax, problems will be minor, and you can use the time for bonding, sharing experiences, and creating quality time together. If you make it a habit to sit down on a weekly basis and discuss everything about your relationship, positive and problematic, and how each of you is doing, you'll find it makes everything in your relationship easier. Set a regular time for your meeting, weekly if possible, on a speakerphone or by IM if necessary. At the meeting, each person present should follow these steps:

1. *Appreciation.* Begin by expressing thanks to each other for anything positive that your partner has done recently. For example, "Thank you for keeping all our phone appointments and working with me, I really am enjoying our teamwork." Or, "I really look forward to our evening phone conversations when I feel so close to you." Or, "Thank you for being responsible for your share of the work as well as making it easy to have fun when we're together." If there are prayers or blessings you use as a part of your faith, this is a great time to use them.

2. *Requests.* Next, each of you can make a request for some kind of change that you think will solve a problem you're having. Make a request, not a demand. Frame it as an idea you've

had to solve a problem. In order to bring up something that's a problem for you, make sure you have some idea of what can be done to solve it, even if you're not positive it will work. The point is to stay away from complaining and move toward problem solving.

3. *Solution development.* If either of you has a problem to solve, you can describe it and then ask for help solving it. You can work together to come up with a solution. (See the problem-solving guidelines that follow.) Be careful not to allow your description of the problem to deteriorate into criticism and complaining. Use factual terms and "I" messages:

- "I get annoyed and discouraged when you're gone and I'm left with all the chores."
- "We've scheduled a lot for next week, and I would like to have more time for just the two of us."
- "I would like an easier way to contact you when I need your help."

When you do this on a weekly basis, even if it's by phone, you'll find that many of the small things that come up will be handled before they become large problems. Most problems can be solved before they become disasters if you deal with them early and work together to come up with mutually satisfactory solutions. These steps will help you meet with any members of your support team whenever you need them.

When you have all the components of you SMART decision in place you'll find that your decisions become much more effective and easier to carry out:

- Self-awareness
- Motivation
- Appropriateness
- Research
- Team support

Make Decisions Together from a Distance

Whether you're in each other's presence or at a distance, following these guidelines will help you reach an agreement when you're struggling with a decision and show you how to avoid having arguments about what to do.

SOLVING PROBLEMS WHETHER APART OR TOGETHER

1. *Make an appointment.* Don't ambush each other with a problem, especially when you're getting ready for bed, about to make love, rushing off to work, or during an intimate telephone conversation while you're apart. If you realize a discussion is building into an argument, stop it by making an appointment to discuss the issue later. To make an appointment by e-mail or IM when you're apart, or briefly in person when you're together, say: "I have a problem I'd like to discuss. Will you have time tonight after dinner (or this weekend, or tomorrow afternoon)?" Make an appointment when you'll both have time to think and respond thoughtfully. Alternatively, if you won't have time to talk in the near future, agree on an e-mail heading (for example, "problem discussion") that will alert your partner that you are asking to work on a problem, then describe your problem as in the next step.

2. *Think through the problem and describe it carefully.* This is not the time to just blurt out whatever comes to mind. Writing it down first is very valuable here. Also, try to state your problem as a problem for you, and do not blame your partner or anyone else. For example, say: "I feel frustrated when you come home late, because I worry that something's wrong." Rather than: "Why can't you be on time?" or "You're always late, and it makes me mad."

   Before your appointment time, think about what the problem is and how to state it so your partner will understand and not feel attacked. Ask your partner to agree that he or she will hear and try to understand what you're saying without interrupting.

Then ask your partner for his or her opinion of what you can do together to fix the problem. Do not get into who's right or wrong, but focus on understanding each other and coming up with a solution. "It doesn't work for me not to know what checks you wrote. I understand you're busy, but can we find a way to fix it? Maybe we can get checks with carbon copies, and then when you're out of town you can read from the copies to me by phone so I'll know what our balance is."

3. *Generate options.* Take turns challenging each other to come up with the best solution for the problem. Have fun with it, don't be afraid to be silly, and you'll free up your thinking so you'll come up with more creative options. "I know, let's win the lotto, then we won't need to know how much we have in the bank!" "Maybe we can have an account with online access, then I can input the checks I write, and you can check the balance any time."

4. *Discuss the possibilities.* When you have enough ideas of what to do, discuss them—which would be best for both of you? Consider how your partner would feel about any decision, as well as how you feel. Try the SMART decisions guidelines on whatever solution you think will work best.

5. *Try it on.* If you're not sure which decision would work, consider trying one or two of them out for a short time to learn from your experience. For example:

- If you're struggling about your time schedule and one of you feels like you don't have enough time together while the other feels pulled by work commitments, try a schedule change that you may not think will work, just to see what you can learn from it.

- If you've been a stay-at-home parent and you want to go back to work, take a temporary job for a couple of months to see how it feels and how it changes your family life.

- If your company wants you to take a job in a different city or state and you have some time to decide, spend some extended vacation time there. Check out the schools, the housing market, the salaries, and recreation activities there. Attend some community events to see how you like the people you'll be living near. Once you've done the research or tried the change on, you'll have a lot better idea of which solution will work for both of you.

6. *Clarify your choice.* It's unfortunately easy to think you've agreed upon something when you actually are thinking two different things. To avoid this problem, when you think you've reached a decision, state it out loud. "OK, so we're agreed: we're going to. . . ." It can even help to write it down, in case your memory is different later. If you find yourself disagreeing about what you decided, you can check with your written agreement.

You can go back and follow these steps any time you're having trouble finding a solution or making a decision. They work great even when a decision you previously made requires renegotiation.

How Do We Act on Our Decision?

Of course, no decision, no matter how carefully made, is worth anything until you carry it out. Once you've created a good, solid decision that will help you be successful in your commuter marriage by following the previous exercises and guidelines, you're ready to develop a plan of attack. Here are the simple steps necessary to reach your goal:

Four Steps to Success

You and your partner have used the SMART guidelines and problem-solving steps to make a decision. Now you need to know how to carry it out successfully.

Commit to the Decision

You may be surprised to learn that you can make a decision but not really be committed to it. Somewhere in the back of your mind may be a little escape clause. That is, you've silently and mentally reserved the right not to really be invested in making your decision work. If you allow the escape clause to be there, you won't be able to follow through on the decision. Do yourself and your partner a favor, and make sure you're both really committed to the decision you made, or, if you find out you're not, ask for a renegotiation.

colette & harry

Colette says: "At first, Harry agreed with me that I would stay here, teaching at the college, and he would take the CEO position, and I think he meant it—he could see it was the right move. But soon he began sabotaging. I'd get a call from a realtor Harry had talked to about selling the house without consulting me. So we went back to the drawing board until we had a decision Harry could commit to. He accepted the idea that we'd sell the house and buy a condo in each place. Once we had a decision he could really endorse, the surprises stopped happening, and we both went according to plan."

Break It Down into Small, Unintimidating Steps

Get the steps as small and easy as you can.

jill & james

Jill says: "I needed some physical activity in my new location, and I like music, so I chose a line-dancing class. Getting started was the hard part. I had to break my goal down into manageable steps: (1) Call around to find out what classes are available; (2) choose a class to attend; (3) enroll in the class; (4) go to the first class meeting; (5) evaluate the class as to whether I liked it. Now I find it really good for my body and my attitude. I love it!"

Jill made her steps really easy for her to do. Her steps may seem simplistic, but that's the idea. Make it as easy as possible to do each step. That way you won't be discouraged by "I can't" before you start.

Do Something

Breaking your goal down into the smallest possible steps makes it easier to accomplish the next phase: do something. Many of us know how to set goals but not how to achieve them, so we've "proved" to ourselves over and over that we're failures. That's not true at all. The failure lies in not having completed the rest of the Four Steps to Success. You've just made the third step to your goal as simple as possible, so there are no reasons not to take it. Focus on the third step only: do something. If you can't get yourself to do it, you haven't made the steps small or easy enough. Go back to step 2.

Celebrate What You've Done (Yes, Every Step)

After you've taken each step, celebrate. Recognition of what you've accomplished is important. If you celebrate each step you take toward your goal as you take it, you won't run out of energy before you achieve success, and you'll keep encouraging yourself and each other as you proceed. Your celebration can be just looking into your mirror and saying, "Congratulations, you've just made the first (second, third) step toward achieving your goal." Or your celebration can be more elaborate, such as toasting your accomplishment with each other and a friend or two. It can even be a major party. The important thing is that you do something to make sure you notice you've had some success, however small. It is this celebration that will give you the courage and confidence to go on all the way in achieving your goal. There is no such thing as too much praise or celebration. Can you overdo motivation? Of course not. Fresh flowers on the table just to say how much you appreciate yourself can do a lot toward making you happier any day. A new trashy romance novel can be a great reward/celebration for reading your required technical books. The important point is that celebration of what you have accomplished already will create motivation to accomplish more.

How to Celebrate

Get creative with your celebrations; have fun. Celebrate a cherished friendship with an impromptu lunchtime picnic and a balloon. The point is that a celebration is fun. You may need to periodically remind yourself of how much you have accomplished on your own. Celebrate your independence, your spirit, and your willingness to be responsible for yourself. Use all the information you have gathered about who you are and what you like to develop celebrations that suit your style or personality. Take a few minutes with yourself every day just for appreciation and celebration. If you make it easy and fun, it will be very effective and you can live every day energized and motivated.

Whenever you find your motivation flagging, look around for how you are doing at being in charge of reaching your goals. Are you using a motivational, supportive style? Have you let someone else take over your authority? Is there some appreciation you need? As you achieve your goal, go back to the Four Steps to Success and choose a new goal, then follow the steps through again any time you have a decision to carry out.

No matter which style of commuter marriage you have, If you know how to make smart decisions, have a successful plan, and create the motivation and persistence to carry them out, you can have the results that you want.

personal and emotional growth
in a commuter marriage

Commuter marriage is a challenge, and challenges can be difficult. If you handle the challenges carefully as they arise and you're willing to learn from them, they can become great sources of personal and emotional growth.

Long separations do not have to limit your growth as a couple or interfere with the development of your relationship. It's your choice whether you grow apart or let your partnership connection and intimacy dwindle. One of the most productive areas of growth in a commuter marriage is your growth as an individual. Because you are separated, you may be forced to grow in areas where your experience and abilities previously were limited, and you have an opportunity to grow in areas where you may have felt stifled. While it is possible that your individual development could take you in different directions, if you manage the changes appropriately the resulting personal growth can add new, exciting dimensions to your marriage instead. In this chapter you'll find techniques and guidelines for growing closer while you are apart, plus guidelines for managing your individual growth and keeping in touch with changes in each other. In this chapter you'll find answers to questions like:

- How can we learn from this experience?
- Are there any benefits of commuter marriage?

- Why is growth important?
- What are the growth stages of commuter marriage?
- How can being apart help us grow as individuals?
- If I become independent, will it hurt our marriage?
- Will we be wise and patient enough to deal with everything that confronts us?
- How can we find those friends and family members who will support us?

Your Personal Growth as Partners

As you go through the stages of growth of your commuter marriage, you'll find it useful to consider the whole experience as a course in personal growth. Like most of us, you are probably quite practiced in taking courses. When you sign up for a cooking or mechanics course, you know what you face: weeks of learning new material and homework assignments consisting of more and more complex problems based on the material you have learned. You may grumble about the homework load or complain about the teacher, but you never think you've been given the problems as punishment; solving problems is part of the educational process. Your commuter marriage will teach you many subjects. If you keep in mind that you are a student and the problems exist to teach you something, getting through the hard parts becomes easier and more efficient, and the new things you learn are a great reward.

What Can You Learn from this Experience?

When you use the problems and opportunities of your long-distance marriage as a learning process and accept that you have something to learn, you'll find solving those problems is exactly the way to learn the skills you need. Assume that each experience, good or bad, comes with a valuable lesson attached.

Even if you don't understand or see the gift right now, it will become clear as you move through your experience.

In your relationship, as in any learning process, if you do not grasp what you're supposed to learn from your immediate experience, it won't go away until you have figured it out and learned what you need to know. You'll understand what essayist Ralph Waldo Emerson meant when he wrote: "Life is a succession of lessons which must be lived to be understood." The problem isn't solved until you learn what you need to know to have a fuller, more satisfying relationship. Instead of feeling put upon and resentful when a problem arises, if you're willing to learn and grow through separations, illnesses, and challenges, you'll find your relationship keeps getting better, and you and your partner will be happier and more bonded.

When a problem arises, stop a moment and think before you get upset or defensive. Ask:

- What was I given this problem for?
- What can I learn from this?
- What do I need to know to solve it?

View the problem as a homework assignment, and figure out what it has been designed to teach you.

Bill, who was left at home when his wife Cindy was forced to commute to a new Navy base, felt that Cindy wasn't giving him enough attention. He merely wants a kind word, a loving touch; it didn't seem too much to ask. Yet Cindy seemed to find it impossible. What could he possibly learn from this problem? Bill says: "It took me a while to figure out that I had relied on Cindy to initiate all our affection and our social life as well. When she was gone five days a week, I was left to my own resources, and I had none. I had to learn about networking, having a circle of friends I could rely on so that Cindy was not under the strain and stress of having to meet all my needs. I began to invite friends and family over. A pat on the back from my Dad and a hug from my Mom felt great. My brother-in-law turned out to be a great buddy; he'd help me work on a project at the house in the evening, and his wife would watch Chloe and their kids while we worked. Then we all had dinner together, and maybe we'd watch a video while the kids slept in the other room. I realized how much I liked the family feeling, and when Cindy got home, I wasn't so demanding and needy, so our closeness improved too. I never realized how dependent I was on her."

How Can Being Apart Help Us Grow?

Here are some possible learning opportunities your commuter marriage might present to you in order to help you grow:

Learn to be happy alone. It's easy to become sad and lethargic when you're home by yourself and your partner is gone. It's also easy to feel miserable when you're away from home all alone. In either case, you may need to develop some skills for being on your own successfully. If you're at home, you have friends, family, and resources to draw on, although many of the social activities you're used to doing as a couple may not work as well as a single. Later in this chapter, there are guidelines for learning to be happy when you're on your own.

Learn the art of appreciation. Feeling and expressing gratitude for whatever contact or time you have together, however slight it may seem, will help you maximize your opportunities and take full advantage of them. Remember that appreciation increases motivation, and thank each other for every possible thing.

Learn to be fully present. The fewer and farther apart your moments together or chances to talk on the phone are, the more important it is to stay focused and take full advantage of every opportunity. This is not the time to multitask. When you have a chance to be together or talk, pay attention and let your partner know you hear what he or she is saying. Don't waste your time squabbling.

Learn to count your blessings and make the most of them. Keep a gratitude journal and list every moment you are thankful for, then share it with each other on a regular basis. If you have a religious or spiritual practice, add a prayer of thanks.

Learn to treat your partner as your best friend. Don't take each other for granted or lapse into bad behavior. Make your moments together about helping each other and learning and growing together.

Learn to have faith. Whatever your religious or spiritual background is, find a way to ask for help when you need it and to follow any wise counsel you are given. Have faith that you and your partner love each other and that the two of you can work through whatever is happening. If you and your partner are having a problem, try saying: "I don't know what this is all about, but I know we love each other, and we both have something to learn from this, and I'd like to find out what it is. Let's pray (meditate, chant, ask for guidance) about it," then hold your partner's hand and see if the atmosphere changes. Most of the time, it will.

Learn to create a blessing on your relationship. Design a ceremony. It could be a talk with your Higher Power, a meditation session done while holding hands, a party with friends who will be willing to support your goals, or wishes written down and ceremoniously burned in the fireplace. Find a way to dedicate yourself and your relationship to learning and growth. If you are married, you had such a blessing when you started out together. Create a new one for this new phase of your relationship.

sara & paul

Sara and Paul have discovered the power of having a special affirmation of the intent of their relationship. Sara says: "I learned it at church, it's from Genesis: 'The LORD watch between me and thee, when we are absent one from another.' We repeat this aloud before we go to sleep and whenever we feel worried about being so far apart. This prayer comforts both of us. It brings us back to the reality of our love and mutual good intent instantly. When Paul comes home, we'll give thanks together every day."

You can use any positive statement from your religion: poetry, a quotation, or a statement from your personal experience will do, especially if it clearly states the intent of your lives together. Some of my clients repeat portions of their wedding vows (especially if they wrote them). In the middle of a struggle, if one of you repeats this meaningful phrase, it will help you remember the friendship and love between you, and your problem will get easier to solve.

Learn to resolve problems and heal wounds. You and your partner are bound to hurt each other's feelings from time to time, and when you're commuting, it's even easier because of the stress level and because you are often rushed. Being close to each other means you can easily hurt each other without meaning to, so it's important to know that all hurts can be healed. You can resolve hurt feelings and apologize once you understand what went wrong. Try bringing it up to your partner and asking for help:

"I've been contemplating my feelings, and I find that the way you tell me of things you don't like reminds of my father (mother, old lover). I was terribly afraid of him, and I don't want to feel afraid of you by association. Will you help me deal with that?"

If your partner agrees, then quite often a simple talk can point out the differences between then and now. Sometimes clarity about what's really happening as opposed to what you're afraid is happening is the healing quality. After sharing and talking, figure out a way to do it better using the visualization exercise in Chapter 6. You'll find that as soon as you know how to protect yourself, all the hurt and anger fade quickly.

Learn to get help. Don't resist getting help if you don't know what to do. Turn to other couples that have successfully negotiated a similar experience, supportive family and friends, a clergyperson or spiritual counselor, or a licensed marriage counselor. Make sure the person you consult has some experience in the area in which you're having a problem. You can look online for referrals, but asking friends or family for people they recommend is the surest route. Before you go for sessions, ask the counselor if he or she has had any success with commuter marriages.

> Sara found it was really helpful to turn to her pastor for counseling and advice. "Paul and I have talked about it, and we've decided that when Paul is home we'll come to the pastor with anything that feels difficult or unsolvable."

Learn to have fun with your commuter marriage. Even though you are going through stressful times and your time together is at a premium, spend some time having fun. It will recharge your relationship better than anything else. Laugh together, be silly, make love, and have a good time together. You'll find more about having fun at the end of this chapter.

Growth Stages of a Commuter Marriage

You might be surprised to learn that the changes you are going through usually follow predictable growth stages. If you understand what these stages are, you'll have an easier time relaxing and being patient with the upheaval of change.

1. *Speculation.* Before you create a major change, like commuting in your relationship, you must have an idea of what changes you're contemplating. This is when you research the

change you're about to make, so you know all the benefits and reasons why the change is desirable. Having a clear idea of the change you want to make, how it will look and feel, and what you will say and do is a great way to try the change on before you actually implement it. The SMART decision process outlined in Chapter 6 shows you how to do this stage.

2. *Exploration.* In this stage you get more deeply into picturing your life after you implement the changes you want to make. What kind of people will you want to have around you? What will you want to do? How will your life look? The visualization exercise is one way to do exploration. It's the research part of the SMART decision process.

3. *Preparation.* Here you begin to break your proposed changes down into steps that you can actually accomplish. If the steps are detailed and small enough, they seem easier and encourage you to believe you can actually accomplish what you want to do. Here your proposed change is becoming more real, and this is a great time to anticipate the support you'll need and where to find it. Do you need new friends? Are there certain members of your family who'll be supportive of your changes? Do you need professional support and guidance? The four steps to success exercise provided in Chapter 6 shows you how to do this.

4. *Dedication.* Once you are clear on what steps are necessary, you're ready to begin. Of course, when you actually make your change and try it out you will learn new things and probably have to go back to the drawing board and rethink some of your original plans. But as you get more experience, you'll find out what works and become comfortable with the changes.

5. *Expansion.* Once you've established your new situation, you'll develop it more fully and deeply. This is a great time for lots of discussion and problem solving about the aspects that are not yet working.

6. *Completion.* If you're beginning a long-term commuter marriage, this is the stage where you've figured out how to make it work, you know you can do it successfully, and it becomes easier. If you're in a short-term situation, this may be the stage where you decide to change back to living together and repeat the stages again to make that transition.

colette & harry

Colette and Harry spent a couple of months in the speculation, exploration, and preparation stages before Harry moved to his new CEO position. They talked about all the possibilities, they visited Harry's new company and the surrounding area looking for possible places for him to live, and they talked to other people who worked in Harry's field. They examined the financial history of the company that wanted to hire Harry. They looked at expenses and weighed them against Harry's new salary and Colette's salary. Once they were convinced the move was a good idea, they moved to the dedication stage and began setting up their commuter marriage. Once Harry was in the new job for a few months, they entered the expansion phase as they decided to sell their house and buy a condo in each place, which made both places easy to care for by eliminating the need for yard work and heavy housekeeping. This took a while, but they're now settled in to several years of commuter marriage with Harry spending his vacation and as much other time as he could with Colette, and she spends her summer vacations and school holidays with him.

Building Your Separate Life

When you and your partner are apart, you'll probably have more time alone than you've ever had. If you're at home and you have children, you'll feel like a single parent much of the time. If you're away from home, you might feel disconnected and at a loss when you're not working. If you're used to being at home with your partner during nonwork hours, it's a big change.

Instead of sinking into loneliness and misery, you can use this extra alone time to focus on your dreams and goals as well as your emotional and spiritual development. Up to this point, your life may have been focused on others and the demands of work, home, and family, and while those responsibilities continue, this is an opportunity to bring your personal dreams into the forefront. It's time to consider what you want to do for yourself. You know how you deal with work, with financial decisions, with family, friends, and your partner. But how much attention have you paid to your relationship with yourself? This is a great chance to develop whatever interests and pursuits you've always wanted—to write that great novel, learn to ride a horse, take cooking classes (really valuable if your partner is the better cook), go back to school, volunteer somewhere meaningful, or learn tai chi. Not only will this fill your time and keep your spirits up, but it will also create a happier, more fulfilled, more interesting you and your relationship will benefit. If you're the one at home and your partner was always the handyperson, you could take a class in simple carpentry, repairs, and electrical to become more self-sufficient.

Whether you've always wanted to heal the planet or just have time to walk in the woods, here is your opportunity to do it. Perhaps you want to learn to live more simply or to get politically active. Whatever your dream, simple or complex, if you allow it to emerge, you can find the strength and skills to actualize it.

Learn to think of yourself and your life as a gift you are giving. As a result of your life experience you have become a marvelous package of talents and skills—these talents and skills are your gift. The skills you already possess may be enough to actualize your dream and make the changes you want to make. Learning to think positively about who you are, and therefore make the best of each of your traits and talents, will enable you to operate at your most powerful and to be truly satisfied with the results.

You may have always thought you were too quiet, too talkative, too aggressive, or too passive, but what happens if you reevaluate "too quiet" to mean that you're a good listener, or "too talkative" to mean you are an excellent communicator? Traits you perceive as too aggressive can be considered leadership qualities, and "too passive" traits can mean you're an excellent support or follow-up person. As you learn to develop those traits and become more self-sufficient, you'll feel better about yourself.

Jill & James

Jill, the editor who moved away from home to take a great job, was at a loss at first. "I didn't know how to fill up my own time, or even if it was OK. I was used to waiting to do something together with James. Once I began thinking about what I wanted to do, and what would be good for me, and to believe it was OK for me to do what I wanted, I started to have fun with it."

Being on your own will highlight the unintentional and unconscious dependency you may either have developed or kept hidden within your marriage—the idea that you need your spouse or someone else to take care of you in certain ways you never learned to take care of yourself. Perhaps you:

- Don't do mechanical or fix-it things well.
- Feel at a loss with your children without your spouse to set the pace or the rules.
- Never learned your way around the kitchen or your mother-in-law.
- Always deferred to your spouse when handling financial decisions or papers.
- Don't feel competent at hiring people to do child-care or household maintenance jobs.

When you make decisions based on what others want or just react and respond to events you're outer directed. If you allow yourself to feel incompetent, anxious, and helpless, you will eventually grind to a halt and become emotionally paralyzed. When you are the one in charge of your life you know your own opinion and you act on it. The opinions of others are helpful input, but your decisions must be your own.

Are There Any Benefits of Commuter Marriage?

As you conquer your feelings of helplessness and learn the skills you need to feel competent and secure when you're alone, you'll grow in:

- *Self-reliance:* You'll feel more in charge of yourself, more able to respond well in unexpected circumstances, and confident you can count on yourself without being helpless or dependent on others.
- *Self-trust:* You'll be able to make a promise to yourself and keep it, as you would a promise to a respected friend, and also extend the same careful consideration to yourself that you would wish from a friend.
- *Self-determination:* You'll decide your own future through planning and careful action.
- *Self-confidence:* You'll gain the security that comes from having a sense of purpose and the confidence to accomplish your purpose.
- *Self-esteem:* You'll recognize your own talents and abilities and that you are a healthy, capable, and loveable person.
- *Self-motivation:* You'll discover a desire to create and accomplish, not only for outer rewards, but also for the satisfaction of accomplishment.
- *Self-love:* You'll become more comfortable with your own feelings, be more able to understand what you're feeling and why, and to focus caring feelings inward toward yourself.

- *Self-nurturing:* You'll understand when, why, and how you need to care for yourself to get the same rest, healthy nourishment, and physical activity and maintenance you'd recommend for your spouse and children.
- *Self-support:* You'll learn to back yourself up when you face difficulties or opposition, to stand up for what's important to you, and to be strong enough to follow through on your goals.

Will Independence Hurt Our Marriage?

Gaining true independence and self-reliance will enhance your relationship with your partner, friends, and family, because when you are self-sufficient you are free to love and give freely.

> Jill says: "The more I do for myself and the happier I get, the better James and I get along. I'm a better partner now because I'm a happier person."

Your ability to respond to life is both an asset and a challenge. To achieve independence you must make a realistic assessment of your emotional and physical needs and act on the results.

Developing Internal Companionship

In addition to knowing what do to in areas where you used to feel helpless, you can learn to be your own companion when you get lonely or needy. Whether you realize it or not, the relationship you have with yourself sets the pattern for how you connect with others. By developing a nurturing way to relate to yourself, you create a personal experience of both giving and receiving friendship.

Best of all, you'll have greater trust in your decision-making ability when you regard yourself positively and treat yourself well. When you become comfortable with a constructive inner dialogue, you can create an inner support system—you'll become more confident in your evaluation of your thoughts, feelings, and options.

Loneliness is a valuable emotional clue that you are feeling abandoned by yourself, because when that happens you also feel abandoned by others. No one else can meet your internal needs for intimacy and love more effectively than you can, because only you always know exactly what you want and exactly how satisfying the different kinds of interaction are to you. When you meet your own needs for conversation, companionship, and attention, you free yourself from anxiety about being alone and simultaneously reduce your neediness around others. Then when you do have an opportunity to be with your partner, you can be relaxed and open. Developing internal intimacy also means you will be free to choose your companions because being with yourself feels so good you won't settle for less from others.

The following exercise will help you discover how you feel about giving and receiving love, and enhance your friendship with yourself, which will help you communicate effectively with your partner. Try it whenever you feel rejected, lonely, abandoned, or unloved.

EXERCISE: DEVELOPING INTERNAL COMPANIONSHIP

1. *Find the source of your loneliness.* When you're sad and lonely, longing for your partner to keep you company, take care of you, or make you feel better, ask yourself what you would like him or her to do for you or say to you. Take some time with this, because it will give you clues about the source of your loneliness. Be as specific as you can, and make a list like the following one.

1. I want my partner to:
   - Make me laugh
   - Tell me everything is OK
   - Share an experience with me

- Protect and reassure me
- Understand my feelings
- Be sympathetic and supportive
- Give me a hug

2. Now that you know what you'd like from your partner, *take a look at how you treat yourself:*
   - Are you supportive of yourself?
   - Do you seek your own opinion or ignore it?
   - Do you consciously talk over decisions with yourself before you make them or worry ineffectually about them?
   - Do you enjoy time with yourself, or avoid being alone?
   - Do you celebrate your accomplishments and successes?
   - Do you motivate yourself to do well?
   - Do you tend to criticize everything you do?

3. *Compare how you treat yourself with what you're longing for from your partner,* which represents how you'd like to be treated. You may be dismayed to find out you treat yourself quite differently from the way you'd like others to treat you, or even the way you'd treat those you love:
   - You might keep promises to a friend but often renege on promises you make to yourself.
   - You may not treat yourself with kindness and respect. Perhaps you mentally nag or criticize yourself.
   - You may never break a date with a friend but keep putting off your time with yourself.
   - You might speak more harshly to yourself than you would to a friend when you make a mistake.

   The best test of your friendship with yourself is: If someone else treated you the way you treat yourself, would you want to be around him or her?

4. *Be a friend to yourself.* Now that you have clarified the way you treat yourself, you can decide to treat yourself better and put your decision into effect by developing three simple ways of doing so. One way to approach this task is to treat yourself as you would treat a good friend or your

favorite sibling. Ask yourself, "What would I do for Maggie if she were in my shoes? What would I say to her?" It's likely that it's easier to think of nice things to do for her. By considering treating yourself the way you treat your friends, you'll begin to develop clear guidelines about how to be your own friend. Write down your ideas about befriending yourself, and put them into action.

Sara & Paul

Sara decided to spend twenty minutes each day having tea in her backyard, among her beloved flowers, to choose one thing each week she wanted to do for herself, such as a facial, and to take a few minutes each morning to give herself a pep talk. "I had no idea how soothing and rejuvenating having tea in the garden would be until I tried it. It gives me something to look forward to every day, and it changes my outlook; if I'm feeling down, I get more hopeful looking at God's creation in the flowers and trees. Now, I wouldn't ever do without it."

5. *Create a habit of internal companionship.* Using these steps, you can create an internal bond and a strong habit of being a good friend to yourself. Learn to treat yourself with care and consideration, and to be a good companion to yourself. Create a list of guidelines for how to treat yourself and post it where you can see it often. With consistent practice, treating yourself well becomes much easier and feels more comfortable, and you'll find you feel less lonely and needy when you're with yourself.

6. *Learn to soothe and comfort each other.* As a good friend to yourself, you'll know how to soothe, comfort, and care for yourself and your partner when you're stressed or tired. Develop a style for recharging and relaxing together.

   • What makes you most comfortable?
   • What soothes you?
   • What helps you relax and recharge?

It can be anything from a bubble bath, a yoga session, or your favorite music to a long walk in the country, a phone conversation with your mate, or a nap. Make a list of your favorite personal rechargers. Make sure the list includes simple things you can do cheaply (such as relax with a cup of tea and read a favorite book) to things that are very special (such as spend a day at a bed-and-breakfast or have a massage and a facial). Keep the list where you can refer to it whenever you feel in need of a recharge, and make use of it often.

When you and your partner are friends to your individual selves, you'll discover that it becomes easier to be there for each other and to appreciate everything you give to each other.

Wisdom and Patience

Going through changes smoothly requires patience and wisdom because no change happens instantly or exactly the way you expect it to. The amount of patience you have in daily life and in relationships can determine how much you enjoy your life.

- Learning to be patient and remain calm reduces and relieves stress and worry.
- Cultivating patience is really learning impulse control—it's an issue in self-control.
- You can learn how to perform emotional maintenance and shake off stress, keep on track of what you want to do, and let go of frustration when something is getting to you.
- Patience is learning how to pause and think before acting and to make sure you understand the options and take control of your own ideas and decisions. It's a growth process, a transformation of self through awareness and learning.
- To acquire patience, you need to learn not to act on impulse; you need to change your thinking and attitude, and reach

out for support and encouragement. To learn the necessary patience and determination to reach long-term goals, practice on small things first and learn how to sort through what is worth being patient for and what is not.

Philosophers have said that the wisdom guiding each of us is available if we just listen and trust what we hear. Inner wisdom is not rational or practical in nature but more intuitive and spiritual. It may make itself clear in one instant flash or gradually by following clues one at a time. Once you understand it, it will still take work and experience to bring it about. It can provide a way to see the big picture or a more detached and objective viewpoint of the issues and problems of life. Each new idea must be tested through practical use to see how it works. Step by step, using both intuitive wisdom and clear thinking, you can bring your inner motivation to the surface and use it to create what you want. A combination of inspiration expressed through action will develop the meaning of your own life. All the experiences of your life, including your commuter marriage, have taught you valuable skills. Using what you've learned in life to help yourself and others can create meaning out of struggle, and every trial that you face has something to teach you and can become a source of wisdom.

EXERCISE: INNER WISDOM

Here's a visualization exercise to help you access your inner wise person:

1. Mentally picture a person of seventy or more, just the kind of elder you admire, the one you would like to become. This elder has a great marriage, is financially secure, in good health, surrounded by good friends and family who care, and is active with lots of interests.
2. Introduce yourself to this elder, and notice your names are the same—this is you later in life.

3. Make an agreement with this ideal older self that you will get advice about what decisions you need to make as life goes on to live to a healthy and happy state of being. Continue your conversation as long as you wish, and ask what your elder's secret is for living to such a lovely old age.

4. Once this contact is established, you can check out your decisions regularly by frequently asking this wise mentor within. Consider:

   • How does this inner counselor react to your life choices?
   • At that advanced age, will you look back on what you've done and think it was worth it?
   • Does your wise self approve?
   • Does he or she think your choice will last?
   • What is the difference between what's important to you and what this inner counselor regards as important?

As you become comfortable with the process, your inner counselor will help you access what you know. It is a very effective tool to help you look at your own life and your decisions from a different and valuable perspective. The decisions you make today affect the rest of your life, and you and your partner are ultimately accountable only to yourselves and each other.

How Can We Find Friends and Family Members Who Will Support Us?

Not only does it take a community to raise a child, but also in our mobile and fast-paced society, a sense of community, family, and connectedness helps us to function more effectively as adults in all phases of life. Such support is especially helpful when you're in a commuter marriage. In Chapter 2 you learned briefly about parenting networks that can help you raise children when you're on your own, and here we'll explore all the other networks that can help you survive living at a distance from each other.

Creating Networks

There are several kinds of networks (connected groups) of friends who can support you and bring harmony into your life.

Your chosen family: Warm friends provide a cushion and a shield in life's difficult times—someone to talk to when you need support or advice and to celebrate your triumphs with you. It's a great blessing to be surrounded by a trusted and trustworthy group of friends who make your life's journeys with you and know exactly how far you've come. Choose established friends, supportive family members, and bring new friends into this group; leave people who criticize and undermine you out.

Your neighborhood family: Friendly neighbors make your neighborhood, your apartment building or condo complex, or your block safer. Their watchfulness will protect you against vandalism and other problems, whether you're at home or away. Get to know your friendliest neighbors and they will call 911 for you, watch your children, take package deliveries, or feed your pets.

Your family of origin: Family is the network we turn to first in times of need, and to share the good times, too. If your family has drifted apart, try building a partial family network with those you like or who live close by, and soon other family members could be drawn closer.

Your fun family: These people enjoy the things you like to do. They can be couples who enjoy spending time with both of you and understand about your time shortages, friends who will go walking with you when you're alone, families who want to do parent/child activities or share your weekends and holidays, or couples who join you for fun times.

By creating networks that feel like family in several areas of your life, you'll have the joy of the give and take of friendship and support that helps you through fun times and tough times. You'll create blessings for yourself when you share your rituals, holidays, laughter, and information. Welcome friends who are alone into your family's good times. With these "chosen" families you can offer comfort in life's difficult times and be a willing participant in celebrating successes. Everything you give will come back to you multiplied in the joy of connection. Sara has strong support from her family, Jill enjoys her book group, and James is close to his sons. The more connected you are with supportive, reliable people, the easier and more enjoyable your life will be.

EXERCISE: STEPS TO CREATING SUPPORT NETWORK

1. *Identify others who have similar goals.* Select a specific goal you want to implement that, ideally, would be easier if done as part of a support group, and find several people who share these goals. Perhaps your common interest is looking for new jobs, learning a foreign language, creative writing, or even an interest in a craft or hobby you can enjoy together. Or perhaps you want to connect with other couples who are commuting. To find people with similar interests, you can talk to friends and family or put an announcement up on a bulletin board at work or school, a community center, the Laundromat, a computer bulletin board list such as Craigslist (*www.craigslist.org*), or the market. You can even place a small ad in a local paper. (Note: if you are contacting strangers, don't give your address, and arrange to meet in a group in public places until you know them a little better.) When you have found at least three or four others who express interest in your project, go on to the next step. You may not believe you can find anyone who is interested in your idea or project at the start, but if you discuss your

interest with others, you may be surprised to discover just how many are enthusiastic.

2. *Agree to meet.* This doesn't have to be formal. Invite a person you don't know well or a work colleague to go for coffee, or invite a few friends who have something in common over for lunch.

3. *Get together regularly.* Whether you have a specific focus or you just want to have a good time together, seek to set up regular times to get together. This will give your group a chance to gel. You can just chat, work on projects, play golf or another game, or go power walking together. Whatever your goal, make it a practice in the group to be as positive and encouraging as possible. To encourage attendance and build closeness, make feeling good and having fun together your group's priorities.

4. *Strive for balance.* In the most effective and lasting networks, giving and receiving feels balanced for everyone involved. You can support and encourage each other with praise, information, and caring. Observe each person's behavior and attitude to discover who fits best in your support team.

5. *Allow the group to develop.* Give each network some time to coalesce. People may come and go, but after a while you'll clearly see who will become a long-time friend and part of your support system.

Following this process, you can begin to look for new friends everywhere you go to build a more informal group of friends.

CHAPTER 8

how commuter couples
find resolution

Even commuter marriages eventually develop a routine. Although you'd never say commuter marriage is easy, you deal with all the changes and stress, and eventually you settle into a system and an arrangement you can live with. It's a relief to have worked out most of the problems, even if this situation will eventually change, because most commuter couples eventually return to living together. In this chapter, we'll see how our commuter couples resolved their situations and how they answered the following questions:

- Is it OK to enjoy being apart?
- What does the future hold?
- Do we have to go through all that change again?
- Can our marriage be better than it was before the commute?
- Who should move so we can be together?
- How do I get reestablished after we are back together?
- What happens when I stop traveling for my job?
- Do we have to develop a new infrastructure for living together?

You'll find the answers you seek about resolution in this chapter.

Settling In: Is It OK to Enjoy Being Apart?

If you learn the skills and follow the guidelines in the previous chapters, and you and your partner work together to make your living apart situation work well, you reach a point where the situation is working, you're experienced enough to know what to expect most of the time, and you actually can relax and enjoy your time alone as well as your times together. Surprisingly enough, this is when insecurity and guilt can set in.

> *Colette & harry*
>
> Colette was surprised and felt a little guilty to realize she actually enjoyed her new situation. She loved her new condo, she and Harry had a great time when they visited each other, and she got a bonus: the most time she'd ever had to herself. "The change was more difficult for Harry than for me. He had a tougher time than I did, because he had to deal with more changes. I just had the commute to see him, but the rest of the time I was at home, with my usual routine mostly intact. I wasn't sure at first that it was OK to be so content in my solitude."

After coming through a stressful time, you might feel uncomfortable when everything seems to be falling into place, your loneliness has subsided, and you've established routines, activities, and companions for when you're both separate and together. Now that you have acquired the skills of commuting and the sense of self-confidence and self-reliance they bring, life becomes much easier. All the chores and skills you needed to learn are now familiar, and you're settling in to this new lifestyle. Things aren't perfect—you still have times when you're frustrated, bored, or stressed—but, all in all, it feels pretty good. Now you may be surprised to find yourself wondering if it is OK to feel this content. In the beginning, establishing a routine is a great relief, and you just relax and enjoy life with a minimal amount of chaos and difficulty for the first time. After your new skills of autonomy became natural and automatic, life is a lot more fun:

- Because you have learned to make effective choices and considered the short- and long-term consequences of your decisions, you no longer go from crisis to crisis.
- Since your life is more predictable and calm, you have the energy to build healthier habits and thought patterns, experiment with new behaviors, and begin to enjoy life more.
- When you are no longer overwhelmed by the demands of the change, exhausted by stress, or feeling incompetent to handle problems, you experience a burst of enthusiasm.
- You feel safer, confident, more playful, and you have figured out how to enjoy yourselves alone and with each other.
- Because you feel more secure, you can experiment with new situations, succeed, or be disappointed, but through it all you'll have the confidence that you can handle the situation and adapt when things don't work out the way you planned.
- You're having more fun with friends, family, and coworkers, and life is less chaotic and more positive and rewarding because you know how to work out problems with effective choice making and negotiation.

When you have done a good job of negotiating the changes, consider it good if you feel happy. Enjoying your time apart is good for you and for your marriage. When you get back together, you'll bring all the strengths and new experiences of your separation back into your marriage, and enjoying your time alone refreshes you and gives you a more positive attitude to bring back home. You've entered a growth phase experienced by each of the couples whose histories have illustrated this book:

Lucy & Josh

Lucy, the homemaker with two children, and her husband Josh, the long-haul truck driver, have settled their arguments about a fair division of labor. Josh is now helping their sons with homework and doing the household books while Lucy has arranged with parents of their sons' friends to keep the boys from time to time, so she and Josh are getting to go on the road, as they did when they were first married. "We are deeper in love, closer, we no longer fight, we have fun together, and life is a lot more fun," says Lucy.

judy & nick

Fireman Nick and his wife, flight attendant Judy, have two children and schedules that don't always coincide. Learning how to make smoother transitions when going apart and coming back together stopped the irritation and disconnect they were feeling. Since they've learned to communicate more frequently and work out problems together, they have more time to have fun and relax together.

jane & edward

Edward, the medical equipment salesman, and Jane, the nurse who is getting a postgraduate degree, have learned to make the most of their limited time together and to support and help each other. They're looking forward to Jane's graduation, when she can get more regular hours as a nurse practitioner, and they can think about having children. Jane says, "I'm very grateful to Ed for all his help and caring. After surviving this, I believe we would be able to work through anything."

gail & charles

Pregnant Gail is waiting for her merchant marine officer husband Charles to come home for the birth. They have learned how to keep in touch and feel close, and Charles has learned how to reassure Gail when she is jealous or frightened. They're both waiting for his retirement in a few years, and he has plans to start a business. Gail says, "We are so much stronger as a couple now that we've learned to stay close, no matter what."

Sara & paul

Sara and Paul have made the difficult adjustment to his deployment in Iraq. They have a baby on the way and a small daughter, so Sara has relied heavily on the support of her sister, her mother, and her mother-in-law while Paul is gone. They have figured out how to keep in touch and stay close while Paul is so far away, and Sara also has the support of other Guard wives. Of course, they'd both rather he was home and are looking forward to that day, but they've managed to make this work for now.

Jill & james

Jill took a coveted editor position at a magazine in another city a few hours away while her husband James, a lawyer, stayed home. James's grown sons at first thought this was the preliminary to a divorce, but James and Jill have managed to create a nice setup, with a condo where Jill stays during the week that James and Jill and their sons can use for a weekend getaway. Jill says: "James and I both think this experience has enriched our marriage. We are closer now, and we value our time together more. I've learned to be more self-sufficient, and I've made friends here that I really enjoy."

Colette & harry

Colette was not willing to leave her tenure-track career and research as a university professor when Harry was offered his dream job in another city. They struggled for a while, but now they've settled into the routine. They sold their large house and bought a condo in each city, and they share time back and forth. Colette has a lot of time off during school breaks and Harry isn't tied to his desk too much either, so they've worked out a schedule of time in each condo, and they're enjoying their time together. Harry says, "I had trouble understanding Colette's reluctance to move at first, but now I get how important the time she's invested in her job is to her. I think she is also enjoying the alone time she has when we're apart, and it certainly has made us appreciate the time we have together. This situation won't last forever, but we're OK with it for now."

rachel & michael

When Michael was downsized from his executive job and finally had to take a position in another state, his wife, Rachel, stayed home, close to her aging mother and their grown children and grandchild. They had a very hard time at first, but Michael lives in California and their children love to visit, and Rachel has come to enjoy her visits too. Michael comes home for holidays and vacations, and Rachel goes to see him as often as she can. "I feel much better staying close to my mom and the kids, who need me. What I didn't anticipate is how much Michael and I would learn from this situation, and how much better our time together would be. It was a rough transition, but we have gotten to a really good place, and Michael thinks his company is opening a branch near here, so he's applying to be transferred back home."

cindy & bill

Navy nurse Cindy and her contractor husband, Bill, were upset when her base closed and she had to commute 120 miles to another base for work. She has four more years to go until retirement, so they're sticking it out. "It's been hard for our daughter, Chloe," says Bill, "as well as the two of us. But we've figured it out, I learned how to cook, and Chloe and I got a lot closer when I became her major source of parenting for several days a week. We cherish our weekends, Cindy trades shifts when she can to get extra time at home on Mondays and Fridays, and it's going OK. We'll all be glad when Cindy is home permanently, but we've worked it out so we do have enough family time, and Cindy and I have bonded more because we've come through this struggle. We've proved we can work together and count on each other when things are difficult."

Susan & Bob

With three children, Susan and Bob were really thrown when the aerospace company he worked for laid him off from his project manager job. He is back in school, learning advanced Internet technology, which they both feel has a good future. This situation has put them in a financial pinch since Susan works as a teacher's aide because it's compatible with the kids' school hours. Bob says, "I work now as a computer tech days and go to school nights, so both of us are working much harder than we used to. But we've figured out a routine that works, I help when I can, and Susan and I have learned to make the most of the little time we get together. We're both eager for me to finish school and start my new career. By the time we get there, we should be so good at using limited time and limited finances that we'll feel like we're on a luxury vacation."

Like most of these people, it may take you a while to learn to trust your newfound comfort and happiness, to believe it will last. Because you're doing something most couples don't do, the security of successful commuting seems fragile, as though the stress of making the changes can come back at any moment. But as you learn that you can correct any errors you make, and sustain your carefully developed ways of living and relating, your feeling of competence and security in your new way of living will grow. The relief of having found a solution to living at a distance can last months or years, depending on the nature of your situation. For a while, it is enough just to have managed all the changes and have an effective arrangement worked out. Relax and enjoy feeling competent and organized again. You've worked hard to get here, and you deserve to celebrate it separately and together. They may have said it couldn't be done, but you've done it. Remember: celebration + appreciation = motivation. Take stock of all the changes you've negotiated together and separately, and congratulate each other regularly on a job well done.

What Does the Future Hold?

Even though you also have been facing life together as a team, each of you has had to do a lot on your own. When you take responsibility for yourself and think for yourself, you begin to discover and expand your own individuality. Once you are independent, making choices on your own, and feeling more competent, an interesting thing happens. When you take care of yourself and create internal and external support for yourself and your individuality, you provide yourself with the secure base you need to grow and to express yourself.

Living on your own, even part time, and making decisions that don't depend on others for approval or acceptance increases your sense of individuality. Each of you has developed a way to view your life with a new sparkle in your eye—a creative, individual approach to life and other people that's brand new. You have used clear thinking and effective choice along with intuition, inspiration, and faith in yourself to take risks, experiment, and create a whole new way of living. Even when you come back to living together, you'll bring all of this learning and growth with you. Both of you will be more open to creative, new ideas and more aware of your feelings and reactions. Your enhanced individuality will express itself in a way that is attractive to others and productive for you.

YOUR INDIVIDUALITY IS ON DISPLAY WHEN YOU:
- Take an idea or event and place your unique stamp on it.
- Create a satisfying marriage that is quite different in form from your parents' marriage or from those of your friends.
- Choose work that is satisfying, even though it may be different from what your parents and friends think you should do.
- Have friends who enhance your life and who like you for who you are.
- Express your true individuality when you eat, wear, and do what is right for you, regardless of the fads and trends of the day.

- Create a home that you enjoy and the decor reflects each of your own individual tastes.
- Express yourself as you wish, making room for your favorite talents, hobbies, and pastimes, as well as each other.
- Solve problems creatively, using your feelings, intuition, and your life experience, to imagine new options and make sure they are considered in a logical, practical manner.

These are the gifts your commuter marriage challenges have given you. The next exercise will help you use your hard-won independence, creative thinking, and self-awareness to face whatever your future brings with more confidence and to look ahead for possible consequences and outcomes. Like a chess master, you can use foresight in your own life to evaluate the results of decisions before you make them. The great masters of chess are masters because they, too, have developed this ability to look at the chess board, work out every possible move that might be made, and then consider all the possible consequences.

EXERCISE: PLAYING CHESS

1. Think creatively and visualize. Like a chess master, imagine the future and how each of your moves and choices will play out. Whenever you're facing a choice or decision, take the time to picture each option available. Suppose you're considering living in two different cities. Before deciding, take the time to gather as much information as you can about each place, then try to picture what the home and work environment would be like. Imagine:
   - Getting up in the morning
   - Going to work
   - Interacting with people at work and in your neighborhood
   - Being in the work environment doing your assigned tasks

- What are the pluses of the move? What are the draw-backs? Do this with each possible choice, creating as complete an image as you can. Remember to consider the long-term possibilities as well as the immediate ones.

2. Evaluate the possible choices. To learn how you feel about your possible choices, ask yourself questions as you would with a dear friend. If you're considering moving to a new city, your questions might be:
    - Is it too far away from friends and family?
    - How do salaries compare to housing costs and expenses in the local economy?
    - What is the lifestyle of most of the people who live there?
    - What neighborhoods and schools would be good, and can you afford to live there?
    - Is this a place you could live in for a long time?
    - Would you be better off as a whole from where you're living now?

3. Sort and evaluate your choices. Try looking at the future from every angle possible:
    - Discuss it with your partner, friends, and family.
    - Arrange your list of pros and cons into two columns on a page for easier comparison.
    - Visit and spend some time there to see how it feels.

4. Get expert advice. To verify the reality of your ideal images and provide environmental support for your search, locate some experts who have firsthand knowledge about the information you are seeking. In our example of moving to a new city, you can:
    - Contact the chamber of commerce to get to know the businesses there.

- Contact Realtors in the area to find out about home costs, neighborhoods, and schools.
- Search the Internet for chat rooms about that city, and ask questions there.
- Ask your medical insurance about providers and facilities there. Do they have the health care you need?
- Call a CPA in the area to find out about local and state income taxes.
- Call utility companies, phone companies, and other vendors to find out what things cost.

5. Allow yourself ample time. Perhaps most important, allow enough time to be able to make a choice. Waiting until the last moment to make decisions deprives you of the opportunity to find out what your options are or gather sufficient information to think about them. The whole point of the playing chess exercise is to take the time to work out and consider all the possibilities, which gives you more autonomous control and a better chance to make a great choice. In the example of moving to a new city, don't wait until you can't stand your commuter situation a minute longer, until the job that's keeping you apart ends, or your children are about to get out of school so you can move over the summer. Begin early to look and compare to give yourself time to choose so you can find a locale that is ideal.

Playing chess will work in every aspect of life where you're facing changes—if you want to go back to school, change jobs, or if your children are going to college or you're facing retirement. The skills you develop playing chess will make every change easier and more successful.

judy & nick

Firefighter Nick found this helpful: "Since learning to 'play chess' I find that it's easier for Judy and me to make decisions. First we try out the variations, and where they'd lead, then we can talk about what we think our experience will be. It worked great when my station gave me the option to switch to two twenty-four-hour shifts and then four days off. We thought through it, projected it out, and then decided it would be easier to coordinate Judy's flight times if I only had two days on in every six."

Do We Have to Go Through That Change *Again*?

Change is a basic fact of life. We grow older, seasons and situations come and go, and the circumstances we live in are constantly in flux. Sooner or later, like most couples, you'll be facing a new change: living together again.

If you think that you've done it before and you'll just go back to what you used to do, you're not taking into consideration all the learning and growth you've accomplished. As we explored earlier, your commuter marriage experience has changed you and caused you to grow, giving you expertise, experience, wisdom, and other gifts in the process. If you apply your skills, wisdom, and gifts to this change of living together again, it will be an easier process than you had before. If you're planning carefully, thinking clearly, and choosing wisely, you can have a brand new future and live life the way you really want to. Once your resistance to change is resolved, you'll find the experience exhilarating, and you'll look forward to it. The prospect of change becomes exciting. No matter what changes you encounter in your future together, you will have developed the skills you need to cope with them. Once you understand the growth and satisfaction that comes from successfully negotiating change, your marriage, even when you're back together, will never become stagnant, because you can always make a change if you need to.

Nick and Judy face constantly changing schedules and days off, but they've grown to like the changes. Judy says: "We've gotten so good at change that we have confidence that when we both get to leave our jobs for something new, we'll do fine."

Can Our Marriage Be Better Than It Was Before?

Deciding or having the opportunity to live together again is a great opportunity to make any changes you want to make. If you had some problems getting along before you went into your commuter marriage, you don't have to go back to them. You can develop brand new patterns for dealing with each other in more effective ways, and you can develop new boundaries, guidelines, and agreements that will create a much better living situation than you had before.

Trouble Signs

As partners in a healthy relationship, each of you is responsible for stating your wants and needs, and for self-monitoring for signs of resentment, disappointment, or deprivation, which indicate that something about your own internal relationship, or something in your relationship with each other, is not meeting your needs.

When these signs occur—as they do when you become stressed, are too busy to pay attention, or some problem activates an old, bad habit—whoever becomes aware of them first is responsible for initiating the effort to make them better. For example, if you're feeling irritable, anxious, and frustrated, instead of blaming your partner, first use an inner-awareness technique (such as the consulting yourself exercise in Chapter 5) to figure out what's wrong. Then, if you want your partner's help in solving the problem, you can calmly discuss it. ("I realize that I haven't been getting enough sleep because I've been staying up too late watching TV with you, can we talk about it?")

If you are too upset to talk calmly, handle your feelings first (on your own) with discharging or time-out (see below) until you are prepared to talk reasonably.

As a healthy couple, you regard fighting as a mistake, not an inevitable part of relationships, and use smart decision-making to find other ways to handle problems.

> If Nick and Judy have a fight, they break it off as soon as possible, take a time-out, and when they've calmed down they discuss two problems: what they were fighting about, and why it became a fight and not a discussion.

The more practice you have in dealing with problems this way, the more you will embrace it, because you know it is the best way to care for yourselves and each other and to ensure a healthy, growing relationship.

Take Responsibility

When you take responsibility for your own feelings and reactions, you know that in an autonomous relationship it's up to you to handle any problem that makes you uncomfortable:

- Become aware of it.
- Discuss it with yourself and find possible solutions.
- Implement those solutions that require only your action.
- If you want your partner's help, discuss the problem and ask for what you want.
- Work with each other until you find a mutually satisfactory solution.
- If you can't find a mutual solution in a reasonable time (an hour or so), you may need to make a temporary decision that you both can agree to and come back later to try again until the problem is satisfactorily solved.

Overcoming Personality Quirks

Because you and your partner are different from one another, with different backgrounds and experience, each of you has small quirks, personality traits, or habits that must be accommodated in one way or another if you wish to have a sustainable relationship. These quirks can include:

- A laugh that grates on your nerves
- Differences in messiness or neatness
- Irritating jokes or stories
- Incompatible work schedules
- Different ideas about TV programs or music, housekeeping, your partner's nailbiting or smoking, what and when to feed the dog, how politely to speak to your children, or how warm the room should be

Little oddities like these are easy to ignore when you are dating or when you live apart and don't see each other too often; however, when you put up with them for months and years, they can feel like a sufficient reason to get a divorce, or even instigate mayhem. Many of these things may seem silly and so insignificant that you feel embarrassed to be so unhappy about them, but if you and your partner can't resolve your frustration, small irritations can create enough resentment over time to become serious problems.

Judy says: "Nick has a habit of leaving his clothes where he takes them off. I know he does this with his boots and pants at the firehouse, so they'll be ready to jump into, but at home it makes me feel like the hired help to keep picking up after him."

Dealing with Your Partner's Personality Quirks

When such small irritations happen, there are four things you can do.

1. *Don't sweat the small stuff.* Sometimes your partner's quirks, such as being messy, picking at teeth, not putting lids back on jars tightly, watching too much TV, or singing off key, are small enough to be easily dismissed by deciding the whole package of your partner more than makes up for the little annoying habits. If you can do this without resentment, your partner's quirks will cease to be a problem, although occasionally you may need to remind yourself of the benefits of being together.

> Judy can decide it's not a problem for her to pick up after Nick because he does so much around the house in other ways.

2. *Fix it yourself.* If you are the one with the annoying quirk, you can voluntarily modify your own behavior (go to the bathroom to pick teeth, screw the lids on tight) to reduce the annoyance to your partner. If you're the one getting annoyed, you can screw the lids on tight yourself and remove the problem.

> Judy can leave Nick's clothes where they are so he has to deal with them himself and maybe also the fact that they don't get washed if they're not in the hamper.

3. *Remove yourself.* You can minimize (by leaving the room or distracting yourself with a project) the impact of your partner's habits on yourself.

> Judy can shove Nick's clothes over to the side to make them easier for her to ignore.

4. *Resolve it between you.* If the previous three steps don't work, and you feel irritated and resentful about a quirk or habit, you and your partner can use the Steps for Solving Problems

Whether You're Apart or Together in Chapter 6 to discuss the problem objectively, without blame or defensiveness, and create solutions that satisfy both of you.

> Judy told Nick that his clothes left around the bedroom were a hassle for her, and they discussed it. Nick said he was OK with putting dirty clothes in the hamper, but when he wanted to wear something again before washing it, he didn't know what to do with it. Judy got him a rack of hooks, and he agreed to be responsible for putting his dirty clothes in the hamper and that she could remind him if he forgot.

By using these guidelines, over time you can create new ways to be partners for a lifetime without getting on each other's nerves and create new options for dealing with the irritations when they arise.

Good Times, Bad Times

You've already survived a lot of good and bad times in your commuter relationship. All relationships go through good times and bad times, and as partners you'll probably face fights, tragedies, betrayal, and struggle in a lifetime of living together. Although you may want very much to believe in "happily ever after," you need to consider the other possibilities:

- What happens if you lose your job?
- How are we going to handle it if we have money difficulties?
- What if one of us gets very sick?
- What if you have more success at your career than I do?
- What if we get more successful than we ever dreamed?

In a lifetime of living together, you and your partner need to be able to handle many ups and downs, such as:

- Problems to solve and victories to celebrate
- Moments of excitement and moments of peace
- Times of boredom and times of stressful activity
- Fights and harmonious times
- Tragedies and blessed events
- Highs of tremendous love and caring for each other
- Lows of distance and irritation

The expertise you've gained in solving problems during your commuter marriage will help you meet all these ups and downs as a team, work together to solve the problems, and celebrate your successes. Each experience that demonstrates you are a team who can remain calm in times of crisis, think problems through carefully, solve them in a way that satisfies both of you, and enjoy your successes to the fullest will strengthen your bond of trust and partnership and cause you to feel more free in your partnership.

Transitions

As you grow older and gain more experience, your attitudes, expectations, and preferences change. Because your relationship is a reflection of the attitudes and experience of both of you, it must change as you do in order to sustain a mutual sense of freedom. A big change, whether caused by circumstances (a new job means you must move to a new city), personal growth (you become more self-assured and want to make some new friends or develop a talent), or an unexpected event (your spouse gets a serious illness) always creates some turmoil and confusion.

As you probably experienced in your transition to commuter marriage, when your familiar way of doing things begins to change, you can struggle, compete, or fight because one or both of you are stressed, insecure, or frightened. However, now that you've successfully made the huge transition to commuter marriage, you can look at big changes as just a series of problems you must solve.

When Michael finally got his transfer to a job near home, he and Rachel were thrilled, but they had to make many new adjustments such as how their plans for Michael's retirement would change, how they would handle their new time schedule and living together arrangement, and whether to keep the condo near Michael's other job location and use it for a vacation home or rent it or sell it.

By solving each of these problems individually, rather than letting themselves see the whole thing as one big confusing problem, they were able to work with a financial advisor and solve their problems. Property values were very high where the condo was, and they were able to make up the losses in their retirement account by selling it. They decided it would make better financial sense to pay for a vacation on the West Coast when they wanted one rather than keep his house for that use.

You and your relationship will continue to grow and change, and you won't always progress neatly from one stage to the next or find an arrangement that is permanently satisfying. Each of you can even be at different stages at the same time! But your skill at making smart decisions and solving problems make each transition an exciting new adventure or challenge instead of a frightening change.

Forgiveness

In a lifetime of living together, you are bound to unintentionally hurt each other's feelings, betray trust, or let each other down from time to time. Some emotional hurts, such as the harsh words or betrayal that might occur during a relationship crisis, will only be resolved through healing and forgiveness. Expertise in problem solving will help you forgive, because once you find a solution to the problem that originally caused the damage, teamwork makes it much easier to let go of the hurt feelings and get back on good terms with each other.

If you find you are holding hurt, anger, or resentment toward your partner, use the seven steps for turning talk into communication outlined in Chapter 3 until you understand clearly enough to communicate the problem that needs to be resolved. Then proceed to solve whatever you feel hurt or angry about as if it were any other problem. You'll find that once you come to a mutually satisfactory solution, forgiving your partner (and yourself) is made easier by the reassuring knowledge that the problem won't be repeated.

Challenges

Paradoxically, the closer you and your partner become, the more you'll face challenges to heal and grow, because partners in intimate, committed relationships often challenge each other in emotionally sensitive areas. When that happens, your relationship can become an arena for facilitating healing and growth. If you or your partner has had a painful past relationship (for example, violence, cheating, dishonesty, abandonment, or financial disaster), wounds may still exist that may cause overreacting in your current relationship. Whenever one of you is being emotionally dramatic or overreacting to a normal marriage problem, the following guidelines will help you diffuse the situation and calm things down.

GUIDELINES: OVERCOMING CHALLENGES

1. *Don't panic.* As painful and overwhelming as this situation may seem, challenges are common in relationships and can be overcome. Do your best to stay calm and use your clear communication skills to find out as much as you can about the problem, and then follow the seven steps for turning talk into communication (Chapter 3).

2. *Be as supportive as you can.* If you (or your partner) are upset, do your best to be emotionally positive and encouraging. Reassure each other that you won't go away or avoid the issue. Even if you have to take a break to calm down, you can still agree to resume your discussion after you calm down.

3. *Get outside support.* Select friends who can support both of you emotionally when you have a challenge, and don't hesitate to let them know when you need help. Having someone who cares, and who can listen and support without interfering, will relieve some stress and help you stay calm.

If you expect to face challenges, understand that most relationships have them, learn to take care of yourself, recognizing that challenges present an opportunity to heal and grow, and know when to get support, you'll be able to overcome challenges and keep them from damaging your partnership. Successfully overcoming challenges strengthens your bond of confidence and trust in each other and in your partnership.

Together At Last!

The final problem faced by couples in long-distance relationships is how to bridge the distance and end the long-distance arrangement.

- Who should move so we can be together?
- How do I get reestablished after we are back together?
- What happens when I stop traveling for my job?

You can see this as an opportunity to redesign your living together situation and incorporate what you learned from being apart. What do you want to recreate the way it was before? What do you want to change? Let's take a look at how and when each of our couples were able to come back together and how they set up their new situation for success.

colette & harry

Colette and Harry were able to move back together after he had a couple of years as CEO and she attained tenure at her university. Harry got another CEO position closer to the university and Colette had more free time when the pressure was off her to publish so much. They decided to try for a baby, which would be another new adventure. Colette says: "We learned so much through our commuting experience about how to solve problems and talk through arguments, and how to listen, that we think we'll be better parents because of it. We plan to eventually buy a house again, but we'll wait until I'm pregnant."

lucy & josh

Josh isn't going to give up driving his truck anytime soon. He loves his work. Their oldest son will be going off to college in the fall and their younger son the year after, so they're looking forward to having the house to themselves again. Josh says: "Because I learned how to stay in touch, I'll always be close to our sons, and I'm proud of them. We've been taking trips on the weekends to look at colleges. But Lucy and I are looking forward to having our twosome back. We've been enjoying the occasional times she can travel with me, and now we'll be able to do it a lot more. Eventually, I'll hang up my driving gloves, but for the next few years, we're going to have a great time together."

judy & nick

Fireman Nick and his flight attendant wife Judy have adjusted to his new schedule, and they are having an easier time coordinating their schedules together. They will be in this commuting situation for a number of years. Judy says: "Eventually, I will apply for a ticket agent job, which will allow me to keep my flying and insurance benefits. My seniority will help me get a good schedule, which should be compatible with the kids' school hours. Nick and I feel that we will be able to handle that change well because we've learned so much about working as a team and coming up with creative solutions to problems."

jane & edward

Jane has graduated and is now licensed as a nurse practitioner. Both she and Edward are relieved that her heavy schedule of nursing plus school is over. She works now in a doctor's office with regular hours, and she makes a better salary than she did as a nurse. She loves her new job, and she and Edward have a lot more time together in the evenings. They're considering having a child and looking forward to being parents. Jane says: "It was really hard work, going to school and working nursing shifts, but it was worth it. Edward was so helpful, and we worked together so well that our relationship has gotten much closer. We're really enjoying this time we have now, because we know that will change when I get pregnant."

gail & charles

Gail and Charles, the officer in the merchant marine, have had their baby, and Charles got home in time for the birth. He stayed home for a couple of months to help Gail, and they enjoyed their time together, but, of course, a new baby took up most of their time. Charles only has a few years to go before retirement, so he's making plans to begin his own business. Gail says: "Wow! I knew a baby would be a lot of work, but the reality s overwhelming. Charles is gone again for several months, so thank God I still have my family for support. "

sara & paul

Paul and Sara have been separated for two years, and now Paul has come home from Iraq. This is a big change for both of them, and they're not sure if he'll be sent back again. Sara says: "I'm so glad he's home safe, but it wasn't easy for him. He's a different person. We stayed in close touch while he was gone, and we're doing pretty well at talking. I have to say, I'm different too, now that the baby has arrived. We have a lot of changes to deal with, but we have a good basis, and we're going to counseling. I still have support from my wives' group and my church. The pastor has been helpful, recommending counseling for us."

Jill & James

After two years on the magazine, its management changed, and Jill left her editor job to come back home. James is very glad to have her back home. They sold the condo, and now they're planning to travel. Jill says: "The editor position was a great experience, and I'm very glad I did it, but I'm also glad to be done. I'm working on a book and as a freelance writer now from home, and I like that. I enjoyed my book group and my line-dancing classes so much that I have found both things here at home. James and I are having a great time being back together. What we learned by being apart is really helping us do better than we were before."

Cindy & Bill

Cindy, the Navy nurse, has only two years to go until retirement, when she can get a civilian nursing job. She is already looking for possibilities near home. Bill says: "We're doing so well. We have learned how to create sweetness in our marriage, and when Cindy can work here at home, things will be great." Cindy says: "I'm grateful that I got such great training and experience in the Navy, and I'll be able to have a great nursing career in the civilian world. Chloe is doing fine, and I'm going to be glad to be home with her every day and not just weekends."

Rachel & Michael

Michael, who lost his job and had to take one in another state, has now managed to be transferred back home to a new branch his company built there. He and Rachel are settling back into living together. Rachel says: "We are doing well. It's great to have Michael back home, and we're spending more time in our individual pursuits than we used to because we enjoy it, and also because it keeps our connection fresh and interesting. My mother is ill now, so it's good to have Michael home to help."

Susan & Bob

Bob, who lost h s aerospace job and went back to school to learn Internet technology, is now out of school and has gotten an IT job that has good benefits with a big corporation. Susan has decided to keep her teacher's aide job because it's so compatible with the children's school schedules. Susan says, "It was tough while Bob was in school, but we made it through. We both learned a lot, and we don't waste time now arguing or bickering. I found I really liked being a teacher's aide, and I know more about how to work with my kids at home too. After the hectic days when Bob was at school, we feel like we have lots of free time now, and we're enjoying each other and the kids."

Do We Have to Develop a New Infrastructure?

The exciting answer is you have the opportunity to create your lifestyle and intimate connection in a whole new way. To do this, you need to understand the characteristics of healthy relationships and have a model for creating a healthy relationship style that is satisfying and relatively easy for you to sustain.

A Model for a Healthy Relationship

As healthy partners, you create your relationship to suit yourselves and each other. Each relationship is therefore unique and different from all others, because as partners you are different from everyone else and you can express your individuality. You do not have to distort yourselves to fit some idea of a relationship. Because every person is unique, there are no rules that apply to all relationships, which makes it difficult to formulate a model for healthy relationships. Therefore, it is necessary to learn to build your relationship from scratch and figure out what works for you. The negotiation and communication skills you have learned here can help you shape your relationship any way you wish, provided both of you are happy with the results.

IN A SUCCESSFUL HEALTHY RELATIONSHIP:

- You feel supported by each other.
- You have help and companionship in the hard places.
- You are aware of advantages and reasons you are together.
- You have goals to work toward and mutual successes to celebrate.
- When either of you experiences difficulties or failures, you know how to offer solace and reassurance to each other.
- You feel empowered, because two people working as a team have more power than individuals working separately.
- You have the strength of commitment that comes from knowing that you and your partner are in the best relationship possible for each of you.
- You are free to let your partnership take any form you and your partner want to give it.
- And, best of all, your way of being together and your personal wants and needs are flexible enough to change over time as you as individuals change and grow.

There are four basic characteristics of autonomous intimacy: a positive connection with yourself, relaxed closeness with each other, shared warmth, and shared humor. You have healthy intimacy when these characteristics are present. Whenever your ability to care for yourselves, be generous with each other, and be relaxed and open enough to enjoy each other is blocked, intimacy will not flow between you.

Positive Connection with Yourself

One advantage of the separation of your commuter marriage is that it forces you to be more self-sufficient, which is a great opportunity to develop and enjoy companionship with yourself. Several exercises in this book, like the inner wisdom exercise in Chapter 7, help you make the most of that opportunity. The caring and responsibility you learn from your positive connection with yourself becomes the basis for your relationships with others. In other words, to determine how well you are doing, you compare the quality of your internal relationship with the intimacy you and your partner share and create a sustainable, satisfying, and successful relationship in which you both relate honestly and reliably. The more success you have with each other, the more trust and intimacy you build together.

Relaxed Intimacy with Each Other

Your mutual trust and intimacy form the foundation for a love that feels free, generous, and flowing. It is not limited, possessive, or controlling. Instead, you each encourage the other to grow and seek satisfaction; you rejoice in each other's joy; you support, love, and teach each other; and you allow each other whatever closeness or distance you need. When you are open and honest with each other, you each feel truly loved for who you really are. This free and flowing love is easy to sustain because it feels so good. Because each of you meet you own inner needs and don't feel obligated to fix your partner, and you both have the skills to solve problems as they happen, you can both relax and be free to have fun together.

ELEMENTS OF YOUR HEALTHY INTIMATE RELATIONSHIP

1. *You're together by choice.* You are not in the relationship out of fear of loneliness, need, helplessness, or so someone else can make it better but because you are good partners, you feel loved by and loving toward each other, and your partnership works. You're in this relationship by choice.

2. *You admire each other.* Your mutual intimacy is based on good self-esteem and respect and care for each other.

3. *You value the results of your connection.* Both of you value the content—that is, the connectedness, caring, commitment, and satisfaction—of your relationship. It is not the fact of the relationship that is important but its results: you and your partner feeling mutual love, respect, teamwork, and reliability.

4. *You do what works.* As partners, you can think clearly, share ideas, and solve problems on the spot according to what works best at the time rather than trying to follow someone else's pattern or model. You deal with issues and problems as they arise, figuring the answers out as you go along, looking at long-term as well as short-term results, and adapting to new situations as they happen in a seat-of-the-pants operating style. Instead of arguing about who's right or wrong, you calmly discuss what will solve the problem.

5. *Your communication is clear and open.* You value honesty and clear communication above protecting yourself or your partner from hurt feelings, although you take care to express the truth as kindly and gently as you can and still be understood.

6. *Your contract for being together is mutual and fair.* You both consider your relationship to be an agreement or contract in which each party has responsibilities and benefits and which clearly states, in advance, what happens if the contract is broken. Try saying this to each other while holding hands: "I will stay with you as long as it is healthy for me, and you agree to do the same. If either of us feels the some part of our relationship is becoming unhealthy or uncomfortable, we will bring it up for discussion. If we cannot solve the problem ourselves, we agree to bring in an objective third party to help. If nothing will fix it, we will renegotiate whether we want to stay together."

   That is, you recognize that your relationship will not survive no matter what, and you each take responsibility for keeping it worthwhile for yourself and for each other. If either of you feels that your relationship is becoming detrimental, you say so as soon as possible to give yourselves an opportunity to work the problems out.

7. *Negotiation is your normal mode.* As with any viable contract, problems, confusion, and changes are resolved through discussion and negotiation. You bring up whatever feels like a

problem to either of you and then you discuss it, use effective decision-making techniques, and work it out together.

8. *Your relationship is sustainable.* You both understand that each of you must be able to do what is necessary to keep it going for a lifetime. You recognize that neither you nor your partner will be able to sustain uncomfortable or self-depriving behavior for years, and you balance your need to be yourself with other considerations of what is good for you.

> Lucy says: "Josh loves country and western music, and I've always loved classical. We used to fight about it, but now he can have all the country and western he wants while he's driving, even when I'm in the truck, and I get my classical music at home when he's gone. We've both relaxed and found ways that we can both listen to classical sometimes and country and western other times, and if one of us gets too much of a style of music, we can just say so and work it out on the spot."

This may sound utopian and unrealistic, but you'll find if you use what you have learned here it is not only possible but it also becomes easy.

Shared Warmth

Perhaps you think a relationship in which each of you is responsible for taking care of yourself sounds cold because the fantasy of romantic love is about being taken care of. But the actual experience of healthy love is anything but cold. Taking care of yourself without a struggle creates security, and the absence of struggle allows you to feel warmth toward each other. Your personal inner security and comfort radiates out from you as the feeling others describe as warmth and generates intimacy that feels warm and inviting. The freedom to love each other without stress, coupled with reality-based mutual trust and lack of pressure, allows warmth to flow between you.

Warmth is a spontaneous feeling of goodwill, respect, pleasure, and satisfaction that arises when intimacy is coupled with freedom and trust. Because you are equals, together by choice and showing your love of yourselves and each other, taking responsibility and solving problems together, you are free from struggle and frustration. You have maximized the good feelings you have when you're together, and over time you'll experience the accumulation of these emotional rewards as warmth—the result of successful intimacy. Once established, warmth radiates in all directions, and both of you will feel bathed in it. You can tell you're experiencing warmth if you find yourself smiling with pleasure and appreciation when you think of your partner.

Cindy and Bill have become experts in expressing their affection toward each other with touch, looks, words, and little surprises. Bill says: "I was never very good at expressing my love before Cindy's job moved and she was gone all week. It's one of the great things I learned from struggling through this." Cindy says: "The warmth between us is a great reward for being more thoughtful and understanding. Just a moment of caring creates hours of good feelings between us. We are definitely a happy couple."

Being surrounded with loving, spontaneous warmth every day makes working on your relationship worthwhile and pleasurable even when outside things go wrong. Undemanding, generous warmth feels equally good to the receiver and the giver. When such warmth and goodwill are present between you and your partner, your relationship becomes precious. You are committed to each other because the warmth is there.

Shared Humor
It may seem odd that one of the characteristics of healthy living is humor, but when you are unafraid to be different and

individual, you are also free to be funny. Healthy partners feel free and secure enough to laugh at silliness in life and in each other, without sarcasm or cynicism. Laughing without criticizing or attacking each other is closely connected to warmth, and it is characteristic of healthy intimacy. It takes a certain amount of self-acceptance to create healthy humor rather than the hurtful kind, but this loving, shared laughter also enhances your self-esteem. It feels good to laugh together. The more you learn about being happy inside and intimate with each other, the less you'll struggle and the more you'll laugh and play. When an overwhelming feeling of warmth and caring flows over you, laughter will arise spontaneously.

Colette & harry

Colette says: "Harry and I were always serious people. Work was important to both of us, and we took ourselves a little too seriously. Being apart gave us a better appreciation for each other, and we both realized that our relationship is going to outlast our work, and that made it more important to have fun together. We like to watch silly movies, we read funny passages from books to each other, and we laugh a lot more than we used to. What a surprise that commuting taught us to laugh together!"

Whether you commute for years or come back to living together after a short time, the skills you've learned here will help you make every day of your marriage a good day. You are blessed to have found each other and to be surrounded by children, families, and friends. You have learned you can make new friends, learn new things, and explore new ways of living. Commuting, when you know how to do it well, can strengthen your bond, as does any difficult life passage you negotiate successfully. You may have commuted to make a dream come true or because circumstances forced you to. Some of your commuter situation has been fun, some of it hard. Now you have the information and tools necessary to make your commuter marriage whatever you want it to be and when you get the opportunity to come back together to make that a great experience also. May you have many happy years of positive connection with yourselves and each other, including shared warmth and shared laughter.

Index

about the author

TINA B. TESSINA, Ph.D., MFT, ASJA (*www.tinatessina.com*) is a licensed psychotherapist in private practice in California since 1979. Her practice includes individual and couple counseling. She earned both her BA and MA at The Lindenwood Colleges, St. Charles, MO (1977) and her PhD at Pacific Western University, Los Angeles (1987). She is a Diplomat of the American Psychotherapy Association and a Certified Domestic Violence Counselor, and is certified to supervise counseling interns.

She is the author of thirteen previous books, including *Money, Sex and Kids: Stop Fighting about the Three Things That Can Ruin Your Marriage*; *The 10 Smartest Decisions a Woman Can Make Before 40*; and *The Unofficial Guide to Dating Again*. Dr. Tessina has appeared extensively on radio and TV, including on *To Tell the Truth, Larry King Live, Oprah*, and *ABC-TV News*. She has been quoted in *Redbook, Cosmopolitan, O The Oprah Magazine, Ladies Home Journal*, and many other magazines and newspapers, and has been published in sixteen languages. On the Internet, she is known as Dr. Romance, the Dating Doctor, and The Love Doctor. She is an online expert, answering relationship questions at *www.CouplesCompany.com* and *Yahoo! Personals*, as well as a Redbook Love Network expert, and has been a "Psychology Smarts" columnist for *First for Women*. She publishes the "Happiness Tips from Tina" e-mail newsletter and has hosted "The Psyche Deli: Delectable Tidbits for the Subconscious" radio show. She also writes the "Dr. Romance Blog" at *http://drromance .typepad.com/dr_romance_blog*.

She and her husband, Richard Sharrard, live in Long Beach, CA, and enjoy their 1918 California bungalow, gardening, and playing with their three dogs.